THE LOHVIAN CYCLE I

The Dray Prescot Series

THE LOHVIAN CYCLE I

Kenneth Bulmer

writing as

Alan Burt Akers

Published by
Bladud Books

First published in 2011 by Bladud Books

Originally published separately in German by
Heyne Verlag in 1991-2.

Originally published separately in English by
Savanti Press in 1995-6.

Published separately by Mushroom eBooks
from the original English manuscripts in 2008, as:
Scorpio Reborn
Scorpio Assassin
Scorpio Invasion

This first omnibus paperback edition published in 2012 by
Bladud Books, an imprint of Mushroom Publishing,
Bath, BA1 4EB, United Kingdom

www.bladudbooks.com

ISBN 978-1-84319-891-8

Contents

SCORPIO REBORN

Dray Prescot

For those unfamiliar with the Saga of Dray Prescot, all that it is necessary to know is that he has been summoned to Kregen, an exotic world orbiting the double star Antares, to carry out the mysterious purposes of the Star Lords. To survive the perils that confront him on that beautiful and terrible world he must be resourceful and courageous, strong and devious. There is no denying he presents an attractive yet enigmatic figure. There are more profound depths to his character than are called for by mere savage survival.

He is described as a man above middle height, with brown hair and level brown eyes, brooding and dominating, with enormously broad shoulders and powerful physique. There is about him an abrasive honesty and an indomitable courage. He moves like a savage hunting cat, quiet and deadly, sudden.

Having won his princess, Delia of Delphond, Delia of the Blue Mountains, and having become the Emperor of Vallia with Delia at his side as Empress, Prescot has renounced the crown and throne. Any thoughts of a quiet life are foolish, as he well knows. Among the many problems besetting him, the most important are uniting the lands of Paz and beating off the viciously hostile raiders from over the curve of the sea, the feared and hated Shanks.

Scorpio Reborn is the first volume of the Lohvian Cycle. Flying a kite one moment, battling through an inferno the next, Prescot is flung headlong into fresh adventures under the mingled streaming lights of the Suns of Scorpio.

Alan Burt Akers

One

Handling a Valkan kite in any sort of breeze demands skill, nerve and strength. Young Inky had the first two in abundance; but the third... Well, now, young Inky was only a little lad, full of fire and spirit and years away from growing into his full strength. Every now and then I swear his feet left the ground.

He was laughing. The wind snatched his curls and tumbled them about his flushed cheeks. The breeze freshened and the kite swayed and rose and Inky really did go up.

That, I decided, was enough. I turned my back on the panorama spread out far below the clifftop. Valkanium's new buildings gleamed in the light of the suns and the waters of the Bay spread in glittering magnificence. Up here the air held the combined perfumes of sea and land, the fresh salty tang mingling with the aromas of shrubs and flowers as the ruby and emerald lights of the twin suns mingled in streaming radiance upon the world of Kregen. Looking at Inky, I turned away, too, from the clifftop fortress and palace of Esser Rarioch, my home.

Inky stared up, fascinated. His bare feet trailed across the turf as the kite pulled. I hastened my stride. If he went over the cliff...!

"Look!" he called, hanging onto the line, staring up. "Look!" His feet touched the turf and his bare toes curled and dug in. The line slackened. I looked up.

With sharp talons hooked over the top bar of the kite, a superb bird, all gold and scarlet, turned his fierce head sideways to glare down upon me. I knew him. Oh, yes, I knew this splendid bird. Inky could see him too and this did not surprise me. The Gdoinye, the messenger and spy of the Star Lords, may sometimes be seen by the innocent at heart as well as crusty reprobates like me. When he spoke, cawing down his truculent message, I do not believe Inky heard anything other than the cry of a bird.

"Dray Prescot! You are required *at once!* The Star Lords in their wisdom afford you this, for their demands are not to be questioned, yet—"

I felt the breath rush from my lungs. A mist fell over my eyes.

"No!" I started to shout, hearing nothing, seeing nothing save an all-encompassing blueness. Above me, gigantic, reared the phantom Scorpion, enormous through the swathing mists, his blueness enveloping me in coldness, darkness and a fate I could not avoid.

Head over heels, spinning, the Star Lords hurled me from the high cliff-top by Esser Rarioch in Valka, hurled me—where?

The Star Lords were in a hurry. As I felt the coldness bite into my bones I knew what that haste meant. Someone had fouled up. A Kregoinye, sent to do the bidding of the Everoinye, had failed. So the Everoinye hoicked out their expendable, their trouble-shooter, the fellow they'd used many times to patch over a hole in their careful plans. I felt heat.

Flames roared and coiled all about me and smoke stung my eyes and choked in my nostrils. The transition had been quick, deuced quick, by Vox! I stood in a burning building. That was the emergency, then, and I had to find the person the Star Lords wanted rescued. Yet the first and most important item I noticed was simply this—I was fully clothed! I wore my decent russet tunic cinctured with my old leather belt with the dull silver buckle. This belt carried various pouches of use. From separate belts hung my rapier and main gauche. I wore no shoes or sandals, bare-footed as Inky had been.

The floor, I may say, was hot.

Wisps of smoke drifted from the floorboards to join the gusts of foul-smelling smoke jetting from the walls and ceiling. This was a sizeable hall with wooden pillars supporting a beamed roof. The wood flamed. The stink of some unnameable substance permeated the suffocating air. Blazing beams bent and collapsed and smashed down in smothering avalanches of sparks. Half-shielding my face and eyes I peered around, feeling as though I was a scrap of meat thrust too precipitately into the fire. Smoke writhed like phantom snakes and sheets and fangs of fire darted everywhere.

Spouting sparks, a beam crashed down making me skip out of the way most smartly. Beyond the hedge of fire two bodies lay in contorted attitudes. This was the reason for my summary arrival here at the behest of the Star Lords.

Trying not to inhale the smoke and trying to shield my eyes I leaped the blazing beam. The man was nearest. He had worn a mail shirt and carried two or three swords and daggers; now he was just charring. I turned my attention to the girl. She had not yet burned and as I bent closer I saw she was not yet dead. She wore an odd-looking outfit consisting of a green slashed jerkin and tights, daggers snugged in sheaths at her waist. Sparks smoldered in her dark hair and I stopped to bash them out. Something bright and golden winked beside the man's curled fingers and swiftly I picked up a golden trinket and stuffed it away in my pouch. Then I hoisted the girl and started to find my way out of the furnace.

A pillar wreathed in tendrils of flame abruptly bent, broke and collapsed. The beam it supported smashed into the floor, through the floor, and took with it the best part of the aisle between the pillars this side of the hall. I suppose I must have looked like a beast at bay as I turned to seek another way out of this blazing bedlam.

Head down, cradling the girl, feeling the heat blistering my feet, I started for the nearest aisle between the columns. Spouts and gouts of flame licked up the wooden pillars, scarlet and orange transparencies, moth wings of destruction. There was no way through there. I hauled up and a beam smashed down to join the burning wreckage cumbering the floor. There was no way out at my back and each side roaring columns of fire blocked off sight and sense. The incessant crackling noise battered at me. I realized I was doing a strange kind of dance, lifting one foot and then the other, performing a weird hornpipe trapped there in the fiery furnace.

No way out through the aisles or doors, certainly no way up—therefore the way out was down.

Smoke continued to jet from the joins in the floorboards. The floor had once been highly polished and the wood seethed with a brown boiling scum. I could see no railing around stairs down. By this time the smoke made seeing even more difficult, to add to the constant half-closing of my eyes against the ferocity of the light and the sheer heat of the place. I began to feel the Star Lords had this time landed me in it far up past my armpits.

"By Zair!" I said to myself. "There has to be a way down!"

Now, I'd no idea where I was. I did not wish to contemplate the awful possibility I might be back on Earth. No, I told myself sternly. No. I was still on Kregen, even if I didn't know where. Buildings are erected in as many if not more styles on Kregen, as they are on Earth. Now where would the logical place be for the cellar steps?

Alongside an entrance hallway, for one. And all the entrances were mere pits of fire.

I took a mouthful of stinking smoke and gagged. From the feeling in my eyeballs I now knew just how two fried eggs feel in the pan.

There *had* to be a way out!

With a crash that vibrated the floorboards beneath my feet a whole section of the floor vanished into a spouting volcano, dragging blazing beams into the pit below. I squinted to see past the hellish uproar, tears distorting my sight and refracting scintillant rainbow colors around the edges of vision. The damned floor had split three or four paces off and if I was right only smoke coiled up there, before the pit of fire began.

There was only one way to test that theory.

Taking a firmer grip on the girl's lax body I took those necessary three and a half paces and jumped.

Even as I sailed down through the smoke-filled hole so a beam burst across above and showered down a rain of stinging sparks. I hit not too clumsily and rolled sideways to shield the girl. Smoke wafted. Ahead the blazing debris from above walled off progress that way; but with a feeling of thankfulness I saw that the opposite direction, luridly revealed in the fire glow at my back, remained clear—for now.

6

The floor above sucked up smoke through the joins, and tendrils of orange fire ran all along under the boards. In almost no time at all that floor where I had been standing would burst into an inferno. I put my head down and ran swiftly through the last of the smoke, heading for the end of the building.

A narrow alleyway led between vast stone vats, rotund and gleaming in the firelight. The pungent smell of wine, full-bodied, ripe, permeated the air. At the end a wheelbarrow containing a spouted pot together with sundry measuring ladles and jugs revealed the purpose of this place.

The air was a trifle clearer here and I paused for a quick breather. Then it was past the wheelbarrow and up the narrow stone stairs beyond the trapdoor in the ceiling. As I mounted so the air grew hotter and the roar of the fire closer. Still, there was no going back. I had to go on.

The stairs turned sharp left and ended at a closed door.

This I kicked open and plunged through, bursting into a sheet of flame and trying to shield the girl as best I could. I roared on and through the flame and burst out into a corridor which was about to explode into fire in the next instant. Like a maniac I raced for the far end. A pair of double doors stood half open. A white and leprous light glowed beyond. The ceiling fell in an avalanche of sparks and spinning blazing brands at my back, making me hurl myself forward for the double doors. The girl moved in my arms and abruptly struggled with shocking strength. For that moment I was distracted, fearing her injured, and something ugly and hard—and hot!—struck me alongside the ear.

I fell down.

The complete blackout could not have lasted long. I was aware of heat and of hands dragging me and of my back scraping along and scratching confoundedly irritatingly on splintered boards. There was no smoke about me. No smoke choked down into my lungs. The heat materially decreased. My back scraped over stone and then grass. Above me lifted a tall blue sky with not a cloud in sight as my eyes cleared.

I was out of the inferno, and—someone had dragged me out.

My head felt as though it was not there, or had been lent out to someone else who had stuffed it with feathers and hung it out to dry.

When I shook my head I did not hear the familiar carillon of the famous bells of Beng-Kishi, rather, there echoed only a dull and empty shushing.

A juicy voice said: "And your friend?"

A girl's voice, very crisp: "He is dead."

I turned that empty noddle of mine to see what might be seen.

The girl I'd carried from the burning building and who then presumably had dragged me out in turn stood looking with an expression I could not then fathom at a stout, florid, important individual with a girth swathed in golden scarves. His face glowed and yet, even in my muzzy state of half-awareness, I sensed there was little of good humor in this man.

In the slanting rays of the twin suns shadows did not stretch far. As a backdrop to the important principals discussing the fire the crowd clustered with that particular air of satisfied fascination peculiar to crowds watching the destruction of a building by fire and flame.

The stink of burning smothered everything with the dry taste of ash. My eyes burned. Just how much skin I'd had burned off I was reluctant to discover. Another voice, hard-edged with habitual command, a woman's voice, said: "I am in his debt, for he carried me to safety. I could wish him alive so that I could reward him."

"I," said the girl from the fire, "could wish him alive, also."

I did not miss that sharp rebuke.

By turning my head and ignoring that dull emptiness between my ears, I could see the woman standing on the other side. Yes, she was clearly important, and not just self-important, either. Clad in a chequered gown of green and yellow with enough gold to indicate her status, she bulked with good living. Her face did not partake of that plumpness of form, being hard-edged like her voice, with a rat-trap mouth and a narrow nose that, whilst it was not exactly a witch's hook, nevertheless gave one that impression.

A few burned rags on the ground at her feet and two slave girls hovering near explained the clean crisp appearance of her gown.

What in the name of Opaz had been going on here? The dead man in the burning building had rescued these people; as far as I had been able to see there had been no one else inside, so why had he gone back and thus caused this spritely young lady to risk her life hauling him out? He must be the kregoinye who had failed, and his friend had gone in to save him and the Star Lords had called on me to assist. Well, all that fitted.

The crowd shuffled feet and remained mostly silent. No one made any attempt to extinguish the blaze. The building was too far gone for that. It stood in an open dusty area by itself, so the flames would not spread. Four wide streets intersected here, flanked by white flat-roofed buildings. Trees grew everywhere, bright green and yet lacking the profusion of foliage of trees in Vallia or Valka. I began to form opinions about where I might have been flung by the Everoinye. Kregen is a whole world.

The important man said to the important woman: "Do not distress yourself, Lady Floria—"

She interrupted sharply: "I do not, Lord Nanji. Although, by Loncuum, when a pleasant evening's entertainment during a long unpleasant journey is thus summarily ruined, one is entitled to a little pique, sus?"*

Despite the fog swirling in my head the woman's words were confirmation that the burning building had been a dancing rostrum. That was easy enough to understand; but the long unpleasant journey? That sounded promising.

---

* sus: nicht wahr? n'est-ce pas? A.B.A.

8

"Assuredly." This fellow, Lord Nanji, let his fruity voice make of the syllables a veritable squish pie. "I will escort you to our lodgings."

Her hard face ridged.

"I think not, Nanji. We have few pleasures on this abominable journey. I intend to take every opportunity to enjoy myself before the lights."

"Very well. Then I shall accompany you—"

"If you wish."

She turned to her slave girls, decently clad in gray frocks with clean faces and not too many bruises, saying: "Follow."

Lord Nanji walked into my sight. He strutted. Well, that was to be expected. Following him a couple of husky guards, well-armed, lounged along as though saying there is nothing in this for us.

A number of interesting items had been learned in this short space of time. By talking of an evening's entertainment when by the position of the suns it was middle afternoon, mention of the lights, and the long journey, made it clear these people were part of a caravan and would turn in early and start early. Problem was: just whereabouts on Kregen was this caravan marching?

The guards' weaponry gave some clues. They carried broad-bladed spears, a weapon often associated with mercenary caravan guards. They had no shields; but then, most Kregans do not carry shields about in civilized towns. Their swords were decently scabbarded, one a thraxter the other a lynxter.

Their harnesses were brass-studded leather with boiled-leather helmets reinforced with iron strips. Perfectly standard attire.

The crowd parted respectfully for them. The dancing rostrum would take some time yet before it burned out. I guessed the people were waiting to see the final crashing fall of the roof, always a high spot in fire watching.

I tried to sit up and could not.

The hollow emptiness of my skull was shared by my bones and muscles; truth to tell I could feel very little of myself right then.

Another voice spoke, a softer voice, yet one without hesitation, a voice accustomed to speaking thoughts well-formed before utterance.

"I add my thanks to your friend, my lady—"

"I am no grand lady. My name is Mevancy."

"Mevancy." Did I detect a tinge of pleased irony? "He pulled me out. He was a brave man. I grieve when the world loses a single person not of Tsung-tan. I shall intercede for him in my prayers. It may be Tsung-tan in his gracious benevolence will smile and admit your friend to paradise. What was his name?" A little cough. "Mine is Tuong Mishuro."

"Rafael," she said. "Just Rafael."

"And you knew him well?"

"Passing well. We traveled together. I grieve..."

By this time I'd managed to get my head rolled the other way and so could see these two. The girl, Mevancy, had her hand to her eyes. Not a nice time, when a friend dies, not nice at all.

Tactfully, the old buffer kept silent. He wore a decent enough gown, dark brown, open at the throat to reveal pure white linen blackened by smoke. His feet were encased in curly slippers in red velvet which delighted me more than I can say at that not auspicious period. His face was just such a face as you may see carved on Buddhas in many temples of our Earth. He wore no jewelry and no cap; probably that had been lost as he'd been carried from the conflagration by Rafael, who was a kregoinye working for the Star Lords and who was now dead in their service.

The thought occurred to me, and not for the first time, that maybe the Everoinye were remembering their humanity. Rafael had died and his friend and companion Mevancy had ventured into the blaze to rescue him and been overcome. With Rafael's work done, there had been no need for the Star Lords to concern themselves further. I was confident no one else remained in the dancing rostrum and Rafael had lost his life searching frantically for others to rescue. I knew what he must have felt. I, too, had searched for the person or persons the Star Lords wished me to assist. Would they, I wondered, have bothered to send another kregoinye after Delia if she had been overcome trying to drag me out? And the thought occurred, yes, perhaps they would. Perhaps the Everoinye were remembering their lost humanity.

With these profound meditations finding tentative lodgment in the vacuum that was my brain, I returned my attention to what was going on now. At the side of the old buffer, this Tuong Mishuro, stood a youngster in a ragged brown robe tied up with string, with bare feet. There was no straw in his hair; I felt there ought to have been. His face was heavy and dark with the beginnings of a beard, and his lips were full and red.

Very humbly, this youngster said: "Master, I must fetch clean linen for you. It is not seemly—"

"Yes, yes, Lunky, I agree. But there are more important things in life than clean linen."

"Of course, master. Good food and wine—"

"I shall fetch my switch, Lunky, if you continue."

"Yes, master."

Mention of wine did not afford a clue to my whereabouts. Well, not much of one. Wine is carried enormous distances on Kregen, of necessity, to those regions which do not grow grapes.

Tuong Mishuro half-turned and spoke in a friendly and enquiring tone of voice to a newcomer just out of my vision. "How are they, doctor?"

"They'll live, they'll live. Thanks to the man who pulled 'em out."

Now I could see the doctor, a short, stout, bandy-legged man with sweat drops glittering on forehead and cheeks. He carried a leather bag, was clad in decent blue robes and was your Needleman to the life.

He saw me. "Oho. You've found some more, then."

Everyone turned as though operated by clever springs to stare down on me. The odd thing was, aware of their stares and that I ought to stand up, I felt no inclination to do so. I just remained sprawled out on my back. Equally, I felt no desire to talk to them. Oh, yes, I wanted to know whereabouts on Kregen the Star Lords had thrown me; but that could wait. Now, if only there had been a pillow under my head I'd be able to nod off most comfortably.

The doctor knelt and placed his bag on the ground. I was aware of his fingers, soft and strong, probing at me. He tut-tutted to himself and when he had concluded his examination, he stood up, puffing with the effort.

"Nothing wrong with him. A big fellow like that, no problem. I'll put some ointment on his feet; but he's not badly burned, not like lynxor and lynxora Shalang." He shook his head. "Lynxora Thyllis will take some time to mend, I'm afraid."

Tuong Mishuro made a deprecatory clucking noise of sympathy. "A terrible tragedy, terrible. Still, in the expert hands of Doctor Slezen both will recover, I feel sure."

"I'll do my best," said this Needleman Slezen. "Do my best."

"And," said Mevancy, who had been looking critically at me. "This fellow?"

"I'd rather he didn't walk just yet. Carry him to your lodgings." At that moment the roof of the dancing rostrum collapsed with an almighty roar and blast of displaced heated air and showers of sparks that gyrated and whirled upwards like an exploding volcano. To my surprise a great cheer broke out from the watchers. Well, fire watching is an obsessional pastime.

Tuong Mishuro said: "That is easily arranged. Lunky, find four stout fellows who wish to earn a silver khan between 'em, and a blanket."

"At once, master."

Now I do not mind spiders as a general rule, unless they're poisonous or any of the many varieties of giant killer spiders of Kregen. So when a spider crawled up my arm and headed steadily for my face I took no real notice. I'd just shoosh him off gently, for I cannot abide louts who stamp on any little scurrying creature they see. He crawled up my chin and circled my mouth. I did not raise a hand to shoosh him off. Just as I thought to lift my hand Tuong Mishuro bent to me, not smiling but immensely polite.

"Llahal. I am Tuong Mishuro. Would you favor us with your name?"

I'd tell them some name or other. By Krun! I had plenty! I thought I'd just brush that little spider off my face first and then tell them the name I'd choose.

My hand did not move. My mouth did not open. I made no sound.

The reason for the lack of sensation all about me and inside my head became at once crystal clear.

I could not move or speak.

I was paralyzed.

Two

"Dribble, dribble, dribble," said Mevancy. "He's just like an overgrown baby."

"With shoulders like that," observed Mistress Lingshi, wife of Nath the Landlord, "overgrown he surely is."

Mevancy wiped soup away with a yellow cloth and then filled the spoon again. Carefully, she tilted it over my mouth and some of the soup splashed between my lips. Thank Zair my inward parts still worked. And, too, I felt supremely fortunate that my eyelids could close and open. Utter torture would have resulted if they'd been as paralyzed as the rest of me.

Mevancy sighed and filled the spoon again and a little more soup trickled down my gullet. It was a soup I had not tasted before, rich but not as thick as it might have been. And it was not hot; these parts, then, shared the fashion of drinking soup cold. All I had seen after being carried here in a blanket had been sky, ceiling and a swift vision of wall and bed when I'd been turned over to be washed. As Mevancy had said to Mistress Lingshi: "I rescued him and so I feel responsible for him."

"But you and your poor dead friend rescued a whole lot of people—"

"True. But they're not like little babies, are they?"

"And you mean to go on with the caravan? The way is very dangerous, particularly at this season."

"Without being disrespectful to your delightful town, Larishsmot is not the place for me. I must push on to the coast—"

"But!" exclaimed Mistress Lingshi. "You can't mean to travel through Tarankar? Never! They fry and eat babies, you know."

"Well," said Mevancy, and a trill lightened her words. "This one here would make a feast for them!"

"Tsung-tan in his majesty preserve us!"

"Well, I suppose I could leave him here—"

"Oh, I don't think you ought to leave him here with us, dear. Much better to be able to keep an eye on him yourself."

"Well, if you think that best—"

"Quite the best. Oh, yes, the best all round." Mistress Lingshi sounded positive, alarmed and relieved, all at the same time. I swear I detected that lilt of mockery in Mevancy's tone.

"It's lucky," said that young lady primly. "I've plenty of money so that's no problem."

"Of course, dear, if you think it better for us to look after him—"

"Oh, no, dear Mistress Lingshi, as you say it's best all round if I take him along. I couldn't impose on you in that way, money or no money."

"We-ell, dear—"

"Here is the soup bowl and spoon. Now I'll just plump up his pillows and then I must see Master Cardamon."

When a woman has a fellow helpless in bed the pillows become objects of desire for her. She is forever plumping them up. And I was paralyzed and couldn't dodge the barrage of straight lefts and right hooks that whistled past my ears. When Mevancy had gone a round or two with the pillows and got them thoroughly cowed and obedient, she let out a snort of satisfaction, and strode off with Mistress Lingshi trailing after.

The door creaked and then slammed shut. Shortly thereafter it creaked open and soft and furtive footfalls approached the bed. I just lay there, rigid as a brick wall. The seamed face of Nath the Landlord hovered over me. He held a spouted wine jug. He smiled and nodded but said nothing. He applied the spout and I glugg-glugged. When he judged I had swallowed enough he looked around furtively and then crept out and the door creaked shut.

Good old Nath the Landlord of the Jeweled Crook.

There are many Naths in the grouping of continents and islands called Paz. I blessed Nath the Landlord who had felt fellow-feeling for a man in distress surrounded by pillow-punching females.

My own feelings of lethargy persisted. I was well enough aware that having accomplished my mission for the Star Lords I could go home. I was absolutely confident this paralysis was merely temporary. All too soon I'd be up and about and this little interlude be over. And, I own, despite the pillow-punching propensities of Mevancy, I enjoyed this slothful lying down and doing nothing. She was an odd one, this Mevancy. Her face was not that of a great beauty; it possessed animation and aliveness. Her nose was finely shaped but her mouth was generous, far too generous for beauty. Her teeth were small and white. As for her eyes, they were dark and unfathomable. Her dark hair, from which I had bashed sparks, was usually caught up in a plain linen band. She habitually wore a slashed tunic and tights. The arms of the tunic were fastened down their length with latches giving a mannish Renaissance look. Her skin visible through the oval openings looked strange, almost granular, yet the skin of her face was real skin, smooth and silky, and nothing like a squamous or pebbled skin.

Nowadays there are two sapiens in our name; we are Homo sapiens sapiens, having recognized our old rivals Homo Neanderthalensis as being sapiens also. Homo sapiens sapiens on Kregen is apim. I wasn't certainly sure this strange girl Mevancy was apim. Just at the moment it didn't matter—unless she was from a race that practiced cannibalism.

When she returned she was practical and businesslike, all starched efficiency and bustle. "Master Cardamon will take us in his caravan and we must leave right away." She stared down at me. "If you do not wish to go with me blink your eyelids twice."

I tried not to blink at all.

"Very well." She turned her head. "Nafty! Pondo! Come and get him."

All I saw of these two was the back of one as they hoisted me, bed and all. By Krun! Mevancy had bought the bed off Nath and was taking it and me!

My own russets lay folded neatly at the foot of the bed and my rapier and main gauche hung from a bedpost at the head. They had attracted notice only as foreign weapons, known to these people. All I wore was the old scarlet breechclout. The money pouch on the belt had not been opened by Mevancy as far as I knew. That belt also supported the scabbarded seaman's knife.

As we went lolloping down the stairs and along the street to the Wayfarer's Drinnik and the blue sky passed overhead, I reflected again on the reasons for the Star Lords to dump me down with clothes and weapons, something that had happened infrequently in the past. Rafael, burned to death and now, I had heard, decently buried, had probably been deposited well-armed and clothed and with money. Well, he'd been wise to team up with Mevancy, for it was clear she was a young lady used to having her own way and with the wherewithal to pay for that way.

If, as I vaguely suspected, Mevancy was not fully apim, that would make no difference. On Kregen, if miscegenation could occur, people looked only to see if true love was involved. Cynics scoffed, of course; but cynics get their kicks from mistrust widely advertised.

The uproar from the Wayfarer's Drinnik was, as was usual and expected, prodigious. Dust smoked under the twin suns. I could see the sky without a scrap of cloud; yet I could see in my mind's eye all that was going on around me with absolute clarity.

The caravan of which Cardamon was Master was due to head west. This town of Larishsmot was more than a mere caravanserai. Here a caravan would rest up to make repairs and buy provisions and get ready for the next stage of the journey. Also, as lady Floria had said, this was a time to relax and snatch what entertainment might be found.

A shadow fell across me and against the light the form of Mevancy showed hard and edged, riding a zorca. I felt relief that this land knew of zorcas and, no doubt, as did everywhere else, cherish the wonderful riding animals.

"You will ride in the cart. It will not be comfortable. The quicker you regain your senses the quicker you'll ride easier."

Mevancy spoke Opaz's solemn truth, by the invisible Twins!

The damned cart was uncomfortable. Hideously uncomfortable. Yet I am an old sailorman trained in the toughest Navy the world of Earth has ever seen. I have been wounded before and carried home in a cart. Getting wounded in a battle is not to be recommended. This despicable example of the cartwright's art disdained springs. I do not believe the wheels were triangular, as might well be believed, but merely square. The thing jolted up and flopped down and threw me about like the ball a child tosses up and down in a handled cup. Now I might be paralyzed so that I could neither move nor talk; I could damn well feel, by Vox!

When this hoity-toity young madam had dragged me out of the fire I'd felt my back scraping along the ground. I reasoned that I must have hit the back of my head and neck on some hard projection thus to become paralyzed. I did not think the falling beam had done this. Anyway, I could feel. And I felt every jolt and jerk of that infernal cart. This was a physical torture to add to the mental torture of my situation.

I shall have more to say on this question of torture, which is often bandied about as though torture is a commodity to be purchased over the counter. Those people who traffic in torture are, of course, sub-human despite overt intentions, as has been exemplified in the teachings of San Iwanhan, who suffered at the hands of well-intentioned torturers. This cart was, indeed, a simple-minded example of torture, to be sure; at the time I raved mentally and cursed all the dark gods and spirits of Kregen for their vile habits.

In the nature of things much of that portion of the journey went away from me as though shrouded in mists. I was sponged down a couple of times, by which I knew the way was waterless. If I couldn't begin to move pretty soon sores would start to appear, and quite apart from the inconvenience to myself, I would shrink from inflicting the smell on those about me.

The two louts engaged by Mevancy to help proved an ill-assorted pair. Nafty giggled and fooled around a lot of the time; Pondo remained silent and surly. Once or twice I was turned on my side and could catch occasional glimpses of the outside world over the side of the cart. Mostly that was low dry hills, a few thorn ivy bushes, and the distant figure of an outrider. Some of these hired caravan guards rode zorcas and some a thumping six-legged waler of a saddle-animal with family connections to the sectrixes. But, mostly, when I lay on my side I could study the whorls and knots and weathering of the timbers of the cart's side and bed.

In that wood were whole worlds, maps of Kregen and of Earth, faces of friends and foes, a picture gallery that my mazed mind pondered for hour after hour. When I was turned over onto the other side I found a distorted mirror image; for my brain transcribed from the wooden markings the same faces and pictures although the maps were different. Then I would be rolled onto my back and so could study the even white blueness of the unchanging sky.

The twin shadows of the suns moved across the cart as the days went by, the jade and ruby lights streaming the mingled radiance of the Suns of Scorpio. Then I caught a few surly words from Pondo and a light bubbly rejoinder from Nafty.

"There'd be total darkness over the land, Pondo, if Luz and Walig waited for you to laugh before they rose of a morning."

So now I knew where I was.

It does occur to me that you who have listened to my story will already have reasoned out where I was. But you must remember I was not myself; I was not the true Dray Prescot, Lord of Strombor and Krozair of Zy, late Emperor of Vallia. I was a poor creature who had been cruelly stricken down with paralysis of body and mind. I was sluggish. I'd seen people around with red hair, and some of the guards carried impressive longbows; but these are found all over the lands of Paz.

Still—Luz and Walig.

I knew the twin suns better as Zim and Genodras, or Far and Havil or any of the plethora of local names. Luz and Walig.

I was in Loh.

Loh, shaped somewhat like a Stone Age hand-axe, point to the north, is one of the continents of Paz and contains mountains, rivers, jungles and deserts just like any self-respecting continent. I could only hazard the guess I was in the south, for the central sections form the jungles of Chem and the northern pointed promontory forms the land of Erthyrdrin. That made me think of my blade comrade, Seg Segutorio, and long for him to be here where in no time his cutting wit would have me up on my feet foaming—and we'd have a wager on it, too! And, too, across to the east lay the land of Ng'groga and naturally that made me think of my blade comrade Inch whose tallness and thinness and lethal axe had figured in many a bonny adventure.

By the direction of travel of the twin suns across the sky I knew I was in the southern hemisphere of Kregen. Well, as soon as this confounded paralysis wore off I'd make my way back home. There was still a kite to fly with young Inky.

That little thought gave me pause. I marveled. Here I could dream of returning home to fly a kite when only a few seasons ago all the cares of the Empire of Vallia crushed down on my shoulders. My Delia, the divine

Delia of Delphond, Delia of the Blue Mountains, had shared that burden with me and now we were both free of it. Drak and Silda had taken over, now they were Emperor and Empress of Vallia—and good luck to 'em!

At the moment Delia was off on one of her secret and hair-raising missions for the Sisters of the Rose. Even if I could return to Valka this very minute, as ever was, Delia would not be there.

"Sink me!" I burst out; but silently, mentally, hotly. "We've got to come to an understanding with Delia and her Sisters of the Rose." But I knew dismally enough that the Star Lords would whisk me off at any time, just as Delia went off with the SoR.

Information of any kind was hard to come by as I lay in that creaking torture-machine of a cart. From odd snippets of conversation I drew the firm conclusion that most of these folk were more religious in outlook than many of the people I had known. They referred constantly to Tsung-Tan in tones of respect, awe and affection and not in the usually Kregen way of a mouth filling oath or three. I overheard one quietly serious conversation in which the speakers sought to establish whether or no the theatres in paradise would close on Tsung-Tan's day, as they did here on Kregen. This paradise presided over by Tsung-Tan clearly was vividly real to these folk. They called their paradise Gilium.

On a day when a tiny cloudlet appeared in the sky early on, to vanish the moment the day's heat began to build, the cart jolted to a stop. I heard someone yelling and someone else screaming. The cart started up again and now it jounced and bounced and threw me about. I could hear the rattling patter of hooves, and more shouting, and smell dust flying up. I could visualize the caravan as rushing along in panic.

A trumpet brayed, hard and brassy, and a thin silver echo sounded some way off. Like a magician's stage trick, abruptly and without warning, a long arrow sprouted from the timber side of the cart directly before my eyes.

The shaft must have shaved over my body. The trajectory was flat. So the bandits were close, then. I could only lie there. All too soon the sound of tinker-hammering broke along the caravan as guards and bandits clashed. I could see it all in my mind's eye. But, as the caravan was attacked and the guards slain, I, Dray Prescot, simply lay idly on my back.

With a great roaring and splintering the cart threw itself over on its side. Helplessly, all atangle, I was flung out.

The ground smacked me across the face. Half on my side, sprawled, my arms outflung and my legs twisted, I lay there and I know I looked like a corpse.

My eyelids were half lowered and I could see slantingly upwards.

Hoofbeats hammered past. Dust drifted across. The last few shrieks scythed the hot air and the raw tang of blood mingled with the taste of dust.

And I just lay there.

If only I could move! If I could get to my feet, snatch up a sword, fling myself on these drikingers, these murdering thieves preying on the caravans! My right arm outflung was turned at the elbow and I could see my right hand. The fingers lay like that fabled bunch of bananas, limp and useless. If I could just move!

Intermittent noises spurted up as the bandits ransacked the caravan. My humble cart, broken as it was at my back, attracted scant attention. I expected the drikingers to take all the water they could lay hands on.

At length, eight tall spindly legs daintily moving up and down, moved into my vision. Two long spirally twisted horns appeared and then the owners of the legs and horns. Two fine blood zorcas, moving with all the lissom grace of that superb saddle animal, halted before me. Their riders were so different from their mounts as to form a blasphemy under the suns.

Yes, their faces were fierce and predatory. Yes, their lips curled with arrogant contempt. And, yes, the veneer of humanity and civilization had been stripped from them. But these are things one expects if one follows the drikinger's trade. Bandits are not nice people. They sat their superb zorcas staring down at the smashed cart at my back and at me, a corpse sprawled in the dust. One lifted his bow and drew the string back. The steel point, a broad flesh-cutter, pointed directly at me.

He smiled, black beard glistening with sweat. I could see one eye along the shaft, baleful, hard. For sport, he was going to skewer me.

"He's a gonner, Naghan," shouted his companion. "Don't waste a good shaft on the cramph's corpse."

The bow string relaxed as this Naghan decided not to waste a shaft. In a heartbeat he could draw and loose and bury that steel head in my heart.

In that tense moment of waiting for his decision I saw a sight that filled me with two opposite emotions. I gleed with a fierce joy and I shook with a shattering horror.

Directly before my eyes my little finger was twitching, was moving, was curling in as the savage impulses to move at last stirred.

I could not stop that little finger moving and I could not move any other portion of my body.

If this rast saw my little finger moving he'd as lief shoot it off as a target shot, and then perhaps slit my throat with his knife.

That little finger curled like a piglet's tail.

"This caravan," Naghan the Bandit said. He lowered the bow. "Not well guarded, Kwang. And why?"

Kwang said: "How should I know, by Lokush the Chuns? We've lost more shafts than we've gained. That I do know."

"Yes. You are right—for once."

"Hai! Have a care lest I lose a shaft in your miserable hide!"

Waiting, head in the dust, eyes half closed, I could feel many sensations—sweat trickling, the awkwardness of my position, the ground pressing hard and unyielding into my hip and back—yet the chief sensation was one of complete helplessness. That betraying little finger curled and stopped and these two zorca riders, Naghan and Kwang, swiveled their mounts and moved off. I knew I'd passed perilously close to the entrance doors to the Ice Floes of Sicce then. The experience was unpleasant—unpleasant!

I do not wish to experience too many like that, I can tell you.

Mevancy had taken my belt away and hung it on the bedpost. That belt held my Kregan belongings; besides the pouches it also held my rapier and main gauche. That belt was missing from the bedpost.

Useless to rage and fume. The thing was gone; so it was gone and one with Beng Dithermon the Gatherer. So I lay there in the dust, abandoned, robbed and left for dead.

Presently the bandits mounted up amid a great hullabaloo. I could hear screams and the sound of blows. Whips cracked. Then that hateful word spat out with all the vicious force of slavemasters. "Grak! Grak!"

The people who had ventured across this waste land in the caravan were now slave. They were being driven off into slavery. And the word to use to make slaves jump, and cringe, and rush to do your bidding was—"Grak!"

If you didn't grak then ol' snake would curl over your shoulders and sting you through to the bone and teach you what grak meant.

The sound of carts and carriages rumbling off told me the bandits had made a haul of plunder even if they were short of shafts. The soft shushing of footfalls mingled with the harder staccato of hooves. Gradually the noises faded and at last died and I was left to silence.

The idea that it might have been preferable for that Opaz-forsaken drikinger to have shot me, to have placed that broad sharp arrow head clean through my heart, could not be allowed into my thoughts. I was not dead yet. Until I was dead I would go on struggling, for that is my way.

So I began to concentrate on trying to move that little finger.

The frightening deadness in my body complemented by the deadness in my brain had to be fought. I felt sweat on my face. This was a matter of mind over body; for Needleman Slezen had pronounced my body as being perfectly fit and healthy. "The knock has done some deep internal damage to his brain. Until that is rectified by an opposite force..." Slezen's opinion was cultivated. "He will remain a cabbage."

My reactions when the bandits appeared had motivated enough muscular energy to shift one little finger. By Krun! What would it take to make me lift that arm? The sack of a city?

A fluttering sighing sound heralded Rippasch's arrival. He strutted into my sight, ruffling his black feathers, turning his head from side to side, and the twin suns glinted in jade and ruby glory from the curve of his sharp and hooked beak. He eyed me. He was very sure I was dead and his belief was shared by a brother or sister. In a great swishing of wings another vulture landed beside the first. Well, that was one eye apiece so far.

I could visualize this scene as it might be witnessed by Rippasch himself as he sailed in the upper air, scanning the ground below. A litter of thrown aside goods all mixed up with broken carts and dead animals, the shafts capable of being loosed again cut out so the blood ran freely. Corpses lying about untidily—there are always corpses lying about after hideous incidents like the one just past. If I lost my eyes I wouldn't be able to see Delia again. That would be a punishment beyond bearing, I thought. Delia had a way of dealing with Rippasch the vulture. Oh, yes, Delia didn't stand any nonsense from them. Even so, I could not find it in my heart to wish she were here. Suppose, suddenly, I regained movement. I was stranded in the middle of the waste land without transport or weapons, without water.

The vultures flapped their wings and moved in closer.

Again I made a superhuman effort to move, and stirred not a single muscle—wait! My little finger. It moved. It curled and uncurled. And as I struggled so I saw the next finger curl and uncurl. The vultures came closer.

They turned their heads to the side and stared at me. Their beaks glittered in the light of the suns. Fluttering his wings with shooting downdrafts of sand spraying everywhere, one—the first one—alighted on my body. He bent to peer more closely at my face.

I couldn't close my eyes.

I wanted to see all there was to see until I saw no more.

I strained and struggled.

With a sensation of every cord in my body tearing free, as though my arm was pulling muscles, sinews and tendons clear out of the flesh, my right arm flapped up and over, like the jib of a crane, and flopped down across my chest. Rippasch let out a surprised and disappointed squawk and fluttered dust all over me as he took off, springing up into the air. His companion joined him and a long Lohvian arrow sprouted from the sleek black body.

A flushed face came into view.

Mevancy said: "So you're still alive, cabbage? Remarkable. I really shouldn't have bothered to come back for you; but you're just like a newborn baby."

I could say nothing. I simply closed my eyes.

Three

Under my nose the dusty sand moved past at a steady walking pace. The saddle of the lictrix was not particularly well-adapted to a man's body slung over athwartships, head hanging down one side and heels the other. And six-legged riding animals—in general—are not as comfortable as four or eight-legged ones.

"Try moving your other arm, cabbage!"

I couldn't snarl back that, by Krun, I *was* trying, wasn't I?

My right arm possessed some movement, although it seemed to move of its own volition. I'd hit myself on the nose trying to wipe my mouth, for example. Now I was working away on the left arm, and hoping against hope that the little finger would vouchsafe me a sign of future success.

I hadn't heard Mevancy and the two lictrixes returning. I put that down to my utter concentration on what Rippasch was about to do, and of my attempts to move my arm. Certainly the vultures had not heard. Mevancy, I suppose because there was no other audience, had fallen into the habit of talking to me. She spoke not quite as a mother to a child, more like a person talking to herself. Now she said: "I dislike killing anything, cabbage; but I thought the vulture was about to feast on your eyeballs."

We rode along towards the west in the wake of the caravan. Mevancy had a filled waterbottle. I could only assume she had managed to escape from the bandits and steal the two lictrixes. Certainly, I warmed to her. She was brave and resourceful, that was clear. And she'd come back for me.

Of course, her tongue was more of a cutting instrument than a bludgeon; but she could deliver a few shrewd whacks with it, nonetheless.

"Well, cabbage, you've lost your fancy foreign sword and dagger. Now if you could use a sword at all we could fix you up with a lynxter, or a Havilfarese thraxter. If you know how to use them, that is."

After a space she went on: "If those Gahamond-forsaken bandits show up again—well, cabbage, we'll run. That's all we can do."

That was an eventuality I did not look forward to. Galloping face down over an animal's back is no fun way to ride.

And notice, please, that that was my first thought. Only second came the thought that I did not relish running away from foes.

I might have won a resounding victory and be able to move my right arm and my left little finger; but my head was still dazed and mazed and stuffed full with chair upholsterer's padding.

"Reminds me of the time old Kervaney the Wand's caravan was attacked. That was up in Snarlendrin. Right in the middle of it the Rains came down. Ha! Talk about mud baths. By Spurl! We were a bunch of mudlarks all thwacking away at one another. Nath the Onker's sword slipped out of his fist and stuck clean through the throat of the drikinger who was just about to strike Kervaney down. Flew through the air like he'd hurled it." Here Mevancy paused and I imagined she was shaking her head in amused reflection. "Old Kervaney couldn't do enough for Nath the Onker who'd saved his life. And it was the making of Nath the Onker, too. Called him Nath the Volscreetz after that."

Whilst the anecdote possessed some vestigial interest, I quite failed to see what beautiful Rains had to do with the dry and dusty desert trail that was slowly desiccating us and sucking us into sere husks.

Like any sensible desert or wasteland traveler, Mevancy allowed no water drinking during the day. At the going down of the suns we could drink.

Surmising that she did not wish to close up too close to the bandits ahead I was not surprised when she ordered an early halt. Caravans are slow by their very nature. I assumed she'd halted just out of sight of the dust cloud up ahead. A few hard dry bushes grew in strips here and there and a couple afforded us cover. This particular species of wasteland had stretches of pure sandy desert interspersed with straggly bushes in strips and clumps as hills broke the flatness of the plain. It was not unlike some parts of Arizona. The people of the caravan had mentioned the Salt Desert to the west with some trepidation, and this I gathered was similar to the great salt deserts of western China.

She said: "One good thing, cabbage. I don't have to threaten you to keep quiet. These dumb beasts that are not so dumb are different."

Dumped off the lictrix I sprawled out on the dust behind a bush. Mevancy gave my head a twist on my neck so I could see along the ground and through the dry branches. I could hear her at my back and one of the lictrixes emitted a snorting whinny cut abruptly short. By this I knew Mevancy was tying cloths about their mouths. So we were in ambush, then...

Soon after that I heard them.

Soft shushing and harder hoofbeats, the jingle of bit and bridle, they were riding with assurance, confident of their own power and prowess. They rode into sight down the little incline past the dry bushes. They rode zorcas. They were mailed and carried slender lances and bows. Their helmets bore clumps of feathers, dyed bright red and yellow. In my life on Kregen red and yellow have been my colors more often than not.

I counted twenty-five of them.

The leader rode a blood zorca of superlative quality. His head was held erect and he laughed openly, a fiery red moustache curling up past his nose and his eyes creasing up in good humor.

"You speak sooth, Hangol. We will have these abandoned of Tsung-Tan by supper."

"And then, lynxor, we shall put them to the sword."

"I suppose so. It is just. Anyway, you will enjoy it."

"Oh, yes," said this Hangol. He rode just that fraction of a space to the rear on the leader's left side. We were to the south of the trail so the party of zorca riders crossed from right to left. I noticed this Hangol held his head a trifle turned away and put this down to a fawning attention on his leader and paymaster. His zorca was fine and his armor resplendent, and among his plethora of weapons, in the good old Kregan way, hung thraxter and main gauche. This told me he was left-handed.

Mevancy stood up, strode out from the cover of the bushes, spraddled her legs, put her hands on her hips and yelled. "Llahal and Llahal!"

They all reined up as though they'd been shot.

I quite enjoyed that. Had I been that leader with the fiery red moustaches paying this fellow Hangol to be my cadade, my captain of the guard, I'd have his hide for failing to post point, outriders and flanks. By Krun, yes!

Bows were drawn and arrowheads glittered in the declining light, all aimed at Mevancy.

The standard-bearer had a little difficulty in handling his zorca, who jounced around and wanted to kick his legs a trifle. The banner, a tresh of red and yellow of intricate design and difficult to distinguish at that distance, fluttered bravely.

"Declare your intentions or you are dead!" shouted up this Hangol.

Mevancy laughed.

"I chose to stand forth and greet you. I could have chosen to shaft you. You do not know how many bows are here with me."

The leader leaned gracefully and spoke quietly to Hangol. Hangol's helmet bobbed and even at this distance and seeing the whole scene on its side, I saw the surliness of that response. The cadade shouted up.

"We give you the Llahal. This is Leotes li Ningwan, Vad of Sabiling, Paol-ur-bliem."

The leader favored Hangol with a swift look of sharp displeasure, and then recovered his good humor. So he was a vad, just one rank below a kov, a duke. Well, he was high and mighty then. Just what the significance of Paol-ur-bliem might be I couldn't fathom. Paol is generally regarded as the earthly part of vaol-paol, the eternal cycle of existence encompassing fate and destiny. Bliem is a word for life.

With her back to me Mevancy's expression might be anything; I rather fancied she was putting on one of her more genial looks.

"Llahal, Vad Leotes. If you're after those Tsung-Tan forsaken drikingers, then I shall ride with you." She made a small gesture with her left hand. "I am Mevancy nal Chardaz. Lahal."

The vad lifted his hand. "You and your forces will be welcome, my lady."

"Now," I said to myself, "Lady Mevancy nal Chardaz, let's see you get out of this one without moving!"

She simply hauled her lictrix from the cover of the bushes, mounted up and flung a word back to me before cantering down the slope.

"I'll be back for you, cabbage. Don't run off."

She must have impressed Vad Leotes, for they spoke together briefly and then they swung their steeds' heads around to the west and galloped off.

I lifted my left arm and shook my fist after this hoity-toity miss.

Then I realized what I had done.

I lifted both arms, and clenched and unclenched my fists.

By Zair!

Now I could get to work on my legs.

My feet were now just about healed and if I could once get up on my pins I had no doubts whatsoever I'd walk. I'd damned well run!

Making muscles obey the dictates of my brain, telling sinews and tendons to pull, forcing my paralyzed legs to move at all—that was the trick.

As I lay there under the sere black bush and struggled to move, the twin suns steadily declined. Zim and Genodras, which here in this part of Loh are called Luz and Walig, cast long and longer shadows, emerald and ruby, smoking in the dusty light. There is no need to belabor my pains. At the time I heard a caravan approaching from the east, I felt the first bendings of my knees. By the time the caravan was in sight and preparing to make camp I was up on hands and knees, and when the first tents went up I went up too, to stand totteringly, reeling, dazed—but up on my own two feet.

After that it was a matter of climbing up onto the lictrix's saddle, a feat rather like climbing a peak in The Stratemsk, and of gently ambling down the incline towards the caravan and the camp. I was stopped very quickly, naturally. A man put a long polearm up at me. I saw it was a strangdja, a weapon of Chem, much feared.

"Whereaway, dom?" he said, in no hostile way, for I think he had the wit to guess from whence I came.

I smiled at him.

"Llahal, dom," I said. "I'm from the caravan that was attacked."

Then I stopped speaking.

What actually issued from my mouth was something like: "Lla—l—mm—mm—cvn—tat—"

So. I was still unable to speak.

The guard—he wore brass-studded leathers and a leather cap—put his strangdja on the ground and reached up. "Here, dom. You need attention, and we've the best Puncture Lady this side of Tarankar." He caught me as I fell off. His nose was ripe and large and possessed fissures like those of a river system as it enters the Delta. His mouth was wide and mobile. I felt the limber strength of him as he caught me. He yelled: "Hai! Nath! Scrimshi! Come and give this poor devil a hand."

Three bulky leather-clad men hauled me up and carried me into a tent where the sweet scent of palines growing in a tub made my mouth water. I suppose the efforts I'd put out just recently had drained some other reserve of energy quite distict from whatever lack caused the paralysis. They gave me a handful of palines and I devoured the yellow berries knowing that in themselves they could cure a mighty lot of Kregen's ills. I stood up, swaying, it is true, and again essayed to speak, with the same dismal result.

The Puncture Lady wore a neat blue dress with a yellow collar and cuffs. She bustled in ready to order, organize and generally boss people about. Her face showed all that in its straight lines its angle of jaw, the tightness of the prim mouth. She started to punch me, here and there.

"Nothing wrong with him," she pronounced. "I'd think him drunk if he smelled of liquor. He's fit. You say he's from the caravan we found?"

"We think so, doctor," said the fellow with the strangdja.

"Where else can he have come from?" said the one called Scrimshi.

The one called Nath said: "Maybe he ran off and hid and pretended to be sick." He nodded wisely. "It is known."

I started to swing my arms about like a windmill in protest. The Puncture Lady grasped both my wrists and put my arms down by my side. She had no difficulty in doing that. I tried to resist and could feel her pressure on my wrists inexorably forcing down my arms. By Krun! I was weaker than a woflo!

"I dunno—" said the fellow with the strangdja. "I wish we could understand what he's trying to say."

"Well, whatever it is, it does not alter the fact that there's nothing wrong with him."

I tried to throw my arms about again and she simply held them fast.

The tent was furnished in this section more as a doctor's waiting room and I supposed there were sick in the caravan. A carpet of a weave unknown to me covered the floor. There was one chair and table of plain bent wood. I could see no paper or writing equipment.

These three caravan guards quite probably could not read or write and so did not think to communicate with me in that way. But surely this doctor would? She looked tired beneath her hard professional veneer. I surmised that Vad Leotes demanded much from his people.

"What shall we do with him, Doctor Fenella?"

"Oh, find him a corner somewhere. If he's run off from his duty the vad will want to see him. Oh, yes, assuredly so."

"Come on, Llodi, give us a hand," said Nath. The man who had first halted me tucked his strangdja under his arm and helped Nath and Scrimshi haul me out of the Puncture Lady's tent.

Already a little queue of sick folk was forming.

Outside, twinned shadows lay long, with that effect peculiar to worlds with more than one sun of each shadow being, as it were, re-lit by the other sun. They carried me along with my head hanging down; I knew where we were going for I could hear the animals, the whicker and snort through wide nostrils, the stamp of hooves and the slap of rope against picket.

"Bung him down among the calsanys," said the one called Scrimshi, and he snickered. I'd marked him as an unpleasant sort of person.

"Naw," said Llodi. "What with him being sick, an' all."

"Then sling him here." Nath settled it by dumping my feet onto the bare ground. I toppled around and fell onto a heap of fodder bags.

"That'll do."

Llodi bent to me. "You stay here, dom. You'll be all right."

"We'll tell the next watch to keep an eye out." Scrimshi breathed in, swelling his chest. "You'd better not run off. The vad'll want you."

They went off about their guard duty. I pondered. Well, now, I was in no state to take the lictrix and make off. Anyway, I didn't really want to. I own I felt unease about the safety of that young female tearaway Mevancy. What she recalled of the fire I didn't know; what I surmised was that she had little memory before she dragged me out. As far as she was concerned, she really had rescued me. I would go along with that.

So I made myself comfortable on the fodder bags—and went to sleep.

Four

"You call me notor," said Strom Hangol ham Finral as I wheeled to a halt facing him with guards either side of me and prodding me on from the rear. "You are accused of deserting the caravan you were sworn to protect."

He sat at a table on which rested a large double-bitted axe and a clepsydra just turned. The water dropping down was stained a pleasant pink color. Around us in the early rays of the twin suns, the caravan breakfasted preparatory to moving off. Smoke and cooking odors wafted. The day would be fine. Also, if this buffoon of a strom sitting in judgment on me couldn't be made to see sense, it could be the day on Kregen I breathed my last. Or, at the least, suffered some horrendous punishment.

I said: "I did not desert," and the sounds were like those of a bosk with his snout in the trough.

"The fellow is an idiot as well," observed the thin-faced ascetic in the blue robe standing just to Strom Hangol's rear. His face would have served as the model for the chunk of cheese one places in the mousetrap.

"Or he just pretends, San Hargon."

As Hangol spoke so the early suns light flashed from the silver mask covering the right side of his face. That had not been visible when he'd trotted past below and Mevancy had stood up. The metal might be a mask; equally it could be a replacement skin.

The easy assumption could be made that the disfigurement necessitating the wearing of a mask had scored deeply into Hangol's sanity, that he would like to serve the rest of the world of Kregen as he had been served. Well, just because easy assumptions are easy, that does not automatically debar them from accuracy. I own I rather wished Vad Leotes had been sitting there in judgment on me; my impressions of him had been cautiously favorable. Whilst I realize the following remark must expose my own overweening self-importance which I deplore and which had been very necessary during my time as Emperor of Vallia, I saw that as an emperor I could have turned Vad Leotes into a useful and loyal noble devoted to the crown. Still, those days were gone. Now I had to manipulate these nobles in other ways.

"Give him a prod, you," said Hangol to the guard on my left. He obediently thrust the butt end of his spear into my side. I was not bound. My hands were free. I moved to slide the blow and ease the spear away and the butt end thwacked me in the side. I let out a gasp. By the Black Chunkrah! I was abso-zigging-lutely useless!

I opened my mouth and gargled, trying to force coherent words out.

The ascetic in the blue robe spoke primly: "An idiot."

"It seems you are right, San. No wonder the caravan succumbed with onkers like this to guard it. It is quite clear the fellow is of no use." He picked up the double-bitted axe. "Take him away and execute him."

I tried to shout and the guards twitched me around with contemptuous ease. Strom Hangol rose from the table, turning to speak in a perfectly normal voice to the ascetic. "I trust our discourse today will yield sweeter fruit than yesterday's, San."

To which San Hargon replied in a smooth and smarmy voice: "It is my intention to take chapter eleven of Beng Loshner's 'Active Principles' as our starting point." The two walked off, already oblivious to anyone else.

So I tried to struggle and was hoicked up like a chicken and carted off feet first.

How incongruous my megalomaniac thoughts regarding emperors and their handling of lords, and my present position, in which a vad hadn't even bothered to sit in judgment on me and had left it to his assistant, a strom!

They took me a little way off among thorn bushes. No doubt they did not wish to disturb the stomachs of the breakfasters. This was the first breakfast; the second, if taken at all, would be taken en route. I saw Llodi with Nath and Scrimshi walking up to the guards holding me.

"I'm not surprised." Scrimshi gave his opinion heavily. "The fool deserves all he gets."

"Better for him, really," said Nath. "To be out of the way."

"I dunno." Llodi's magnificent fissured nose shone in light and shadow like a mountain range. His cheeks were leathery, fissured, and shone in a similar if less formidable way. "Pity for him, being an idiot an' all."

"You wanta do the job," snarled one of the guards holding me. "You do it. Otherwise push off, schtump!"

Scrimshi snarled in reply: "I'll have your liver and lights one day, Nalgre the Pock!"

The guards were no longer holding me. They dropped me onto the dusty ground. As I fell I managed to twist so that I might have a grandstand view of the coming brawl. I quite cheered up.

These caravan mercenaries were sensible enough not to draw weapons one against another. No doubt long held resentments had to break out every now and then. Human nature is petty at times, and as these guards were all apims they could knock one another down with a gusto that had nothing of inter-racial prejudice about it. Dust rose. I managed to stand up and started off for the shelter of the nearest bush. I saw Llodi give a big bull-headed fellow a roundhouse to the jaw and then jump and kick him in the guts and I winced. Scrimshi was down and Nalgre the Pock was sitting on him and bashing his head against the dirt. I nodded sagely.

Once I had the bush fairly between the brawl and me, I paused to try to think what to do next. By Krun! I was in a pretty pickle and no mistake!

The animal lines were busy as the outriders saddled up. Breakfast fires were being doused. Tents that before had risen in considerable numbers were now absent, and the last few were coming down in billows of canvas. Noise and smells and dust and slanting suns shine, all was a flicker and a bedlam to that side; this side lay only the open wasteland.

I had aims in life.

Quite apart from the necessary aim of staying alive, I had grand visions of what might be made of our grouping of continents and islands called Paz upon the surface of Kregen. I wanted diff and apim to live together in harmony in all the lands, and not just in those already with liberal policies. I wanted to make sure the evil cult of Lem the Silver Leem was abolished never to be resurrected to the torture and destruction of little girls. I wanted to make of the Kroveres of Iztar a band of people devoted to furthering these grand aims of making of Kregen a better place—given that better in this context meant what I and my friends considered better. Perhaps above all I was committed to resisting the invasions and wanton slaughter by the Shanks, the fish heads from over the curve of the world. In this last, I knew, I had the blessing of the Everoinye.

Oh, yes, by Zair, there was so very much I had yet to accomplish in this terrible and beautiful world of Kregen, four hundred light years from the planet of my birth.

I stared at that open wasteland.

To venture out there, even if I had health and strength, a fleet zorca and a full water bottle, would be an enterprise fraught with peril. No. Despite all seeming, I had a better chance within the caravan—if I could so arrange matters to my own advantage.

The brawl roared on, blood flowing from noses, eyes closing, fists lashing, knuckles skinning. Nalgre the Pock was down with Llodi sitting on his head as Scrimshi scrambled up, blood flowing from his nose, roaring. Nath gave his fellow a shrewd blow betwixt wind and water and, suddenly, it was all over. Llodi let Nalgre up and he and his two fellows ran off.

"Well," said Nath, feeling a newly loose tooth. "I quite enjoyed that, by Lohrhiang of the Waters."

"I'll do for that Nalgre one of these days," growled Scrimshi, exploring his nose. "And we're left with the prisoner."

"Is that our business?" demanded Nath.

"Fambly! Of course it is. We've stopped a detail carrying out a duty and we'll get it in the neck when Strom Hangol finds out. So—"

"So," said Llodi, and he spoke heavily. "We must carry out that duty ourselves." He looked around. "At least, we can send him off to the Death Jungles of Sichaz all clean and tidy. That lot would've played with him first, the shints."

The Death Jungles of Sichaz. That was what folk down here in Loh called the Ice Floes of Sicce.

"Aye," said Nath. "Unhealthy folk, those."

"They get pleasure out of it," said Scrimshi, wincing as he felt his nose. "Well, we'd better get on with it."

They picked up their strangdjas and walked across to my bush and I realized how ludicrous and pathetic had been my attempt at escape.

So I stood up. In that moment blazing anger was replaced by black amusement. That I, Dray Prescot, with all these resounding titles and all these fabulous deeds to my name, should be chopped in the dust of some forgotten desert somewhere in Southern Loh. Well, wherever death finds you out, that spot does tend to figure large and importantly in your scheme of life.

"I just hope he don't make a fuss," mumbled Llodi.

"He's big and ugly enough for two, anyway," said Nath. "I'll hold him."

Scrimshi took his strangdja in two fists and gave a couple of preparatory swings. The strangdja varies in form, pattern and size; essentially it is like a large holly leaf fashioned from honed steel cunningly sharpened and mounted on a shaft. It is, indeed, in skilled hands, a feared weapon.

The ferocious holly-leaf shaped head glittered blindingly in the light of the suns as Scrimshi swung the weapon up. Beyond his upraised arms I saw a small cavalcade of riders pace into view past the thorn bushes. In the lead rode Vad Leotes deep in conversation with Mevancy. The riders looked disheveled, many no longer had their lances, and some were wounded. They headed towards a marquee that had not so far been pulled down. This would be Leotes' tent, I surmised. I opened my mouth and croaked garbled sounds.

Nath said, sharply: "Get on with it, Scrimshi! There's the vad and we want this done before he finds out."

As he spoke Nath gestured vehemently, releasing me.

For me to try to shout was totally useless. I could not run, for I could barely totter. I just hoped my strength was up to the trick that was all I had left to play. These three would butcher me without thought as a duty that must be performed. I bent down.

There was no time to be fussy. I picked the first stone to hand, stood up as tall and straight as I could, and hurled the stone. It struck Leotes on the side. I gasped. Thank Zair my aim was good! Scrimshi roared in frightened anger and slashed the strangdja down.

With a tiny fragment of my Krozair skills I managed to stagger sideways and the blow missed. Nath jumped for me to pinion me like a chicken for the chop. Scrimshi was making a frightful noise through his squashed nose.

Leaning sideways I surged the other way and had as much chance of avoiding Nath's clutching arms as a ponsho has of evading the jaws of a leem.

Twisted around and held fast, I saw the glitter of the strangdja. I tried to kick and could not. The leaf-shaped spikes would rip my head off.

"Stand perfectly still, strangdjim!"

The brilliant head wavered, descended, and then held steadily aloft.

I swallowed down.

By Krun!

"Bring him over here."

Llodi was the first to obey the vad's orders. He took me by the left bicep and ran me across to Leotes. I say ran, I tottered and Llodi held me up.

Up on his zorca and blazing in the early light of the suns, Leotes looked impossibly tall and resplendent. His red moustaches curled splendidly.

"Is this the man, Mevancy?"

"It is, Leotes."

Oho! I said to myself. They're on first name terms already, without the lord and lady. Very cozy!

She leaned from the saddle and looked at me.

"We have been searching for you for a long time, cabbage. I told you not to run off."

"For your sake I am glad the man is found. Now, by Beng Trunter the Nosher, I am famished! Let us eat both breakfasts in one before we resume our journey. The caravan may proceed ahead of us." Leotes lifted his gauntleted hand. "Give this man food and drink and clean him up and bring him to me when I rejoin the caravan."

"Quidang, lynxor! At once, lynxor!"

Oh, yes, this Leotes ran a tight ship, all right!

Mevancy favored me with a long downdrawn look; but she said nothing further. She looked just a little frazzled around the edges, a mite tired. I own I had to feel genuine gratitude for her actions. Clearly she'd returned with Leotes from their attempt to rescue the captives from our caravan and, not finding me where she'd left me, had persuaded the vad to search. Yes, a resourceful, persuasive and most high and mighty miss, this Mevancy!

There was no difficulty in guessing why the three strangdjims took such good care of me after that. They had been deputed to care, so they did. Also, and with my knowledge of the tricks of a soldier's or mercenary's life, best exemplified by the mythical figure of Vikatu the Dodger, I could see by devoting themselves to me—on the vad's orders!—they got out of other and much more unpleasant duties.

So we all settled down to a splendid feast of the left-overs from the cooks' tent and when we'd bloated ourselves out I had a dry-wash and my hair was brushed and I began to look presentable.

The last few carts were trundling off and only the beasts and carts that would take the vad's gear remained. Nath went off, to return shortly with one zorca, one lictrix and two preysanys. Here was revealed a distinction between these three mercenaries. They were all three ordinary mercenaries; none wore the silver pakmort or golden pakzhan at throat, pinned up with silk. Scrimshi mounted up on the zorca and Nath on the lictrix. So that left Llodi and me to straddle the preysanys.

These three might be only ordinary mercenaries, hired caravan guards; they knew the ropes. When the vad at last indicated that he was ready to proceed we trundled gently along with the other riders and carts, and these three hadn't done a stroke of work in getting the caravan under way.

They'd stick to this duty like glue, keep out of everybody's way, and hope their lazy life would continue for as long as the journey.

A corpulent, choleric, contuming Deldar rode up astride a zorca and started shouting. Well, of course, that last remark is superfluous. All Deldars shout. It is habitual to them to pass on the orders from the higher officers to the men.

"You three lolly-gagging layabouts! I'll have you Where have you been hiding? Get on about outpost. You, Scrimshi, take point! Bratch!"

"Can't do it, Del." Scrimshi sounded as though he was in pain, so much was he enjoying himself. "Direct orders from the vad. Gotta take care of this fambly. Daren't let him outta my sight."

"Do what?"

"That's right, Del," amplified Nath, expansive with good humor. "The vad detailed us special. Can't leave him."

The Deldar's leather harness swelled. His beetroot red face went redder. He took another rib-straining breath. "I'll give you three heart beats to get on duty. One! Two!"

"Del!" interrupted Llodi, urgently. "Don't say Three! It's true. We've gotta take this fambly to the vad soon's we rejoin the caravan." He gestured. "Well, look at him. He ain't all there and what with the vad's new fancy lady looking out for him an' all—"

"Yeh," said the Deldar. "I saw *her.*"

"You see?"

"You've got away with it this time. But there'll be a next time. I'll have you three. I'll have your ears toasted for breakfast."

After the Deldar had taken himself off to rouse out some other unfortunates to ride point and flank, Scrimshi and Nath rolled about in their saddles laughing. Llodi laughed, too.

They were chortling so much they were quite unprepared for the presence and the voice that flayed across like an icicle knife.

"What is this creature doing here, alive, instead of dead and Rippasch meat?"

The change in demeanor of the three strangdjim was remarkable.

Their laughter ceased abruptly. Their faces tautened. They stiffened up in their saddles. They made the rote response.

"Lynxor!"

"I asked a question, shints! You—" he pointed at Llodi. "Speak!"

"Yes, lynxor. We must care for him—"

"I gave orders that he be executed at once." The voice softened. "Why did you disobey my orders?"

"The vad, lynxor! He told us. We must report to the vad with him."

The streaming mingled lights of the Suns of Scorpio flashed off the silver mask covering the right side of his face. That glorious suns light looked cold as though the reflection drained the color and brilliance.

Strom Hangol ham Finral stared at me. He was arrogance personified, of course, a person who revelled in power over others; now the name of Vad Leotes held him in check. His look would have withered the stoutest heart of the wrongdoers paraded before him for punishment.

"I shall not forget this," he said, and his voice shook with passion. "I shall remember you, rast, and see you are put where you deserve to be. By Lem, I'll not be thwarted by the likes of a yetch like you!"

With that he slashed with his riding crop full at my face.

Oh, yes, I was suffering from the effects of the paralysis, I was weak, without strength; all the same, I remained a Krozair of Zy. I still possessed the old Krozair skills, even if my puniness diluted their shattering effectiveness. I moved my head sideways and the blow rattled down on my shoulder. I reached up to take the crop away from this fellow; but he was far too quick and the crop whistled up beyond my reach. Then his zorca reared and he fought the reins and clung on.

Llodi called: "Your pardon, lynxor! We must take him to the vad in good condition!"

Hangol's nostrils pinched in. His helmet framed the viciousness of his face. Oh, of course, one can see his point of view. His authority, he would think, had been undermined, without thinking beyond his own immediate self-importance. But had he been your proper officer in the first place, this humiliating contretemps would not have arisen.

Without another word he galloped off.

"A nasty one that," said Llodi, shaking his head. "If he's your enemy, then may the wise and good Tsung-Tan have you in his keeping."

Five

"Get your tongue up behind your teeth, cabbage! No, no—shut your black-fanged winespout! If you stick your tongue out again I'll bite it off!"

"Th—th—" I mumbled.

"It's not th you great fambly! It's t—t—t!"

Some people would welcome the preliminaries to Mevancy biting their tongue off. That was my incongruous thought. The tent Leotes had placed at her disposal had belonged to a stromni who had died of blood-poisoning some way back east. The tent was comfortable, well-furnished and pleasant. I sat on a figured rug and drooled, trying to learn to speak all over again as I had done at my mother's knee all those years ago four hundred light years from Kregen.

Although I had no personal stake in the people who had been taken by the bandits, I was pleased that Leotes had rescued them all. I did not enquire what had happened to the drikingers. On Kregen one knows what happens to the bad guys in general, because for all its beauty and culture there is on that wonderful world this old barbaric streak that demands an eye for an eye. Now all those people I had met in Larishsmot after the fire who had gone with Cardamon's caravan had been incorporated in Leotes' caravan. Well, no doubt they would be asked to pay. There is little one gets free on Kregen, as on this Earth.

What I had received free from Mevancy was truly splendid, although I might have paid ahead of time in carrying her almost out of that fire. I wondered how bashing the back of my head and neck when she dragged me so that I became paralyzed would appear in the balance of payments. Still, that thought was churlish, and not worthy of a Koter of Vallia.

"Try again, cabbage. T—and get your tongue well in."

I tried. "Th—th—"

She threw a cushion at me. "Never mind. Maybe it'll come back of its own sweet will, some day. Let's look at your muscles."

She walked over to me with that lithe swing of the hips that can so injure a fellow. She wore a casual lounging robe of blue silk; I noticed she had chosen one from the wardrobe of Leotes' women that had long sleeves. She took my left bicep between her fingers and rolled as though kneading dough.

"It feels strange, cabbage. Like a bladder that instead of being blown up hard is flat and flaccid. H'm. I'd guess you once were quite strong."

She dropped my arm. That is a correct description. I managed to get enough power into my muscles to stop the back of my hand hitting the carpet. She snatched up the paper and writing implements. "Now, cabbage, tell me more about yourself."

I'd written a theosophical pack of lies about my history. At the first shot at writing communication I'd been pleased that these people of Southern Loh used one of the universal scripts of Kregen that reflected the universal Kregish, imposed from Outside forces. I'd been a fool of course; incautiously in response to a request for my name I'd started with: 'Dra.' I advance for my stupidity my state of mind, the paralysis and the fuzziness of my thoughts. There was little chance that these people would not have heard of Dray Prescot, the puissant Emperor of Vallia. And I didn't want the hassle of claiming I'd been named for the emperor. So I used one of my familiar use names. I simply added Jak to the Dra. I was Drajak. Then, out of homesickness, I suppose, I wrote that I was Drajak ti Zamran. I felt any references to Vallia or Valka would be inopportune. Zamran was a pretty market town in my island kovnate of Zamra, just north of Valka. Mercenaries traveled the world of Kregen; origins oftentimes were less important than current loyalties. Oftentimes; not always, by Krun!

"Zamran," she'd said. "No, I don't know it. I know Zamrarn, of course, where the black pearls come from."

I'd scribbled a swift little story about being swept overboard in a storm and the subject of just whereaway Zamran was was buried.

So, now, I elaborated on my fictitious history and was able to use a number of real events that had occurred in my life. When I asked about her she laughed and refused to be drawn.

One item that intrigued me Mevancy answered casually.

"Paol-ur-bliem," she said, reading where I had written. "Oh, I'm not sure. Something to do with their religion. Leotes was reticent."

So Mevancy didn't come from these parts, then.

She made me exercise cruelly.

I had to pump my legs away, run on the spot, lift weights. Weights, ha! It took all my strength and effort to lift a chair from the carpet. As for an amphora of water—no chance. Mevancy persisted; I felt no answering increase in muscular powers.

The two louts she'd hired on, Nafty and Pondo, had not been slain when the bandits attacked. Now Nafty stuck his head around the tent flap and in his laughing way said: "My lady." Mevancy went out at once.

By the time she returned the caravan was packing up for the next portion of the journey across the wastelands.

"You'll have to ride the preysany Leotes was good enough to find for you, cabbage. You lost the lictrix of mine—" She stopped herself, and laughed in an odd way. "The lictrix you were riding."

Mounting the preysany, whose name was Tuftytail, proved easier this day than it had been yesterday. I took no false comfort from that. Mevancy would ride with the vad. Scrimshi, Nath and Llodi had been relieved of their special duty and gone back to riding escort. My interview with Leotes had been short and—given the circumstances—sweet. He'd simply consigned me to the jurisdiction of Mevancy nal Chardaz with firm orders that her instructions were to be obeyed. The black look on Strom Hangol's face at this might have been rewarding; it was also a thundercloud warning of difficulties ahead.

During this period of travel through a portion of the wastelands that was relatively pleasant, we could find water and ample wood and grazing. Also, during this period, Hangol began to get the hang of being unpleasant to me in ways that outwitted Mevancy. He didn't mark me, of course. Every attempt on my part to prevent him was swept aside as an adult with a child. He took to being ingratiating with Mevancy. And, a sight that saddened me, I saw all three of those strangdjim, Scrimshi, Nath and Llodi, stretched out on the flogging frame. They were not flogged jikaider, for which small mercy I was thankful. But they were given a regulation number of lashes for some supposed dereliction of duty. Everyone knew this was Strom Hangol in his mean way getting his spiteful revenge.

Truly, when a great lord puts power into the hands of his cadade, it behooves him to choose wisely and well!

I'd asked Mevancy for full details of the rescue from the bandits, and from the way she replied I gathered she'd played a large part in that venture. When I asked about my kit and the rapier and dagger she shook her head. My belt had been found, around the waist of a headless corpse; Mevancy said she'd not seen the weapons. As I have said, no fighting man ought to rely on just one special weapon or set of weapons. Your true warrior can snatch up any weapon and get on with the fight. All the same, I was sorry to lose them, for they were a finely matched pair given to me by Prince Varden, a blade comrade.

As we traveled towards the west it was noticeable how the folk tensed up. They were bracing themselves for an unpleasant experience.

Between us and the city of Ankharum lay the Great Salt Desert. Deserts are often unpleasant places; salt deserts almost invariably so.

Unable to admit to any joy in traversing so inhospitable a place, I nevertheless at this time took delight in discovering the sobriquets of the three mercenary strangdjim.

Back home no doubt they'd be called spearmen, rather than strangdjamen, and they were among the lowest paid of all mercenaries. Scrimshi, I discovered, was known as Scrimshi the Sturr. This, remembering the Moder, enchanted me. Nath was called Nath the Arm. Well, as it is said, there are as many Naths in the world of Kregen as stars in the sky. I'd known a Nath the Arm before, a kaidur trainer for the Jikhorkdun in Huringa in Hyrklana. Much later I heard he'd managed to retire on his winnings to a little farm out by Halphen, an area noted for first quality Pombolims. Mind you, I'd never have believed he could ever leave the excitement of the arena and of shouting for the Ruby Drang. As for the here and now, Llodi rejoiced in the nickname of Llodi the Voice.

Mevancy deigned to answer my scrawled questions and told me that Llodi possessed a fine tenor voice. He'd sung in his local temple's choir in his youth and had then run off very sharpish when the priests had wanted to castrate him to preserve and encourage his splendid voice. I didn't blame him.

On the journey with Leotes' caravan, when the dust did not rise too thickly and we had filled water bottles with the prospect of a water hole or oasis ahead, Llodi would sing as we rode along.

And, indeed, his voice was surpassing beautiful.

He was fond of 'Carnation Pink and Iris Blue' a song of Houdondrin in Loh. He had an extensive repertoire. I jotted down a note to Mevancy, and she sniffed and went off to find Llodi the Voice. So, to my request, he sang all through that famous old song 'The Bowmen of Loh.' If I thought of Seg then, why, you will understand, I am sure.

Then, just before we were due to essay the crossing of the Great Salt Desert, another Opaz-benighted band of drikingers attacked our caravan.

A riderless zorca pelted in, all that was left of our point.

Immediately a tremendous hullabaloo started up.

Mind you, as I thought then, this attack showed the lamentable lack of intelligence of these creatures who had taken up the bandit trade. Had they waited until we'd crossed the Great Salt Desert we would have been in poor shape and in no great case to resist their attack. That is what I thought then, without experience of the Great Salt Desert.

They rode in with a whoop and a holler, driving their lictrixes hard. A shower of javelins produced a few casualties. Dust smoked up and already it tasted salty on the tongue. Our bowmen shot in their superb Lohvian longbows and took out mount and rider. Dust gouted. Shafts crisscrossed. Despite my undignified position aboard a preysany near the tail of the caravan, I saw more than one heroic deed. The bandits closed in near my position and I felt my fingers twitching. I'd be as useful as a week-old baby out there right now. I saw Nath the Arm whirl his strangdja and a bandit's arm fall off. There was no sign of Scrimshi the Sturr or of Llodi the Voice. I trusted they were still in the land of the living, even Scrimshi, who had lived up to his cognomen of the Sturr. As for Nafty and Pondo, if they were not defending their mistress, the Lady Mevancy, with their lives, then I'd have to have a word with them—and this I thought, then, in the heat of the fight when I was still half paralyzed.

Strom Hangol roared past cutting a swathe from the flank through a bunch of the bandits. He actually took time out to notice me. And as he galloped on he sneered. He actually thought it important enough in the middle of a brisk little action to show me his contempt.

By this time, having heard other folk talking in unguarded moments, I had to come to the conclusion that Strom Hangol was not worth contempt.

This conclusion is always saddening, however just. One does not like to lose a human being in the sight of whatever gods may be believed in.

The drikingers fought viciously and hard for a time; then the fire went out of them.

Right at the end, a bandit flogging his zorca on roared in towards me in the final throes of the battle rapture that gripped him. He was a Rapa, beaked and feathered, and his sword glittered as he swung it down towards me. I saw Strom Hangol past the Rapa in a perfect position to give the killing thrust with his lance. Hangol hauled his zorca back. His face was a mask of glee. Here was where without effort he repaid the slights he imagined he'd suffered at my hands. My paralyzed hands, by Krun!

That half silver mask of Hangol's with the mingled emerald and ruby lights splintering from its edges, covering only the right side of his face, complemented the glee transfiguring the fleshly half of his face.

The bandit screeched in unholy gloating as he whipped his sword down at me. I tried—of course I tried!—to slide the blow as the Krozair Disciplines aided me. I was looking straight at the Rapa. His feathers bristled green and red. The sword glittered. He was gloating in this last moment of killing lust before he made his getaway.

Crimson spurted from his left eye. Instantly crimson spouted in a gout from his right eye.

I watched, fascinated.

The Rapa screamed. He dropped his sword and clawed at his face.

He could not see. His eyes were ruined beyond redemption. I fancied

I could see a thin stick-like object, like a needle, sticking out of each of his eyes. He was screaming and yelling and rocking about on his zorca, clearly a man without hope in this world, and it was a mercy for him that Mevancy rode up and sliced her lynxter neatly across his throat.

The Rapa fell off his zorca, spraying blood everywhere. Strom Hangol rode off in urgent pursuit of the remnants of the bandits. Mevancy reined up by me.

"Why can't you keep out of trouble, cabbage? You are a sore trial to me."

I said: "You just wait!" but all that came out was: "Yo-js-tt."

"Oh! You Drajak!" she said.

She slid a slim leg over her lictrix and jumped to the ground. She was highly capable with the dead Rapa's zorca, seizing the bridle reins firmly, letting the animal see who was his new master, gentling him, stroking his nose at the root of the proud spiral horn—zorcas love that. He quietened down. She turned a flushed triumphant face to me.

"Hai! Now I have a mount!"

I nodded and pointed to her lictrix.

"Oh, yes, cabbage, of course—only do try not to lose this one."

Just then, Vad Leotes rode up with his escort. He looked puffed up with excitement, bursting with rich blood running through his veins, and his red moustaches fairly bristled.

"My Lady Mevancy!" he called. I gathered he'd been worried about her in the fight.

"My lord!" she said, laughing, mischievous.

Instantly he was himself. He smiled and bowed gallantly. "I see you have won a fine zorca. You may keep him, if you wish."

Now Mevancy wasn't fool enough to go shouting that she'd won the damn beast and so therefore of course she'd keep him. She knew as everyone else knew that any loot obtained by people of the caravan belonged to the vad.

She smiled. "Why, thank you, Leotes. It is a generous gift."

He made some fustian gallant reply but I wasn't listening. I had my mind set on climbing up on that lictrix and of essaying a few swings of Mevancy's lynxter. Mevancy mounted up and, indeed, she cut a fine figure. Nafty appeared and was told to transfer her kit from the lictrix to the zorca. This took no time at all and then she and the vad rode off followed by the escort.

Well, I tied old Tuftytail to a cart and took hold of the lictrix. I managed to mount him without too much trouble and I sat back, taking a breather, wondering and hoping that this was the beginning of the end of the paralysis.

A little breeze began to blow warmly from the northwest, bringing with it the unmistakable tang of salt. That made me feel pleased that the idiot drikingers had made this lictrix available for me to ride through the Great Salt Desert. I gave him a little rein and walked him about and began to feel quite at home. The caravan was getting itself back in order now and the calsanys were quietening down. Some of the slaves were already preparing graves for the dead of the caravan; what they would do with the dead bandits I did not know. There was a quantity of shouting and a few trumpet calls. This activity and the new mount had taken my mind off an investigation I had intended to carry out as soon as possible.

Now I rode back to where Tuftytail was tied up and dismounted. The dead Rapa lay where he had fallen, weltering in his own blood. I bent to that beaked vulturine face, not without a quiver of ironic appreciation that this vulture-headed man had perished through the loss of his eyes. I looked. The orbits were already congealing with blood, puss dribbling. If I had seen a small stick-like object it was not there now.

As I straightened up, Nath the Arm walked up. Blood stained his legs.

"Hai, onker," he said, heavily. "Scrimshi. I had to—he was sore wounded. He begged me. D'you understand, onker? He begged me!"

I gargled out stupid ineffectual words.

"Oh, shut your black-fanged winespout, if that's all you can do!" Nath the Arm had been badly affected. "Well, he's well on his way through the Death Jungles of Sichaz. I just hope the spectral syatras don't get him."

Scrimshi I had put down as an unpleasant person on first acquaintance; still, he'd improved with time and I felt sorry for him.

I didn't try to speak again but pointed to my mouth and then did an imitation of a man singing.

"Huh?" said Nath the Arm. Then: "Oh, I see. Dunno. Last I saw, he was in a right old ding dong with a couple of Fristles. By Yakwang! He put one down so fast with the strangdja hoicking off his arm the other shint ran off screaming. Then I had a pestiferous Brokelsh to deal with after he'd done for Scrimshi. Well, I suppose Tsung-Tan might have him in his keeping if you believe in Gilium."

Nath the Arm went off trailing his strangdja, that wicked holly-leaf shaped head glistening thickly with blood, not all of it red. I knew he'd start to clean and polish that up soon and I also knew—well, trusted more than knew for a certainty—that he'd soon be over the death of Scrimshi. The mercenary's trade brings passing comrades and death in liberal portions.

The caravan's Saddler, a little Och called Tanki the Stitch, did not tut-tut overmuch when presented with the new saddle requirements. Most folk of Kregen with the wide array of splendid saddle animals are philosophical about the different saddle requirements. They cope without fuss with saddles of different specifications. All the same, it was more convenient for Mevancy to swap the Rapa's saddle for one more suitable for a lady. Her old lictrix saddle, again, would not suit, as it was adapted for a six-legged animal. It was a tight fit for me and Tanki the Stitch altered it for me-Mevancy paid.

Certainly, I'd had my belt back from the bandits who'd stolen it; the pouches were empty of money and most of the bits and pieces a fellow carries around. Unable to work, penniless, I had perforce for the moment to rely on Mevancy's generosity. She must have been clever and quick to have got her own money back when she escaped from the drikingers.

One of the guards, Deldar Gurong, that same Deldar who'd tried to order Scrimshi off to point duty, rode in carrying a parcel of weaponry taken from dead bandits. Among the swords, so Mevancy told me later, were weapons belonging to the lords Tawang and Shalang. This trading of weapons is commonplace among any fraternity of fighting men or sorority of Jikai Vuvushis—even if their trade is banditry. I felt a spark of interest and wrote my question and she raised one round shoulder. "Can't say, cabbage. I saw no rapiers or daggers."

She saw my face and said roughly: "Well, cabbage, it was only a thin sticker of a sword and a clumsy great dagger. That scum Hangol wears 'em, I notice, though I've yet to see him use 'em in a fight."

I didn't bother to write that often it is better to use a stout fighting sword rather than a rapier in these kind of rough-house combats.

Vad Leotes might have employed a miserable specimen for a cadade; his choice of Caravan Master couldn't be bettered. Master Pandarun held that dark aloof dignity of those who spend long periods out in the great wastelands of the world. His face was not as seamed or craggy as that of Llodi's; but it reminded you vividly that this man had slept under the stars more often than under a roof. He wore loose flowing robes of a fawn color and a mass of white cloth perched on his dark hair. When he spoke his caravan crews jumped.

Master Pandarun told us that in Meimgarum, the oasis city on this eastern side of the Great Salt Desert, we would spend a few days preparing for the crossing. His thin mouth curved only slightly as he said: "All the saddle animals are sold there and we hire—"

"All sold!" exclaimed Mevancy. "But my fine new zorca!"

"It would be cruel to try to take him across the Salt Desert, my lady."

Her lips compressed. Her nostrils flared. She glared at me and said: "And you needn't laugh, either, cabbage!"

I couldn't say anything sensible. "But," I said to myself, "by the disgusting putrescent protruding pot-belly of Makki Grodno! The injustice of the woman! I wasn't laughing at her discomfiture, by Krun!"

Truth to tell, there was precious little to laugh about at all as we trailed into Meimgarum between white flat-roofed houses and drooping trees. And to cap that, of course, as everyone said, the Great Salt Desert was no laughing matter at all.

Six

Well, as I may have remarked before, any desert is unpleasant to the unwary and salt deserts are worse than most. This specimen of salt desert was referred to bitterly as the Gleek Frankai. The good folk of Meimgarum made a living preparing travelers to cross the desert and of repairing them once they had crossed from the west.

All our saddle and draught animals were sold and the carts and carriages with them. No great noble would bring his own personal coach on this journey knowing it must be sold. We hired slounchers, animals that, I suppose, must be regarded as Loh's form of camel. Being of Kregen, of course, they had eight legs and three humps; but otherwise their morphology followed the necessities of desert living, like an Earthly camel. Some were exceedingly bad-tempered and others docile. It was known that they would kill anyone who attempted to molest their young. As a consequence slouncher handlers had to be a tough breed of people when it came to training time in a young slouncher's life.

As for clothes, we all bought light airy robes, and massy turbans, and sand scarves. In this part of Loh sand scarves were called flamins. We all dressed up and looked one another over critically, and there was a quantity of high-pitched, nervous laughter at our appearances.

I remained pathetically weak and had a deal of trouble scaling the high side of the mount allotted to me for the crossing. He was called Flamdi and I hoped against hope he had a placid temperament.

Mevancy dealt with her slouncher unhesitatingly, and the animal seemed to me to understand the rider on his back would take no nonsense from him.

Despite my weakness and inability to speak coherently, when I heard that on the western side of the salt desert a large river ran southerly through Ankharum, I made up my mind to take it down to the southern coast of Loh. There was bound to be a port and shipping and I could arrange passage home. I brushed aside any consideration of the problems involved in that course of action. I had finished the work the Star Lords had brought me here for. The quicker I got myself home to Valka the better.

The thought had not escaped my attention that Delia might also have finished her work, for the SoR, and be high-tailing it for Esser Rarioch.

"By Makki Grodno's disgusting diseased left eyeball!" I said to myself. "That's the plan, and the plan will work!"

Oh, well, as they say in Sanurkazz, Zair lays many a trap for the unwary feet of the boastful.

We did not, of course, carry very much money across the desert. The family with whom Master Pandarun dealt were known to him from previous transactions. We sold our carts, carriages and animals to the representatives of the Nuong-Hi family in Meimgarum, and received bonded receipts which would be redeemed in Ankharum for conveyances and animals of similar quality. The force of greed might well impel bandits to operate within the desert if a caravan was foolish enough to carry the money it had received in the sales. Families like that of Nuong-Hi materially lessened that risk.

I do not wish to make a song and dance about the desert crossing. It was difficult and it was unpleasant but only three people died, and two of them through their own fault. We emerged dust and mica smothered, encrusted with salt and longing for baths and drinks. Perhaps the most impressive aspects of the Gleek Frankai were the solid pillars of salt forming white cathedral aisles, a bewildering maze of alleyways stretching fingerlike, fashioned by the twin powers of erosion and wind. Yes, an unhealthy place, that Great Salt Desert of southern Loh.

Why some people are as they are is a mystery of life, known only to Opaz the Fashioner. Everyone agreed with Master Pandarun that we should spend a few days in Ankharum recovering. For his part, the salty crossing appeared to have made no difference to him at all. So we saw about buying fresh conveyances with our bonded receipts. Mevancy obtained a good class zorca for herself and a nice lictrix, called Swiggletoe, for me. Lord Nanji Tawang could be heard from here to the coast, I shouldn't wonder, as he bellowed his outrage.

"My rig was first class, a genuine Porstheimer! Now, by Loncuum, you have the effrontery to offer me this rubbish in exchange!"

Languin Nuong-Hi spread his brown hands in apology. A thin and lugubrious individual, he had done his best to provide us with kit similar to that we had parted with to his cousin in Meimgarum. "It may not be a Porstheimer, lord; nevertheless it is a first class rig."

"It is rubbish! I demand proper recompense!"

"There is not a Porstheimer in all Ankharum at this moment—"

Lady Floria said: "And these people have the effrontery to call themselves honest merchants. They are cheating you, Nanji."

"I know. Well, they will rue the day they started that trick. You, tikshim! I demand a cash settlement of the difference."

Again Languin Nuong-Hi spread his hands. "If that is your wish, lord. The difference is fifty mings."

"Fifty mings! Fifty gold pieces! Are you makib, bereft of your senses!"

"No, lord. This rig is a Merkaller, the equal to a Porstheimer. The difference in cost is fifty mings."

Mevancy caught my eye and jerked her head. Leading our animals we walked outside Master Languin Nuong-Hi's establishment. I'd not much idea of the cost of either a Porstheimer or a Merkaller. That wasn't important. This petty incident, despite Nanji Tawang's real cause for annoyance, showed the fellow up in a bad light. He was a trylon and so of some exalted state, between a vad and a strom. He was the Trylon of Fuokane. His rantings displeased Mevancy.

"A boring boor," she pronounced, nodding her head. "They'd give cramphs like that short shrift back in Chardaz, I can tell you, cabbage!"

I managed a smile. I knew my folk of Valka would do likewise.

However they settled that matter between the family of Nuong-Hi and Trylon Nanji na Fuokane, settled it was, for the fellow appeared sitting in the coach and wearing an expression of constipated disgust. What intrigued me was to see that the Lady Floria Inglewong shared the coach with Nanji. Well, I would be rid of them in a couple of days once I could arrange transport down the River of Oneness. Written enquiries elicited the information that flatboats, barges and fast packet slikkers, boats similar to dhows, plied the river, and with gold passage was easy to obtain.

I wrote for Mevancy: "When we finish this journey, where do you go then?"

She said tartly: "The journey has to be finished yet, cabbage."

Patiently I wrote: "Yes." I wanted to know where I might send money in repayment for that I had had from her. Also I would like to repay the cash I intended to borrow or steal from her in the immediate future. "I have to know where to send to repay your generosity."

She said, roughly: "Don't worry your head about that."

I started to scrawl: "But I do—" when her firm tanned hand closed over mine and squeezed. I had no strength to resist. She looked at me, gave me a twist of her supple lips that approximated a smile, and almost snarled: "I said it doesn't matter. Forget the gold!"

She flounced off, then, and I stared at her shapely back and legs as she vanished among the zorca lines. She did care for the beasts she employed. The thought occurred that she regarded me as just another beast to be looked after.

Llodi the Voice walked up head turned from where he'd been watching Mevancy. I'd been really pleased he had not been chopped in the bandit raid; but along with Nath the Arm he had become subdued after Scrimshi's death. Now he turned back to look at me. "I'd make myself scarce, if I was you, Drajak." He hawked and spat. "Strom Hangol's on his way over here."

The avoidance of a confrontation with that rast was imperative. I gave Llodi my parody of a smile and took myself off.

One odd thing about that brief period in Ankharum was the growing feeling of doom surrounding this caravan. There seemed to me no rhyme or reason for this feeling; yet I sensed that Llodi shared it, and Mevancy, too, by her sudden abruptness at times. We'd made a successful crossing of the Great Salt Desert. Our financial standing was good, despite the tantrums of Nanji and Floria. We had a top class caravan master in

Pandarun. We had a powerful noble and his retainers as escort. Yet—yet no one seemed light-hearted, not even Nafty. As for Pondo, his surliness turned his face lemon sour. No one could find a good word to say about our prospects of onward travel to the west. Doom and disaster permeated everyday life in our caravan.

All this merely strengthened my determination to go downriver. I could not work for lack of strength, and could not really cope with the job of a stylor, for although I could read and write, I could not tell what I read or carry on a conversation—although, come to think of it, maybe they were exceedingly good reasons for me to be employed as a private secretary. Mulling this thought over in my still sluggish mind took a couple of the days we were due to spend in Ankharum. I'd have to make a decision soon, and find finance.

Do not imagine that I was blind to the ironies of my present situation when compared to what it had been such a short time ago!

Whilst I thus fretted over my best course and made firm decisions one day only to scrap them for something else the next, a freak storm swept the city. Ankharum, whose wide avenues, cluttered back alleys, houses with flat roofs and white walls, presented a pleasing sight, was further graced by many ancient trees. Tall serene trees lined the wider avenues, and all the courtyards had their own ornamental or shade trees. The gale broomed brutally across the city. The houses mostly escaped unscathed except where trees fell on them. The trees were mercilessly scythed down. They lay in droves as though brought low by the reaper's sickle. They looked like pathetic giants fallen from grace.

The gale lasted for most of one tormented night. From our lodgings we could hear the wind bellowing and blustering and shaking the whole building. Casements rattled dancing skeletons. I suppose that to a fellow like myself from northern climes the absence of rain in all the uproar and violence of the storm gave it its most macabre aspect. The wind howled and roared and next morning clearing away of the trees began slowly. Nothing like it had been known for season upon season. No one could even remember hearing of a similar storm in the past.

Mevancy put her head in the door, beaming most evilly, to say: "A wonderful great tree has fallen full on Trylon Nanji's Merkaller. Squashed it flat. Such a shame."

And I said: "Such a shame."

What came out, what sounded, was: "Susha shame."

"Cabbage!" exclaimed Mevancy, delighted. "You're making sense!"

"Sense but no strength," I more or less said.

"Keep trying. Keep the old tongue mobile!"

"Yesh," I spluttered.

The loss of Nanji's carriage delayed the caravan's departure. This I welcomed for I could thus postpone the final decisions about my own plans. Despite incredible exertions and body-shattering exercises, I gained no strength. I remained as weak as a woflo.

"Still," said Mevancy in her newly-rough way, "you can talk a bit now and you can lift a pen. You'll do. I'll give you the gold you need." She screwed up her eyes at me. "I don't feel responsible for you any more, Drajak."

"I give you my thanks," I mumbled. "I will arrange passage."

"Well, if you change your mind, do it soon. Master Pandarun won't wait for laggards who can't afford to pay for the privilege."

So I went down to the levee and fixed up a passage aboard a flat-boat.

Now I had no inkling. I'd done my work. I was not myself as a result of that task, and resented that, I can tell you, by Krun! I said goodbye to Mevancy and I own I felt a pang. I owed her much, a damn-sight more than mere gold. She gave me a nice lynxter and the sword was a parting gift I knew I would treasure. We made the remberees and I walked off towards the river.

"Remberee, Drajak, cabbage!" she called after me again.

I turned. "Remberee, Lady Mevancy nal Chardaz!"

The words sounded almost as though uttered by a human throat.

Llodi appeared at my side and said he would stroll down to the levee with me, as the Deldar had gone off with a local girl for the afternoon.

A giant of a tree lying athwart the roadway was being cut up by gangs of slaves. It had fallen just short of the river and its leafy branches spread their debris alongside the landing stage where was moored my flat boat. Llodi stood back for me to pass around the stump end of the tree. This had been wrenched out of the ground to form a round saucer-like mass of earth and broken roots. Incongruously, still adhering in a ring to the flat surface, now on its side, neat rows of flat pavement tiles formed a wall instead of a road. So I inched my way around past the earthy bottom of the tree and a brick wall. The passage was narrow by reason of the gaping semi-circular hole the uprooted tree had left in the pavement.

That it should be at this precise point that I collided with Strom Hangol came as no surprise whatsoever to me.

This confrontation had been long in the making. This seemed a spot picked by the invisible referees of the Hyr Jikordur for the ritual initial insults.

Hangol simply snarled: "Out of the way, shint."

Well, now. I stood still and silent for a moment, and in that tiny space I heard Llodi call soft and urgently for me to withdraw. I supposed in that moment of indecision and self-mockery that, indeed, I would have to withdraw. I was in no case to fight this cramph now.

He took my indecision as a calculated insult.

He slashed at me with his riding crop.

To say that I dislike people who go around hitting other people for no reason, with riding crops or anything else, is a grave understatement. In the normal course of affairs I'd have taken the whip away from him and wrapped it around his head. But, as before, I was slow and weak and he caught me a slicing slash across the shoulder. Instead of staggering back, I thought to be clever and use an old ploy. So I gave a stentorian bellow of pain—and the fakery in that was minimal, by Krun!—and surged forward as though falling helplessly.

He was very quick.

He stepped back sharply so that I ran stumbling on, almost losing my balance, for five or six long paces. As I went past him so he hit me again.

I regained my balance and turned. Llodi came into view around the uprooted tree stump, a look of intense sorrow on his face. Hangol faced me and slowly thrust his riding crop down his belt and drew his sword.

"I have suffered under your insolence, you rast, and now will repay you."

There was no point in my hanging about. Already I was late for the flat-boat, delayed by fallen trees, and I knew I would not last two passes in my present state if I allowed this brawl to develop into a sword fight. As I reached that insalubrious conclusion Hangol advanced on me, sword poised.

He wore a plain yellow tunic, with a fawn robe carelessly caught over his right shoulder. His face expressed the most lively anticipation of enjoyment.

He dropped his sword. He clapped his left hand to his neck, and he let out a surprised yell. I thought—I was not sure—I spotted a tiny stick-like object protruding from the side of his neck between his fingers.

Someone yelled fiercely: "Run, onker!"

So I ran.

I helter-skeltered down the side of the fallen tree to the levee. The master of the flatboat stood at the top of the jetty steps looking back. When he saw me he waved an urgent arm and I fairly flew along and clattered down the steps into the boat.

"You come finely on your time, dom," he growled and his crew poled off.

Seven

I, Dray Prescot, Lord of Strombor and Krozair of Zy, was far from a happy fellow that evening as I sat dangling my legs over the boat's bows and watched the twin suns go down.

Strom Hangol had run after me, yelling and waving the rapier he'd ripped from its scabbard. I had not waited. Rendi the Keel, the master, had decided he would not hang about, either. So, I had run off from a foeman. Well, I've run away before, and by Vox I don't doubt I'll run away again in the future. I am no longer the headstrong Dray Prescot who first came to Kregen under the Suns of Scorpio. All the same, it rankled...

And I can be even more headstrong and violent now than ever I could. The passage of the seasons has tended to channel the direction of those efforts.

The river burbled on and I settled into a fresh acceptance of my lot. The banks were flat and varied greatly in height. All away to the east lay flat desertland. The irrigations of the city persisted some way along the margin of the west bank, interspersed with buildings and little villages. They would soon peter out. I supposed this River of Oneness to have its sources in some vast range of mountains among the jungles of Chem. If it carried me down to the west of the South Lohvian Sea I could then sail eastwards and visit my kingdom of Djanduin. That appeared to me a particularly appealing prospect.

In floods and sheets of crimson and jade, of orange and emerald, with spears of gold and umber striking upwards, the twin suns sank. Luz and Walig vanished beneath the horizon and still light bloomed in the sky as the stars came out and the two second moons of Kregen eternally orbiting each other cast down their fuzzy pink moons light. The scent of Moon-blooms reached me from the eastern bank. The smell of the river, dark and pungent, secret with secrets old before man ever sailed these waters, wafted upwards as the prow cut southwards. Well, then, I was sorry to part with Mevancy; but I would force myself to be content with my fate in that, and press on with what had to be done on Kregen.

In the last clash of colors as the final rinds of suns sank and the stars winked out and the Twins circled above I saw vaguely through the green and the crimson and the pink a wash of blueness steal between me and the stars.

The blueness swelled and bloated above me and the gigantic form of the phantom Scorpion leered down. I felt coldness. I was lifted up, gasping, for a crazy topsy-turvy instant seeing the flatboat sailing along over my head, and then down I went, splat! into the dirt.

My first action after I spat to clear the dust from my throat was to feel for the sword. It still swung at my belt. The blueness vanished and with it the spectral Scorpion. I sat up. Now where was I?

"By the revolting dangling left eyeball of Makki Grodno!" I said, breathing hard. "Now what the merry hell are the Everoinye playing at?"

For I was sitting in the dirt of a village street and from the shape of the church or temple at the water's edge I recognized a village we'd sailed past just a short time ago. So the Star Lords did not wish me to leave.

But—not leave what? I did not groan as I got to my feet; but I'd felt that thumping great arrival here. Was I supposed to stay with the caravan? With Mevancy? Here in Ankharum? Or perhaps one of the folk in the caravan was the target of the Star Lords concern. I just didn't know.

As to that, then, as I started to walk back, I'd find out.

With sensible rests and a good pace and a careful lookout the walk back through the narrow alleyways through the irrigations and past the occasional village took me round almost to the rising of the suns. I crawled into our lodgings and found a straw-heap by the downstairs door and flaked out.

Something hard and pointed jabbed into my ribs and I rolled over and saw it was a toe with a round pink toenail trimmed and shining.

I looked up. Past the pretty pink toenail the rest of a shapely foot and then a perfectly turned ankle and a calf of superb curve and proportion led my gaze to the edge of a violet towel obscuring the balance of a rich thigh and a swell of hip.

She said: "You nurdling great onker! That shint Hangol has sworn—he was foaming—he'll kill you on sight. You utter nincompoop! What the hell have you come back for?"

The fact I noticed was the smooth shining silkiness of her skin. I looked up at her face—a face not remarkable for beauty but noteworthy for strength of resolution and conviction—and saw black thunderclouds there that would have brought a whole regiment of aerial cavalry down in flames.

"Well," I said, and then paused, and said, again: "Well," and so said no more.

"Well?" she snapped, twitching the violet towel more securely around her. That smooth loveliness seemed somehow different on her forearms and the grainy look caught the light differently.

I'd absolutely no story prepared to explain my return, and I could not think of one on the spur of the moment. She saw me looking at her naked arms and her face flushed up—making her look suddenly vastly more attractive.

"Oh, you!" she flared out. "All right, cabbage. We'll have some breakfast and then I'll have to see Rikky Tardish. It might just be that I can save your bacon for you, you get onker you!"

So after she had dressed we had breakfast in the upstairs room and fine fare it was, too, to a poor wretch like me who had marched famished all night. The sleeves of her tunic were fastened more tightly than usual so that only small oval shapes of grainy skin were visible. If she'd suffered some accident as a child, say a nasty scalding, she ought not to be ashamed of that. Somehow I had the firm impression that had she suffered an accident and been disfigured she would not be ashamed but angry and defiant.

"Don't you care what happens to you, cabbage?"

"Usually," I said, equably. Truth to tell I was pleased to be able to join in conversation again, even though I've always been more of a listener than a talker. "But there are priorities. At the moment, breakfast is the top priority. After that I'll start thinking of ways not to get killed."

"I have already thought. You must keep out of Hangol's way—look at you! You're hardly strong enough to slice that loaf!"

She exaggerated; but not, by Krun, by much!

She went on, her nostrils pinching and flaring: "We have to cross the Farang Parang to reach the capital. Once we get there we can—"

"P'raps we'd better think what to do when we get there when we get there."

She glared.

Then: "You, Drajak, are damned rude. But I suppose you're right."

"Who's this fellow Rikky Tardish?"

"Ah!" She perked up and I caught a distinct impression of a small girl planning mischief. "He thinks of himself as a sly rogue; but everyone takes outrageous advantage of him. He runs a traveling entertainment troupe."

So, at once, I saw what she planned.

I did not exactly groan. So far I'd avoided the old cliché, found in so many stories of Earth and of Kregen, of the famous hero or heroine hiding in a circus or troupe of players. The nearest I'd come had been with Rollo the Circle and his artists. I am not enamored of circuses. Still, she had the right of it in this: I had to steer clear of Hangol for a time yet.

"You will have a green face and a red nose, with ears of a size."

She did not exactly smack her lips at this prospect; but her eyes were bright and her lips curved in such a way as to show her deep mocking enjoyment.

"You," I said, trying not to snarl, "are worse than a Witch of Loh."

Of course, I did not mean that in any literal sense—naturally!

Her face clouded. "Do not," she said, and she spoke seriously. "Do not speak of the Witches or Wizards of Walfarg to Rikky Tardish." She blew out her cheeks, and added: "He was englamoured of a Witch of Walfarg once, and did things he tried to forget, things that give him nightmares."

I thought of Kov Vodun Alloran who had been englamoured of a witch and had caused grievous harm in Vallia before Drak and Silda had saved him. Kov Vodun had raged against Hamal, like Cato and his refrain delenda est Carthago. Now Vallia and Hamal were allies, delenda est Carthago—or Hamal—was long put aside.

This reminder of the outside world did not depress me. The Star Lords had sent me here for a purpose which was still unfulfilled. Here in this vast stretch of country in Southern Loh the people were isolated from the greater outside world, it is true; but they had their ways and civilization and religious beliefs. They were not barbarians. What might depress me quite apart from the weakness upon me was the notion that I couldn't get away from here until I had first discovered what the Everoinye wanted done—and then doing it. For a time yet, I, Dray Prescot, was prepared to be patient. After that, mind you...!

"If," I said heavily, "this Rikky Tardish has been fooling around with a Witch of Loh, a Witch of Walfarg as you call 'em here in Loh, then he deserves everything he gets."

She eyed me sharply.

"You sound as though—"

"Oh, no," I said, somewhat hastily. "I'm not that much of a fool."

I was not prepared to go into details of my own war with Csitra, a Witch of Loh. And, by Zair! Didn't that seem a long time ago now!

"Well," she said brightly, popping a paline. "Let us go and find the green paint for your face. And ears as large as maybe." She rose from the break-fast table, brisk and businesslike. With a groan, I followed.

When a girl can't thump your pillows for you she'll find some other way of devilry to torment you. A Green face! And Ears!

Well, I thought sturdily as I trundled along abaft Mevancy, I'd damned well take comfort from the red nose, by Zim-Zair!

Rikky Tardish was all the things Mevancy had said. Lively, sparkish, thinking of himself, as a later age would express it, as one hell of a guy, he was three times ripped off even in the short time Mevancy and I talked with him. Once a decrepit object borrowed silver and went off whistling. Once a girl said she had a headache and was excused and was later seen with her lover in a low tavern. Once a coper swore the mytzer he was selling was in perfect condition, and that draught animal later expired of advanced colic.

"All the time, Mevancy?" said Tardish.

"All the time," said Mevancy, with great firmness, "until you reach Makilorn."

I opened my mouth to speak and Mevancy snapped: "Shut your black-fanged winespout, Drajak. All the time! Dernun?"

"But," I got out. "The ears? Not the ears!"

"The ears, cabbage."

I groaned. This strong-minded female lady was condemning me to walk about by day and sleep by night with a green face, a red nose, and wearing enormous ears. Quite apart from the ludicrous costume I must wear.

"Strom Hangol, in the short time I have had the misfortune to know him," said Rikky Tardish, "strikes me as a—a—"

"He's all of that," said Mevancy. "And he will strike you, as Tsung-Tan is my witness, with or without the slightest excuse."

"A green face," I said. "Jeehum!"

"As I said, cabbage, I no longer feel responsible for you. If you continue to improve and keep your red nose out of trouble, by the time you reach Makilorn you should be recovered. I repeat, I want no recompense. Now—"

"You're leaving!"

"That's right. I'll bid you Rememberee, Drajak. I'm sailing downriver. My flatboat's waiting and I'll be gone long before the hour of mid."

Eight

I, Dray Prescot, Lord of Strombor, Krozair of Zy, King of Djanduin, Hyr Kov of Zamra, Strom of Valka, Vovedeer (and a lot else, Opaz forgive me!), ex Emperor of Vallia, solemnly daubed green greasepaint all over my face, donned a large and scarlet false nose, and finally hung huge donkey ears about my own. I dressed myself in a confection of red and green and yellow and blue, of bows and folderols, of laces and ribbons, and, finally, I took up a parti-colored stick with an inflated bladder attached.

Thus armed, I strode out onto the stage to entertain the good folk of the caravan.

I was, as you will readily perceive, the butt of the farce.

Very quickly my bladder was taken from me by a succession of actors and actresses and I was thoroughly and repeatedly hit over the head with it.

In the natural course of development, Theatre on Kregen varies widely. And, as you know, at this time when I refer to Kregen I am really talking about our grouping of continents and islands called Paz. Here entertainment has progressed at different speeds in different parts and stands at varying levels within nations as well as between country and country. Shadow plays are popular, mimes and dance, a whole slew of weird singing plays are known and loved. The Italian commedia dell'arte gave rise to subsequent greatness—who greater than Jean Baptiste Poquelin?—from its knockabout beginnings. So here farce and comedy and tragedy mingled and gave rise to the great works of Kregen dramatists. Some of these and their works I have mentioned from time to time.

Do not for a single instant believe that the sublime dramatic works that are the glory of the Kregan stage were even dreamed of by Rikky Tardish's traveling company. Oh, no! A green face, red nose and a pair of donkey's ears—why, yes, that was the level. And that was the level Rikky Tardish intended to keep. He knew the majority of his audience. I guessed that Leotes and one or two of the others merely humored the mob in thus sitting prominently in the front row and applauding—just a fraction of a second after the other groundlings. Strom Hangol was lapping it up. Yet, the rast, he'd appreciate other more refined fare. And, even as I leaped about and cavorted and tried to avoid the bladder blows, so I knew that this farcical stuff was good of its kind. Improvisation upon a basic scenario was all; the more inventive the comicalness the louder the audience applauded.

Tiny Tanch pranced on in a piebald outfit to hit and be hit. He hailed from Ng'groga and was scraping eight foot tall. A quantity of tomfoolery ensued between him and Fat Naghan and I could step back for a moment. The smell of greasepaint, the tang of dust and oil and the mere hint of sweat combined to form a bouquet to remember. I looked at Hangol. If one wished to be uncharitable one would say he laughed the loudest at someone's misfortune. His silver mask flashed. He was enjoying himself.

The whole caravan had turned out for this show, glad that Tardish's Troupe was accompanying them and hopeful of a fresh show each evening.

I'd overheard Hangol talking in a bitter raving kind of way to his cronies. He'd been reviling Vallia. It turned out he'd taken his facial wound at the Battle of Ovalia. I remembered that fight—well, by Vox, would I ever be likely to forget? My Vallian Eighth Army had bested and beaten the iron legions of Hamal and their fanatical allies. We'd swung the thorn ivy trap on them and shattered them. Their commander had been Kapt Hangrol in the alliance with the traitor Layco Jhansi. Well, they were all smoke blown with the wind now.

In what would be the orchestra pit, Tardish's little band scraped and blew away. He had no less than three punklinglings, melodious instruments, and they should not be called plunkings as some ignorant folk do. There were tabors and trumpets and in all the band produced interesting sounds. The girls danced on in their frilly skirts and beads and little else kicking their legs, arms across one another's shoulders, smiling. Oh, yes, Rikky Tardish insisted on the chorus girls smiling, smiling...

Strom Hangol slouched back in his chair and spoke out of the side of his mouth to one of his cronies, a beetle-browed fellow with black hair and a bad skin, known as Gandil the Mak, who habitually carried sword and axe.

After the girls had done their dance I was to be hit over the head again. Tiny Tanch, towering up and up, slipped over and fell on his bottom and drew a roar from the audience. He struggled up and swung a sword at me. I dodged. I flung up my hands and looked all about, trying my best in the pantomime, and the audience picked this up quickly and started yelling.

"A sword! A sword!"

Rikky Tardish himself trotted on, smirking, swishing a sword about. I do not think there was a soul in the audience who did not know I was the fall guy and no matter what I did I would come out with the sticky end.

Then I saw the weapon Tardish proffered me. I ought not to have been surprised. After all, the bandits' loot had been recovered, and here was my own rapier. It was perfectly clear why this particular weapon should be chosen. I was the clown. Therefore I could have an odd, foreign, unfamiliar and therefore funny weapon. Strom Hangol leaned forward, shouting something, and Leotes called out and Hargol sat back.

A girl—she was Fashti, a shapely Fristle maiden—ran out and hit me over the head with her stick and the bladder caught one of my ears and knocked it off.

I think, even in that moment, I knew Strom Hangol would recognize me.

His attention had been drawn by the rapier and no doubt he had protested that such a weapon should be used in so low a farce. Touchy, he'd be, the cramph, about that. He edged forward, staring at me. Then Tiny Tanch, eight foot tall, took a swipe at me, making a grotesquerie of it, and caught me a whack across the buttocks with the flat. I jumped. They were falling about down there in the audience. My green face and red nose and one ear told them I was the butt of all this. The remaining ear fell off. Strom Hangol rose from his seat and I, of course, like the veritable onker I was, stared at him. Tiny Tanch gave me a buffet that knocked my stupid stuffed hat off.

I saw the expression on Hangol's face.

There is the old tradition that members of the audience in some of these congregational farces join in the action. No one would have been vastly surprised when Hangol jumped up onto the stage. Perhaps Leotes might have felt a stab of mystification in this act of his cadade. Hangol flourished his rapier.

"Let one who knows show you!" he bellowed.

"Strom, strom!" the crowd bellowed. "Teach him! Teach him!"

This suited Hangol's book.

He shickered his blade before my face. Then he said in a hissing fashion: "Shint! I know you! Rast—you are going to die!"

I didn't bother to waste breath on him. I was in poor case here. Oh, yes, I held a rapier I knew. I did not have a left hand dagger. My strength was such that at the first pass Hangol would brush my blade aside hardly noticing the beat or the pressure.

Just how good a swordsman was he, anyway?

Since my escapade with Mefto the Kazzur, all my old feelings about sword fighting had been enormously reinforced. No longer was it a case that one day I might meet a better swordsman—I'd already met him. So, maybe, this Strom Hangol was another. Unsettling, that kind of thought.

53

If I was to have any chance at all in this fight then that chance would come only from my skill. If this bully boy was any kind of fist with the Jiktar and the Hikdar, the rapier and main gauche, then I'd not escape without serious injury, a ghastly maiming or, if he wished, my quietus.

I grasped the rapier awkwardly. When I tell you the thing felt as though it weighed like one of those monstrous two-handed swords of the Blue Mountains, you can gauge of my weakness and muscle-power. I swished it about.

The crowd applauded. Hangol laughed. He said: "I shall not kill you at once. Slowly is the way to do it."

Abruptly he drove in and with a flickering glitter of steel he slashed down and a bright green bow fell off my gaudy costume.

Well, a beginner can do that after he or she is shown how.

"Parry him!" yelled Rikky Tardish from the side. "Make a show of it!"

"I shall make a show of you, rast," said Hangol in his vindictively genial way. "I shall enjoy this."

I swashed the rapier before me as he struck again and his blade knocked my own away and seared on to remove a yellow bow.

I did not have a main gauche. He had not drawn his as yet. Well, that was an advantage. I got my left hand onto the knuckle bow of the rapier. I gripped the pommel and knuckle bow in a clumsy grip, a pathetic apology for the two-handed grip I'd use on a Krozair longsword.

Perhaps, just perhaps, if I had sufficient skill then a rapier used in two hands might just get me out of this scrape in one piece.

It was vitally necessary to do a great deal of prancing about the stage. I kicked my heels up and danced this way and swung that, managing to keep my two-handed grip, swashing the rapier around in exaggerated circles, and the audience howled. Hangol breathed hard. He wanted to get in a few pretty strokes yet, to toy with me further; but in very short order I had sussed him out. His skill was average. He had not, I fancied, swaggered as a Bladesman in the Sacred Quarter of Ruathytu. And he most certainly had never, ever, been to far Zenicce to face the Bravo Fighters there.

So, what with all this skipping and jumping, and the use of all my poor strength in that extraordinary two-handed grip, I kept his blade out.

Oh, yes, it was known for a rapier fighter to grab hold of his hilt and slash two-handed; that would not go far if the opponent kept his head and used his skill and so thrust home.

What would my Krozair Brothers have made of that exhibition!

The farce could not go on long. For one thing, the audience would rapidly tire if some satisfying knock-about conclusion was not quickly reached. Always the crowd hungered for new sensation; after the girls had danced and Slender Varankey the juggler had done some tricks, they'd be ready for another bout like this. As it was, knowing this, Hangol would press hard to finish it. As it was, knowing this, I had to finish quickly before all my puny strength leached away.

One of the strangest things about that strange fight as Hangol whipped out his left hand dagger and brought that into play, was the use of two-handed Krozair sword artistry with a rapier versus a rapier and main gauche. I discovered some new tricks there, by the Blade of Kurin!

He was really trying now. I wondered just how many people in the audience realized this Strom Hangol was really trying to thrust home, was really trying to finish me. None, I'd guess. Even Leotes was unfamiliar with rapier work. The uproar was prodigious. People were stamping their feet and yelling and applauding. I could feel what little strength I had draining away.

In the end I used a half-complex routine from the Seventh Circle of the Artifices of the Sword written by San Zefan some two and a half thousand seasons ago on the island of Zy in the Eye of the World of Turismond. San Zefan, Krzy, did not fail me. As I completed the preliminary movements I checked the second passage in which Hangol's sword would fly from his fingers. Instead I transferred the pressure and so, letting out as loud a shout as I could manage in my state, and stumbling forward with a tremendous bustle, I stuck the rapier through the rast's right thigh.

Instantly I endeavored to withdraw and, of course, the pesky thing wouldn't come out cleanly with my level of strength. If he had the courage and strength of will now, he could finish me.

Instead he let rip a scream of pain, dropped both rapier and main gauche, and staggered back, thus freeing my blade, and clapped his hands around his thigh from which the dark blood welled. I managed—and to this day it is a marvel, by Krun!—I just managed to stop my blade striking for his throat.

I turned away, capering like a loon, and Leotes was bellowing and Rikky Tardish was catching me by the elbow and yelling that it was all a mistake. His face sheened with the sweat of fear. He dragged me off, as Hangol's cronies leaped to the stage and carted the strom off. For a space there was considerable confusion and uproar and then, with his showman's gifts fully deployed, Tardish had his girls out there prancing with flashing limbs and flaunting feathers and the inevitable dazzling smiles.

Tiny Tanch leaned down.

"You'd better clear off a bit, dom. Let things simmer down."

I shook the rapier and a drop of blood flew.

"You are right, Tiny, and I thank you."

Truth to tell I felt as though I'd been pushing a sixteen ton load up a hill for ten years straight. I wheezed. I felt my muscles burning. By Krun! What a burden on a fellow it is in life to be weak!

Rikky Tardish hove up, sweating, shaking.

"Make yourself scarce, Drajak. Oh, that I listened to the smooth tongue of that Mevancy! I knew she'd bring me trouble—"

"Blame that shint Hangol!" I said, sharply. "Mevancy paid you gold."

"Aye, aye, by the mercy of Tsung-Tan she did. Now clear off, schtump!"

Nothing loath I took myself off and wandered among the tents and carts. I could still feel the reaction after that ludicrous fight. My Val! To fight like that! It was a wonder I wasn't stuck clean through.

Out past the last line of tents I walked along, swishing the rapier about, looking for a proper clump of grass or a wide-leaved bush to clean the blood from the blade.

Blueness grew in the air. I sucked in a startled breath, looking up.

Blueness, high in the sky, washing down in a broadening belt of blue radiance... "What in a Herrelldrin Hell do the Everoinye want with me now?" I said. "I suppose, you Scorpion, you've come to dump me down where Mevancy has gone."

The shape of the enormous phantom Scorpion glowed above me in fire. I knew I'd never seen him from quite this angle before. He seemed somehow removed from me. The shape dropped lower. All the ground before me radiated blueness. Yet I could hear the chirp of insects in the grass and feel a gentle breeze. The shape of the giant Scorpion wavered before me, pulsating, diaphanous. The shimmer melted, flowed, dissipated and within three heartbeats the phantom Scorpion of the Star Lords was gone.

I let out my breath.

I was standing quite still, and staring, and not believing. Oh no, by Vox. I certainly didn't believe this.

For out from where the blue radiance of the phantom Scorpion had died a woman walked towards me.

As I stood with my eyes sticking out like organ stops, Mevancy walked out from the Scorpion of the Star Lords.

Nine

"It really does look as though I can't go off and leave you, cabbage, without you running your fool neck into trouble. I was *sure* the shint wouldn't recognize you in that remarkable get-up."

"Well, he did." I mumbled something about Tiny Tanch and the Fristle fifi Fashti. We sat in her tent. But I was not really there. I was still standing out there on the edge of the plain as the blue radiance died. I remember with absolute clarity that the scent of Moonblooms mingled on the air with someone frying momogrosses. A girl was singing in a tent close by. She sang "Oh for the Sword of my Lover", which is a sad little ditty filled with long cadences and the drawn out vowels of sadness. Whenever I hear that song I am transported back to that dusty grass plain outside Ankharum where I first saw another being moved through space by the Star Lords.

How well aware I was of the importance of this occurrence!

I had met other kregoinye laboring for the Star Lords.

Once Pompino had staggered back to me, thrust there to do his duty. But this—this was altogether different. And, into the bargain, this was no kregoinye. This was a kregoinya.

Mevancy nal Chardaz was a kregoinya!

I shook my head, there in her tent, and heard as through a veil her testy words. "I cannot go down to the coast now, cabbage. So I'll just go along with you to Makilorn."

"To be sure," I mumbled, and then found I was not at all sure of what I was sure about. She'd certainly hauled me the last few feet out of that damned fire. I'd thought that had conferred responsibility upon her by transference. All the time it had been her duty from the Star Lords. They wanted me to look out for Mevancy, I believed. Now, it appeared, they wanted Mevancy to look out for me.

I thrust that idea aside.

This was turning out to be more like the jobs Pompino and I had done together. The Star Lords recognized the need for a team, at times; in some of the more tricky situations they threw their kregoinyes and—now—kregoinyas.

"You're mumbling, cabbage. I thought you were getting better."

"It is very good of you to come all this way back to look out for me, Mevancy." I thought I'd try a gentle boot in. "I can't imagine why."

"How do you know it is all this way back?" she demanded.

"I just supposed."

"H'm. Well, just be thankful I was able to persuade Leotes that it was all just an accident. Hangol was—upset."

"He tried to stick me through, to kill me."

"No one, if you bray that out, will believe, will they?"

I breathed heavily. "Llodi would, for one."

"Of course. But everyone else will question why a high and mighty lord, a strom no less, should worry his head over a clown."

"It is known—"

"Yes, it is. And if you get Llodi involved, then his head will roll."

"Well, I'll just have to watch out, that's all."

"You'll watch your front and you hope Llodi and me will watch your back?"

I mumbled around that one, and she got the drift I was grateful.

"It is quite clear this shint Hangol will try to kill you or have you killed. If we can reach Makilorn safely we'll stand a chance."

On that rather insubstantial note she said she was retiring and told me to clear out. Her cart, tent and gear were all here correct. She had worn her proper clothes when the Star Lords had brought her back from her trip downriver. I wondered if a folk tale might grow of people who took passage on flatboats down the River of Oneness and then disappeared.

As I bid her goodnight I reflected that the Everoinye looked after those kregoine they favored. Me, they'd fished up out of a Savanti reject. The old feelings I'd had of the Star Lords, that if they'd supplied me with a shield and a helmet and a spear, I'd think the less of them, seemed now, whilst still true in the savage barbarian code, hardly applicable to Mevancy.

I found myself a corner and a bit of straw and slept the sleep of the mightily abused of the world.

All the same, as I awoke, my second thought was a gleeful reminder that I'd kept the rapier. If you do not know my first thought by now, well, as it is the same as the last thought of all before I sleep... and if you still do not know, I can only say...!

Mevancy seemed to me a trifle down as we ate the first breakfast. I surmised this might be because she'd been dragged back here by the Everoinye to nursemaid me when she clearly had other plans. Mind you, Pompino's other plans always went up in smoke if the Star Lords called on him.

The sense of doom surrounding the caravan had been lightened only temporarily by last night's entertainments. Mevancy just toyed with her rasher and loloo's eggs. "You'll have to keep well out of the way, cabbage." She heaved up a sigh. "I suppose I'll see some more of Leotes, now. He at least among these people appears a person of culture and—" She interrupted herself sharply as she caught my eye. "And you needn't mock, you fambly!"

"Mock?" I said. "Mock? What, me mock a grand lady like you?"

She threw a piece of bread at my head. I caught it, reached for the butter, spread it, said: "Why, thank you," and popped the morsel into my mouth.

She sniffed.

"At least your reflexes are improving."

I did not feel in the mood to explain to her that they and skill were the only things that had kept me alive last evening.

Following on that thought convinced me that Mevancy had not been flung back by the Star Lords to take care of me. Had they considered that then she would have arrived before Hangol began his antics.

So, therefore, that line of argument carried me, what difference was there between this last return of Mevancy's—not to rescue me—and the occasion when she had returned in time to knock off the vulture—clearly to rescue me? Or was I wrong in that, too? Her explanation of her escape from the bandits rang hollow, a matter of biting through bonds and sneaking out and of finding the two riding animals. Oh, no! The Star Lords had hoicked her out of the bandits' camp, provided her with animals, clothes, weapons and money. Truly, I had been a starveling beggar where the Star Lords were concerned. Well, I could see changes there, startling changes, as you shall hear.

"You look as though you've lost a zorca and found a calsany," I said, a trifle sharply. "I do appreciate your concern for me, but—"

"But nothing, fambly! Oh, you! You remind me of old Pontior when I was looking after him and I had to dress him up as a woman." She put her head on one side, sizing me up. "No. I can't imagine you dressed up as a woman."

"I have done so," I said, equably. "And no doubt will do so again." Then I essayed a nasty shaft. "Do you make a habit of going around taking care of people?"

Her head went back. The piece of bread, butter and marmalade halted before those ripe lips. "And if I did, does that concern you?"

I felt a mean beast.

Just why I had not told her outright and at once that we both worked for the Star Lords I can only attribute to my natural secrecy where my hide depends on caution and a testing of the way. I would tell her, clearly, one day. Right or wrong, I judged that day had not yet dawned.

"Not my concern," I agreed, which was a lie.

Llodi popped in to tell us that Strom Hangol had taken to his litter. His wound was turning septic and the needleman was concerned that septicemia would set in under the difficult conditions of the journey. Llodi did not smile when he told us this—well, not outwardly.

"It's a shame for him," said Llodi solemnly. "Him being a lord an' all."

"That Hargon—oh, yes, I know he likes to be called San—" snapped Mevancy. "Him and Hangol are thick as thieves. Leotes is too easy going."

"Yes, my lady," said Llodi. "Hargon was beside the litter early this morning. What they talk about an' all, I dunno."

"I've a nasty feeling I could make a shrewd guess not too far from the truth."

She sounded heated. How far, I wondered, had the friendship between her and Vad Leotes prospered?

With the incapacitation of the strom helping us we were able to arrange matters for me to keep out of sight, what today would be called a low profile. I continued to help Rikky Tardish; I was not called upon to venture upon the stage again. When I say I was heartily glad to be rid of the green face, the red nose and the donkey's ears, I understate my feelings. And yet—and yet, if farces are demanded and paid for then someone has to dress up like that. Why should I imagine I was above that? What! I'd been the buffoon for a damned long time and only very recently had I been gaining a different view of the Star Lords, an understanding a little better than an inkling of their purposes.

The caravan wended its way westwards across southern Loh. Far to the north sprawling across the equator lay the jungles of Chem. South of them were the savannah type lands, grassy and open plains, filled with a teeming wildlife as well as roads and cities and civilizations. As the character of the land changed, its vegetation, its soils, its climate, people adapted themselves. This trail we were following, the Old Lorn Trail, traced a course at the interface of grass and desert. I asked questions, naturally, and was told the peoples of the north compressed these folk of Tsungfaril so that their homes were built along the rivers and in the oases. They ventured in guarded caravans across the true deserts to the south to reach the broad and fertile coastal plains to carry on a lively trade. Ng'groga, Zamrarn, Din'nagul and other nations, prosperous countries all, were regularly visited in the way of trade. To the west, to Tarankar, the folk of Tsungfaril did not go. Was it not well known that the evil beasts of Tarankar roasted and ate human babies?

Despite this trading activity, and also despite its scattered nature, the land of Tsungfaril was relatively cut off and isolated. The people kept to themselves. Well, that is known. My Djangs do not often care to venture abroad save on the most urgent of errands.

During these questions the name of people referred to as paol-ur-bliem cropped up. My natural queries were met by averted eyes, a shake of the head, and either silence or a change of conversation. Llodi did say, before walking off rapidly: "You must speak with a dikaster, him being a diviner an' all."

"Where do I find him?" I shouted after Llodi.

"I couldn't tell you."

"Couldn't or wouldn't?" But he vanished around the lictrix lines and I did not follow, for Strom Hangol's tent wasn't too far off and his cronies were to be reckoned with in my puny state.

To refer to that side of this trip for a moment, Mevancy had spoken to her friend Leotes and the word had gone out. Hangol and his cronies' hands were stayed for now.

All the same, Vad Leotes was far too easy going. His red moustaches bristled up in fine good humor, and he laughed endlessly. Well, by Vox, he had every right to, didn't he? He was rich, pampered, was served hand and foot, didn't do a stroke of work, and from what I gathered could do nothing at all he didn't want to do—save in one thing.

"The queen sometimes presses him hard, cabbage." She shook her head. "Leotes is vastly loyal to her. Why, why else do you think he'd venture out on the Old Lorn Trail if it wasn't because she sent him?"

"Is he married?" I said brutally. I knew marriage as an accepted form of union existed in Tsungfaril.

"He was. His wife died. He has children, though—"

"Then I'm doubly sorry for him, and also glad."

I knew she had the wit to understand what I meant. She cocked her head on one side. "You have children, then."

"Yes." I wasn't prepared to tell her that Drak was the Emperor of Vallia, Zeg was the King of Zandikar, and Jaidur was the King of Hyrklana. Nor that Lela was still prancing around Prince Tyfar of Hamal, the pair of them a couple of loons. Nor that Dayra was—well, where was Dayra, Ros the Claw, and what was she up to? And little Velia—well, little Velia was no longer little but a full fledged member of the Sisters of the Rose along with Didi.

Oh, yes, I had children all right; yet I felt young, young, and could still act with all the thoughtless enthusiasm of youth when I forgot the cares of empire. She gave me a long look, and the subject was dropped.

We crossed the Farang Parang, sticky but nowhere as unpleasant as the Great Salt Desert. In somewhat better land to the north, a ferocious nation of nomads effectively barred the easier route. Sometimes those who attacked the caravans were not just disaffected bandits but members of these nomad tribes, the Glitch Riders. They were also a pain to the civilized lands to the north.

What she did say, once when referring to children, was that Vad Leotes' children seemed unimportant. Singularly unimportant, Mevancy said.

The subject of children came up when I tackled Rikky Tardish about the missing left hand dagger to the rapier he'd given me.

He spread his hands, soulfully.

"The vad had all the loot from the bandits, as is his right."

Somewhat crustily, for as close to the main gauche as this I was annoyed to be baulked of it by some damned vad, I said: "And I suppose it'll stay in his family for generations and his kids will have it—"

"Yes and no," said Rikky Tardish.

"What's that supposed to mean?"

"Here in Tsungfaril," he said, and averted his eyes, "we praise Tsung-Tan and we would prefer not to talk about the paol-ur-bliem—accursed to foreigners. Even those of good heart."

He would not be drawn any further so I took myself off wondering why Leotes, as he was one of these mysterious paol-ur-bliem people, should be accursed.

Rikky Tardish's long eight-wheeled plains wagon dropped its front two off-side wheels into a stone-strewn gulley and smashed the pair of them to flinders. The twelve mytzers hauling the wagon were unhitched after they'd hauled the wagon out and Rikky stared glumly at the wreck. Leotes sent word that the caravan would camp for the night here and now, as he wished to visit the abandoned city of Ivory Lorn. Rikky puffed out his cheeks.

"The vad is a good man, Drajak."

"Aye," I agreed.

As a world Kregen is a remarkable place. Yet geography and natural causes, unless interfered with by savants, operate in much the same way as on Earth. The River of Drifting Leaves ahead of us on which stood Makilorn had once flowed southwards here. Its course was still broadly marked in the dust. Once both banks of the river had flourished with vegetation, rich with produce and fat cattle in the water meadows, the irrigations giving life to support the splendid city whose ruins now exerted so powerful an attraction upon the mind.

Mevancy, glowing, said: "Leotes and I are going to explore the ruins, cabbage. I suppose it is no use you trying to help Rikky?"

"Not much."

She laughed and walked off with that lithe swing of her hips and I saw her and Leotes mount up and gallop off towards the abandoned city. Well, if that was the way of it, then it was no business of mine. I felt that little itch of puzzlement over Mevancy; I still wasn't sure she was apim. Not, of course, that it would make any difference if the races were compatible.

The short day's travel left me feeling restless and it was in my mind to have a look at these ancient ruins myself. When the river changed course the people had simply taken what they could carry and left what they couldn't and traipsed off to find the river again to the west. The city left in the dryness still stood, in surprisingly good condition. Some of the temples remained impressive buildings, towering against the afternoon sky.

The lictrix Mevancy had provided, Snuffles, gave me a leery look as I unhitched him from the lines to which he'd only recently been led. He pawed the ground; but he used his near side middle leg, so he wasn't too upset. I had my foot in the stirrup when Master Pandarun hurried up, calling: "Drajak! A moment. Have you seen the vad?"

"He went off to the ruins."

"I know but—"

"Yes, I saw where he went."

"Zorca riders have come in. There is an urgent message from the queen. The vad must be informed at once. Will you—?"

"Of course." I mounted up, touched Snuffles, and set off thinking only that this was a reasonable excuse for me to have a look at the ruins.

The city of Ivory Lorn must have been a tremendous place. I found myself comparing the pile with lost cities of two worlds. Ivory Lorn ranked high. As I rode gently down a broad dust-choked avenue flanked by the facades of still impressive edifices, I spotted two figures high on the flank of a temple. They'd tethered their mounts and climbed up to get a panoramic view. They were sitting close together, dangling their legs over the side. I found myself thinking that Vad Leotes wouldn't mind if I shouted up.

A projecting cornice obscured the two figures as I rode on, and when I'd passed that building and cleared the cornice away, there was no sign of them.

My feelings were not wholly of annoyance. I wouldn't mind climbing up and taking in the view. I tethered Snuffles and started the climb which was easy.

Always I walk with a light tread, as silently as I can; it is a habit. A noise of a slide of loose stone took my attention back to the avenue. Three figures ran out and vanished into shadows opposite. I frowned. One of those men was Gandil the Mak, the second Sar. Hargon and the third another of Strom Hangol's cronies, Nalgre the Frunicator. I went back to climbing with great urgency. I felt a thickness in my throat. By Zair! If... I stopped that thought and climbed frantically.

When I reached the place where I'd spotted them, there was no sign. I called: "Mevancy!"

A voice directly ahead called back: "Cabbage!"

I moved forward cautiously on that high platform and looked over the edge. Mevancy clung to a narrow ledge, a decoration in the stone, just an arm's length below. She had the fingers of both hands hooked onto the ledge. Leotes had his arms wrapped about her waist and hips, hanging from her body. The avenue stretched a killing distance below them. Mevancy's fingers slipped. There was not much time. Her head tilted and her face looked up, taut, strained, yet she said: "Lahal, cabbage. Can you do anything?"

I lay down on my stomach, stuck my head over the edge, staring down. We were a long way up. One slip and it would be squashed tomato down there.

I put both my arms down and could just reach her wrists. In the instant I grasped her, her fingers slipped again. She gasped. I felt her weight pull on me and my body scraped three inches forward over the platform.

"We will pull you over too!"

"Just hold on, Mevancy—"

"My fingers are done for—"

"I'll hold you."

"You, cabbage! With your woflo strength!"

I felt myself slide forward again. There was absolutely no way on Kregen I was going to pull them up. There wasn't even a decent toe hold.

For the first time Leotes spoke.

"We will pull us all over. I do not want you to die, Mevancy."

She took what he meant instantly.

"No, Leotes! You can't! Help will reach us—"

"You forget I am paol-ur-bliem, my dear." He tilted his head back and I could see his fierce upturned red moustaches. "I just regret the time wasted. Still, youngsters grow fast when there is a reason for it."

I didn't know what he was burbling on about. I did know that if help didn't come damned quickly then I had a most horrendous decision to make.

With a kind of snorting gasp I managed a hoarse bellow.

"Help!"

Mevancy took up the shouts, fiercely: "Help! To the vad! Help!"

Leotes cut in. "We are slipping down. Help will not reach us in time."

She stared up at me and blood rushed into her face. "Don't you dare drop the vad, Drajak! Don't you dare!"

She must have felt some movement of his arms about her, for she screamed again, almost incoherently: "No, no! Leotes! No!"

My body scraped forward again, nearer to the edge where I would topple helplessly over.

I'd be a red puddle down there unless I let go.

And, truth to tell, I could feel the strength leaching away from my fingers and wrists. In all Opaz's Truth, I couldn't hold on much longer.

I think Leotes saw that in my face.

What he couldn't see was the guilt I would bear for ever after, for I knew without the shadow of a doubt where my loyalty lay. The noise of my belt scraping over the stone sounded hideously. In only a moment or two I would have to act or die.

Mevancy calmed down. She said something in a low voice and Leotes laughed—a weird jolly laugh, full-bodied and without mockery, devastating for a man in his position. "You will wait, my dear?"

Mevancy said: "Of course, my love."

And Leotes let go and dropped down and down and splattered on the pavement.

I felt the difference at once and knew I could hold Mevancy.

So that was the way they found us when rescue at last arrived.

Ten

Mevancy said: "There is no one in the caravan we can rely on who has power sufficient to hold the shint. Hurry, fambly! We must ride for the city and lose ourselves there as fast as maybe."

She was upset and hurt, that I could see. I believe she had a little cry in the privacy of her tent before she blazed into action. She was not distraught. She acted, and the impression I gained was clear, as though there had been an interruption in her plans.

A tragedy of this dimension, one would think, would drive her crazy with grief. But, no, she remained calm and firm, taking control and organizing us for our flight through the desert to Makilorn.

Master Pandarun had found us, and the zorca riders from the queen had hauled us in. There was no chance, given the scene, that we would be thought guilty of the vad's death. That, of course, would not stop Hangol; for a space he would have a free rein and he'd revenge himself. I, I may say, packed very smartly for the off.

We felt little surprise when Llodi the Voice said he would fly with us. Strom Hangol had Llodi marked for destruction just as we were.

We didn't bother with the cart and Mevancy found a lictrix from somewhere for Llodi. We took plenty of water, enough food, our weapons and ourselves and we set off, running for our lives.

I do not know by how much we scraped clean away before Hangol's cronies started vengefully to find us; it must have been by precious little, by Krun!

We rode hard and sharp into the night, heading west for the River of Drifting Leaves and the great city of Makilorn in which we would hide.

What had passed between Mevancy and Leotes was privileged to them; I had heard only scraps. If I couldn't make head or tail of this information yet, that is not to be wondered at. Ideas drifted around in my skull; but nothing seemed to make sense. This concern must have been the reason that I completely missed the obvious. I failed to see what was going to happen in our lives with sudden and unopposed authority.

Poor old Llodi! He would, as I knew, probably see nothing.

In the event it turned out somewhat differently from what one would expect, given their ways.

The Maiden with the Many Smiles was up, shining refulgently down upon the waste of the Farang Parang. Stars glittered in their multitudes. The night was cool but not unpleasantly so and the hooves of our mounts thudded muffled in the dust. Ever and anon I threw a searching glance back.

Reivers of the Glitch Riders might be out on a night like this, hoping to take a caravan by surprise. Ordinary bandits operated in this area also. We might spot dark shapes under the Moons and not know who they were. We'd know only one thing; they did not wish us well.

Mevancy had said that San Hargon had laughed most cruelly when the other two villains had pushed her and Leotes over the edge. He'd looked down and at the obvious question had answered that the two victims should be left to fall on two counts: one that the deaths would be accounted accidental, and, two, that he would enjoy the thought of the suffering before death.

A cold, reptilian creature, this ascetic Hargon.

So, when it happened and I finally got the message into my stupid old vosk skull of a head, I let out a shattering bellow of mingled chagrin and rage.

And, as I have said, it happened as it had never happened to me before.

The phantom shape of the giant blue Scorpion bloated above us. Llodi rode on, head thrust down, completely oblivious; he might have been asleep.

I tensed, expecting the coldness, the rushing sensation of falling, the thump of landing elsewhere. Suppose, just suppose, the frantic thoughts cascaded through my head, just suppose they hurled me back to Earth!

The silent, invisible uproar ceased. Llodi still rode on ahead; there was no sign of Mevancy.

The blue Scorpion had vanished.

Instantly I reined up. Hell's Bells! I'd have to ride back now.

I needn't have bothered.

The blue Scorpion re-appeared, vast, filling the sky, leering down on me. Expecting, this time, to be snatched up and whirled end over end I was once more astounded to find myself still astride Snuffles. Together, we went up and end over end. Just what the faithful lictrix thought of this behavior I didn't know; I damned well knew what I thought of it, by Krun!

We came down with a thump, not too demanding on Snuffle's six legs.

Against the stars reared the dark outlines of Ivory Lorn. Directly ahead stood the rows of tents, the animals lines, the carriages. So, this proved the point absolutely. The Star Lords required Mevancy and me to protect someone in the caravan. Problem solved.

Ha!

Looking about carefully in the pink moonslight I saw no trace of Mevancy. Now, where would the girl go? Probably she would discard the idea of going to her tent or cart. She might sneak into the marquee where the body of Leotes lay in state. That would be dangerous; it would be like her. Then I took the notion that from what they'd said the corporeal body was of small importance once dead. Mevancy was not of Tsungfaril; I fancied she'd taken up with Tsung-Tan.

What a mess! Here we'd made a perfect escape, got clear away, and the damned inconsiderate Everoinye had just tossed us back into the fire!

Rikky Tardish—well, that was the best bet.

He'd be shaking in his shoes and not liking it one little bit; I thought he'd care for Mevancy, even if he turfed me out.

His girls lived in the eight-wheeled plains wagon and it suddenly struck me that Rikky might hide her there. The other performers lived in their own vans or in tents. I didn't want to hitch Snuffles to the animal lines for a saddle would stick out like a sore thumb there and, just in case we had to gallop off hurriedly, I wanted Snuffles all saddled up. If we did ride off, this time I'd damn-well shout up that we were trying to preserve our necks for the sake of the fool Star Lords. So I pulled the reins over his nose, patted him, and said in his ear: "There's a good fellow. Now, stay!"

We Clansmen of the Great Plains of Segesthes have ways with animals...

Leaving the lictrix standing still I crept off through the fuzzy pink moonlight towards Rikky's tent. Two of the minor moons were up, hurtling low over the surface of Kregen. In the shifting illumination I saw shadows moving, and then, sharp, stark, poignant, a voice: "By Spurl! You cramphs all deserve to die, you Gahamond-forsaken bunch of shints!"

She sounded fierce and brave. A coarse laugh answered her, and then Strom Hangol, rich and fruitily unpleasant:

"Take the shishi to my tent—" He saw me in the instant I saw him.

He rode a zorca and his leg stuck out. His cronies surrounded him, bold, swaggering, ruffianly fellows who'd slit a throat more for the love of it than for the gold. "Take him," he said, and he spoke quite softly.

Rough hands seized me. I struggled. That was like a bird in a wire snare. Mevancy called: "You onker!"

Hangol lifted above me astride his zorca. He carried a blatter, a nasty stick for hitting people, rather like the balass rod of office and chastisement carried by some foremen. The zorca curveted. Hangol handled the animal adequately and reined in beside me. He stared down.

The fists grasping me were not to be dislodged by muscles of milk and water. Hangol gloated openly. "Now," he said, "now we can redress the balance. Bring him along with the girl. We shall listen to them scream for a long time, I think, by Lem, yes!" He lifted the stick. "And this to keep you quiet, shint!" The stick slashed down at my head.

I tried to duck and turn away. The blow smashed down on the back of my head. I felt it. I felt the stick strike down into the base of my skull and the top of my spine. I yelled; I couldn't help that, and fell forward in the grip of the men holding me, unable to move.

As I toppled I saw as it were the stars going around in a circle, I saw the Maiden with the Many Smiles floating serenely away up there, I saw Mevancy with her arms cruelly twisted up her back, I saw Strom Hangol laughing and riding off, grand astride his zorca, swishing his stick.

Then I felt as though I had been tossed into a vat of boiling oil.

My body jerked. My mouth opened in a rictus of agony and no sound came forth. My limbs shook. I vibrated like the plucked string of a harp.

And boiling oil washed all over me and pain lapped me and exploded in my skull like a bursting shell of Earth. I shuddered and trembled, and then I screamed. I yelled. I shrieked. Silence came back as I forced my mouth shut, to be followed by the laughter of Hangol's cronies holding me.

Gandil the Mak and Nalgre the Frunicator stood in front of me as their two colleagues held me. I brought my arms in together, dragging the two men with the movement. I twisted my wrists. My hands were free. I took these two unhappy wights around each one's throat and bashed their heads together. I dropped the bodies and started for the two in front.

Gandil the Mak just ran.

Nalgre the Frunicator was either slower or more stupid. I twisted his neck and dropped him and started off after Gandil the Mak.

So far the knowledge of what had happened was simply there, in my skull, not yet to be thought about, studied, gloated over. By Zair, though!

Strom Hangol's tent was indeed a splendid affair. Well, naturally it was, since up until this evening it had been Vad Leotes' marquee.

Two of his cronies stood guard before the flap of the opening as Gandil ran up, yelling. They were both armed with strangdjas. Gandil vanished into the marquee. The two guards leveled their weapons at me as I ran up.

I didn't even bother to draw the rapier the Star Lords had so considerately left me. I ducked the first strangdja, kicked the other fellow betwixt wind and water, smashed the first's face in, and turned back to finish the one who was doubled up and whoofling.

Without pause I went on past the flap and into a wide canvas-floored area, clearly the ante-room to the marquee where boots would be cleaned before stepping onto the Walfarg weave carpets and rugs of the interior.

Strom Hangol and Gandil the Mak were just emerging from the far curtained opening. They saw me. They moved forward over the canvas and Hangol unlimbered his rapier and main gauche, the only weapons he wore. Gandil drew his thraxter, the straight cut and thruster of Havilfar. They advanced on me.

"Your death shall be even more painful for you and edifying for me," quoth Hangol, his dark eye bright, the silver mask glittering in the light of the samphron oil lamps. "You and the shishi will prove greatly entertaining, and, by Lem, you will be sorry!"

I suppose the old intemperate, hot-headed, headlong and harebrained Dray Prescot must burst out now and again, Opaz forgive me. I freely admit to a vice that I abhor overcoming me in this situation. I played to the audience—oh, the audience wasn't either of these two bastards. The audience was invisible, in my head yet perfectly visible there all about me, watching what went on with small shakes and nods of the head, pursing of lips, murmurs of approval—or not, by Vox, given that they knew me, they knew me!

The old sailor knife over my right hip slid out with only the faintest of hisses of oiled leather. In the next heartbeat the knife was in the air and in the next its broad blade was buried in Gandil's throat. He fell down.

"By Lem!" screeched Hangol. "You yetch! I shall teach you—"

Reflectively, as I drew my rapier, I said: "You nulsh! I have burned many temples to Lem the Silver Leem."

He goggled at this, and then he cursed, vilely, and bore in determined to win quickly, to disable me, and then to enjoy his torturing fun at his leisure. I was not naive enough to imagine he cared a whit for his dead cronies.

Because I played to that invisible yet immanent audience I knew I would not slay this kleesh. He was a mediocre swordsman, and I do not care to slay in cold blood. I have signed Execution Warrants. I know. So I swirled a circle with my blade and we set to.

He was absolutely confident—well, he would be. Was he not a notor of Hamal? Was I not a clown? Did he not know the rapier and main gauche, the Jiktar and the Hikdar? Was not the rapier I wielded a weapon of ridicule?

Yet he must have puzzled over my reference to Lem the Silver Leem.

Mind you, I rejoiced in the feel of the blood singing through my veins, the sensation of muscles responding, the whole corpus proper to a fellow.

Truth to tell, I was disappointed that this evil rast Hangol was so poor a hand with a rapier. I would have welcomed a hard fought fight. Still, I have my own philosophy when it comes to the arcana of sword fighting. I know what I know. I wouldn't deign to play with him, even though the feel of blade against blade and the screeching chingle of metal aroused all the fire in me: no. I'd just use a simple passage, twirl him around—like so, as his rapier flew through the air—then grasp his right wrist with my left, striking past his dagger—as the dagger in his right hand tried to degut me.

Because he was left handed, because he wore a silver mask on the right side of his face, he was kack-handed. Instead of a clean disarm, he suffered, through his lack of experience of fence, a blade through him. I withdrew at once, feeling annoyed. He did not immediately fall down. He stared at me, his one eyebrow drawn down, both hands holding his guts. No blood yet stained his lips.

I didn't even bother to kick him as I ran past.

Three carpeted openings further in, Mevancy lay bound on a divan. There was no one else around. I breathed a shaky sigh, shook my head, and started on her bonds. Her eyes flashed enormously upon me above the gag. Studiously, I worked away at the ropes holding her wrists and ankles. Even then, even in that moment, I noticed the granular, smooth yet spikey effect of her forearms.

When her right hand was free she ripped the gag away.

"Oh, you! Cabbage!"

"You're all right, then."

She drew a breath.

"Strom Hangol?"

"He might be dead, he might not be. I'm not sure."

"Oh? We'd better know, or else—"

"There was a deal of confusion outside," I said, telling the truth and knowing I used it to lie. "You get ready. I'll go and look."

Before she could protest I hurried back to the entrance. Gandil the Mak still lay there and I put my foot on his face and pulled the sailor knife free. Hangol had gone. Thoughtfully I cleaned the sailor knife and sheathed it. The rapier had more than half-cleaned itself as I'd withdrawn from Hangol's body on his clothes. Yet he was not here. Was the cramph still alive, then?

As I stared about, Mevancy joined me.

"Good riddance to offal," she said, looking at Gandil's corpse.

"Hangol was wounded," I said. "I thought sore wounded. But he is not here, as you can see."

"What army was it?" she said, in a half-joking fashion, half-serious. "Or did the drikingers attack again?"

"I couldn't say."

"And how did you get here so rapidly—or know where to come?"

"Easy enough to guess—" I began. Then I stopped. This was footling.

She was staring at me, hard, her face tight-drawn.

I said: "The Everoinye sent me."

Eleven

She reacted to that.

Her face, taut as it was, tightened still further.

"Well, you hulu! Oh, you!"

"There's no time to explain now—" I began, using the time-honored formula. "We have to—"

"I agree explanations can wait." She had had a shock. Well, that was easily understood. By Djan! When you found out somebody else besides yourself served the Star Lords, was a kregoinye, well, that came as a body blow, believe you me! "You've kept this from me all along. Still—" here she glanced towards the exit. "Still, it does explain a great deal. All right, cabbage. If the Everoinye have sent you along to assist me, then assist! We'll have to clear out of here right now."

With that I perfectly agreed.

I said: "The worry is Hangol. It seems we must remain with the caravan. That is clear. If Hangol—"

"I'll do the thinking. What I cannot understand is why the Everoinye should employ a weakling, and why, by Spurl, they should saddle me with him."

She gave me no time to answer. She padded over to the outside flapped opening, glanced through, didn't turn her head as she said: "Come on, cabbage."

Shades of Strom Irvil of Pine Mountain! At least Mevancy hadn't thought to call me a body slave, as Strom Irvil in his bluff numim way had, and into the bargain calling me Zaydo, as he called all his body servants Zaydo.

She slid through the opening and again I admired the slim suppleness of her, lissom and lithe, straight after being lashed up like a carcass.

She of the Veils had risen and washed down her pink and golden light as I followed Mevancy. The camp was relatively quiet, with the stamp and snort of beasts, the odd noises that seem to have their origins in no known source, a dog barking—that was Lady Floria's obnoxious little white thing, all belly and jaws. She stepped over the two guards, daintily, without a word. The questions I wanted to ask her boiled up in my head as, clearly, the questions she wanted to ask fizzled in hers. Well, all that could wait. We had to decide what to do—rather, Mevancy the kregoinye was going to decide what to do!

In one sense the most important thing to know was—just who did the Star Lords wish us to protect?

Mevancy headed off to her own tent and cart, abandoned when we'd cut and run.

Over her shoulder she snapped: "Get your gear. We'll take what we need and follow the caravan at a discreet distance. If anything happens we'll be within striking distance."

Yes, well, and of course. That was one solution.

For all her hoity-toity ways, this girl was a genuine; I sensed that. I liked her anyway. So I gave up any notion of a showdown to see who was boss.

"Right," I said, and cut along to where Snuffles still waited.

Mounting up I swung his head around and trotted towards Mevancy's tent.

Now I wouldn't have been in the least surprised if, when we rode out, the blue Scorpion had arisen balefully over us and thrown us back into the camp.

That did not happen.

Maybe the Everoinye could understand what we were doing. Maybe they just trusted Mevancy far more than they had me. Although, mind you, that last was changing. I'd ask her if she'd been in that confusing place of metal boxes.

"This'll do until the morning," she said, reining up and dismounting. "If we stay behind this ridge they can't see us. I'll take the first watch. Get to sleep. I'll wake you when it's your turn."

I looked at her, and then dismounted. "Mind you do," was all I said.

Sleep came easily enough and I awoke to her hand on my shoulder. By the stars and the Moons I knew she'd judged half the night. I said: "Mind you sleep, my girl—"

She lay down and spoke in a composed way. "I am not your girl, and you will speak with civility. I can manage without your assistance, so do not forget that." She turned over and in a changed voice but one she knew I could perfectly hear, she finished: "What rubbish the Everoinye do employ!"

It indicates a great deal of my feelings that I immediately took it that she teased me. I didn't think she was built of vindictive stuff.

All the same, her earlier remark remained true; she was running this show and I was content that it should be so.

Nothing happened for the rest of the night and in the morning we breakfasted cold as we watched the caravan pack up and get under way.

"They will take Leotes back and bury him with great pomp," she said. "I shall attend the ceremony. That is settled. You need not, cabbage."

I said: "I'll just reserve my decision."

She swallowed bread and picked up a handful of palines. "Tell me, Drajak, whilst we wait, all about yourself and your life. And this time, tell me the truth!"

So I told her a farrago, a lot of it true, and mentioned the time I'd had to rescue old Mog from the Manhounds of Faol. "I wasn't sure who I had to hoick out of it, and took out a number of the wrong people. The Everoinye allowed me to see each to safety before dumping me back among the Manhounds."

"Reminds me of the time old Suringlas couldn't make up his mind who was the target—"

"Suringlas was a kregoinye?"

"Well, of course, fambly! We stopped a gang of footpads bashing the kov, and all the time it was the kovneva we had to look out for."

I thought I'd essay a little test. "You'd think, would you not, if the Everoinye are so all-fire powerful and wise they'd have the common sense to tell us who they want—"

"Cabbage! Have a care!"

Her face expressed a lively appreciation of imminent catastrophe. I sighed; but to myself. Here was another like Pompino, then; devoted to the Star Lords, believing they could do no wrong, kow-towing all over the place. Pompino thought they were gods. I had an idea Mevancy might not believe that. What she did believe was written on her face; the Everoinye were above criticism. They demanded absolute faith and obedience and they got them. Queyd-arn-tung!*

She composed herself and was about to speak when I said: "Have you discerned any pattern in your work for the Everoinye?"

---

* Queyd-arn-tung: No more need be said! *A.B.A.*

"Pattern? I'm not sure I know what you mean."

I judged she had not been a kregoinya for very long. And, it was clear, she'd been out as Number Two. This Suringlas and poor Rafael who was dead, had been in command. Now she was compensating for that, and taking command of this new team. I didn't mind that.

"Some of the people I've rescued have done things that revealed why the Star Lords wanted them kept alive."

"We-ell," she said, screwing up her eyes. Then: "No. No, I can't say I've noticed anything like that."

"For instance, a religious teacher and prophet I saved has been getting a better deal for the gentler kind of diffs. They don't get put on so much now."

"That was not in Loh!"

"No. In Hamal."

"Oh," she said. "That's in Havilfar."

So I gathered a new impression; Mevancy hadn't been to the great continent of Havilfar across the sea to the east.

Talking of this reminded me of Strom Irvil again and his wondrously amusing numim ways; amusing to me only, of course, for he was very strict with his body slaves, as he said, very often. And the thought followed from what Mevancy had said in her immediate comment that that had not been in Loh. There was more food for thought there...

We talked more as we waited for the caravan to move off; both of us were cautious in what we revealed. At last the carts and carriages rumbled off and the lines of pack animals trudged rhythmically through the dust. Two figures still stood where the camp had been, each holding the reins of a Lictrix.

"What are they waiting for?" demanded Mevancy, fretfully.

I stood up.

She started to rap out: "Get down you—"

I said: "That's Pondo and Nafty. They're waiting for you."

"What!"

She couldn't believe this. She started to say something, changed her mind, stood up, shaded her eyes to stare at her two employees.

"What in the name of Gahamond the Wise do they think they're doing?"

"Earning their hire. Looking out for you."

"But nobody knows we're here, you onker!"

A shadow fleeted across the dust and grit, over the ridge, flattening towards us, separating into two shadows as it neared. The twin suns cast light into the other's shadow: one flying object threw this twinned shadow.

I said: "Here is someone else who knows we're here."

She looked up.

That expression on her face! It mirrored the expressions worn by Strom Irvil, by Pompino, when they thus stared up at the Gdoinya, the spy and messenger of the Star Lords.

She swallowed. Abruptly, she looked radiant. Then she astonished me. She waved cheerily at the giant raptor, glistening up there in his golden coat of feathers, scarlet and black, proud and arrogant, circling in hunting circles above us.

The Gdoinye planed lower, wings stiff, and then he swept upwards with tremendous velocity. He let rip a single squawk. Then he was a dot and then he was gone.

"The Gdoinya," said Mevancy, letting out her breath. "We are in good hands!"

She said Gdoinya quite clearly, using the female form. That made sense. I'd always suspected that there was more than one spy for the Star Lords, and already had some evidence for that. She, like myself, knew that Pondo and Nafty could not see the Gdoinya. Now she went on: "Well, that is good. Let us find out what those two famblys want."

With that she looked at me. "Well, cabbage? What are you waiting for?"

So I trailed off down the back slope and brought up her zorca and Snuffles.

We mounted up and rode towards her two men. Nafty greeted us with a laugh and Pondo even managed not to growl too much.

"Lahal, my lady!" called Nafty. "We are to tell you it is safe now."

"How did you two hulus know I was there?" demanded Mevancy.

"Why—we were told, my lady."

"Who by?"

"Tuong Mishuro," said Pondo. "The creepy one."

"He's not creepy!" protested Nafty.

"Well, how did he know?"

They started a wrangle, and Mevancy snapped, hard, "Shastum! Silence!" Then she said: "Tuong Mishuro told you I was out here, and to say it was safe?"

"That's right, my lady," said Nafty, somewhat subdued.

"Like I said," repeated Pondo as we started to trot after the caravan. "The creepy one."

Neither of these two fighting men expressed surprise at their employer creeping off into the wasteland, apparently hiding. They'd kept clear of involvement with Hangol. They were not slaves, being caravan guards hired for pay; but what their lady employer did was what she did. That was no business of their's unless they had to draw sword to protect her.

This line of thought made me say quietly to Mevancy as we trotted along: "I hope Llodi is all right. He'll be wondering—"

"If he's got any sense he'll ride on to Makilorn."

"Probably."

"And what does that mean, Drajak?"

Had I been other than I am, I'd have laughed easily, casually, and made some light evasive answer. As it was, I said: "I value good comrades."

She rounded on me like a spitfire.

"Do you mean to stand there and suggest I don't—"

"I'm sitting in a saddle," I said in a mild voice.

By Vox!

She let me have it, as we'd say on Earth, she let me have both barrels. The feathers flew.

After a space she halted to draw a breath. Her face was flushed clear to the hairline. She had a strong face, not beautiful but pleasant with her wide generous mouth now compressed into a thin line after she'd drawn breath. Her eyes were bright. The flush of color in her face was high, very high. The red pulse of blood under the skin surprised me with its brilliance.

I decided to try to calm things over. Ha! I, Dray Prescot, decided! It makes me hoot with laughter to think of it. I said "Calm down, Mevancy. You'll burst with blood pressure."

My Val!

She started all over again, ranting and raving and calling me the lowest of ingrates, the stupidest of onkers, the most heinous of hulus. In the end I touched my heels to Snuffles and cantered on ahead a space and joined Nafty and Pondo.

"And don't think I won't let *them* know!" she yelled after me.

As far as reporting me to the Star Lords was concerned, which was clearly what she referred to, she didn't understand my relationship with those mighty and lofty but essentially lost superbeings. They knew by now they could discipline me. They flung me back to Earth for twenty-one miserably awful years; because I disobeyed. Now I felt I'd reached a better understanding. All the same, they knew how I contumed them, them and their Gdoinye. Oh, no. Poor Mevancy with her awe of the Star Lords had no conception of the way I treated them.

Mind you, it was probably true to say that I was the onker in these relationships. Past humanity though the Star Lords were supposed to be, it seemed to me they still retained enough petty humanity to treat me as they habitually did instead of in the far more generous way they treated Mevancy. Again, I could be completely wrong in this mean estimation of them; and I suppose to be honest in my heart I realized I was. Perhaps, I promised myself, perhaps next time I might not indulge in a slanging match. Mind you, that perked up the old bloodstream no end, by Vox!

This silly squabble with Mevancy meant that I could not ask her the questions about Leotes and what he had meant just before he willingly fell to his death.

Anyway, the hoity-toity miss probably wouldn't tell *me*, a weakling onker wished on her as a stupid assistant.

We rode gently on and caught the caravan and Tuong Mishuro, half-smiling, did not explain but simply said that San Hargon had spurred ahead to the city. Hangol had been hurt and they sought better medical attention than that afforded by Doctor Slezen and Doctor Nalgre the Needle, Leotes' doctor. There had been unexplained murders and everyone was a little jumpy. Still, we should reach Makilorn soon, and then everything would be all right.

"Who did the killings?" demanded Mevancy.

"No one knows," replied Mishuro. "Also, I do not think anyone cares."

As you may imagine, that depressed me. When I was Emperor of Vallia I found out what I had known before. It is everyone's duty to care about what happens in a country. It's no good leaving it to the other person.

Mevancy said: "Thank you. Lynxor Mishuro—"

"You may call me san," Mishuro interrupted mildly.

"Of course." Instead of a lord, this Tuong Mishuro was a san, a sage or dominie, master. Mevancy went on: "Thank you, san. We will sort things out when we reach the city."

So we went on our way and in the fullness of Tsung-Tan's time we reached the River of Drifting Leaves and the great city of Makilorn built upon its banks. I, for one, rode in wondering what the hell happened next.

Twelve

"I must make a list," quoth Mevancy nal Chardaz. She spoke with a fine confident ring of authority. We sat in the upstairs room of Lulli Quincy's lodging house. The remains of the first breakfast lay upon the table, the radiance of the suns slanted in the square windows, and Mevancy was all business.

Shades of G&S! I said to myself. I've gotta liddle list!

"This is serious, cabbage. I've not forgiven you yet for—"

There must have been a curve to my lips, thinking of G&S and their liddle list, that she mistook for a smile. "I agree it's serious," I said, and I tried to make my tones portentous. "Can you remember all of them?"

"Of course, fambly."

"If you recall, I was lying flat on my back, rigid."

"Oh, I remember dragging you out all right."

I started to say what I'd done, and then stopped. That was not what a gallant koter of Vallia would say to remind a lady. Instead I said: "I picked up a little gold or brass ornament poor Rafael was trying to reach—"

"You did! Well, where is it?"

"Drikingers."

She started to swear in her ladylike way and then checked. "That means it could be with the gear Leotes brought back from the raid on the bandit camp. You know, when we got that rapier you carry about like an onker."

"What's so all-fired important about the trinket?"

She frowned. "I don't know. And that's the truth. But San Tuong Mishuro was very upset that he'd lost it. He kept on about it."

"H'm. Well, he's on the list, then."

She wrote the name down at the head of the paper. "And Lady Floria."

"The Lynxora Floria Inglewong, yes. And Lynxor Nanji na Fuokane."

"Nanji Tawang," she said, and made a face. "Yes, I suppose so. Him too."

"There was mention of a lynxor and lynxora Shalane."

"Oh, the obese Thyllis. They remained in Larishsmot."

"So that's all—?"

"No. If you wish to work for the Everoinye you must be smarter than that, Drajak. There were the servants and slaves. Also there were Olipen, a merchant, from Guishsmot, a young newly-married couple, Listi and Larrigen Parfang of Makilorn, Margon the Ron, a zhanpaktun, and mistress Telsi, a lady of uncertain occupation. They were all with the caravan."

"And were safely rescued?"

"Of course."

"Well," I said, a little stuffily. "It's not a liddle list anymore, is it?"

She tapped the paper. "One of them has to be protected..."

I spoke up. "In my view it has to be San Tuong Mishuro. He is the obvious kind of person the Star Lords look out for."

"Your views will be taken into consideration when I make my decision," she said with grave equanimity. I did not burst out laughing.

I busied myself with the pottery dish of palines. At least, they were real in this situation which, in my view, was rapidly becoming unreal.

All the same, this was reality. I knew that if I fouled up the Star Lords would have no compunction in flinging me back to Earth.

And yet—and yet, as I had been thinking recently, maybe they wouldn't...

"Yes," she said. "I rather think our zhanpaktun, Margon the Ron, fits the bill."

Carefully, I said: "Have you had much experience with mercenaries?"

"I know a person who wears the pakzhan glittering gold at the throat is a great fighter and renowned as a warrior."

"Well, some of 'em."

"Oh, you!" she flared up. "What does that mean—besides sour grapes?"

"You mean am I jealous of 'em—no." I felt my lips ricking back. "Oh, no."

"Well, we'll find out where he's lodging and see what is to be seen."

"As the leader of the expedition," I said, "you can't say fairer than that. Lead on, my lady!"

Now this great city of Makilorn was remarkably small by the standards of cities I knew—Ruathytu, say, or Vondium or Zenicce. There were probably not more than a hundred thousand or so inhabitants. The city stretched out on both banks of the river, a place of architectural surprises. Many of the buildings reminded me of the tomb of Genghis Khan: domed, jutting of eaves, eight or six-sided, solemn—what one would call po-faced. Yet they were not tombs but the bustling homes of a busy people. The tombs were out in the wasteland which here barely merited the description of desert. The land rose in an escarpment and following customs old before mankind left the caves, the folk buried their dead in mausolea and tombs cut from the living rock. When I visited the city of the dead out there in the wasteland I was not reminded of the majestic tombs of Egypt; rather I called to mind the mysterious city of Petra and the riches there to be discovered. After all, Jean Louis Burckhardt, rightly credited as the first European since the crusades to see legendary Petra, was there for only one day, sacrificing a goat to Haroun. Some of the glamour brushed off on Makilorn. Oh, yes, in the fuzzy pink Moonslight of Kregen, the place was easily mistaken for 'the rose-red city half as old as time.'

For, by reason of the ivory City, this city was relatively young.

Mevancy lost no time. Brisk, smart, she set about her work for the Star Lords in fine style.

Perforce, I tagged along after.

Yet I felt cruel, even then, in the way I mentally mocked the poor girl. She was a natural. This thing had to be done; ergo, she would do it perfectly.

There weren't many flowers in Makilorn. The folk used every square inch of land to the utmost in growing food, either crops or animals. Some of the grander places might have a few earthenware tubs with flowers growing in grudgingly provided dirt. Palines, of course, were the most common pot plants. Some of the temples were enormous. Tsung-Tan, the universal deity, was well-served. When I saw processions wending along I thought of back home where the great processions traverse the boulevards and avenues beside the canals, and the fervent chants of *OO*-lie *O*-paz! *OO*-lie *O*-paz! rise in long sonorous waves to set the doves twirling among the towers. Here, the religious beat gongs and rang bells and chanted for Tsung-Tan, yet the religious practices were worlds apart. In Vallia, Opaz and the spirit of the Invisible Twins is a deity revered as the great beneficent overlord of humanity, with ramification upon ramification in the devotees' interpretations and practices. Here in Makilorn in Tsungfaril, Tsung-Tan was revered as the great provider who had reserved your place in the paradise of Gilium. The people did not go so far as to claim that the experience of life here on Kregen was the experience of living in hell, not in general. There was one large schismatic sect which did so claim. There was little friction between adherents; everyone agreed that to be taken up to heaven into the place reserved for you in Gilium by Tsung-Tan was the sole aim in life.

This tended to create a lack of interest in the here and now much beyond satisfying immediate needs.

The folk of Tsungfaril appeared to Mevancy and me to be gripped by a lassitude that extended into every aspect of life.

Foreigners bustled and got things done, in employment or on their own account. I'd tackled Mevancy on the subject of paol-ur-bliem, conscious that I trod painful ground in talking of Leotes. Yet he bustled, and he was of Tsungfaril. She'd put me off. "I expect one day I'll tell you, cabbage."

Some of the foreigners in the city were from Walfarg. Walfarg had once conquered all Loh, Pandahem, vast lands in the east of Turismond. Now all that sprawling and splendid Empire of Loh was swept away. Pockets of culture and custom survived here and there. Tsungfaril showed a few evidences. But their religious beliefs and isolation maintained a distinct and different culture. I saw women walking with veils of many patterns and colors covering their faces, women from other parts of Loh. In the city there was an enclave of houses built in the Walfargian style with hidden walled gardens where these veiled women might rest and relax.

The idea that Mevancy might need to wear a veil struck me as comical.

The Old Lorn Trail continued on to the west and arrangements existed at the southern end of the city to provide a proper ferry service. The area which in a normal city would be the Wayfarer's Drinnik had here been grudgingly provided, just like the dirt in the flower pots. If you couldn't grow food on any piece of ground it was worthless; if you could then you grew food. Oh, no, the folk of Makilorn understood this. They charged sky-high rates to cross the River of Drifting Leaves. You could quite see their point. Mevancy didn't, and got into a heated shouting match with the ferry operators.

I wandered across and leaned on the stone wall and looked over the river.

"Outrageous!" Mevancy was leading off. "Just two people, with no baggage, and returning this afternoon, a guaranteed double passage? And you try to charge me a whole ming! Are you mad? A whole gold piece?"

"You may swim if you wish, lady."

The ferryman wore a lopsided turban of some grayish cloth; he was not slave. The slaves tailed onto the lines with which the ferries were hauled across. Flat bottomed rafts, really. When a vessel wished to sail up or downriver past the ferry the lines were slackened off and dropped to the bottom. There was a fair amount of traffic, and slikkers were racing one another just for the dare of it, their sails billowing.

Mevancy choked and pointed to the water. "Swim? With them?"

The twinned black fins cutting the surface did not look inviting. There were not a lot of them; one of them would have jaws enough to make swimming a one way affair.

Shades of the River of Bloody Jaws! I stopped myself thinking of Seg and Milsi and adventures along the Kazzchun River.

Mevancy snapped out: "And how much for a single person, you black-hearted drikinger?"

He didn't look in the least discomposed. His brown face, seamed and cunning, sized Mevancy up. "You need not lay your tongue to me, my lady, for I am Aron the Ferry, son of Aron the Ferry, and my belief in Tsung-Tan is unshakeable." Then, like a striking risslaca: "Forty five silver khans."

I thought Mevancy would have a stroke. Her face bloomed with blood. She shook her fist under Aron the Ferry's avaricious nose. She stuttered and spluttered. "There are sixty silver khans to each gold ming!" she raved. "You are a—" She whooped in a breath and waved her arms about. She whirled about and stared balefully at me, leaning on the wall.

"And you needn't stand there looking smug, cabbage!"

I had the sense to say nothing.

The last of the carts and animals and passengers for this trip of the ferry were crowding onto the flat deck only a foot or so above the water. Aron the Ferry stretched and hitched his fawn robe about himself. He had a nasty-looking curved dagger at his belt, somewhat after the fashion of a Havilfarese kalider. That could slide in your guts and burst your heart.

"You must make up your mind. We cast off now."

The flat and ugly crack of a whip smacked into the hot air. The slaves groaned and got themselves together and laid onto the lines.

I had to remove my sensibilities quickly. There was absolutely nothing I could do, here, about the detestable institution of slavery. One day, Opaz willing, my friends and I would eradicate it everywhere in Paz.

"Oh, by Spurl! Very well, then. You robber!" With that, Mevancy fairly hurled a gold ming at Aron and pushed roughly past. I followed.

I said to Aron: "Will it be a ming to return?"

"Assuredly, walfger." He did not address me as lord, walfger being one of the Lohvian words for mister, equating with the Havilfarese horter and the Vallian koter.

I wasn't fool enough to threaten him, or to say I'd make enquiries about the ferry prices the other passengers were paying. I'd find out.

The west bank differed subtly from the east mainly, I fancied, because there were fewer temples and more laboring areas. There did exist the maze of narrow streets and alleyways that are to be found in most cities; but here this tangled confusion of living and working accommodation hardly merited the description of the aracloins, the all-embracing term for the warrens and souks.

We found the address, a large lodging house with almost as much style as Lulli Quincy's establishment, and as we went in I pondered on this fresh revelation of Mevancy's character. She must be paying very near the top price for our lodgings; she protested at a single gold ming for the ferry. Mind you, I felt pretty convinced Aron the Ferry, spotting a likely pigeon, had swooped.

I knew all the people on our little list—or I should say Mevancy's list—from the days spent with the caravan. Mevancy had told me that she and Rafael had herded most of them out in one parcel, finding a way through the fire which, so far, had been mostly smoke. Later the flames had bitten.

A large slatternly woman chewing cham told us that that hulking great brute of a paktun had taken himself off and good riddance. Now I own here that I was vastly satisfied at this news.

Not sure just what Mevancy intended by this visit I'd envisaged a nasty scene. I mean, did the girl intend to mount a day and night guard on Hargon the Ron? She stood there watching the woman's fat cheeks go round and round with the cud of cham. At last, quietly, she said: "Thank you, walfgera," and walked away as calmly as you please.

I said: "Strike one off."

"I assume so. He's gone. Had he been the target we'd have been sent after him by now."

"Yes."

About to continue with a casual: "Who do you fancy now?" I was interrupted by a sharp: "The Parfangs. Listi and Larrigen. They are newly married and their resources are slender. They lodge this side of the river."

With that comical caution that was becoming habitual when I suggested something to this hoity-toity miss I fancied she'd overlooked, I said: "They will not welcome busy bodies watching them all the time."

"I would imagine the honeymoon is over by now."

Cynical with it, then, this young lady!

"Lots of marriages founder, do they, where you come from?"

She simply ignored that and walked on with her lithe swing towards the narrow street where the lovebirds were lodging. What this Larrigen Parfang did for a living, I'd been told, suited his mild temperament. He was a stylor who organized the lading of vessels plying the river. He'd been to Larishsmot to see his bride's parents. I sensed a romantic story there, given the distances involved. Caravan masters demanded and obtained high prices for their services, and then there were all the gear and animals to buy or hire. No wonder the newlyweds were living in reduced circumstances. Could they be our target? The answer to that was: very easily! They could have a child who could revolutionize some aspect of this civilization, cause destruction and the death of millions, turn the course of history.

They were out when we arrived, and Mevancy bit her lip.

Cruelly, I said: "What now, my lady?"

"Oh, you!" she snapped; but the snap lacked fangs.

"Think I'll take a stroll down to the wharves. Might find them there."

"Very well." Her head went back. "I shall go and—"

I interrupted. "I think it would be best if we stayed together."

"Cabbage, I've told you, I do the thinking."

There was no shifting her. I suppose I should not have gone down to the riverbank by myself; at the time I felt that a little time on my own would prove productive. As they say, "the selfish sow sour seeds."

Because Makilorn was accustomed to the sight of strangers as they passed through, I was spared much of the xenophobia found in many parts of this Earth, although noticeably less so on Kregen. The Suns of Scorpio glittered off the water. Further along there was considerable activity around the fishing sheds. I turned to look back up the bank; there was no sign of Mevancy. I went along to the fishermen and without any unseemly haggling soon arranged that Kang the Hook would be happy to take us across the river in his boat for a silver khan.

"The ferrymen are a bunch of grasping stranks," he said, jerking a brown thumb at the twin fins cutting the water. "I've known 'em push folk in who wouldn't pay the fare."

"It's the carts, d'you see," said a whiskery fellow smothered in the net he was repairing.

"Aye," confirmed Kang. "It's the carts and animals."

"I'll be back in a bur or so," I said, and went off to find Mevancy.

The bank here, just before the fishing sheds, had been raised with trimmed stone blocks. The fisherfolk, despite their importance to the city, had been relegated to a muddy patch fronting the sheds. That made launching their boats easier, of course. My views were that the Star Lords would make sure we were in the immediate neighborhood of the person we had to protect if that person ran into trouble. Running about all over the city was fruitless, in my view. But how to get that point across to madam?

A number of people moved about their business, and back from the raised bank the warehouses lofted brick built walls. In one of those places Larrigen Parfang spent his days writing down the ladings of the vessels.

I kept a sharp eye open.

Presumably Mevancy had seen the fatuity of her intended course of action for here she came, stepping smartly down towards the stone bank. I watched her, admiring the lithe swing of her walk. Then I yelled.

"Mevancy! Behind you!"

She whirled about instantly. The three plug-uglies who broke from a passing group of warehousemen lifted cudgels, blatterers of heavy wood. They were dressed in clothes little better than rags, and their faces were filthy. They leaped for Mevancy, alone there on the stone bank.

She stretched both her arms straight down her sides. Then she lifted them up to forty five degrees. I saw the latchings of her sleeves burst open. The leading thug reeled back, screaming, clawing at his wrecked face. Blood spurted everywhere. The second tried to dodge and his face, too, was ripped into red ruin. What looked to be a mat of needles covered their faces as the blood and puss flowed. The third thug bundled down and on and crashed headlong into Mevancy.

She tried to dodge that frenzied attack.

Almost she swerved away. The thug tried to grab her and I saw how his right eye vanished in a wash of shining crimson. But the effort overbalanced her.

The plug ugly was screaming, clawing at his face, stumbling about bent double.

I ignored him.

Mevancy stumbled, tottered, tried to regain her balance and failed.

Without a cry she tumbled headlong into the river. Immediately two pairs of twin fins cut the water towards her.

Thirteen

My old sailor knife slid out of its oiled sheath and I was running along the stones of the bank and taking a long flat dive slap bang into the water.

Well, yes, I am accounted a fine swimmer and can stay underwater for what seems an incredible length of time to onlookers. I went in and at once saw Mevancy rising to the surface flapping her arms and legs.

Beyond her in the brilliant water the lean lethal shape of the strank showed dappled gray and green and pink, twin fins stiff, jaws agape.

The second was a mere blue farther off.

I corkscrewed my legs, dived under the strank seeing his two black eyes like marbles fixed on the thrashing form of the girl. Up in a ferocious kick and the sailor knife went in and along slitting his belly. His scaly skin was tough; the blade was keen and my muscles were impelled as much by fear for Mevancy as evil joy in using them again.

Blood spilled into the water.

There was no time to waste on that one for the second was finning in and aiming directly for me. He'd hold on to his course. The blood in the water would affect him, that was true; but that would be after he'd chomped me.

After that his brothers and sisters and cousins would turn up...

Again, I swirled under him as he made his pass. He tried to thrash back but the sailor knife went in abaft his gills. I hewed the knife about. He rolled away and blood stained spreading in the water. I wrenched the knife free and kicked savagely for Mevancy.

I came up under her and caught her about the waist, lifting her. That was, of course, not only foolish, it was asking for trouble.

She tried to hit me about the head and then we broke the surface.

I whooped in a gargantuan breath, yelled: "Rope!"

The stone face of the bank lifted before me, green and slimy. Up there, foreshortened, a row of torsos and heads peered down. Somebody had the nous to throw down a line.

Before I did anything else I ducked down and peered back through the water. There was no sign of a strank—yet.

I hitched the line about the girl as she spluttered and tried to speak. "Shut up, girl, and hold the line." I lifted my old foretop hailing voice. "Haul away, handsomely now!"

Mevancy went up in a wet clinging smother.

Again I didn't hang about. Another huge breath and I was under the surface, knife in hand, looking for stranks.

This time a cousin turned up and I dealt with him as I had the first two.

This time when I stuck my head up through that dancing silver sky I saw the rope dangling against the stones and so gripped it in my left fist. The sailor knife went between my teeth, my right fist got a purchase on the line, I shoved my feet flat against the stones and went up there like a mountaineer.

I swear to this day I heard the snap of strank jaws just abaft my heels.

Mevancy was flat out on the stones and a girl was jumping up and down on her and driblets of water were coming out of Mevancy's mouth.

The clamor surrounded me as the people expressed surprise and horror. I looked for the three thugs. Their bodies were missing.

With a noise like a blocked sink freeing itself of a month's garbage, Mevancy got out: "You! Oh, you!"

The girl stopped jumping up and down on her.

I said: "Thank you, walfgera."

She wiped a strand of hair from her face, her mouth pursed. Then she said: "It is always difficult to know what to do best. But you are foreigners."

"They might," shouted a crone with a shawl about her head, "have been converted to the glory of Tsung-Tan, Ysbel—we don't know."

Ysbel snapped back: "No, we don't know, mother-in-law."

I said: "Walfgera Ysbel, you did right, and I give you thanks."

Mevancy whoofled a bit and shook her head and spat and swallowed and generally regained the centre of attention. When she stood up the crowd considered the entertainment over. No one commented on what had happened.

Very soon they'd all gone back about their business, leaving Ysbel and her mother-in-law staring at Mevancy.

"Your arms—" said Ysbel, at last.

Mevancy had pulled the broken-open sleeves over her forearms; but the wet cloth could not conceal the pitted state of her skin.

"Oh," said Mevancy, tossing her head. "It's just the water." She turned on me like a chavonth. "Well, cabbage? Are you going to stand lollygagging here all day? We have work to do."

I spoke directly to Ysbel. "I thank you again. There should be gold between us, I think." Then I added: "To the glory of Tsung-Tan."

Ysbel's mother-in-law cackled.

Mevancy ripped open her purse and shoveled mings at Ysbel. I turned away. I was beginning to appreciate the problem Ysbel had faced when confronted with the apparently drowned corpse of a stranger.

Looking up quite frankly, Ysbel said: "Thank you, lady. Now had you been a paol-ur-bliem you would not be thanking me at all!"

Mevancy's lips tightened. She did not reply.

With the polite remberees between us we parted and as we walked along the bank Mevancy said harshly: "Hangol's work, I judge."

"Probably," I said. "We can't be sure."

"Ordinary footpads, those?" She shook her head. She had recovered with feline speed and grace. "No, I do not think so."

When I conducted her to Kang the Hook's boat she tossed her head, said not a word, stepped aboard and paid over the silver khan without so much as a blink of her eyelids. All that was equivalent to her: "Oh you!"

The pull across the water took little time, and Kang burbled on about my foolhardiness in diving into the water, and how much the lady must be loved and how much she must love me in return. I could see Mevancy would explode like a stoppered kettle soon; thankfully we reached the opposite bank and disembarked before that catastrophe occurred. Still and all! It amused me.

As we walked along to the lodgings she said: "Tomorrow is the funeral."

I wasn't stupid enough to ask her if she was going.

I said: "Probably the others from the caravan will be there."

"Possibly."

"Yes. I think I will mingle with the crowd."

"As you please."

I said: "Aron the Ferry saw you coming. You were a pigeon, plump for the plucking. No, it does not please me to mingle with the crowd. But I fancy we'll stand a better chance if both of us are not stuck out like sore thumbs."

She swung about and halted. "You! Cabbage—remember who—"

"I remember very well—Pigeon," I said, and walked quietly on.

She did not speak to me again until we had eaten and sat back in the upstairs room to contemplate what was left of our first day in Makilorn.

Suddenly, she said: "Cabbage!"

I looked up. "Yes, Pigeon?"

She breathed hard through her nose, very hard. Then: "You were looking at my arms."

"Aye."

"I suppose I must tell you, then. Anyway, I must eat a great deal now."

"I noticed you were stowing it away."

"I must replace the lost tissue as quickly as possible. I expended just about all my bindles."

"They were what stuck all over their faces?"

"Naturally."

"And in the eye of that Rapa, and what stung Hangol by the tree?"

"Down there by the river I was startled, I was extravagant. I shot off far too many. Far too many."

"You did rather make a mess of the cramphs." I picked up a paline and turned the yellow berry in my fingers. "May I—?"

"I suppose so. Here." She held out her right arm. The smooth and silky skin ended at wrist and elbow. Between lay a pitted skinscape, rather like a honeycomb. There were only a dozen or so of the deadly little sticks, her bindles, remaining in their slots. These gave the granular effect. She went on: "They are shot off by blood pressure. It makes it easier if I'm angry; usually I am. More often than not I'm frightened."

"Join the club," I said.

She pulled her arm back. I own I was fascinated by this fresh glimpse of the way nature had developed on Kregen. Still—maybe this was not natural evolution but another example of the way the ancient savants had interfered with nature?

"Everyone is like this back home?"

Her wide mouth widened into a smile.

"Oh, no. Only the females."

Well, that explained some of her hoity-toity ways, then.

"Tell me, Mevancy, where away is this land of yours?"

Truth to tell I didn't expect her to answer. But I suppose some dam had been released by what had occurred, for she said simply: "I come from Sinnalix. We were once as advanced in culture as any nation of Kregen;

but we were overtaken and now we are little better than barbarians. It is a great shame."

I'd heard the story. The Sinnalixi inhabited a portion of Loh south of Murn-Chem, north and west of where we were. So she wasn't too far from home, then. The country had been part of the Empire of Walfarg; evil days had fallen on the people and whilst there are barbarians and barbarians, I knew what Mevancy meant. I hadn't known about this remarkable ability of the Sinnalixi women to defend themselves by shooting miniature darts with great accuracy into the eyes and faces of evil kleeshes who attempted them. I found that, in general, I approved.

She'd come, she said, from a good family who had fallen on bad times. Well, by Zair, and who hadn't! After the spread of barbarism over Sinnalix, a barbarism of material and spiritual significance, the country had gone wild. Life had been hard. Mevancy's father, and I gathered he'd had some holdings in the local community that demanded obedience, had prospered, married a wealthy girl of a friendly tribe. Perhaps the seasons-old blight of ignorance across the land might be lifted. The legacy of Walfarg's empire might yet yield good.

"I attracted notice as a person not dealt with lightly." She spoke without looking at me, playing with a paline around and around her plate. "My mother died in a raid on our hold, and that was the beginning of the evil times."

I thought of Jilian Sweet Tooth. The two girls were remarkably different, one from the other, yet they might have been sisters in adversity.

"Suringlas had a job to do and I helped him. One thing led to another and eventually I was overjoyed to be taken on full time for the Everoinye."

Such a flat matter-of-fact way of describing being taken up by the Star Lords astounded me more than anything else she said.

"So you've just been working for them ever since?"

"Ever since Suringlas came to Sinnalix."

I decided not to ask how long that was. I judged it was not long.

She said: "How long—?"

I said: "I have not always seen eye-to-eye with the Everoinye. Sometimes I have disobeyed them and they have punished me."

She sniffed. "Well they would, wouldn't they, cabbage?"

There was no arguing with that statement, by Krun!

Choosing my words with some care and speaking as casually as I could, I leaned back in the chair, and said: "Now that Pondo and Nafty have chosen to return to Larishsmot, the question of employees has come up."

It is, of course, a gross exaggeration for me to say that had she shot off her remaining bindles at me I'd not have been surprised. As it was, she stiffened up her back and gave me a piercing look. Then she said: "You mean, had we had them down by the wharf I wouldn't have fallen in the water?"

"Possibly."

"H'm." She looked away and played some more with the paline. Just before she popped it into her mouth she said: "Very well."

"That's a relief."

"My purse is not bottomless, you know."

Taking this as a matter of comment and not of criticism I could say easily enough: "I suppose the Everoinye provide you with funds?"

"From time to time."

This casual attitude to what were marvels to me still took a bit of getting used to.

"Well, you shouldn't starve, then."

"As you are my assistant, then neither should you, cabbage."

"Thank you, pigeon," I said, humbly, and I really had to screw up my face not to allow the smile plastered all over the inside to show on the outside.

"You feel sick?"

"No. No, thank you. Just a passing fancy."

"Well, let it pass off, if that's what it does to your face."

"Quidang!" I rapped out in best military style.

"Yes," she sniffed. "Oh, I'd guessed you are a paktun ages ago." She eyed me meanly. "More likely a masichieri—bandits pretending to be honest mercenaries." She was working herself up now. "And I suppose you are high and mighty and way above a mere mortpaktun—oh, no! You are a zhanpaktun, a hyrpaktun, and wear the golden pakzhan on its silken cords at your throat!"

I admit I felt not so much embarrassed or annoyed, or even sorry for her, as an acute puzzlement. There was one highly unsavory explanation for her behavior. I dreaded that. Dreaded? Well, then, by Vox, did not welcome, did not welcome one little bit. I'd developed a keen sense of self-preservation when it came to dealing with predatory women lusting after what was not theirs. And so, then, wondering if that was the explanation, I did feel sorry for her.

Her eyes were bright. Her breast rose and fell. And her color was high—very high. That color, evidence as I'd thought of a somewhat unhealthy blood pressure, was now explained. And she did eat! Her body was hard at work growing fresh bindles to take their places in the clustered slots on her forearms. I knew very keenly that I wouldn't like that little lot of nastiness chinking into my eyeballs, no, by Djan!

That afternoon I went down and found Mistress Quincy and asked her a few pertinent questions and then went back to Mevancy. I said to her: "Will you lend me four gold mings, please?"

"Oh?"

"I need to buy an outfit suitable for Makilorn. A fawn cloak—"

"Popinjay time is it, now, cabbage?"

Patiently, seeing the way her red lips quivered, I said: "I intend to mingle with the crowd at the funeral and I shall keep a sharp eye on you, pigeon. It will be easier if I am not marked as a foreigner."

"Yes, yes, I see that. Here, cabbage, here." She fairly flung a handful of gold and silver coins at me. They rang and chingled in the upstairs room.

I began very moodily to think that maybe I was going to have trouble with her. What a tragedy! We ought to be a smoothly functioning team working for the Star Lords. So, of course, this had to rear its ugly head.

Deliberately, for I really couldn't believe what I'd just been thinking, I said: "We shall all miss Leotes."

She was clearly brooding on something else, for she spoke without thinking. "Oh, he'll be about, he'll be about."

Fourteen

The funeral of Leotes li Ningwan, Vad of Sabiling, turned out to be entirely different from what I'd unthinkingly expected.

Given that Kregen is a huge conglomeration of peoples with widely varying customs, one would still expect rituals and respects, however oddly at variance one with another they might be. Leotes, it seemed to me, standing in the shadow of a squat pillar in a gloomy domed hall, was just shuffled off.

His body still wrapped in the canvas in which he'd been laid in the caravan was brought in by four slaves and placed on the pyre. His children walked up and looked—I thought perfunctorily—and walked away. San Hargon was there, astringent as ever, apparently in a supervisory capacity. Strom Hangol was not present. Mevancy stood to the side, pale, tense; if Hargon attempted violence now, I had already decided to be as ruthless as he was. Tuong Mishuro and his apprentice, Lunky, stood near Mevancy. There were no signs of anyone else of the caravan. So much, I thought then, for the camaraderie of the journey.

Slaves waited deferentially. Hargon gave an impatient sign and torches were thrust between the thin scattering of wood. Flames bit up, blackening the canvas shroud, flickered and died.

Clearly there was nowhere near enough fuel to form a pyre to consume a human body. Smoke lifted thinly. No one spoke or moved until San Hargon lifted the little golden staff he carried. Instantly the slaves hustled forward, took up the singed canvas bundle, and marched out.

A voice spoke breathily in my ear: "They used a lot of wood on him. A lot. Well, they would, wouldn't they, him being a rich vad an' all."

Without turning around, I said: "Are you in one piece?"

"More or less. It's been touch and go, what with dodging about an' everything."

"What happens to him now?"

"Why, they'll take it across the river and just put it in his cave."

"Just like that?"

"Well, by Lohrhiang of the Five Palms, it's only his old used-up body."

"I'd have thought they'd show a little more respect."

"Well, they have, haven't they? Look at all the wood for the funeral pyre."

I saw I wasn't getting anywhere here. Still without turning, I said: "I'm keeping an eye on Hargon. I think he will seek to harm Lady Mevancy."

"I'll shaft the shint first."

"We were sorry to have missed you on the ride in. I know Lady Mevancy will be overjoyed you are safe."

"Safe, aye, and hungry!"

His attitude to Hargon intrigued me, and I filed away my ideas on that. Now the slaves carrying Leotes's body had left, San Hargon followed. He did not look at Mevancy, and he did not see Llodi and me in the shadows. He went out.

Mishuro moved towards Mevancy. His voice was low but clear.

"You are brave but foolish, my lady. I believe you to be in great danger."

"I believe you are right, san."

"Well, then?"

"If I am foolish it must be because I am a foreigner and not used to your ways. I wanted to look on Leotes's face once more."

"I shall soon be arranging that, as I have informed you, since you are in a privileged position. The trouble is that Hargon will be the guardian."

"I do not know—I am not sure—what I can do about him."

In my ear, Llodi whispered: "Shaft the shint!"

I said: "Perhaps later. Now, would you shaft those fellows creeping—"

"I see 'em!"

I heard all the sounds of a man drawing a bow, letting fly, reaching for the next shaft. The arrow flew true. The first of the men in dark clothes creeping from the shadows past the far doorway screeched as the arrow punched in. There were four more of them and these leaped forward, still silent despite that they had been discovered. Swords glittered in their fists.

Llodi let fly with his second shaft and took one of the assassins out temporarily, the arrow through his arm.

Buying the new fawn robe gave me the ability to move among these folk without attracting attention. I had to keep the rapier hidden, of course. So I ripped out the lynxter Mevancy had given me and jumped forward.

The first assassin was pawing at his eyes. Blood and muck spattered his cheeks.

That left two for me to deal with.

These assassins were not dismayed by their losses. They were real professional stikitches. Their dark clothes, their silence, their swift onrush, all proclaimed that. The one with the arrow through his arm had now recovered and as I closed with the two before me I lost him beyond them. Their blades flashed before my eyes.

Mevancy screamed: "You onker, cabbage! Keep out of it!"

She'd drawn her dagger and she knew how to use it. Of course! She hadn't believed I'd knocked over Hangol's guards to rescue her and she thought I was still as weak as a woflo, a camouflage I intended to keep up. But, here and now, with Mevancy's life in danger? Not likely, by Krun! No subterfuge was worth the life of this hoity-toity little madam for whom I cherished a lively affection. She had to be saved, no argument.

I slid the first blow and twisted and thrust and so recovered, the lynxter glistening red.

Mevancy hurled her dagger. It whistled damn close past my ear and went twunk! into the face of the second assassin just about to engage me.

As this black clad unhanged villain collapsed I saw past him the fellow with the arrow through his arm now sported a second arrow through his neck. Llodi had finished what he had started.

"Well!" snapped Mevancy in an exasperated voice.

I said: "These stikitches are professionals. They are not high quality—"

"Because they failed, Walfger Drajak?" said Mishuro.

He looked unruffled, calm, in control of himself. Lunky hovered.

"Yes, as well as their lack of masks and body armor."

"Assassins vary over Kregen," said Mishuro, somewhat sententiously. "These five were quite good enough for me, thank you."

And Mevancy laughed.

"You were right, san." She caught my eye and I frowned and then gave the universal expression of questioning. I meant—was she the target, or was he? Was he the person the Star Lords wanted us to protect? I was more and more convinced that he was. She did not stick her tongue out at me; her expression indicated that she had done so, and I deserved it.

"I think they would have slain me, into the bargain," said Mishuro. "Stikitches do not respect much in this world of sin."

"Nor does that shint Hargon," I said, somewhat heatedly. "He and that cramph Hangol sent these hired killers. You know, san, it was Hangol's men and Hargon who pushed Leotes and Lady Mevancy off, don't you?"

"This is what Mevancy says. It is her unsupported word." As I was about to let rip with a volley of invective he went on: "I believe her. But nothing can be done in any legal way." He let it hang there.

So, all right, then! He might look like an ancient Buddha, serene, self-less, above petty mortality's envy and strife; he wanted something done here. I am not an old leem-hunter for nothing. I sensed immediately the wheels of plots turning here. San Hargon might have been pleased San Mishuro was killed in the unfortunate assassin attack; vice versa operated here, and no mistake, by Krun!

People were coming in to find out what the commotion was about. We left them to sort out the bodies and clean the place up. Mishuro insisted we go with him to his villa.

As we walked along, Mevancy in a most serious tone of voice said: "You were fortunate that fellow rushed straight onto your blade and skewered himself, cabbage. Otherwise your head would have rolled."

"Very fortunate." So my footling and petty-minded disguise of still having no strength remained! Very well, then. Let it remain!

I'd cleaned the sword on the black clothes of the corpses. I noticed that Llodi retrieved two of his arrows, the third being broken. His bow was the great Lohvian longbow. In the continent of Loh as I was, that is not a stupid remark, for flat and compound bows are prevalent there as elsewhere in Paz. As to Llodi's skill with the bow, a strangdjim as he was, I could only surmise. Had he been a bowman of quality, one would think, he'd be employed as a bowman, not a spearman.

If he could be persuaded to take employment with Mevancy, I, for one, would welcome him.

Mishuro's villa was a place of cool arcades and walled gardens and high comfort. He had a small army of servants and slaves. This did not agree with the appearance he had made in the caravan. Then there was only Lunky, his apprentice. Now there was a villa full of people. I did notice that he employed only a token force of mercenaries under a cadade, fat and sweating, whose chief function appeared to be superintending opening and closing the big front door.

"Naturally enough," he said in reply to my query. "No one would even dream of harming me."

"It's unthinkable," said Llodi. "Why, Diviners are like the Todalpheme. Sacrosanct."

We sat down to a splendid meal and I came to the reluctant conclusion I must insist on having a few answers to the questions I wanted to ask, questions I feel sure you who listen to my story have already asked yourself, questions to which you have already found the answers. I can only say in mitigation of my blindness that I hadn't really sat down and thought the situation through.

I said: "I understood that Diviners—and forgive me, san, when I say I've no idea what a Diviner is or what he or she divines—were most secret."

"Indeed," said Mishuro. He leaned on the table, peeling a squonch with a small gold-handled knife. The rich juicy smell filled the small eating room. "Indeed." He stared fixedly at Mevancy and then switched his gaze to me. But it was to and of Llodi that he spoke. "I sense here something strange. I ask you, Llodi the Voice, to take employment with me as a bodyguard. As for my secrets; yes, they are real. I am not called a Diviner, a dikaster, for nothing."

Mevancy opened her mouth to speak but he went on: "There is mischief here. Evil, that I can sense, and evil that fills me with foreboding."

"There is sorcery involved?" demanded Mevancy.

"I—I am not sure—"

"A damned Wizard of Loh!" I said. And added: "I mean a Wizard of Walfarg."

"No, I do not think so." Mishuro stopped peeling the squonch and wiped his forehead with the back of his hand. "No. If it were, we were in far worse case. I have the strongest feeling evil is at work. I ask you to help me."

A scuffle and a breathy voice, more squeaky than hoarse, said: "I am here, master."

"Yes, yes, Lunky. You are a good fellow. But I think a strong arm is required now. Llodi—"

"Strong arm!" burst out Lunky. "Why, Walfger Drajak is like a woflo—!"

"Quite!" said Tuong Mishuro, dikaster, and Lunky subsided, chastened.

Thinking that this man was the target the Star Lords wished us to protect, and therefore he was assisting us in our duty, I was happy to accept. I should have remembered that the Lady Mevancy headed up this team, by Vox!

"We-ell," she said, pursing up her lips. "We have heavy commitments, san."

He put that heavy Buddha-like head on one side, regarding her from under heavy lids. "Yes, I quite see that. I can offer you the hospitality of my house, as well as what protection that affords, as you assist me."

I said: "The san speaks good sense. There is evil about. This solution to some of our problems works for me."

"Yes, yes, cabbage. Do let me do the thinking."

Llodi was ungentlemanly enough to emit a snort through his nostrils. I, although no gentleman, remained silent, looking at this girl not in anger or in sorrow, rather in admiring wonder.

"Yes, well, san," she said at last in her brisk voice. "I would be happy to accept your kind offer." She frowned at me. "As will Walfger Drajak."

Llodi was only too eager to join in, and he'd be paid! So the deal was concluded and the simple bokkertu made

Tuong Mishuro sent a parcel of slaves under a lesser majordomo to Mistress Lulli Quincy's lodging house with a note to collect our belongings, scanty enough though they be. That, I felt, could not be helped. Anyway, if

Hangol or Hargon decided to deal with us they'd very soon find out where we were. I found myself wondering if that great rast Hargon, the Ascetic, came from Hamal like his companion in crime Hangol.

As for the evil involved, if it was not sorcerous in origin then we ought to deal with it adequately. If it was sorcerous, I harbored the gloomiest forebodings that San Tuong Mishuro, Diviner or no, was not your regular thaumaturgist who would go up in magic against a Wizard of Loh. Mishuro had suggested that if sorcery was involved it was not the work of a Wizard of Loh, or Wizard of Walfarg as he ought rightfully to be called here in Loh. There were many other cults and secret societies of sorcerers. Even if it turned out to be one of these lesser mages, I still doubted Mishuro's competence to handle him.

My two comrades who also happened to be Wizards of Loh ought to help from wherever they might be in Paz. Khe-Hi was in Valka and Deb-Lu had gone across to Vondium in Vallia over a matter for Drak, the emperor. And when I say ought to help, I mean, of course, ought to be able to help. Wizards of Loh, comrades or not, are highly touchy in the most odd ways about arcana the ordinary man or woman completely fails to grasp. As for Ling-Li, well, she'd be with Khe-Hi, and she was a comrade who had assisted us in our sorcerous struggles. Now I just devoutly hoped these three Mages of Loh would help again.

With the aroma of squonch in our nostrils we went off to see about our gear and accommodation. I felt I'd unraveled a little of the conflicting threads in this business of Diviners and dikasters. The man or woman might not be secret; the secrets lay in how they performed their work. In violent societies it is always a surprise to find anyone willing to agree not to lay hands on anyone else. Yet Kregen shares this odd habit with parts of Earth—a parcel of priests can walk unharmed through a battlefield. All the same, sacrosanct or not, Mishuro feared for his life. That, I felt, was certain.

Was that great rast Strom Hangol dead or not?

A little reflection assured me that San Hargon was the greater menace.

Yet he was not a sorcerer. At least, the few enquiries I'd been able to make and Mishuro's own opinion suggested that. He could be hiding his light under a bushel, boxing clever as I was supposed to be doing. The outcome of this affair seemed to me murky, most murky indeed.

Later that afternoon Mishuro was visited by a group of serious-faced people. They were closeted with him for an hour or so and when they had gone he told us that nothing had been discovered concerning the identities of the assassins. Well, that didn't surprise anyone, by Krun! He went on: "I shall be extremely busy for the next week. All my time will be occupied." His face expressed a concentration of effort, as though he strengthened himself for an ordeal ahead. "For all our sakes I believe it would be best if you accompanied me."

Without thinking, I started to say: "To do what—?"

Mevancy cut in like a chisel. "Wait, cabbage!" She half turned to Mishuro. "This is for Leotes, san?"

"Yes."

"Then, of course, we will go with you."

And, still, I hadn't grasped what the background to all this was! I suppose that knock on the head had addled my wits even further. Everything was now so obvious that a blind man ought to have seen it. Oh, well, as I thought then, I'll just soldier on and see what happens.

Of course, sometimes doing that, by Makki Grodno's diseased disgusting dangling left eyeball, is just like sticking your fool head into a leem's jaws!

Fifteen

The woman said: "Lord, the baby died."

Mishuro studied the woman attentively. Her face showed tired lines and her hair draggled and her mouth, pale and weak, drooped in defeat. She stood at the open door of her house, a mud brick dwelling, one of many, between the edge of the cultivations and the desert. Her dress was a simple sack-like garment, once a cheerful yellow and now a washed-out ochre. She wore no jewelry. Her man was in the fields, laboring, and she would have been there but for the recent birth of this baby who had died.

Hargon, brittle, cutting, said: "The woman lies."

Tuong Mishuro's face expressed nothing. "Show us the grave."

She waved her hand over towards the river and the true desert beyond.

"No," said Hargon. "No, I do not think so. Stand aside."

The smell of the cultivations, mud, crops, the wetness of things, smoked from the earth. This family lived and worked here all their lives. I thought the death of a baby could be a serious set back, or a blessed relief. At the time I didn't know. What I did know and should have thought was that each family would be different, anyway, whatever the circumstances.

The woman made a pathetic gesture to prevent Hargon pushing into her hut. A mercenary, one of Leotes's men, pulled her aside. I noticed he was not unnecessarily rough. Hargon went in, followed by Mishuro and Llodi. Mevancy looked across at me. I guessed her thoughts. What the blazes were we doing operating this close to that shint Hargon? We were those who could bear witness against him in the case of the murder of Vad Leotes. He had tried to have us put out of the way, and no doubt he'd go on trying to kill us. This task was a most uneasy affair.

The Suns of Scorpio slanted their mingled radiance across the fields and glittered from the irrigation ditches. The woman was crying now, shiny tears just silently rolling down her cheeks. Mishuro appeared at the door. His face had not changed expression.

"Kling Koo," he said, for that was the woman's name. "This is not the one."

The woman fell to her knees, her hands raised. Her face was radiant.

"All praise to Tsung-Tan!" she cried. "All praise and glory!"

Hargon stepped out, looking mean. "The woman should be punished. She calls on Tsung-Tan, yet she defies Tsung-Tan. The college is given express powers to demand inspection without exception. She must be punished."

"I don't believe that really is necessary in this instance." Mishuro spoke firmly; I sensed he knew he was on shaky theological grounds. "No harm has been done. You can quite see why the woman lied."

Hargon's fist descended to his dagger. I'd have the cramph's head off before he had time to get the point within an inch of Mishuro.

"Yes, some do, some do not. There is shame in it, they think." He had a flush along his cheekbones. "I shall report this to the college."

"That is your privilege." Mishuro half turned to Lunky. "Where is the next?"

"A house on the north wall, master. The son of a watchman."

"Very well. Let us get on, then."

We all moved off, walking sedately after the two sans. I'd noticed Hargon appeared to have no apprentice; the reasons for that I didn't know. If you imagine that walking like this with a murdering cramph gave me an itch up my back—then, by Vox, you are right!

The whole situation was, to me, highly strange and charged with emotions and passions, desires and demands. These people were like kettles coming to the boil. Anybody who got in their way was like to be scalded.

Thinking these confused thoughts and trudging after the others I wondered: Could Mishuro be the target the Star Lords wished protected? Mevancy did not think so. She was, reluctantly, coming around to the idea that the target was one of those unpleasant people, lord Nanji or lady Floria.

As we went off something made me turn to look back at the woman who was so ecstatic that Mishuro and Hargon had not chosen her baby. As I have said, the soldier who had served in Leotes's retinue had dealt with the woman as kindly as one might expect; more kindly, given the nature of these things. As I turned I saw a soldier, newly engaged by Hargon, walk past the woman as she knelt by her doorway. What he did seemed natural to him, I suppose. She was not really in his way as he marched past with his strangdja over his shoulder.

In his way or not, he gave her a thumping great kick as he went by, knocking her over with a crash against the doorpost. He laughed.

I stopped. I just stood there. I waited as the others walked past me and this woman-kicker approached.

He lifted his head and gave me a quizzical look.

"What's up with you, dom?"

I didn't bother to speak; at least, not at first. I hit him clean on the chin and knocked him down. He was still conscious. His strangdja clattered off his shoulder. He stared up at me, his face a blot of anger.

I said: "You kicked that woman. This is what it feels like."

And I kicked him, hard, where it hurt.

He was messily sick.

I just walked on after Mevancy and the others.

There was no feeling of self-righteousness in me, or, Opaz forfend, of pleasure in kicking a nasty specimen. Anyway, the poor slob had no doubt been kicked many times in his life and knew exactly what it felt like. All the same, I'd given him that experience to chew over afresh.

The incident had occurred at the tail of the procession and no one had noticed. Moving on casually I caught up Mishuro's tame slaves carrying gilded boxes filled with papers and books. Lunky was punctilious in supervising these ancient tomes. Mishuro appeared to have little need of them to refresh his memory; he did beckon Lunky over and had him produce a book bound in risslaca scale when we reached the watchman's hut on the wall. He studied for a moment, then went inside with Hargon. Lunky, holding the book, followed with Llodi. We waited outside. The suns shone. Presently Llodi came out and made a flat gesture with his hand, so we knew that whatever it was we sought had not been found here.

The next port of call, Lunky told Mishuro, was a timber merchant down by the wharves. Hargon had been receiving and sending messages by slave runners most of the time, rather like a bookie taking bets and laying-off. Now he took the lead and bustled off towards the river. Following along, Mishuro fell into conversation with Mevancy and I was content to trudge along a little in rear. Soldiers tramped in their harness and nailed sandals, their weapons slanted over shoulders, their faces sweaty and dusty and blank.

The fellow I'd kicked gave me a look; he said nothing.

"Now why is he going this way?" enquired Mishuro of no one in particular.

Going down to the river whichever way made no difference to me. We walked on in the mingled light of the suns. The street Hargon chose to approach the wharfside led past tall buildings, blinding white in the light, dedicated to the pleasures of life.

Now I do not think it is a sixth sense in the general understanding of that mysterious power. I am an old fighting man and apart from keeping alert and having my wits about me, it is habitual to keep everything going on about me, as it were, under constant review. The pattern of activity about me is registered, updated, and the information filed, dealt with or ignored.

I did not ignore the statue of the strangdjim standing on the parapet of the next building. Many statues adorned the walls: dancing girls, musicians, clowns, soldiers. Mevancy and Mishuro, talking, walked close beneath and the statue of the soldier rocked, toppled, fell full towards them.

I didn't bother to yell.

I just leaped forward, got an arm around each waist and rushed on against the wall.

And the damned fool soldier marching along at the side just marched on, and by the time he'd started to react it was far too late. He ought to have jumped very smartly away. As it was Mishuro and Mevancy slammed into the wall, the statue smashed down with an awful crashing noise, and the soldier walked straight on under it.

When we turned to look there was the stone soldier and an arm and a leg of the flesh and blood soldier sticking out underneath. There was, of course, a quantity of blood dribbling across the stones. Well, maybe I should have yelled. My decision had been not to shout and thus not to run the risk of startling Mishuro or Mevancy and making them do something stupid so that it would be much more difficult to grab them. Maybe I was wrong.

There was quite a lot of shocked gabbling as what had happened penetrated.

"Thank Tsung-Tan you are safe, master!"

"Yes, Lunky, and thank also Walfger Drajak."

"You were quick, cabbage."

Thinking to be cunning, I rubbed my arms and said: "I thought my arms were coming out by their roots."

They'd had a shock, all right. Also, Mishuro, slowly, said: "So this is why he chose to go down to the river this way."

"The shint!" spat Mevancy with great feeling.

I said no more. I had made up my mind on a course of action.

As it turned out, the timber merchant's son was not right either, and, this weird business apparently being concluded for the day, we all trooped off. Mishuro shook his head as we watched Hargon and his retinue walking off.

"I find it impossible to believe that he would raise a hand against a Diviner. Particularly as he is a Repositer. No, he tried to kill you, my dear."

I wasn't at all sure about that. Hargon had tried to catch two birds with one stone there. But I said nothing of that.

So, having made the necessary enquiries with a casual air of mere idle curiosity, and learning what I wanted to know, I waited for Mishuro's household to quieten down for the night. Eluding his watchmen was easy enough and I went over the wall like an eel. I wore the old scarlet breechclout under a plain gray tunic, and I carried the lynxter and rapier. I was, I confess, in a somewhat ugly mood. I could imagine with horrible clarity the arm and leg sticking out from under the statue belonging to Mevancy instead of that soldier. Mind you, if he hadn't kicked the woman, and been kicked, he might not have had his mind on thinking evil of me, and so been more alert.

She of the Veils was up and shedding her rosy golden light upon the city. With the directions clear in my head I went quickly along, passing without notice among the few people about in this residential quarter. A watchman at the gate could safely be ignored. I went around the wall to the rear and as I'd exited from Mishuro's property, so I entered Leotes's. Hargon lived here.

He had no idea in the world he stood in any physical danger from me. In any judgment it would be his word against Mevancy's, for I had not witnessed the crime, and who would believe some strange foreign woman against the word of a respected san, and a Repositer into the bargain? The law was all on Hargon's side.

A soldier standing guard by a gate went to sleep standing up and I eased him to the ground. I knew him from the caravan. Prowling on I found a door into the rear quarters of the villa. The place, as befitted a vad, was splendid. A deep silence hung over the halls and corridors and the explanation for that I found in the third or fourth room I looked into. This was an antechamber to a bedroom, and thinking Hargon might be beyond, I entered warily.

A woman slumped half asleep in a chair. She did not stir as I passed. In the bed in the room beyond lay Strom Hangol.

His face had the color and sheen of a moldy candle. It shone with sweat, the skin translucent, the closed eyelids heavy with shadows. He barely breathed. I stood looking down on him for a space, then I heaved up a sigh and took myself off. Even in that state he still wore his silver half-mask.

Two doors later I found San Hargon.

Two pretty boys lay on the carpet where I'd knocked them. They had not seen me; Hargon certainly had for he started up in the bed. He tried to yell. I reached him in a couple of violent bounds and gripped my fist under his lower jaw. His mouth stuck out. He made a funny mewling noise; he certainly could not shout for help. His eyes goggled.

"Listen, you kleesh, and listen good," I said into his ear. I shook him to make him understand I meant business. He lifted his right hand from under the bedclothes and—lo!—it held a dagger. I took the dagger away with my free hand and stuck the point into his throat—a bit.

My fingers and thumb bit into his cheeks and I didn't care if I crushed his teeth in. "I said listen, not play silly onkers with daggers." His eyes rolled. I spoke clearly. "You have been trying to kill the Lady Mevancy. You will not succeed in this; but you are an irritant, like a pestiferous fly. Do not try again. I shall not kill you now. Believe me, if you make any further attempt upon the Lady Mevancy you will die as sure as Luz and Walig rise in the morning." I felt proud that I had kept my temper so admirably. But a vision of Mevancy's arm and leg sticking out under the statue, a vision of Mevancy in the jaws of a strank, a vision of Mevancy bound in Hangol's tent, abruptly afflicted me with a shuddering shake. I threw the dagger into a corner of the room and I put my fist into San Hargon's eye.

He jerked back and I released him and then, as a leem strikes, clipped him across the jaw. He flopped back onto the pillows, out like a light.

Well, so much for being the new moderate wild leem of a Dray Prescot.

Leaving was as much bother as entering. I went back to Mishuro's feeling very small, with that damned itch up my spine, and without any firm conviction that San Hargon would heed my sage words of counsel.

Sixteen

The city guards came for me as Luz and Walig rose into a limpid Kregen sky.

Well, of course!

San Hargon's temper was such that he wouldn't lie down under the insult, the assault and battery, I'd done him. I did not doubt the moment he recovered his senses he was raving for his people, calling out the city wardens, going to the queen if necessary, organizing my arrest, imprisonment, trial and punishment. That punishment would be death.

I went over the back wall as the guards came in the front door. Llodi shouted: "I didn't warn you so you could go by yourself. Wait for me!"

"No, Llodi. You stick by Mevancy."

"We-ell, by Lohrhiang of the Straight Path! All right!"

So, off I went, haring out into a new day in a city that would buzz with the hue and cry for my hide.

The good folk would be outraged at my impiety—at least, I imagined so. I fancied a Repositer was in the same league as a Diviner, in which supposition I was wrong.

With me, apart from my weapons, I had the gray tunic under the fawn cloak. I had a few golden mings and silver khans left from those flung at me by my hoity-toity lady. I wouldn't starve, at least, not straight away. So

I put on a straight and simple face that would not hurt too much. Since Deb-Lu-Quienyin had taught me the secrets of changing my face subtly, fooling by misdirection rather than heavy alterations, I had progressed in the art. I looked a simple sort of fellow, with little substance and much air between my ears.

That, by Vox, was the sort of fellow I felt myself to be!

All the same, everything was not lost. I could still keep an observation on Mevancy and Mishuro from, as it were, the crowd. If Hargon, or Hangol if and when he recovered, tried to get to them, I'd be there. That I promised myself as much as the Star Lords.

With the mass of white cloth turbaned on my head and the rapier hidden under the fawn cloak I looked as much like the next simple fellow as could be. I just mingled with the crowds gawping at what went on in Makilorn on the River of Drifting Leaves. By its nature the city was long and narrow, with two extensive waterfronts, a number of parallel avenues and many cross streets. Before long I'd drifted into a section that bore the marks of poverty, avarice and vice. I inspected what was going forward there even at this early hour, and then wandered back towards Leotes's villa.

The smells of this place changed subtly. Down by the river, mud and weeds dominated; further along there would be the tang of spice, the reek of curing smoke, or the subtle aromas of scents from a woman's souk. As I have said before, the marvelous air of Kregen varies from continent to continent; I thought I'd know the air of Loh again.

As I reached the front gate I joined a small crowd watching the notables emerging. I munched a handful of sticky dates, wishing I had a piece of bread slashed across and stuffed with onions and vosk rashers, so that I mingled admirably. The guards marched out and then slaves and stylors. San Mishuro walked along in quiet conversation with Mevancy, with Llodi hovering near. I didn't notice Lunky. Guards brought up the rear and they all went off along the cross street to join the avenue—this was The Avenue of the Seven Trees—where they turned off to the right. Moving slowly with the bunch of hangers on I felt pleased. Llodi had looked right at me, and past me, without recognition. So, I walked along and heard the rapid patter of footsteps running up from the rear.

I half turned to see Lunky, clutching his scrip with papers fluttering, pelting along from the gate to catch up.

As he ran past he panted out: "You've stirred up a hornet's nest, Drajak. Hargon is one boil of fury. You'd better take care."

I felt chagrin. A little sharply, I called: "You think you know me, dom?"

He slowed a fraction and flung back: "Do what? Oh, you're wearing a funny face, I see. Well, Drajak, San Mishuro says I will be a greater Diviner than he has ever been, and not too far off, either!" And he sprinted off.

The chagrin slowly changed to amusement. There was more to this awkward Lunky than appeared. I felt pretty sure that Mishuro had not recognized me as he walked past. He might have done, of course, and given no betraying sign. Mevancy had been looking at the san and not at me.

Keeping the procession in easy sight I followed as they were joined by San Hargon and his people. They all went off to an overly decorated building with a green dome and high-jutting eaves and the principals entered.

They came out and there was much shaking of heads. They all went along the Avenue of Splendid Arches and at the second cross street they halted and I could make out that they'd been joined by another procession of similar character. Easing forward through the crowd which quickly gathered I saw the magnificently adorned figure of a woman at the head of her retainers. Her face was shadowed by a gem-encrusted turban of feminine style, quite different from male turbans. Her clothes were stiff with gems. Jewels winked on her fingers. I took her to be the queen.

Presently from the people following her a short, stout man joined her in conversation with Sans Mishuro and Hargon. Everyone else stood back. This fat little fellow had as many gems and jewels as the woman. I'd not heard of the queen possessing a king; still, perhaps this was the fellow.

The decision not to ask the scar-faced fellow standing next to me who this man and woman were was reached without difficulty. He carried a nasty-looking curved knife in a sheath, and his dirty robes smelled. The next person was a cheerful woman with a pot on her head and a child at her side. I decided not to ask her, either. If I knew the rast, Hargon would have placed a reward on my head. These folk would love to earn gold that easy way.

The woman beckoned in no particular direction and immediately Lunky and another lad and a girl walked to join the group. The glitter of gems about the persons of the two women and two men contrasted with the simple attire of Hargon, Mishuro and Lunky.

So the apprentices had been called to the conference. I began to suspect that this overdressed couple were not the queen and king but dikasters.

As we stood watching these high and mighty important people in conference with the bustle of a city in our ears, I had time to think that perhaps I'd been far too hasty last night. I kept an eye on Mevancy. I made up my mind that I must buy a Lohvian bowstave and a score of good shafts. I'd been far too confident in allowing myself to be parted from her. And, she'd be worrying about me, wouldn't she?

At last the processions got under way again and they all went off and led us to a fisherman's hut some distance from those near Kang the Hook's section.

When Mishuro came out of the hut he held a shawl-wrapped bundle high in his two hands.

So I saw they'd found the baby they were looking for.

The baby's mother, clad only in a torn gray shift and with bare feet, slunk along after the san, half-crouched and looking up. I couldn't read her expression; there was fear there, and regret—I thought also she looked jubilant. Her hair straggled across her face and she patted it back with a stunningly graceful gesture.

A fisherman with silver scales across his back standing near me said: "Siloni lost her man two days ago, the stranks got him. If the Repositer deals justly with her—"

A woman with a wide cloth-covered basket on her head, cut in to say: "Don't have to do anything for her. That's the laws."

"Still an' all—"

"And that's San Hargon. You know what he's like. Pity last night—"

"Hush your mouth, woman!" And more than one pair of eyes glanced fearfully about.

Again, I was not fool enough to risk my neck on the mere supposition that the woman's chopped-off words meant they'd all cheer for me. Oh, no, by Krun!

The baby was placed in a cradle and slaves lifted it on poles. Hargon turned to leave. The woman approached him, almost crouching like a dog, and stared up, speaking to him. He glanced down and then turned away without any acknowledgement of her presence. She fell prostrate in the fish-smelling mud.

Mevancy caught her up under the armpits.

I tensed, ready for violent action and hoping it would not happen.

It did not, for San Mishuro stepped up and spoke to the gem-encrusted woman, with a slight side nod to the gem-encrusted man. Slaves moved forward to take charge of the baby's mother and she went off with the procession.

The woman near me with the basket on her head sniffed.

"Like I said. At least it'll save him the cost of a wet-nurse." She hitched up her skirts and walked off, saying: "May Tsung-Tan have her in his keeping."

The fisherman turned away, shaking his head. He saw me and said, as it were, half to himself: "They ought to give the Diviners just that bit more power. Still, it's in the accursed laws, so it can't be altered now."

He didn't pronounce the word accursed as though it were an adjective, given the Kregish sentence construction. The accursed—they must be people.

I made up my mind—and confoundedly late, too, by Vox!—to do something positive at last about the questions seething in my head.

First I went off to the Street of Bows. Well, now. I was in Loh. The Bowmen of Loh are the pre-eminent archers in most people's opinions, although I'd had many a lively discussion with my comrade Seg over the merits of the reflex compound and the crossbow. In the Street the signs clustered thickly. The Trade of the Hork flourished here. I wandered along, savoring the atmosphere and looking in the various windows where the reed shutters were drawn back.

Wood was precious along here where a thin strip of green cultivation grew between the river and the desert. The long log rafts might swan down-river from the forests of Chem; wood here was not grown on your front doorstep. The freak storm that had destroyed many of Ankharum's fine trees would have been a total disaster here in Makilorn. Ankharum and Makilorn, two cities on rivers, and now by conquest in the same nation, were very different cities, vastly different. In the end I chose a little inconspicuous shop whose sign proclaimed:

TWANG AND DAUGHTERS
BOWYERS AND FLETCHERS

The place held that familiar smell I had so often encountered entering Seg's rooms. I snuffed, remembering.

The proprietor smiled as I went in, saying: "Llahal. May I be of service?"

He wore a decent tunic of yellow linen and his face was brown and experienced, his eyes gray. I saw that the fingers of his right hand were missing, and understood why and the vile practice that was. I nodded.

"Llahal. A bow, if you please."

He started to bring out cases of bowstaves and I began to make an initial selection by eye only, and carrying on a casual proprietor-customer conversation. Presently we got onto the pleasant business of stringing one or two. When I had half a dozen I thought choice he said: "I see you understand." He spoke in a friendly tone. "Although you are not a Bowman of Loh."

"I had lessons from a man from Erthyrdrin."

"Ah!" Well, of course, that 'ah' meant it all. Of all the Bowmen of Loh, those from Erthyrdrin are the finest.

We went out into the yard at the rear of his premises. The butts stood at the far end. Twang brought a score with him and I selected one shaft, fitted it to the string, drew and let fly. I hit the chunkrah's eye.

After three shots from each bow I picked one up.

Twang smiled.

"Quite. Perhaps you would care for some refreshment."

It was not a question and when we went back into the shop a pretty girl who was obviously his daughter was just bringing in a tray and the cups. I sat down and said: "Have you tried a steel loose, Walfger Twang?"

He lifted his cup. "Yes. And horn and ivory, bronze and wood. They serve. That is all one can say for them." I could imagine. An archer whose fingers have been amputated is in sorry case; an artificial set of fingers, a loose made of cold material and not flesh and blood, could not compensate for the loss. He saw my expression. "My four daughters build the bows. They are the finest fletchers I have ever known. Their mother is with Tsung-Tan, whose name be praised, in Gilium. Meanwhile, as I wait to join her in paradise, our daughters build the finest sets in all Makilorn."

I finished the cup, thanked him and then broached the subject of price. He told me.

I said: "I do understand that bows cost a great deal here. Unfortunately I did not realize just how much." I spread all the money I'd left over from that given to me, hurled at me, by Mevancy. "Will you take this as a deposit, keep the bow for me until I return?"

"You do not haggle?"

"Not for a bow whose worth is such as this."

"I see. I will keep the bow safely for you, walfger."

"Chaadur," I said, using a name I've used before.

"Chaadur the Horkandur, perhaps?"

"No, Walfger Twang. I leave that to my comrade."

When I went off I did not have a bow. I felt inspired by this man Twang, useless in the profession he had trained in since his grandfather's time, creating a new life out of the wreckage. Brave deeds are not all on the battlefields of Kregen or of Earth. No, by Opaz!

Thus thinking, wearing my strong simple face, I went off towards the sumptuous villa of San Tuong Mishuro.

A certain misty miasma that had been hanging around my head since the fire and my paralysis appeared to me to be clearing. I thought I could both see and think with a great deal more clarity.

And, by Krun, I needed to for what lay ahead!

Seventeen

"But, cabbage, what did you *do* to the beastly man?"

As she spoke she laid the baby back in his cradle. I'd waited until his mother had finished feeding him before climbing in through the window. There had been no difficulty whatsoever in re-entering the villa, and now I intended to have a right royal heart-to-heart with Mevancy.

"I told him to steer clear of us. Apparently he did not heed the warning."

"Oh, you! Did you expect him to?"

I wore my own face. I spoke in a suitably apologetic tone of voice that would have vastly amused some of my more disreputable friends.

"Well, I'd hoped—"

She sighed. "What am I to do with you? Anyway," and her voice sharpened, "I doubt if you've the strength."

"I see they found the baby they were looking for."

"Oh, yes. And Leotes is such a dear sweet—"

"Leotes? You give him that name—a fisherman's son—?"

She looked at me. Again she sighed. She wore a long pale lavender gown that clung to her hips and breast. Her arms were covered in her usual way and I wondered how she was getting along with growing her bindles. "I suppose you ought to know. The Everoinye must have given you to me for some reason."

"Whatever reason that might be."

"They are above criticism, cabbage! Well, I will tell you. Perhaps it will help us find our targets. I confess I am puzzled."

"Chances are it's Mishuro. Anyway, just tell me."

She might have flared up at this; instead she gave me a low look under her eyebrows, her eyes bright, and said: "The baby is Leotes."

"If that's what it's been decided to call him."

"Oh, you! You just don't understand. This *is* Leotes!"

I suppose some inkling of what had really been going on before my eyes must have made me realize what Mevancy was saying was true. At least, in the eyes of those who worshipped Tsung-Tan. The accursed needed explanation, as did paol-ur-bliem. But I had experience enough to grasp at what was going forward here. I said: "Why is the baby here and not at Leotes's villa?"

"The mother had to see to him, and Mishuro has rights until the going down of the suns."

"Then he goes to Leotes's villa?"

"To his own villa, yes."

"Yes, well." I drew a breath. "I see some of it; a lot, I suppose. You'd better tell me all. The Everoinye are not meddling here for nothing." I tried to keep from my voice and manner the habitual briskness that would have bristled her up. "Mishuro seems all at sea. One minute they're out to get him, the next and he's back to the inviolability of a Diviner. If the Everoinye want us to do a task here, then Leotes, Mishuro, Hargon, must all be mixed up in it."

She bit her lip. Then: "But how?"

"Tell me about Leotes, about Paol-ur-bliem, about the accursed."

She motioned me to follow her into an inner room. "They'll be coming to take Leotes to his villa soon. We have time." She threw herself on a chaise longue and stared up at me. "Now, cabbage, the story goes like this."

She was visibly tense, yet she spoke evenly. "Three thousand seasons or so ago the new-fangled religion following Tsung-Tan was making its way into these areas. This part of Loh is cut off from much of the bustle. Tsung is the godhead, his word was preached by a fanatic called Tan. When Tan died he was taken up to Gilium to become part of the godhead. These people believe absolutely and without a single doubt that after death they will go to Gilium, to paradise, if they deserve that good fortune."

"Otherwise they'll wind up in the Death Jungles of Sichaz."

"Just let me tell you, cabbage—if you wish to hear."

I let her get on with it. Apparently, Tsung-Tan's new religion had not swept all the old allegiances to other pantheons away; there had been some bloody battles. One particular god, Loctrux the Lame, had priests who motivated constant antagonism to Tsung-Tan. But, over the years, Tsung-Tan won over all the inhabitants and the last hard core of the Loctruxites was expelled.

"Then an evil wizard whose name has been completely expunged from the records raised up treachery. He repudiated Tsung-Tan and demanded the return of Loctrux. He gathered followers and they committed many atrocities, acts of barbaric savagery. Well—" She broke off and then said: "Well, I understand that well enough from Sinnalix. In the end a great priest of Tsung-Tan called Lohrhiang conquered and saved the religion. There were one thousand and one people taken up as prisoners who rejected Tsung-Tan. The college pronounced sentence on them, confirmed by Lohrhiang in a miraculous appearance of the godhead, Tan, himself.

"The one thousand and one were given a chance in the mercy of the god. Instead of being destroyed they were sentenced to live one hundred lives before being admitted to Gilium."

I closed my mouth. This was something like the situation I had expected; but not exactly so. By Krun, no! At last I'd worked out a simple reincarnation theory, given that paol referred to the terrestrial half of paol-vaol, and bliem is a word for life. Life on Kregen, reincarnated for a hundred times, as punishment before one could enter paradise! No, this was no simple reincarnation plot at all.

"So Leotes knew he couldn't be killed."

Very sharply, she said: "That does not make what he did any less brave!"

"No. It would not have been nice."

"And the paol-ur-bliem, the accursed, can be killed so that they do not return in another body. That terrible knowledge is reserved to few."

That knowledge would be dangerous. I suspected it involved a ritual similar to those familiar on this Earth. Tribesmen cut off the heads of their enemies to stop their spirits haunting them. Here the ritual ensured your enemy did die and was not reincarnated.

"You mean he goes straight down to hell, and no Gilium?"

"Yes."

"And Mishuro—the Diviners?"

"They serve for a lifetime. You know, cabbage, these folk really do believe that the accursed are forced to return to this world, time after time, as a punishment. The Diviners are trained from youth to be able to detect in a newly born baby the spirit of the paol-ur-bliem who has recently died."

"It's complicated, I suppose?"

"Very. Yet it has power to move emotions of awe and reverence. You really do feel that San Tuong has arcane powers able to discern the personality of the dead in the body of the new born. It is uncanny."

She spoke with feeling, not looking at me, and her fingers twined like a fisherman's net in her lap. I was not going to ask her if she believed.

"And the Repositers? This rast Hargon?"

"They are guardians. They live with the family, observing all that goes on. When the paol-ur-bliem dies and is reborn, the Repositer draws forth from the child's mind memories of earlier lives."

I said: "More likely stuffs the kid's head full for the first time."

She was pale. She nodded. "That interpretation of the Repositer's function occurred also to me. I just do not know. Everyone is so—so intense about it all."

"So the baby next door is really Leotes. And you are going to wait for him to grow up?"

"I—" She stopped herself, and swallowed. "I do not believe I gave an undertaking that would bind me. Leotes and I—" Again she stopped herself. Finally, rising to her feet, she said: "If you hang about here much longer—"

"Yes, yes. Look, pigeon, I have a plan. I'm going to—"

"Cabbage! I plan around here. You know that."

"I'm going to disguise myself and join Mishuro's bodyguard. When I turn up to be signed on, make sure you urge the san to take me on."

She was white to the lips.

She said in a choked voice: "The Everoinye—"

"You are quite right, pigeon. I don't intend to hang around here." I crossed to the window and then remembered another important reason for my visit. "I'm negotiating to buy a bow. I need some more gold."

Her head was held so far back I thought her Adam's Apple would pop.

"Why don't you take it out of your mercenary's pay from San Tuong?"

I felt my lips rick into a smile. She was, in truth, a hoity-toity lady! I said: "That's the chicken and the egg."

"Yes, I quite see that." Her color was returning and her breathing steadying. She put a hand to her breast. "I suppose I shall give you the gold."

Quite sincerely I thanked her as I shoveled the mings into my pouch.

I had compassion enough to add: "It will serve us better if I am engaged as a bowman rather than a spearman."

"Yes. Now you had better—"

"I'm going. Oh, and pigeon, if you allow yourself to be killed when I'm not around I shall be wroth, most wroth indeed. Dernun?"

And with that rather impolite demanding question hanging in the air between us, I wriggled through the window and took myself off.

The name given to the secret ritual which ensured that a person was truly dead and on the way to the Death Jungles of Sichaz was Kaopan. I was cynical enough to believe that any of these one thousand and one folk condemned to live a hundred lifetimes would prefer that punishment to being shuffled off to dance a measure with the ghostly syatras of the Death Jungles. Anyway, didn't this explain how wealth would accumulate! Hargon now ran Leotes's villa and estates, all his people and slaves, controlled his treasury. This had been going on for generation after generation. Power would centralize. The queen was probably a paol-ur-bliem, was almost certainly so.

She would also be, I had no need to guess, a genuine Lohvian Queen of Pain.

Another daughter served refreshments this time as Twang and I sat in courteous converse, discussing this and that, and in particular, bows.

"I do not decry the crossbow, as so many do," said Twang. "It has its uses."

I said: "I would have thought the queen might employ a few crossbowmen."

He pursed up his lips. "She holds to the traditions."

The refreshments being finished and the bow packed, spare strings placed in their waterproof pouch and a score of arrows fletched pale red in their quiver, I handed over the gold. Arrows stood in vases about the shop like banks of brightly colored flowers. Twang's daughters would dye your fletchings any color you wished. The queen's bodyguards, I learned, always used yellow feathers.

"Remberee, Master Twang."

"Remberee, Walfger Chaadur."

So I went off with a new face to seek employment as a mercenary with San Tuong Mishuro.

Mishuro's fat and sweaty cadade, a fellow hight Chiako the Gut, grumbled away to himself as the slaves hauled open the big front door.

"All these new men. Anyone would think the san needed them."

It was quite clear he'd grown used to the easy life and did not relish any end to the quiet time. I said: "It will be an honor to serve the san."

"Well, we really don't need you."

I moved forward into the courtyard. A few plants drooped in pots and the outside stairs looked colorful with hanging rugs. Mevancy walked out from a door under the stairs talking to Mishuro. Looking across the yard she saw what was happening. At once she started across, with Mishuro, looking amused, following. Mevancy hauled up before me and the captain of the guard.

"No, we do not need you, dom. I have a new man coming in this afternoon."

Mishuro gave me a searching scrutiny. I'd no idea if he recognized me.

"He looks useful, Mevancy. I'm sure we can find a place for him."

"Very well, San Tuong. But we do need this new man this afternoon."

"Of course."

Mevancy hadn't taken any notice of the clothes, for they were like anyone else's. The bow was new to her. The rapier was hidden. The lynxter she had given me, a serviceable weapon, was, again, unremarkable. No, there was no reason she would recognize the face I wore as that of Drajak.

Did I feel a pang of disappointment?

With a slight nod Mishuro walked off and Mevancy followed.

"Right, dom," I said to the cadade. "Where—?"

He interrupted in a splashy, frothy torrent of words. All they boiled down to was: "You call me Jiktar! Dernun?"

Jiktar, captain of a company, in this case captain of the guard, was a hard won position. I nodded. "Quidang, Jik!"

He shut his mouth and breathed out hard through his nose; but he said no more. I marched off to the guard barracks built against the wall and found a straw pallet I could claim. Well, it is a humdrum life, that of a guard. I've done it enough times, Opaz knows, and no doubt will do it again—many times.

They issued me with a spear from stores. Not a strangdja. This was a normal custom; any lord would have a store of spears for people he employed. Their other weapons were their own responsibility. So I, a bowman, stood guard at stairways and gateways with the spear at the correct vertical.

I yawned.

Then I stopped very quickly as down the inner stairway came walking the fat jewel-smothered man I'd seen previously talking to Mishuro. This time he was gesticulating excitedly, his face sheened with sweat.

"But, Tuong, she is determined on it!"

"Then you are, also, Yoshi. I understand. All the same, my view is unaltered. Vad Leotes did not commit suicide."

"Then how else did he fall? The woman was found hanging from the man. I hesitate to suggest they murdered Leotes, as you have taken them into your house." The sweat glistened from ridges of fat in his neck. "But what else is there?"

Mishuro stopped with his back to me. He spoke with measured force.

"The woman and the man did not murder Leotes. He did not commit suicide. He is fully entitled to the deduction of one life from his sentence of paol-ur-bliem."

This fat fellow, Yoshi, shifted from one foot to the other.

"If they did not kill him and it was not suicide, then it was an accident."

"It was not an accident, Yoshi."

The man made a gesture, his palm up and fingers spread. "You are telling me someone murdered Leotes? You have hinted at this before, Tuong."

By this time I felt that Mishuro had divined who it was lurking behind the face of his new bodyguard called Chaadur. He'd stopped here to have this conversation so I could overhear. I quite saw that if Leotes committed suicide, that wouldn't count as a life against his punishment of one hundred lifetimes. Immediately, many schemes for cheating the dikasters' in their surveillance of the sentence occurred to me.

Every one had been thought of and countered, as I discovered.

Yoshi rubbed his roseate nose. "Well, the man is being hunted by Hargon." He smiled. "He won't get far."

I formed the conclusion that if the fat woman controlled this Yoshi, Yoshi was being paid off by Hargon. From things that had been said, positions taken, from a knowledge of human nature, by intuitive leaps, I began to sense a pattern to the plot. I could now see the likely course of events here. What I didn't know—and that was the most important item in the whole shooting match, by Zair!—was why the Star Lords were involved.

That was a detail that Mevancy and I would have to work out PDQ.

Eighteen

What I needed at this juncture was to sit down quietly and think about the situation and try to decide what to do. What I got, by Makki Grodno's pendulous pustular nose, was red-roaring bloody action.

I'd just relieved old Nath the Lump, named for a monstrous growth on his neck. He'd worked for Mishuro for many seasons, standing guard, for whilst the person of the Diviner might be sacrosanct, his property was not. Thieves would have found rich pickings in the villa had they been allowed a free run. The gate whose watch we shared stood at the back of the villa in a brick wall covered with a pretty pale yellow flower that yielded sweet fruit later in the season, sweet rispas, and the guards watched the fruit as well come the time.

A fellow with a seamed face lounged up along the narrow alleyway separating this property from the next. He wore the usual fawn cloak, slung casually over his shoulder, and his left fist rested on the hilt of his sword. As he approached I sniffed. I'd been enjoying the perfume of the flowers; now this fellow exuded a stink I couldn't place.

"Hai, dom," he said in a surly tone. "We bear you no ill will, so stand aside."

I didn't bother to answer him. Two more ruffians appeared and strolled up. One carried a strangdja.

"Come on, come on, shint!" rasped the first. "And you can tell us where the bitch is. We don't have all day."

Again I did not reply.

"The dikaster's employing the deaf and dumb," observed one of the new-comers. "Keeps his secrets safe."

"Naw, Lefty," said the first. "This rast is insulting me."

The one with the strangdja grunted out: "Chop the cramph and get on!"

He slashed the vicious weapon at my ribs, clearly intending to finish me off with a single blow.

The sidestep I made was quick—well, by Krun, it needed to be!

I stepped in closer and the spear went through his ribs.

The other two roared in fury and ripped out their swords. The first one took the withdrawn spear through his ribs as his blade cleared scabbard. Lefty tried to be clever.

He circled around and then flashed his lynxter and slid sideways and slashed back. I caught the blade on the spear and twisted and Lefty, open-handed, received the full force of the spear butt, like a quarterstaff, on the forehead. I'd intended to knock him unconscious so he might be questioned. But the knowledge they'd come especially for Mevancy must have nerved my muscles, for the spear butt smashed the fellow's head in like a fruit under a boot heel.

Looking down at them, I felt the disgust. What a life! What a way to earn a living! All the same, the threat from Hargon, and by implication Strom Hangol, was now far too serious for us to be stupid about it.

I remembered the little promise I'd made Hargon.

Well, boasting has never been my game. Now, I would have to honor that promise.

Some of Mishuro's tame slaves cleared away the bodies and I growled at the poor devils to cart the rubbish into the yard and dump it until the master had decided what to do.

When I was relieved, early, by Tongwan the Slow, I was called before San Tuong Mishuro to explain what occurred. I told him, simply, with-out frills.

"We have not heard the last of this," he said, uneasily. Mevancy stood at his elbow. Her face was shadowed, and I didn't like the lines creasing down her forehead.

"I have to leave the city, in any case," she said. "Something has to be done about San Hargon, I agree. But if I am not here for a time—"

He gave no indication in his heavy Buddha-like face that this news meant anything particular to him. But to me, by Zair, it meant a great deal!

"You will always be welcome here," he said.

"And I thank you, san, deeply." Her voice sharpened. "If only my cabbage was here now. He could be useful, even though he's a bit of a hulu."*

"Oh, I expect he'll hear, wherever he is."

The heavy crescent-shaped lids lowered over the eyes and he did not look at me. I was convinced he recognized me now.

I said: "San. May I leave now, please?"

Mishuro waved me away and I took myself off. This time I made enough alterations in the way I wore the ubiquitous fawn cloak and robes to differentiate the paktun Chaadur from the paktun Drajak. I wore the rapier outside and took off the massy white turban-hat. Then I put on my own face and went back in.

"Cabbage!"

"You are welcome, Walfger Drajak. But I cannot protect you for very long against the just demands of the law. Your return is fortuitous."

I swear he was laughing at me.

"I am glad to see you well, san." I nodded my head to him.

"It's just as well you've come back, cabbage. I've been waiting for you. What happened to your wonderful plan?"

"I—uh—I was delayed."

"Well, we have to go to the Springs of Benga Annorpha."

I managed to stop myself from snapping out: "Why?"

I suppose she must have seen something of that in my face, which I tried to smooth out, for she said: "Nanji and Floria. That's where they're going."

I couldn't help it. "They're not important!" I brayed. "You know—"

Well, she just cut me down with a look. All these first person pronouns I'd been flinging about put me in entirely the wrong light. If she really thought Nanji and Floria were the people the Star Lords wished us to protect, then quite apart from seeing her point of view I felt I had to support her. Looked at calmly, Mishuro, although the obvious and important person to protect, was already protected by his profession of Diviner. I thought back to the conversation after the funeral, and felt I could have overreacted. Mishuro had confidence his life was not in danger through the habits of a lifetime. It would have been easy for me, an old fighting-man, to misconstrue his words. Even the idea that he'd countenance an

---

* hulu: Someone who is part fool and part rascal, whose villainous schemes usually result in their own discomfiture. A.B.A.

attack on Hargon in retaliation, now, seemed in retrospect most unlikely. Mind you, he had blown hot and cold. If Mevancy was right, Mishuro had nothing to fear and therefore no need of our protection; if she was wrong, then—well, then, I refused to contemplate that.

And the unpleasant pair of Nanji and Floria were just the people the Star Lords, in their inscrutable demands, selected for protection.

Just how much insight a Diviner had into people I didn't know; Mishuro sometimes showed an uncanny knack. Now he spoke quietly, almost reflectively.

"Hargon is an unpleasant creature, this is true, as Tsung-Tan is my witness. I confess I harbored doubts. But it is too far-fetched to believe he intends to harm me. In fact, I shall discharge this new man, Chaadur, I have taken on." He made a gesture. "He used my spear remarkably."

So now I knew he had recognized me.

When I say this gave me an uncomfortable itch up my spine, I am sure you will understand.

Mevancy and I made protestations of gratitude which were perfectly genuine and then we went off to prepare for the journey. The gold she had had from the Everoinye was holding up; it would not last forever.

"Anyway, pigeon, why are they going to the Annorpha Springs?"

"Same reason everyone else goes. Floria has a swollen ankle and the waters are a renowned cure."

The Springs of Benga Annorpha were situated in the oasis town of Orphasmot a few day's ride to the west. Sleepy, dusty, white, the town in these days existed only for service to the visitors to the Springs. As to the efficacy of the waters, mistress Telsi declared in glowing terms that they could cure anything.

"Including a broken heart?" enquired Lunky, gloomily.

Mistress Telsi looked at him under her long curling lashes and then turned to stare across the Wayfarer's Drinnik to Walfger Olipen. He had not gone to his home of Guishsmot. He had remained in Makilorn in passionate pursuit of the butterfly beauty of Telsi. She had refused all offers. Still, now that lord Nanji and lady Floria were going to the Springs, well, this might be the time she would change her mind. This, naturally, depressed the good Lunky. He had thought—and only a humble apprentice—and then the rich merchant had appeared, and, well, Lunky wasn't sure just what he ought to do.

San Tuong Mishuro, unsmiling, said: "In this I cannot give you counsel, Lunky. You must work out the vicissitudes of the heart yourself."

"I'll go and be a Todalpheme," he said, savagely.

Mevancy and me, hidden in the back of a cart, felt for poor Lunky. Still, our decision to go with Nanji and Floria made, we now found mistress Telsi and the merchant, Olipen of Guishsmot, in the company from the old caravan. If our target turned out to be one of those two I'd not be surprised. Not now, after all my dealings with the Star Lords.

"If there is another death, Lunky, I will send word."

"Yes, san. And thank you."

"I have a meeting with two of the queen's Repositers. So I will bid you remberee and take my leave."

"Remberee, san!" they called and Mishuro walked off with his heavy stately walk. I noticed Chiako the Gut and half a dozen of his men were there.

Eventually the little caravan got moving and we trundled off westwards. It did occur to me to wonder if we'd ever return east to Makilorn.

Mevancy dug me fiercely in the ribs as we lay side by side under the sacking in the back of the cart driven by one of Mishuro's slaves. "Well, cabbage. And what of your famous idea? Your disguise?"

"All I can do now is to pull my flamin over my face." I twitched the sand-scarf up. "We'll have to emerge and mingle soon if we are not to—"

"Yes, yes, of course. Have you seen anyone you think might belong to that shint Hargon?"

"No."

"H'm. Well, neither have I. And that means nothing, by Spurl."

She was right.

She turned over restlessly and this time her elbow dug in although she had my full attention. I growled: "I feel sorry for the poor devil you marry."

She sat bolt upright. She glared at me and the blood in her face glowed scarlet. "You! You!"

"Oh, I didn't mean it, pigeon. My ribs'll be blue now."

She breathed hard; but eventually she quietened down. I own, I am an uncouth boor at times. Not all the time, only sometimes.

Presently she said: "I am surprised there is this liaison between Lunky and Telsi. It is—"

"Would-be liaison, don't you think?"

"Oh, yes. I hope Lunky wins over Olipen, although he's quite nice."

"I saw a sweet little girl with Llodi the other night when he was off duty. Black hair in ringlets, slender legs, a sprite. Llodi was quite—"

"Quite, cabbage! I'm not sure I want to hear!"

"Come on, Mevancy! Llodi's entitled to a romance, isn't he? This Pulvia—Pulvia the Ringlets, I believe—might be good for him. I don't know. I just hope so, that's all."

"Yes, of course."

Funny thing, that. Our Mevancy was a bit of a straight-laced lady, more than a little correct. I found that charming.

Nineteen

"By the Black Chunkrah!" I said, and gave the sand a thumping great kick. "I wish I knew what to do!"

"I've told you, cabbage—we are—"

"Yes, yes, pigeon. Yes. But I don't like leaving Mishuro alone—"

"Llodi—"

"I know. Llodi will cope. But, just suppose, pigeon, just suppose it is Mishuro."

The day was on the wane and the twin Suns of Scorpio, Luz and Walig, dropped down the sky ahead of us. Massy banks of ochre and chocolate, of gold and vermilion, a swirl of colors high up and level banks below, filled the sky with a rainbow confusion. Shadows, red and green, streamed behind us.

"Just suppose."

"Then the Everoinye will take us back, Drajak!"

"There have been arguments between me and the Star Lords. They're not so all-fired hell-on-wheels. They make mistakes."

"Cabbage! Have a care, for the sweet sake of Gahamond!"

"All I'm saying is they could take us back too late." I walked on across the sand beside our cart in the little caravan. Camp would be made shortly and I felt the greatest unease. "If the Star Lords don't act soon—"

"Then that will prove Mishuro is not the one."

"Not necessarily! I've told you. The Everoinye make mistakes. They're old. They've dropped me in it before this—"

"It would not surprise me if they decided to discipline you—"

"Oh, they've done that. But, right now, I'm trying to work things out their way." If there is one thing among the many I do detest, it is not being able to make up my mind. I like to decide and then get on with it.

I said: "Right, pigeon. Our target could be Mishuro. It could be the Nanji and Floria connection. It could be anybody of those you pulled out of the fire with Rafael—"

"Yes! And that includes you!"

"Yes, and that includes me. There are two of us. You stick with what you think right and I'll stick with mine." She glared at me. "Mishuro is clearly the most important person involved—"

"And, as you've said and we know, that need have nothing to do with it."

"I agree. If you look at all the runners, anyone—"

"Yes, yes," she snapped. "So?"

"So I'll toddle off back to Makilorn and keep an eye on Mishuro."

She'd been walking along sturdily, striding out, head up, kicking the sand out of her way. Now she favored me with a quick upward glance, like a bird. "If you think that best, cabbage. My bindles are almost full-grown now. I do not want to quarrel with you or give you orders you think unjust."

I shut my black-fanged winespout with a snap. You see! How could I be nasty to her? She was doing a job, and trying to do it well. And here was I, a hairy old graint, a leem-hunter, a ferocious fighting-man, a zhanpaktun, and much more besides, lumbering along like a self-destructive avalanche ready to engulf her in my bad temper.

"We-ell—"

"If you think that right. I admit; I worry about San Tuong."

"Give me an animal, any animal, and I'll trot back."

Then, surprising me—but in a pleasant way—she laughed.

"Very well. And if I'm wrong and the Everoinye act, I'll be in Makilorn before you!"

"By Zair! You're right!"

Only when I was riding back astride the dinky little white-haired prey-sany Mevancy had cajoled a flushed-faced merchant into selling did I consider that the Everoinye might well not act. Mevancy ought to be able to cope on her own, surely? Almost I pulled Blanky around to ride back; then the thought of Mishuro gripped me again. Mevancy just had to be able to cope if fate should pick on her.

Ahead the desert glowed with the pink and golden light of She of the Veils. I'd always felt a special affinity with this particular Moon of Kregen. A reflective mood overtook me. In the spirit of that mood, now, I can mention that in reality the Moon called She of the Veils is the largest of Kregen's moons. It is her distance from the planet that reduces her apparent diameter to less than the Twins and the Maiden with the Many Smiles.

Shadows flitted under the Moonglow.

For only a single moment I tensed and grasped my sword; then I saw the untidy procession of Umblers just beginning to halt and think about making camp for the night. A funny lot of diffs, Umblers—erratic, incompetent, leaving behind them a trail of accidental damage. The noise they were kicking up as patched tents were pulled out and firewood searched for and children ran screaming spread across the desert. The wonder was with their notorious incompetence how these Umblers ever succeeded in reproducing. Truly, Kregen is home for an astonishing and splendid array of diffs!

Shaking my head I rode on and quite soon threaded my way through the irrigations of Makilorn.

Umblers like to keep out of the way of other folk, keep to themselves. The generally-held belief is that if they tried to build houses for themselves every single one would fall down, brick almost leaping off brick. There is only one known activity in which the Umblers possess skill, and that is a world-renowned skill. They can breed and produce the most marvelous goats. There are many varieties of goat on Kregen with a multitude of names. Umblers can husband them all superbly.

No one inhabiting the land of Tsungfaril was at this time expecting any direct military invasion from any direction, so the walls were lightly manned here in Makilorn. Moonglow and star glitter reflected from a few helmets along the parapets. I headed for the Pancheen Gate. The waft of perfume from moon blooms sweetened the air past an open drain. I heard the noises as I caught the stink.

Very familiar, those noises, very commonplace on Kregen and very dreadful. The slither of steel on steel, the slurring stamp of sandaled feet, the soggy thumps and the abruptly choked off scream of agony—oh, yes, this was the Kregen I knew.

Like phantoms the brown-cloaked figures rose from the shadows and the moonlight threw black and silver stains across the glitter of their blades where the pinkly-silvered steel darkened with blood.

A fleeting glimpse of hook-nosed faces, dark and narrow, the flaring swirl of a cloak, a distinct view of ornate glittery badges in their turbans— that was all I saw. The assassins vanished.

The poor devil they'd done for was past worrying about his fate here on Kregen. He would be concerning himself on the best ways of getting safely past the specter syatras and the stifling spirits of the Death Jungles of Sichaz. This was the hard and vicious face of this wonderful world that sometimes lay dormant so that one could forget the horrors. Eventually the lurking beast would spring forth, snarling and shaking the blood drops from fangs that had bitten deep, tearing the life from brightness. I rose to my feet, promising the corpse's ib that I would send a party to secure him a proper burial. Then I went on and shouted up at the watchmen and they let me through the postern by the Pancheen Gate.

The sense of urgency that had hurried me on through the night forced me into a run as I neared Mishuro's villa. Suppose the san had been murdered whilst I was away! I fairly raced up to the gate and saw the figure of an armed man turning back from the little sentry box. I whipped out my sword.

"Hai, Drajak! No need for that—it's a long watch, me bein' on me own an' all. Pulvia's just keeping me company, like."

The glitter of bright eyes in the moonlight, the glint of teeth, the sense of a swirl of black ringlets—yes, this Pulvia would be a luscious armful to while away a tedious and uneventful watch. All the same...

He must have caught the expression on my face, for he said quickly: "I know, I know. But there's nothing doing since lady Mevancy went away, an' it being so quiet and everything."

The reflection that it was no part of my business to reprimand or discipline Llodi made me relax. He was a good comrade. I said: "I bid you

Mellow Moonlights," and went on towards the villa. Mellow Moonlights is just one of the many Kregen ways of saying Good Evening.

The servants told me San Mishuro was safely tucked up in bed.

I checked this information, personally, to find it correct.

Absolutely no feeling of anticlimax could find lodgment in my head. The dash across the desert among moon shadows, the bloodcurdling incidents of the night, the momentary heart-stopping apprehension at what might have become of Llodi's antics with Pulvia, and then the subject of all this concern to be sleeping like a baby simply fuelled the fires of concern. The tension screwed tighter. There was no release from the pressing sense of encompassing danger. If anything, my feelings of anxiety increased.

The next two or three days passed as though life was running along normally. Mishuro accepted me again into his household with elegance. We ate and drank, slept and walked, played Jikaida and discussed erudite topics, all just as though nothing was amiss with our existence. And the screaming heebie-jeebies clawed away at my nerves and threatened to turn me into a shredded husk.

No word came from Mevancy.

On a morning when the twin suns' radiance was fuzzily dissipated by a high thin drift of vapor pretending to be a cloud, Mishuro asked if I would care to accompany him to the villa of Lord Kuong. Glad to get out I readily agreed and we set off in that strange multi-colored light. Mishuro told me that Kuong Vang Talin, the Trylon of Taranik, had recently reached the age at which it was considered proper for him to take up the reins of management of his estates. As a Paol-ur-bliem he had grown to manhood under the guidance of his Repositer, San Caran. I received the impression that Mishuro did not much care for this San Caran. "He still has many lives to lead on this sinful world," said Mishuro. "But that is his punishment. Kuong is a likeable lad, though."

Trylon Kuong, indeed, turned out to be a cheerful, personable young fellow. His eyes were clear, his cheeks ruddy, his lips firm. I fancied that plenty of girls would take to the cut of his jib. He welcomed us warmly and just as San Tuong opened the conversation, San Caran marched in.

Well, now.

Rub a cat's fur up the wrong way and watch the sparks fly.

Yet the whole encounter was handled with exquisite manners on both sides. San Caran as good as told San Tuong to shove off and stop interfering in things that were not his concern. San Tuong replied that he was not happy at the way San Caran was handling the trylon's affairs. It was all prettily done but at the end I took the clear impression that Caran, having run the estates for so long, was not prepared to hand over his authority to this slip of a boy he'd raised from babyhood.

With self-mocking cynicism I could well understand how Trylon Kuong would be happy and well fed and chased by girls. After all, by Krun, he had money, and estates, and so why shouldn't he enjoy himself? If leading this kind of life was his punishment, one might think, you'd have folk queuing up to be punished. The reality, of course, was quite the opposite. No one of Tsungfaril was prepared to wait about for lifetime after lifetime before being allowed to enter Gilium. However marvelous a life the paol-ur-bliems might lead here, the paradise of Gilium offered unthinkable delights.

This San Caran was having his cake and eating it.

He was partaking of the delights of a sumptuous lifestyle here and now, and his passage to Gilium was assured and booked.

Oh, no. He was not prepared to give up his power and luxury to a youngster.

As for himself, San Caran wore a snuff-colored robe, with green slippers and sash, and wore on his long face a mournful expression. I couldn't make up my mind if that pained expression was that of a martyr or someone sniffing an unpleasant smell.

Absolutely nothing came of that visit. Kuong had just returned to Makilorn from Taranik over to the west and San Tuong, shaking his head, grumbled to me that there was going to be trouble, big trouble, in that quarter. "And in the not too distant future, too!"

"I suppose San Hargon and San Caran are bosom friends?"

"Assuredly."

I said: "Perhaps too much power is collected into the hands of a Repositer under the present system." I spoke carefully.

"That is certain sure. The queen has listened sympathetically to arguments in favor of altering the laws. But that always takes time."

"So in the meantime—"

He interrupted me, a following thought in his mind breaking out. "Caran is well aware I am trying to influence the queen to have the laws changed. Hargon with a new Paol-ur-bliem to care for will support Caran and the other Repositers. Yet it is the queen's policies with regard to Tarankar that should concern us all at this time." He sounded out of breath. "Well, that is not for us to meddle with. What the queen wills, the queen wills."

Later that day Mishuro had to attend a meeting and I was left at a loose end. After a few practice shots with Master Twang's fine bow, I felt in need of a wet. The evening trade was beginning to buzz, although this city of Makilorn was vastly different from Ruathytu or Vondium, and even more vastly different from Sanurkazz, as Mother Zinzu is my witness!

They did have clouds around here, once or twice in a decade, I guessed, when some freak meteorological conditions prevailed. The early wisps had not been burned off but had thickened enough to cause evening to arrive earlier than usual. Just as I passed Tongwan the Slow, who'd been told off to stand guard at the doorway, a flurry of drapery rushed towards us.

We saw a shock of dark hair, bright eyes, lissom legs flashing under lifted skirts. "San Tuong!" cried the girl. "It is murder! They are murdering Try-lon Kuong!"

Tongwan grabbed her and twisted her around. I recognized a girl who'd brought in refreshments when Mishuro and I visited Kuong. Tears glittered on her lashes; but she was fierce as a leem.

"Hurry, hurry! Send men!" She tried to wriggle free from Tongwan but he held her fast. "You great lummox! What do you wait for?"

"Tell the san," I rapped out. "I'm on my way."

With that I sprinted out from the villa and tore off along the road to Kuong's.

As I ran, this particular plot came clear in my mind. Mishuro had rattled San Caran who'd decided to act at once. If Trylon Kuong was dead, then a new Trylon Kuong must be found. Caran, as the Repositer, would care for and guide the baby. Mishuro had mentioned that the binding oaths all dikasters took to serve Tsung-Tan faithfully and truly in the matter of Repositing and Divining seemed not to bind Hargon or Caran. He'd sounded sad at this falling away of standards. Mishuro probably couldn't fully comprehend that a person who swore in as a dikaster might not truly believe in paol-ur-bliem. What that kind of person would believe in would be the power and wealth accruing. By Krun, yes!

One or two folk glanced at me curiously; no one offered to stop me.

I welted into Kuong's front gateway to find no sign of guards. Caran had had seasons to suborn them to his service. I began to feel I must be too late.

In the event, what Caran had arranged smacked of the over cautious. Instead of getting the trylon's guards to despatch him, Caran had hired professional assassins and seen the guards were removed from the vital posts. That way, no accusing finger could point to the Repositer.

So confident was Caran, and—evidently—so mean, he'd hired only two stikitches. Well, as I burst into Trylon Kuong's rooms, these fellows looked highly colorful in their black robes and masks and assortment of lethal cutlery.

What did surprise me was to spot San Caran in person skulking beside a tall jar packed full of petals. The subtle perfume scented the rooms sweetly.

"Get on, get on!" he was shrieking as I rushed in. "He is only a boy!"

The boy had a sword in his fist and was putting up a doughty defense.

San Caran screamed: "Kill him! Kill him!" He was practically foaming at the mouth, wrought up with passion and impatience. When he saw me he screeched: "Your backs! Another one! Slay them both!"

Although I had no great respect for the professional competence of these local assassins, they at least did not allow me to leap on them from the rear in total surprise. One continued to foin with the trylon as the other swung about to deal with me. He was not quite quick enough and he went down as I withdrew the lynxter from his throat. At this Caran let out such a screech I imagined he'd ripped his own throat out and hurled himself forward, a long dagger a bar of glitter in his fist.

Kuong took a scratch across his cheek and he fell back, panting, and dashing the hair out of his eyes with his left hand. His assailant pressed forward in silent triumph as Caran reached us. There was no time to think. I saw the way of it, and the two targets, the two tasks, and acted.

A vicious leap bundled me bodily into the side of the assassin as Caran struck and my sword deflected his blow. The blade snouted forward as it were of its own accord and slid between Caran's ribs. At the same time my left fist came around and clouted the assassin behind the ear. He did not fall down. Caran let out a gurgling sigh and as the lynxter withdrew sank to his knees. The assassin took all this in as he swung about from Kuong, recovering his balance.

He made what must have seemed to him the right decision and he began to twist about ready to run off. My blade whistled around, low and flat, and sliced all across his abdomen. He let out a single shriek and collapsed.

"That was—" said Kuong. "You are very quick."

"Well, now, trylon," I said. "We have one dead Repositer on our hands."

Kuong visibly recovered himself. His face began to resume a semblance of normal color. He put a hand to his forehead. Then he said: "Do not fret, Walfger Drajak. Caran has forfeited by his actions any honor and protection his position would have afforded him. You have nothing to fear from the college."

I own I felt genuine relief at that. Messing about with other peoples' laws and customs is a risky business. Look what had happened before, and then I'd only spoken a trifle sharply to a Repositer!

Kuong was fully recovered by the time a crowd of guards and servants from Mishuro's burst in. Tongwan slashed his spear about, looking fierce. "I wasn't slow this time, by Yakwang!"

I agreed he had been commendably quick and then, looking about, said: "Where's Llodi?"

"He has been left to guard the main inner door," snapped out Chiako the Gut. He was anxious to make his position of authority plain in these important affairs. "I do not neglect my duty."

Just about at that point I saw the horror.

I knew.

Without bothering to shout, without a word, I rushed madly from the room, knowing already the plot had worked and I was a blind and stupid cretin.

Twenty

A blind cretinous fool! An onker, an onker of onkers, a get onker! I ran. By Zair, how I ran!

I didn't even bother to change my face from Drajak to Chaadur. There was no time for subtlety now, no time to disguise myself from the wrath of San Hargon. The time had passed and I'd been sucked in like any green coy. Now I had to race for San Tuong Mishuro faster than a speeding crossbow bolt—and bearing the shriveling knowledge I was already too late.

Because his guards had rushed off to the assistance of his friend the trylon, Mishuro's gates stood unguarded. Like a maniac I roared in and through the villa charging for the inner doors where Llodi the Voice stood on duty.

He lay on the floor, his hand spread against his side. Dark blood welled between his fingers and stained the rugs across the marble pavement.

"The san—" he choked out, scarcely able to speak. His eyes glistened. He stared at me with the awful knowledge of what had been accomplished here distorting his features. "Pulvia—"

"Rest easy, dom," I said as I ran on without breaking my stride. "I'll get help to you afterwards."

He choked out a groan and slumped back and the dark blood dribbled between his fingers from Pulvia's treacherous dagger stroke.

As I sprinted I saw that my earlier feeling that the name Pulvia was too heavy for a light-minded flirtatious girl had substance. Except that the reverse was the case. The merry ringletted girl was the disguise; the heaviness of the name suiting the dark treachery that had struck Llodi down in his own blood.

My legs flew over the rugs and the tesserae. From Llodi's condition I judged that little time had elapsed since Pulvia ran through these corridors brandishing her bloodstained dagger. She might have had to take time to open the doors to admit accomplices, fellow stikitches. I took heart. There was still a chance to reach Mishuro before they did for him!

A vast and rotund ceramic jar stood jutting from the corner of the corridor ahead and I took absolutely no notice of the designs patterning the glistening surface but just hurled around, giving the jar a thump as I rushed past. It toppled over and burst with a thunderclap. Shards of china flew everywhere.

That thunderous noise echoed between the walls, and the booming crash framed in sound the apparition that confronted me, waiting for me.

I skidded to a halt.

My breathing remained even and steady. I looked at the man sitting in his skin-covered chair. That chair with its broad armrests and curved legs engulfed him in skin and scale comfort, with peacock feathers ready to wave a wafting zephyr against the stinks that clearly stank in the places where he habitually lived. The predominant color among the streaks of green and black of chair and robing was red—red! It was not the brave old scarlet of Strombor but a smoky sullen red like the banked furnace fires of hell.

His robes streamed away from artificially widened shoulders, revealing a scaled shirt, with many golden adornments and a broad golden collar. His hands were bone white and grasped the haft of a double-handed axe resting between his knees. A little scaled creature with a silver collar crouched against his booted right leg and a half-naked girl with flowing yellow hair clasped his booted left leg. And so I looked up at his face.

Incongruously he wore a thick brown beard—but no moustache—to adorn the utter pallor of his face. White, like freshly-scraped chalk, that face of horror. The bone structure clearly showed through paper-thin skin. The lipless mouth revealed a double-row of fang-like unhuman teeth pressing outwards from the wide jaws. Nostril slits only pulsed regularly above that trap mouth. And the eyes! Not utterly black, yet all the blacker for that infusion of dark blue, eyes that bulged and glistened with the uncanny red glow of rhodopsin; eerie, dominating, demanding, the eyes of a devil...

In complete silence the chair lifted from the carpets, rose into the air to hover a pace above the floor.

There was much much more to this man and his chair; at that time of our first confrontation I was in a hurry to pass and took notice only of what I have described. I drew in a breath and took a first tentative step forward.

From the wall at the side of the chair a thing emerged into the corridor. It slid through the solid wall as though passing through a cloud.

Diabolically-formed, this thing. On two scaled legs it stood man high and with a torso and a squat, flat head with bone ridges above the eyes. But the thing that took all my attention waved undulating before it as it advanced. Instead of arms this monstrous creation possessed four tentacular appendages. Each had a pseudo-head at its tip, a bulb-like growth containing two eyes set beside the fanged mouth. Each mouth opened and closed as the thing bore down on me, each seeking individually to rip away portions of my flesh to gulp down its intestinal tract to join the other mouths' offerings in this thing's stomach. Oddly, there was no stinking stench in a miasma about the thing.

Of course not—this thing was an apparition, an illusion. It had just oozed through the solid wall; it might be real, and of that I had my doubts; it most certainly was not here in this corridor before me.

A voice like the whine of a draught under a door spoke from somewhere.

"Wait, Arzuriel."

The scaled horror before me halted, and the fanged mouths wove patterns in the air.

From a haze of smoky-red blackness at the rear of the chair two white arms emerged. They were the rounded arms of a woman and the plump hands held a convoluted and massive crowned helmet above the man's head. Slowly the arms descended to place the crown upon the man's hairless head.

That helmet told me many details, and all were of horror and despair.

The helmet lifted high above the man's forehead, bigger than his own face. The crown segment was formed from a curved rank of tridents. As a visor, the shape of a barracuda's head had been fashioned in gold to shield the man's eyes. Silver fish-faces crowded in sculpture around the helmet. A brown drapery was just visible swathed around at the side. The central portion at the front represented a ferocious fish-head, needle teeth exposed, malevolence personified. A swift and scared glance would easily confuse—was this creature a man wearing a fish-faced helmet, or was he a fish with a man's face as a neck adornment?

I own I was glad I'd seen the bastard before the white plump womanly arms had placed the helmet upon his bald head.

The vision of Pulvia running through this corridor carrying her blood-stained dagger nerved me. She might have accomplices. This thing before me, this Arzuriel, was just an illusion. I leaped forward.

A fanged mouth at the end of its tentacle swept for me. I ignored it and plunged on.

The damned mouth closed its double-row of teeth on my left arm and ripped away a mouthful of skin and flesh. I yelled. Absolutely furious I slashed the lynxter down and the severed mouth skipped from the green-stumped end of the tentacle. The dratted thing was real! Another mouth gaped for me and the lynxter beheaded it and then sliced around to complete the foursome.

Arzuriel slobbered from his wide mouth and lurched forward onto the blade of the sword. I wrenched it about a bit before I withdrew. If this damned fellow in his chair was real I'd have him, too, the cramph! By Krun, yes!

I leaped the wallowing Arzuriel and plunged for the chair. I saw the man's face. Scraped white, with black and redly-glaring eyes, mouth ricked into a snarl, it bore the utmost malice. I'd give the rast malice!

My sword slashed down—and through the man and so sliced up a floor-carpet. I hauled it up again, breathing heavily, and glared upon the true apparition.

The man's keening voice whined: "You will never succeed, Dray Prescot. For I am Carazaar. Already my plans are past your powers to interfere. Farewell, prince of fools!"

And with a blink and a wink this bastard of a Carazaar was gone.

I span about. Arzuriel had gone, too, and his severed mouths, gone off to practice more deviltry with his master Carazaar I did not doubt.

What an unhealthy couple!

This Carazaar and his pet Arzuriel had delayed me. But I refused to believe I was really too late. I rushed on, haring along the corridors and bursting past the doors to slide at last into San Tuong Mishuro's bedchamber.

Just as San Caran had been unwilling to trust tools to finish his job, so San Hargon had been unwilling to trust either Pulvia or his hired assassins. Two poor little serving girls lay butchered on the rich rugs. Their slender limbs and light draperies looked pathetic as they lay there, wantonly cut down. This kind of unnecessary slaying always infuriates me. Two black-clad fellows were turning away from the handmaids and before I did anything else I lit into them like a hurricane.

They both went down, chopped as they had chopped the girls, before they knew what was happening. One minute they were engaged on striking down pretty happy doomed little girls; the next they were trying to figure out a way past the deadly syatras of the Death Jungles of Sichaz. Bad cess to 'em!

San Hargon glared across at me from the inner doorway leading to San Mishuro's bedroom. He screeched something indescribable and ran back into the inner room. The door slammed shut.

I just charged full tilt at the door.

I bounced.

San Hargon had planned, and planned well, and it was down to me to thwart the fellow. No stupid lenken door was going to stand between me and doing whatever had to be done on the other side—no, by Vox!

Had I been a Vengali Sorcerer from Vinkleden I'd have worked up a spell and hurled it at the wall around the door, turning stone to mud, so that the door would fall forward—slurp!—from the wall. As I was not one of those mysterious beings, a Vengali Mage of Vinkleden, I took ten measured steps back, set myself, whooped in a great lungful of air, and hurled myself forward.

Mentally, I was shouting: *"Cha-a-arge!"*

That door was damned hard. I hit it full tilt and felt the impact all along my shoulder and side and then with a screeching ripping splintering the door fell inward off its hinges and I was stumbling forward off balance across soft carpets.

Something went *whick!* past my ear.

The dagger—it wasn't a terchick—hit the wall beside the ripped-off door and fell unseen to the floor. It did not tinkle on those thick soft carpets. San Hargon glared at me from beside the bed, half-crouched, the other dagger in his fist glistening red, red in the mellow light of the lamps.

Pulvia lay at his feet, face down. In the lower centre of her back a red splodge glistened like a flower, crimson petals spreading across her gown.

The rast had stabbed his instrument of murder to silence her for ever.

So I looked at the canopied bed.

"You're done for, you shint!" screeched Hargon. "Done for! You will take the blame for all this!" He panted with the violence of his emotions.

On the bed the limp figure of San Tuong Mishuro lay sprawled. One arm dangled loosely down from the edge of the bed. His face lay in shadow.

Beneath that face his throat was a mere red splodge.

Pulvia had slit his throat as he slept.

I felt the ice creeping along my limbs.

Mishuro was dead. I had failed. This was disaster—yet I could barely comprehend yet what that disaster meant.

San Hargon had won and his will had been carried out and he had slain Pulvia, the instrument of that will. No doubt he would have more guards at hand to summon, to arrest me, to carry me off to torture and to death.

I threw the sword up in the air and caught it between forte and hilt.

I stared venomously at Hargon.

"At least, you kleesh, you will not benefit from your treacherous murderous ways!"

The sword flew true. The point took him in the throat and the blade crunched on and almost—almost!—the hilt smashed into his chin.

There was no need to take any more notice of San Hargon.

I stared sickly at the bed, and the dead form of San Tuong Mishuro.

Disaster? Utter, complete, dreadful disaster!

I had failed the Star Lords.

I straightened up, breathing deeply, smelling the raw stink of freshly spilled blood. Utter disaster!

Into that closed bedchamber crept an insidious blue radiance. I stood straight, stony-faced, empty-handed, waiting for whatever fate would be meted out by the Star Lords.

Even then, even then in that moment of utter horror—and especially then in that moment of utter horror—I felt my thoughts twine lovingly to Delia, to my Delia of Delphond, my Delia of the Blue Mountains. Agony awaited me, I thought, the sundering of four hundred light years from all I held dear.

So, straight and despairing, I waited for the Star Lords' sentence.

SCORPIO ASSASSIN

Dray Prescot

Dray Prescot has been described as a man above middle height, with brown hair and level brown eyes, brooding and dominating, with enormously broad shoulders and powerful physique. There is about him an abrasive honesty and an indomitable courage. He moves like a savage hunting cat—swift, sudden and lethal.

The superhuman Star Lords have brought him to Kregen where, in pursuance of their schemes for that marvelous and terrifying world, he has managed to be successful on his own account. Reared in the harsh conditions of Nelson's Navy he was not successful on Earth. Now he has abdicated the throne of the Empire of Vallia. The empress, the divine Delia, agreed wholeheartedly in this decision—but she has been busy about affairs for the Sisters of the Rose, and Prescot has been sent on a hair-raising mission for the Star Lords.

Down in the southern half of the continent of Loh, in an isolated desert land where the belief in reincarnation as a punishment is firmly accepted, Prescot and a new comrade battle intrigue and assassins and attempt to follow the desires of the Star Lords. This new kregoinya is Mevancy nal Chardaz, a most spirited lady who means to keep Prescot thoroughly in his place.

Not completely sure if the guardian Tuong Mishuro is the man the Star Lords wished protected, Prescot and the guards have been hoodwinked. Prescot races to Mishuro's assistance, to arrive too late.

At this point the volume called *Scorpio Reborn* ended. Now this volume, *Scorpio Assassin*, takes up the tale.

Alan Burt Akers

One

Absolute dismay gripped me. I had failed the Star Lords! Utter disaster!

Those unpredictable and intolerant superbeings did not tolerate failure.

Blueness grew around me in that bed-chamber of death. I swear blueness grew and thickened around me. I stood there, empty-handed, my sword still buried in the throat of San Hargon who slumped by the bed. Beside him, the still form of Pulvia lay face-down on the floor. On the bed rested the body of San Mishuro, freshly slain, the man I believed the Star Lords required me to protect. So I stood there waiting for the enormous spectral blue form of the Scorpion to materialize and seize me up into the whirling coldness between the stars. The Everoinye would send their Scorpion to snatch me back to Earth, to leave all I loved on Kregen—perhaps forever.

I swear that bedchamber was irradiated with the blue radiance.

Perhaps I could defy the Star Lords, not as I once had done, stubbornly, foolishly, and so been banished to Earth for twenty-one years. Perhaps I could this time fashion those defenses of the mind I had been working on to deflect the wrath of the Star Lords, divert their desires? As I stood there, panting, seeing the corpses and the blood as through a blue mist, I screamed silently inside my head: "No! No! I will remain here on Kregen!"

After all, the Star Lords required my help here. They had told me that. There were so many things to be done the problem was where to begin.

A voice, shrill with passion, ripped through my tangled thoughts.

"There he is! He has killed the san! Cut him down!"

The blueness vanished and the mist cleared.

Through the open door of the bedchamber leaped two black-clad men disguised in black masks and brandishing swords. San Hargon, sprawled by the bed with my sword through his neck, had, indeed, brought reinforcements, and here they were ready to avenge the death of their employer.

The sword sticking in Hargon was a local weapon, a Lohvian lynxter, given to me by my fellow kregoinye Mevancy. The two assassins must have seen my empty hands as they rushed on me, and no doubt this pleased them.

I must admit I felt the blood in my head. I ripped out my rapier, a foreign weapon in these parts, and charged full tilt at the assassins. I admit it. I yelled with ferocious venom, charged with the awful anticipation of a horrendous future parted from Kregen, I shouted like any frightened spear-carrier in the ranks. I was considerably wrought up. I still believed I was due to be hurled contemptuously back to Earth and I didn't intend to land up there badly wounded, no by Vox!

So I just tore into these two assassins, stikitches of some quality, and our blades met in that spine-tingling screech of steel on steel.

They quite clearly had no conception of rapier work. Their cut and thrusters faltered and fell short as I showed them a few sword tricks that probably would not be of the slightest use to them where they were going. The rapier slid on—one, two—and I stepped back. The bodies slumped to the thick carpets. I own I felt very little shame—far less than a similar performance in other circumstances would have warranted—very little at that petty performance. There would have been no point in trying to question them. What had happened here was plain to see in the blood-smeared corpses.

The rapier was wiped clean on a black facemask, then I crossed to Hargon and retrieved my lynxter. Standing like that, running the black cloth up and down the blade to remove every last smear of blood, I heard the trampling noise of armored men advancing along the corridor towards the bedchamber.

There was probably a secret way out; there was certainly no time to search for and find the hidden catch to open the secret door. Somewhat like a savage beast at bay I glared around, determined to smash a way through these confident armored men, and belting them left and right tear off into the darkness. That was the plan.

The first man through the door was Trylon Kuong.

My sword described a brief arc in salute, then I thrust the clean blade back into the scabbard.

"What goes forward, Drajak—?" he began, and then saw the shambles, and so checked. Men closed up to his rear and all stopped, staring into that bedchamber of death.

"We were tricked, Kuong." I spoke harshly. He was a trylon, an exalted rank of nobility, and I wanted to get on simple straightforward terms as soon as possible. I did not intend to kowtow to him. He was very young still, and I had taken a liking for him. With his clear eyes, ruddy cheeks and firm lips he looked every inch your high-spirited young tearaway, a rip-roaring bladesman, a noble spark. I fancied he might be all of these things, given time; but his upbringing so far at the hands of his guardian, San Caran, had produced a young fellow more moody than he should be, even allowing for the peculiar circumstances of his many lives on Kregen.

"San Tuong is dead—and so is San Hargon—Drajak—what—?"

I gestured around the room. The raw stink of spilled blood has always been offensive in my nostrils, although, Zair forgive me, I have smelled that stink often and often. The warmth of the place clogged. "As you see, Kuong, San Hargon used this poor woman as a tool. She tricked her way past the guards and stabbed Tuong Mishuro to death. Then Hargon stabbed her. When we all rushed off to your villa to stop your precious San Caran killing you, that was half of the plan. This half worked." I eyed him. I had no compunction in reminding him of his debt, for I saw his use to me and to the plans of the Star Lords for the future. "The half that entailed your death, thankfully, failed."

"Thanks to you, Drajak!" he said at once, impulsively, openly. "You have my thanks and gratitude. If there is anything—"

"First we must think what to do with the corpses. You are sure no retribution will fall upon us for slaying dikasters?"

He laughed scornfully, and I am sure he was reliving those fraught moments, only a short time ago, when the assassins tried to slay him. His laugh sounded brittle. He put a hand to his cheek where the bright blood showed the nick he had taken in the fight in his villa. "Absolutely sure, Drajak. By their actions, Hargon and Caran are no longer fit to be considered as dikasters. They took their oaths to the college to become Repositers and faithful to the dictates of Tsung-Tan. They broke those oaths. I doubt if they will even receive a perfunctory burial."

Chiako the Gut, the dead Tuong Mishuro's captain of his bodyguard, having so signally failed in his duty, blustered. "Throw them in the river!"

The River of Drifting Leaves on which stood the city of Makilorn contained among many varieties of fish the twin-finned and voracious stranks. Anybody attempting to bathe in the river would rapidly become a strank's lunch.

"Aye!" rumbled those crusty guards clustered in the doorway.

I was not surprised.

The dikasters, both Repositers like Hargon and Caran, and Diviners like Tuong Mishuro, were regarded as sacrosanct. Poor Mishuro had not believed that any dikaster would break his solemn vows. Now the plot's hatching was complete, he was dead of his trust.

Again Kuong fingered his blood-dappled cheek. "It is very warm here," he said. I leaped and caught him as he fell. His eyelids fluttered.

"Water!" I bellowed.

The collapse of the young trylon seemed to break the spell of that bedchamber of death. Chiako, no doubt consumed with anxiety for his personal future, took charge. He acknowledged me as Walfger Drajak, a friend of Mishuro's. He did not recognize me as Chaadur, a name and disguise I had adopted, and he bustled around organizing. Trylon Kuong's own guards carried him back to his villa. I was sympathetic. The events of the evening were enough to cause a grizzled veteran to topple over, given that the basic tenets of these people's religion had been violated.

Only then was the realization borne in on me that I was still in Mishuro's villa, in the city of Makilorn on the River of Drifting Leaves, in the land of Tsungfaril in the continent of Loh on the world of Kregen.

By this time I'd quite expected to find myself chucked down naked in some far and forgotten corner of Earth.

The Star Lords most certainly had started the blue radiance in the room, I felt sure of that. But I had not been transported between the stars back to the planet of my birth. Yet San Tuong Mishuro had been the most likely candidate among the score or so for the position of the person we had to protect. I call Mevancy a fellow kregoinye; she was of course a kregoinya, a lady employed by the Everoinye to carry out their tasks. She might crow a trifle that I'd been wrong about Mishuro. She'd feel damn sorry the old boy was dead; but she'd be all the more keen to find out who our real target was. The Star Lords wanted us to protect someone around here; now it had turned out not to be Mishuro—so I thought—then who was it?

I took a breath outside in the arcade. I must see that Llodi the Voice, a comrade stabbed by Pulvia before she went on to stab Mishuro, received proper attention. Then I would travel back across the desert west to the Springs of Benga Annorpha and find Mevancy and bring her up to date with the news.

Oh, yes, she'd be mighty cutting about my views that Mishuro had been the target. Mind you, he might have been and the Star Lords might be biding their time before they punished me. The Everoinye were unaccountable. They had once been human beings and now were advanced far beyond the normal state of flesh and blood. I'd no idea what they looked like, how they lived, if they still needed to eat and drink. I did know they made mistakes. If they were as old as I thought, and they admitted to being old, perhaps they were becoming senile? That, as you may well imagine, was a most uncomfortable thought. Most, by Krun.

They wanted Mevancy and me to do something down here in Tsungfaril in Loh. Now I could see how gullible I had been in the past. I'd simply taken my lead from what the Star Lords presented. I'd attempted to defy them and they'd hurled me back to Earth for twenty-one horrible miserable years. Could my desperate attempt to thwart their efforts to send me back have succeeded? I decided not to bank on that. Rather, my work for the Star Lords was not over and I was still of use to them. That, I reasoned, was a far more logical explanation of events.

So it was imperative that I speak with Mevancy as soon as possible.

One result of the death of San Hargon and the understanding of his villainy was the calling off of the law from my neck. I was no longer a wanted fugitive. I own, I felt grateful for that. Having to disguise myself, having to keep under cover, while interesting pastimes, tend to add unnecessary difficulties in doing the job for the Everoinye.

Llodi's splendid fissured nose did not glow with its usual brightness as I found him lying on his back on a couch. A Needleman was working over the dagger hole in Llodi's side, concentrating on his work, his yellow smock already stained with Llodi's blood.

I said: "Will he live, doctor?"

"Hey!" yelped Llodi. "Don't shuffle me off so fast, dom."

The Needleman spoke without turning. "The wound is not serious."

"Thank Tsung-Tan for that."

"And no thanks to that murdering she-devil!" burst out Llodi.

"You heard?"

"I heard."

"I do not think she was essentially an evil woman, Llodi, just misguided and easily led into evil ways."

"She fooled me with her pretty ways, that's for sure."

"Well, you must get well soon. I do not think this affair is finished. Not finished by a long chalk, by Zair."

He nodded and then yawned as the Needleman neatly inserted a needle and set fire to the herbs at its tip. Llodi felt no pain. Once his side healed up he'd be good as new. Llodi's eyelids closed.

The doctor stood up and brushed his knees.

"He'll sleep twelve clepsydras. Then he'll be on the mend."

"Your name, doctor?"

"Wei Fwang. I care for Trylon Kuong."

"You will not be insulted if I ask you to accept this trifle of gold?"

"I might have been, when I was young. No longer."

I gave him the gold. He was alert, thin-faced, with surprisingly large bags under his eyes for so thin a countenance. He was apim like me.

He went off smartly to see about Kuong's fainting fit and I walked slowly towards the main gate of Mishuro's villa.

There was no chance of starting for the Springs of Benga Annorpha tonight. I'd have to go along to Wayfarers' Drinnik and see about finding a caravan going west to the springs. I pondered. Perhaps I could chance the journey alone astride a good mount. Perhaps. I'd ridden in from the springs alone and had not been killed, so there appeared no good reason why I shouldn't return. Apart from one. There had been rumors of raiders from the north filtering down along the river, and at least two caravans had been attacked. The lone traveler was asking for trouble.

Well, I'd leave that decision for the morning.

Now it seemed to me with the people of Mishuro's villa busily clearing up that I stood in dire need of that wet I'd been about to take when the alarm had sent me haring for Kuong's villa. Well, I'd calmed down a trifle now and could look more reasonably at what had transpired. They'd tricked us beautifully. The attack by Caran on Kuong had brought us all rushing there with me in the lead, and the way was left open for Pulvia to stab poor Llodi—no doubt in the act of kissing. Then Hargon and his bully boys had burst in and the end result was the bedchamber of death. All that followed the laws of logical reasoning. What did not follow was the inevitability of the incident now being closed.

Caran and Hargon had been in it together, in cahoots, as they say.

I felt most strongly that there were other and more powerful forces and personalities involved. Shadowy figures, hovering in the background, pulling the strings that worked their puppets. Puppets like Sans Caran and Hargon!

The nightlife of this riverside city of Makilorn, while not like the raucous nightlife of Vondium or the riotousness of the Sacred Quarter in Ruathytu, was highly colored and racketed away under the stars. What it most certainly was not like was the night life of Sanurkazz. By Zair! Is there any other place on Earth or Kregen quite so rowdy as Sanurkazz when the swifters pull in?

I went along to a stucco-fronted place where people sat at small round tables drinking the local beverages. You could get imported wines, of course; but they cost money. Also imported ales were popular in this land of near-desert aridity, whose soul was the river. I took a flagon of Shenlitz and sat in a shrouded corner and watched.

My back itched.

That meant something I couldn't quite bring to mind was troubling me.

Very well. The Star Lords had pitched Mevancy and me here in Tsung-faril. I'd bet that we had to protect Mishuro and now Mishuro was dead and I was still here so that proved me wrong. There were the others who'd come in with our caravan who had been rescued by Mevancy and who therefore logically could qualify for further protection.

That was elementary. I felt with the utmost conviction that the Star Lords were interested in this remote country with its steadfast belief in a heavenly paradise to come. Why the Star Lords should be interested I didn't know. What they knew and what they did, they knew and did. What it all boiled down to was this: Mevancy and I had to find the person or persons the Everoinye wished to care for and protect them with our lives.

Simple.

Ha!

The things to do were to finish up this flagon, find a bite to eat, and then crawl back to Mishuro's villa, find my pallet, and go to sleep.

Everything would come clear by morning.

The last drop of Shenlitz went down glug-glug and I stood up from the table, the flagon still in my fist.

A man clad in the universal fawn clothes, with a yellow turban above a swarthy face, brilliant eyes and a hooked nose, halted by the table.

I noticed the brooch gathering up a corner of his cloak, a glinting bauble representing a swordfish in a hoop. In the next instant his brown hand shot from the sleeve of his robe and I caught the evil glitter of steel. He threw with unerring accuracy. The dagger flashed straight for my throat.

Two

The flagon in my fist whipped across in a purely reflexive action. The dagger chingled a single gong-chime and span away in a flash of silver. In the next heartbeat the flagon flew the intervening distance and crashed full against the forehead of this unpleasant dagger-throwing fellow. He gave a tiny grunt and simply fell, collapsing from the knees. His face smashed into the table edge.

In the hubbub around only a few people noticed the byplay.

A gaunt Gon at the next table said: "That was quick, dom."

"Aye."

"Either finish him now or clear off schtump."

The advice, given the circumstances, was good. I nodded. "You are right, dom. Remberee."

He nodded in reply and lifted his flagon as I walked quickly to the door. The fellow wearing the swordfish in a hoop badge might have friends. I had no desire at this juncture to brave perils unnecessarily. When I knew a great deal more about the machinations behind the scenes would be the time to sort out this bunch of rogues.

The startlingly uncommon clouds that had darkened the city earlier in the evening persisted. The narrow streets lay in shadow. It did not rain for that would have been so startlingly uncommon as to defy belief. One of the more interesting stories of this part of the world related how a certain Naghan the Cheerful, being so much in love with Cheryl, the daughter of a prosperous jewel smith, asked for her hand and was brutally rejected by the jewel smith, Hwang Wei, who said: "My daughter will never marry a penniless sandalmaker's son! Begone!" Naghan and Cheryl were in despair. Out of desperation they decided to elope. They unhitched Hwang Wei's best lictrix and riding bareback with two water bottles set off to cross the desert and begin a new life. Their hoof prints lay in the sand for all to see. Hwang Wei would have no difficulty following them with his relatives in hot pursuit. Then the miracle occurred. It rained. The storyteller would pause at this dramatic point and allow his audience time to exclaim in wonder at this unheard of marvel. When all this took place is a matter for scholars.

It did not rain on this night in Makilorn.

The stars were already breaking through the overcast and once the twin suns, Luz and Walig, rose, the few remaining wisps of cloud would vanish as though they had never been.

But, during this short period, the night was as dark as a night of Notor Zan, even though She of the Veils was floating high in the sky above. The Moon She of the Veils is often called She of the Blushes in Loh. As I felt my way along from torchlight to torchlight in the street I felt quite pleased that my favorite Moon's light was cut off for the moment. I needed to get away without assassins dogging my footsteps.

Just at the moment it was useless to try to figure out who had sent the dagger thrower. Hargon and Caran were both dead and once the people they had paid had finished that contract, nothing more would be done for Hargon or Caran. Those two were effectively out of the reckoning.

My earlier decision to find something to eat and then turn in now seemed to me unsatisfactory. I felt restless. Well, by Krun, that is no new thing in my life!

A flaring becketed torch over a doorway illuminated a beam from which hung a flagon. People were passing in and out. I recognized The Tavern of Lush Bonhomie. That decided me, so in I went.

The outer walls were sheer and unpierced, the entrance leading onto a courtyard surrounded by booths, open windows, doors, all shedding golden lamplight into a wonderful brilliance. I blinked. The place hummed. I suppose other pleasure seekers in other times and places would say the place jumped. Many of the young people here enjoying themselves wore half masks, many of the women wore veils, all were well dressed, sumptuously dressed in many instances. There was wealth here, on display and openly flaunted. The scents of wine and perfume coiled and mingled. I suppose the most strange defect in that glittering display to me might seem odd to some observers: I was immediately aware of the odd effect created by the absence of rapiers swinging at the sides of the young bloods. Thinking of some of the hellions I had known on Kregen, I shook my head. By Krun! To ruffle it during an evening's entertainment without your rapier! Unheard of! But, of course, rapiers were strange foreign weapons down in this part of Loh.

They didn't even have some of the stickers the Krozairs wore for a night out when they left their great longswords at home.

There were lynxters and daggers and knives aplenty. I moved quietly in, intending to find a wet and a snack whilst I made the final decision to set off for Annorpha and Mevancy at once.

My firm intention was to stay out of trouble.

Ha!

A laughing lad lurched into my path, and almost fell, and clung on to me, spluttering, saying: "My apologies, dom! I own I am grievously at fault. It is all that Leone's doing, the wanton."

He wore a fashionable red half mask and his face peeped out, flushed, bright, merry. His hair stood in spiky disarray. "There!" he spluttered out. "There is my character witness!"

His free hand pointed at the table; his other hand clung on to me with a grip of death. Another youngster and two girls sat at the table laughing at their companion. The two lads were well-dressed and daggers swung at their belts, everything smothered in gems. The two girls wore light silk and silver-tissue chemises, long skirts—one maroon, one saffron—and much jewelry. Their faces were half hidden by veils and their hair was piled high with much artifice.

"Llahal," I said, and I could hear the ridiculous formality in my voice. "A pleasant evening to you." And, deftly, I foisted this youngster clinging to me onto the nearest chair. He collapsed, still spluttering his good-humored laughter.

So, filled with good intentions, I turned away after favoring the ladies with a nod of parting each.

Here in the Tavern of Lush Bonhomie people intended to enjoy themselves. That these folk of Tsungfaril devoutly believed that when they died they would go to Gilium, a heaven and paradise of unimaginable delights, did not alter their desire to enjoy themselves in the here and now. This was in marked contrast to many of the people I'd already met who merely drudged through this life on Kregen with every ambition and thought centered on the life to come in Gilium. I'd received the impression that the people of Tsungfaril merely tolerated this life, and had not suicide prevented them from going up to Gilium, there would be a mass holocaust as everybody slit their throats and went off to enjoy themselves for eternity.

Naturally, the accursed, the paol-ur-bliem, who had been condemned to live a hundred lives on this world of Kregen before they would be allowed to enter the paradise of Gilium, looked at living these lives somewhat differently from other folk. If they had to spend a hundred rotten lifetimes down here, then they'd jolly well enjoy 'em! There was a great deal more to learn about the paol-ur-bliem yet.

A shrill scream at my back brought me around, hand on sword hilt.

The lad who'd clung onto me—his companions had called him Wink— was falling back clutching his side. Dark blood welled over his fingers. The knife that had caused that damage was wielded in the fist of a man in dark brown evening clothes. His face held a tight intent look of utter concentration. Instantly I looked at the small brooch he wore high on his left shoulder. It was not a swordfish in a hoop. It looked to be a chavonth and wersting, I couldn't be sure. What he was was amply demonstrated by what he was doing.

The girl called Leone screamed again as the strong and supple brown

140

fingers of the thief hooked her necklace away in a single skilled jerk. She tried to struggle up from the table and the thief pushed her down—hard—and with his right hand grasping the necklace back-handed the other youngster across the face. The knife in the thief's left fist made a single threatening gesture, and the lad flinched back, eyes enormous over the mask.

This all took place within the compass of half a dozen heartbeats.

The thief, satisfied with his booty and ignoring the rest of the jewelry on display, swung about and started to run off

It was perfectly clear that Wink had tried to stop the thief snatching the necklace and had been stabbed for his pains.

At my side people were shouting, still sitting at table, and other people were setting up a racket. No one offered to stop the thief. Blood glistened thick and black-red on the knife blade.

I picked up a thick pewter plate from the table and skimmed it back-handed. Like a discus it flew spinning through the air. It struck the running thief clean on the nape of the neck. He stumbled forward, arms flinging wide, legs tangling, and then he fell down.

Spilled wine scented the air with expensive perfumes. I walked forward past shouting people at table towards the prostrate thief. He was not unconscious, let alone dead, and as I reached him he was making motions like a swimmer. In a minute or two he'd be up. They make professional thieves out of tough material on Kregen.

The knife was still clutched in his hand. So was the necklace in the other hand. Again, professional thieves of Kregen do not lightly give up either their weapons or their booty.

I put my foot on his right wrist. I pressed. He gave a soggy gasp and his hand opened. The necklace tumbled free.

"Thank you, dom," I said, and bent down and picked up the bauble.

"By Diproo the Nimble-Fingered, dom. What did you hit me with? A whole flaming table?"

"The flagons fell off," I said.

"I'd never have noticed."

"They're coming for you, dom. If—" I released my foot.

Why I spoke and said this I have puzzled over. He rolled over and sat up, staring at me. His face looked like a walnut.

"They call me the Dipensis." He stood up, warily, like a cat. "I'm off, dom. This time I'll catch the table and throw it back."

I shook the necklace. Other people had been scarcely aware of this byplay, so little time elapsed—the thief fell down, I picked up the necklace, and he ran off. I did not pursue but returned to the table where three worried young people were regarding the fourth's bloody wound.

I said nothing but hoicked Wink up over my shoulder and started for the exit door.

The other young fellow, very upper-crusty, said: "Hey! Wait a minute! What are you up to?"

"This laddie needs a doctor." My voice was harsh.

The girl with lighter-colored hair than normal down here said in a shushy voice: "Yes. Come with me. We'll take him home."

"You have a Needleman or a Puncture Lady there?"

"Oh, yes, of course."

"Lead on."

The other young man—I gathered his name was Prang—offered to assist. I said: "I can manage, thank you. Here, give this to Leone." I passed across the necklace that had been the cause of all this turmoil.

Leone, she with the lighter than normal hair, grasped the necklace and stared sickly on Wink.

"Will he die?" She fluttered alongside as I took long strides to get clear of this place. "Poor Wink! Tell me he won't die, please!"

I found myself saying: "So he's not a Paol-ur-bliem, then."

"Oh, no. No. I am, but poor Wink isn't."

The sky already showed a healthy smattering of stars and the pinkly golden light of She of the Blushes wafted down most gratefully as we sped quickly along. They led me to the narrow postern gate set in a high stucco wall. Leone had a key and she let us in. They acted in a furtive manner, so I guessed they were not supposed to be out enjoying themselves on the town in the evening. One reason for that, clearly, was what had happened to Wink. Young nobs, I surmised, all breeding and money and spirit, and as far from the workers in the irrigations as it was possible to get.

"We'll have to tell them," said Prang. His voice was a strangled gasp. "Have to. Leone—you see that!"

"I suppose so." Her voice sharpened. "And if they want to blame anyone then I'll take the blame—"

"Oh, Leone!" broke in the other girl, Ching-Lee. "It wasn't you!"

"I won't have them blaming poor Wink, not like this. No. I'll take the blame. Now, Ching-Lee, hurry and fetch the Puncture Lady."

We went through shadowy grounds where bushes and flowers grew in an abundance that showed how rich this place was. Through a door, along corridors, up stairs, into a hall sumptuously furnished. I began to surmise this was a palace. In a small room papered with blue and white volail flowers I put Wink down in a couch smothered in gold fleur-de-lys, and so stood back, and looked at these young tearaways. Ching-Lee came back then with the Puncture Lady, so I was not called on to comment on the tears in Leone's and Prang's eyes.

"Tut-tut," said the Puncture Lady in her brisk professional way. "Now what mischief have you young scallywags been up to?" She bent at once to Wink's injured side.

"Oh, Mistress Lingli! You wouldn't tell her majestrix, would you?"

Leone's piteous voice would have melted a granite mountain.

Mistress Lingli, carefully cutting away Wink's bloodstained shirt, did not look up. I heard the soft affection in her voice. "Why, Leone, would I be so cruel?"

"We-ell—we were out—"

"I don't want to know." Skilled hands inserted acupuncture needles. One thing—Wink would feel no more pain. "What you tell the queen is your business. Mine is making Master Wink well again."

"Oh, thank you, Lingli! You are a gem!"

"H'mff!" sniffed the Puncture Lady, and got on with Wink.

After that she turned on me.

"Hold still," she said in her no nonsense voice. Carefully she unwrapped the grubby bandage around my left arm. The mouthful of flesh ripped from my arm by Arzuriel, a most unhealthy and uncanny monster with four fanged mouths at the end of his arms I'd encountered just before the debacle of poor Mishuro's death, would, I knew, grow back swiftly enough. This Puncture Lady could not know that. She tut-tutted again in a most aggressive fashion.

"Playing with your pets, have you?"

Her attitude and the conceit pleased me.

"I'm not a cannibal on a self-catering holiday."

"Aha. It's your business. Hold still!"

She wanted to stick needles in me to ease the pain but I assured her I felt no pain now—which was not strictly true. She fixed me up in her neat way and patted the last knot of the bandage.

"You'd better see your own doctor tomorrow."

"Quidang," I said in meek agreement.

"Lingli—you are sure Wink will be all right?"

"Yes, Leone. Look, he is sleeping like a baby. If you do not wish to be discovered you must—"

"Yes, yes!" cried Leone. "Prang, you must carry Wink to his bedchamber. We'll—"

"Call the slaves," said Prang, off-handedly.

"Oh, you fambly!" said Ching-Lee, looking exasperation personified.

Patiently, Leone said: "The slaves will talk, Prang. We must carry Wink —and we must hurry."

Prang started up, eyebrows raised and mouth open. "Of course!"

About to offer my services as a Wink carrier, I desisted. They could handle this between them. I'd better be off. Prang lifted Wink and Ching-Lee bustled alongside as they left this pretty room. Doctor Lingli, after a look from under lowered eyebrows at Leone and me, sniffed and followed.

"I won't ask," I said, and I admit I spoke somewhat drily, "how you'll explain away the hole in Wink's side."

"I will think of a story. I am quite capable of that!"

"Well, I'm off. Remberee." And I made for the door.

She caught me up as my hand fell on the latch. She looked up into my face and put her hand on my arm as she started to say: "I owe you a great deal, walfger, and no pappattu between us."[*]

She saw the expression I instantly quelled, and glanced down, and saw her hand gripping onto my bandaged arm. Brilliant blood suffused her face.

"Oh! Oh—I am sorry! Tsung-Tan! How thoughtless—"

"It is of no consequence. My name is Drajak."

"Then Lahal and Remberee, Drajak."

When I was once more out in the streets of Makilorn under the stars, I reflected that this Leone had more to her than the mere empty-headed chit of a thing she appeared to be. Anyway, I felt I could like her.

Three

I, Dray Prescot, Lord of Strombor and Krozair of Zy, stepped out of the palace gate like any silly woflo ripe for the snare.

There was time to notice that a torch by the gate pillar was no longer alight. There was time to notice that the shadows fell thickly across the path. There was even time to hear a soft footfall at the side.

Finally, there was time for me to turn swiftly to face this unseen threat.

After that there was time only to feel a smashing great thwack on the back of my head and to pitch into the enfolding darkness.

When I regained consciousness those famous old Bells of Beng-Kishi were ding-donging away inside my skull. As I may have previously remarked, getting hit on the head happens with distressing frequency on Kregen.

Blearily I managed to get my eyelids to unglue themselves.

The light from a cheap mineral oil lamp was not too bright so I could bear the brilliance of scratching illumination on my eyeballs. I blinked. Directly before me sat the thief I'd felled with the pewter plate.

I caught a vague impression of shadows shrouding the brick walls of this small square chamber, of a table and of other men and women lounging on the edges of my vision. I tried to turn my head to see more clearly and found myself securely bound in a chair with my head between a metal vice.

If I saw anyone wearing a badge of a swordfish in a hoop I'd know I was in for serious trouble. This fellow's badge I could now clearly see was

---

[*] walfger: gentleman, herr, mister. Pappattu: introduction. *A.B.A.*

indeed a representation of a chavonth and a wersting, claw to paw, in a fanciful pairing. The dark serious eyes in his walnut face studied me somberly. The knife that had stabbed Wink glittered as he turned and twisted it idly between his nimble brown fingers. I eyed him stonily.

"Well now, dom," he said. "Now you're awake you can tell us what your little game is. Dernun?"

That dernun demanding to know if I understood him did not spit with the usual venom of that intolerant word. He sounded almost pensive.

"Well now, dom," I said, and my voice sounded thick in my ears. "The necklace was the property of the lady. That is all."

"Tut-tut," he said and—in that situation—I, Dray Prescot, almost laughed out loud. He was aping Mistress Lingli, and the juxtaposition amused me enormously. Something might yet be made of this little thief.

"You do not wear a schturval." The way he spoke was an accusation.

His schturval was the chavonth and wersting. That this was the badge of some kind of thieves' guild I did not doubt.

"No."

"You took the necklace, yet we did not find it on you. So you have already disposed of it."

"That's right."

He leaned forward and the knife flicked up. "Do not misunderstand me, dom, just because you let me go."

"I let you go because I did not wish to see a fellow creature thrown to the stranks in the river. They have nasty jaws."

"Agreed. So where is the necklace?"

"With its owner."

"You gave it to the queen?" He sounded shocked.

"No. To the lady from whom you took it."

"Oh, her. Silly chit." He hesitated. Then he said: "Not that I would relish her punishment at the hands of the queen."

I said: "So it was the queen's necklace and the lady borrowed it for an evening on the town."

He shook his head. "No, dom, if I read your thoughts aright. She was not in league with us to acquire it. More's the pity."

I hadn't been thinking that Leone had taken the necklace so that it might be stolen by accomplices, thus bringing punishment on her head but exculpating her from charges of thievery. She, I felt absolutely confident, would have treated any approach of that sort with the utmost scorn.

A throaty voice from the shadows spoke with a snarl.

"The scheme worked and this shint spoiled it. What are you going to do about that, Kei-Wo?"

"When I have decided, Fing-Na, I will tell you. Until then, keep your black-fanged winespout shut. Dernun?"

This time the word spat with vicious power.

The little thief, Kei-Wo the Dipensis, leaned forward. "No idea whose necklace it was, returning it, no schturval." He leaned back and he spoke at large, addressing that shadowy company of rogues. "We have here, fanshos, an innocent. He is not of our profession, no, and Diproo the Nimble-Fingered would not own him! Haw!"

Coarse laughter burst from the others and there was a clearly felt relaxation of tension.

They'd belatedly reached the conclusion I was an innocent passerby and not a thief from a rival guild.

All the same, I'd done them out of their booty. No doubt they'd want to take payment out of my hide. A number of people on Kregen have desired that and tried to perform the deed in the past. Most of them have regretted the foolish decision.

The bonds restraining me in the chair felt as though a good heave would burst them. The steel vice around my head was a different matter.

A woman's voice with an unpleasant cutting edge sounded from the shadows. "Let me tickle him up a bit." She used a phrase to describe me that combined insult, obscenity and contempt. "He'll soon tell me what we want to know."

Before anyone else could speak up I said in a low but penetrating voice: "So the filth on the floor in here actually can speak. Remarkable."

Kei-Wo's walnut face creased into a broad smile. He sat further back in his chair and crossed his legs. Then the woman's angry shrilling burst out. Kei-Wo spoke to me directly over that incoherent torrent.

"Now you've upset Sooey. I must warn you, she does know how to use her little knife exceedingly well." The devil was thoroughly enjoying this and perfectly prepared to let what might happen happen and glee at whoever won this confrontation.

Or—was he? Was I wrong to detect a strain of amused lightness in him? He owed me nothing apart from his life. He probably owed this gang and this Fing-Na and this Sooey a great deal. They were his people. It seemed to me I had to get clear of this contretemps under my own power.

The woman's silhouette bulked against the lamp and her shadow fell over me. She moved aside to pass Kei-Wo in his chair and the lamplight fell on her lank black hair, the side of a scarred face, the cheek sunken and marked, and a single bright eye. She wore shapeless rags. Her fist lifted, sinewy, knuckled-ridged, yellow. The knife was small and cunningly curved. The lamplight fell on the blade and glittered into my eyes.

I said: "What was your question?"

I could hear her panting. I'd expected the others in the room to be shouting and yelling and urging her on. Everyone sat silently.

"No question now, shint! First I'll have one eye—"

The knife moved forward slowly, turning as she sized up the orbit of my left eye. I used my muscles, broke the bonds, reached up and twisted the knife away. She screeched like a banshee and staggered back, her lank hair flapping about that narrow vicious face.

"So far I have been merciful to you, Sooey, for I did not break your wrist. Do not meddle with me again." I threw the knife into the shadows of a corner. Then I cocked an enquiring eye at Kei-Wo the Dipensis.

He uncrossed his legs, swiveled and gave Sooey a kick up the rump.

"Clear off, Sooey. This is no business of yours."

She hissed and drew her rags about her; but she withdrew.

The little thief looked back at me. "Your name, dom?"

"Drajak."

"Perhaps. It should be Drajak the Sudden, I think."

"If you will it so."

"If I do so will, then it will be so!"

I felt around the metal vice. "Does this damn thing come off without taking my head with it?"

He wheezed a laugh at that. "The latch in the back, right hand."

I flicked the latch and the metal sides opened and I was able to move my head again. I said: "I shall stand up now."

"Very well. Naghan the Chik will put his knife through your eye if you make—"

"Naghan the Chik may rest easy." I twisted my head about on my neck. I must admit I'd had a few nasty moments wondering if the blow on the back of my head would bring back the paralysis from which I'd suffered previously. After the paralysis I'd been as weak as a woflo, and Mevancy still believed me to be without muscles. "I shall not make a silly move."

"No. No, Drajak the Sudden, I do not think you will."

I rubbed my neck. "I was on my way to eat and drink when we met. As you will readily perceive, I have had neither since."

He lifted a hand and called: "Valli!"

Just what might transpire now I was not sure. The situation had been retrieved. I was not for the immediate chop. Much of these people's immediate fate rested on how well Kei-Wo controlled them. If he could not keep them under control and they started in on me then a lot of them would die.

I wondered if he would comment that I'd chosen to make my attack on a woman. Fing-Na had merely voiced a hoarse query about my general fate. This rag-and-bone woman, Sooey, had offered to tickle me up a bit and into the bargain had used a most coarse expression which I am not at liberty to repeat. She just happened to be female, that's all.

The shadows clustered and jumped as the lamplight flickered. This claustrophobic atmosphere caught in the throat. I was not out of the wood yet. A slip of a girl with a shy, averted face brought a bowl with bread in flat round cakes, dates, figs and a linen bag of some soft and oozing cheese. She wore a simple shif-like garment and her feet were bare. At the sound of her name, Valli, I felt a pang of homesickness.

Kei-Wo picked up my rapier. My lynxter and all my possessions were spread on the floor beside him. He withdrew the slender blade from the scabbard and moved it experimentally about through the air.

"I have heard of these swords. Rapier, they call 'em. I'm told they are quick. Still, I don't believe they have the strength or weight to do much damage in a fight." He gave me a quick lowering look. "Well?"

"Depends on the fight."

"Would you face a good swordsman's lynxter with your rapier?"

"What are the odds?"

A coarse laugh came from Fing-Na. Kei-Wo leaned back and smiled. A calculating look passed across his thin walnut face.

Someone from the shadows called: "Set Fing-Na on the boaster!"

A bulky form moved forward more clearly into the light. He was splendidly built if a trifle thick about the waist. His clothes were the usual fawn robes. His face possessed a magnificent pair of moustaches, pointed and waxed, standing out well beyond his cheeks. He looked competent.

I said: "No, I will not fight. I have no quarrel with Fing-Na despite his words earlier. And I would not wish to slay him."

Fing-Na bristled at this. Kei-Wo laughed. That laugh was calculated theatre. I began to believe he could keep these ruffians in order.

"Yes, we do not need blood spilt here. Valli! The wine, girl, the wine!" He gestured expansively. "We will drink together and we will talk of ways of taking the queen's necklace."

Valli returned with a tray laden with goblets and as I took one I said in as casual a way as I could manage, given the circumstances: "What's so all-fired important about this pestiferous necklace, then?"

The wine was a thick green Pimpim from Chem, cloying as syrup. Kei-Wo saw my grimace as I sipped.

"The wine does not please you?"

"It's not that. Just I would have preferred something lighter and more refreshing. Also I think you have fortified this."

"Of course. Best quality dopa in there, dom. Still, if you don't like it... Valli!"

By the time I was sipping a light crimson—I believe it was a Niliin from downriver and not a real wine at all—I thought I understood what all this palaver was about. Kei-Wo was a professional thief leading his band of rascals. Someone had employed him to obtain the queen's necklace. Of the four young people out on the town, who would have so arranged matters that the pleasure-loving and giddy girl, Leone, would be able to borrow the necklace? So, in addition, who were these four young people? That must have been the queen's palace where I'd taken Wink. I did not think they were serving folk; they were of the gentry all right. Nobs. Yet someone had arranged for Leone to wear the queen's necklace, and for Kei-Wo to steal it.

These notions tumbling through my head were half right. Kei-Wo quickly showed me where I was wrong.

He spoke matter-of-factly; I did not miss the steel in his words.

"You, Drajak, stopped me from carrying out what I have promised to do and have been half paid for. That silly girl will not again be allowed to wear the queen's necklace. Anyway, I imagine she has had a shock and will be far too frightened to borrow it again."

I said nothing. I'd been talking far too much just lately. And I wasn't at all sure that Leone would be frightened. She struck me that she might be a giddy girl; but she had a streak of courage I recognized.

Kei-Wo went on: "Our information told us she borrowed the necklace. As soon as she wore it, it would be ours. Yet you happened along."

Again I said nothing.

"So what must be done is quite clear. If you do not do as I wish, Naghan the Chik will put his knife clean through your throat wherever you happen to be. I am saying your life is forfeit if you fail and you cannot hide from us."

I was sensible enough to recognize this threat as one perfectly capable of being carried out. I couldn't guard every second against the assassin's flung knife, although I might deflect it more than once.

I said: "I suppose you will eventually tell me what you want?"

His face blackened with anger; then he flung back his head and hooted with laughter. "A right one we have here, fanshos! A right one!"

"I'll probably put my little Sklitty through one of his eyes first," snarled Naghan the Chik. "I'll enjoy that."

"Only if he fails us, Nag, only if he fails."

"By Chikitto the Unerring! If he does!"

"Aye." Kei-Wo returned his attention to me. "So you understand. Good. I need the queen's necklace. It will not leave the palace again around the neck of a silly shishi. You took it back, and that onker who stood in my way. They must love you in there. You can enter as a friend. You will do that and obtain the necklace for me. *Dernun*?"

Four

In a fetid alley in an unpleasant part of the city Naghan the Chik used his knife to cut the ropes from my wrists. There had been no alternative back in their hideout. I had been blindfolded and bound and led off along twisting alleys and up and down narrow steps so that all direction was lost. I'd not find my way back there easily.

Naghan showed me his knife. He shoved it under my nose.

"That's for your eyes, one after the other. Then your throat, shint. Best you do not fail Kei-Wo the Dipensis."

"The Chik's knife is very deadly," quoth another of the thieves, a runt of a fellow with a yellow-scarred jaw and bad teeth, called Ping.

The knife was not a terchick, the throwing knife of my clansfolk of the Great Plains of Segesthes, being heavier and, if my eye did not deceive me, of inferior balance. Still, I did not doubt Naghan the Chik's boasts. He had a belt of these knives around his thick waist.

I had to get free of this unpleasant company. There were schemes afoot beside their desires to steal the queen's necklace.

With that in mind as I chafed my wrists I stared about in the light of the moons. Whilst the bazaar area and the maze of alleyways here in Makilorn were hardly representative of the aracloins—the uproarious, fizzing and generally hell-on-wheels form of life in many of the cities I knew—they did have their own low-life vitality. Here villainy was a way of life. Here dark desires could be satiated. Here rogues could hide from the law in the confusing maze. Here life was cheap.

I felt I wanted to lash out a trifle. I said: "Can Naghan the Chik hit the narrow target every time? Every time? And never miss?"

"You try me, shint!" snarled Naghan.

"Any time, sunshine, any time."

He'd have started something then; but Sindi-Wang, a woman of enormous development casually displayed between the folds of her dress, breathed: "You harm him before he's done his work, Nag, and you'll lose yours."

No one was indelicate enough to enquire just what Naghan would lose.

"Kick him out!" bellowed the Chik. "Set him away from me!"

"Go on, Drajak," ordered Sindi-Wang, waving her arm and shaking like a jelly. "Just remember. Every mur of your life is observed by us."

Now this I was quite soberly prepared to believe. These rogues knew the city. They knew their part so well they'd never be caught and they'd know other gang's stamping grounds well enough to be able to keep me constantly under observation. I had to get free of them. Doing just that was going to prove a sticky problem.

"I'm going," I said, in a truculent voice, a voice I made stupid with a bravado of no substance. They snickered as they had every right to do. They'd formed their opinion of me, an innocent abroad, ready enough to stop a thief taking a necklace but a fellow who would cave in the moment his own life was in danger. I shook my shoulders, stripped the last of the rope from my wrists, and glared at Naghan the Chik.

"Don't get lonely," he said, and giggled at his own conceit. "You'll never be alone in Makilorn until you bring the necklace to Kei-Wo."

I stared him in the face.

"I'll always know where you are, anyway, Naghan. By the smell."

He tried to hit me; but I ran off.

If you feel this is highly unlike Dray Prescot conduct, you are right. I wanted to give the impression of a high-spirited person who'd fold up under the first real pressure. This would fit Kei-Wo's belief about me to a nicety.

It would also serve me if I was going to deceive them.

She of the Veils, rosy and refulgent above among the stars, had been joined by the Twins. These are the second Moons of Kregen, eternally revolving about each other. They are revered by many people in that intriguing and puzzling world for their suggestion of Twinship. There are many twins born on Kregen. Whole cults are devoted to ascertaining just what the Twins mean to individuals on every day of the season. Down here in Loh the Twins, who have many names all over Kregen, are often called the Dahemin which is an exceedingly ancient name for them. Most often in Loh the Twins are called Holi and Hola.

As I slowed to a brisk walk and moved into a cross street where the becketed torches were near enough to one another to provide almost continuous illumination, I reflected on names. Thieves all over our part of Kregen, called Paz, swear by Diproo the Nimble-Fingered. By his name the credulous swore he had eleven fingers and thus could steal with consummate ease from purse or pouch. Given that many races on Kregen have more than four fingers and a thumb on each hand, the asymmetry of roo—eleven—adds an intriguing dimension to this belief. What concerned me was to go on doing what I had to do here and go on living to do it. Thieves, nimble-fingered or not, expert knife-throwers or not, could not be allowed to interfere.

Pretty soon I'd picked up the tail they'd set on me. A number of possible reactions would have been proper. I could have become indignant at this affront to my dignity. I could have been contemptuous. I could have let red roaring rage take over and striding back have knocked the fellow's head in. The reaction I felt proper to the occasion was to estimate if they were being clever. Were they letting me see this tail deliberately, so that other trackers could follow me unseen?

So I came to what I considered a proper decision.

The idea of going along to the palace straight away was instantly discarded. I'd toddle along there bright and early in the morning. I'd go in wearing the face of Drajak and by using the techniques taught me by my comrade, the Wizard of Loh Deb-Lu Quienyin, I'd walk out with the face of Chaadur. Also, I did not relish returning to the Mishuro Villa.

So that left one course of action.

Around the next street corner I sidestepped and then waited quietly. My shadow dutifully followed me and as he came around the corner abreast of me I seized him by the throat and an arm. I twisted him a little; not much for I did not wish to damage the goods.

"Hey, hey!" he gasped. "You're not supposed—"

"I don't mind you following me, dom. Although I know some folk who'd have had your tripes all over the street by now." His answer was a gurgle as I tightened my grip. "I am going to find a bed for the rest of the night."

With a supple rotation I twisted him around upside down. I shook him. Sundry objects fell off his person, his legs waving wildly over his head. "I just need lodging money, that's all, dom. These will do nicely."

I picked up three silver khans, bit them, and tucked them away.

He rotated again and landed thump on his feet. His face was dark with congested blood in the light of the Moons.

"What'll—?" he began.

"Just tell Kei-Wo to put this trifling sum on my account."

He goggled at this but I turned around and gave him a thumping great kick up the rump and sent him staggering off. I bade him a pleasant good night and then sauntered off the other way in search of decent lodgings.

In the event I soon found a reasonable lodging house and dickered for a bed for the night. I didn't care to patronize the more expensive lodging houses catering for visitors to the city. The place was clean, a meal was provided, and I was not disturbed by prowlers seeking portable property to claim as their own. By the time I'd finished eating a huge breakfast I really did feel a new man, or, at least, a less damaged one after the events of the evening before.

The Twin Suns of Scorpio, Luz and Walig, were streaming their mingled opaline radiance across the city as I emerged onto the street still chewing the last of the palines. My shadower was readily visible, a fellow lounging across the roadway and picking his teeth with a splinter. I did not wave to him. I simply walked slowly off in the direction of the palace.

The idea that this man was the up front tracker and the shadows were filled with other thieves watching my every move was probably correct. They had complete confidence in their abilities to have let me go walking off. Without the knowledge I had of disguise it would have been enormously difficult to escape detection.

Just walk boldly up to the front gate of the palace? Well, yes. That method probably would serve best.

So I did.

Ornate and over-dressed guards stood woodenly outside the open gates. Many people were jostling in and out and I gathered from their openly voiced hopes and fears that the courts were sitting. The queen's palace served as her place of judgment. I caught the impression that folk were unsure if they'd be happy or not if the queen in person sat in judgment on them. She was fair but strict. There was no possibility of bribing her as, lamentably, there was with the lesser magistrates. The noise of the people and the acrid smell of dust, the glisten of sweat along forehead and cheek, these sights and smells were as old as people built cities and created civilization.

The outer corridors and chambers had been designed to impress. Here people were guided by flunkeys to the courts where their appearances had been commanded. I went on directly and the first flunkey who stopped me, gorgeous in yellow robes and much trailing silver-laced cord, answered my question.

"Lord Wink? Certainly, walfger. You will find him in the Chambers of Luxurious Rest—the old Chemzite Chambers. So along this hall to the stairs and through the courtyard beyond." He gave me instructions and I found my way through the warrens of the palace without difficulty. I recognized the last set of halls and corridors. Here I had hurried carrying Wink, with Leone and the other two hovering anxiously. The direction from which I was coming was the way Ching-Lee had scurried off to find the Puncture Lady.

Where last night a door studded with brass nails had simply been pushed open by Leone, today a tough-looking guard stood alertly. He hefted a strangdja, and that vicious glittering weapon could take my head off.

"Llanitch!" He spoke and meant what he said. Llanitch is a word meaning Halt; but it is more than that, for it carries the clear implication that if you do not stop stock-still in your tracks you will probably wake up in the Ice Floes of Sicce pondering your mistake.

I stopped stock-still.

"Drajak to see Lord Wink!"

I spoke as a military man, snapping it out.

He slammed the butt of his strangdja twice on the door and it opened and Ching-Lee's face peered through.

"Drajak to see the Lord Wink!" bellowed the guard, not taking his gaze from me.

Ching-Lee saw me, and fluttered her eyelashes. "Oh, it's you! Well, you'd better come in. And don't make a noise."

The guard swished his strangdja out of the way and I went in.

We did not stop in the pretty room papered in blue and white volail flowers but went on through the way Prang had carried Wink. We found him in his own bed in his chambers within this wing of the palace, The Chemzite Chambers, now renamed in the florid Makilorn way the Chambers of Luxurious Rest. He was propped up with a mass of pillows and was playing Jikaida. His opponent was a lean, narrow-faced man who, whilst clearly a man who did not pamper himself, was, I judged, not your full fanatical ascetic. He was smiling at Wink as he moved a piece on the board, saying: "I will put your lack of concentration down to your injury, Wink, my boy."

"Your sarcasm does you credit, san."

So this fellow was a san, and you don't get called a master or dominie or sage on Kregen without very good cause. His smile made his narrow face more attractive, and by the laugh lines around eyes and mouth I fancied he liked to enjoy the quiet joke or three. He wore a soft lounging robe of yellow silk and his slippers—and here I found myself heaving up a sigh— were bright red velvet and with huge curled up toes.

Wink made a move and then slumped back against the pillows.

"You are in pain?" The narrow face lost its smile.

"No. No, San Chandro. Just itchy. Perhaps—"

"Of course."

San Chandro stood up and saw Ching-Lee and me entering. "Wink needs the Puncture Lady. I'll—"

"I will go, san," said Ching-Lee. "This is Drajak." And she hurried off back into the palace.

"Drajak!" called Wink. "They told me, and I remember. I owe you my thanks."

"Oho!" quoth San Chandro. "I understood you to say you accidentally fell over on your knife, Wink. What is this about Drajak here?" Then he turned to me, his smile returning, to say: "Llahal and Lahal, Drajak. I am remiss in my manners, I fear."

"Llahal and Lahal, san. What Lord Wink says is so. Believe me."

He gave me a mighty shrewd look. Then: "And is it just Drajak alone?"

"I have been called Drajak the Sudden."

"Drajak the Sudden. You will care to finish Wink's game for him?"

Jikaida, the principal board game of Kregen, is played everywhere, continuously, obsessively. This San Chandro didn't even stop to consider if I could play. It was taken for granted that any educated person played Jikaida. There are those who cannot fathom the fascinating intricacies of Jikaida, and who must therefore make do with games like Jikalla and the Game of Moons.

I nodded. "I am at your disposal, san."

Mistress Lingli swept in already brandishing her box of needles, and so with a few words San Chandro and I were able to take ourselves off into an adjoining room where a table and chairs were all we needed. Chandro corrected me on that as he rang a silver bell. A most beautifully-formed Fristle fifi came in, smiling, ready for anything.

"Parclear and Sazz, miscils and palines, Fansi."

Fansi said: "At once," and with a flick of her tail, around which a red bow was artfully tied, went out.

Chandro had not spilled a piece from the board and as I studied the game situation I saw that Wink had been lax. Chandro was almost in an unassailable position. There was just a chance. As you know, I have studied Jikaida under masters. My son-in-law Gafard, now dead, had been a Jikaidast. I had played Death Jikaida and Kazz-Jikaida. Extricating Wink's pieces from the carefully prepared trap and then going on to a winning position would prove an interesting challenge. And I was in no mood to go racing about after the queen's necklace for a bunch of thieves.

There was Mevancy out at the Springs. I'd have to tell her that Tuong Mishuro was dead, I knew that, and I didn't care for the job.

"Are you ready, Drajak the Sudden?"

"As I'll ever be, san."

"Then it is your move."

I did what was necessary to rescue my almost-lost paktun and restore the situation on that side of the board. Chandro hummed a little tune under his breath, fingered his lips, hesitated, and then moved. I knew he had been forced to move a piece different from the one he'd planned to throw in. He glanced up at me. "You have a plan?"

"An old one, san. But it might serve."

"I see."

I didn't feel it necessary to say that whilst the plan was an old one it had been extensively modified by Naghan Furtway, who had once been the Kov of Falinur. Chandro was playing the blue, and Wink, and now me, played the yellow.

The situation was retrieved for the yellows as Fansi returned with a laden tray. I was glad of a little throat-moisture and drank off a glass of parclear with relish. I popped a paline and made the move that would start an attacking drive that, if all went well, should see yellow victorious.

San Chandro did not make the correct response.

I said: "I would ask you to bare the throat, san."

He raised his eyebrows. "So soon? You are very sure. I do not see it."

I explained.

He pushed back in his chair. His eyebrows drew down and together. His face looked thunderous. Then the black scowl cleared, he threw back his head, and laughed. Tears squeezed under his eyelids.

"By Tsung-Tan the Mighty! A veritable coup!"

He looked at me, still laughing, and spluttered out: "Aye! Aye, I bare the throat. And well done, Drajak the Sudden. I shall remember that plan. I have in mind a certain San Yango who needs to be humbled in the sight of Tsung-Tan."

I made a few further observations about Furtway's plan, elaborations to counter the opposite diagonal thrust. He drank his Sazz and popped a paline and looked quizzically at me.

"Were you not with San Tuong Mishuro?"

"I was."

"I heard the ghastly news this morning. And Caran and Hargon, too." He licked his lips. "Tuong mentioned his unease. But neither he nor I believed anyone would harm a dikaster." He shook his head and there was not the trace of a smile on that narrow visage.

I had to speak carefully, for meddling in other folks' religious beliefs is always a chancy business.

"San Tuong told me that many of the old beliefs had fallen away. That there are people who will kill a Diviner or a Repositer is obvious from these awful happenings." He was studying me attentively. I took a breath. It was quite clear he had not heard all the news; there hadn't been time for that. I felt a liking for this narrow faced old buffer. And—methought Dray Prescot the old leem-hunter—he could be useful to my own plans. So I went on: "Hargon and Caran plotted to kill Trylon Kuong and San Mishuro. They failed in one instance and, heartbreakingly, succeeded in the other."

"Yes? Go on."

"I was there when Caran attempted Kuong. I stopped him. I was too late with Mishuro. But not too late for Hargon."

He sucked in a ragged breath. He put a shaking hand to his lips.

"You! You killed two Repositers!"

"Trylon Kuong put the situation succinctly. Those two murdering cramphs forfeited their position as dikasters."

"Yes, yes. I would agree. But, you slew two Repositers!"

"I stand in no peril from the law. That I am assured."

"Kuong stands well with the queen at the moment. She is strong-willed, some would say self-willed. I applaud that, for I trained and guided her and watched her grow to womanhood. She is a remarkable woman."

As he spoke, his fervency revealed to me how much he loved the queen.

He picked up a paline but did not pop it into his mouth. "Will you tell me the truth about the death of Vad Leotes in Ivory Lorn?"

"I have already told all there is to know; but I will gladly repeat myself." I saw his eyes suddenly widen on me and realized I'd put on something of a scowl at the idea that I'd got to go all over this old ground yet again. I said: "My comrade, Mevancy, and Leotes were pushed over the edge of a high building by Hargon and Strom Hangol's bully boys. Leotes fell. All those rasts except Hangol have paid the price."

"They are all dead. Yes. And Strom Hangol lies abed of a wound and is near death so I am informed."

He favored me with another of his shrewd narrow looks. "There is a mystery about that. Are you the man who gave Hangol his wound?"

"Aye."

He stood up and started pacing up and down. I can tolerate folk who do this in order to get the blood flowing through their brains so they can think, provided they don't trip over my legs or walk on my belongings. He marched up and down, looking thoughtful, hands clasped into the small of his back. His curly red velvet slippers made hush-shush-hushing sounds on the thick carpets of Walfarg weave.

At length, still pacing, he said: "You are a man of parts, Wr. Drajak."*

I said nothing and listened.

"Tuong Mishuro was not mistaken in you. You are well named Drajak the Sudden. I am confident I can trust you. Will you help me? Will you help my cause and the cause of the queen?"

He stopped directly before me and spread his hands.

"I will insult you by offering gold. You will not insult me and you will accept. I need your help. I would like to employ your special talents. How say you?"

Five

I sat there pretending to think, seeing the pieces on the Jikaida board's blue and yellow squares, and Chandro's tipped-over Queen. There was no need to let him see how pleased I was at this turn of events.

I stood up and he lifted his face to stare into mine.

"I accept your offer, San Chandro. Thank you."

He smiled and looked pleased and relieved. "I am glad. Good. Excellent. Now we can plan how best to circumvent the queen's enemies."

The cynical thought occurred to me that now he knew I'd seen off a number of villains who'd run across my path, was he using that word circumvent as a euphemism for a darker thought?

"There are five of us Queen's Repositers," he told me. "San Nath the Uttarler is our chief. He tries to be just and fair and finds that hard. San Nalgre Hien-Mi is my friend and we think alike in the queen's service. I have mentioned San Yango in connection with your splendid Jikaida plan. He stands against us. With him is San Ranal Sharg-Li-Po known as the

---

* Wr.: Abbreviation for walfger, herr, mister. A.B A.

Kaour, the Death Dealer. If Ranal hadn't been a Repositer for most of his life he would have been knocked on the head seasons ago."

As I digested this information, Fansi came in flicking her tail to say the queen was abroad and wished to see San Chandro at once. Fansi gave me a saucy look, tossed her head, and let her tail curl up around her waist. The red bow stood out brightly against her silver-gray fur. She walked out with that kittenish swaying movement young Fristle fifis employ to infuriate susceptible males of other races of diffs.

Chandro started for the door at once, then caught himself and paused, turning to me with a lop-sided smile. "Your pardon, Wr. Drajak. As you see, I must go. The queen calls. Tell no one of our new arrangement. You understand?"

"I understand, san."

When he'd gone I picked a handful of palines and went back quietly through the bedroom where Wink was snoring away like a volcano. I went out and Leone came hurrying up, looking annoyed.

"There you are!"

This morning she wore a pale blue gown with silver leaves patterning the hems. Her light hair was neatly combed back. Her face was not—quite—petulant in expression. I had seen evidences of courage in this girl. She might be a spoilt palace brat; her spirit was all right.

"Here I am, Leone."

Her eyebrows went up.

Before she could answer I went on: "Is there a place more private than this corridor where we might talk?"

Without a word she marched off, shoulders held very squarely, and I tagged along. We landed up in a small antechamber furnished in simple style, mostly fragile wooden and rush pieces. The double doors to the chambers beyond were closed. An eagle was carved and painted on each leaf.

"Well?"

"First, Leone, the necklace."

"Yes?"

Neither of us had seated ourselves. We faced each other almost as antagonists in the arena. Her breathing quickened.

"Is there a copy made?"

"A copy? You mean a fake?"

"Yes."

"I don't know. Why? Is it important?"

"Yes," I said. "Yes, Leone, it is important."

"Well, I can find out, I suppose."

"Good." I gave her a small encouraging smile and deliberately walked across to a comfortable if fragile chair, and sat down. She frowned at me, puzzled. I stared back.

After a couple of heartbeats I said: "Well. Leone?"

"Well what?"

"Why, go and find the copy of the necklace and bring it here."

Her face flushed with blood. She half lifted her right hand and the pale slender fingers clenched.

"You mean—?"

"Of course. Right away. Now."

"Why should I? What's so important?"

"They mean to have the necklace. They'll kill to get it. I don't yet know why it is so vital. I intend to find out. I am supposed to steal the damn thing from you and give it to the thieves, or they'll kill me."

Her hand flew to her mouth. Her eyes widened.

"But they'll know it's a fake!"

"Eventually. I just need a little time to move, that's all."

"I'll go at once!"

As she started for the door with a swish of her blue gown I said: "There is another matter to discuss when you get back. I will wait here."

"All right! All right!"

The courage I had seen in her must be matched by integrity and intelligence. Although I could not be sure, I fancied Chandro would want me to do some dirty work for him. If that work coincided with my own plans, then quidang. And, of course, my plans were those of the Star Lords'.

When Leone returned her color was up, her eyes were bright and her ripe pert mouth was tightly clenched. She wore the necklace.

A small furtive movement under the table attracted my attention as I stood up.

A reddish-brown scorpion waddled out from the table's shadow.

His tail curved arrogantly over his back and his legs, bent and braced, glinted. His eyes regarded me steadily. I checked, holding my breath.

Leone released that tightly-held clamp on her mouth. She spoke in a controlled breathy voice.

"I have been thinking, Drajak. Thinking that you are trying to trick me. But why, I cannot understand, for if you wanted to steal the necklace you would not ask for a copy. How can I possibly trust you?"

I looked at the scorpion. Leone ignored him altogether. This, I felt sure, was not because she was wrapped up in her own thoughts and worries, but simply because to her he was invisible. He waggled that stinger at me. He was from the Star Lords, no doubt about it. They were keeping an eye on me. My original feelings of despair that I had failed them had been materially dissipated. I had not been flung contemptuously back to Earth. But—here was the scorpion of the Everoinye, watching me. Perhaps my punishment would still be meted out.

"Well? Why do you not answer?"

I roused myself.

"You do not know for sure if you can trust me. I accept that. All I can do is assure you that what I have told you is true. Is that the fake?"

"One of them."

"Oh?"

She walked across to a fragile couch and threw herself down so that the rush seat squeaked.

"Oh, Drajak! I don't know! I want to trust you. I feel—I feel something—odd. Something about you I do not wish to know—I think."

"You have nothing to fear from me, Leone."

"Perhaps not in the way you mean. But—but I feel—I think perhaps I do!"

The damned scorpion stood there drinking all this in. I wondered if the Star Lords—who once had been as human as Leone or me—I wondered if they still remembered how a young girl's emotions fluttered about like a bird in a cage.

That I felt sorry for Leone goes without saying. Still, I had a job to do that, once done, would free me to return to Delia, my Delia of the Blue Mountains, my Delia of Delphond. And why on Kregen I ever allowed myself to be parted from her for a single second longer than necessary I could not understand. Only duty, damned duty, kept me from haring off to Vallia and telling the Sisters of the Rose what I thought. Then Delia and I would fly off to be by ourselves. By Zair! I own I almost turned around and marched clear out of that palace in Makilorn and started for home.

But, if I did, the Star Lords would send their gigantic blue phantom Scorpion to fetch me back here where I was needed to further their schemes.

I blinked my eyes and the scorpion was gone.

I let out a breath.

"All right, Leone. Tell me about the necklace."

"The queen was most amused."

"Oh?"

Her lips began to tighten up at my tone and I readied myself for a scornful blast. Then she shook her head and said: "She knew that I borrowed some of her jewelry from time to time. She did not know I borrowed this particular necklace and was at first angry and upset. Then she—it was a strange effect—she smiled and became very friendly, almost as though she was enjoying a joke."

"At whose expense?"

"She showed me a cabinet. Drajak—there were nine necklaces, all the same!"

She unhooked the necklace and handed it to me.

"We thought the necklace was important. Well, this proves it is most important indeed." I took it from her fingers. "Thank you, Leone."

"Yes."

"But they would not all be the same, would they."

"But they were, Drajak. All nine exactly the—oh! I see!"

I turned the necklace over in my hand. The gems were linked by double strands, alternately gold, silver and dudinter which we on Earth call electrum. The gems looked splendid and although I could not give them a full test I had the ticklish feeling that they were real. The centre pendant contained within a golden trelliswork a large ronil, a purple-red jewel of great price. I felt convinced this was real and not paste; but the jewelsmiths of Kregen are fantastically capable of producing imitation gems that will fool all but the most expert scrutiny. If there were seven others like this, and the genuine article, someone had gone to a very great deal of trouble to disguise that same genuine article. Maybe it was not in the cabinet the queen had shown to Leone but was locked away separately. Perhaps there was no original at all but simply the nine matched necklaces.

Whatever the truth, the fact that there were nine identical trinkets in existence must mean a mystery was attached.

The door opened silently and a half-grown Sybli girl wearing a gray slave breechclout crossed to the side table where the sand glass showed the last few grains tumbling down. She stood perfectly still, her soft features expressing nothing whatsoever as she waited. As the last grain slipped through she turned the glass with a single expert motion and set it back on the table. With the smooth young gait of Sybli girls she crossed to the door and closed it silently behind her. Leone just had not noticed the hourglass change at all. Slaves lived and moved among the lords and ladies like fish in the water, there but unseen, unnoticed.

Well, you know my views on slavery.

Also, it is worth mentioning that in this desert area sand glasses were commonly in use. The thought crossed my mind that the water from a clepsydra might come in handy one day. And, another point, the queen's palace provided a glass changing service even to a small room like this. Just how many slaves went around changing the glasses? Well, the palaces of Ruathytu and Sanurkazz and those of Vondium before the destruction made this desert palace look like the lodge by the side gates. Ah, well...

A feeling for the passage of time is buried in most people and Kregans are no exception. Without any connection with the slave girl's turning of the sand glass, Leone looked across and saw the bur was gone. She moved to the door and half-turned her head to look at me, a most graceful movement.

"I told you the queen was amused. After she'd got over being angry. She has commanded you to the first lunch. She wishes to inspect the man so involved with the necklace he is willing to risk his neck. We'd better go now."

Without answering I walked across and we went along the corridors and through the halls together. The place was splendid, all right, and I stopped comparing it with other palaces I had known. At last we reached a pleasant room furnished with tables and chairs where the first lunch was taken.

Apart from the guards with their Lohvian longbows and yellow-fletched arrows, the only other person present with the queen turned out to be the court wizard. Well, now!

He wore dazzling robes, a tall hat, curly yellow slippers, and his face revealed nothing of his thoughts save one. That face knew secrets, that face concealed secrets, that face gloated with the power of secrets known.

As for the queen—she was breathtaking. I gave her a polite bow, making a leg. If she wanted me to go into the full incline, I might consider it carefully before I rejected such slavish foolery. Her face was pale. Her eyes were large and clear and softly brown. Her mouth seemed to tremble with controlled passion; I decided I did not wish to find out what emotion motivated that passion. Her robes were simple, sheer laypom, and her hair neatly curled and piled and threaded with gems. There was no doubt about it: this woman had presence.

"Majestrix," spoke up Leone. "This is the man, Drajak the Sudden."

Lifting my head from the bow I said: "Llahal, majestrix."

She nodded, not smiling, her mouth wet and red and full. She motioned with her hand to chairs at the table. The wizard was already at the food. I seated Leone and then sat down. The queen broke a bread roll between her fingers, staring at me. I picked up my bread roll and got on with it. If she wanted to talk she'd do it in her own sweet time. In the interim, like any good Kregan, I wanted to eat this one of the six or eight square meals a day that are de rigueur on that world.

When she did speak her voice held an attractive quality I liked. She began with general enquiries about me, which I answered with the standard set of Dray Prescot lies. These lying stories were far simpler than the truth, by Krun! Then she said: "Can you lead my guards to where you were taken by the thieves?"

"No, majestrix. I was unconscious going and blindfolded leaving."

"A pity. Still, we can have the thieves taken up as you hand them the Skantiklar."

The wizard stopped chewing, looked me in the face, and said: "You did not hear that, tikshim."

Ordinarily I don't worry over insults people hurl at me. I take notice only when it serves my purpose. Now the word tikshim, which means something like 'my good man', is considered normal by those of the upper class who use it and infuriatingly insulting by the lower classes to whom it is addressed. So that didn't worry me. The attitude of this wizard was clear, frighteningly clear. Consumed with his own position and power he was in mortal fear of losing both. I took notice of the symbols spattering that dazzling gown. I'd find out about this fellow, never fear.

"Well?" The word was positively snarled.

"I heard," I said, casually, and continued eating the salad.

Leone kept her head down over her plate.

The dark blood rushed and collided in the wizard's face.

"You shint! Did you not hear me tell you to forget you'd heard?"

"That's what I just said, I heard."

His lips compressed and went white, scarring that dark aquiline face.

"I'll—"

And the queen laughed.

Leone glanced up, startled. The queen sat back in her chair and laughed. She put a slender white hand to her lips. Her eyes were bright.

"I think, San Chang-So, you must admit Wr. Drajak has the right of it."

He managed to get his lips unglued. His voice held an ugly note as he said: "Of course, that is what he meant. He does not seem able to express himself clearly."

As for me, as I went on eating the first lunch, mostly salads, I was cursing away at myself. What a fool! This man was an ugly customer all right, with prestige and power, and I'd made him an enemy on sight. If I knew men of his stamp—as I did, I did!—he'd seek to do me an injury to avenge his slighted honor.

By Makki Grodno's disgusting diseased liver and lights! Why couldn't I keep my black-fanged winespout shut?

Six

The first lunch proceeded in something of a silence after that.

Eventually the queen tapped her lips with a square of yellow linen and said: "Palines, I think. And then, San Chang-So, you will do what must be done. Have you discovered anything further about this new wizard?"

He said: "He comes from Whonban." Chang-So's voice held barely suppressed venom and envy. "From Nik-Whonban. Even so, this makes him a real Wizard of Walfarg."

I perked up at this. By his robes and general demeanor he hadn't impressed me as a genuine Wizard of Loh would. Here in Loh there were as many different sorts of sorcerers as there were in any other parts of Kregen, probably more, apart, perhaps, from Balintol. The real genuine Wizards of Loh came from Walfarg. After all this time I fancied I'd have trouble trying to remember to say Wizard of Walfarg instead of Wizard of

Loh. Still, by Vox, this choice specimen Chang-So would not possess the amount of kharrna and the consequent sorcerous power as your true Wizard of Walfarg.

"Well, keep an observation upon him."

"I do. And he knows it. By Hlo-Hli! I feel his power!"

The queen glanced sharply at him. Sweat sheened on his forehead.

"You are well, San Chang-So?"

"Perfectly, thank you." He recovered his poise. "If this new sorcerous shint is here in Makilorn because of the necklace, then—"

"Why, then," exclaimed the queen brightly. "He will be on a fool's errand!" And her light amused laugh filled the room with silver sound.

As for me, I wondered just how well this Chang-So had sealed this room against a real genuine Wizard of Loh's power to see and hear at a distance.

Mind you, there were many different gradations of accomplishment among the real Wizards of Loh. I had known some in much reduced circumstances and others who could perform what were to ordinary folk genuine and frightening miracles. Power was relative to other power; well, that is a truism.

The queen stood up and we all immediately rose. Chang-So glowered at me. "Is he to come?"

"I think so. After all, he is taking the necklace."

Leone started to say: "I will retire now—"

The queen said most pleasantly: "Stay and keep me company, Leone, dear."

"Yes, majestrix."

We all trooped out and along a corridor with only two guards at our backs. Naturally, these people didn't know what that maniac Dray Prescot could do in circumstances such as these. Still, this game looked to be worth the candle, so I dutifully trotted along with them. We entered a small antechamber and then through draped dark blue curtains into a narrow although lofty temple.

Pillars of black marble upheld the arching roof, dark with mystery. The walls, carved with mythological scenes from the life of the great Tan, were illuminated by lamps so that the figures seemed to be alive. The altar was modest. I saw no signs of a black iron cage, for which I was glad.

The floor of black and yellow hexagons stretched bare to the altar rail. As we walked down with our footsteps ringing the hollow echoes, three young girls wearing flowing draperies and not much else ran out with three light cane chairs which they positioned before the altar. They fluttered off and the queen motioned to us to be seated. Chang-So walked on towards the altar. Here appeared to be a weird mixture of religion and sorcery. This temple was dedicated to Tsung-Tan well enough and yet wizardry was clearly taking place.

A lad scuttled out of the curtained shadows on the left side carrying an enormous cope on a frame. I had to keep a straight face as between them they got the thing around Chang-So's shoulders. It glittered with gems. It gave him a spurious air of dignity and command.

He stood by the altar and a certain amount of mumbo-jumbo followed. This, I imagined, must be the religious aspect of the ceremony. He passed on to the thaumaturgical aspect and as he did so all the damned lamps in the place flickered. Sheer co-incidence or a parlor trick, I told myself.

The queen said: "Take the necklace up, Leone."

Leone flashed me a scared look. I handed her the necklace and she walked haltingly to the rail.

Chang-So took the necklace and hung it on a tripod so that the dependent jewel, the great ronil, swung just above the surface of the altar block.

He stood back. He must have pressed some secret lever for the top of the block began to slide sideways. The instant the slab revealed the opening beneath, a brilliant coruscating beam of radiance flashed upwards. I blinked and water filled my eyes.

When I could see clearly again I made out the hazy shape of the ronil bathed in the incandescent shaft of light from the pit beneath the altar. Chang-So stood to the side, silently. There was a greater magic here than any words he might chant. A swift glance at Leone showed her cowering in her chair, trembling. The queen sat straight, shoulders back, chin up, a veritable dandy fighting lady.

At length Chang-So released the lever and the slab hissed shut. The radiation died and the shadows came back, the lanterns totally unable to light the gloom. Our eyes would take some time to adjust.

Chang-So unhooked the necklace and almost before the queen spoke Leone was up and walking forward to bring it back. She handed it to the queen.

"Yes," said the queen, reflectively. "It is warm and it holds power. How long will it deceive them, Chang-So?"

"The thieves, probably for ever."

"And the sorcerer?"

"It is impossible to say."

The queen turned the necklace in her slender fingers. Then she accepted the reply. I fancied Chang-So just didn't know and didn't have the power to find out. "Leone, give the necklace to Drajak the Sudden."

The thing positively radiated energy. It tingled in my fingers. I'd be prepared to swear the jewel was crammed full of magic, by Krun!

"You will have a chance, Drajak." The queen bent her brows to look on me. She half smiled. "You will be able to get away, at least."

"You are kind, majestrix."

"That is one duty laid on me as majestrix."

I let that go. It could be mere flannel, rote description of the queen's position, propaganda. Still, I felt she believed it. I caught the idea that perhaps she was not a Queen of Pain of Loh. Perhaps she tried to rule wisely and well. If so, it would make a refreshing change.

"Then you will have the thieves taken up, majestrix?"

The words were hardly out of my mouth before the wizard snarled: "That is for the queen to decide, not you, tikshim."

Leone gave me a quick look and then away. I said nothing.

"That is all." The queen lifted a hand. "You may go."

I said: "Majestrix. Tell me—when Leone brought the necklace to me in the anteroom, did it not cross your mind I might walk out with it then?"

Chang-So started to make a snarling grunting but the queen waved a hand at him. To me she said sweetly: "Yes. You were under observation at all times. You would never have reached the inner gates." Her voice bubbled with laughter.

And I, Dray Prescot, laughed with her.

On that pleasant note I was able to retire and make my way out of the palace. There were still many aspects of this affair to be explored; but I was beginning to resent the amount of my time all this nonsense of thieves and necklaces was stealing away. I did admit it had been quite pleasant to meet the queen. I wasn't fool enough to imagine that at the moment she had any especial interest in me to account for her actions. Oh, no. She and that damned wizard of hers had other fish to fry, and the new wizard who had just arrived in Makilorn and who wanted the necklace was one of the fish they'd like to see sizzling on the griddle.

Leone trotted along at my side to the main gates past the courts where the throngs still moved backwards and forwards. She touched my arm.

"You will be careful, Drajak?"

"I always am." A thought occurred to me. "Tell me. What is the queen's name?"

"Leone."

"You are named for her?"

"Yes. We are related. It is all complicated, quite apart from being paol-urbliem." She sucked a breath. "Don't you think she is splendid?"

"Oh, yes, very splendid."

My neutral tone did not invite further comment. We said the remberees and I went swinging out into the mingled radiance of the Suns of Scorpio.

In no time at all my tail had picked me up and I had spotted her.

Now, I told myself, just before I go and sort out Mevancy at the Springs, I'll go into business on my own account. I'd find out a bit about these thieves and this new mysterious Wizard of Loh that will owe nothing to Leone or Kei-Wo the Dipensis or this splendid Queen Leone of Tsungfaril. By Vulken the Insinuator, yes!

Seven

With my shadow dutifully following me I walked out of the main gates of the palace. The kyro beyond was filled with clamor and movement as people passed about their business. Many sideshows here added to the color and din. I noticed a group performing on carpets, lifting one another up on poles by their hair. That has always struck me as a painful way to make a living. Still, I suppose the children are born to it and have the roots of their hair strengthened from the time they begin to grow the first fuzz.

Just past them a fire eater was having a flaming second lunch. Jugglers were throwing things about, including themselves. I always detest those shows which include animals, so I turned away from a poor half-dazed creature with a chain about his neck dancing to a pipe.

Any thoughts of hitting his owner over the head and breaking the chain were, of course, fairy stories out of children's books. Interfering with people's pleasures and entertainment—so-called—has to be done on a long-term and authoritarian scale, as we had banished slavery in Vallia.

My sharp turn away did not fool the girl following me.

What it did do was bring me slap bang face to face with Naghan the Chik.

He was completely startled, and started back, knocking over a passing slave. He didn't notice that and the slave ran off—silently.

"You shint!" he got out, gobbling.

Fing-Na closed in from the side. His enormous waxed and pointed moustaches quivered. These thieves did not like to be caught on the hop.

I said in a bright tone: "Why, Lahal. Are you ready to take me to Kei-Wo now?"

"You got it?" growled Naghan the Chik. The knives in the belt around his thick waist were concealed by a flap of his fawn robe.

"That's for me to tell Kei-Wo."

"If you've got it, give it here. We'll take it"

This did not suit my plans at all.

Of course, I was fully aware of the risk involved in taking the necklace into the thieves' kitchen myself. They'd as lief knock me on the head after I'd handed it across as give me a thankyou.

"Give it here!"

"No."

"Wha—?" No one would know what Naghan the Chik had been about to say for I struck him neatly on the chin and he fell down, just as the slave he'd knocked down tumbled over. The difference was Naghan didn't get up at once. In the same action my foot hit Fing-Na in his capacious gut and as he belched and doubled-up I rabbit-punched him down. He lay slumbering beside Naghan the Chik.

Turning like a leem-hunter I fastened my fingers on the neck of the girl who'd shadowed me from the palace. If there were any more followers they'd have to be dealt with when they turned up—if they did.

"Now, girl, I mean you no harm." I spoke gently and walked her rapidly away from the scene of the fracas. No one had taken overmuch notice and I had a story ready, in case of question, that they'd tried to abduct her.

No one stopped me. Her feet barely touched the ground. I don't think she was so much frightened as shocked. After all, Naghan and Fing-Na were among the most formidable rogues in the band. And she'd seen what happened to them. Away around a corner I slowed down and set her on her feet.

"Now, young lady, what's your name?"

She stammered it out, shaking. "Falima—"

"Falima. A nice name. Now I have something to give Kei-Wo so we'll just go along and see him now." My voice tried to be gentle and, I own, it was not the old Dray Prescot growl of savagery I'd lived with all my life.

"Yes, master, yes. Please don't hurt me."

I felt injured. "Have I hurt you?"

"Well, no—"

"So that's settled. I might find a silver khan for you, too."

She perked up at this and seemed to gather herself for she started off along the avenue. I followed with a friendly hand resting on her shoulder.

Now this had not been the plan I'd envisaged. I seriously doubted if I was doing a wise thing. As we went along I began to think that I was your thick-headed barbarian oaf to the life. I was running headlong into a peril that was nothing to do with me, for no profit, and at danger of a life that was spoken for elsewhere. And all out of perverse pride! "Sink me!" I burst out to myself, silently. "I'll not get myself killed out of pride!"

I fished in my pouch and found a silver coin, one of the few left.

"Here," I said, stopping and halting Falima. "Here is the khan I promised. And here is the necklace Kei-Wo wants. You just take it along to him, Falima. Keep it safe. Feel the magic in it. Tell Kei-Wo that Drajak the Sudden honors bargains. And if he meddles with me again he is a dead man." I looked into her little screwed-up face with the staring enormous eyes. "Do you understand?"

"Yes." She clutched the khan and the necklace and then in a swift practiced movement they both disappeared under her simple brown dress. "I will tell Kei-Wo. And about Naghan the Chik and Fing-Na!"

Her feet were bare. Dust caked up along their sides. On naked flashing legs she ran off and I wondered if this second trumped up plan was any better than the first.

I followed her until she rounded the next corner. Still hurrying along I took off the mass of cloth on my head that wrapped into a turban shape and thumped it into a different shape. This was not your rounded dome-shaped turban but your flat pancake type that might droop here and lump there. I pulled my fawn robes around so they crossed differently. And I did as my comrade, the Wizard of Loh Deb-Lu-Quienyin, had taught me and altered the planes and angles of my face so that a quite different face from that of Drajak looked out. I held an arm up to hide that particular process as I went on; there were few people along here and no one noticed.

Falima was just disappearing into an alleyway ahead and I doubled along to keep up.

We were penetrating into the more insalubrious parts of Makilorn now and the people here looked furtive, with averted faces and downcast heads, their hands gripped around the hilts of knives or swords. Falima appeared to have no fear of them, and I surmised that trouble would start only if you started it. Once we entered the real warrens, the dens of thieves and assassins, live and let live as a rule would probably prevail. These people preyed on those who lived in the wealthier areas. All the same, trouble would flare up from time to time, and then the corpses would be dragged out, their late owners' ibs gone to investigate the Death Jungles of Sichaz.

The face I'd chosen to wear was not the simple-minded idiot-like face I often chose. In view of possible unpleasant happenings I'd chosen a face that was not mine but was if possible even more hard, vicious and malevolent. I looked a villainous desperado as I followed Falima through the greasy alleyways.

She would be a capital tracker here, I knew; I have some skill in that direction and she was not aware that she was being followed.

She led me across a litter-filled place where two alleys crossed leaving a wider expanse, although nothing that could be called a kyro, to a stucco-walled structure with a flat roof and enclosures at the sides. The door was low and narrow and an amphora swung on a beam above. I simply waited on the shadowy side of this little square and watched.

Half a dozen miners swaggered into the square, laughing and pushing. They wore tattered finery and were clearly in from the workings. A great deal of mining activity took place north and south of the trails leading to the city. Emeralds in particular were found in abundance; but many other fine gemstones could be dug up out there, as well as the more common minerals that fed the forges of countries downriver. Makilorn gained much of its wealth from trade and mining. These jolly diggers tumbled into the tavern and I guessed they'd be there as the Suns declined and through much of the night.

Those same Suns crawled across the sky and the heat of the afternoon mounted. At last, here they came, shambling along like a pair of disgruntled graints seeking to sink their claws and teeth into anything that moved. They pushed people out of their way, and the pushees after a single glance did not argue. They looked most unhappy. They crossed the square and ducked down to enter the tavern. I wondered if the miners would fall foul of Naghan the Chik or Fing-Na. I own I felt quite sorry for the diggers.

Very very quickly, but not surprisingly quickly, the first miner came flying through the doorway headfirst. He squelched on the cobbles outside. Almost immediately another followed and then another and after that the rest of the diggers ran out on their own feet, yelling blue bloody murder. Oh, yes. Naghan the Chik and Fing-Na worked their ill-humor off and loud were the crashings and bashings thereof.

Still I waited.

Patience is not so much a virtue in a hunter as a prime necessity.

Eventually, as the Suns were declining in a welter of reds and greens, the gang slouched out of the tavern. Kei-Wo headed them as they went off along narrow alleyways and up and down the rickety ladders leading from level to level. There were still people about, enough to give me cover as I trailed the gang. Had the queen decided to arrest the thieves she'd left it too late the moment they entered these runnels, havens of villainy.

The gang finally came to rest in a four-storey block that looked to be a fortress in its own right. Few windows pierced the outer walls and these were more like arrow slits than decent civilian windows. The shadows dropped down in the alleyway where I watched the last of the gang sidling through a narrow door opened in a re-entrant angle of the wall. If the queen sent her guards along here they'd have a tough time breaking in.

Houses crowded in on all sides, looming over the alleys and forming a confusing jumble. I'd be able to find my way back here all right even so. I felt strongly there was no point in hanging around here any longer. Kei-Wo would deliver the necklace to this new mage on the morrow. The Wizard of Loh would not come down here. The meet would take place in more salubrious surroundings.

So I decided that as this affair was really of no concern of mine I'd take myself off to bed. If it became necessary to find out about the new wizard, I'd ask around. And, there was always Queen Leone to ask...

The stinks of the alleyways had to be ignored; but the truth was the effluvium mingled into a disgusting brew that would take the skin off your throat and nostrils. I was glad to get back to the fresher air outside and I deliberately took a little stroll by the river. Fins cut the surface, rippling pink and gold, and very soon I tired of this and went off to the lodging house I'd patronized the previous night. Just before my last thought of the night, which is the same as my first thought of the morning, I realized I felt more than a vague dissatisfaction with my day's doings.

In a very real sense this had been a day wasted.

No matter how long a life you have, you cannot afford to waste a single day, not a solitary single one.

Tomorrow I'd find out what San Chandro wanted done in the spying-on-the-queen's-enemies line. When that was done I'd see about Mevancy. With these good intentions neatly made and filed and my last as ever thought, I went to sleep.

Eight

The guard slammed the door shut at my back and as I walked into San Chandro's rooms the Repositer looked up and said: "Hai, Drajak! You are just the man. Come and join me in the second breakfast. There are schemes afoot."

As we ate he told me that he wanted to know how deeply Yango and Ranal Shang-Li-Po had been involved with the two dead Repositers, Caran and Hargon. "You see, Drajak, if it was just those two villains on their own, why, the damage is dreadful but not anywhere near as awful as it will be if Shang-Li-Po and Yango are mixed up in it."

"The queen has five Repositers," I said. "There must be a great deal for her to learn as she grows up."

He gave me a quick glance. He nodded. "So you have fallen under her spell? I am not surprised; I would have been surprised had you not done so." He heaved up a sigh. "The man she decides to marry will be—well, were I—" He chopped his words off. I felt sorry for him, of course. Also, I wasn't about to tell him that much as I admired Queen Leone she was nothing beside Delia. Well, that is a stupid remark. No one is anything in the way he meant it beside Delia.

Carefully, I said: "The queen is a charming and remarkable woman. And, yes, the man she marries is going to be fortunate beyond his wildest dreams. But I was thinking of the burden she carries."

I knew the chief Repositers and Diviners formed a college to deal with all matters pertaining to the Accursed, the paol-ur-bliem. Now Chandro explained that they also had a large hand in government, planning and advising the queen and making sure the administration functioned smoothly. He went on: "Whilst the queen is growing up each time, of course, the college runs the country."

"Those two dead Repositers ran the estates whilst the young nobles were growing up. Their greed was such that they wanted to kill the nobles so that they would be reborn as babies, and the Repositers would retain the power."

I gave him a hard look. "Does the queen stand in danger?"

He sucked in his cheeks.

He looked abruptly haggard as he said: "I dare not believe so; but, yes. Yes! Horrible as it is, I believe she does!"

"And you think it's this Yango and Shang-Li-Po?"

"I—I do, Tsung-Tan forgive me the thought."

About to follow the logical if unpleasant thought through I was stopped as he burst out: "They must not be harmed! Quite apart from their position as dikasters, more scandals would ruin the queen's reputation."

"Better for the queen to have a little scandal than to be murdered."

He was shaking with the violence all mixed up inside him. Almost absently, thinking of something else, he said: "Not really. She would be born again and would have served one more life here on Kregen."

They really believed that the paol-ur-bliem, the Accursed, condemned to live a hundred lives, really did come back again and again to live out their punishment until, at last, they could enter the paradise of Gilium.

"So you think it better for the queen to get herself murdered as many times and as fast as she can?"

His head went up at my tone. His eyes cleared. "No, no, of course not. The college laws expressly forbid that."

"I'll spy on these rasts for you."

"Good. Excellent. Here—" He moved breakfast things out of the way and spread a plan of the palace. "Here are the secret passages."

He pointed out the apartments inhabited by Yango and Shang-Li-Po. Secret passages riddled the walls all over the palace, a usual part of palace, temple and fortress building on Kregen. The queen's outer apartments were marked on the plan. No indication was given of any secret passages there. And the centre of the queen's area was a blank.

I made no comment on this, and Chandro did not need to give the obvious explanation.

I had determined to be brisk with this Queen's Repositer. I said: "I don't intend to hang about all day skulking in passages. I'll have to know the places the villains will be and the times they will be there."

He accepted my tone, saying: "Of course. I can tell you that."

Like many similar institutions, the palace ran on a regular routine. During the hours of duty the Repositers would be in known places. Outside of that their time was their own and they might be anywhere within a circumscribed round of pleasure. Creatures of habit, some of these high and mighty ones.

When I had digested all the information and got it firmly wedged in my old vosk skull of a head I felt I had a chance of eavesdropping successfully. Undoubtedly I felt a keen admiration for the queen. She was a splendid woman. She might believe that when she died she'd return to Kregen as a newborn baby; I wasn't at all sure I believed it, no, by Krun! Further, I felt that if these villains harmed her, then scandal or no damned scandal, it would go hard with them.

Well, that is what I thought then, and as they say in the Eye of the World, men sow and Zair reaps.

We talked a little further, generally about the situation, and I was able by a few casual remarks to assure myself he knew nothing of the queen's necklace affair. If Leone wanted to tell him, that would be between them. At last he suggested I ought to be lodged in the palace; there were rooms enough in his own apartments. I accepted and asked that my belongings be brought round from Mishuro's villa. "There is a particularly fine long-bow I just bought from Master Twang. But I don't think that will come in down these passages!"

He smiled, a little wanly, and gave orders for my stuff to be brought round. I took a handful of palines and stood up. "I'll make a start."

That first little recce down the dusty flang-infested corridors hidden in the walls yielded precious little. I orientated myself and checked on three or four quick routes back to Chandro's apartments. I might need a quick getaway if affairs went wrong. I looked in on a number of interesting tab-leaux; but as they had nothing whatsoever to do with the plot, I refrain from mentioning them.

For, plot there was. And a damned ripe rascally plot, too!

The thought did cross my mind that the Star Lords wanted Mevancy and me to protect the queen. That notion was rapidly discarded. The queen had not been in the burning dancing rostrum. Once I had done my stint of spying this afternoon when Yango and Shang-Li-Po would be together to sign papers, I'd really clear off and go see Mevancy.

As the afternoon wore on I found myself pacing restlessly up and down Chandro's carpet of Walfarg weave. This shiftless kind of existence did not suit me. Oh, yes, there were many irons in the fire and lots of skullduggery was going on in the background and blood curdling action could erupt at any moment; all the same, I could not stifle the feeling that time was slip-ping away and nothing done.

Leone came in to see me and demanded to know what had happened. As she said, hotly: "The queen wants to know, Drajak!"

I told her that the necklace had been delivered safely to the thieves. "I expect they'll hand it to this new wizard today and collect their hire money. How long it will fool him, I don't know, nor does that posturing idiot Chang-So."

"Drajak!" She was shocked. "You can't... He is a famous wizard!"

"He's scared stiff of this new one. What's his name, anyway?"

"Na-Si-Fantong."

I didn't like that Si in the middle there. It reminded me uncomfortably of another Wizard of Loh with a Si in the middle. Well, he was dead now, thank Opaz.

"Na-Si-Fantong. Well, it's my guess, although I don't know, that he'll discover the gem is not the one he wants quite quickly. Just who will get the blame is an interesting speculation."

"Not you, Drajak, surely!"

Trying to lighten the conversation I made a bad gaffe. I thought Leone was taking this far too seriously, so I said off-handedly: "Oh, they're bound to blame the queen."

She rounded on me like a leem. "So you've become her slave, too, like everyone else! You've seen her once. We've known each other for a very little time, yet I know you are—"

"No, Leone, no. I am not. And you are not to say so. As for the queen, I think she is a wonderful woman and that is all." I drew my eyebrows down at her. Her hand went to her lips. "Just stop all this foolery, Leone."

This girl was easily led, that I knew. She could be told what to do, asked, ordered, begged, phrase it how you will. Yet she had courage. She flared back at me: "It is not foolery, Drajak! I know what I feel! You are the man—"

"I am the man devoted to a lady who does not live in Tsungfaril."

Her face went white.

Then she ran from the room.

Chandro came in with his head twisted on his neck. He regained his poise and walked across to me, saying: "A whirlwind, a veritable whirlwind of the desert! She almost bowled me over. What have you done to her?"

"She harbors delusions more suitable to a schoolgirl."

"Ah, yes. She is very—pliant."

"Will you have a word with her? Tell her to find her own man?"

"If it will do any good. Now her cousin, Kirsty, is quite different. If anyone is going to do any telling, it's Kirsty."

"She sounds a likely lady," I said, not really concerned, thinking of all the annoying consequences that might follow on this Leone nonsense.

"Oh, yes. Very likely."

A glance at the sand glass told me the time was near when Yango and Shang-Li-Po would be together ostensibly signing documents. If they were planning treachery then I wanted to hear.

So, ensconced among the dust and cobwebs I peered through a little grille and listened and the two Repositers signed papers and barely exchanged half a dozen words. When they rose and stretched and left the room I felt absolute disgust. What a waste of time! On my return Chandro expressed himself as pleased I had carried out an observation without being seen. If he was satisfied, I most certainly was not. I broached the subject of my going off to the Springs of Benga Annorpha to visit a comrade.

"Oh, I don't think so, Drajak. If we are to penetrate the secret plotting of these villains... No. You'd best stay here."

Now, of course, I could simply have ignored all that and gone off to see

Mevancy as I had kept on promising myself. But I liked the old buffer and if he felt there was a genuine danger for the queen from these villains, why then—you see!—damned duty held me fast here.

So the next couple of days passed. I got to know the corridors in this part of the palace very well. I ate enormous meals. And I did not leave the palace environs. I did put in a spot of archery with my new bow. This took place in an indoor butts used by the queen's bodyguards.

After the shooting rounds we went off to their mess where they celebrated the birthday of a young Hikdar. The drinking was moderate. Then, like good Kregans, they started the singing.

Very naturally we sang 'The Bowmen of Loh' and this was followed by 'When a Wizard meets a Wizard, Sailing through the Air.' After that we sang our way through many of the ditties of Kregen and one or two new to me; Lohvian songs and a plaintive little number from Tsungfaril: 'Asleep by the Desert Lily.'

I didn't count that short period wasted.

When I returned, Chandro was about to sit down to a slap up meal and I joined him. He mentioned that I did not keep any body slaves. To go into that prickly subject at that time seemed to me inopportune. Instead I said I had a comrade who had been wounded in the attack on Mishuro. This Llodi the Voice, I said, I felt responsible for. Nothing would satisfy Chandro but that Llodi must immediately be brought here and Mistress Lingli must care for him. I was happy to accept this munificence.

He waved a hand. "Gold is mere metal. A good heart weighs heavier in the balances. I could wish the queen—well, never mind that."

All these half references from him and Leone didn't add up to a whole. Whilst I was prepared to spy on villains, I was not prepared to allow complicated situations concerning young ladies to arise. There was no doubt Leone was easily led and influenced, so therefore let some nice respectable young man, with the approval of the Repositers, court and win her.

Llodi was well on the mend, thank Opaz, and his magnificent fissured nose positively glowed. He would take time to get over the treachery of Pulvia and the death of Mishuro. Meantime, he lay in bed and ate like your true Kregan.

On the next occasion Chandro told me a meeting of the villains was in progress, I went quietly along the dusty secret ways and once again spied on them.

Again, they barely exchanged half a dozen words. When they left the room my dissatisfaction was such that I went on exploring further than I'd been before out of the sheer desire to do something to stifle the frustration. The corridors all looked the same, narrow slots built within the walls. By the time I cooled down and decided I'd best return before I was lost, I discovered that I was lost.

There was no cause for alarm. I could always peer through one of the many concealed grilles to find an empty room and then open the secret door. Once through that chamber and into the corridor beyond I'd ask my way back. No problem.

Except that, well, yes, there was a problem.

The chambers beyond the secret observation grilles were furnished magnificently. Luxury breathed everywhere. I saw why I was lost, and why I didn't recognize these passageways. It dawned on me that these secret runnels had not been marked on the map Chandro had shown me. That meant I was prowling around between the walls of the queen's apartments.

If I barged out into a corridor here I'd be strung up before I could get the first Llahal out.

Refusing to be worried over the situation and trusting to my bump of location, I began to work steadily in one direction. I passed a hallway shimmering with mother of pearl, no doubt brought all the way up from Zamrarn, and the next observation grille showed me the chamber beyond the mother of pearl hall. Alabaster columns upheld a glittering ceiling. Many fans worked by rope through high pulley-holes waved languorously to and fro and the perfumes wafted dizzyingly through my spyhole. A marble floor scattered with rugs surrounded a pool of water tinted a clear pale blue. Steam rose in wisps and I felt how sensuously attractive it would be to plunge in and relax in that warm and perfumed water.

The bathing pool was completely deserted and even in my hidden corridor I could sense the feeling of waiting that assembly rooms have just before a meeting. This was like a stage set. At any moment there would be the sound of voices off, and the shuffle of feet, and then the beginners would step out and the play could begin.

Carefully, I moved along the flang-infested corridor. The odd thing was, I found I could see very well in the dimness. This darkness was artificial, in the sense that it was caused by material objects blocking out the light of the Suns or the Moons and not natural in that the Suns or the Moons were absent from the sky. Lamplight, in a weird way, appeared to make no difference. There was no time to puzzle over this strange phenomenon at the time. I kept looking for footprints in the dust and found none save my own. I couldn't backtrack my own footprints for a number of the corridors had been swept clean. This puzzled me at first, until, coming across stone steps leading upwards, I went up to find a long clean corridor without a single observation grille. Instead ropes led from holes in the wall to wooden cylinders with iron handles. No one was up here and I realized this was the punkah operating room for a chamber below.

Pressing on I descended and quickly found myself back in the dusty narrow channels between the walls.

At a corner a pile of yellow bones lay in confusion. I looked with some sympathy for the poor unfortunate lost and trapped here, and saw the rusty dagger through one eye orbit. By the tusks sticking up at each side of his lower jaw he had been a Chulik. What, I wondered as I went on, was his story?

The passage turned again and perforce I had to follow, aware that I was being forced in a circle and was going back in the opposite direction on the other side of the bathing pool chamber. Light cut across the corridor ahead from a grille set in a concealed door. I stopped and looked through.

Amid much laughter and splashing girls were disporting themselves. Some dived in and swam about, splashing, their bodies shimmering in the wisping mists rising from the warmed and scented water. Others lay languorously on couches or rugs bordering the pool. The scene presented a spectacle of beauty that touched me, a grizzly old leem-hunter, with an awareness of what life could and should be. And, yet, of course, many poor people worked long and hard hours in the irrigations and sweat shops so that these pampered ones might enjoy sybaritic luxury.

A cluster of handmaidens parted at the edge of the pool and the queen rose from the water, glistening, rosy, superb.

Well, this was no place for me. My spying brief did not include the part of a Peeping Tom. So I began to turn away to continue my search for the exit and from the corner of my eye I saw the quick feline movements and the glitter of swords as killers burst into that warm and scented chamber.

There were half a dozen of them, clad all in black, with black scarves about their heads. The feral glitter of their eyes matched the glitter of their swords. At once all was pandemonium and uproar. Girls screamed, and choked on their screams; girls ran and died as they ran.

The queen drew herself up, shining, resplendent, breathing deeply. She stared upon her death. Paol-ur-bliem or not, that experience must have scored into her mind. She faced the assassins bravely, boldly, her fists resting on her hips as the scented water ran down and I could swear a small contemptuous smile touched her soft lips.

My sword was in my fist and I hurled myself at the grilled door.

A curtain of blue radiance dropped before me.

Through that shimmering blue veil I saw another scene. I didn't believe what was happening, what I was seeing; but I saw another scene, a different scene yet one horribly the same.

Black clad assassins went racing forward to cut down the shrinking form of a young woman, and a lad with empty hands stepped out bravely before her. Shadows from the twin suns streamed ruby and jade across the desert sand. I could see both pictures with equal clarity: the queen standing firmly on the edge of her bathing pool as her handmaidens shrieked and scuttled, and the young woman cowering back as the young man stepped before her. The scenes were superimposed and both were touched by the blue radiance before me.

I hurled myself forward to smash the door down and go roaring across the marble into that secluded bathing chamber. I would fight for this woman, this Queen Leone of Tsungfaril. I would do what I could to protect her.

The door was not there.

Shattering coldness gripped me. I gasped with the shock of recognition.

Two women in peril, black clad assassins about to cut them both down... A curtain of blue radiance, sent by the Star Lords, a fragment of their phantom Blue Scorpion... I rushed on, sword pointed.

But—to whose rescue was I rushing?

Nine

Sand gritted under my feet. The late afternoon heat from the twin suns smote down.

The cloying scents of the bathing pool vanished. The icy grip of the radiant blue portal sent by the Star Lords fell away and as I rushed forward with poised sword there was just time for one single scarlet thought of regret for Queen Leone.

Now she had used up one more of the hundred lifetimes she had been condemned to spend in this sinful world before she might pass into the heavenly paradise of Gilium.

Thoughts of the queen and of being condemned to life as a punishment were swept away by the young people's peril. The lad stood bravely enough as I knew he would. I saw that I would not reach him across the sand before the first assassin chopped him down with ruthless efficiency.

The hilt of my old knife snugged into my hand and I drew from the sheath over my right hip and threw in a single flowing motion. The blade twinkled once as it flew. Running, I'd missed the target I'd aimed for. The knife smashed into the fellow's face below the glaring eyes, ripped through the black facemask, laid his cheek bare. My clansmen would tut-tut at that, well enough, knowing I'd aimed for the throat. The assassin did not tumble over straight away. He dropped his sword and put his hand to his face.

The second assassin collided with the first and I heard his savage yell of anger. These stikitches, although well able to slay defenseless women, were not top class professional assassins. There were three of them and as the first reeled about trying to stop the blood pouring from his face the other two turned to face me.

They were shouting now, some rigmarole about their patron saints and bolstering their courage with rote liturgies from their no-doubt secret assassin disciplines. There was no time for nonsense of that sort.

The fellow with my knife through his face at last collapsed, trying to scream and producing only a bloody froth and sickening mewling sounds. They tried to meet me together, two blades to one, give them credit for that. So I circled, drawing them away from the two young folk, and made a sudden and savage dart at them.

That devilish screech as steel blades meet and cross, slide and chingle! Ah, well, swordsmen know what they know, by the Blade of Kurin!

From these two I expected good quality swordsmanship, for despite their lack of professional stikitche know-how they should, at least, know some of the arts of the sword. I was not disappointed.

So we set to.

After a few passes it was established between the three of us that their skill would not match mine. Therefore, all things being equal, they were dead men.

Things in this valley of tears, of course, are not equal.

Knowledge of the sword, great skill in its use, vast experience, all may in certain circumstance avail nothing before a less skilled opponent. Well, didn't I remember Mefto the Kazzur! Resolutely I thrust thoughts of that unhanged villain away and let my self flow into the blade so that I could have fought these two blindfolded.

After a few more passages they realized the truth of the understanding we had established between us. They stopped fighting and sought to escape.

The heat of the suns blistered up from the sand and the light, all pervasive, blinded in a jade and ruby dazzle.

Whether or not I would have let them go I cannot now say.

The young man, who I now realized was Lunky, picked up the fallen stikitche's sword from the sand and with a loud and angry shout, rushed at these two trying to escape. He was coming in from the side and rear and they'd be perfectly able to chop him down as they ran past.

"Get away, Lunky!" I roared.

I don't suppose he heard me, for his blood was up. The young woman, who stood exactly where Lunky had left her, was Mistress Telsi. Her face glowed passionately, suffused with blood, and her fists were clenched over her breast. No wonder Lunky was fighting mad!

There was nothing else to do but try to disable these two assassins before it would be needful to stop them permanently from harming Lunky.

Again I shouted: "Keep away, Lunky!" and went racing after the two black clad forms.

In the event, as one turned to face me again, Lunky thrust home.

The other one I managed to twinkle his sword up out of his fist and then, moving rapidly, swung him about, tripped him and so kicked him down.

"No, Lunky!" I yelped and used my own blade to flick Lunky's captured sword from the assassin's tenderest parts.

"I'll have 'em!" he shouted. "Murdering shints! They were going to kill Mistress Telsi! Let me at him!"

"Hold on, hold on! Now listen. We want to find out who sent them, don't we? Well, don't we?"

As I spoke I rested my foot across the throat of the prostrate stikitche and if he wriggled I pressed down to emphasize my words.

Lunky's young face twisted. I'd never seen him like this before, wrought up with blood lust. It was not a pretty sight. But then, of course, we were not dealing with pretty subjects.

"Well, I suppose so, Drajak." He lowered the sword. "All the same—" His dark heavy face looked sullen and his lips, always very red and full, glistened as he licked them. Then he burst out: "These must be the shints who murdered San Tuong!"

"Probably. When did you hear?"

"Riders came in today." He made a gesture across the sand. He still wore his brown robe tied up with string but on his feet he wore sandals against the hot bite of the sand. Suddenly he threw the bloodied sword down in disgust. He shook his head, said: "All right, Drajak. Do what you have to. Make him tell us," and walked across to Mistress Telsi.

She put her arms about him in an unaffected gesture. I guessed she had had an almighty fright, a shock that she might take some time to get over. Her long curling lashes swept down over her cheek as she shut her eyes, holding Lunky. When I'd left them here it had seemed that Mistress Telsi, who after all was a lady of uncertain occupation, had determined to marry the merchant Olipen. He had followed her to the Springs of Benga Annorpha as had Lunky. No one fancied Lunky's chances, an acolyte versus a rich merchant, and yet here Telsi was clearly concerned for Lunky.

The stikitche under my foot wriggled and I looked down at him. I used the tip of my sword to flick his black mask free. His face was brown and taut, marked with deep lines in which blue pigment traced patterns that must mean something to him. As I glowered down on him he flinched back. I suppose that old Dray Prescot look that people call the Devil's Look must have flashed into my ugly old beakhead. I said in a neutral voice: "You heard. Just tell me."

He swallowed and I eased my foot up to assist him. He said: "You know I may not do that."

I sighed. They didn't breed a quality class of stikitches in these parts, that was for sure. Why, some of the assassins I'd known—and seen off, by Krun!—would have tears in their eyes with contempt for this lot!

He ought to have said that, naturally, he had no idea who had set the contract. I'd probably have believed that. As it was, by saying he wasn't allowed to tell me, he was admitting he knew.

He might have been a low class stikitche with a little sword skill; he was enough of a professional to handle himself after a fight. I heard a gasp and a little cry and swiveled to see Mistress Telsi trying to support Lunky. He was gradually slipping down out of her arms. He'd have the shakes and get over them, I rather fancied sooner than later. There was a great deal to this young fellow.

"Drajak!" called Telsi. "Help me!"

"Let him lie down, Telsi. He'll get over it."

"Why—you!"

"Are you going to keep an eye on this fellow, then?"

By this time Lunky was almost horizontal and Telsi was leaning down over him, her arms outstretched. She twisted her head to look up at me. "You have no heart, Drajak, no heart at all!"

No sensible answer being available to me, perforce I said nothing. Thinking this byplay was his chance to escape, the assassin gave my foot an almighty heave, twisted aside and leaped up. He started to run across the sand.

Now fear and panic lead people into strange actions. To escape pursuit until night he would need to run out into the desert away from the white buildings around the Springs, and then sneak back to retrieve his mount and make sure of his water and rations.

He ran straight towards the buildings.

His head was down and his black robes streamed out abaft his flying figure.

He ran headlong into a party of men walking out towards us. They recognized him for what he was. They saw Lunky lying on the sand and Telsi bending over him. So as this poor stikitche ran into them their swords flashed and they chopped him.

Lunky's hoarse voice reached me. "Did he tell you?"

I did not think it necessary to mention his attack of the shakes and Telsi's instinctive reaction. I was glad he was coming back to us.

I said: "No. It was not really necessary. Those two villains Caran and Hargon plotted to kill San Tuong Mishuro and now it seems you were included in the plot."

He started to rise and Telsi helped him, not looking at me.

"I find it hard to accept that dikasters would order anyone murdered." Lunky brushed sand from his brown robe. "But I do accept it. San Tuong Mishuro was a good and fair master. Now he is dead I joy for him that he has at last reached Gilium but I feel saddened at the way of it."

As he spoke I decided human nature is so intractable a creature as to defy logical analysis. Already I'd established that if you suicided you would not be admitted to the paradise of Gilium. That would include paying a stikitche to kill you. What a weird and wonderful world it was, this planet of Kregen! Like any normal human being you'd struggle to stay alive and yet all the time, here in Tsungfaril, you were longing to go up to Gilium and live in paradise for ever!

Much of the country wore this apathetic air of caring only for the afterlife. This obsession was not really like the attitudes of religious folk here on Earth who believe they will go to heaven when they die. Oh, yes, there were similarities but they paled before the intensity of the obsession with Gilium.

I said: "San Tuong was a good man. But I think you will be just as good a man, and probably a better Diviner."

"Oh, yes. That is generally accepted," he said quite matter-of-factly.

"And you will take over?"

"The college will swear me in. Yes, I shall be San Lunky Mishuro."

So that was it.

The Diviner's Apprentice, the Acolyte, had been the target Mevancy and I had been sent by the Star Lords to protect.

In that case, then, where the hell was Mevancy?

That odd feeling I'd had when I'd been transited here through the Star Lord's blue curtain of radiance had not been caused because of that very transference. Although different, it was enough like being shifted by the phantom Blue Scorpion as to be familiar. And I'd recognized the feeling when it happened. No—the oddness was that the time was now late afternoon. Between my leaving the queen's bathing chamber and my arrival here time had elapsed. My leaving and arrival had been instantaneous, I believed most devoutly. So the Everoinye had deliberately done this.

Just as I reached this disturbing conclusion a hail brought my attention to the party from the town.

"Hai! We thought the San was dead."

Lunky waved an arm and as the party came up he said: "I live, praise Tsung-Tan in his infinite wisdom."

"The stikitches were observed," said the bluff, red-faced fellow who stood as their leader. "And as sure as my name is Hung-do the Ron, we smelled out their mischief."

"We came as fast as we could," piped up the little fellow with a spear taller than himself, his buck-teeth protruding.

"I give you my thanks, walfgers." Lunky spoke slowly, his voice deeper than I remembered. Already he was settling into the position of a Diviner, one whose task in life was to seek out and proclaim the spirits of the paol-ur-bliem in new born babies. He'd be good at it. No doubt of it. "I shall speak of you to the college."

Whatever that meant, or, rather, whatever might come of it, the people showed their pleasure at the promise. Being a cynical old hare I surmised there would be money and rewards accruing.

Mistress Telsi, holding onto Lunky with a possessive grip, said: "I would like to go back where I might lie down—"

"Of course!"

At once everybody sprang into action and they'd have carried her back if necessary—or if she let go that death grip on Lunky.

The situation here, crystal clear in itself, had no need of Lunky's few words in explanation.

The news of Mishuro's death had reached the Springs this morning. Arrangements for Lunky's departure were made at once, the start back to begin on the morrow. This changed the romantic situation. Now, instead of a lowly acolyte serving and studying a man who would live for years, Lunky was himself the Diviner. Now he stood in a much better position than the merchant Olipen. And, clearly, Telsi really preferred Lunky. Olipen had received his marching orders, and the two lovebirds had taken a little stroll out from the Springs to discuss their future. The assassins had ridden in this morning, too, and chose this opportune moment to strike.

That was all easily understandable.

What puzzled me was the absence of Mevancy. She was here, at the Springs. Why hadn't the Star Lords just hoicked her out of whatever she was up to and dumped her down here to protect Lunky?

Half-carried, Telsi was being taken off and Lunky trotted alongside. He turned to me, his heavy flushed face not really smiling but shining with benevolence, to say: "We owe you a great deal, Draj—"

Startled into speech, I burst out, drowning what he was saying. "My debt is to you, san." Then, quickly and low enough so that only Lunky could hear: "You remember once you saw me with what you called a funny face? So that I was disguised? I would esteem it a favor if you would not call me Drajak—"

"What should be your name, then?" He was amused at the conceit.

"Oh—Nath the Twist will do."

"Very well, Nath the Twist, so be it."

"And Telsi also."

"As you wish."

I offered no explanation. People on Kregen are often under the necessity of sailing under false colors. Names are important, and more than one lame brain has lost his head because a name was not remembered. If Lunky would not grasp the necessity for this stratagem, Mevancy most certainly would. By Vox, yes! She would see at once that I would have to explain how it was that I was in the palace one moment and across to the west at the Springs of Benga Annorpha the next. How, the question would be asked, how was that possible? Black magic? Sorcery?

Some explanation would have to be concocted for Lunky and Telsi if they asked. Otherwise I'd stay mum.

Once we reached the cluster of white buildings, Telsi could lie down and recover. The bodies of the assassins were brought in and they would be disposed of. The attitude to assassins hereabouts was ambivalent. It was accepted that these fellows earned a living doing what they did, and the nature of their occupation would not necessarily bar them from Gilium. All the same, a very natural and understandable revulsion towards stikitches was apparent. In general—not always—they received short shrift from me.

The excitement died down and Lunky and I found some refreshments. The Suns would soon be gone and the multitude of Kregan stars would burst across the desert sands. I wondered if I ought to play a trick on Mevancy when she at last put in an appearance. Still, she would have to know what I'd been up to, as I most certainly wanted to know what she'd been getting into lately. So I decided to let my own old Dray Prescot face show when she arrived. And—I knew what her first word to me would be! Oh, yes!

When the door opened on a gust of sand and she stomped in, I lifted my jug to her in friendly greeting. She stopped, put her fists on her hips and glared at me from under down drawn brows. She said:

"Cabbage!"

Just as I'd known she would!

Ten

As far as Mevancy nal Chardaz knew, I was still a weakling not fully recovered from injury, or recovered but without strength.

This state of affairs had just happened; admittedly I'd done nothing to disabuse her of the notion. It wasn't really important. This was why she continued to call me cabbage.

Now she stood glaring balefully as Lunky said: "You are welcome, Mevancy. Come and sit down and take a glass. You have heard the news?"

She had to force herself to regain her composure and be polite to Lunky, who was, after all, now an important personage.

"Yes, and I must call you san now—"

"When the college so decree."

"There will be no problem over that. I am sorry that San Mishuro—I mean, he has gone up to Gilium; but—"

"I know. Here." Lunky handed her a glass of the clear straw-yellow wine as she sat down. She wore a new outfit rather after the fashion of the near-universal men's fawn gown and cloak, except that it was unmistakably styled for the female figure. Her arms were covered by sleeves gathered in a series of loops and the oval shapes of skin already showed that her deadly arsenal of needles—her bindles—were well grown back. Anybody who tried to attack Mevancy would get a shower of needles in the eyes and face.

She gave me a look. "Well, cabbage?"

Carefully, I said: "The plot was cleverly managed. It was—ah—fortunate that I was on hand to help Lunky defeat the stikitches."

She took my meaning at once.

She sipped her wine delicately and glowered on me from under her eyebrows. Her dark hair had been caught up in a web of brilliants—all artificial, as I well knew from the state of our treasury. She wanted to ask me all about it; and could not because San Lunky sat there between us.

Not a beautiful girl, our Mevancy; but alive and quick and passionate. Her mouth was too wide and generous and her chin strong and her ways abrupt, and because she was the leader of our team and was a trifle insecure and anxious not to go wrong, somewhat arrogant, imperious and a lady for whom I cherished a lively affection that caused me not to chop her down to size. Given the inscrutable ways of the Star Lords there was a good chance that one day Mevancy might be honored to meet Delia, ex-Empress of Vallia. In that case, I fancied Delia would act with such graciousness that Mevancy would blossom into real womanhood.

"Cabbage? Are you ill? Your face has all gone like putty."

"You really do look—strange," put in Lunky.

I roused myself. "I was thinking of a lady."

"Oh," Mevancy sniffed. "That one."

I gave her a look and she flushed up. Poor Mevancy! Because she was a Sinnalix she could shoot deadly darts from her arms into the eyes of enemies. This was done by blood pressure. As I said, poor Mevancy—she flushed all too easily.

Lunky's skill as a Diviner, one who could find the spirit of a person in a new born baby, was easily equal to smoothing over little difficulties of this nature. He lifted his glass. "If we are to start for Makilorn in the morning, it is bed for me." He drained the glass and Mevancy and I stood up as with wishes for a good night's sleep he went out.

When we were alone she took a deep breath, plunked herself down and in a menacing voice said: "Well?"

"We were both wrong. The target was Lunky all along."

"The Everoinye brought you here to save him?"

"Yes."

She put a finger to her lips, pressing, thinking.

"I had to deal with a thief who tried those two unpleasant nobles, Nanji and Floria. He'd have slit their throats as they lay in each other's arms." She gestured. "When that happened I was certain they were the targets."

"So if you'd been brought here by the Star Lords to defend Lunky those two would have died?"

"Oh, yes, certainly."

I felt anger and suppressed it. Nanji and Floria were unpleasant people, that was true. They were nobles, a lord and lady, and they acted in the worst traditions of nobility. All the same, they were people and Mevancy had done right in saving their lives. All the same, when I thought of what had gone on here, of the transaction, the balance, the weighing in the scales, it was all I could do to stop myself jumping up and rushing blindly out into the night, swearing at the top of my voice and swishing my sword about in violence and savage baffled fury.

"You look..." she said, and then: "You'd better tell me."

"Aye," I fairly snarled. "Aye, I'll tell you. Stikitches attacked Lunky all right. I was dragged here just as I was about to prevent another pack of assassins from doing their murderous work—"

"Oh? Who was their target?"

I breathed in and out. "The queen."

Mevancy put her glass on the table. She lost some of that high color. "She is all right?"

"I do not know. No, Mevancy, no. I am sure she is not all right."

"The queen is dead? But—if you were there—?"

"Oh, aye, I was there. And a blue curtain dropped before me, a part of that damned Scorpion, and brought me here. If the queen is murdered then the responsibility rests squarely with the Everoinye."

"I suppose—"

"Suppose nothing! The damned Star Lords don't care about ordinary individual people. I wouldn't put it past them!"

"Cabbage, have a care!" She was agitated, squirming on her chair. She looked about the room almost as though she expected to see a Star Lord walk in, or, more probably, fly in. "Drajak, you mustn't say such dreadful things about the Everoinye!"

I fumed away, and, truth to tell, I thought myself a pretty poor kind of fellow. I was letting off steam like this, and poor Mevancy was taking the brunt of my ill humor, because a fine woman had been so wantonly killed. That she and everyone else believed she'd come back as a new born baby made not the slightest difference. Did I believe it?

I looked across at Mevancy. I could feel for her, no doubt of it, feel compassion and affection and a little remorse. I wanted her to succeed as a kregoinya, an agent of the Star Lords. She shared the same fanaticism as Pompino, my kregoinye comrade. She believed—and I did not want her to fail. I knew what my Delia would say if I was unkind to Mevancy.

By the Black Chunkrah! My Delia would go through hell and high water to avoid being unkind! And she had a way with her of making sure I acted likewise. By Vox, hadn't I climbed down a damned great hole at her command to bring out a Wizard of Loh who was now our comrade?

Oh, no, make no mistake. Delia of Delphond, Delia of the Blue Mountains, did not tolerate unkindness although she would be the first to forgive and start afresh. I thought: If I don't see Delia again soon I shall do more than swear at the Star Lords!

Speaking more calmly I told Mevancy of the situation in Makilorn. "San Chandro seems a decent old buffer. I thought spying for him would prove an excellent opportunity—"

"I see. It is a pity I was not there to do the thinking for us, as usual. Now you have unwanted explanations to offer." Her voice rang tartly.

I ignored that. I wondered if I'd asked her what she would have done in the circumstances what her reply would be. I went on carefully: "The queen's Chief Repositer is Nath the Uttarler and it seems he is not a strong personality. Two of the queen's Repositers, Yango and Shang-Li-Po, stand directly in opposition to Chandro. It is possible they ordered the queen's death."

"You were much taken by this Queen Leone, Drajak. That is clear."

"There is also a matter of the queen's necklace. Her bumptious wizard, Chang-So, is a fellow to watch out for." I told Mevancy what had transpired and finished: "Whatever is the secret of the queen's necklace, it seems to me nothing to do with our duties to the Star Lords."

"I shall make that decision, cabbage. Now we must turn in to make an early start tomorrow."

She was back in command again, poised, ready to be cutting or gracious to me. I didn't smile. This whole imbroglio looked to be far more complicated than anything Mevancy could dream of.

I said: "Better not say anything about the queen. We'll—"

"Quite, cabbage!"

By which she meant I ought not to have got myself embroiled with Chandro and spying and the queen to the detriment of our work for the Star Lords.

She went on in a different tone of voice: "This reminds me of the time when Rafael and I had a child to care for and there was a hue and cry for a thief down the aracloins up in Shangsha—terribly hot and humid—and we had to lie our way out of it." She pursed up her lips. "Well, we had to, cabbage, you see that? So I fancy we'll forget about the queen's necklace if I say so. All these baubles are overpriced, anyway."

There seemed little to say after that so we went off to our respective bedrooms and I, for one, slept soundly. A stout old campaigner has to get his hours of sleep in when and as he can.

As she was in the habit of calling me cabbage, because of my helpless paralysis after the fire, I called her pigeon, because of the way she'd been overcharged by the ferryman. I realized I'd not called her pigeon once during our charged conversation.

The morning and the first breakfast brought news of an unwelcome kind.

Chiako the Gut sweated as he told us. I eyed him with some disfavor. He had been Mishuro's guard captain and whilst you couldn't blame him for Mishuro's death, unfortunately for him mud sticks. As a cadade he had the safety of his master in his care. His master had been murdered—ergo, Jiktar Chiako the Gut, cadade, was at fault. As he told us the news he was, I am sure, sweating over what Lunky's decision would be. Lunky, I felt, was too gentle a soul to sack the cadade on the spot.

Just before we'd gone in for breakfast Mevancy had told me in her decision-made-no-argument manner that we must get back to Makilorn as soon as possible. That way, she reasoned, we might be able to avoid awkward questions about my being in two places at the same time. As I'd been lost in the palace labyrinth I could say I'd been knocked on the head by someone and only now found my way back. I'd said: "Lunky—" and she'd said: "Leave Lunky to me."

So now, unhappy about her so-called plan, I listened as Chiako the Gut said: "The Glitch Riders have been reported moving south. It is not yet known if this is a raid or a nomadic movement."

As the Glitch Riders inhabited a stretch of land to the north of Tsungfaril and were nomads and reivers, this news was not good. Chiako went on: "It would be wise to delay our return to Makilorn for a few days until we know how dangerous a threat the Glitch Riders are this time."

That made sweet sense. Not to Mevancy, though—oh, no!

If she wanted to smuggle me back into the city and bluff it out then this interruption was fatal to her scheme.

She did take things with intense seriousness!

"This is a nuisance," said Lunky. He shook his head. "I really do wish to return as soon as possible. There are many things to be done now that San Mishuro is gone, things I would rather do sooner than later."

"Yes, san," said Chiako, sweating, "but—"

"And Mistress Telsi will be coming with us." Lunky didn't smirk—well, not exactly—but he looked like the little boy who's found the biggest sweet in the jar.

Chiako half raised his hands from his leather-clad sides and let them drop. Clearly, he was saying, this is the last straw.

Mevancy said: "You are mighty tender about your lord now, cadade. Where were you and your men last night when the assassins struck?"

I held myself still. This was a sore point. Chiako's heavy face blackened with anger. His gut quivered. Yet he controlled his manner so that his words sounded neutral. "The san slipped out without telling me. No one knew he had walked into the desert."

I felt that to be the truth of it. And, yet— "It is your duty to watch the san at all times, cadade!" flashed Mevancy.

He wriggled in his armor, already hot in the growing heat of the day.

"You have had an easy life in your position as captain of the guard to San Mishuro. You oversee the slaves as they open and close the main doors. That about sums up your duties. Well now, cadade, life has changed. Now," and here Mevancy rolled the words around savoring them. "Now you will have to earn your hire. Your life is forfeit if harm comes to the san."

"But—" began Chiako, blustering a little and yet with common use on his side. Some societies would punish guards who failed. "My contract—"

"May be terminated if you wish."

Lunky said in a nervous voice: "Well..."

A change had gone on in the relationship of Mevancy and Lunky since I'd been away, that was crystal clear. She was acting with an authority that surprised me. She ought to have told me if Lunky had given her authority.

"We shall be leaving for Makilorn directly after the second breakfast." Mevancy made it crisp. "Be ready. Now you may go."

He gave her a sloppy salute, his face murderous, and took himself off.

"Gahamond-forsaken idiot!" she said. "By Spurl! That man needs a lesson!"

"You are sure, Mevancy? I mean, Mistress Telsi—"

"Quite sure, Lunky—san. You have power now. Don't forget that. We'll take good quality zorcas, travel light, and we'll be there in no time."

"If you say so, Mevancy."

So that was the way of it.

I knew why I wanted to race back to Makilorn as fast as the fleetest zorca in all Kregen could carry me. I could still see the picture of the queen etched into my memory. She stood on the edge of the pool, the scented water running down her body, glowing, shining. Her fists on hips, her head high, she stared with contempt upon the assassins. Could she have survived, somehow still be alive? I did not think so.

San Chandro had said the queen's Repositers must not be harmed for the stability of the state. I do not believe in blind revenge. But, if Yango and Shang-Li-Po had ordered the queen murdered... As our little party mounted up on blood zorcas I knew then I didn't know what I would do.

So we rode back to Makilorn through the streaming mingled lights of the Suns of Scorpio.

Eleven

We traveled light and we rode fast. Being what my Terran friends call an old hare I'd taken the precaution of taking along a bow. This was a splendid Lohvian longbow obtained by Chiako the Gut at Lunky's orders. I hadn't paid for it. The superb bow I'd bought from Master Twang remained among my possessions with San Chandro.

Our small party rode fast but after a time it was necessary for us to dismount and walk along leading the zorcas. Zorcas are wonderful saddle animals, tall of spindly leg, close-coupled, full of fire and spirit; they are not magical and they need to be treated properly like any other riding animal. The desert about us drifted with an occasional lift of sand as a random breeze wafted. I had the uneasy feeling we might be in for a storm. If that were so then it was imperative our zorcas were kept fresh and strong.

So, walking along over the sand leading our mounts, we pressed on for the river and Makilorn. And, of course, it was as we were thus walking that the Glitch Riders struck. Naturally!

They came whooping over a dune off to our starboard bow. Clearly one of them had been lying invisibly there and watching us approach.

"Mount up! Mount up!" Chiako screamed it out. He was in trouble with his zorca, the animal rearing and lashing out with his hooves as Chiako held onto the leading rein. "Hold still!" he yelled, and: "Mount up!"

Well, the cadade was trying to live up to his job and do what was required. No doubt he could still hear Mevancy's stinging words sizzling his ears. Lunky was trying to help Mistress Telsi mount up, and Mevancy was interfering and trying to help Lunky. Some of Chiako's guard detail were already in their saddles, others were unhandily trying to climb aboard.

Before I mounted up, I decided, I'd essay a shaft.

Because the longbow was of Lohvian manufacture and style it was first class. It was not in the same class as the bow I'd bought from Master Twang—that was premium class and no mistake. I nocked the first shaft and quite unselfconsciously thought of Seg. I said silently to myself: "To you Erthanfydd the Meticulous the cast," and let fly.

The shaft flew true. It struck the leading Glitcher and with a wailing screech he flopped sideways out of his saddle. The next shaft was already winging on its way and the third was in my fingers. Compared to any normal archer, I suppose the shooting was quite good. Seg would have feathered four shafts before you could blink.

An unholy racket was going on at my side and between the soft shuffle of zorcahooves on sand and the stupid yelling I made out Mevancy calling: "Stop that at once, cabbage! Mount up instantly! Unless you wish to be left alone!" I loosed the third shaft.

Well, by this time she was right. There were about twenty Glitchers, and three were down. Had we all shot we could have drastically thinned their numbers. As it was—I stowed the bow, grabbed my zorca and swung up into the saddle.

Now we were going to gallop off, running for it. Again I suppose Mevancy was right, for we had Lunky and Mistress Telsi to concern us.

I anticipated no problems in running away. We rode zorcas and the Glitchers rode narrow-flanked, spiky-headed, six-legged saddle animals called wegeners, with desert-yellow hides and mean eyes. We could out-run these wegeners with ease—well, that is a foolish remark. As I believed then a zorca could outrun any animal on Kregen.

The Glitch Riders swung parallel, whooping and brandishing their weapons. They used the yellow wegeners on their raids because of their camouflage color. Their own lands were marginally desert and grassland and there they'd use any of the wonderful array of riding animals available to Kregans. One or two loosed off after us; no one was hit.

For all my joy in the longbow and my knowledge of its powers in the hands of a competent bowman, let alone the marvels a master like Seg can achieve, I am aware that there are cases where a shorter bow becomes useful. You see, even now I hesitated to say was better. The short compos-ite reflex bow as used by Valkan Archers was the weapon from the saddle. What Seg might say about the large composite reflex with its cunning sinew and horn pulling and pushing I did not care to contemplate. But that was a thing for the future. Right now as we galloped over the desert with the shushing thump of hooves, the jingle of harness and the savage yells of our pursuers in our ears, was the time I fancied I'd try a few shots.

Mind you, all this smart talk about short bows for cavalry to use more easily than long bows—well, a cavalryman handles a long spear or lance well enough, and a bow can be canted to avoid hitting the animal—I dropped to the tail of the rout and nocked an arrow. Like your true Par-thian I turned in the saddle and shot in the longbow. The leading Glitcher tumbled from his mount and I selected the next arrow.

"You fambly, cabbage—concentrate on riding!"

I picked the next Glitcher and loosed. As I could not think of anything polite to say to Mevancy I kept my old black-fanged winespout shut.

"Oh, you!" She was riding alongside now and a return shaft thunked into the sand between us. So, thinking of something useful to say I snarled out: "Ride further up the front and look out for Lunky."

A single quick glance at her face showed me a Kregan sunset with the red sun dominating all the sky. She was spitting angry. My third shot knocked over a Glitcher and I reached for another shaft.

"You do not talk to me like that, Drajak! You forget, I am the one cho-sen by the Everoinye to lead—" She didn't say any more because her zorca abruptly pitched over. The creature let out an agonizing sigh. He toppled over, sprawling forward and furrowing the sand. An arrow stuck up, ugly and obscene in that beautiful animal. Mevancy went head over heels in a flurry of garments and landed splat on her back.

I'd been using my knees to control my zorca, an old clansman's habit, and now I reluctantly lowered the bow and gentled the animal with my right hand. I spoke to him as a clansman speaks to his animals and we skidded to a halt, and pirouetted, no doubt making a most pretty picture of fountains of sand and swirling draperies, and circled, heading back to where Mevancy was just standing up and pulling out her sword. The Glitchers whooped in triumph and came sweeping down, weapons glittering.

There was just time. It was going to be nip and tuck; but if she didn't argue and if she climbed up directly, we should just get away in time.

Well, of course, as I reached her, being Mevancy, she wanted to argue.

Leaning over I clasped her around the waist and violently heaved her up. She was not light; but she was not as heavy as I'd expected. She nearly nicked me with her sword and she was swearing and yelling and generally carrying on dreadfully.

I slapped her face-down before me and started the zorca into motion.

An arrow whipped past my nose and another hit a stirrup.

The zorca responded strongly and we went bounding away.

He was a splendid animal; his name was Sandeater and he lived up to it in fine style, and we hurtled across the desert. The ferocious yells of the Glitchers bounced after us. Ahead our party still galloped on and not a single one of them had turned back to our assistance.

"Let me up! Let me up!"

She wriggled around and hit me a thumping great clout with her leg as she swung across to sit astride. She hadn't dropped her sword and she scabbarded the blade; I wasn't foolish enough to say anything about my approval of that excellent conduct. Now a zorca is very close-coupled. A single rider can sit comfortably in the saddle. When two ride fore and aft the limited space forces them to sit packed tightly together. This close and intimate contact didn't bother me, and I didn't really give it much thought. The Glitchers were still following and still shooting although their shafts were falling short, and what would happen if they hit Sandeater was uppermost in my mind.

Mevancy wriggled about.

"Try to sit still, pigeon. Sandeater—"

"Let me have the reins, then, fambly."

They'd been hitched up out of the way when I'd been shooting. As she was sitting in front of me it seemed logical she should have the reins. She kept her balance superbly; but again she wriggled and swayed. I took my feet out of the stirrups and said: "Use the stirrups."

After that we raced along in fine style. No more arrows dropped near us; but a cautious turn to look back revealed the Glitchers still stubbornly following. They were no doubt calculating that an animal bearing a double load would soon tire.

We weren't out of the wood yet, no, by Krun, not by a long way!

Sitting this close to Mevancy enabled me to smell her perfume, subtle and rather nice. Perfume used with skill is charming; overdone it is repulsive. Again I looked back to see our pursuers riding on. Funny though she was, this Mevancy nal Chardaz, her fate would not be funny if she fell into their hands. Perhaps if I tried another shot...

"Sit still, cabbage! You'll have us both off!"

Sandeater bounded along, it seemed effortlessly; but he'd tire in the end. And, then— "If you will lean forward, pigeon, I will try a shot at them. Every one less is—"

"Yes, yes, I know that. But you can't shoot like this!"

Patiently I said: "If you just bend a little and give my right elbow some room. Yes, like that. Good." I nocked the shaft, turned and loosed at the leading pursuer. I missed.

Mevancy's eye gleamed as she looked back. She opened her mouth and just then Sandeater—who was clearly as much taken by Mevancy as was I—gave a sudden extra leap on and Mevancy gasped and clutched and nearly fell off.

By the time she'd got herself straightened up I had another shaft in my fingers. I said: "Hold still and bend over, pigeon!" and this time my shaft hit the fellow leading the pursuit. I heard his screech as he tumbled off. All the same, by Vox, the others continued to ride on.

Useless to think the obvious thought that occurred to me to enter my brain. How grand to have Seg riding alongside! He'd feather the whole bunch of 'em back there before you could blink. And Inch, with his axe, to lop a few heads of any who continued to hang about. Well, the Star Lords had snatched me away from home and comrades and I had to soldier on as best I could without them.

Mevancy, looking back over my shoulder, said with a very sharp snap: "You have only nine shafts left."

I said: "Ten, I think."

It wasn't a case of thinking; any bowman worth his salt knows how many shafts he has left in the quiver. But I didn't want to be unkind.

"And there are thirteen of the shints left."

"I don't think they will continue to pursue if we reduce their numbers a trifle more."

"You're very damned confident, Drajak! I wonder your arm has the muscles to pull a bow."

In all the uproar I'd forgotten I was supposed to be a weakling.

"It's a knack, I suppose."

So, of course, my next arrow missed.

"If," she said, fairly spitting it out. "If those shints up ahead stopped and we all shot together—"

"We'd still have to come to handstrokes. And there's Lunky."

"And he can only think of Telsi. What a mess!"

"There's no discredit in a man wanting to look after a woman," I said, somewhat more tartly than I'd intended. "Nor a woman looking after a man. Even if the person being looked after somehow fancies it demeans their self-respect." I felt the way her back went up; but she didn't interrupt. "I don't forget how you cared for me, pigeon."

"And you don't think I did that just because the Everoinye—?"

"No, I don't. Oh, sure, the Everoinye tasked you with saving my skin. I think you'd have acted as you did in any case."

Then she showed her spirit and my stupidity. In an even voice she said: "You're getting maudlin, cabbage."

My Val! And wasn't she right!

I turned around, feeling her back against my side, and loosed a shaft with considerable venom. Another Glitch Rider hit the sand.

The folk up ahead were drawing steadily further and further away. A quick glance in their direction told me that and also showed me Lunky leaning around and looking back. As I swung back to let another shaft go at the devils pursuing us, Lunky seemed to me to wave his arms around. My arrow hit and I reached up for another shaft.

The whole desert tilted, the world of Kregen went upside down and around and around and I went up with it and came down smack and just managed to roll and break the violence of the fall.

Mevancy let out a muffled shriek. She landed on top of me.

Sand in my eyes and in my nostrils, sand clogging my mouth. I spat and clawed up. I shook my head and the famous old bells of Beng-Kishi clanged a single gong note in my skull. A furious swipe across my eyes and I could see the Glitch Riders roaring on, sand kicking away from their mounts' hooves, their weapons glittering, their sand scarves streaming in the wind of their onrush. They looked a ferocious bunch. Mevancy rolled off me and struggled in the sand like a fish in a net. The longbow was not broken—thanks be to Opaz!—and I snatched it up and nocked a shaft.

One—two—three—and then it would be handstrokes.

In the event I managed to loose off four—and had a flashing notion that Seg would take delight in his old mocking way—and then it was time for handstrokes.

The longbow pitched into the sand. The leading rider leaned far forward over his mount's ungainly neck, his spear held low. The point looked decidedly nasty.

Abruptly he reared up, shrieking. His face was a mask of blood. I caught a glimpse of Mevancy at my side, her arms extended before her. Her face, flushed with blood, held such a look of concentrated fear and loathing I began to feel a mite sorry for these importunate Glitchers. The following rider collided with the first and the wegeners sprawled sideways, sand spurting, and went down in a tangle of limbs.

There was no point in hanging about for the next one to get a clear run at us, so I let out a shrieking kind of yell, an incoherent screech, and leaped forward.

A fellow who wore a leather helmet under his riding hood tried to spit me and I slipped his spear, grabbed it with my left hand, jerked, and as he somersaulted out of the saddle, slit his throat.

Mevancy was yelling. "No, Lunky, no! Keep away!"

There was no time to see what the hell was going on there. I could guess, though, by Vox!

The next rider hauled up, and the wegener's hooves slashed sand in a flat arc. He pulled away and started to gallop around to the side and I swiveled with him. As he did so the next in line hauled out to the other side. So that was to be the way of it!

They'd ride circle about us and shaft us as we stood. I might down some of those remaining; they'd get us in the end. It was quite clear these Glitchers came from a society that did not overvalue human life, their own or other peoples'. They'd kill Lunky and me and take the girl.

I stuck the sword in the sand and dragged up the long bow.

"Lunky! You fambly! You'll be killed!" Mevancy sounded more cross than frightened now, so I guessed her reactions had settled down. She'd let rip with her bindles, the deadly darts from her forearms, and she'd got one of them; the others would stay out of her range.

Lunky said: "I could not ride off and see you slain, Mevancy."

He came up and slid off his zorca. Poor old Sandeater struggled on the sand beyond us, an arrow through a hindquarter. If we could get him to a vet he'd recover well enough. I eyed Lunky's zorca.

"Pigeon! You and Lunky must ride off! Now!"

"But—"

"By the Black Chunkrah, girl!" Then I let rip. "If your everlasting Everoinye knew what they were doing they'd send their damned great Blue Scorpion to hoick us all out of it!"

"Drajak! Have a care how you talk of them—!"

"What, now?" I snarled a choking kind of laugh. "Now when we're all about to get the chop?"

The Glitchers swung about us, kicking sand. They presented targets they no doubt considered difficult to hit. We were in the open. "Get yourself up by the zorca. Make Lunky go as well." The old devil flamed in my voice, for she grabbed Lunky and shoved him up against his zorca. I stepped before them. Now we had only one side to worry about, from incoming arrows, and we'd have to watch out for a sneaky attacker creeping up beyond the zorca.

The Glitchers took a fatalistic approach to life and death. No doubt the remainder of the warband circling about us had not spared a single thought for their dead comrades. Whilst the girl was there for the taking each one would fight for her. As they rode about us, and the first shafts came in, I considered this was neither bravery nor stupidity but simple cupidity.

The old Krozair techniques of knocking arrows out of the air would preserve my life in this situation. I could use either sword or bowstave in those cunning twists and deflections. So I'd be all right. Mevancy and Lunky—well, now, I had to save them and so would have to leap about in front, and I'd have to be mighty careful that a deflected arrow didn't hit the zorca. So whilst I was doing that an arrow could all too easily come flying in and go thwunk into me. I set myself and began knocking arrows out of the air.

Lunky was having none of this.

He stepped up beside me, sword in fist swishing about and making me skip out of his way.

"Lunky!" yelled Mevancy.

She pulled him back and he shook himself like a dog shaking off water. An arrow went whick! into the sand at his feet as I knocked it down.

"Let me at 'em!" he was shouting, waving the sword, foaming.

What a circus! Each time I deflected a shaft I could see the picture we made. Also, I was glad some of my comrades couldn't see that farcical scene. Turko! My Val! He'd never let this choice example of Dray Prescot idiocy rest. Not likely!

Quite clearly this could not go on much longer. Either I'd miss an arrow and one of us would get killed, or Lunky would break free from Mevancy and go charging out to be feathered. In the event the ending turned out to be so mundane I felt all that humor boil over. The Glitch Riders stopped circling us, turned tail, and galloped off. Shortly thereafter a troop of cavalry charged past in pursuit. Trylon Kuong and his retinue halted before us. He was vastly surprised to find us in the desert like this and as he dismounted and greeted us he said: "I have come to fetch you, San Lunky Mishuro. The college is assembling." His voice sounded bleak. "The queen is dead."

Twelve

Lunky took his duties as a Diviner with the utmost gravity. This was what one would expect both of him and of a Diviner. Together with the other two Diviners, they must now discover the queen in the body of a new born baby.

The funeral ceremonies, given the beliefs in reincarnation of these people, were lavish. Not one but two bundles of wood were used for the queen's cremation fire, and the coffin, which was painted tastefully with scenes from Gilium, actually had a corner quite badly burned.

I, for one, did not miss the irony of the paintings of Gilium on a coffin containing a paol-ur-bliem, a person accursed, sentenced to return a hundred times to Kregen before being allowed into the heavenly paradise of Gilium.

Trylon Kuong, well-recovered, proved himself worthy of taking up a political position in the life of the city during this time. He was going to prove a most likely and useful person to have on our side in the struggles to come. For there was no doubt that the dikasters were split, in opinions and beliefs. Even more importantly, when it came to push of pike, they were bitterly and personally opposed to the extent of murder—as we had seen.

A new Repositer would have to be appointed for Kuong, to replace Caran. Kuong would have a considerable say in the selection and he spent a considerable amount of time interviewing candidates from the college's training academy. The position was slightly complicated by the need for a Repositer to replace Hargon for the instruction of Leotes, and here continuity was not, of course, possible.

As for myself, I decided on a bold course in dealing with San Chandro. He'd seen me off into the secret passageways of the palace, and then I'd turned up in the retinue about Kuong and Lunky.

Mevancy went off with Lunky and Telsi and they would take up residence in the Mishuro villa. I went off to report to Chandro.

Because I had the entry permit I was able to see him, and he was more than anxious to see me. We met in the small room where we'd first played Jikaida, and the board lay on the table, set for a game. Chandro greeted me eagerly. There was no smile on his narrow face and he looked more gaunt than ever.

"So you see, Drajak." He spread his arms. "Even the queen."

I nodded, for clearly I couldn't say: 'May her soul rest in peace,' for her soul was being reborn in an infant.

He gave me a sharp look. "And where have you been?"

So I played it, as I said, boldly.

I made an expansive gesture. "San, I do not understand much of what passes here in Makilorn. I know of the power of Tsung-Tan. All I have learned tells me the wizards are mighty in power." I paused for effect, and went on in a hushed, heavy voice: "I can tell you only this. From being in the secret passageways I found myself in the desert." I held up a hand as he opened his mouth. "I do not understand. I may have been knocked unconscious and carried there. But, san, you will know. I believe the might and majesty of Tsung-Tan drew me from the palace out into the sands of the desert."

I put an awed look on my face. Even if I do say so myself, I fancy I put on a fine performance. And, anyway, in a society riddled with the kind of beliefs they had here in Tsungfaril, my story ought to be swallowed hook, line and sinker.

Poor old San Chandro put a hand to his mouth, his eyes widening. Then: "This has happened to you? Yes, yes. It is a miracle vouchsafed of Tsung-Tan, highest in heaven. It has been known, it has been known." He was working himself up into a frenzy of religious fervor now, his narrow face flushed and glittering with sweat. "Praise be to Tsung-Tan!"

He'd said that this kind of experience had been known before. Could, my natural thought prompted me, could the Star Lords have had a hand in that one, too?

Or, as was perfectly possible on Kregen, had a wizard exercised his command of thaumaturgy? And, the experience could have been what Chandro believed—a purely religious phenomenon.

He ordered up parclear and sazz and miscils and palines. For a few moments I think he even forgot the queen had been murdered.

I ate and drank with relish, thankful that my ruse had worked.

Reality could not be kept at bay for very long. Chandro heaved up a sigh and said: "What I feared happened. The queen and her handmaids were all slain."

"Were the—?"

"No. They got clean away for no trace of them was found."

"Professional stikitches."

"Yes."

I took a paline. "And their employers?"

He moved his lean shoulders irritably. "I can guess. But we cannot know for sure."

Two things I recalled. One, Chandro saying the death of the other Repositers now would destabilize the college and government, and, two, my vengeful promise to myself if the queen came to harm. Vengeance is a thankless task, anyway. Sometimes there is a dividing line between Justice and Vengeance. Opaz knew, I'd had to tread that line often enough in my career on Kregen. So I made up my mind how to handle both sides of this equation, and used patience to bide my time.

"You look," said Chandro, rather sharply, "you look as though you contemplate murder. That is—"

"I know, san, I know."

"There is no proof."

"As you say, there is no proof."

He gave me a queasy look so I changed that conversational subject.

"I believe San Lunky will prove a first class Diviner."

"Oh, yes, that is certain sure." He stirred the few remaining palines in the bowl. "Yoshi and Vasama are good, no doubt of it; Lunky will prove superior. Tuong always said so."

Yoshi was the fat fussy man and the fat fussy woman was Vasama. I believed Yoshi to be controlled by Vasama. Right then I couldn't see any problems in tracking down the queen. Which just goes to show. Kregen is a wonderful and terrible world and infinitely capable of complicating the simplest issues and causing mayhem over just about anything.

An enquiry about Leone elicited the news that she, with Wink, Prang and Ching-Lee, were still dazed with horror at the queen's murder. Their positions in the palace hierarchy were secure, for under the guidance of Chandro they would serve the same queen. But the horror remained.

Each of the queen's Repositers was responsible for a small cadre of youngsters like this, and Chandro said that fights between them were becoming distressingly more frequent.

I said: "And because San Nath the Uttarler is weak he fails to moderate between you and San Nalgre on our side and Yango and Shang-Li-Po on the other. So who will train and guide the queen as she grows up?"

"I hope I remain unbiased enough to say I pray to Tsung-Tan it will not be Shang-Li-Po."

That seemed a fair enough comment to me. "My spying efforts proved a disaster. They never once discussed anything except the work they'd met to do. If they plotted then they did so elsewhere."

"Oh, they plotted all right."

"So—"

"I stand in danger, as does San Nalgre. Yes, I accept that."

He remained calm but the glitter of sweat on his face came now not from wonder and joy at a miracle but from a more sinister reason.

How long, then, could I wait?

With the care habitual to me now in talking to him, I said: "Lunky has dismissed that buffoon Chiako the Gut and his crew, and rightfully so. I thought criminal proceedings would be brought against them for not honoring their contract. They—"

"They have already applied to me for employment."

"And?"

"Oh, I refused. I told them had Lunky been killed they would all have been guilty." He managed a half-smile. "Anyway, Llodi mends each day and he is anxious to get back into harness. No, Chiako and that juruk are disgraced and Lunky feels that is punishment enough."

Chiako, as cadade of the juruk, would have to take them off somewhere else to find employment. That might not be easy. Scandal spreads.

"So you are going to take on a few more guards?"

He nodded, a reluctant nod. "I fear so."

"Lunky is probably right; but he is a trifle soft-hearted."

"The teachings of Tsung-Tan," he began, and went off into a short sermon, to which I listened politely. That brought him back to my transit from the palace to the desert. He waxed eloquent. It was, in very truth, a marvel. "You are not of Tsungfaril; but I believe you stand high in the estimation of Tsung-Tan. The Godhood has looked upon you and smiled."

Obviously, there was nothing I could say to that.

He went on: "We face perilous times. With the queen still in the body of a child, needing to relearn everything, strong and ruthless people seize their opportunity. I just hope Lunky can sway Yoshi to choose aright. It is certain sure Vasama stands with the other camp."

We talked further, and then, I suppose with a flash of that old leem-hunter intuition, I said: "Would you expect Tsung-Tan, whose name be praised, to transport me about again, san?"

He pursed up his lips in that lean face. He looked judicial. "It is not beyond the bounds of possibility."

How many times people say that when they don't know and want to play both ends against the middle!

"So if I suddenly disappear then you'll know."

"To you the honor, for you have been selected."

I'd been selected all right. By the disgusting putrid nostrils of Makki Grodno! I'd been selected, but not by his Tsung-Tan, oh, dear, no. The Star Lords had more work for me to do down here, that I knew with a dark foreboding, as though my old sailorman's nose had sniffed out a coming gale.

Chandro left for a meeting and when the Blue Scorpion appeared, impossibly huge in that room, and seized me up in cold and vertigo, I experienced the weird and trembly sensation that I had foreseen this occurring just that moment ago. I'd anticipated this happening before it happened.

There was grist for the mills of the mind here.

Head over heels, up I went, as the phantom Blue Scorpion flowed over me, and heels over head I went down, splash! Warm water engulfed me. For an awful instant I thought the Star Lords had thrown me into the River of Drifting Leaves to let the stranks get their teeth into me. I was naked. That had been usual up until recently. Still, for the moment it didn't matter as, rising to the surface and flinging the water from my eyes, I saw I was near the edge of a sizeable pool filled with naked people all splashing and swimming and enjoying themselves.

My first instinctive and ugly thought was the last time I'd seen a swimming pool the Star Lords had dragged me away. So, what was it this time?

The noise boomed up to bounce from a gracefully arched roof built cunningly from several spans joined and supported by slender columns. I saw that I'd been thrown into the water close under an array of diving boards and the next instant a naked young lady hurled herself on top of me. I dived out of the way, to surface and see her swing her hair out of her eyes, laughing, laughing. Then she rolled over and swam off into the throng, to become just another pair of flashing arms among a forest of arms and legs.

The splashing and commotion racketed up across in the corner past the diving boards. By this time I knew I was back at the Springs of Benga Annorpha and this was one of the smaller baths. In the corner the noise spurted up, hard and ugly, and a woman screamed.

I swam across to see the familiar faces, if not the forms, of Nanji and Floria, those two unlovely nobles Mevancy had already rescued. She had been firmly convinced they were the people we had to protect until the attack on Lunky. Now it seemed she was right. They appeared to be arguing with another couple, the man a striking redhead and the woman darker and with an intense, angry, contained face.

The pool grew shallower to the corner in a series of steps. I stood up. There was blood in the water and a body thrashing about. The four struggling together were trying to climb out. Clearly, the woman who had screamed was now drowning and bleeding to death.

She came up in my arms limply, a floppy, naked, pathetic bundle.

A single glance showed me she had no chance of life left.

A wriggling movement in the water drew my instant and concentrated attention.

The beastie was not a true snake, for it had eight limbs and a fish's tail like an eel's. It had hinged jaws and fangs all the way up to its throat. It was about three feet long. And it was wriggling straight for me, jaws agape.

The woman had to be given up for lost; there are few snakes on Kregen, thanks be, but there are poisonous animals. This thing was a Chasserfic, unhealthy, quick and lethal. The woman was as good as dead.

With a quick prayer for her to Tsung-Tan, I hurled her pathetic body straight at the wriggling Chasserfic. She made a tremendous splashing confusion. Shallow though the water was, I could duck under and swim leanly between the stone step and the pool's surface. Blood choked everywhere. Through its coils the woman's body flopped away ahead and the squirming shape of the Chasserfic rolled away, pushed by the massive water disturbance.

Before he could flap his tail and wriggle himself into forward movement I pounced.

His scaly neck just about fitted my fist. Gripping him just abaft that vicious poison-fanged head of his I stood up. The noise shattered off the roof as people panicked. Nanji and Floria and the other two were half-way out, struggling to get up the marble lip. The raw stink of fear smoked over the pool. When the nearest splashing people saw me rise from the water grasping the sinuous lethal length of the killer the screams redoubled.

The Chasserfic was trying to lap his body around me as though he was a python. He had no chance of that, by Krun! He was a water breather. That meant someone had brought him here in a pot of some kind. Now I had no liking for him at all. But it was in his nature to bite people and thus poison them. He was probably just as frightened as the folk milling about trying to clamber out of the baths. On Kregen, of all places, is the spot to recall the frog and the scorpion. So I waded across to the edge and thrust his head under to give him a chance of a breather.

There was a jar. A ceramic pot of a suitable size, painted with mermaids and sea serpents. It stood a pace or two beyond the edge beside one of the columns. Whoever had organized this murder had preferred the subtle ways of nature to the crude knife or arrow of humans.

I started to climb out of the water still holding my poisonous little friend.

"Are you mad!" The voice slapped in, hard, high, intolerant. "Kill the beastly thing at once!"

The woman who spoke so intemperately stood arrogantly fronting me now the danger was past. Her hair was much darker than the norm and water plastered it to her skull. Her face had a curious intense look as though all her features had been drawn forward. She was, interestingly enough, really beautiful; but normal beauty was overtaken by the intensity and driving force of her expression.

"Did you hear? Kill it at once!"

Nanji and Floria, dripping and looking forlorn, gabbled on urging me to kill the horrible thing. They were so consumed with their own fears they hadn't recognized me. Well, that was not surprising; they were nobles and I was a nobody.

I lifted the lid of the pot. There was water there. With a swift and I hoped skilful enough movement, I thrust the Chasserfic in and slapped the lid down. There were plaited cords to hold it securely.

The man with red hair, a splendid specimen of a fighting man, said: "He's safe enough now." He looked at me. "You did well."

The intense woman interrupted. "I want that awful thing killed. Rodders! Smash that damned pot!"

He gave me a lop-sided grimace. "Llahal. I am Ron Dang Fang—friends insist on calling me Rodders—and you, walfger?"

"Llahal. Drajak. I leave the decision to you, walfger. I will fetch that poor woman out." And I dived in. I didn't want to get involved in a domestic argument, and I didn't want wantonly to kill the animal.

The woman was dead and I put her down gently. Reddened water ran from her to drip into the pool. The ceramic pot painted with mermaids and sea serpents lay in pieces, shattered, and the Chasserfic was contorting in the last few automatic reflexes of death.

The dark-haired woman now had a yellow towel draped about her. Her shoulders were very high and square. The red headed man took his towel from the attentive slaves, goggling at the last dying floppings of the Chasserfic. Nanji and Floria were hurrying off. It seemed to me the Star Lords had brought me here to protect them. That was not as important a detail as finding out who had tried to kill them.

I took a towel and said to the man: "Have you any idea who would bring such an animal in here? And why?"

He wiped the back of his neck with a corner of the towel. "They are scarce animals; thankfully they are dying out. But as to who would do such a dreadful thing—"

The woman suddenly shivered, interrupting. "I may be a Paol-ur-bliem. I would not like to die like that."

The man, this Rodders, put his hand on her shoulder and murmured a few soft words of comfort I did not listen to For an instant she let his hand rest there, her head drooping a little sideways, then she straightened those square shoulders and threw his hand off, swinging about to give a shard of the broken pot a vigorous kick.

"If I catch who did this he'll go headfirst into the river."

There was no doubt she meant it, and no doubt—at least in my mind—that she would carry out the threat.

"I want the Puncture Lady to take a look at you," said Rodders. He turned to face me, smiling his lop-sided smile. "I give you my thanks again, Wr. Drajak." He swung back to the woman. "Now let's go. Come on, Kirsty."

Thirteen

Yes. Indeed. This was the Kirsty whom San Chandro had spoken of, a cousin to Leone. She was sharp. Very. Her nose was small and with flared nostrils. This was unfortunate, for she seemed always to be wearing a contemptuous expression towards the rest of the world. She'd determined to have the Chasserfic put out of the way for the thing had scared her in a fashion she found unsettling and unpleasant. She was a lady who did not have upsetting experiences happen to her. The Chasserfic had died.

Marveling at the way creation brings forward these different characteristics in people related to one another, for Leone and Kirsty were like the famous chalk and cheese, I put Kirsty out of my mind and cast about for a way out of my predicament.

Here I was, in a fashionable watering place, without clothes and without money. Ha! The Star Lords might even find amusement in my plight if, as I believed, they retained that tiny scrap of sense of humor.

In other spots of Kregen there would be no problem. I could go to the local Vallian consul, as I had done before. I could contact a merchant with trading links with Vallia, or Djanduin or, these days and remarkably, Hamal, and take out a letter of credit. In the last recourse in hostile lands I could knock some poor wight on the head and help myself.

Finding some clothes proved not too difficult. With the yellow towel draped about me I wandered along to the changing rooms. Circumspection was necessary. Any thoughts of going to Nanji and Floria were put out of my head as soon as the ridiculous notion occurred to me.

A little Och slave with a shriveled left middle sat at a table. A pottery bowl before him held a collection of coins, all copper. I marched in past the table without even looking at the Och. The room was long and narrow and there were cubicles lining each side. This, then, was indeed a high class establishment, for many changing rooms were just an open room and everyone got on with it. However upper class the place might be, the arrangements made it more difficult. There did not seem to be any system of presenting a tally to secure your clothes from your cubicle. This was a case of pot luck.

A couple of men walked out, talking, engrossed. They remembered to drop a couple of copper coins in the bowl as they went. Now the place was empty apart from the Och slave attendant. I took a breath and started for one of the doors in the row.

Footsteps slapped on the marble and a voice called: "Wait for me, walfger. We must take a glass together."

I span about. Ron Dang Fang, who was always called Rodders, walked in briskly toweling his fiery red hair. He strode along and halted beside me, half-turning. His clothes were in one of these cubicles, then, in any one of those to left and right. I managed a grimace that passes for a smile. "You are very kind, walfger."

"Call me Rodders." He put a hand on the door latch of the cubicle directly before me. "Don't be long." He opened the door and went inside. When the door closed I let out a breath. I could smell water and salt and vinegar and those mingled scents inseparable from the baths.

These were mineral springs, not the Baths of the Nine. So we were here for health purposes. There might well be establishments here catering to the sybaritic desires of honest folk; certainly there would be a place where a fellow could slake his thirst.

I dived into the opposite cubicle and saw at a glance that the clothes might fit a dwarf; not Dray Prescot.

Tumbling out I cast a glance at Rodders' cubicle. He might well wonder at my antics. The next cubicle along contained a hideous bright green gown with the ubiquitous fawn cloak. I remembered I was Dray Prescot. This play-acting lately must be eating into my brain. I slammed that door shut and tried the next.

Here a decent set of fawn gown and cloak fitted me well enough. There was a curved dagger in a plain sheath, a pair of sandals, and a scrip containing coins. There was no time to check them for a voice lifted outside: "Come on, Drajak! My tongue is afire!"

Rodders swung about as I emerged. "Ah! Let's go!"

I pitched a copper coin into the Och's bowl after Rodders, and we went out under the arcade. The Suns slanted in, glorious in mingled jade and ruby. The scent of flowers from the court and the tinkle of water came very restfully to me.

"The Puncture Lady said she would be all right. She had a shock."

"A nasty business—Rodders. Any idea who—?"

Expansively he put a hand on my shoulder. He was as tall as was I. "Not in the matter of names I would repeat, Drajak, no. But I surmise. Ah, yes, I surmise!"

If he thought the threat had been to him or Kirsty, my feelings were that Nanji and Floria had been the targets of the assassination, the kitchews as stikitches call them. I wondered what Madam Mevancy would say.

This Rodders was powerfully built, a fine fighting man. At his waist he carried a lynxter and dagger. His clothes were not ornate. I fancied he'd been a mercenary in his time. Probably he'd been a zhanpaktun, entitled to wear the golden pakzhan at his throat, a mercenary of renown. He carried himself lithely, and he would not be easily surprised.

So that made me realize that, like many men, his panic-stricken concern for his lady had robbed him of his habitual toughness and common sense. He told me she had a mind of her own, and had insisted on returning to carry on her affairs as normal. He made a lop-sided grimace. "So here we may sup a while. The H'siung Garden is refreshing at this time of day."

The establishment was surrounded by a small garden lushly green, a result of ample water, and Rodders led in briskly. When we were seated he drank down quickly and called for more. I drank sparingly.

He began to tell me about himself and I listened out of politeness. My plan—transparent as ever!—was to hitch my fortunes to his until I could get back to Makilorn. Every heartbeat that went by I expected to feel a heavy hand on my shoulder and a voice: "Those are my clothes!"

Rodders was, indeed, a mercenary, a pakzhan. He smiled wryly as he said he habitually kept his golden pakzhan with his baggage. He was a Bowman of Loh from Walfarg. Wandering from hire to hire he'd met Kirsty in the line of business, and she'd done his business for him. He recognized her prickly qualities, the sharpness of her, her ruthlessness; but, as he said: "That's Kirsty."

His voice fell silent and in that vacuum, for the sake of something to say, I piped up: "She is cousin to Leone, I understand."

The Bowman of Loh downed his drink and slammed the glass onto the table. "Aye. The little milk and water miss shivers every time she sees Kirsty. Leone—she has no idea what being a woman means."

"She seemed very pleasant," I said. "She is always very kind to me."

"You know her well?"

Alarm signals buzzed in my brain. I drank a little of the sazz to cover my hesitation. Then: "We have just met. I was able to do her a small favor." His eyebrows rose. I plunged on. "Young Lord Wink—"

His powerful face creased into a knowing smile. "Say no more. That young tearaway and his cronies will cause a sensation one day."

"He was a trifle—elevated."

Rodders laughed. "And their mentor, San Chandro?"

"I played him at Jikaida."

He nodded. "I see you are a man of parts." He finished his glass and rose from his chair, looking at me. "I have enjoyed this short talk, Drajak. Now I must look in on Kirsty and then see if Erthanfydd smiles on me. Then it will be an early night and the Annorpha Aigrette on the morrow." He shook his fawn cloak straight. "Where do you lodge?"

Ah! I said: "I put up at a caravanserai—"

"Nonsense, Drajak! You must lodge with us. Kirsty would not forgive me else. And we can talk!"

I wasn't so sure about that self-centered lady's forgiveness; but this solved my problems of food and lodging—as I had planned, by Krun!

We went along to the private butts and shot a short round. He was a splendid bowman. Just because Loh is the home of the Bowmen of Loh does not mean that everyone in that continent is a superb shot. He was good. I shot circumspectly, reserving my fire, as we say on Earth. He told me he was agog to shoot in the tournament tomorrow, the winning archer to receive the Annorpha Aigrette and a handsome purse. At once I saw a way to fill my pockets, and my first task would be to buy fresh clothes and dump these in a convenient spot to be found and returned to their owner.

The rest of the day passed slowly enough. We went to his lodgings—very comfortable—and ate and drank moderately and talked and then turned in early ready for the competition the next day. The more I learned of this Rodders the more I found I liked him and the more he seemed to me to be a complete man. He admitted to faults. His temper was quicker than slower. He'd broken the nose of a man who stared insolently at Kirsty.

The moment I could kit myself out and either buy or steal a zorca would be the moment I could take off for Makilorn.

Just what was going on there now, Opaz alone knew.

The problem of the Glitch Riders I trusted had been dealt with by strong forces from the city. The party who had chased after the survivors of the Glitchers who had attacked us were the advance screen. Just how effective Tsungfaril's military forces were was something I could not be sure about. News of the queen's death would reach Annorpha soon and then no doubt there would be a mass exodus as people rushed back to the capital.

The temptation to remain with Rodders and enjoy myself in shooting and singing and bathing and then return with everyone else was mighty powerful, mighty powerful, by Vox!

After all, Madam Mevancy could look after herself. She'd proved that, and, into the bargain, could look after the folk the Star Lords required to be protected. It occurred to me—belatedly—that perhaps I ought to stay here at the Springs to keep an eye on Nanji and Floria. The Everoinye it seemed to me were conducting this operation in ways different from any I'd encountered before. Yes, there were some similarities with the time Pompino and I had operated together; the differences were what counted.

When duty and inclination coincided was the time, by Vulken the Insinuator, to be watchful, vigilant, and ready for something squashy and unpleasant to drop on you from a great height.

During my time on Kregen many strands of life had threaded their tangled webs and people had appeared and disappeared, as you will have heard in my narrative. Many resolutions had taken place that I have not mentioned because they happened, as it were, off stage, and events had overtaken them. Happy—and unhappy—outcomes had taken place to many of the problems I have mentioned in the past and if these tapes hold out I hope to tell you who listen to me all the details. As it is now, I must press on with the tangled webs being woven in Tsungfaril in Loh.

The next morning in a mood of laughter and enjoyment Annorpha Springs witnessed the Grand Tournament for the Annorpha Aigrette.

The arrangements for the shooting itself were simple enough. Sightseers clustered. Marshals waved their wands. Music played and flags fluttered. The targets were set at stipulated distances and entrants were required to shoot their set number of arrows. A miss resulted in instant dismissal from the competition. In an atmosphere of tense excitement the better archers were whittled down until the final half dozen were left to shoot it out.

In the continent of Loh, what more natural than an archery competition?

Relaxed and confident, Rodders said to me: "I feel I am in great form, Drajak.

207

Huang is the man to watch. You shoot well; but—" he spoke in his easy way, "but I feel I have the beating of you, with all due respect, you understand."

If Seg were here and inevitably betting on the outcome, he'd put all he could on me. I knew I had the beating of Rodders and this Huang, who was not as good as Rodders imagined. This is not boasting, which I abhor, but simple professional assessment. A little wind puffed and died and the flags blew out and then hung limply. The crowds kept up their animated chatter. Vendors went around doing a brisk trade. About to make some noncommittal reply, for I just intended to shoot and win and so take the purse—the Aigrette itself could also be sold, I judged—I was stopped in my tracks at Rodders' next words.

"By Hlo-Hli! I am determined to win the Aigrette for Kirsty. She will be queen of the ball this evening, as the Hork guides my shafts!"

The expression on his face left no doubt that he meant every word. Even penniless as I was, in my precarious position, with my hopes resting on his goodwill, could I risk beating him out of the Aigrette he so coveted for his lady? By Makki Grodno's disgusting diseased liver and lights, what a confounded unwanted complication this was!

Fourteen

What a mess! This was a completely unwanted complication. There was absolutely no question of my winning, of keeping the purse I so desperately needed for myself, and of presenting the Aigrette to Rodders for his lady. That would demean his honor. Oh, no. Where honor and pride in shooting skills are concerned, you walk over live coals.

I have very little truck with pride, as you know, and as for honor: mine may be a chameleon beastie, it remains intact in those areas of importance to me.

So, I made up my mind on a course of action.

Yes, very well. I, Dray Prescot, Lord of Strombor, Krzy, etc. etc. etc. ad nauseam, chickened out.

Huang and Rodders were left to shoot it out as my last shaft hit the spot at which I'd aimed, a spot a good thumb outside the aiming mark.

"Ha!" exclaimed Rodders, his red hair fairly bristling. "You see!"

The crowds yelled and cat-called, a single hyena-note made up of individual shouts and cries and curses. The Suns shone. Young boys ran everywhere scattering perfumed water to slake the dust. I held my face admirably still and noble, letting Rodders see how chagrined I was at missing the mark.

"You will win, Rodders, and my very best congratulations."

He nodded to the flags drooping on their staffs.

"You over estimated the breeze."

"Aye."

He smiled and turned back to finish his conquest. I let out a breath of relief. Not until he mentioned the breeze could I be certain he had been fooled by my shooting. Offering him the Aigrette after I had beaten him would have been bad enough; to have let him see I allowed him to win would have been disaster.

In the event he squeaked home over Huang. The prize was presented by a fat woman, the wife of a high official. She smirked and simpered and Rodders took the spray of gems and feathers into his brown fists. He lifted the trinket high and the audience yelled. Then, with the conscious solemnity of the occasion, he gave the trophy to Kirsty. Her face was a picture. She was pleased. There was no doubt of that. That she should be accorded this favor fitted well with her feelings of her own superiority.

I managed a brief: "Congratulations, Kirsty." Whereat a tiny frown dinted in between those heavy eyebrows before she dazzled me with her smile. "Thank you, Drajak." I wasn't having any kow-towing and inclining where this lady was concerned, no, by Krun!

After that, it was all a helter-skelter as the final preparations were made for the Grand Ball as the Suns went down.

The oasis town of Orphasmot in which the Springs of Benga Annorpha rose so magically and refreshingly to the earth's surface might be drowsy, dusty and suns-baked, it provided capital entertainment. Here the division of status was clear and simple. There were the people here for the cure, as at any spa, out to enjoy themselves, and there were those many more, slave and servant, here to serve. As the last of the preparations were made, I wondered, not without an ironic smile at my own expense, just which side of the divide I belonged. A fellow with all the lands and titles I had amassed—and all he had were the clothes he stood up in!

The third half—if I may use that typically shorthand Kregen way of expressing a complicated thought simply—of the people here was well represented. These were the merchants and traders. They'd sell anything to make a profit and the folk taking the waters were in the holiday mood where they'd buy anything.

There'd be no expensive fancy dress for me tonight. I'd probably buy the cheapest mask I could find and leave it at that. What little cash was left had to go on filling my stomach.

As for the fancy dress that turned out as the twin suns, Luz and Walig, sank in their suffusions of light—it was fancy. Highly ingenious and decorative, the costumes dreamed up by the people responsible created a riotous confusion of color and glitter, a never-still river of fantasy and delight pouring through the town.

On this night the folk of Tsungfaril threw off their usual air of lassitude, of waiting to go up to Gilium, and threw themselves wholeheartedly into enjoyment. Much was the wine drunk and many the dances danced and songs sung. Drifting along with the crowd, wearing my silly little black mask, I just absorbed impressions. Later I was to meet Rodders and Kirsty. The scenes of laughter and jollity all about inevitably drew my thoughts to far off Vallia. How often we had rioted through the avenues and along the canal banks! And in Ruathytu and Sanurkazz, too, folk had seen their fair share of hedonistic enjoyment. So I began to think of my comrades and the times we had had.

Many societies of Kregen—and I suppose some of Earth, too—fervently believe that thinking of an event or person will attract that event or person to you. Talk of the devil, as they say.

My old comrade Wizard of Loh, Deb-Lu-Quienyin, along with Khe-Hi-Bjanching and Ling-Li-Lwingling, had many times shrouded a thaumaturgical shield over me. Of what value a warrior's puny sword against the ferocious might of a wizard's sorcery? So, as I put my foot upon the lowest rung of a ladder leading from this roof level to the next higher level, I stepped back to allow the man bundled in the blue cloak to descend the ladder first. Just how he'd appeared so suddenly above me I couldn't fathom. I'd been about to go up and the next instant, there he was, on the ladder and descending.

The scent of Moonblooms wafted from a doorway at the side where the flowers grew in a rotund ceramic pot. The light of the Moons fell aslant the doorway, and a man slumped there, fast asleep, his turban slipping.

The fellow on the ladder stomped down, heavy brown boots descending the treads with clumsy authority. A smell of rank fish coiled among the scents from the Moonblooms. I stepped aside and saw the ladder above through the blue cloaked body of the man. Through his body. He was not fully realized.

As I reacted to this piece of information, the man reached the tiled roof beside me. He moved with a heavy ponderous swing of wide shoulders and thick waist. He half-turned to brush past.

I saw a wide sullen face, heavy, with pouched eyes half-hidden by the drawn-forward cloak hood. He sucked in a breath. "The necklace," he said. His voice gusted ludicrously thin and reedy from such a gross frame. He sucked another breath. "You have one more chance. No more."

The dark blueness of the cloak was fading. As he spoke so he appeared to need to shake his body, perhaps to shake out the words. He was becoming faint, drizzle-thin, was vanishing into thin air. No doubt he calculated that the evanishment of an apparition would scare me sufficiently to rush off at once to secure the necklace for him.

He was gone.

A voice from the side said: "Very pretty, Dray. I really believe we may have Discovered an Adversary in him." The slumped man with the slipping turban in the doorway was sitting up. "Friend of yours, Dray?"

Turning slowly to face Deb-Lu's apparition, I said: "Hardly. That was Na-Si-Fantong. I've never met him in the flesh." Deb-Lu's creased old face smiled up at me under that vast and toppling turban. He smiled. That, I can tell you, cheered me in a most heart-warming manner.

"I suppose you have Contemplated the Si in His Name?"

When Deb-Lu spoke with Capital Letters, it behooved the listeners to listen.

"Aye."

"H'm. Well, since you disappeared from Esser Rarioch we've been searching all over for you. And now I've found you it is Distressingly Difficult to Maintain Contact."

His form wavered as though seen through a column of hot air. He was somewhere up in Vallia in person, and in that mysterious and magical state of lupu had sought and found me down here in Tsungfaril in Loh.

"Tell Delia I'm all right, Deb-Lu—"

"Naturally. She Has Spoken Somewhat and At Length upon your Disappearance. You are detained here?"

"Yes."

"Ah."

What Deb-Lu-Quienyin knew or suspected of the Star Lords I wasn't sure. What I did know was that any Wizard of Loh walked circumspectly anywhere near the ambiance of the Everoinye. He was aware of my disappearances from time to time. He and his comrade wizards erected defenses for my comrades against unhealthy sorcery. Even if Deb-Lu could only maintain a tenuous contact with me I felt vastly reassured. Na-Si-Fantong wasn't going to turn me into a little green frog—at least, not without a struggle!

"By the Seven Arcades!" said Deb-Lu. "This plane is most confoundedly dismal!" His form fluctuated, and brightened and darkened.

He'd explained to me that on the surface of Kregen two places might lie many miles apart yet on another plane they would be cheek-by-jowl. So if you wanted to go from one to the other you crossed as many intervening planes as might be necessary until you found yourself on the right one. The trick here was that the 'you' of the quotation would need the many years' training and experience undergone by an initiate of the Cults and Orders which possessed the knowledge. At that point in my knowledge of Kregen the pre-eminent colleges of thaumaturgists were those of the Wizards of Walfarg, better known to the outer world as Wizards of Loh.

Deb-Lu's spectral form quivered like a reflection in water.

"This is difficult, Dray. Please Excuse Me."

Quickly I gave him the few details I had concerning the queen's necklace. This was Wizard's work. As his form at last dwindled and expired, his final words were: "Prospects and Interesting Possibilities open up before us, Dray! I shall return! Remberee!"

"Remberee," I called; but Deb-Lu was gone, hurtling back across the planes to far Vallia.

The thought occurred to me that Loh was Deb-Lu's birthplace. He was a renowned Wizard of Loh—a Wizard of Walfarg. Something must be going on somewhere to account for the difficulty of communication quite apart from the distance involved.

The flat roof suddenly filled with a crowd of people, all fluttering scarves and feathers, flushed faces, laughing eyes. They sang and danced their way across rooftop after rooftop and gathered other folk until the procession broke up into fragments along the main streets. Well, this was not the usual behavior of those seeking to enter Gilium. The atmosphere of general pleasure and the visitation from Deb-Lu combined to put me in a happier mood. I would see Delia again, soon. I knew, and with a sudden somber shiver, that Deb-Lu was right. There were vast possibilities in the future—possibilities and perils, by Vox!

Fifteen

"You kept yourself well out of the way of all the trouble, cabbage. Well, I've got news for you. We have a crisis on our hands."

"That's news?"

"Oh, you!"

As predicted, when the queen's death became general knowledge in Orphasmot a mass exodus ensued. My simple-minded plan had worked and I'd tagged along with Rodders and Kirsty. Now, taking a chance on San Chandro, I'd trotted along first to the Mishuro villa to find Mevancy. I'd found her all right. She lost no time in bringing me up to date with the dramatic events that had taken place in Makilorn whilst I'd been away.

Lunky had in some way managed to persuade his fellow Diviner Yoshi to become an ally. Maybe some emotional tangle had caused Yoshi to fall out with Vasama. The importance of this became apparent when not one but two babies were discovered with claims to housing the spirit of the queen.

Vasama, 'quivering like a jelly' according to Mevancy, had stated that the baby of the noble lord Pling-Fe-Hwang had been chosen to receive the spirit of the reborn queen. She had proudly brought the baby forth from Hwang's villa to display to the multitude.

At the very same time across the river Lunky had divined the queen's spirit in the baby of Tsun and Hosifi Shiang. They were potters and the baby's cradle was formed from half of a smashed pot. Lunky brought the baby out of the pottery kilns and across the river to the queen's palace to be confronted by an enraged Vasama clutching her choice.

Two factors determined the outcome.

One, that Yoshi had fallen out with Vasama and was willing, out of spite, to side with Lunky, seemed to the college to be the lesser reason.

The important reason was simply that Lunky was already recognized as a Diviner of great power. There were politics simmering away in the background, as, by Krun, there usually are! The upshot was that Lunky's choice, the Shiang baby, was judged to hold the queen's spirit.

"Presumably, cabbage, that was why the Everoinye wished us to save Lunky."

"It would seem so."

"All would have gone as the Everoinye wished, only—"

"What?"

"You remember I told you about Kaopan?"

"Oh, no." I felt a pang, for the baby, for the queen, for Lunky.

"Yes. Someone had the Shiang baby killed according to the rites of Kaopan." She shook her head. "The queen is now truly dead. She will not return to Tsungfaril in another body. She will not go up to Gilium in glory. She will go down to the Death Jungles of Sichaz."

I said nothing. I really didn't know if I believed all this mumbo-jumbo about the accursed, the paol-ur-bliem, returning to Kregen for life after life as a punishment. On Kregen there are enough weird and wonderful things, by Opaz the Eternally Veiled, to last many a lifetime! The whole story, the religious beliefs, the reincarnation, all of it, all could be true.

"That damned lot led by Shang-Li-Po," I said. I heard my own voice. I heard the snarl. Snarl! If I were a free agent and the constraints imposed by San Chandro brushed aside, I'd do more than snarl. I could feel the blood pounding in my head, and I had to hang onto this new Dray Prescot whose image I had been so assiduously creating. To rush off and deal with Shang-Li-Po and his cronies, in memory of the queen, would serve no one. I had to remain cool, calm and collected. For Dray Prescot even in this latter day that was asking a lot, a whole lot, by Krun.

I could still see the queen standing by the pool's edge. Vibrant, superb, quivering with all the eagerness of a girl embracing life to the full, she limned indelibly in my memory. As the scented water ran in wanton rivulets down her body and the black-masked assassins padded towards her, their naked swords ready to kiss her naked body, so she lifted that rounded chin in a haughty stare of utter contempt. If only...! But, paradoxically, what happened next was mercifully veiled from me by the blue veil, the very blue fragment of the Scorpion that dragged me away.

"Your face has gone putty again, cabbage."

"I was thinking of the queen."

She shook her head, her cheeks flushed. "And what would your—?"

Her mouth closed with a snap, the sentence unfinished, for she had seen my face and I know, to my despair, that the old devil look had flashed there. What she had been about to say troubled me, for I thought she was over her silliness. A trifle breathlessly she said: "Well, there it is, then. The queen is truly dead. Now they have to find a successor."

"That is college and council business. I suppose the Star Lords will have to put their oar in."

"Cabbage! Must I keep telling you? Have a care."

"The Everoinye wanted Lunky's choice to be queen. She would be, as it were, on our side. Given that San Chandro represents our side and Shang-Li-Po heads up the opposition."

"The Everoinye will not take a rebuff lightly."

"Of course not, pigeon! There will be plenty of work for you and me, never fear!"

She bit her lip and turned away. I was wrought up enough not to feel proper compassion for her until after we'd parted to go about our different tasks. Then, as I headed for San Chandro, I did feel I ought to have been more gentle with her where her sensibilities regarding the Star Lords were concerned.

As for Queen Leone—what a tragedy, what a waste!

In addition—and most darkly, most deeply dreadfully darkly indeed—Queen Leone had been slain because the Star Lords had snatched me away.

Could—and I dared to think the thought out of anger and compassion—could the Star Lords have wanted the queen slain to further their own unfathomable ends? And were those ends now confounded by the fine Italianate hand of Shang-Li-Po? Was there more horror to come? Well, this was Kregen, and however wonderful and beautiful that world truly is, horror formed all too potent a part of its makeup.

Leaving the Mishuro villa I went the long way round to the palace, striding out, breathing deeply, trying to bring myself under control. Many thoughts jostled inside my cranium. There was the affair of the queen's necklace yet to be settled, a damned sorcerer to be dealt with, a gang of cutthroats to be cut down to size. There was the ever-present urgency of getting this whole imbroglio over fast so I could return to Vallia and Valka. There was the mystery of Carazaar and his minion Arzuriel. Lurking like some monster of the deep below everything else the hideous problem of the reiving Shanks from over the curve of the world remained. They would not go away until everyone of Paz united to drive them off.

By the time I had waited for my name to be sent in to San Chandro and his authority of admittance returned I had quietened down. I had left my admission with my clothes as I'd been hoicked up and out of here. I'd go along with the same story to San Chandro, and, in sooth, he must have heard of the disturbance in the pool at the Springs of Benga Annorpha and the peril of the Chasserfic.

He had heard. He greeted me kindly, although clearly abstracted by affairs of state, and was galvanized into eager demands to hear more when I explained what had happened. He was convinced the Chasserfic was a part of the greater plot. At the moment I couldn't accept that; but I didn't argue. I made a casual mention of the lord Nanji and the lady Floria; he hadn't the slightest interest in them. His spies had reported their presence in the city, and their movements, and that was all.

"No, my boy, it is that Tsung-Tan-forsaken Shang-Li-Po! He and his evil schemes are at the bottom of everything."

"I thought San Lunky did well—"

"Yes, yes! Of course. But events have swept past now. We must look to the heir. Whoever is pronounced queen will need the Repositers to guide her in ways quite different from what we have done before."

Aware of the importance of the answer in his eyes, I asked: "Who is the heir?"

He pursed up his lips, that narrow face shrewd. "There is confusion in the records. The lines of descent were tangled at the best of times, and that time was a long time ago. As the college sees it, there are three people who have legitimate claims to be the closest next of kin."

I waited as he heaved up a sigh. He could see the troubles ahead that would accrue from arguments and confrontations.

"The three are, one: the lady Kirsty, two: the lady Thalna and three: the lady Leone."

"That is our Leone?"

"Yes. And her cousin, Kirsty. You met her, of course."

"Of course."

"My best judgment is that Thalna will be knocked out of the running first. Her claim is the most tenuous of the three."

"And the best?"

"That will have to await the adjudication."

He gave me a stare. "You may wonder why I am so free with you, Drajak. I fear dark times are ahead. The old order is crumbling. I need a man like you at my side."

Again, I waited. I didn't want to ask the question burning my tongue which he might well consider impertinent. He was, after all, down here in Tsungfaril, a very important personage.

He cocked an eyebrow at me. "Yes, Drajak, I see your tongue is commanded by your head. You would like to know who I support?"

"Yes."

He stood up from his chair and walked across the room, turned and walked back. He eyed me like a sparrow sizing up a crumb of bread.

"Your reticence is as important as your assistance. You know how much I care for Leone. She is of the spring, warm and young, green and growing. She is not cut from the same cloth as Queen Leone was." He stopped by the table and picked up a Jikaida piece, turning it over in his thin fingers. It was the Yellow Pallan. Then he placed it down firmly beside the Yellow Princess. He gave me that fierce sizing-up look.

I drew a breath.

"Then you will support Kirsty."

He nodded. "Aye."

"I understand."

"If I thought you would not then I would not have told you, neither would I have sought to employ you. You do follow, Drajak?"

Now it was my turn to nod. "I follow."

Sixteen

In ordinary times one would quite have expected San Chandro to have trumpeted the stunning news that a mortal man had been blessed by Tsung-Tan and had been moved through time and space at the whim of the godhead. As it was, Chandro hugged this information to himself. My best judgment was not that he was obsessed by the imaginary power this information gave to him alone but that he sought ways of using it to further his plans for Kirsty as queen.

In a very short time arrangements were finalized for the adjudication which would take place in the college palace. Mevancy went off to join the crowds whilst I stayed in the Mishuro villa.

One person who was delighted Chandro wished Kirsty to become queen burst in to see me beaming. Trylon Kuong had been kept busy lately; now he had taken time off on the day of adjudication to come and congratulate me and thank me for Kirsty's life.

"That's a rather melodramatic way of putting it." I waved a hand at the refreshments on the side table of this small room Mevancy and I used as a sitting room. "There were other people involved—"

"Oh, yes, true! But it was that damned traitor Shang-Li-Po, the Kaour, behind the plot. And he wanted to kill Kirsty!" Kuong was outraged.

In as casual a way as I could manage—I made play with a paline in my fingers as I spoke, carefully—I said: "Kirsty and Rodders are well matched. Leone is unattached. As, trylon, are you."

Such a match, apart from creating a splendid marriage, would have solved some of my unwanted problems too, by Krun.

He ducked his head in that way people have of telling you they understand what you are saying.

"Leone is—well, Leone. My love-life is well catered for at the moment. Most." A look one can only describe as self-satisfied came over his bronzed face. "Highly spiced. Oh, no, Drajak, nothing like that."

"Lucky you," I said, keeping the bitterness out of my voice with difficulty.

"No, it's damned politics again. The western boundary of my trylonate of Taranik runs along the eastern boundary of Tarankar. At one time we had friendly relations with them. They are a strange lot, in any case, and now apparently a new lot of diffs have moved in. The upshot is that they refuse to trade, they have assassinated my merchants and returned the queen's ambassador's head in a sack."

I made a sympathetic noise and added: "A cause for war?"

"I detest war. But Vad Leotes and I were trying to persuade the queen to take a more positive attitude. San Chandro, also, is of our mind."

"If Shang-Li-Po counsels no war he will be popular—"

"That is true. I find it distasteful that I am in the warmongering party. As you know, the Queen's Repositers are split; Nath the Uttarler is unable to make a decision even concerning the Queen's Matrons." He checked himself there, and shook his head. The Queen's Matrons provided the queen with information about her past lives unknown to the male Repositers. Kuong went on speaking in a slow and wondering voice: "You know, Drajak, now there is to be a new queen, where is the need for Repositers or Matrons?"

He sounded like a man who had just discovered a new planet among the stars of heaven.

I said: "The Repositers will be required to store information for all future queens, as has been the case in the past. Their feathers may be clipped; they'll still fly high in Tsungfaril."

He gave me a quick look. "You sound—hard."

"When I first became interested in all this political mélange here I assumed it was the usual thirst for power, with half-crazed people killing and bribing their way to positions of authority. This remains true, of course; but reincarnation, the paol-ur-bliem, adds a new dimension and creates a profoundly different situation. Whether or not you believe the old chestnut about absolute power corrupting or not, once most people gain positions of authority with the wealth and privileges attached they are drastically disinclined to give it all up. Now you have power blocs continuing from generation to generation centered around the very same person."

"Except for this situation now with the queen—"

"Aye, Kuong, aye. And Kirsty will need good friends."

The sound of rapid footfalls reached us from the hallway and we turned as Mevancy marched in.

"They're still at it," she said, not breathlessly but in a rush. "They've been closeted for half a day now."

Kuong said: "Even if the outcome is already decided, they have to make the proceedings appear difficult and important. And, anyway, I expect Nath the Uttarler has held things up humming and hawing."

The college and the council would, so Chandro had assured me, not fail to choose Kirsty as queen. After all the votes had been tallied up, Chandro said there would be a difference of one vote. And that would be enough. That, he had said confidently, also took into account the probable vote of Nath the Uttarler—if he managed to rouse himself to remember to cast his own vote—for Shang-Li-Po's faction.

"Shang-Li-Po's faction," I said. "The party of peace."

Mevancy said: "Shang-Li-Po's faction. The sell-out party."

"That is true." Kuong frowned. "They'd sell anybody to save their own skins."

The whole city of Makilorn waited. A new queen was being chosen. Lassitude might mark most of the dealings of these folk as they prepared themselves for the delights of Gilium in the afterlife, already I had seen the way they could throw off constraints and enjoy themselves at times of celebration. Now another absorbing conundrum had been presented to them and they threw themselves into the fascinating pursuits of guessing and discussing and gambling on the outcome.

We here were in possession of confidential knowledge. The folk of Makilorn knew there were three contestants, and so they judged them on what was known and according to predilection. Kuong judged that most people favored Leone. This seemed natural. After all, she was young, beautiful, eager, with a dazzling personality. Kirsty was dark and hard and would suffer no nonsense. As for Thalna, very few inveterate gamblers would take odds on her victory.

The time ticked by and the sand dropped in the glasses.

The twin Suns of Scorpio, Luz and Walig, passed across the sky.

Kuong strode up and down. At last he burst out: "I cannot stay here like this! I'm for the college."

"There is a huge crowd—" began Mevancy.

"Oh, yes, of course. They're all hanging about, waiting, betting, listening to the most ludicrous rumors, eating and drinking, like a crowd of vosks all waiting for the swill to pour out."

"Can we get through?"

"I am, after all, a trylon."

"Um," I said.

"Well, cabbage, it's better than sitting here."

"Very well."

Truth to tell, I welcomed the activity, even if it could have no influence on events. We prepared ourselves and then went quickly through the deserted streets to the palace that housed the college.

The rumble of the crowds swelled like thunder as we approached. True to his word, Kuong led us around to the rear entrance and was able to gain entrance without trouble. The palace was sumptuous. Guards stood everywhere. We were shown to a waiting room where other notables sat tensely or walked up and down, and even here the bets were being laid.

The inner chambers were sealed off and the college and council met in utmost secrecy. We heard that Ortyg Hanshar, the chief priest, had gone in looking pale but firm. Nath the Uttarler had been found wandering in a picture gallery admiring the portraits and been led gently in to do his duty. No news reached us. The golden doors remained fast shut.

"What is the delay?" demanded a rascally-looking fellow emptily.

"They merely prove their own importance," snapped a waspish woman with considerable venom.

A man with the brown face of the desert, lined and harsh, said: "The due rituals must be observed in the light of Tsung-Tan." He was a strom from a distant oasis and clearly believed completely in Gilium and the paol-urbliem and the fitness of the college and council. "It is beneath my dignity to place a wager on so important a matter. Had I done so I would have unhesitatingly placed a fortune upon the choice of the lady Leone."

Kuong made a little grimace at me. "You see?"

One of the high-ranking guard commanders who waited with us half-turned at this. He was a Khibil, smart and well-turned out, and wore the pakmort at his throat. "I would choose the lady Kirsty," he said with a military snap. "There are hard days ahead for Tsungfaril."

"Then you will lose your wager, chuk."

Just as the Khibil chuktar rapped back: "No one can know for sure until the trumpets sound," the silver pealing notes of the trumpets rang out, high and brilliant. Utter silence fell. The golden doors shivered, and moved, and opened wide. On the heated air the cloying scents of much perfume clogged the nostrils. Priests appeared in procession, walking with stately self-conscious tread, gorgeously appareled. Under a golden canopy borne by armored acolytes Ortyg Hanshar looked every inch the most important priest serving Tsung-Tan. His granite face, marked by years of uncontested authority and set in lines of inflexible purpose, demanded and commanded absolute obedience from all those who lived in the hope of Gilium.

"The die is cast," breathed Tuong. "Queen Kirsty will—"

Then he stopped speaking as though he had fallen over a precipice.

Following the canopied high priest and borne by two dozen yellow-dressed slaves a throne-chair rode high in the air. Every eye in the chamber fastened on the throne and its occupant.

High she rode above the throng. Surrounded by the images of her power and symbols of royalty she sat upright in the chair, hands resting firmly on the silk-covered arms, her face a glowing wonder.

From the crowd a deep chant rose, controlled and ordered, the words distinct and striking to the heart.

"Hai, Queen Leone! Hai Jikai!"

Mevancy's grip on my arm crushed through to the bone.

The procession marched on as the crowd parted for it. The doors at the far end were flung open. As the nobles and high ones in this antechamber shouted for the new queen, so, as she proceeded, the crowds waiting outside took up the acclamations. The din was prodigious. After all, when had there last been a new queen in Tsungfaril?

"Leone," said Kuong. His face had lost color.

"San Chandro," said Mevancy, on a breath. "It has gone wrong. Where is Chandro?"

"There," I said, and nodded my head at the notables following the throne. Nath the Uttarler led off, supported by two slaves. He was followed very closely by a tall figure dressed from head to toe in red. So closely did this person walk that he was almost abreast of poor old doddery Nath. His face bore marks of granite that made of the granite face of the high priest a mere child's simpering countenance. Shang-Li-Po gloated in his victory. Dogging his heels walked his crony San Yango. Chandro trailed along at the rear of the group of Repositers. His head hung down and his face lay in shadow.

"I see him," snapped Mevancy. "And San Nalgre?"

"No," said Kuong. "He is not there."

The Queen's Matrons followed with the Diviners. Lunky's face expressed repressed sullen fury. He did not look up as he passed.

"So that's the way of it," I said.

There was no sign of Kirsty or Rodders, or of the lady Thalna come to that. Kuong rolled his shoulders like a man drowning.

"I cannot stay here!" he spat. Without another word he barged his way through the crowd heading for the small doors at the side. Mevancy gritted out: "Follow me, cabbage," and we headed after Kuong.

Outside the palace we moved along the streets trying to avoid the crowds. Makilorn gave itself up to celebration. Not one of us could find the heart to speak even when we had reached the Mishuro villa. Kuong kept striding up and down in fury. Mevancy, it was clear, was consumed by apprehension at the reaction of the Star Lords to this disaster.

Later on, when Kuong still simmered with helpless fury, San Chandro turned up. He looked exhausted, shrunken. We guided him to a chair and pressed a goblet into his shaking hands.

He stared up at us, his eyes unfocussed. "All the plans," he whispered. "Utterly wasted. Shang-Li-Po struck through to the heart. He prevailed upon San Nalgre. Nalgre voted for Leone." He tried to drink and the wine slopped. "Nalgre could not resist the pressure. Shang-Li-Po had him taken away somewhere under guard and the threat of instant death—"

"This behavior from a Repositer!" shouted Kuong.

"Shang-Li-Po has gone above the law. He has taken the reins."

"Then he must be taught—" I began hotly.

"No, Drajak!" Chandro shook. "Any visible conflict between the members of the college will result in untold harm."

"That is perfectly correct," came Lunky's voice as he entered the room. He was pale and nervous. "Tsungfaril cannot support any overt violence."

"But—" said Mevancy.

"There is no but." Lunky dropped into a chair. "Nalgre has been taken to one of Shang-Li-Po's secret villas. He has girls there. There is a tunnel and a shaft from the villa to the river—"

"If Nalgre was free," Mevancy spoke more calmly. "He could cast his proper vote, could he not?"

"But he is not free. And there is no way we can free him."

"But if he was?"

"Well, yes, to speak of the impossible. This vote could be declared invalid and a fresh one held. That is true."

"Well, then," said Mevancy with a note of triumph in her voice. "We must go there and rescue him!"

At this both Chandro and Lunky protested, horror in their faces and voices. It was impossible. Any use of soldiers was quite out of the question, could not be tolerated by the state, the priesthood.

"We are beaten." Chandro leaned back and closed his eyes. "All we can do is hope to influence Leone."

"You were her mentor, san," I pointed out.

He waved a weak hand, his narrow face filled with pain. "All that is changed. Shang-Li-Po has the power now."

"A small group of us could break in," protested Mevancy.

Kuong shushed her. "That is not possible, if I know the kind of place San Lunky means. You'd need a small army to break in there."

"And the army would refuse to attack a Repositer," said Lunky.

"Well," I said, my voice eerily cheerful in that room of doom and gloom. "If the paktuns and the army are useless we'll just have to use a different sort of army."

Seventeen

The narrow door set in the re-entrant angle of the heavy walls gonged dully as I thumped it. They must have seen me walk up in the last of the radiance of the Suns. They kept a sharp lookout from the arrow slits. Nothing happened. Just as I lifted my fist to give the door another thump it opened. It did not creak. It swung open on well-oiled hinges. They needed to get in and out of here fast at times, I didn't doubt.

A mass of hair sprouting around a bald pate confronted me in the light of a lantern held aloft in one raggedy arm. A mouth opened among the hair. I gave the doorkeeper no time to speak.

"Take me along to Kei-Wo the Dipensis right away, sunshine, or you'll taste ol' snake."

"By the snaggle-teeth of old Snorribunder Himself, dom! Easy! Kei-Wo is expecting you—"

"So what are you hanging about doddering for?"

He belched a tuneful belch, hitched up his gown, and started off along the brick-walled corridor. The effluvium rose ripely all around.

"By Lohrhiang of the Five Palms," he grumbled to himself, slouching along ahead with the lantern light striking weird shadows from the slimed walls. "I jes' hope old Fing-Na an' Naghan the Chik gits aholt o' yourn!"

And he hawked up a noisy gob and spat, accurately if splashily at a scurrying little thing of eight spindly legs.

He led me into the chamber in which I'd awoken to find myself tied in the chair with my head in a metal vice. The smells were much the same. A fellow now sat in the chair with his head fixed rigidly looking sorry for himself. Kei-Wo lolled back in his chair, picking his teeth. Most of his gang seemed to be there. I identified Sooey, Sindi-Wang, Naghan the Chik, Fing-Na and a few others whose faces I recognized.

I didn't want to give this Kei-Wo any chance of taking the initiative. I nodded to the man bound in the chair and said: "Unless his crimes are too heinous you'd better release him. You're going to need everyone you've got for this night's work."

He went on rocking himself back and forward with his foot on the floor. He wasn't in the least discomposed. "You are anxious to die?"

I fixed him with a stare. "If you do not do exactly as I say you will surely wish to die when Na-Si-Fantong starts on you."

He stopped rocking. Everyone stood stock-still. Utter silence fell.

Oh, yes, make no mistake. Like any onker I was gambling. The first result was totally in my favor. The whole gang were petrified.

At last Kei-Wo managed to get words out. "The sorcerer? You have talked to him—he was mighty wroth about the trick—"

"He and I deal now, Kei-Wo. You obey the mage or—" I waved a hand. "He requires the Queen's Necklace. We are going to get it for him tonight."

The smells in the chamber increased in ripeness. Young Valli was crouching by the door, fascinated by what was going on. I had the oddest conviction that if, by some evil chance, Na-Si-Fantong was spying on this savory gathering he might derive amusement from my ploy. All he wanted was the necklace. As far as I was concerned, the necklace was of no importance. In that, by Vox, as you will see, I was very far adrift from the realities of what went forward.

Kei-Wo was a hardened hulu, no doubt of it. He bounced back. "We looked for you, Drajak the Sudden, so that Naghan the Chik might hurl at you. The wizard had difficulty restraining himself from turning us all into little green frogs."

Here in Loh, as a stranger, I spoke with all the pseudo-authority of the newly-informed. I said: "Some mages can do some things, and others others."

I knew what I knew. Sorcerers spent a great deal of time learning their arts. They tended to specialize. If one mage was hell-on-wheels at turning people into little green frogs—which I doubted—then he would be less successful when he went into lupu to spy on people at a distance. This meant that any wizard who boasted of what he could do, and did it, might well be useless in the remainder of sorcery. Of course, that little word 'remainder' could embrace details of the thaumaturgical trade quite unknown to ordinary mortals. This was one reason why, as the one-time Emperor of Vallia, I welcomed having three mages actively working for Vallia. There were likely to be more in a few years' time. Khe-Hi and Ling-Li were off in Whonban seeing about the proper rituals and ceremonies attendant upon the birth of their children.

So, now, as the tough leader of a city gang, Kei-Wo could say: "That is true. But if a wizard commands, you do well to obey."

I nodded. "Exactly so. Prepare yourselves. We break into a private villa tonight. There are guards. We must use whatever force is necessary. Na-Si-Fantong expects our success."

The buzz of animated conversation in the chamber had to be allowed. I was confident that not one of these folk would go against a wizard. The only peril, and it was a real one despite my feelings, was that Na-Si-Fantong, assuming he watched us, would not go along with my plan.

I wondered at what distance he could detect magic. There had been no time for me to see Leone—now Queen Leone—and have the court wizard, Chang-So, cast magic upon another fake necklace. That could have been a useful ploy; as it was, these villains would have to burst into Shang-Li-Po's villa in furtherance of my schemes, and to the utter confusion of theirs and Na-Si-Fantong's.

If Fantong took an interest in the midst of all these proceedings, I fancied his reaction might well include little green frogs.

The gang prepared in a mood not exactly sullen; but not eager, either.

Because I have been a bit of a reiver in my time, a roamer, a fellow who has had to live hard in the face of enmity, I suppose the feeling that I was still Dray Prescot made me unwilling to use these gullibles too harshly. So, I said: "You will all search assiduously for the necklace. Anything else you find of interest—"

Kei-Wo interrupted with a bitter laugh. "Oh, we understand. We must fetch out the necklace and nothing else—"

"No." I raised my voice. "Anything of loot you find is yours and you may bring out what you can carry."

At this their reactions took on an altogether different aspect. They made a fair old hullabaloo of gratified anticipation as they prepared.

I even caught Fing-Na, in between fingering out his huge waxed moustaches, whistling a scrap of the old Lohvian song 'Her Hair as Red as the Robin's Breast'.

There's nothing like a spot of loot in the offing to perk up your true reiver, no, by Peetir the Sequestrator!

There was no need for me to advise or instruct these villains in methods to be adopted of attacking and robbing a villa. True, they would not in the normal way even consider burglarizing a villa in the respectable quarters; in the matter of raids and assaults against other gangs they were past masters. They had all the equipment: ladders, ropes, scaling irons, axes. Their methods began with the subtle and if that failed ended with a straight bash-down and raid.

When I say they wouldn't normally consider burglarizing a respectable villa, I refer to the expedition we were on tonight. Of course, for a few cunning thieves to break in and steal what was lying about was a normal way of life. In truth, I had no need to feel tender about this pack of light-fingered gentry—or ladies, come to that.

When the twin Suns of Scorpio were finally gone and the sky lost the last of those ruby and emerald bands and the stars pricked out we set off.

She of the Veils would shine down upon our enterprise later; I felt She would avert that rosy gaze from our proceedings. So we padded silently through the early evening streets, going in ones or twos, until we reached the riverside location of Shang-Li-Po's secret villa. Here he kept his ladies.

Kei-Wo hauled up sharply, his hand on my arm. "We are observed!"

Two dark cloaked figures emerged from the shadows of the wall.

"You did not, did you, cabbage, think we'd let you go off alone?"

And Kuong said sturdily: "If it must be done it must be seemly done."

Smoothly I said to Kei-Wo: "These are friends who would not wish to see me in the river."

Hewing to his purpose at heart, Kei-Wo snapped out: "I suppose they want their share!"

"There is enough to gladden the heart of the meanest man in Makilorn."

On that we went forward. The gang's locksmiths went to work as others squirmed over the walls. Kuong said fiercely to me: "I scarce credit what goes forward here! But if we must, then—"

"You have already said, Kuong, that by his actions Shang-Li-Po has forfeited all right to the status of a dikaster."

"That I believe to be so. Ah!" He pointed. "They open the doors."

"Lunky," said Mevancy, "was concerned about the Kaour's guards. Apparently they are formidable. Vankaris, he said they were."

Vankaris I knew about, a race of diffs of powerful physique, of practically no forehead, of spatulate nose, of wide gap-jawed mouth, of a stooped posture that emphasized their brooding hunched menacing aspect. Like many a member of the poorer folk they chewed Cham all the time. They were reputed to be fond of Fristles, and the Fristles did not reciprocate, which amused everyone except the Fristles.

"Tough," I said, as casually as I could manage. "Kei-Wo's ruffians are tough, too. They'll handle 'em."

"If only we could have brought in the army," said Kuong, and his voice was not altogether steady. "This is all so—so—"

"So underhand and horrible," I said for him. "Brassud! We're going in!"

"Hold on!" came a breathy voice from the shadows to our rear. "Wait for me. I'm not so fast right now, what with my wound an' all."

Mevancy swung about at once. "Who said you could get out of bed?"

"Well, now, my lady." Llodi the Voice marched up, and I swear his splendid nose had grown in size and number of fissures. He had been stabbed in the side on the same occasion I'd had a chunk of my left arm ripped off. Because Llodi had not bathed in the Sacred Pool of Baptism in far Aphrasöe he did not mend with the magical speed I did. I didn't know if I was pleased or not to see him here.

Kuong was already running fleetly towards the opening door. Llodi gave his strangdja a heft and, as it were, sidled past Mevancy and trotted off after Kuong. She stared after him and then turned on me.

"He's not fit yet. You knew about this?" She was all set to accuse me and pronounce judgment.

"No. We'll just have to keep an eye on him, that's all."

"Well, come on, cabbage. Stop lollygagging about there like a movong waiting for an offoce!" With that she turned and ran across to the door.

Kei-Wo's villains knew their job. Directly inside the door the body of the guard slumped against the wall. Lamplight lit the corridor. The raiders flitted through like shadows. I ran along with them, wishing Lunky had had more information about the layout of this villa.

San Nalgre Hien-Mi could be kept prisoner anywhere. My guess was the cellar complex.

So far no sound had betrayed us. Just as I reached the head of the cellar steps a clang of metal on metal and then a frightful shriek told us all that we had been discovered. Now the raid would begin in earnest.

As I clattered down the brick steps I wondered how long each one of the gang would search for the necklace before cupidity overcame Kei-Wo's orders and the fear of the sorcerer. There was precious little light down here. I reckoned the gang would search patiently for a considerable time judging by their terrified reaction to the name of Na-Si-Fantong.

My first impression of the darkness down in the cellars was swiftly succeeded by an awareness of the edge of each tread below me, of the grimed and greasy walls, of the brick floor cumbered by rubbish. I was concentrating on listening for hostile Vankaris or for a possible cry for help, so I just padded silently down the stairs and cautiously ventured across the floor to the opposite door. This was of flimsy reed construction, reeds forming a common building material considering the scarcity and price of wood. I gave it a gentle push, ready for an immense guard to rush roaring at me.

Nothing happened save dust floating from between the reeds. The cellar beyond was empty of anything except more rubbish and a pervasive smell of river mud.

Philosophically I went silently on, searching in all the cellars to find them uniformly the same. The longer I looked the more clearly I could see. Eventually I climbed back up the stairs hoping the others had had better fortune.

From the head of the stairs I could hear a tremendous racket above with the clash of metal mingled with shouts and shrieks and the screaming of women. The light from the lanterns hurt my eyes and I blinked.

Nalgre had to be somewhere in here. Lunky had said so. Most of the noise crashed down from the next floor and the stairs here were covered by carpet. Up I went to burst out into a wide hall. Here the Vankaris had made a stand. Kei-Wo's gang must have fought like leems, for there were more dead and dying guards than ruffians.

Well, I have had my fill of stepping delicately over the human debris of a battlefield. Some of the gang were crawling out of it, trailing blood, and I had to hope they'd make it safely outside. Time was running out for us. Quickly I ran through the hall looking past open doors into the rooms beyond. Kei-Wo's people were busily ransacking everything that looked as though it might contain treasure.

The next flight of stairs led past a pile of mingled corpses.

A quick glance up showed me Naghan the Chik snatching a knife from his belt and hurling it clean at a Vankari guard who screeched and fell away with the knife through his throat. Another guard screamed incoherently and clawed at the ruin of his face. Amongst the red pudding many little needles stood out like porcupine quills.

Mevancy swung to face me, her forearms extended.

"Pigeon!"

"Oh, you!" she shouted, annoyed. "He's not here anywhere!"

"Next floor."

"Right."

Naghan went lumbering across to the nearest door. So far he had not stopped to loot. Mevancy and I raced for the next stairway as Fing-Na tumbled down it, swearing horribly, his sword a red bar and a great gash across the side of his face.

"My moustaches!" he shrieked.

And, indeed, it was so. Now he had a magnificent single whisker sprouting from the uninjured side of his face.

Mevancy and I pushed him aside as he stumbled back. We went haring up the treads. The ceiling here was painted in a representation of one of the more obscure legends of Kregen; Mevancy pointedly ignored the pictured scenes. Three guards leaped on us. Mevancy splattered the first with a shower of her deadly bindles and as he clawed his shattered face I sliced up the next one and whirled to catch the blade of the last on my edge. A quick turn of the wrist and a thrust and he went down.

Below us the noise of combat died down. No one screamed any more.

"If we don't find him soon," panted Mevancy, "the whole city will be up."

These rooms formed a suite, well furnished, and we rushed through door after door. In the lamplight a man sat with his back to the wall, holding his guts. He was the fellow who'd been imprisoned in the chair with his head in the metal vice. A single look convinced me he had been better off then than now.

Just beyond him a Vankari guard was trying to stand up, and failing because of the blood pouring from his right leg. Mevancy gave him a kick as we ran past and into the last room.

The place looked like a shambles. Bodies lay everywhere. I saw the sinewy form of Sooey sprawled out, her lank black hair dabbled with blood, her single bright eye closed for ever. Kei-Wo was just finishing off his opponent. Llodi stood sweeping his strangdja about him and two Vankari guards tumbled back. Kuong slid his blade deftly and took his man. The noise that a moment ago had racketed to the ceiling ceased. The raw tang of blood smoked on the close air. Kei-Wo swung about to glare at me.

Before he could say whatever he was thinking, Kuong shouted: "Too late! Too late!"

Mevancy rushed across to the outside wall. Here a round opening with its covering panel swung back told the whole grisly story.

"Just shoved him through," said Llodi, slamming his strangdja down and leaning on it, breathing hard. "Like an old sack of rubbish. Dumped him down the chute and into the river, and him a dikaster an' all."

Eighteen

Queen Leone queened it in Makilorn.

With the disappearance of San Nalgre Hien-Mi there was no chance the adjudication could be overturned. Queen Leone was queen of all Tsungfaril.

A new Repositer would take Nalgre's place and continuity would be maintained. The incoming dikaster, man or woman, could have no influence on past decisions.

Queen Leone, a bright, outgoing personality, a beautiful young girl, was welcomed ecstatically wherever she went. She was popular. Everyone wholeheartedly supported her—except for us few ingrates.

"So that's it, then." San Chandro sounded so despondent. If it were not for his automatic exclusion from Gilium he'd have slit his throat, there and then.

"I can say goodbye to my lands of Taranik." Kuong heaved up a sigh. "And it isn't just for that I supported Kirsty."

"Surely," snapped Mevancy as she slammed her cup down, for we were at the second breakfast. "Surely the people of Tsungfaril will not allow those awful diffs of Tarankar to attack them and steal their lands without fighting back?"

"The people will do what the queen tells them. And she does what Shang-Li-Po tells her to do." Chandro spilled palines as he spoke.

"You were her mentor," I pointed out.

Chandro's narrow face twisted in mortification. "She told me she does not hold a grudge, and I believe her, for she is a bright forgiving girl. But she no longer trusts me. After all," and here Chandro waved a finger in bitter anguish, "did I not betray her? Did I not vote for her rival Kirsty?"

"As you would again, san," said Kuong.

"Aye. Aye, as I would again, Tsung-Tan forgive me."

I caught Mevancy's eye and nodded my head sideways. She stood up. We were both about to make our excuses to leave, for although we had talked incessantly about the disaster to our plans, there was yet more to be said.

Kuong was sitting bent forward with a paline half in and half out of his mouth. Chandro's head was turned awkwardly as he looked up at Mevancy. Neither moved.

Very quietly, Mevancy said: "I am frightened, cabbage."

There was nothing sensible I could reply. We both waited as Kuong and Chandro sat stiff and unmoving. We waited for the Star Lords.

The coldness gripped the room and passed. The Gdoinye flew in at an open window, circled around and alighted upon a high cupboard. He cocked his head on one side and surveyed us through one piercing eye.

Presently the Gdoinya flew in and joined him. The two superb raptors perched there, claws biting into the plaster of the cupboard, their golden and scarlet feathers sheening in the brilliance of the early suns.

The raucous squawk battered down on us; but which bird spoke we could not say.

"You have failed the Everoinye."

In a cool, calm, modulated voice I said: "We have not failed the Evero-inye. We preserved the lives of Lunky and of Kirsty."

"Onker! Kirsty is not queen!"

"So you did have Queen Leone murdered, you rasts!"

"Drajak—" Mevancy's voice was a stifled moan.

"No! That was not the doing of the Everoinye."

"No? You snatched me away when—"

"When the old queen's time was numbered, it was numbered. You had the new queen to protect."

I shook my head. I couldn't remain cool, calm and collected much longer, not when I recalled the passion and beauty, the warmth of the dead queen. Mevancy cleared her throat.

"The evil work was taken out of our hands." Her voice whispered.

The two gorgeous birds shining refulgently in that upper chamber of the Mishuro villa shifted their perches, almost as though they communed together. Mevancy was trembling. I felt growing anger that the Star Lords in their high and mighty aloof way could so thoroughly frighten the girl.

At last they spoke in their raucous squawk. "Yes, that is so. There is still work to be done. Other hands must take up your task, and when they have done what must be done, you must finish the task."

"Other hands?" Mevancy's color, always high, had practically vanished. Now spots of crimson glowed in her cheeks.

"Hands more sure." Was there a smug knowingness in the harsh tone?

"Tell us what to do next, you pair of nurdling great onkers!"

At this outburst I couldn't stifle, Mevancy collapsed back into her chair. She covered her eyes, as though expecting me to be blasted on the spot. Well, by Krun, that wouldn't have surprised me, either.

"You will be told when the time—"

"Is right!" I shouted up. "It's always the same with you! If you want to do something useful why don't you get this maniac Wizard of Loh, Na-Si-Fantong, off my back?"

"Your ridiculous escapade with the Skantiklar is your concern. Fantong has decided this gem is not available for the moment and has gone."

"Gone? Where?"

"When he arrives we will know. He is not for the moment important. Your concerns lie in other directions."

If I was surprised to learn the Star Lords had even that little concern for my skin, the next words of the twin birds astonished me completely.

"You have served us well in the past. Mevancy is loyal. We have no wish to lose your services, selfish though they may be. We are holding the evil influence of Carazaar at a distance. But more failures will inevitably increase his power."

I shut my open mouth. I swallowed down. What I was about to say I've no idea, for Mevancy interrupted, speaking in a hesitant vague way. "Yes, I am loyal. I do not understand what you are saying; but I am loyal!"

In a biting tone I said: "Perhaps you had better tell me about this Carazaar. At least I've done for his henchthing, Arzuriel."

The birds did not exactly laugh; their cackle was perilously close to mocking laughter. "Arzuriel is a multi-dimensional being. You have not finished with him or seen the last of him."

"I stuck him—" I started, hotly.

"One dimensional representation only. As for his master, Carazaar, your bungling here increases his influence. Do what must be done here and then we will—"

"If we'd had more co-operation," I fairly yelled up, "things would have been different! The bungling is all yours, you and the Star Lords!"

Mevancy put a hand on my arm. "We will do as you command." She spoke up firmly, her voice clear and controlled. I admired her more in that moment, for I understood her feelings—at least, I thought I did.

With lazy, arrogant beats of their shining wings, the two raptors flew through the open window, and their last squawks floated down.

Chandro said: "Take great care, Mevancy." He finished his turning movement to look up at her. His eyebrows drew down. Clearly, he could see the change in her face caused by an occurrence of which he was entirely ignorant. "You do not feel well?"

Kuong popped his paline into his mouth as Mevancy brushed a hand across her forehead, forcing a smile for Chandro. "Oh, all this business would upset Benga Serenmefa."

With that Mevancy and I were able to leave. We had a lot to discuss. We were, as they say in Clishdrin, in a pretty pickle.

"At least," I said to her as we walked down the stairs to the villa's side exit, "we don't have that idiot Wizard of Walfarg Na-Si-Fantong on our backs."

"On your back, cabbage!"

Oho, I said to myself. So madam is recovering her spirits. Good!

She went on: "You'd better explain the other things—Carazaar?"

"An apparition. His beast follower, Arzuriel, apparently is not dead, which in itself is a crime against nature. They seek to do me mischief."

"If they are connected with the Everoinye—"

"I had assumed not. I was surprised when those damned birds—"

"Cabbage! Really! You must moderate your tone. Who knows what could have happened to you?" She turned her face to me, glowing now with her natural high color all returned. I felt a real mean sort of fellow to cause her distress. But, I'd been slanging the Gdoinye now for years and he returned my insults with interest. As with the Star Lords themselves, I had established a rapport and a kind of accommodation with the Gdoinye.

"Yes, well," I said, mumbling a bit. "Those uppity birds fairly get up your hooter." We walked out into the radiance of the Suns of Scorpio. "Let's go and find a cool drink of parclear. I'm parched."

"After all you drank at breakfast?"

"Too right."

There is always an odd feeling in a fellow when he walks along with a pretty woman and nearly all the passing men turn to stare at her. This is not rudeness, at least as I see it, rather it is a form of homage to beauty. Of course, if the lady is restive, if her escort feels the stares to be too oppressive, then perhaps action must be taken. All the same, you really cannot legislate against the thoughts in a man's mind—at least, not until these prophecies of thought police and control become realities.

So Mevancy took absolutely no notice of the man who stared openly at her from across the street. I gave him a hard look. He was of middle height, with dark brown hair and eyes. His face appeared to me to be pleasing and regular of feature, although marked by a couple of spots here and there. Like most folk of Makilorn he wore the ubiquitous fawn gown and cloak and his left hand rested inside his robes. When he saw me staring at him he swung away and vanished down an alley. No thought of following him crossed my mind. Mevancy, head up, strode on ahead.

One—just about the only one, by Vox!—good thing to come out of the victory of Shang-Li-Po's party, as far as Mevancy and I were concerned, was that we were off the hook of assassins. At least, I had taken that view, one concurred in by both Kuong and Chandro. The sight of this smart fellow, well set-up, watching us with more than simple admiration for Mevancy, worried me. As I have said, Mevancy was not your raving beauty of a girl. Her attractiveness came from her vitality and aliveness more than the configuration of her features. So, what did this fellow want?

We found a small open-air counter on the corner of a building with apartments above and drank our parclear. At least, I did. Being contrariwise in the accepted way of womankind she demanded sazz. She chose a bright green drink. That didn't bother me one iota.

We discussed the apparition of Carazaar, and I said that it hadn't needed the Gdoinyi* to tell me he was evil to his backbone.

"If he is connected with the Everoinye in any way, cabbage, then he is my business, too."

"Assuredly."

"Oh, you!"

Well, I said to myself, she may not be the prettiest girl in two worlds, she has a fire and spirit anyone would admire.

By this time she'd tumbled to my gentle mockery, my idiotic leg-pulling, and would flash me a glance from those eyes of hers that was designed to cut me down to size and put me in my place.

She did not mention the man who had stared at her.

I turned around to lean back against the counter with my elbows on the bar, watching the passing parade. The suns slanted in and there was the usual taint of dust on the air. A party of the Queen's Guards marched along and as this was in Loh and the old imperial traditions still persisted they marched all in step with a swing. The yellow fletchings of their arrows caught the light and shone brassily. At their head a Hikdar with an anemic face and too much gold lace about him walked, I thought, rather too mincingly for a soldier. He called a command in a high-pitched voice and the party came to a crashing halt opposite the refreshment counter. I shoved up straight and I couldn't prevent my hand going to my sword hilt.

"None of that, tikshim!" The reedy voice had a nasal twang. "You are Drajak known as the Sudden?"

"Who wants to know?"

"Cabbage!" came the fierce whisper at my side.

"Hikdar Vangli ti Trishnar, shint! You are summoned!"

With that the guard party closed up about me.

There was no way even Dray Prescot was going to cut free from this little lot, particularly as the Lohvian longbows came off shoulders and the sharp steel arrowheads all aimed at my midriff.

I said: "Who summons me?"

No way or not, if the wrong answer was given I'd have to make the effort.

"The queen, shint! Now, *Bratch!*"

That was not the wrong answer. At least this unpleasant person had said Bratch and not the slave-driving Grak. I moved quickly forward until I stood by his side. He blinked. He opened his mouth, which was thick-lipped and purple, and I said sharply: "What are you waiting for? Let's go." And I pushed past the two nearest guards and started off.

He pattered up alongside, trying to match my stride. I did not turn my head. If Mevancy—as we moved along I heaved a sigh of relief. She had had the sense not to cry out or make a scene. As far as Vangli ti Trishnar

---

* Gdoinyi: Prescot spells this out. It is the plural form. *A.B.A.*

232

could see she was just a woman at the counter and nothing to do with the man he'd been ordered to bring in.

So we all swung along in the dusty sunslight toward the palace.

You had to give Leone the credit. She looked every inch a queen. My escort wheeled me into a chamber that, whilst it was not large or conspicuously grand, was not your simple ante-chamber. Leone sat in what can only be described as a mini throne, glittering with gold and cool with ivory. She wore a queen's ransom of jewels about her person. Her light-colored hair was coiffed up and threaded with gems. Her face—well, that pretty face glowed with color and her eyes looked brilliantly upon me.

"Drajak!"

"Majestrix."

She waved the escort off and Vangli hesitated. "You may rest easy, Hikdar. This man is a friend."

He bowed and took his guard party off.

Leone frowned at me. "I call you a friend, Drajak, yet you ignore me."

"You have new friends now, Leone. San Chandro—"

"Oh!" she burst out. "And are you going to whine on his behalf?"

"He loves you dearly—"

"And a fine way he has of showing that!" She was breathing rapidly and the jewels adorning her bosom glittered. "And you, Drajak, do you love me as much?"

The thought occurred to me that she had the power to order: "Off with his head!"

I stared into her face, seeing the high color, the brilliance, and the little betraying tremble of those soft lips.

"Well, Drajak?"

"You know the answer to that, Leone."

She bit her lip and sank back in the throne. A little silken-slippered foot tapped the ivory rail. "You would be my consort."

"This is impossible. I would spare you the indignity—"

"Indignity!" She flared up, leaning forward and sitting bolt upright. The jewels positively coruscated about her. "Shang-Li-Po has said certain things about you, and about San Chandro. Had I a mind to..."

In a hard and hating voice I fairly snarled out: "Shang-Li-Po is no friend to you, Leone! He had Nalgre murdered. He will have Chandro slain if he can find a way. He cares only for himself."

She was shaking with passion. "You cannot speak to me like that!"

"I just have. And there is more. If you listen to Chandro—"

"After his betrayal!"

Clearly you couldn't expect her to understand, still less accept Chandro's support for her cousin Kirsty. I said: "Just remember, Leone, Chandro and Lunky and Kuong are your true friends."

We might have gone on wrangling like this for some time if Wink hadn't walked in with Prang and Ching-Lee. At least I'd got her off the subject of me. Her friends crowded in, laughing, calling: "He is here!"

She was almost as glad as I was at the interruption. Also I was glad to see she had remained on intimate terms with her palace companions. There was a great deal to admire in Leone, as I knew. Now, I surmised, she'd regain her composure and have another go at me later on.

She rose gracefully from the mini throne. "You may go now, Drajak." I didn't smile at her tone. She'd picked up the knack of giving orders quickly enough. "My portrait is to be painted and the artist is here."

I favored her with a small bow and she lifted her head and went out with her companions, all chattering in the old way.

Finding my way out was not difficult. Guards stood here and there and the palace corridors were familiar. I suspected poor old Chandro missed the comfort of his quarters in the queen's palace over at the Mishuro villa. The penultimate corridor before the chambers leading to the side doors lay before me empty of guards. At the far end I caught a glimpse of movement instantly stilled at the rear of one of the huge ceramic jars. So I was ready as I walked down. This, I felt completely confident, was not Leone's work. This was the dark hand of Shang-Li-Po. The fellow down there, a damned assassin, I felt sure, had been hurriedly summoned the moment Hikdar Vangli had reported my presence in the palace. I trod on steadily, ready to catch the first blow and stick the stikitche in return.

A few paces only remained before the ceramic jar. A bulky man wearing black robes toppled out from behind the jar, sprawled face down. From his back protruded the handle of a dagger.

I stopped stock-still, and now I drew my sword.

"You won't need that, dom. He's done for."

The voice was light and self-assured. The man I'd seen staring at Mevancy stepped out from the shadows of the doorway. He strolled up, bent down, and retrieved his dagger, wiping it on the black robes.

He looked about. "We'd better put some distance between us and this pathetic stikitche, Drajak. Through here."

Without further ado he pressed a panel in the wall and a secret door slid open. "I found this only this morning. It was so simple it would make you cry. These folk really aren't up to much."

If he'd intended to kill me he'd have done it by now—or, at least, died trying. I nodded and we went into the secret passage and the door closed. A lantern burned at a corner corresponding to the turn of the outside wall. Here stood two doors, both closed.

He put his hand on the latch of the left hand door, and nodded to the other one. "That leads outside. Now I must cut along to the queen. It won't do to keep her waiting at the first sitting."

The door did lead outside into an inner courtyard, as I knew from my explorations. This artist was certainly a lively fellow.

He didn't open the door. He half-turned to me. "You are Drajak the Sudden, surely?" His hand grasped the dagger handle.

"Aye. And you?"

"Caspar Del Vanian. Lahal."

"Lahal." I felt a genuine shock. I didn't know him. A superb artist who'd painted for Delia's grandfather, the Emperor of Vallia, had been called Caspar Del Vanian. If this fine young fellow was the great grandson it was clear he'd never seen Dray Prescot when I'd been Emperor of Vallia. In addition, Caspar had been made a trylon, the third highest rank of nobility after a kov and a vad—not counting a Vadvar—not only for his enormously brilliant artistic achievements but for financial assistance to the crown. Things had gone wrong for the Del Vanians and whilst I did not know all the details, I had heard they'd lost their trylonate and little had been heard of them at the beginning of Vallia's Time of Troubles. Now it seemed this latest scion of the line intended to regain his family's fortunes by more than the brush and paints.

"You don't," he said, continuing his line of thought, "appear alarmed that you were nearly assassinated."

"I was just thinking that you were a pretty cool customer yourself."

He smiled at that, showing even white teeth. "It's a trade."

"Oh?"

He shook his head at my tone. "No, no. I'm not your ordinary run-of-the-mill assassin."

"I can't say I care for the breed, myself."

"I understand perfectly what you mean. But, you must admit there are people in the world who'd be better off out of it."

"Yes," I said, thinking among others of Shang-Li-Po.

"There you are then." He really had an attractive smile. "I must be off. This first sitting won't take long then I'll come to see you and Mevancy at the Mishuro villa. The Everoinye made it quite clear you needed other hands."

Nineteen

"Other hands! You mean to say, cabbage, the other hands belong to an assassin?"

"And a very smart well set-up young fellow he is, to be sure."

"Caspar Del Vanian? What kind of name is that, for the sweet sake of Gahamond?"

No doubt the good Vallian name sounded odd down here in Loh, she was just making a fuss because she'd been surprised. People of Kregen are well accustomed to hearing and using all manner of weird and outlandish names.

"He must come from some country to the north. You'll have to ask him when he gets here."

"By Spurl! I'll ask him a lot more than that!"

Her color glowed in our sitting room. Carefully, for she was running this show—was she not?—I said: "No doubt he will make it look like an accident. But in any event Chandro must—"

I had not been careful enough.

She flared up, in a way different from but reminiscent of the way Leone had flared up in her throne. "How many times must I tell you, cabbage? Leave the thinking to me. Of course we must not let San Chandro find out this Del Vanian's profession. D'you think I'm an onker?"

"There's no answer to that, pigeon."

"Oh, you!"

"All the same, when Shang-Li-Po is out of the way, however this Caspar manages it, Chandro will have to seize his chance."

The ramifications here extended hazily so that any attempt to foretell what would happen was completely useless. Chandro had been insistent that any violence between or against the dikasters would result in catastrophes within Tsungfaril. If Caspar simply knocked Shang-Li-Po over that might precipitate the disasters. My feelings were that the Star Lords would not choose anyone less than totally expert at their craft to serve them. And this, mind you, after my meetings with other kregoinye who had amused me.

In this little silence as my thoughts twined around, Mevancy had clearly been thinking along parallel lines.

"If Shang-Li-Po dies of an accident or of apparently natural causes, then San Chandro must pounce at once. I shall tell this Caspar that he is not to assassinate Shang-Li-Po like any common stikitche."

"Oh, he's not common."

"I shall go and put on some nice clothes." She gave me a sudden and dazzling smile and in that smile she was truly beautiful. "After all, it's not every day I have my portrait painted by an artist who paints the queen!"

"Oh, I shouldn't bother," I shouted after her, feeling devilish. "He'll probably want you to take all your clothes off."

She swung about, leveled her right arm and in the next heartbeat one of her bindles flew past my ear and stuck quivering in the plaster. "Crude," she snapped. "That's all you are, Drajak, crude." And, with that, she stuck her nose in the air and swept out. That, by Krun, is the only way to describe her decisive exit.

Perhaps I ought to have elaborated on the circumstances of my meeting with Caspar Del Vanian, stikitche extraordinaire. After all, if that damned fellow in black waiting for me in the corridor meant business on my account then he might have friends contracted to deal with Mevancy. Llodi the Voice came in to say that Wr. Caspar Del Vanian had arrived and was waiting to be admitted. I nodded and in a twinkling there was Caspar, still dressed in the ochre robes, half-smiling, walking forward.

"Lahal, Drajak. Mevancy? Is she here?"

"Lahal, Caspar. She is under the impression you are about to paint her portrait." I couldn't help adding: "No doubt using the very same brushes and paints as those you used to paint the queen."

"Capital!" he exclaimed. "A splendid idea."

"Ah—yes," I said, all the wind knocked out of my sails.

When Mevancy joined us the wait was well worthwhile. She looked marvelous. She wore a light chiffon costume of some exotic kind, with, very naturally, heavier material looped along her arms. Her hair was brushed and shining. Something cunning had been done to her face. There was absolutely no doubt that cosmetics had been applied, but so expertly that I could not swear to detect them. The result was that she glowed. By the time I realized that I was feeling very pleased for her the lahals had been made and she and Caspar were engaged in a lively and bantering conversation. All the same, some of the smartness and alertness seemed to me to have deserted Caspar. Why?

"What's up, Caspar?" I interrupted. "You look as though you've lost a zorca and found a calsany."

He shook his head, frowning. "No, Drajak. Quite the opposite."

"Oh?"

"Yes, by Vox. I've lost the damned calsany and found a beautiful zorca."

At his bitter words I felt uneasy. Mevancy rattled on ignoring what we mere men discussed, saying: "I do hope there will be time for you to paint both portraits, Caspar. It must be so wonderful to have such a divine talent."

"Talent," he said, trying to rouse himself. "And hard work."

"Oh—of course!"

"The queen has commanded me to wait on her in the morning. We have the rest of today and tonight to decide how best to go about it."

As he had brought no painterly equipment with him I judged he did not intend to begin on Mevancy just yet. We sat down and stood up and walked about, helping ourselves to light refreshments from the side table as we talked. Mevancy wanted to know all about Caspar.

He told her that he intended to recoup his fortunes. He painted portraits of the high and mighty ones of those lands he visited. He had strayed a long way from home following various commissions and, I guessed, at the commands of the Star Lords. He said with vehemence: "I detest the lot of them—well, almost the lot of them. My real work lies among the poor folk, in the warrens, the souks, the aracloins. There I find so many subjects that I regret every moment I must spend painting some fat fool of a lord or lady."

He was a real painter in the sense he wished always to be trying something new, attempting to capture the most difficult subjects, trying to put down on canvas the inner truths that his eyes saw.

In the next instant he showed how much I underestimated him. He had not brought easel and palette and brushes. Instead from his robes he took a sketching block. The paper was very good quality; it was not the paper milled and distributed by the Savanti. He eyed Mevancy keenly. He used a stick of charcoal and began quickly sketching.

She said: "How do you wish me to pose, Caspar?"

"Oh—just continue as we are. I wish to catch as much—" he stopped. Then: "It must look like an accident."

"That is true," I said.

"And," he went on. "How can that be achieved? I was informed of the situation here, as you know. I am the other hands required. But if the dikasters are to be defeated the corpse must receive the full rites of the Kaopan. That sounds disgusting to me. But the Everoinye command. The corpse's disfigurement will clearly disprove any idea of an accident."

I felt a whirl of bewilderment. Mevancy gasped.

"But Shang-Li-Po is not a paol-ur-bliem! No one will question his death if it is accidental."

He looked up from his sketch pad. His face looked abruptly haggard. "Shang-Li-Po, Mevancy?" He shook his head and the stick of charcoal snapped across with a crack. "No. My target is the queen."

I stood absolutely perfectly stock-still.

Mevancy opened her mouth, said nothing, clamped her lips.

Caspar went on heavily: "The Everoinye wish Kirsty to be queen."

On the wall hung a pretty picture of the river with boats and the twin sunsets. I looked at it. I could say nothing.

Now I knew why Caspar did not look so jolly.

And, also, I knew without the shadow of a doubt he would kill Leone, disfigure her body in the rites of Kaopan, and obey the Star Lords. This, after all, would be the quickest and simplest way of crowning Kirsty as Queen of Tsungfaril.

At last Mevancy got her breath. "No," she said. Her voice shook. "There has to be another way."

I did not tell her; but I knew another way. This bright spark of an artist would have to be put out of the way first. That was all.

"If another way could be found then I would be happy." He was perfectly genuine. He might go around assassinating people on the orders of the Star Lords. The people he disposed of needed that treatment and left Kregen smelling sweeter by their absence.

I said: "I have not heard of the Everoinye employing a kregoinye in this fashion before."

"I am not a kregoinye—"

"But you must be!" flashed Mevancy.

"I am a kaogoinye."

The aptness of the name was not lost on Mevancy or me. Kaogoinye.

"There must be another way," repeated Mevancy.

I felt sympathy for her. Damned Star Lords! They were putting her in an impossible situation, yet one which, by the very nature of the Star Lords, could not be impossible. What they commanded would be done.

The Star Lords had once been human. That was a long long time ago. I believed I had detected remnants of humanity, a sense of humor, even, as I had come to know them better. And, now, this. As was perfectly obvious, to achieve their ends meant putting Queen Leone out of the running and this agent of theirs, this kaogoinye, was the simplest answer.

Caspar had stopped sketching. "The problem is not insoluble. Afterwards, people must think the queen met with an accident and some other hand inflicted the rites of Kaopan. Will that succeed?"

"Hardly." I spoke so that Caspar swung sharply to stare at me.

"Then you have a better idea?"

I didn't say: "Yeh! Tip you in the river for the stranks."

Anyway, if that happened the Star Lords would send someone else. Also, they would punish me. They'd hurl me back to Earth, four hundred light years through empty space, contemptuously fling me down all naked in some benighted spot. Then they'd leave me to rot. They'd done that to me before. I'd spent twenty-one awful years on Earth before clawing my way back to Kregen. Oh, no! I wasn't going to let that happen to me again.

I said: "Yes. But Chandro will have to be brought into the plot. We have no influence here in Tsungfaril; Chandro can arrange what is necessary." I bore down on them with a stare. "The details are going to be unpleasant."

"But Leone—" began Mevancy.

"I regret the necessity," put in Caspar.

"Nobody is going to hurt Leone," I said. "She may be a silly little girl, but she has courage. All this paol-ur-bliem nonsense may be true. Either way, nobody is going to chop Leone up."

"That is for the Everoinye—" began Caspar, somewhat stiffly.

"Aye. And what goes on here is for us."

"Hadn't, cabbage, you better tell us this marvelous plan of yours?" Her voice shivered with icicles. "I remember your last plan."

"A fair hit," I acknowledged. Indeed, a palpable hit. "We must first get hold of the body of some poor dead girl and that's where Chandro will come into the plot. Llodi will help, Kuong too."

"I see. And we substitute some poor dead trollop for the queen?"

"Yes."

"You cretin! You onker! Don't you think anyone will see the difference?"

"Kaopan."

"Oh!" she said, on a gasp, and was silent.

I turned to Caspar. "I suppose the precious Everoinye told you how to carry out this disgusting procedure?"

"Of course."

I suppose, being Dray Prescot, I couldn't have stopped myself on two worlds from saying: "Sooner you than me."

He nodded, his frank open face sheened with sweat, set hard. "It is the necessity only, you understand."

When Chandro and Kuong joined us, Llodi was sent for. The atmosphere of anxiety, subterfuge and defiance enclosing us seemed almost palpable in the room. Chandro was horrified that anyone could dream of harming Leone, let alone disgustingly preventing her from entering Gilium in the fullness of time when her punishment ended. We knew he drew the line even at dealing with Shang-Li-Po. When he heard the details of the plot within a plot he shook his head, his narrow face like a sparrow's, turning from side to side as he sought a different solution. In the end he had to agree. There was no other acceptable way.

I refrained from suggesting to Mevancy and Caspar that perhaps the Star Lords were watching and listening to us. What would their reaction be? To my way of thinking, if we achieved the result they demanded then how we did it was up to us. Certainly, that had been my experience.

Nervous and tense with forebodings though we were we managed to eat a bite like good Kregans. Llodi, armed with a note from Chandro, went off with an escort to the city watch tower some distance away. You will understand the fraughtness of the situation and my feelings when I say that had Llodi taken to the profession of Burke and Hare, which was as well known on Kregen as it was on Earth, I would not have been surprised.

The dreadful thought occurred to me that were the girl alive that would make it much easier to bring her along with us. For the sake of sweet Opaz rather than any Makki Grodno curse! Corruption can eat the soul.

That thought, banal though it was, brought me to a fresh realization of the cunning lethality of the punishment given to the Accursed. Surely, the idea must have gone, a person can commit enough sins in one lifetime to make hazardous their entry into Gilium. How much harder, therefore, to enter Gilium having to run the gauntlet of a hundred lifetimes open to all the sinful temptations that will drag the sinners down to the Death Jungles of Sichaz.

To keep her mind occupied in something other than fretting over the hazardous task that lay before us, Mevancy began to ask Caspar the questions she had promised.

"Home?" he said, trying to be polite. "Oh, I've strayed a long way from home."

"Vanian," she said. "I've heard of Varnion, where the mussels come from. Although by the time they reach here they're mostly inedible."

"Vanian is the family name, not my location." He sat down opposite Mevancy and leaned forward. "No, my home is in Vallia."

"Vallia! But that's dwaburs away north—right over the equator."

"We use airboats to fly vast distances."

"So I have heard. You must tell me about them and about the emperor." Her voice fell to a conspiratorial whisper. "And is the empress as beautiful as word has it? The most gracious lady—"

"Drak and Silda. Yes, I have painted both their portraits. I admire them both vastly—"

"I have not heard of Drak and Silda. Are you sure? You are not confusing Emperor Nedfar of Hamal?" She was just like any empty-headed girl listening to gossip about the great figures of the world. "I thought the emperor and empress of Vallia were called Dray Prescot and Delia."

"Oh, they were, they were. But they abdicated. Opaz have them in his keeping."

"What on Kregen would they do that for?"

"The latest information is that they are to be rulers of all Paz."

"We here are in Paz," interjected Kuong who had been listening. "How can they claim to rule us?"

"Oh, they don't claim it, trylon. The task is being thrust upon them by forces no one can resist. The Force of Destiny, if you will."

"That's all very well—"

I said: "The point is all the islands and continents making up Paz have got to stick together to fight the Shanks. And it would seem some poor pair of idiots have got to be elected figureheads."

"Cabbage! You shouldn't speak so disrespectfully of Dray and Delia Prescot! Why, if you'd read all the books about them I have, you'd understand!"

This surprised me. Of course, any Vallian bookseller would be only too happy to sell his wares overseas. There were many stories about me circulating in various gaudy guises, most totally untrue. Also, Mevancy didn't come from this cut-off part of the world.

Feeling mean and devilish at the same time, I said: "You must lend me one some day."

"Oh, no!" she snapped. "I don't lend books. They never come back."

"You can say that again," said San Chardro.

"Figureheads," said Kuong. "We-ell, it makes sense." Then he proved he was a most sensible man by saying: "It's certain sure I wouldn't want the job!"

Presently Caspar got onto more interesting details of Vallia, to which Mevancy listened fascinated. Kuong was interested, too. I lapped up a deal of news I was grateful to learn. Drak and Silda were keeping the old country on an even keel, thanks be to Opaz.

When the next glass had been turned Chandro stood up. "I am for bed. There will be a great deal to do and I need my rest."

He was right.

In a splatter of mutual Mellow Moonlights, we all trailed off to our bed-chambers, the Mishuro villa having ample accommodation for all.

About to get my head down I sat up sharply in the bed.

A blue haze shimmered against the opposite wall.

If the damned Star Lords had been listening in and had come to impose some discipline, I was in for a nasty confrontation. Then I let out a sigh of relief.

The friendly familiar features of Deb-Lu-Quienyin appeared as his image solidified from the haze.

"Lahal, Dray. Again this plane is awkward. My apologies."

"Lahal, Deb-Lu. All is well?"

"As May Be Expected. I have news of the Skantiklar."

"Ah!"

"This Na-Si-Fantong would appear to have vast ambitions."

"He certainly scares those he meets."

"Yes, I was fortunate enough to have half an eye on your escapade with this poor Naghan fellow they slid down the chute. Unpleasant."

He put up a hand to straighten his ever-toppling turban. Light glowed on him from a different angle from my small lamp. He went on: "The facts are easily established and quite simple. It is the interpretation that will present the puzzle. A long time ago, accounts vary, a great Wizard of Walfarg died. You now grasp the distinctions between a Wizard of Loh and a true Wizard of Walfarg, Jak?"

"Um, I trust so—although—still, no matter. Go on."

"His power was truly great. There was an object—some say a bracelet, others a necklace, others a plastron, containing nine gems. Each gem looked like a ruby and was identical. With these nine jewels came the source of unimaginable power." Here Deb-Lu stopped with one of his dry chuckles. "Well, Jak, unimaginable to most non-sorcerers, I suppose."

"I see. So Na-Si-Fantong intends to collect all nine and set up as a master mage."

"The power is very great, in sooth, very great."

I realized I had been deceived by his manner. When he called me Jak, as he more often did in remembrance of our adventures together, he was relaxed and easy going. His struggle through the planes to reach me here and my obvious pleasure in seeing him had caused him to revert to Jak. But he was deadly serious. He mentioned power and he meant power. This Skantiklar was no apprentice sorcerer's plaything.

His figure began to waver. I could see the wall through him.

I said: "Fantong has left Makilorn and given up the attempt to take the gem here. I do not know where he has gone."

"I shall seek him and apprize you. I fear I must take my leave."

Without a remberee he vanished.

Some force I didn't understand and over which, it appeared, Deb-Lu had only partial control, must be interfering with his jaunts through the planes.

As for the story of the Skantiklar, interesting though that might be, it had no bearing on my nefarious dealings to come. The notion of an article of power being broken up and scattered and of some great wizard seeking all the parts, and joining them, and so making himself a master mage, whilst not new still retained a certain charm. As Deb-Lu had said, that was not the puzzle. The puzzle was just what Fantong wanted the power for. Still, at the sound of his name, I got that itch over the 'Si'.

I stretched out and lay down and woke up to find Llodi shaking my shoulder. "Breakfast and Wr. Caspar is ready to go."

So there was no need to ask if Llodi had been successful.

Chandro turned up late for the first breakfast, having had his religious observances to attend to. Mevancy kept smiling and looking brilliant yet she was clearly ill at ease. Llodi, who joined us, took things in his phlegmatic way. Kuong couldn't sit still. Only Caspar appeared unconcerned, eating and drinking comfortably.

Somehow or other he and Mevancy got onto talking over the weapons an assassin might use. Caspar showed her the dagger he carried concealed in a scabbard under his robes. "This is a peaker. See, it has grooves for poison. Deadly in the right hands." He resheathed the narrow blade. "Folk sometimes call me Caspar the Peaker."

"Caspar the Peaker," she said. She hadn't liked that dagger. "Yes, it has a ring."

Making sure I downed a handsome breakfast—there is something unwholesome about going into action on an empty stomach—I found myself idly wondering how Mevancy was reacting to her cabbage not only having an idea but actually persuading her amongst the others to go along with the plan. If there was going to be any silly nonsense about who was in command, I'd let them get on with squabbling. I didn't want to have to come the heavy hand. But, by Krun, if I had to I would.

The way we agreed to work it was thusly: Llodi would act as assistant to

Caspar, carrying his painting equipment. Kuong and Mevancy would wait for my return from my audience of the queen—and a pretty yarn I was going to have to spin Leone—with the body. Then we would go in and rendezvous with Caspar. It sounded simple; it would not be, inevitably.

"All the marks have been removed from my gherimcal."*

Chandro's voice quavered. He was most unhappy at all this. Mevancy attempted to reassure him; but he shook that lean face, unhappy.

"A small quantity of wine, I think, even at this hour," said Caspar.

They each had a thimbleful; I didn't bother. I stared at Caspar.

"I do not envy you your task, dom. But I must ask again. Are you fully instructed in what is necessary? You are aware of the situation here in Makilorn, I know. But, in such a secret matter as the Kaopan?"

"They gave me full instructions."

My val! I said to myself. What a difference in treatment! Could this incredible disparity simply be the result of my own intransigence? Surely, I'd slanged the Gdoinye and the Star Lords enough times, always believing them to be aloof from petty human emotions. Still and all—had I held them in awe, as Pompino and Mevancy and the other kregoinyi did, what might have been the result? We had aims in common. We ought, then, to work together. Since the last great defeat of the Shanks at Yumakrell, capital of Yumapan in Pandahem, little had been heard of them. Knowing them as I did I had no illusions they had sailed away to their own mysterious lands over the curve of the world. They bided their time to strike again. And the Star Lords had sent Mevancy and me, and now Caspar, to Tsungfaril.

I swallowed down. "Caspar—what did the Everoinye say of the Shanks?"

Clearly his mind had not followed the train of thought of mine. He was still wrapped up in the unpleasant business of mutilating the fresh corpse of a young girl. "Shanks?" he said, not looking up.

"You know, Shanks, Shants, Shtarkins, Schnooprins. By Vox, dom, you must have heard of them!"

His head snapped up. "Naturally—by Vox!" He made the oath significant.

I forced myself to pick up a biscuit from the dish. It was a Sweet Ordum, octagonal and nice. I chewed. Then: "Well?"

"They are also known as Schturgins and they come from Schan, the grouping of continents and islands on the other side of Kregen from Paz."

My astonishment was at once quelled. Of course, the Star Lords would tell their favorite assassin far more than their most disregarded kregoinye. I went doggedly on: "Is there more known of them after Yumakrell?"

"There were more than that one band operating." He looked at me as surprised I knew so little if I was a kregoinye. Mevancy, listening intently, had

---

* gherimcal: small carrying chair, sedan chair. A.B.A.

the sense to keep silent. "Another evil lot of Fish Heads are still attempting to subdue Mehzta."

"I am glad to know they have not yet succeeded."

"Yes, well, how long that can go on for, Opaz alone knows."

"Yumakrell?"

"The Leem-Lovers retreated in great disorder. Luckily for them some of their airboats were still operational. With those and their ships—weird but wonderful craft—they made good their escape."

All that had happened after the Witch of Loh, Csitra, had given her life in misguided love. Loriman the Hunter had gone in pursuit of the Shanks—well, he could be trusted never to give up a hunt.

"Did the Everoinye tell you where the Shanks had gone?"

He looked oddly at me again, and shook his head. "I begin to wonder if you are a true kregoinye or not! By the Blade of Kurin, Drajak! What is going on?"

"I don't understand you."

He made a little gesture with open palms as of resignation to a fool.

"Why d'ye think we're all down here in this Opaz-benighted place?"

"Because the damned Star Lords sent us, that's why, confound it!"

By the putrescent glistening eyeball and pendulous dripping nose of Makki Grodno! This fine fellow who knew it all had better spit out what he knew, and damn quick, by Zair!

He heaved up a sigh. "If they didn't tell you there must be a reason. I can't tell you if they don't permit."

If I'd been wearing a hat I'd have torn it off, thrown it on the floor and jumped up and down on it. By the tangled and nit-infested locks of the Divine Lady of Belschutz! What a carry-on!

Kuong and Chandro over at the other end of the room looked across at the sound of our raised voices. Llodi walked in half hidden by the easel and cases of paints and brushes. He called out: "All ready!"

Lowering my voice I said: "Look, dom. We're all in this together. I'd like to know why I'm risking my neck. I mean, know particularly."

As I spoke I think I began to gather in enough details to fill in the picture. I could see all the little pieces fitting together.

Slowly, I said: "Tell me, Caspar, is it not true that after we beat the Fish Heads at Yumakrell they fled southwards and passed between Loh and Havilfar, and rounding southern Loh landed somewhere along the west coast?" I studied him, and added quickly: "Or, they fled northwards past the Hoboling Islands and rounded Erthyrdrin and sailed south in the Cyphren Sea and, again, landed on the west coast of Loh."

Kuong called across: "All set?"

"Ready," replied Mevancy. Then, in a fierce whisper: "Whichever way the Leem Lovers went, they're on the west coast of Loh. They're in Tarankar!"

"Well, of course," said Caspar, moving off to pick up his scrip. "And they'll be in Tsungfaril soon if we don't get a queen and college who will stand up to them. Wenda!"*

So out we trooped about our nefarious business, not just to save Leone and put Queen Kirsty on the throne but to start the process of saving all Tsungfaril and surrounding parts of Loh from the marauding and merciless Shanks.

Twenty

The smells off the river wafted rich and pungent even this early in the day. Slaves would be sweating their insides out all over the city, hauling and lifting, cleaning and scrubbing. The ever-present tang of dust in the air slicked a gritty film on tongue and lips. All in all, as we walked on to Queen Leone's palace, an average day in Makilorn.

So this was all about the Shanks! Well, I suppose I ought to have known that, to have realized earlier that the Star Lords would not abandon the crusade we had struck up together to halt and throw back the reivers from over the curve of the world.

As for this fancy Caspar Del Vanian, Caspar the Peaker—the name Peaker made me imagine that he ought to run a chain of restaurants—his intrusion into the schemes was welcome and meant that the Star Lords were bringing in the heavy weapons. I'd known for a long time that I was their boy they threw in when other folk fouled up—as in the fire where I'd met Mevancy.

Mevancy at the moment was garbed in a long man's robe, a burnous-like garment, and was at the back end of the gherimcal. Kuong carried the front end. He was clad in simple clothes, with nothing of the lord about him. I walked at the side, one hand steadying the chair. In the chair sat the corpse.

Much as we were all acting as a group of automata, appearing just to go on straight ahead without reflection, in reality each one of us remained supremely aware of what we were doing. Our own desires, our own fears, had to be put aside. If Shang-Li-Po could not be erased from the problem, then the queen must be changed to one who would boldly front the Shanks. As far as I was aware, and I had had extensive experience of the Fish Heads, there was absolutely no question of parleying with them. They did not talk to the inhabitants of Paz. They slew them. Sometimes they took a few slaves to ease their daily burdens. I often felt the poor unfortunates taken as slaves would wish they had been killed first.

---

* wenda! Let's go! A.B.A.

Being a cautious old leem-hunter I was well aware that I could not altogether trust Caspar. Like all the other servants of the Star Lords I had met, he stood in mortal fear and awe of them. And, rightfully so, I supposed. He'd agreed to go along with the plan. I knew without the shadow of a doubt that he'd plunge his poisoned peaker into Leone if that became necessary in his view.

The closed ochre curtains of the carrying chair concealed the occupant. I must admit as we trudged along that I felt profoundly thankful that Llodi with Chandro's influence had found a dead young girl easily enough. I didn't stop to wonder what I'd have done had no corpse been available and the conspirators taken up a living girl. I know what the Dray Prescot of seasons ago would have done, and been banished to Earth for his pains.

Luz and Walig shone down refulgently this early and twinned shadows lay sharp edged in ruby and jade. There was no wind. I tasted the dust in the air and hardly noticed the smell of the few flowers allowed to grow in the square before the palace. Kuong led around the kyro to a rear entrance.

The guard here was a Fristle. The cat-man looked bored out of his skull and his scimitar, the Fristles' racial weapon, remained scabbarded.

The admission Chandro had signed and sealed got us in without the slightest hindrance. Quickly we passed through a gaggle of slaves carrying water jars. We pushed on deeper into the rear quarters of the palace until we reached as far as it was sensible to venture. I knew the layout here and without any fuss, seizing the opportunity when the corridor was empty, we passed through a secret door into a cobwebby passage parallel to the main corridor. Here the gherimcal was set down

Kuong licked his lips. "I can only wish you good fortune, Drajak. May the beneficent Tsung-Tan smile on you."

Mevancy said: "Cabbage! May Gahamond have you in his keeping— and, by Spurl! Take care!"

What she didn't say, because Kuong listened, was something like: "And don't make a mess of it for the sweet sake of the Everoinye!"

Making sure the corridor was clear I slid out of the secret panel and set off for the queen's quarters.

By this time, according to the plan's calculations, Caspar should be setting up the easel and organizing his paints and brushes, making a show. He'd do a preliminary sketch first. Llodi would stand in attendance.

The guard slapped their strangdjas in a cross before the silver-bound doors. I said: "Pass word to the queen. Tell her Drajak the Sudden craves audience on the matter we discussed. She will see me immediately."

I put on the harsh domineering manner so unpleasantly easy to me. They jumped.

All too soon one came panting back, calling: "Pass Drajak the Sudden through! Bratch!" Then he added: "The queen took fire at his name!"

Well, poor soul, I was duping her. I'd have to apologize most abjectly afterwards—if we were all still alive. As for Dray Prescot apologizing, well, in this case that was no marvel, by Zair.

With a couple of Khibils as escort I stomped through the elaborate passageways and ante-rooms until a door of ivory was flung open and I was ushered into a smallish room where a skylight admitted an opaline radiance.

The easel was set up. The boxes of paints were thrown open. Caspar looked up. Llodi was standing in a corner, motionless. Leone, dressed in a simple shift-like white garment, sat on a plain chair. To one side stood a wicker frame draped with a gown smothered in an emperor's fortune in gems. This was all to plan.

At each side of the gemmed gown stood a Khibil guard, alert, ready to protect the gems. At each side of Leone stood two more, equally alert, ready to protect the queen. This was not in the plan.

By the Black Chunkrah! I said to myself. We couldn't plan our way out of an earthenware pot!

Ergo—the plan must change.

"Drajak!" exclaimed Leone, her color high, her breast heaving, her eyes bright, her breath short—all the Clishdrin descriptives applying to a poor girl in her infatuated condition. "I am glad to see you—" About then she realized she had an audience. "Leave me!" she commanded, waving one slender hand at the guards.

At the sharpness of the command Llodi jumped forward and slammed down the lid of the nearest paintbox, all set to clear out. The guards did not move. Caspar remained at the easel, his bright eyes watching, calculating.

The room was smallish. That meant in a palace it was four or five times the size of an ordinary mortal's dining room. From the shadows of the far end emerged the columnar figure and granite features of Shang-Li-Po. The redness of his robes blazed in the room. His chain of office coruscated about his neck. Here was a man who knew full well the power he wielded and who intended to maintain and increase that power no matter who might be crushed underfoot on the way. The granite lips barely moved.

"It would not be wise, queen, to dismiss the guards."

His gaze rested unflinchingly upon me. He knew who I was all right! By that, I do not mean he knew I was Dray Prescot. In me he saw an adversary employed by his enemies.

Leone's face flushed even more deeply. Her head lifted. "San Ranal," she said, her voice husky, and I had to remind myself that Shang-Li-Po was San Ranal the Kaour. "This man is a friend—and, soon, to be more than just a friend!"

"That may be so, queen. Also, many a wight has aspired and found his ambitions among the stranks of the river."

You couldn't say fairer than that, by Krun!

She half-turned to the dikaster, flustered, not quite sure how to react. She was held, too, by her nature of obedience. I fancy Kirsty in similar circumstances would have told Shang-Li-Po where he could go.

I said: "Please forgive me, Leone. I had not realized you were so engaged. Allow me to leave you—for now."

She bit her lip, then: "And you will return? As you promise?"

"Oh, yes, Leone, I shall return."

Caspar rustled his paper. "Can we get on, majestrix?" He was perfectly the temperamental artist, absorbed only in his work.

Shang-Li-Po watched narrowly as I gave the queen a polite if perfunctory bow and then took myself off. I let out a breath. We had not foreseen this contretemps in our planning. What, I wondered, would Mevancy have to say?

The trouble was, I had absolutely no desire to slay the Khibil guards. They were just soldiers, earning their hire. Of course, when great affairs of state are at risk, the lives of a few cheap soldiers mean precious little. That, disgustingly, is the way of two worlds.

I went off to the corridor and when it was empty slid past the secret panel. Kuong and Mevancy had already taken the gherimcal to pieces.

When I told them what had transpired, Kuong said despairingly: "Then it is all for nothing. We are beaten!"

"Not so!" snapped Mevancy. "By Spurl! We'll just have to—"

"Yes," I said. "And you will not shoot your bindles. That would betray us absolutely. It is cold steel. And if we can, we will not kill the haughty Khibils. Now, let's get the blacks on."

She gave me a ferocious look; but said nothing in reply. We changed into the black stikitche clothes taken from the assassins who had previously attempted us and sequestered by Chandro. Mevancy and Kuong carried the dismantled carrying chair. I carried the corpse.

We could have left the chair by the secret panel for collection on our way out; we might be forced to take another route and so needed the gherimcal with us. My audience of Leone had been vitally necessary to discover where she was in the maze of the palace. I knew the way there in theory. In practice I took a few false turns. In the end we found ourselves in a narrow filthy passage hidden behind the wall of the room where Leone was having her portrait painted.

Watching through a spyhole I saw the damned tall red figure of Shang-Li-Po hovering like a blood-sucking bat.

We pulled the black masks over our faces.

It would be three to four until Llodi and Caspar joined in.

Sword in fist I moved up to the secret door and prepared to burst through. I just hoped we wouldn't have to slay the guards.

Kuong tapped me on the arm.

"It is my duty to go first, Drajak."

"Uh," I said, like a loon, completely caught off-balance. Then: "Of course, trylon. After you."

As he set himself, facing the panel, I had time to reflect on all the other and far superior ways we could have managed this business. There was a case for kidnapping the queen and having the disfigured corpse found elsewhere. That had seemed to us not a water-tight scheme. We were stuck with what we had—and Kuong thrust the panel wide and leaped into the room.

Mevancy bundled me aside and jumped through second. She had to be allowed to do this, for her sake. I whistled through very quickly after her, very quickly, by Krun!

The Khibil guards had no time to react. Their attention was centered on the gown and on the queen. Only one was slain. Kuong caught him as he swung about, and the poor devil took the blade through the guts. I saw Mevancy knock a guard down with a full blooded blow from a blatterer then I slammed the hilt of my sword into the third's chin and whirled to the fourth to see him stagger under Kuong's onslaught, so I hit him as he went down.

Leone was trying to scream and emitting only choked squeaks.

Shang-Li-Po had his own secret entrances and exits within the palace and he'd tried to scuttle off into the shadows of the far end of the room. He hadn't moved from the spot; he was struggling and tugging, trying to tear free from the dagger that pinned the hem of his red robe to the floor. His granite face broke and shivered in terror as Kuong leaped on him.

"A neat throw," observed Mevancy.

Caspar said: "I'll have my dagger back."

I said: "I'll fetch the girl—explain to Leone."

When I re-entered the room with that opaline radiance falling across the recumbent guards, Leone was saying: "But I am the queen!" Her voice was at once petulant and filled with bravado. I truly felt sorry for her.

"Try to understand," Mevancy said in a patient way. "You cannot be queen, for they will kill you, Kaopan, you understand?"

Caspar said: "I'll start over there, by the chair. You don't have to watch."

"But I like being queen! You don't dare kill me! I shall call the guards—"

"Leone," I said, and she jumped, flinching. I took her upper arm into my fist and led her across to the chair she had vacated. Caspar was already at work. "Look, Leone," I said. "That is you."

I caught her as she fell.

"At least that'll keep her quiet," snapped Mevancy, who carefully, very carefully, did not look at what Caspar wreaked. "You were hard on her."

The stink of spilled blood permeated the room.

"There will be a lot of blood," commented Caspar, working on.

He had rolled his sleeves up and put on an artist's smock. That might have been an affectation, down here in Loh; in the present circumstances it was highly practical. He covered his arms and hands with a pair of long stockings. Letting Leone gently to the floor I ripped off her shift and underthings and threw them across to Caspar. Mevancy tut-tutted at the sight of the limp naked body and took out the clothes we had brought.

I walked over to the unconscious form of Shang-Li-Po.

"This shint is called the Kaour." I bent and dragged him across. "Let's make him earn the name."

Caspar did not look up. "A capital notion."

"What—?" said Mevancy. Then: "Oh, I see."

The sound of heavy breathing and a clearing of a throat was followed by Llodi saying: "What about me and the artist, an' all?"

"Knocked over by assassins," I said, cheerfully.

"Oh. Right. Mebbe I'd better be the one to wake up and rush out to raise the alarm and everything."

"Be my guest," said Caspar, delicately allowing blood to stain Shang-Li-Po's robes.

The cruel and pathetic irony for this poor girl lay in this: she had in life been one of the hungry masses, in death she was the queen.

Caspar took his time, and finished without undue haste. I guessed he had in reality worked fast. He cleaned his knife and we arranged the tableau.

We pulled Shang-Li-Po's form across and dabbed his gown in the blood. We put his own dagger in his right fist—and Kuong knew he was not left-handed—and the poor dead girl's heart in his left. We smeared all with blood. Anyone finding that revolting scene would not doubt that Shang-Li-Po had killed the queen and had then performed the rites of Kaopan upon her naked body, and as a result had been overcome. If Llodi timed it right he would bring in the guards answering the alarm at just the moment the dikaster was regaining his senses. That would be nice...

I didn't think we'd hang around to find out.

Caspar took off his bloodstained smock and rolled it up carefully. I had to help him pull off the stockings. I didn't mind a few spots of blood on my clothes if none stained Caspar's. He arranged himself comfortably on the floor, by the easel, and relaxed. "I'm ready."

I remained doubtful. I studied him. I couldn't see any obvious blood on him. Modern forensic science had not yet been developed sufficiently on Kregen to discover the blood that indubitably was to be found on his person. I said: "You sure? You're taking one hell of a risk."

"That cramph didn't see who threw the dagger. I'm safe enough. Anyway, a life without risks—who wants that?"

I didn't burst out: "I wouldn't mind, by Vox!" But I felt the attractions of a peaceful life, by Zair!

That ridiculous notion had no chance of ever becoming real, anyway, on Kregen, for me or for a whole lot of other folk. Life's problems stuck with us. Many of us might not have to worry over where the rent and the money for food were coming from, and those problems are of the very real variety, Opaz knows! We had the Shanks to fret over, to fear, to try to deal with. Whilst the confrontation with the reivers from over the curve of the world remained unsolved the whole of life continued risky for all of us living in Paz.

Llodi took up his position halfway between Shang-Li-Po and the door. When the Repositer stirred Llodi would run out to raise the alarm—an' all.

"I can't," he said with an uncharacteristic loquacity, "say life hasn't been interesting an' everything since we met up, Drajak."

Mevancy snapped: "Get out of the blacks, and hurry. We don't have all day."

When we were back in our ochre desert robes and the blacks and Caspar's blood-stained clothing stowed in a bag all safe, we said a quick remberee and decamped past the secret panel into the passage. Mevancy sneezed as dust puffed up. The panel closed. Through the spyhole we could glimpse Llodi standing, poised. He gave us a cheery wave. Yes, it is refreshing and mighty comforting to have good comrades on Kregen!

The other two carried the parts of the gherimcal. I had Leone slung over my shoulder and the clothes bag clutched in my other fist.

By the time we reached the door through which we must exit onto the open corridor we were dusty and cobweb-smothered. It was therefore vital to clean up before venturing out. The carrying chair went together easily enough and we put the clothes bag in on top of Leone. Mevancy fussed over arranging the curtains to conceal everything.

"All set?" demanded Kuong. With some pleasure I realized that apart from the mutilation of that poor dead girl he was thoroughly enjoying himself.

And, too, I realized that for one of the Accursed, one who was paol-ur-bliem, the sight and remembrance of just what Kaopan meant must come as unwelcome and downright frightening.

"Wenda!" said Mevancy, and out we went into the empty corridor.

Retracing our steps though the palace we quickly came upon crowds of people hurrying about their business. No one spared us a glance.

We had just entered a long gallery flanked by statues. A column of heated air rose from the nearest corner. Kuong and Mevancy padded past without hesitation. I hung back. The shimmer tried to solidify, and gusted about, wavering. I saw clearly, and for an instant only, the features of Deb-Lu-Quienyin. He was trying to get through the planes to me.

Garbled, distorted, his voice said: "Jak! A source of weak kharrna* lies ahead. There is a strong personal animus..." The voice died and the spectral shimmer of the projected lupal image of Deb-Lu vanished.

Instantly, I said in a penetrating whisper: "Kuong, Mevancy! Take the next turning to the right. You can rejoin the straight way out a few rooms ahead."

"Cabbage—what are you on about?"

"Just go on, pigeon. I'll see you back at the villa."

Kuong recognized the urgency in my voice. "Come on, Mevancy!"

She turned her head to give me a hard look and I gestured irritably.

"Oh, you!" she said, and perforce swung right to follow Kuong, the gherimcal swaying between them.

If Deb-Lu said there was trouble ahead there was trouble ahead!

No genius of deduction was required to guess what that trouble was. Na-Si-Fantong, besides having left Makilorn, would not, in my view, be a source of weak kharrna. So the troublemaker ahead had to be the court wizard, Chang-So, the fellow who nursed a grudge against me. I'd known he'd make an attempt on me. It had to develop just now, just when our scheme was coming to fruition and we were making good our escape. Still, that's the way sand castles are washed away, as they say in Clishdrin.

Their eyes wide and blank with fear, a parcel of raggedy slaves ran past. Chang-So could scare them easily enough. When I rounded the corner into the next gallery Chang-So in his dazzling robes and tall hat was carefully standing to the rear of half a dozen hulking bully boy guards. Quite clearly he had been apprized of my presence in the palace and was now here to exact his vengeance for the slight I had put upon him.

The guards carried swords, lynxters, and it was borne in on me that Chang-So wanted me dead.

I had far too much to do to allow that, by Zair!

The guards charged. I ripped out my own blade and met their rush in a chingle of steel. They were solid professional workmen of the sword. They'd get the job done without anything fancy. They would be, I judged, only on distant nodding acquaintance with Kurin.

All the same, there were six of them and if I was stupid they'd stick me.

In a very real sense, as I may have mentioned before, every fight is different and every fight is the same. They circled to get at me from both sides. They were not all apim; I didn't wait to check up on all their diverse racial stocks. I just went slap bang into the nearest, chopped him down, kicked his comrade and sliced my blade across the next and so was through, leaving the three who'd circled me gasping. I faced Chang-So.

He had struck me as a man who gloated in the secrets he knew. Now the most important secret in his life was no longer a secret and that told

---

* kharrna: sorcerous power, thaumaturgical energy. A.B.A.

him his life was no longer his life. He really believed I was about to cut him down.

He staggered back. He lifted his arms and the fingers tried to form some magical symbol. He tried to croak words, and his tall hat shook and fell off to roll on the floor. I gave him a gentle push in the shoulder.

Instantly I had to whirl and catch the quickest guard's blade on my own. There was genuine regret in me as my sword slid his and sank into his body. Still, he took pay for this work and payment came in death as well as coin.

The next hesitated, waiting for his comrade to join him.

I reached around and got my left fist wrapped around Chang-So's collar. I lifted him a trifle so that his heels left the floor. He was gobbling and spitting and tears streamed down his cheeks from rage and frustration and, I daresay, fear. He was not used to being treated like this, no, by The Seven Arcades!

"Look at him, doms," I said in my harsh way. "This is the specimen you'll get yourselves killed for. It's not worth it, as Tsung-Tan is my witness. Schtump! Clear off while you still have the chance."

Three were down and three were left. Blood ran greasily on the floor. The wizard looked to them as though he wouldn't live long enough to pay their hire. One of them, a Fristle, spat out: "Let us take Herkin away with us. You have only wounded him. By Odiflor! You are quick."

"Take Herkin." I hoicked Chang-So up and threw him bodily onto the two corpses and the wounded form of Herkin. "And take the wizard also." With that I sprinted somewhat sharply around the next corner.

Not a shred of doubt existed in my mind that Kuong and Mevancy would succeed. They'd take Leone to the villa, we'd all meet up, and take counsel on our next moves. If our work was over in Makilorn there was equally no doubt in my mind that the Star Lords would soon find fresh work for us.

That work would most probably lie over to the west, trying to deal with the Shanks in Tarankar. Kuong, as Trylon of Taranik, might be very useful. And Caspar the Peaker? Would the Star Lords find someone else they wished removed from Kregen?

The amusing thought occurred to me that in all these calculations about what might happen in the future, in which 'we' would do this or that, the 'we', the 'us', simply included Mevancy as a normal part of life.

That made me realize I had a most wonderful opportunity ahead. By Vox! If only I could manage it! The Shank threat in Tarankar was so serious that I had every right to demand all the help I could summon. The Star Lords should see that. So should the Sisters of the Rose. I'd arrange for a message to go to Seg. He'd contact Milsi and she would contact Delia. Then—then this forsaken part of Loh would see what a real empress looked like!

I was so taken up in anticipatory joy at my own cleverness that the rustling voice addressing me spoke a whole sentence before I located the speaker.

"You, Dray Prescot, have disobeyed the Everoinye and failed to do what you were commanded to do."

Crouching by the corridor wall, a reddish brown scorpion, glinting of body and arrogant of tail, spoke to me, spoke to me directly from the Star Lords. Nothing else moved in the corridor. I breathed lightly.

"Of course I haven't failed! Kirsty will be queen!"

"Nevertheless, you disobeyed!"

"You stupid eight-legged onker! That's nothing to do with it! Kirsty is going to be queen and she'll see to it that Tsungfaril is defended from the Shanks. That's the object of all this."

"It is not for you to tell the Everoinye the objects they pursue."

"Well, if they think I failed then it's time someone told them—"

"Enough, Dray Prescot!"

"And another thing! You can tell your precious Star Lords it's about time I went home." Here I hesitated for a fear-filled fraction of time, and hurried on very very quickly: "Home to Valka! Then we can deal with the Shanks."

"You will deal with the Shanks, Dray Prescot." The rustling voice like dead leaves blown scraping over gravel spoke menacingly. "Before that you will answer for your disobedience."

I opened my mouth to shout in baffled rage that this cretin of a scorpion couldn't understand, and, then, I understood. Disobedience was the issue here. The blue radiance grew about me. I looked up to see the gigantic form of the phantom blue Scorpion hovering. Chill smote me. In an icy blueness, I swept away into blackness.

SCORPIO INVASION

Dray Prescot

Dray Prescot has been described as a man above middle height, with brown hair and level brown eyes, brooding and dominating, with enormously broad shoulders and powerful physique. There is about him an abrasive honesty and an indomitable courage. He moves like a savage hunting cat, swift, sudden and lethal.

The superhuman Star Lords have brought him to Kregen, four hundred light years from Earth, where, in pursuance of their schemes for that marvelous and terrifying world, he has been successful on his own account. His education in the horrendous conditions of Nelson's Navy stood him in good stead in his early days on Kregen; now he has won lands and estates and has recently given up the job of being the Emperor of Vallia after putting the island empire together again with the help of the divine Delia, the empress. A fresh mission for the Star Lords has landed Prescot in much skullduggery and political intrigue, and a deal of skull bashing.

Down in the southern part of the mysterious continent of Loh he has with the aid of the kregoinya Mevancy nal Chardaz and of the kregoinye Caspar the Peaker, with the assistance of Trylon Kuong and of Llodi the Voice, kidnapped instead of killing Queen Leone. The Star Lords want a high-spirited lady called Kirsty to be queen, and have ordered Leone killed so that she cannot return through reincarnation.

The conspirators are hustling through the palace having succeeded in their plan. Now some resistance will be made against the hostile Shanks, Fish Faces raiding from over the curve of the world.

Crouching by the palace wall a reddish brown scorpion, glinting of body and arrogant of tail, speaks to Prescot, speaks directly from the Star Lords, from the Everoinye.

"You, Dray Prescot, have disobeyed the Everoinye and failed to do what you were commanded to do."

Now Prescot must answer for his disobedience, as he tells us in this volume, *Scorpio Invasion*.

Alan Burt Akers

One

"You will deal with the Shanks, Dray Prescot." The rustling voice, like dead leaves blown scraping over gravel, spoke menacingly. "Before that you will answer for your disobedience."

I opened my mouth to shout in baffled rage that this cretin of a scorpion couldn't understand, and, then, I understood. Disobedience was the issue here. The blue radiance grew about me. I looked up to see the gigantic form of the phantom blue Scorpion hovering. Chill smote me. In an icy blueness I swept away into blackness.

Blackness and blueness swirling all about me... Headlong tumbling with the breath knocked from my lungs... The freezing grip of icy chains lapping my limbs... Oh, yes, I knew all about these sensations. The high and mighty Everoinye, the Star Lords, were summoning me to their presence—and this time they were going to discipline me for what they considered disobedience.

Streaks of lambent blue fire shot through the blackness. My body felt black and blue too, by Vox. Instead of having Queen Leone assassinated and then, through the disgusting rites of Kaopan, making sure she could never be reincarnated, I'd saved her and switched in some poor pathetic dead girl to take her place. No one here in Makilorn apart from we plotters would know that. The Star Lords wanted Kirsty as queen, and now she would be.

As I thus hurtled helplessly through a maelstrom of supernatural forces I, Dray Prescot, Lord of Strombor and Krozair of Zy, felt that perhaps all my modulated feelings for the Star Lords had been misplaced. I'd thought we'd been getting onto a better footing where we might understand more of one another's problems. Now, particularly after they'd sent Caspar the Peaker to assassinate Leone so that Kirsty might be queen, I fancied all my old hatred and contempt would flare up uncontrollably.

That, as I knew to my cost, would be a mistake.

Maybe, just maybe, the Star Lords' plans could exist within the framework of decency. Perhaps, just perhaps, absolute power had not corrupted them past redemption.

Below me through the swirling mists I saw a patchwork of green.

Peering more closely I realized I was looking down from a great height upon fields and forests and hills.

This amazed me so completely that I stared without believing.

Never before had I seen anything outside the blue outlines of the phantom Scorpion as I was whisked up to meet the Everoinye or to be tumbled headlong, naked and unarmed, into some dismal spot of Kregen to sort out a problem for the Star Lords.

Arms and spirals of blue, like contorting tentacles, waved all about me. I could hear a vast rushing, as of the wind at the end of the world. A blustery gale swung me up, twisted me about so that for an instant I was staring directly upwards.

Like a lance thrust, a glittering streak of brilliant viridian green slashed across the heavens. I heard the discordant clashing and hissing as the vivid green streak sliced into the blue mists about me.

In the next instant I was right way up, looking down, and seeing my sword and harness falling through thin air below me.

With a single flicking lick of a blue tentacle, a line of blue radiance reached out, snatched the sword and harness, withdrew into the main bulk.

I knew who controlled that acid green. That was the Star Lord called Ahrinye. He might be a million years or so younger than the other Everoinye; he was at once impetuous and icily contemptuous and he wanted to run me hard, so hard that I believed I'd have little chance of survival.

The ground below was coming up mighty fast.

Seeing that ground, and the falling sword, continued to astonish me. When I say I'd not seen anything outside the blue Scorpion I mean ordinary earthly objects of Kregen; I'd seen plenty of fireworks as the Everoinye squabbled among themselves, and as Zena Iztar with her mellow golden yellow light tried to mediate.

The blueness was fading. Without a single doubt the blueness was thinning and vanishing. And I was still high in the air and falling straight down!

"Hey!" I shouted up, feeling the wind gusting about. "Hai! Star Lords!" I bellowed, feeling the wind now as a rushing force upon my falling body. "What are you doing?"

What they were doing was perfectly obvious. They were doing nothing.

"Help!" I hollered up. "I'll be squashed flat! Hai!"

Down and down I plummeted. The ground was confoundedly near by now. "You bunch of miserable onkers, you crew of cretins! Catch me!"

By the pustular nose and infected warts of Makki Grodno! The stupid phantom blue Scorpion had dropped me!

I twisted my head around to look up. Maybe I did that because I did not wish to stare at that frightening ground swishing up so rapidly.

Up there a dim redness washed away to one side. Red was often the color of the Star Lords when they argued with Ahrinye and his acrid green.

"Star Lords!" I bellowed. Still, down and down I fell.

The only explanation I could see for this contretemps was that Ahrinye had attempted to take over control of me and had not quite succeeded but had caused the Scorpion to drop me. The phantom blue Scorpion had fumbled.

"Ahrinye!" I yelled up. "Do something, you stupid great onker!"

Down below the ground looked a patchwork of green, and there were the roofs and towers of a town some way off by a river. I was going to hit and go splat! In a very very short time.

"Star Lords!" I shrieked. "Ahrinye!" And then, with desperation and cunning caused by despair, I yelled up: "Zena Iztar!"

She had been off on her own work far removed from Kregen, or so I had been led to believe. If the Star Lords were unable to agree to save me, my only hope remained Zena Iztar. She had promised her patronage and support for the schemes I wanted to implement for the good of Kregen. If I was dead I'd be of no further use to any of 'em, by Krun.

Down below the ground was so close I could see walled gardens filled with greenery and flowers and fountains. Low red buildings bordered the gardens. In the next instant I'd go squash! and that would be the end of Dray Prescot, lord of this and that, etc, and prince of onkers.

Inevitably, my last thought would be of the one person in two worlds who matters more than anything else—including the damned Star Lords.

I thought of Delia, Delia of the Blue Mountains, Delia of Delphond. I'd not been as attentive to her as I ought to have been, as I desperately wanted to be, in the sweet name of Opaz. The Everoinye called me away from Delia. Still, the Sisters of the Rose called her away from me, too...

I composed myself for oblivion.

Two thin streaks of fire reached down from the heavens.

On one side the acrid green of Ahrinye smoked down to coil and lap beneath me.

On the other side the glorious golden yellow radiance diffused a cushion under me.

"Zena Iztar!" I gasped.

The sensation was like falling upon a fireman's safety sheet. My headlong descent checked. The torrent of wind past me ceased. I was still falling, but slowly as immaterial superhuman forces caught and cushioned me.

The water felt hard enough as I went bodily into it, by Krun!

Down and down I went, turning, ready to begin the ascent to the surface. Great, fat, golden fish swam lazily away, flicking their transparent fins insolently. The bottom of the pool, all green and clean, showed me I was in one of the carp pools of cultivated gardens. Lily stems twined away above. I gave a look of dislike to the tangle of stuff; a couple of flipper strokes drove me safely past and now I began to rise. Able to swim underwater for a long time, I was in no discomfort whatsoever from lack of air.

Although Zena Iztar and Ahrinye had slowed my fall, I'd still been traveling at a good rate of knots when I went into the water. The following rise in balancing compensation saw me shooting up swiftly. I felt a vast wet and floppy mass cushion above my head and then I popped up out of the water into the air with a lily pad balanced on my skull.

I must have shot up over man height before flopping back like a porpoise. In that fragment of time I saw an encircling red brick wall, a green and blossoming garden, an iron gate—and standing each side of that iron gate an armed and armored guard leaning on a spear.

In a lightning swift vision, that whole scene as it must have appeared to an observer etched itself on my brain. Sink me! It must have tickled up those two drowsy guards. There they were, standing guard duty with the sound of the party going on in the next garden. They were bored stiff, itchy, thirsty, and half-asleep. Then like a thunderbolt a thing falls straight out of the sky and goes splash! smack into the middle of the carp pond.

Before the guards have time to close their astonished mouths up leaps a fountain of water and a monstrous naked man like a salmon leaping the weir. Sploshing and splashing, down he goes into the water again. Just where he's come from, the guards really don't wish to think about. All they know is that he's fallen in the water.

That scene, bright and brittle, and wet, was good for a laugh in after years, especially with the lily pad balanced on my skull.

By the time I'd spouted water like a whale and got rid of the lily pad and swum to the bank, the guards had managed to close their mouths and were waiting on the edge ready to prod their spears at me.

I checked my stroke a few feet from the pond bank, treading water, and looked up.

"Hai, doms," I called up. "It's a nice day for it."

Bored, insensitive, callous though these guards most certainly were they remained guards with a job to do for which they took pay. They wore uniforms of a cut and style unfamiliar to me. There was altogether too much flowing drapery, and gold lace, and looping cords and feathers. These were clearly gala uniforms, put on in honor of the party whose sounds were now clearly evident beyond the red brick wall. Two ornate pole arms slanted down at my head. I was not fool enough to imagine those fancy halberds would not be honed to razor sharpness.

"You're a dead man, dom," said the left hand one. His face, brown and seamed, strip-bearded, wore no particular expression. Bored, he'd kill as a mere part of his duty.

"You know no man is allowed in here," confirmed the other, whose face might have been his companion's twin.

The streaming mingled lights of the Suns of Scorpio slanted in across the pond and the ruby of Zim and the emerald of Genodras struck sparks of fire from the wicked spiked and bladed halberd heads.

I spouted some more water and pondered the situation.

If this amazes you, it should not. By this time in this my narrative you should be well aware that I, Dray Prescot, abhor violence and killing. Behavior of that kind has been forced on me by the force of circumstances and—I own it, I own it—by the arrogance of my own resentment and resistance to unjustified and cruel authority.

"Now, see here, doms—" I began.

They were having none of that. The sweet scent of fully blooming blossoms drifted across the carp pond. The suns shone. The air, that glorious fragrant air of Kregen, filled my lungs. And these two talked indifferently of killing.

"No good arguing," said the left hand one. "Stick him, Lin. Them's the orders."

Obediently, Lin thrust his halberd at me.

There was no difficulty in evading the spiked halberd head. I paddled a little way off, regarding these two in frustrated sorrow.

"He wants to play clever," observed Lin. "Better send for a bowman, Hwang, and get it over with." He yawned. "We're off duty in half a bur."

Guardsmen can usually judge the time they stand on duty and know when their reliefs are due.

Hwang nodded and propped himself on his halberd. "Off you go, then."

Now this I did not want. I paddled toward the bank until I was within reach. Lin turned, waiting.

"Giving up, dom?"

I put a hand on the brick facing and looked up.

Hwang sucked a breath, stood upright, swiveled his halberd and thrust hard.

With a sinuous sideways movement I slid the blade, took the haft in my fist, and jerked harder than he'd thrust.

With a loud yell of rage and surprise he went headlong into the water. Lin shouted his own anger and swung his halberd down in a flat arc. This time I was not as clean in my response and Lin toppled sideways, staggering under the impact of his own halberd. Ignoring the splashings and frothing from the man in the water I hefted up onto the bank and as Lin attempted to rise put the hard toes of my right foot into his throat. He emitted a gargling gasping groan and collapsed.

Amidst a great deal of splashing and foaming Hwang spluttered: "You fool, dom! Now they'll..." His words were chopped off as he went under again.

Lin was unconscious. I looked at the pond as Hwang surfaced, spouting, and now his yells were of an entirely different character.

"Help! Help! I can't swim!"

"By the Black Chunkrah!" I said, fairly spitting with annoyance. "What a carry on!" And, feeling like a buffoon, I dived in, stroked swiftly to him as he went down again, and probably for the last time, got a fist into his fancy folderols of uniform, and hoicked him up. By the time I'd towed him to the bank and dragged him out his face held a beautiful tinge of green. I thumped him down where he groaned and vomited. I looked at the pair.

"The Divine Lady of Belschutz undoubtedly has a few words for you two," I said. Working swiftly I stripped off a length of cloth of a reddish color and wrapped it about me, drawing the loose end up between my legs and fastening the makeshift breechclout firmly with Hwang's belt. He wore a second belt equipped with a sword, a lynxter of an ornate fancy pattern, and a dagger. This belt I buckled up about my waist. I looked about.

The noise we had made must surely bring more guards running.

These two lovelies were out of the reckoning for the moment. Now I had to find a safe way out of this infernal place. The noise of the party beyond the gate indicated that that was not the way to go.

In the opposite wall across the pond stood another gate. That way, then.

Leaving wet footprints that would dry rapidly in the heat of the suns I padded around the carp pond, heading for the gate.

I stopped stock-still. I must be growing senile. Was I then so wrapped up in the legends of Dray Prescot that I must always prance around half-naked clad only in a scarlet breechcloth and brandishing a sword?

I ran back very sharply to the prostrate guards and relieved them of all their weapons and Lin's uniform—which was dry. When I leaned over and stared at my reflection in the water I looked a proper fancy guard.

Then I retraced my steps around the pond to the farther gate.

This led into a further garden whose walls were covered with espaliers.

The colors and scents of flowers wafted most pleasantly across the central grassy lawn. A two-wheeled handcart carrying a rotund water tank was attended by two old Ochs who were painstakingly watering the borders. They looked up indifferently as I ran past. The jet of water did not waver by a hair's breadth. Making for the gate opposite the one I had entered by, I reflected that the old Ochs were slaves and they were females. The next gate led into a walled garden crammed with flowers.

By this time I had a shrewd suspicion that where I had touched down after the Scorpion dropped me had landed me in very hot water.

That made me look back for an instant at the spectacle I must have made tumbling out of the sky, going splash! into the water and then spouting up again with the lily pad balanced ludicrously on my head. Well, yes, I suppose it was comical. Had those two dozy guards, Lin and Kwang, been more awake they might even have found a little chuckle, if not going to the extreme of actually laughing.

More walled gardens followed, gate after gate. A few more female Och slaves barely looked up as I went by, intent upon their labors.

Given that the sound of the party ought to come from the central portions of this damned maze of gardens, then to keep on going directly away from the party should bring me to the outside wall. That, at least, was the theory. Ha! You who have followed my narrative will know how theories have the diabolical habit of mercilessly tripping up one hight Dray Prescot.

So far the guard uniform had brought me through without question. Slaves do not normally stand up when a guard passes and challenge him with a "Who are you?"

Other guards might, though.

Two other guards did. Directly, harshly, slanting their spears at my midriff. They were tough, hard-faced, wearing curved leather armor and polished metal helmets flaunting red and yellow feathers. They marched smartly in through the open gate towards which I was walking and simply marched straight up to me, pointed their spears, and challenged me in a most decisive and unmistakable way.

They did not speak exactly as Lin and Hwang had done; the burden of their message was exactly the same.

"There is no excuse," said the left hand one in a clipped, tight voice. "You are not allowed here."

The right hand one said: "We shall take you along to the guardroom. Now just come along quietly."

To reinforce the words she used her spear to tickle my ribs.

"Now look here—" was as far as I got before the spear jabbed again.

"Get moving, you loveless spawn of Holpo the Blasphemer!"

Well, as many folk have said many times, if ladies wish to put on armor and act as soldiers, jikai vuvushis, and wield weapons, they are perfectly entitled to do so. In the struggles in Vallia during the Times of Troubles, I, myself, had cause to be thankful to the gallant regiments of jikai vuvushis who had fought so well for us. I had shuddered away from their use and had only reluctantly come to realize that girls, no less than boys, must be allowed to do what they wish and are able for the good of all.

All this being so, the obverse is also so.

I took the spear haft into my fist, pushed and then snatched it cleanly from the girl's grasp and used it to parry the second girl's automatic stroke. Then I tapped both as gently as I could under the fancy helmets just above their ears. I tried to catch both as they fell, but as I am an apim, Homo sapiens sapiens, and have only two arms, one of the poor girls pitched over onto the path. I lowered the other to her side and stepped back to view them. I shook my head. This happening is the obverse of the bright colors and armor and glittering weapons and flaunting feathers. They both slumbered peacefully.

When I moved off I did so very smartly.

Which was just as well.

A long blue-fletched Lohvian arrow sprouted from the thigh of the nearest sprawled girl.

Without thought, without hesitation, instantly, I hurled myself sideways, ducking away, fleeting over the ground.

More arrows flicked past. When a Bowmaid of Loh shoots at you, you must deflect the shafts, run and dodge the shafts, or let the shafts shaft you to death.

"By Makki Grodno's pustule-covered armpits and leprous biceps!" I said to myself as I leaped from side to side and raced on zigzagging to save my life. "They're mighty sharp around here."

I went roaring past the open gate and immediately cut along to the left beside the wall. That pitiless rain of arrows dried up. I took a breath and scuttled rapidly along by the wall heading for a narrow door at the far end of the path. I ignored the opposite gate this time; it seemed to me that would only admit me onto more trouble. I could hear a few high-pitched shouts from the rear and guessed the Bowmaids would be running after me, their long legs flashing in the suns-light.

The door proved to be unlocked. When I opened it, slid through, and slammed it at my back I assumed the girls, seeing this garden empty, would realize I hadn't had time to cross to the opposite gate and therefore know I'd gone through here. In that case... I slid the bolt firmly, snicking it into its socket with a click.

I turned around. The walls in this garden were completely bare of the vegetation of all kinds that graced the walls of the other gardens. The whole expanse was covered in coarse gravel of a reddish orange tint. In the centre stood a brick fountain with water gushing up and falling into a stone basin. A number of indentations here and there over the gravel thickened near the fountain. Each little scoop looked to be the size of a large animal's hoof, and the further indentations around the central one looked unmistakably and unpleasantly like the mark of giant claws.

The only other exit in this walled garden lay opposite and in the centre of the wall. The door stood wide open. I crossed to it.

To have rushed in through the open doorway would have been highly foolish. I loosened one of my swords and, leaning against the wall, poked an eyeball around the edge of the doorway. This garden looked perfectly normal. Perhaps there were a few more trees than usual and more pretty little birds, otherwise the flowers banked in profusion and the air was filled with their perfume. I took a breath and stepped past the edge of the doorway. At the side an opening had been formed. This was a double wall, creating a long alleyway between the gardens. The alleyway was floored in the same reddish orange gravel. Also, I had not failed to notice the size of this doorway, and the width of the alley between the walls convinced me the animal who lived here and was brought here to drink was of a considerable size.

I shoved my sword back firmly in the scabbard and prowled on.

So far I'd managed to avoid the cluster of roofs visible over the walls. Red tiled roofs, with flat terrace and balcony connecting features, they seemed to me to denote that this place was a luxurious country villa. In that, of course, I could be wildly wrong. By the movement of the twin suns I saw I was in the northern hemisphere of Kregen again. All these walled gardens would appear to indicate I was still in the continent of Loh.

From these conclusions and from what had happened to me since I'd arrived it was now quite clear just where I was. Whilst it is no doubt a splendid and magnificent thing to die young for some great cause, it is, as San Blarnoi points out, far more comfortable to support the great cause without getting killed. And, as the soldier poet Kapt Larghos the Lame observes in his military rhythms, you can get just as dead in a petty skirmish as you can in a full-scale battle. He should know—he got himself killed in an ambush fifteen hundred seasons ago.

The need at the moment was to find the outside wall and go either through a gateway or over the wall and get clear of these gardens. They were highly unhealthy—for unwanted men.

Going on cautiously I crossed three more enclosed spaces of flowers. Apart from that mad dash to the left away from the arrows, I believed I'd kept to a straight line. Unless the villa possessed grounds of enormous extent I ought to be nearing the outer wall, surely, for the sweet sake of Opaz?

Or, perhaps I was running along this series of gardens parallel to the outer wall? "By the Black Chunkrah!" I said to myself. "That is not one of your more helpful notions, Dray Prescot."

The next garden contained a pool clearly designed for people to go swimming. The place was deserted, but from beyond the far wall floated the happy sounds of laughter and the clink of glasses. I stopped and listened. You may believe me when I say I listened most carefully, most carefully indeed, by Krun!

Over in the jungles of South Pandahem we'd encountered the Cabaret Plant. This little beauty grew in the form of a large gourd with tendrils. It had the happy knack of making sounds as of a party to lure its victims to a carnivorous end. Seg and I had experience of the horrors which the dinkus of the forest call the Naree-Giver for they obtain the poison with which they tip their blowpipe darts. So, I stood and I tried to identify the merry sounds and the clink of bottles and glasses.

One thing was sure, I couldn't afford to hang around long. Those ferocious Bowmaids of Loh were after me and they'd shaft me on the spot. The idea that there might be Cabaret Plants growing here to yield their poison came as an ugly thought. Although, mind you, I didn't believe a Bowmaid of Loh needed to tip her deadly arrow heads with any poison.

Taking great care, I stuck an eyeball around the corner. Truth to tell, perhaps, the sight of a Cabaret Plant might have been more welcome than the scene that confronted me.

With caution I could have walked around and past a Cabaret Plant. There was no way I was going to pass this little lot. They were having a party, they were enjoying themselves, and they'd welcome me to their festivities as the human sacrifice to be offered up to whatever dark gods they worshipped.

The women wore precious little in the way of ordinary clothes. Sumptuous silks flowed from their shoulders and trailed them across the grass. They wore artificially-high-heeled shoes. Their navels were bare and many wore jewels there. Their hair piled high in artful mountains of gems and loops of pearls. There was a great use of blown glass as ornament, glittering in the radiance of the Suns, twining around neck and arm and thigh. Every woman was veiled.

"I knew it!" I said to myself. "That damned gerblish onker of a Scorpion! Dropped me down into a harem. Right into a seraglio. This is where I'll lose portions of my anatomy first, before they chop me up." I felt quite warm. "That idiot Ahrinye and the Star Lords between 'em are out to do me down." This was not strictly true, as I knew; but, as I say, I was somewhat warm by this time.

The harem women moved in loose graceful poses. The veils were light chiffon-like drapes, heightening the beauty and mystery of the concealed faces. Most of the poor creatures would be slave, and there was a very great deal of money parading about there. And, they were drinking and listening to the music from an enclosed balcony, and appeared not to be too displeased with their lot.

Time to go. I drew back cautiously and turned about. The other gate in this garden would have to lead somewhere useful, by Krun!

Padding off towards the gate and keeping my head turning I saw the lissom figures appear above the wall to my right rear. Here came the Bowmaids!

Running fleetly over the grass and jinking from side to side, I managed to avoid the lethal arrows sleeting in. If they brought up any more girls they'd put down a barrage no one, not even a Krozair of Zy, was going to run through unscathed.

With a last burst of energy I roared through the gateway. The ground here was uniformly covered by reddish orange gravel. No fountain sparkled at the centre. Instead a monstrous form towered up, shaggy, shambling, its six arms forming a wagon wheel of colossal power. Its four legs supported it in a half-upright position. Its eyes were large, like saucers, round and staring—staring at me! A red tongue licked out past rubbery lips and the gleam of yellow fangs was enough to put a breeze up anybody's spine.

The thing shambled over the gravel towards me. The six arms reached for me. High excited shouts at my rear told me there was no way back.

"By the Blade of Kurin," I snarled to myself, and ripped out my sword. "If this is the way of it, then I'll make a jikai of it!"

Two

The thing advanced towards me, shambling. Something red shone in one of its hands. I cocked up the sword, braced and ready to rush in.

"Nnng—nnng—" The thing mouthed incomprehensible words, slobbering. It stopped stock-still. "Nnng—bbl—" It threw the red object from one hand to another and I saw it was a child's ball.

Ready to leap forward and deal in my usual way with monsters, I paused. The thing turned its grotesque head to one side, and I felt that movement was one of puzzlement, almost of pleading. Once more it threw the ball from hand to hand. Then it threw the ball at me. The rubbery lips writhed over the words. "Bbl—play!"

The ball bounced towards me.

I caught it in my left hand and threw it back. Instantly the thing assumed a crouching position, six arms waving. For a sick moment I thought I hadn't played the game correctly. The thing swayed from side to side as the ball flew towards it and I saw it was playing. It caught the ball cleanly and emitted a high chirruping noise of triumph. That sound was echoed by the menacing shouts of the Bowmaids chasing me.

The thing tossed the ball up again and threw it at me. This time I used the sword. Grasped in two hands, it swung like a bat, caught the ball on the fly and fairly belted it into the far corner of the garden.

That shot was worth a home run or a six over the pavilion any day.

The thing let rip a snorting squeak which I took to be pleasure and started off after his ball. Running around in the other direction I skirted along the wall and fairly sprinted for the distant gate.

The thing lollopped over to the ball and picked it up. When he swung back to where I'd been, he emitted a pinging sound of puzzlement.

Then my movement caught in the corner of his eye and he turned. What he was going to do now I didn't know—had I spoiled his game? Was I ready to be dealt with as monsters habitually deal with folk they don't like?

He let rip a squeak and hurled the ball at me. I noticed that he threw it ahead, allowing for my movement. Obligingly I used the sword and gave the ball a square cut that drove it past wide of his six arms. He started lolloping off after it. I went skidding non-stop through the open gateway.

The Bowmaids would know the animal and wouldn't be halted. I had to run like stink to get away before they shafted me.

Now the cluster of red roofs lay to the rear and the sounds of the party faded. These gardens were mostly given over to vegetables. At this I took heart.

My beliefs were justified shortly when, past a garden with the bright shoots of momolams sprouting healthily, I saw ahead a wall taller than any so far encountered. This jolly-well had to be the outer wall!

There were, naturally, no doors or gates visible in the entire length.

Suddenly, and with an icy chill, I heard among the shouts of the girls the growing howling and barking. I recognized those ululations. Werstings! A pack of the killer-dogs had been let loose on my heels. They'd follow me remorselessly until they were all slain—or, if I were extremely lucky, until I could shake them off. And that, by Krun, was extraordinarily hard to do.

Running through the nearest gateway into the next garden I looked about for some means of scaling that damned wall.

This was the outer wall and they were not stupid enough to grow trees or vines conveniently placed for intruders to enter—which meant they were useless to me trying to get out.

The menacing growls and sharp barks of the werstings appeared to me to grow louder and louder.

One aspect of these walled gardens that had impressed me from the outset was their tidiness and well-kept appearance. I'd seen female slave gardeners on my chase through here; but I'd not seen any of those little gardener's huts one finds in gardens where the tools of the trade are kept. The obvious answer for that was the slaves were issued with their implements from a central source by an overseer. Slave owners do not like stores of potential weapons lying about ready for the first disaffected slave to snatch up. No, sir.

With that in mind as I entered the next garden I saw the solution to my problem, along with, of course, further problems to obtain that solution.

These walls contained an orchard. The trees were not overly tall and in my state of urgency I didn't bother to notice what kind they were. What I wanted was one of the ladders the slaves were using to climb up to the tops of the trees. One of those ladders ought just to reach the wall.

Making sure my borrowed uniform was in correct order, I strutted up to the nearest tree. A woman was working away at the top of the ladder and a group waited below. I put on my harsh voice.

"Get that ladder down at once! Bring it over here! Grak!"

"Yes, master," said the slave with a yellow headband. Slave she might be, she had her meed of petty authority, even if not up to the class of the balass stick.

The slaves wore the gray slave breechclout. The one at the top of the ladder slid down as neatly as a snotty would slide down the backstay. As I stood importantly, scowling at them, four of the slaves took up the ladder and the overseer looked expectantly at me.

"What are you waiting for?" I bellowed. "This way." With that I started off strutting through the garden gate towards the outer wall.

They followed me, marching in step. They must have heard the sounds of the pursuit by now, the howling of the werstings and the excited calls of the Bowmaids and Jikai Vuvushis, but they gave no visible sign of interest.

That kind of thing was not their concern. Truth to tell, it struck me that they probably associated noises of that kind with escaped slaves.

We reached the wall and I made a sharp and contemptuous gesture and up went the ladder to clatter against the top of the wall. It was short by about two feet; that would present no problem.

The slave overseer raised her dark eyes, fearfully, to glance at me.

The habit of instant obedience was so strong that, even if she believed what she saw, she couldn't question me. Clearly, in this section of the gardens, past the monster who wanted to play ball and here in the vegetable patches, male guards were allowed. All the same, I did not want to see these poor slaves punished on my account.

"I shall need the ladder. Go back to work. Schtump!"

They trailed off and I went up the ladder fast. A quick heave at the top and I was seated astride the wall. An arrow flicked past my ear.

The pursuit burst into the garden, Jikai Vuvushis brandishing spears and swords, Bowmaids of Loh running and stopping to take aim, and, foremost of all, the horrific pack of werstings, black and white striped hellions.

I knocked an arrow aside with my forearm. The werstings would not be able to climb the ladder; the ladies most certainly would. So, I bent, got a good grip, and heaved. Up came the ladder just as the foremost wersting made a savage leap. He fell back, baffled. The ladder balanced on the wall. With a swiveling motion I had it around and down on the outside. Down below lay a dusty lane, and another damned tall wall across the lane. Instead of as I'd expected dropping from the wall like a sneaky assassin, I was able calmly to descend the ladder like a respectable burglar going home from work.

The opposite wall looked just like this one, and was clearly the outer wall of the next-door villa. The lane looked the same in both directions. The taste of dust on the tongue was brought by a little breeze that whiffled along the alleyway. So, then, which way? In a mere matter of heartbeats my pursuers would come howling through the main gate and tear after me.

I went to the left.

There was a gate on my left, closed, and if that was the one the Bowmaids intended to use I'd better run as fast as I could, for the confounded lane ran straight as a die towards a further cluster of buildings beyond.

Now having werstings on your trail is strictly bad news. They are smart, although not in the same league as a Manhound. If I was to fool them I needed to be both clever and lucky. One thing I decided; it would not be a good idea to stroll into the town ahead wearing these guard clothes.

The folderols came off thankfully enough. If I had to chance local customs, I would have to do so. I kept a tunic-like upper garment, and with the red breechclout that would have to suffice. I made the castoff clothing into a ball and carefully teased out one end of a scarf to trail. With a good throw I sent the lot over the neighbor's wall and the trailing tail caught on the top and clung, hanging down. Good!

If that did nothing else, it would split the wersting pack.

After all, they had nothing of mine to sniff for the scent.

Running swiftly on I reached the end of the lane as a swimmer must reach the rocks just as his lungs fill with water. I nipped around the end of the wall. Like a trumpet, the lane magnified the horrid sounds of the werstings snuffling after me. I roused myself, took a breath, and sized up where I'd got myself into now and what was my best next step.

Generally, not always, civilizations that go in for private walled gardens with houses without outside windows also go in for a public face on their municipal buildings. I expected to see arcades and pillared porticoes, openness, squares and probably shade trees and fountains.

Four hundred light years away through empty space no doubt those expectations might have been realized. But I was on the splendid if horrific planet of Kregen, in the continent of Loh, and I could expect nothing to be familiar. We all spoke a language imposed on the territorial grouping of Paz, modified by local usage. Beyond that—well, as I turned about I saw that a common language was one thing, fashions in architecture quite another. One could call that style of architecture 'Ornamented Fanciful' for like a lavish wedding cake it sprouted tiers and balconies and dizzying perspectives of red tiled roofs and white colonnades. Yet the whole tended to an upward perspective. Beneath there were indeed arcades; but these held shadows and mysteries and were not, I judged, the sites of impassioned rhetoric and legal argument. I stared, pondering the best place to hide.

The ululations of those damned werstings howled on apace and it behooved me to get a move on.

Whether by ill chance or good fortune, I could not say, but just at the moment only a very few folk walked between those weird buildings.

Moving rapidly I crossed the intervening area and plunged into the shadowed arcade leading directly away from the hunting pack.

All this running about was distinctly annoying. I had work to do. That damnfool Scorpion had dropped me into some petty rushing about adventure when I ought to be about the business of Paz, the business of resisting the ruthless invasions of the Fish-Faces, the Shanks, from over the curve of the world. Many people of the grouping of lands called Paz wanted me to become what they called the Emperor of Emperors, the Emperor of Paz. Needless to say I didn't want the job but felt it imposed on me, not only by the will of the people but by the desires of the Star Lords. They had suggested, it seemed to me, that this Emperor of Emperors nonsense was why they'd put up with me at all, why they'd brought me to Kregen.

The Star Lords used me in this vile way because I had the yrium, that special form of charisma that caused ordinary people and extraordinary people to lay down their lives to serve me. Oh, yes, I felt ashamed, I felt diminished. Yet, if the damned Shanks were to be prevented from murdering every woman, man and child in Paz, someone had to be found who could weld the disparate countries of Paz into a common union of resistance.

And, as you see, that onker was me, plain Dray Prescot.

The problem was, the divine Delia would become the Empress of Empresses. Of course, no one was more fitted to hold that office. But, all the same, I fretted over the potential dangers to which she would be exposed. Of course, that was a laugh. Dangers and Delia went hand in hand. Was she not a Sister of the Rose? Did she not flaunt off adventuring for them and on her own account? Yet I own if aught happened to my Delia, my Delia of Delphond, my Delia of the Blue Mountains, then all of Kregen and of Earth could go hang.

These fretful thoughts were more important to me at that moment, incongruously, I suppose, than the howling pack of slavering werstings and the Bowmaids of Loh and the Jikai Vuvushis out for my blood.

The arcade stretched ahead, patched with shadow, implicit with menace.

Just before I started off into those shadows a brief but excruciatingly brilliant vision of the shaggy monster and his red ball flamed before my eyes. My Val! He had the strength to rip my head clean off my shoulders. His six arms would have been the very devil to counter and beat. Powerful, dominating, a monster—and he'd wanted to play ball! Whew!

Forcing the image out of my vision I raced into the shadows of the arcade.

The wall to my right was pierced by a few tall narrow doorways, all shuttered by solid iron-barred wooden doors. Overhead the roof curved from column to column. To my right the radiance of the Suns of Scorpio threw light as I reached the corner of the building and scampered across to the next series of arcades. The dusty square over on the left remained empty and I felt that however strange and foreign this city might be, one would expect more people than that. A distant murmur like summer bees from ahead, I felt sure, would explain the mystery.

Again I crossed the shafting mingled lights of a cross street. The noise increased. Two men and a woman ran out from a door, which slammed as they left, and raced on ahead. Little detective work was needed to deduce they were running to join the crowd making the noise. I followed on.

Soon other people joined in and I was going rapidly along in quite a little crowd. No one took any notice of me. The men wore strange and fanciful costumes, all draping scarves and tassels, and multi-colored feathers in their wide and floppy hats. A few men wore brilliantly colored loincloths with bare legs, and had swords swinging at their sides. The women all wore veils. These veils were larger and thicker than the flimsy seductive bits of flimsy worn by the girls in the harem. We all ran along to join the procession.

Debouching into a kyro of some size surrounded by the spiring buildings founded on their arcades, the procession wound around and around the square until everyone had joined in. I was near the stern of the mob.

This suited me. Whatever morsel of scent the werstings had picked up must be obliterated and lost in all this throng.

A woman climbed onto the pedestal of a statue of a Khibil holding a Lohvian longbow aloft. The statue was twice life size, one of a number dotted about the kyro. She raised her arms and with surprising promptitude the crowds fell silent. She began to speak in an impassioned haranguing way, all about the lost glories of Walfarg, of the ancient Empire of Walfarg which the barbarian people of the outer world called the Empire of Loh. "Just as," she cried, shrieking, "the benighted fools call the accursed Wizards of Walfarg Wizards of Loh!"

I felt the shock of that. I felt a distinct shock, not to say a tremor of dire chill. By Vox! To call a Wizard of Loh accursed! I stared in fascination at this woman, half expecting to see her turned into a little green toad.

Her face was of that strong hard variety that, nevertheless, is womanly handsome. She could not be called pretty; her appeal came from her inner strengths. This reminded me of Mevancy, although the two were vastly different women in appearance and in the nature of their inner strengths. She wore fancy silken robes attached to her shoulders and trailing; but they were flung back to reveal the curved leather armor across her breast and the pteruges covering her upper thighs. Incongruously, her navel was bare. She wore two swords, a lynxter and a short sword of that type which is called a laiker in Loh. Both weapons had over-ornate hilts. Her feet I could not see for the heads of the crowds between us. Her head was uncovered and her bright red Lohvian hair gleamed in the radiance of the suns.

To say this woman intrigued me must be an overstatement. What she had said and why she had said it—that interested me, by Krun!

Now she was ranting on about the absence of life and energy in the land. People were slothful. People were all sinful. All they thought of were their bellies, their beds, their money. "We must rise up," she declaimed. "Rise up and take back what once was ours!"

A few thin shouts of approval lifted. A few harsher voices of dissent growled away. Most of the crowd remained dumb or talking in undertones between themselves.

So, I reasoned, the people had not raised themselves from their lethargy to run and see and listen to this woman. Oh, no. They were here to see her brought low. If that was not done by a Wizard of Loh then no doubt the agents of the local police or watch would soon swoop. The crowds were looking forward to that pleasurable entertainment.

I felt disgusted with them.

Now she was delivering herself of pent up fury and resentment at the judgment of history. She was blaming the fall of the Empire of Walfarg on the Wizards of Loh and also on the incompetence of Walfargian military men. "We must have boats that sail through the thin air!" she screeched. "We must breed giant birds to carry us on their wings into battle to bring us the victory!" At this the catcalls spurted from the crowds. "We must have these things! We will have them! As I stand here, I, Mul-lu-Manting, swear it! By the Seven Arcades I swear!"

This was heavy metal. The Seven Arcades, whatever they were, were words on the lips of Wizards of Loh when impassioned or inflamed to rage. Maybe this girl was some kind of Witch of Loh, maybe she'd failed her exams or had been defrocked. That would account for her attack on the Lohvian mages.

A stir in the crowd near me and the unmistakable tramp of iron-shod feet heralded the expected fun and games. There was no chance that I could intervene to help this woman. I felt that, had I the opportunity to do so, I would. The mass of people shrank away from the guards, clanking along. By the time they were within reach of the statue of the Khibil with the upraised bow, Mul-lu-Manting was long gone from the pedestal.

"The incompetent fools!" A shrewish little woman was scolding the miserable looking man at her side as though he were responsible. "The vile blasphemer, she got away from them. Now if I had her here—"

"Yes?" questioned a deep, resonant voice at my side. "And, lady, you would do exactly what?"

I sized up the speaker. He was muffled up in a light silken cloak, and his flat, floppy hat hung down around his ears and forehead. His eyes were bright and sharp enough. Before the shrewish woman could answer, her husband piped up: "This is no business of yours, walfger—"*

The woman shut him up with a rattled-out string of nastiness. Then she snapped: "Why, I'd teach her to mind her tongue and her manners!"

The slim figure of a girl in light draperies pushed forward and grasped the arm of the owner of the deep mellifluous voice. He was about to launch into what anyone could recognize as a sermon. The girl spoke swiftly. "It is no use, san. Come away, please, come away now."

He turned his head to regard her and I saw more of his face—a drawn, ascetic countenance, with the harsh lines of suffering etched around the mouth and eyes. "Yes, Xinthe, I suppose you are right. But have I not told you time and again about calling me san?"

The shrewish woman was lapping this up. Now she burst out: "You are one of those dreadful supporters of the witch Mul-lu-Manting. Call the guards! Help, help!"

---

* walfger: mister, monsieur, herr. A.B.A.

Moving with enough speed to get there without loss of time I stepped up behind this unpleasant, little lady and placed my fingers on her neck at precisely the right spot. My other arm encircled a waist more pudgy than pleasant as she toppled unconscious. I pushed her at her husband—if indeed he was that unfortunate person.

"The lady has fainted," I said. I spoke to him as an overseer might speak to a slave. "Take her home before she is injured."

"Yes, yes, master," he gabbled and dragged her off, heels draggling. I wished him well of her.

The girl in the flowing draperies gasped. "I saw that!"

I let my head nod in the briefest of bows. "Better all around, my lady. Now let us take this walfger to a safer spot."

She gave me a hard shrewd look from bright hazel eyes. Her face was of the sort described as elfin; but there were the first faint traces of the lines of responsibility upon her forehead. She came to a decision.

"Very well. I thank you. Now we must get away before the guards find us."

As she spoke I heard that hateful howling of the wersting pack.

Three

We three moved smoothly and without undue haste away from the crowds, and avoiding the further series of arcades struck down a side street. The mingled streaming lights of the Suns of Scorpio flamed into my eyes. Shadows lay to our rear, not overlong shadows, for here in Walfarg we were not too far north of the Equator. The heat was appreciably lessening as the afternoon turned into evening.

"And not a Llahal between us," observed the man.

"Llahal," I said at once. "My name is Drajak," giving the name I'd used most recently down south in Tsungfaril. "Drajak ti Zamran."

"Lahal, walfger Drajak. I am Wanlicheng, Ornol Wanlicheng once of Paramdan and now a wandering scholar—"

"Oh, San Ornol! You are a great teacher," burst out the girl, Xinthe. "Yes," she went on, half scolding half laughing in resignation, "and well you know it!"

"And this," said Ornol Wanlicheng in his mellifluous voice, "is, as you can see, my strict but patient student, Xinthe."

"Lahal, Wr. Drajak.* Now, I think it best if we hurried," and she urged Wanlicheng along. With that fearful howling following us I needed no urging to scamper on with them.

---

* Wr.: Abbreviation for walfger. A.B.A.

Then the obvious and unpleasant thought occurred to me. If the werst-ings were still on my scent—and I really felt that now to be unlikely—they would follow this couple. I'd be bringing a wersting pack down on San Ornol Wanlicheng and on Lady Xinthe. I felt that to be something Dray Prescot would not do. So I told them I'd been followed by a wersting pack.

Xinthe, still hurrying on, shuddered. "They are terrible when aroused. Although the puppies are sweet."

"That is quite all right, Drajak. I have that which will remedy the situa-tion." Wanlicheng spoke quite casually, as though the problem were both simple and academic.

Apart from the central square where the buildings had been reasonably open and impressive, this town appeared to consist of a maze of twisting alleys sometimes bordered by arcades, more often the further we went on bordered only by tall blank walls. Shadows slanted across the bricks from the opposite wall. I would not care to say I saw the top of a single tree over any wall. Careful, then, these townsfolk.

The doorways were universally tall and thin and the doors of solid iron-banded and studded wood. The door which Xinthe unlocked and opened had once been painted blue; now it was mostly back to bare wood, dry and cracked. We went into the courtyard and Xinthe, after a look back, went to close the door. Wanlicheng stopped her.

"Just a moment, my dear, let me place a simple Seal of Passing." He moved out into the alleyway again and Xinthe obstructed my view of what Wanlicheng was doing. "There, that should suffice." He came back into the courtyard and Xinthe slammed the door.

Whether the werstings had missed my trail or whether Wanlicheng's Seal of Passing did the trick I couldn't then have said. Whichever, we were not troubled by a visit from the wersting pack or their Hikdar.

The courtyard was surrounded by buildings, all with mean little win-dows. Directly ahead an arched opening clearly led to the inner courtyard. To the right lay the stables, with the usual litter scattered about. There was about this courtyard a miserable, dingy feeling.

Wanlicheng led off through the arched opening into the inner courtyard. If I expected a blaze of color from gardens, spirited fountains, statuary, I was singularly disappointed. The inner courtyard was just a bigger version of the outer. Certainly, the windows were a fraction larger. Wanlicheng waited whilst Xinthe unlocked one of the narrow wooden doors in the row of doors all around the courtyard and we all went in and immediately climbed a blackwood stair in gloom made darker by our abrupt entrance from the last of the sunlight. At the top lay a chamber spartan in sim-plicity, furnished as a living room. I did not see a single cushion. The bentwood chairs looked hard and uninviting.

"Pray make yourself at home, Drajak. Xinthe, my dear, would you?"

"Red, white, or rosé, or your usual?"

"My usual for myself, I think. Drajak, your preference?"

"It makes no difference, San Ornol; but red would be nice."

"Ornol, please. I regard the word san as a vulgar form of ostentation, along with princes and kovs and the like. I do admit they sometimes have their uses, in the right place and the right time. But Walfarg has suffered too much from her sans and her Queens of Pain."

I could quite see his point. The once great and puissant Empire of Loh, ruled ruthlessly by the famous Queens of Pain, was now gone and crumbled away, blown like smoke in the wind. If the people, as that screaming girl Mul-lu-Manting had said, blamed the Wizards of Loh and their own rulers for the catastrophe, then they wouldn't much care for sans and queens.

Xinthe brought the wine in pottery jugs and readying myself for a tart and vinegary concoction I was pleasantly surprised to taste a smooth and bracing red. Wanlicheng observed my reactions. He smiled, that austere face breaking amazingly into an attractive beam. "Yes, I believe that wine and blood have an affinity, and therefore a good quality is essential."

"A sound principle," I observed, and drank.

Xinthe disappeared and I assumed she was preparing the meal.

Etiquette was more likely than not to be entirely different here. Using what little conversational skills I have I quickly established that Xinthe stood as student, nurse and cook to Wanlicheng and that, thank you, walfger, you may assist with the washing up.

The meal was simple, good, perhaps a trifle too frugal for my taste; but then, an old sailorman like me is used to drawing in his belt buckle.

Wanlicheng, when we had finished eating and the washing up had been placed in its wooden racks, said: "Now, Xinthe, the preparation for the tenth corner."

"Yes, master—which Path do you mean?"

"Impudence!" His thin lips curved into a smile as he spoke. "You well know, tikshvu."

I felt a jolt at his joking use of that word tikshvu, which I have previously translated as missy. Usually it threatens and cows a young girl who has been rebellious. These people made their own rules, it seemed.

She spread her hands in her lap and nodded. "The Path of the Ib."

That is to say, the Path of the Spirit or Soul. Wanlicheng pursed his lips. "In the Path of the Ib, the tenth corner holds a special significance. It is similar to the importance of the seventh corner in the Path of the World."

"In the Path of the Flesh—" began Xinthe.

"Two Paths are enough for the moment." He spoke sharply.

"Yes, master."

"Now, hold your attention to the ninth corner." As he spoke he leaned down and placed his two thumbs over her closed eyelids. The shadows in the room lay deeply now as the suns sank. There was one cheap mineral oil lamp that remained unlit as Xinthe concentrated on her exercise.

I sat very quietly. Both Wanlicheng and Xinthe had the red hair of true Lohvians. Presently he stood back and without a sound sat down in his chair. The silence grew oppressive. I did not drink the fine red wine. I wondered what was going on in Xinthe's pretty head. As for her tutor, his gaze remained fastened upon her face.

At last her lips moved and in a whisper she said: "The corner is true. I am holding it. Fast."

Wanlicheng said: "Good. Fix it and then return."

When at last Xinthe opened her eyes the smile with which she favored her teacher was a wonderful sunburst of beauty. "Yes." she said. "Oh, yes!"

His austere face revealed pleasure. Whatever his history might have been in the recent past, here was a man who understood the finer things of life. Speaking in that well-modulated voice he began a general conversation. Like most people meeting new acquaintances, he wanted to know all about me. For, as he observed: "One can tell you are not of Loh."

Xinthe continued to sit and I surmised she was recovering from whatever she had been doing inside her own skull.

I gave my usual farrago of lies concerning myself and then ventured a question about the scene I had just witnessed.

"There is no such thing as the One True Path. You must find your way as best you can, using whatever means you are able. This sometimes means you may have to deny a certain god, or embrace another. So far no one has been able to convince me that One True God exists, any more than One True Way." I did not wish to contradict him on his point about gods; but I admit I felt this to be a serious chink in whatever theory he was expounding.

He went on to say that his belief in magic and in gods had failed him so often that he had looked around for a better way. He had been fortunate enough to meet a wise woman—he called her Lisa the Forthright, although that was not her real name—who had opened his eyes to Alternative Magic.

"We call our movement Alternative Magic, for it is that, in a real sense. But it is much much more than a mere alternative to magic and gods. We seek to perform the same work as that done by sorcerers—magic—and by gods—miracles—solely through our own human powers. This may sound impious, blasphemous, even. But I assure you, Drajak, a man or woman has the power there in their heads. Through the Paths we move forward to our goal. We can unleash the powers of the human mind and spirit and have no need of sorcerers. As to gods, they have other uses."

"There are then many of you?"

"Not as many as we would like. We have a goodly number of members, all the same, scattered about here and there."

"And you are not persecuted?"

"No, why should we be, since we do not spout our beliefs from statues in the main kyro of town."

Xinthe threw me a sharp glance. I shook my head.

"All this is completely new to me, Lady Xinthe. I am no spy."

Well, it wasn't completely new, of course. There are the two well-known ways to God: Rejection of Images or Affirmation of Images. In addition I had spoken to Kregen philosophers and mystics who recognized the three Paths Wanlicheng had mentioned plus the Path of Afflatus. What this mystic was trying to do was the new thing. If he could perform magic and miracles without any mumbo-jumbo straight out of his head, then he would, indeed, be a remarkable fellow. And Xinthe and the mystic he called Lisa the Forthright would add their peculiarly feminine slant to the proceedings. If between them they could win through all the corners on the paths then I'd be the first to be interested.

They called themselves the Pilgrims.

Sometimes they were known as Wayfarers or Pathfinders.

They were out to perfect Alternative Magic for the good of humanity.

I wished them well.

Then I asked about the woman fanatic Mul-lu-Manting.

"She seeks to achieve her desires by ranting, preaching, trying to arouse the people to past glories. I fear she has no joy in her task."

What Mul-lu-Manting wanted was a new Empire of Loh. She reveled in the luxurious thoughts of the power and prestige once enjoyed by Walfarg. All that had been swept away, she claimed, by the failure of the Wizards of Walfarg and because the governments had failed to provide airboats. Because at the time the empire began to break up a king was on the throne, Mul-lu-Manting blamed the men for the catastrophe. With a return to women, ruling as Queens of Pain, then the Empire of Walfarg, the Empire of Loh, would return!

"People in Loh are too apathetic to bother about such a return to imperial glories." Wanlicheng shook his head. "That thing is best forgotten."

"All the same," observed Xinthe, "you cannot deny it was when Loh was ruled by kings that the empire broke up."

"In certain circumstances, denying a self evident truth can obliterate the truth for subsequent generations. So, missy, have a care!"

She happened to be eating a handful of palines and she threw one of the yellow berries at him. He caught it expertly enough, so I guessed this was not the first time. I was pleased that despite his austere appearance he was no stuffy old prig of a dominie. And if he could move mountains merely by using his head...!

I stood up.

"Thank you for your hospitality. Now I must be on my way."

"You will stay the night here, Drajak. I thought that was settled."

"That is kind of you—"

"You are a stranger in Changwutung. Apathetic the people may be; we have high walls. The alleys are not safe at night."

"I take your point and I thank you again. I shall be happy further to impose on your hospitality."

Xinthe threw a paline at me.

I caught it, popped it, and chewed pleasantly.

I looked forward to an enjoyable evening of civilized conversation.

Four

By the time we retired I had not been disappointed in those expectations.

This apartment boasted two bedrooms, a kitchen and toilet facilities and the living room. I bunked down on the living room floor with an old, and, I am forced to report, a somewhat thin and threadbare blanket. To say that to an old campaigner such things are commonplace is surely redundant by this time in the narrative of Dray Prescot. The rest of the apartments in this building were on the same frugal scale. Household slaves would remove the night soil in the morning, and water would be brought up.

When I tackled the question of slavery, I was partially mollified to hear Wanlicheng express the opinion that one person ought not to be able to own another. To this Xinthe nodded approval; but then in her feminine practical way, she added: "It would be inconvenient to lift and carry things oneself, up and down these stairs."

There were very few people in Paz who had not heard of the Shanks. In an odd but totally believable way it seemed the further away from the coast the stories were told the more hideous were the reports of the Shanks and their atrocities. The apathy into which Walfarg was sunk would, said Wanlicheng, make any Shank attack almost certain of success.

This was just the kind of information I needed—and, of course, by Krun, just the kind of news I did not want!

I went on to say: "Have you ever heard of an entity, a spirit, a ghost—some horrific supernatural being—called Carazaar? And, not to forget his repulsive multi-dimensional assistant, Arzuriel?"

They shook their heads. No, they hadn't.

"Or of a Wizard of Loh—I beg your pardon, a Wizard of Walfarg—called Na-Si-Fantong?"

"Fantong? Oh, he hasn't been heard of for some time. The last news with any pretensions to authority placed him in Kothmir. Rumor had it that he was mixed up in some unsavory trickery involving a necklace."

"As I heard it," amplified Xinthe, "he had to leave Kothmir very rapidly with half the kov's army on his heels."

"But," I said. "He had the necklace?"

"No. It was recovered."

I felt relief at that. Whatever this Fantong wanted all the gems of the Skantiklar for, one would get you ten they were for no good purpose. There were nine gems to be collected. He had failed to snatch the one from Queen Leone in Tsungfaril. I'd been involved in that affair. Just how many had he? Then, the unhealthy thought occurred to me.

I said: "Was the necklace intact?"

"Strange you should ask. There was one jewel missing. Quite a big one, from the account I heard."

So the scheming sorcerer had at least one ruby gem of the Skantiklar!

By the time we'd eaten and I was ready to leave I found I'd grown a healthy attachment to these two. What their relationship was outside the teacher student one was not my business. They slept in separate rooms.

Wanlicheng, strongly supported by Xinthe, suggested I stay for a time and study the various Paths to Alternative Magic.

Now, I admit it. I was tempted. If it could be done!

But—there were Tsungfaril, Mevancy, Tarankar, Taranik, Leone, not to mention Kuong and Llodi, down south. There were my immediate concerns, even if returning to Vallia and Valka remained always my ultimate objectives.

I expressed my regrets in such a way that they saw I was genuine. They wished me well on my journey.

And there, of course, was the rub. How was I to contrive transport all those dwaburs south?*

One notion occurred to me, an obvious one. I was too scared to use it. Oh, yes, I, Dray Prescot, Lord of Strombor and Krozair of Zy, was far too conscious of the risks involved even to think of chancing going the other way, going home, and waiting for the Star Lords to seize me up and dump me down in the land of Tsungfaril where my labors were required.

Not, as they say in Clishdrin, not on your nellie!

So, then, how?

And, another little item in the account book before I left the subject of the Everoinye and their clever phantom blue Scorpion—could I trust the thing any more? The gerblish onker had dropped me, hadn't it? Right in it? Well, then!

"You look, Drajak, as though you have lost a zorca and found a calsany."

---

* dwabur: five miles. *A.B.A.*

I twisted up my lips in some kind of ferocious smile. "If there was a time to use your Alternative Magic, it's now. Then I could fly through the air down south."

"One day, one day," said Wanlicheng, comfortably.

Between me and my destination lay the jungles of Chem. In those dank depths lurked animal monsters and plant monsters like syatras and slaptras. Probably the jungles were swarming with head-hunting cannibals, waiting for me to provide their daily rations.

Well, if I couldn't reasonably walk there, couldn't fly there because there were no vollers, was too frightened to get the Star Lords to shift me, I'd have to go by ship.

As an old sailorman who'd been the First Lieutenant of a Seventy-Four, I anticipated no trouble in finding a berth, particularly as I had commanded swifters on the inner sea of Turismond, the Eye of the World, and swordships in the outer oceans, with particular reference to the Hoboling Islands and Pandahem. To coast down the western seaboard of Loh might be a pleasant experience. It might be ghastly. Either way, that was my path.

They accompanied me down to the levee where a number of river craft were tied up. They offered to pay the fare to the coast; but this I refused, and before long I was fixed up as a deckhand aboard a broad-beamed vessel going down loaded with goods for the towns to the west.

At first I thought I was lucky that the stupid Scorpion had dropped me much closer to the west coast of Loh than to the east. A little reflection made me revise that opinion. The west coast country of Tarankar was, we believed, infested with the Shanks. Their superb ships would patrol the sea approaches. H'mm. It would clearly have been safer, if longer, had I gone east about around Loh.

When we parted, Xinthe suddenly leaned forward and kissed me on the cheek. "You'll come back one day."

The lines were cast off and the vessel nosed out into the brownish waters. I bent to my sweep and then looked up and used one hand to wave to the shore as the vessel cleared the levee.

"Remberee, Ornol! Remberee, Xinthe!"

"Remberee, Drajak!"

Then I put my back into the sweep and hauled and we glided off into the pungent brown smell of the river.

The master, Tsien-Ting, a small nervous man with a bad facial blemish, delegated most of the work to his bosun, a hulking Khibil, Pondro the Pin. No sailorman needed to ask what kind of pin that was.

As the vessel, *Quaynt's Fortune*, glided down, way could be kept up easily by a few regular strokes from the sweeps. The large square sail was generally only used on long straight reaches running free. There was a set of fore and aft sails to be bent on when the vessel tacked up river. The life was strenuous only episodically. There were no voracious fish or monsters in the river, The River of Glinting Charm, which was mightily fortunate for the Khibil bosun, Pondro the Pin.

When he was fished out at the end of a boathook, he glared murderously at me.

What he said I couldn't have heard said better on any stage throughout Earth or Kregen.

"I'll get you for this!"

All I said was: "Next time don't try to use your pin on a defenseless head belonging to a fellow half your size."

The little Och, the vessel's cook, who'd caused the trouble, peered fearfully from the open top half of his galley door. I suppose, truth to tell, he was used to being knocked about by Pondro; but, well, that unfortunately is my way, to go interfering between basher and bashee.

Tsien-Ting bustled up, trying to act with authority, and squeaking like a woflo in a trap.

I felt annoyance. Remarkably, my irritation was not so much for myself as for the unwanted situation. There was nothing much else I could have done, as I saw it.

"Back to work, shint!" snapped Tsien-Ting.

This was quite uncalled for. I ignored him and grasped my sweep to assist us in negotiating the upcoming benc.

Why can't I, Dray Prescot, shut my eyes to injustice and petty terror, to the abuse of authority and to the injury of the weak? I can't; but had I been able to do so I'd have had a smoother life and a few less lumps to show, by Vox!

Sleeping with one eye open is a knack more or less essential to an adventuring kind of fellow on Kregen. I awoke instantly to the soft footfall and so was able to take Pondro's ankle in my fist and twist him over. Once more he went into the river. This time it was night. I hesitated. The splash had aroused no one, since everyone was asleep except for the Brokelsh deckhand, Bargray the Tumbs, and he thought the splash was me going overside. So, I hesitated. But I couldn't.

So I shouted: "Man overboard!"

Mind you, I drew the line at diving in after the rast.

By the time Pondro was fished out *Quaynt's Fortune* was alive with shouts and curses and lanterns and running feet. Once again Pondro opened his mouth to tell me my exact fate. I looked at him. He shut his mouth, quickly, gulped, and turned away.

Oh, well, that dreadful Devil Face of Dray Prescot sometimes comes in handy, I suppose.

All the same, I was not fool enough not to change vessels when the next sizeable town hove up around a wide curving bend. The place looked not too dissimilar from Changwutung at a distance; as is the nature of places, I expected many differences of detail. I was wrong.

This town of Ternantung was the twin of Changwutung.

Just about all that the outside world now knew of Walfarg in Loh were its mysterious walled gardens and veiled women. Perhaps, the notion occurred to me, perhaps after the fall of the empire, those were all there were.

Now it is not my intention to go into great detail concerning my journey down The River of Glinting Charm. There were the smells, rich and fruity close to the shore, surprisingly fresh in midstream. There were the never-ending delights of wild animals, and birds and fish. There were settlements along the banks and here my new vessel, *Garrus*, pulled in to buy and sell the goods she carried. The master, an apim called Nath Hsienu, known as Nath the Bollard, ran a much tighter ship than the ineffectual Tsien-Ting. There was no trouble aboard *Garrus*. In addition, Nath the Bollard was addicted to the game of Jikalla, and we had a number of interesting games, although, as you know, my main interest in that department is Jikaida.

Nath the Bollard warned me that finding a ship going south would be difficult.

"I've heard rumors of a great deal of nasty business going on along the coast there. My cousin twice removed, Naghan the Omurdour, sailed out with a fine crew of fellows. They were never seen again."

"And the rumors?"

"Those devil ships that helped destroy the empire. They've been seen again flying over the coast." He looked at me meaningfully. Because of his work as a vessel's master he was nowhere near as apathetic to events as the majority of his countrymen. "Over the west coast. You know what that means."

I knew—or assumed I did. Those would be the Shank vollers. But it was clear Nath the Bollard was referring to the vollers of Havilfar and Hyrklana, the airboats that had contributed to the defeat of Loh.

"You've not seen them?"

He shook his head. "And don't want to. Some poor devil was fished out of the sea clinging to a stump of mast. He'd seen 'em. Oh, no, if you see them ships flying through the air that's about the last thing you'll see, by Lingloh!"

This news was really more than rumor. The chances of finding a ship to sail south were looking more remote by the minute.

"Cheer up," said Nath the Bollard, setting up a new game. "We're sailing all the way to Sardanar at the mouth of the river. If you manage to find a ship and sail out to get yourself killed, well, then, dom—at least you'll have had the time between then and now to play Jikalla!"

Five

As it turned out, fate or chance took a hand. Take your pick of those two imposters; one or t'other will trip you up when you least expect it. In the event I didn't get to Sardanar on that trip; the place is not so much dire as lacking interest. It does have massive sea walls and fortifications dating back to the early days of the Walfargian empire Those sea walls would prove of little use against an aerial armada.

On the succeeding days as we glided down the River of Glinting Charm we passed a considerable traffic going upstream. Nath said there were more vessels of all kinds breasting the current than usual at this season.

"I think," I said, as I hauled my sweep to steer clear of a lopsided craft packed with people and bundles lolloping along and zigzagging wildly as the helmsman sought the westerly breeze, "I really do think I can guess why there are all these vessels going upstream."

"Aye," said Nath the Bollard, taking his straw hat from his red hair and bashing it against his thigh. "Aye, by Hlo-Hli!"

The bosun, a lively fellow with a meaty jaw and a meaty fist, said: "You reckon it's them Fish Head devil worshippers?"

"Practically certain, Larghos."

Larghos the Bosun spat overside. "Reckon they're running too far."

I agreed with him. The plan of campaign the Shanks were probably following would call for their complete domination of the coastal seas. Only after that would they gather their forces for a push inland. The continent of Loh was so vast that they were likely to be swallowed up in its immensity, so they'd plan with Fish Headed cunning. Mind you, for the poor folk of Loh who happened to inhabit the areas chosen for invasion by the Shanks the invasion would mean the end of normalcy.

We hailed a passing craft and heard a garbled shout about fires.

"The devils are probably raiding up and down to strike terror as far as they can." My own thoughts were that the already existing invasion of Tarankar would form the locus for their main thrust.

The next day not a single vessel plied upstream; on the next another bunch appeared, and the day after that only a trickle.

"The faint-hearts," said Larghos the Bosun with large contempt.

I did not say: "Have you met a Shank yet, Larghos?" for that would have been insulting and cruel. But the thought persisted.

Other riverine craft sailed downstream and we generally kept a nice convoy distance between vessels for safety's sake. Looking ahead as I came on deck for a breath of air, having been soundly thrashed by Nath the Bollard with one of his favorite Jikalla tricks, I saw a vessel ahead closer than I liked. I mentioned this to the helmsman, Chang-So, and he snarled out: "They're luffing and hauling like a pack of famblys."

Nath and Larghos joined me on deck and we watched the movements of the vessel ahead.

"Ah!" said Nath. "There's the reason!"

A dark bundle flipped up from the deck, turned over in the air, and came down splash into the river.

Immediately the vessel picked up speed, spreading more canvas, and glided along to resume a safer distance. I craned overside to see what had been thrown overboard. A man was thrashing about in the water, going under and then rising in a spouting bubble. I threw off my tunic and dived in.

There was no need to knock him unconscious. I got a grip on him, said: "Hold still, dom," and then as he instantly lay limply, swam back to *Garrus*. They'd swung the yard to back the course and there was no difficulty seizing the line and looping a bight around this young fellow. He went up streaming water, his red Lohvian hair plastered to his skull. I followed and shook myself like a dog. The radiance of the Suns would soon dry us off.

When he'd recovered, with a tot inside him, Nath the Bollard asked the obvious questions.

"Lahal, all," the young lad said. He was young, at that, with a glint of fuzz on cheeks and chin. "My name is—Nath the Ready."

Instantly I disbelieved that. There are very very many Naths on Kregen and the name is so often used when it does not belong to the giver of the name that it's almost a totally useless pseudonym.

"Why'd they chuck you overboard?" demanded Larghos.

"They said I was unlucky."

"Oho! Then perhaps we'd better return you to the river!"

The lad flinched back, and then I saw in his face and eyes a defiant flash of anger, as though he was sick of being pushed around.

"Hold hard," I said. "Just why are you unlucky, dom?"

"Oh, I threw the slops against the wind—"

"Ha!" burst out Nath the Bollard. "A menace!"

"Chuck him over again," counseled the helmsman, Chang-So.

I caught the lad's eye and tried to give him an encouraging smile. What kind of expression I'd put on I wasn't sure; he gave me a hard stare but there was no more flinching back.

Nath the Bollard decided to keep this Nath the Ready aboard. As he said: "When we reach Hinjanchung around the next but one bend we will put ashore. That lot ahead will be there, too. We can ask them then."

For a moment I fancied the lad was going to speak out with the truth against certain discovery; he remained silent. I guessed he was hoping to slip ashore and make his escape. He wore a simple yellow tunic girt by a narrow belt from which hung an empty dagger scabbard and a scrip. His legs were bare. He wore a red breechclout which predisposed me in his favor.

As to his face, clearly it was as yet unformed by adult problems. There was a clarity in his skin, a breadth to his forehead most pleasing. Yet, at the same time there was a rebellious set to his jaw, a recklessness in his bearing. I fancied his history, short though it must necessarily be, would prove of interest.

In the event we went ashore in Hinjanchung. Nath the Bollard had Larghos the Bosun confine the lad to his locked cabin. When we'd found the crew of the vessel from which the lad had been thrown—in a sleazy tavern of dubious delights, the Zinul and Queng—the mystery was rapidly explained.

"A damned Wizard of Walfarg!" declared Hwang, the master. "We got rid of him the moment we found out the truth."

"In that case—" said Nath the Bollard, doubtfully.

Chang-So burst out: "Chuck him in!"

At that point the workings of fate, or chance, became more apparent to me. Had that unpleasant rast, Pondro the Pin, not been so unpleasant and I had been able to stay aboard *Quaynt's Fortune*, then I would have been well down the river, and would not have fished this young Wizard of Loh out of the water.

Not for a single moment did I believe the Star Lords or the Savanti had anything to do with this meeting.

I said: "Let me have a word with him."

No one objected. Back aboard *Garrus* I let the lad out of the bosun's cabin. I frowned at him, and he remained still.

Now if you are already way ahead of me in this my newest design I am not surprised. When I'd been counting up the ways of reaching Tsungfaril, far down in the south of Loh, I'd completely overlooked this obvious way.

"You are a Wizard of Loh." He flushed up at this, but kept his mouth shut. I decided to test him. "Why didn't you turn the people who threw you overboard into little green frogs?"

"Oh," he began airily, with all a spirited young man's arrogance. "I would have done so; but—" He saw my face and stopped speaking. He took a breath, and then in an entirely different tone of voice said: "I believe you know why I did not."

"Yes."

"So what do you want of me?"

"That is simple for a Wizard of Loh. If you would be so kind as to oblige me, I would ask you to go into lupu and contact a friend."

He made a face. "Lupu. That was an exercise I always—"

"Was?"

There were as I knew a number of ways a sorcerer could go into lupu, that magical trance-like state in which they could communicate and spy over vast distances. What did he mean, 'was'?

He looked down at his feet. "They threw me out."

"Threw you out?" I repeated like a loon. "What do you mean, they threw you out?"

"What I say. I didn't pay enough attention to the lessons. I failed to pass an interim exam." He looked up, hotly. "It was all the fault of that Pynsi! She promised me and then she gave her favors to that lout, Ul-ga-Sorming!"

"By the disgusting despicable deliquescing bowels of Makki Grodno! You mean you're a damned Wizard of Loh and you can't get into communication with a brother or sister wizard?" I fairly howled with mortification.

"Not really. Anyway, I've given it all up. I am going for a Bowman of Loh."

"And I suppose you failed in an examination to hit the Chunkrah's Eye!" I flamed out bitterly.

"No! I can shoot in my bow with the best!"

"And a fat lot of good that'll do me now!"

"Well, if that's the way you feel, I suppose you'd better throw me in the water again!"

I controlled my breathing. "Anyway, what's your name?"

"Nath the Ready."

"Yes, yes. Your real name, fambly."

Again he gave me that appraising glance. I suppose I was a trifle wrought up. Just as I thought I had a capital scheme to reach my friends, this jackanapes ruined it all because instead of studying his lessons he'd been mooning after a girl. I didn't have a hat on; if I had I'd have ripped it off and thrown it down on the deck and jumped on it. Too true, by Vox!

"I am Ra-Lu-Quonling."

"Ha!" I was already working out what to do with this fine fellow. "D'you know Deb-Lu-Quienyin?"

"Not personally. He left Whonban long before I was born."

"Ah—then you're related."

"All Wizards of Walfarg are related." That was said with a little sniff, not so much of contempt as of recognition of my ignorance.

"I suppose so, more or less. D'you know Khe-Hi-Bjanching, or Ling-Li-Lwingling?"

"They were arriving in Whonban as I was leaving."

Quite seriously I said: "Are they both well?"

"As far as I know. You know them, then?"

"I do. Deb-Lu-Quienyin is at the moment somewhere in Vallia. You've heard of Vallia?"

Again that little touch of arrogant contempt. "Of course."

"Well, if he's too far away, you'll have to reach Khe-Hi or Ling-Li." I reconsidered. "Better make it Khe-Hi. If Ling-Li's heavily involved with reproduction at the moment she won't want a fambly like you breaking in."

Icily, he said: "They have twins, a boy and a girl."

"My Val!" I felt the pleasure. "I have been out of circulation."

"I told you. I don't do lupu very well." He was verging on the petulant. "Anyway, even if I was as good as Khe-Hi-Bjanching, I told you, I've given up being a wizard. Thaumaturgy and I have parted company. I'm going for a Bowman of Loh."

"I'll break your damn bow over your head, you ingrate! Didn't I fish you out of a watery grave?"

And he laughed.

And I laughed with him.

"Well, now," I said, presently. "Come on, Ra-Lu-Quonling. It's vitally important I get a message through."

"We-ell, I suppose I could try. You know, I heard the stories concerning the mages of whom you speak. I know what they do these days."

"Oh?"

"They are among the most successful. They have as clients the royal and imperial house of Vallia."

That was the way a Wizard of Loh would see the relationship, and, as I never forgot, it was the correct way. Khe-Hi and Deb-Lu were true comrades, that is so; but they remained Wizards of Loh.

"So I believe," I said, casually.

"As I said, we are well-educated in Whonban. Even if I skipped some lessons, I never skipped current history. And I read widely."

"Good for you, Ra-Lu. Now, you did say you would try—?"

"Yes. I will try to contact Khe-Hi-Bjanching. What message would you like me to give him, Dray Prescot?"

Six

"Ouch!" I said. Then: "My name is Drajak ti Zamran, known as Drajak the Sudden. I would esteem it a favor if you could remember that. Anything else could prove embarrassing." I added, menacingly: "For those who found out."

"Very well. If you remember that I am Nath the Ready."

"Oh, come on! Find a better name than that."

"Well, yes, perhaps."

"As to the message, ask Khe-Hi to contact Deb-Lu and arrange to send a voller—an airboat—down here. Send two so the pilot of the one I use can fly home. Have you got that?"

"Airboats," he said, and the disgust dripped.

"You'd better also recommend that they don't tell anyone apart from the Lord Farris. Otherwise we'll have an invasion down here."

"I don't quite—"

"Never mind. Now, my lad, do your stuff—and you have my thanks."

"I shall need a little more room."

"Of course." The clean crisp air of Kregen, only partially sullied by the smells of the river, whiffled up my nostrils most beautifully as we came up on deck. I breathed in. By Vox! This young feller-me-lad of a Wizard of Loh was going to fix my ticket, was going to arrange passage back to Tsungfaril, Mevancy, Llodi and all the others, back to intrigue and danger and death. Now he had committed himself he was spry about it.

We found a clear space at the rear of a ramshackle godown where the mud was not too thick. No one was about or could spy on us without being detected. Ra-Lu-Quonling squeezed his eyes shut, opened them wide, flexed his fingers, took three deep lungfuls of air, said: "Right."

He squatted down and lifted his hands to his eyes, threw his head back, remained silent and unmoving. I watched him gravely. He began to tremble, his lithe young body vibrating under the yellow tunic. Slowly he drew his hands down his face. His eyeballs were completely rolled up so that his eyes were mere white blots in that tanned young face. His breathing slackened. Quietly I waited for the next stage in this process. With a strangled cry, a gasp almost of physical pain, Ra-Lu-Quonling staggered to his feet. The shaking of his body ceased. His arms lifted until they were horizontal and like a scarecrow caught in a wind he began to revolve, faster and faster, a whirling dervish spinning in the mud. Abruptly, his whirlwind motion stopped. He flopped down onto his haunches and put his hands flat on the mud. His head tilted back.

Both of Ra-Lu-Quonling's eyes opened, not together, but one after the other. He stared balefully at me. I recalled the first time I had seen this process by which a Wizard of Loh went into lupu, when I had derided the whole notion, back then when with good old Seg I'd searched so desperately for Delia. The frail and not very competent Wizard of Loh Lu-si-Yuong had been unable to find her for me—and I struggling against what everyone said, that she was dead!—but he had warned us about Thelda's danger. He had been an old man; this young whippersnapper was young. Yet both used almost identical methods of attaining lupu. Deb-Lu or Khe-Hi would go into lupu and wander around Kregen through the various planes as you or I might open a door and walk from one room to another.

That very expertise in thaumaturgy ought not to disguise the weirdness of it, the spine-tingling uncanniness of what these mages could perform.

Although, to be sure, Deb-Lu had been experiencing difficulty in getting through down in South Loh. Still, I had every confidence that this self-named Nath the Ready could reach Khe-Hi. After all, although I'd no idea where Whonban was situated in Loh, it couldn't be all that far away from here, could it?

Quonling stared at me. He ought now to be coming out of it, having sent the message. He began to shake. I frowned. This, I did not remember. He opened his mouth.

A harsh rattling voice, deep in the bass register, issued from the lad's mouth. "I see him. So that is the fellow." The boy's eyes were fixed burningly upon me. "After you treat your instructors with contempt you have the impudence to attempt to utilize your imperfect learning! You should know by now the way back for you is hard, very hard. Now go—"

All Quonling's young features writhed and his tongue darted out to lick his lips and I realized he was trying to speak to the owner of that harsh and merciless voice.

"I am a Whonbim!" His own voice gasped the words. "I am merely trying to do a favor for San Khe-Hi-Bjanching. He will vouch for me!"

"San Khe-Hi does not know of your existence, outcast!"

So I saw what had happened. My Val! Young Quonling was doing his best in lupu to contact Khe-Hi and his message had been intercepted by this interfering, officious, overbearing jumped up Wizard of Loh teacher!

"Please—san—San Khe-Hi-Bjanching will—"

"Enough! By the Seven Arcades! Am I to waste my time prattling to a rebellious youngster who has no respect! You—"

I stepped forward and grasped the lad's shoulders. I stared deeply into his eyes. On my face, quite without my own volition, that Devil Mask flamed out, that evil domineering look that has quelled many a proud spirit. Do not think I take any pride from that, quite the contrary; but the demon look of Dray Prescot has proved useful from time to time. As now.

"You do not give me a Llahal," I said in that gravelly menacing voice of Dray Prescot. "You are a teacher who has failed with Quonling. I think it will go ill with you if you fail to pass my message to Khe-Hi."

There was no immediate response from the harsh rattling voice. I was prepared to wait only for a certain number of heartbeats for a reply.

He clearly couldn't know that; but he timed it so there were but three heartbeats to go.

"If you are who we believe you to be, your message will be passed."

I said: "It is not for you to quibble. I am not in the habit of repeating myself, even for Wizards of Walfarg. I will say to you, you without a Llahal between us, you know what is said about teachers. Now contact Khe-Hi and send my message!"

The gasp from Quonling's mouth could have come from the lad himself or his officious damned teacher. Either way, my words must have had some effect. Quonling pitched forward and put his young face into a patch of the more liquid mud we had tried to avoid. I caught his tunic and heaved him back. He was shaking all over now, and that was pure physical fear and reaction and not magical. By Krun! The poor lad had had a time of it!

He gargled a bit and I wiped the mud off. I wanted to know if that idiot teacher had sent the message.

At last he said: "I know what happened. I heard. But I do not believe. No, by Hlo-Hli herself, I do not credit it!"

"Has he sent the message, boy?"

"How should I know? I was disrespectful and disobedient, I know that. But I never went around uttering threats—"

"I seldom threaten. If it has to be done, I do it. Anyway, if you don't know we can only find out by waiting. Who was that onker, anyway?"

"That? Oh, that was Gal-ag-Foroming, one of the head tutors. He has the heaviest and springiest cane in all Whonban."

"Sometimes," I said, "sometimes, I suppose, that is necessary. If he was any good as a tutor you'd pass your exams without the need of a cane."

Although I told the lad this, I am well aware there are exceptions in the case of the genuinely thick. Not the cane, of course, but the passing.

"Oh, he's clever, no doubt of that. Just that, well—"

"Some do, and some don't," I said. "In that game trying hard is generally not good enough. What is accomplished is far too important to have people who fall down on the job." I looked at him, and saw he had regained his color. He was pulling bits of mud out of his red hair. "I thank you for going into lupu, Ra-Lu. You were taking a risk I did not appreciate. I shall not forget that."

"Yes, well. I am more concerned about those plug-uglies who threw me in the water. They are aware my powers are strictly limited; yet they know I was to have been a Wizard of Walfarg and therefore they can punish me."

"What for?"

"Many people, not all, pile the blame for the loss of empire upon the sorcerers of Whonban. That and the lack of airboats and saddle birds."

"I'd have thought a Wizard of Loh could take care of himself. They strike mortal fear into the hearts of folk outside Loh, believe me."

"Why do you think we always seek to practice overseas?"

"That makes sense. And if you're half-trained, then—"

"Oh, I'm more than half-trained. The interim exam I failed was a mere trail-blazer for the finals. Those, I could have sailed through."

"Says you."

"I cut classes, yes, chasing that fickle Pynsi, and my frustration made me disrespectful. But I studied hard to catch up when Pynsi betrayed me."

"H'm," I said, using that old quarterdeck procrastination. "We'd better decide what we're going to do with you, hadn't we?"

I unbuckled one of the swords I'd taken from those two dozy guards, Lin and Hwang, after I'd disposed of the lily pad on my head. Both weapons were lynxters, the straight cut and thruster of Loh, and there was nothing to choose between them. I handed the sword to the lad.

"Here, Ra-Lu. It does not do to go unarmed on Kregen."

"That is true." He took the lynxter. "Still, I'm more of a dagger man. Although the bow is the prime weapon of all."

You can't argue with the Bowmen of Loh over that question.

He buckled the sword on and suddenly looked up.

"All right, then, Dray Prescot, Drajak the Sudden. I shall call myself Rollo. From Ra-Lu—see?"

I nodded. "A fine name. I knew a splendid artist, Rollo the Circle. He could draw a—"

"I know. So could our art master, Tun-du-Haffyien. Perfect."

I was taking to this young scamp. He knew who I was, and had read those outrageous romances about the Dray Prescot in the scarlet breechclout and ferocious Krozair longsword who went swinging about the world of Kregen righting wrongs, defending the weak and rescuing damsels in distress. Yet he treated me with indifferent ease as an equal. I liked that. Also, he may have dodged classes; he was almost a fully-fledged Wizard of Loh. He still had a very great deal to learn and master in his arcane arts. Even Deb-Lu and Khe-Hi and Ling-Li developed their skills as time went by. But he was not the loutish ignoramus deserving of being thrown out of Whonban.

"All right," I said. "Rollo what?"

"Oh, I'll think about that later."

Maybe that was one of his problems. That he put things off.

"I have," I said, changing the subject to one of vital importance. "I have just one gold piece, two silvers and seven coppers. You, I take it, have no cash." This was what was left of the guards' purses.

He shook his head. "You take it aright, Drajak."

"If the message got through to Khe-Hi and if Deb-Lu gets it, and if so when the Lord Farris sends the two vollers—well by a Herrelldrin Hell! We may have a long wait ahead of us, Rollo my lad!"

He nodded, suddenly glum. In truth, the prospect was not pleasing.

"Anyway," I said, voicing an itch that had been worriting away at me. "How did that lot find out you were a Wizard of Loh?"

He looked resentful. "I had a bad dream and started up, yelling damn fool things that branded me. There was no denying it."

"Well, don't have any bad dreams around me, sunshine!"

"Not if I can help it, Sudden."

As I say, a sprightly young spark.

The plan I concocted was simple. Keeping out of the way we found cheap lodgings. I'd have preferred to have found another boat and gone on downriver; but we had to stay here to await the airboats. The nightly charge was one short silver. One of the silvers I had was short, the other broad, so that was three nights at least. We'd have to eat on the coppers and use the gold, changed into silvers, to keep a roof over our heads. "We will have to pull our belts in, my lad."

"I've been hungry before."

One scheme I'd immediately thought of and then reluctantly discarded was to march out into the country and camp rough. Decadent and decayed though Walfarg was, they continued a strong patrol and watch force and vagrants were harshly dealt with. This is not uncommon. I did not wish to spend the time waiting in the local lockup, which looked unhealthy.

If it came to it, mind you, we'd have to do that. We'd be fed. And we'd have to break out when the vollers arrived.

If they did.

The time it would take for a voller to fly down from Vallia would depend on her speed. I felt I could rely on Farris to send the fastest he could spare. The problem lay in what he could spare. There continued to be trouble in voller manufacture. Emperor Nedfar of Hamal was doing what he could, and his son Tyfar, and Delia and my Lela were out there by the viciously hostile Mountains of the West of Hamal trying to sort out the problem. I fretted over their welfare.

So Farris might not be able to send of the best. Our money was down to four silvers, only one of which was broad, and we were using the silvers to feed ourselves as well as pay for the lodgings. If nothing arrived soon, I'd have to think again.

The lodging house, not a real inn at all, was known simply as Mother Molly's. The smell of cooking permeated the place. The stairs were a greasy death trap. Still, this was far cheaper than an inn or tavern.

We had to get out for a breath of fresh air. Well, who could blame us for that? Inevitably, one day someone from the crew spotted Ra-Lu-Quonling. We started off running up the street and immediately there was a pack of them howling on our heels. Ra-Lu ran. As we skidded around a corner and headed past the fish market, he panted out: "I know what I shall call myself. By the Seven Arcades! I shall be Rollo the Runner!"

"Save your breath, Runner, for honoring your name."

A whole screaming foaming pack of them were streaming along after us and another bunch appeared ahead. No one drew a weapon. The mobs from the fish market joined and now a ring formed about us. The cat-calls centered on one subject: "A Wizard of Walfarg! Blatter him into the ground! He's only a novice and knows nothing!"

"And his companion, the shint!"

"Can you do nothing, then, Rollo the Runner?"

"Nothing."

I looked about at the taunting crowds ready to beat us to a pulp. We could expect no mercy. There was no way out. I looked about—and then I looked up.

"Thank Opaz the Punctual!" I said, and waved my arms delightedly.

Seven

They do not mess about, my lads of the Guard Corps.

Directly before the mobs advancing on us a massive burst of fire and smoke blossomed. Almost immediately another fire pot dropped over on the other side of the ring. The crowds halted, open-mouthed. A fishmonger ripped off his scale-coated apron which had caught alight. He flung it from him with a yelp, and two more bursts of fire and smoke smashed the crowds back. Even then, even then, so unaccustomed were Lohvians to fliers that many did not think to look up.

Perhaps they put the gouts of flame and smoke down to the wizardry of the sorcerer of Whonban. I looked up again in great relief. Rollo the Runner, as I will now call him, looked up with me. He said: "Oh!"

Two airboats circled, and with delicate precision dropped a few more fire pots to keep the crowds at bay. I did not think these folk cared to dare the perils of having combustibles flung down on them from above.

Whilst one voller kept the ring, the other touched down delicately. She was a clean-lined craft possessing that sweet petal shape of all good quality small and medium sized airboats. She was, I judged, a smallish ten seater, as was her companion aloft. A voice hailed.

"This way, jis! Step aboard!"

A hulking fellow in a bright yellow uniform appeared clambering down the short ladder, turning on the last step to wave me on. I said: "Go on, Rollo. Run."

He started off at once for the voller and the large fellow in the yellow uniform clambered back over the side. He fairly hoicked Rollo up off the ground and hurled him over the gunwale. I followed smartly and clambered aboard. The crowds were yelling now, in anger more than fear.

"Take her up, Loptyg!" bellowed the giant in the bright yellow uniform. He turned to me and bashed his right fist over his heart with force enough to make his kax vibrate. "Majister!"

"Lahal, Ornol Skobog. And am I going to have trouble with you?"

"Me, jis?"

"Aye, you rascal. You."

He looked down and his face was as red as my breechclout. "You know the chickens were strays and would have wandered off, jis, had I not saved them."

Very gravely, I said: "That is undeniably true; but Opaz preserve me from their fate." Then I held out my hand and we shook Vallian fashion.

The voller climbed steadily and took up station with the other. Faces were staring over the gunwales. Now Sko means left and Bog is the name given to a fellow handy at bashing evildoers. This Ornol Skobog was an old kampeon in the Emperor's Yellow Jackets. I guessed that the Loptyg at the controls would be a rascally fellow called Loptyg the Muncible, serving in the Emperor's Sword Watch. Trust the two premier guards regiments to send men matched, one for one. I said: "This is Rollo the Runner."

Thus briefly we made the pappattu. Rollo was gripping onto the gunwale not looking over the side, and his face was the color of moldy cheese.

Ornol roared out: "Queasy in the gut, youngster? Haw!"

Rollo said in a faint voice: "I am perfectly well, thank you." His voice quavered. "Are these contraptions safe?"

Now he didn't know it; but a few seasons ago that would have been a question of the utmost significance. These days we could buy reliable vollers from Hamal. "Safe?" bellowed Ornol, his whiskery, leathery face creasing in enjoyment. "If she breaks down you can always get out and push."

Rollo closed his eyes and clung on.

I said: "Who's in the other voller?"

He told me their names and I groaned. A bunch of hulus all right, tough, hard kampeons, fanatically loyal to me. Somehow or other enough of a word had got out so that these lads had flown down here. I'd have the devil of a job to persuade them not to fly with me but to go home.

"Where are we going, jis?" demanded Loptyg from the controls.

"For a start, Loptyg you fambly, you and all the rest are going home to Vallia. You belong in ESW and EYJ and not lollygagging about Loh."

An uncanny silence followed.

They were up to a scheme, no doubt of it. The jurukkers in my Guard Corps, guardsmen of superlative worth, toughened by seasons of campaigns and a score of battles won, formed a *corps d'elite* I had not wished into existence. They had formed themselves to protect me, the Emperor of Vallia. Now I'd shuffled off that job onto Drak he had his own guards. Whatever titles might be used, the units that formed the old ESW and EYJ now considered they served me, personally, and not Drak as emperor. And, by Vox, there was nothing sensible I could do about the situation.

They'd have to go home; I couldn't have even this handful traipsing about Tsungfaril. Later, probably inevitably, they would be called on.

Ornol coughed and said: "You will take us, jis? When you go adventuring?"

I fixed him with my eye. "You know I can't, Ornol. What are you now?" I glanced at his rank badges which are different in the emperor's juruk from those in use in the general army. That was my attempt not to have lower ranks in a guard corps counting as higher than those in the line, a system of some dubiety. "A ley Hikdar? H'm, you've flown high lately."

"But—"

"You are a ley Hikdar serving in the Emperor's Yellow Jackets. Your duty lies to the emperor—the Emperor Drak. I am no longer the Emperor of Vallia." I spoke firmly but as kindly as I could. "And how did you find out I was here?"

"As to the second point, majister,"—suddenly very formal—"you know I cannot break faith. I can say the word slipped out as a new born babe slips into the world. As to the first point, the Emperor Drak, may Opaz have him in his keeping, has his own faithful juruk. We are your juruk. We guard you. We are EYJ—oh, and ESW, of course—and you are an emperor still, for all know the truth of the matter. You are the Emperor of Emperors, the Emperor of Paz."

There it was again, the idea spreading that some idiot had to take the responsibility of welding Paz together to resist the Shanks, inter alia.

"And how do ELC and EFB feel about this?"

"They and the other regiments may be new in the guard; they are with us."

"And I suppose the Empress's Devoted Life Guard is of the same mind?"

"With Chuktar Karidge in command, who can doubt it, jis?"

"Well, I agree with that arrangement, at the least."

"So we can come with you—?"

I breathed in and I breathed out. If this great rascal of a faithful guardsman thought I was caught in my own spring trap—for they can't be hoist by their own petards on gunpowderless Kregen—he'd have to be proved wrong.

"Didn't the Lord Farris assign pilots from the Vallian Air Service?"

Ornol suddenly looked shifty at this. I said: "By Vox! Don't tell me you chucked 'em over the side!"

"We wasn't very high up, jis." Ornol spoke defensively, and Loptyg chipped in: "Not high up at all, jis."

I groaned. What would Farris say about my crusty guardsmen throwing his smart young fliers over the side?

Now I could see most of the way of it. After all, it is human nature to boast if you are confronted with comrades of a different service. Human nature, yes; but boasting and Dray Prescot parted company before they were acquainted. Farris, on receipt of the message from Deb-Lu, had quietly detailed a couple of his young Air Service fellows. And they couldn't help talking, boasting, over a wet in the local tavern—probably the Taylyne and

Flea—and a few of my rascals had been in there too, slaking their thirsts. So the inevitable had happened. This little lot, led by Ornol Skobog, had kept their own silence successfully. They must have done. Otherwise I'd have had a sky full of vollers carrying ESW, EYJ, ELC, EFB, EZB and probably one or two more of the newer formations in the Guard Corps.

Rollo groaned.

"We'd better set down, Ornol, and let poor Rollo ease his inward parts."

"Quidang, jis!"

At least Rollo's discomfort could get us to alight without an argument.

Below, forested land swept past. The red roofs and walls of Hinjanchung had vanished over the horizon. In every direction stretched forest and open spaces, threaded with the glint of watercourses. Few countries of Kregen are populated to a limit that would be imposed by the land. As for overpopulation, yes, that does exist, and to our woe, as you will hear.

"There," said Loptyg, pointing, and he nosed the flier down.

In a regular circular shape a patch of bright green showed ahead among the trees. The two vollers curved sweetly down and landed in the center.

"I," quoth Ornol, "with your permission, jis, will step overside. By Vox! I need to stretch my legs."

This was understandable, for he'd flown all the livelong way from Vallia.

"Blotto!" rapped out Loptyg. I killed my instinctive smile. Blotto, which is Kregish for ditto, I always find amusing.

The two guardsmen jumped down and started to sprint about and turn, running and high-stepping, getting the cramps out of their muscles. The rascals in the other voller hopped over and did likewise. I turned to Rollo.

He said: "Can I open my eyes now?"

I said: "We are safely on good old Kregen."

He gave a shudder and opened his eyes, staring at me. His face began to resume its natural bright color. "By Hlo-Hli! What an experience!"

"You'll get used to it."

He looked over the side. At once a remarkable change came over him. He stiffened up, staring, eyes wide. Then: "No! No! Tell them, get back at once! Hurry! Bratch!"

Now my lads of the emperor's jurukkers are not infants at war and battle. So they were running about and getting the stiffness out of their limbs. They did not neglect elementary precautions. We might have spotted not a single sign of life among the trees or in the open. That did not mean that danger might not erupt upon us from the trees. After all, we were on Kregen, where immediate peril is a daily fact of life.

A fellow—I did not know his name—from First Emperor's Zorca Bows had his compound reflex bow strung and an arrow nocked as he exercised. Other guardsmen were clearly ready instantly to form a battle line if attacked. There was, as far as I could see, no sign of danger.

"Hurry!" screamed Rollo. "Come back! Come back as you value your lives!"

Ornol and the others heard. They looked toward the airboat.

I shouted in that old foretop hailing voice: "Back aboard! All of you. At once. Bratch!"

They clumped over and Ornol, out of that sense of duty that seems to ingrain itself in the officers of the Guard Corps, shoved the others on ahead. He would go last. If there was danger, then it was his duty to confront it as the folk under his command scrambled to safety.

He nearly made it.

A sound as of gruel slopping in a bowl, a sucking slobbering noise as of dregs running down a plughole burst up with a disgusting stench. The ground beneath Ornol caved in. At once he was engulfed to his thighs.

"It's a shuckerchun!" Rollo looked distressed. "It will suck us all down!"

As in any seafaring ship, there were coils of rope aboard the voller. I seized one up and hurled it at Ornol. He bighted a loop around his waist and immediately waist and line were sucked down. "Heave!" I shouted.

We tailed on and hauled. With gruesome sucking sounds Ornol started to lift, and then fell back.

"The shuckerchun will drag us all down!" Rollo was more than distressed now. His face was gaunt with the terror of his knowledge. "They can creep under houses and engulf them. We're done for!"

"Loptyg! Get to the controls. Lift off!"

He didn't bother with a Quidang. He jumped for the levers and slammed the lift control over. The voller lurched. I could see the brilliant treacherous green flowing up the side of the other voller like a tide.

"Lift off!" I bellowed.

Loptyg thrust the lever over all the way. The airboat shuddered. She quivered like an exhausted stallion. Ornol's head was going under.

"Come on! Come on!"

With a sound not quite like a cork coming out of a bottle, or that sound magnified and added to by a sloshing sucking, the voller leaped skywards.

Ornol dangled below, his powerful hands gripping the line, looking up.

"By Vox!" he said, and spat. "It tastes worse than a dopa den's floor at chucking out time."

Rollo sagged back. He saw me looking at him.

"I was sure we were all done for. No one can escape a shuckerchun."

"Unless they fly."

"Unless they fly."

Ornol was hauled in over the side. He stank.

"For the sweet sake of Opaz," he said, spitting overside. "Find a river." Then he said: "I give you thanks." To him, the peril was over and now he wanted to clean up. Hard, the men of my juruk.

As for Rollo, he was only too pleased to be flying through thin air.

Eight

I, Dray Prescot, Lord of Strombor and Krozair of Zy, have led a rackety picaresque life on Kregen. This has been forced on me not entirely through the machinations of the Star Lords. Duty, inclination, self-interest, have led me from country to country and continent to continent. I have made many friends and many enemies on that gorgeous and horrendous world four hundred light years from the planet of my birth. My own true inclination is to settle down with Delia in Esser Rarioch, our palace home in Valka. Well, perhaps one day that ambition may be fulfilled. As it is, the Everoinye put tasks into my hands that, for the good of Paz, must be fulfilled.

Once the Star Lords had regained contact with me—and the concept that they didn't know where I was on Kregen came as an intriguing supposition, as a shock, by Krun!—they'd hoick me up out of wherever I happened to be and dump me down somewhere else to get on with my destiny.

That damnfool Scorpion had dropped me. Well, to be fair, he'd been unsettled by the acrid green thrusts of Ahrinye. All the same, I regarded with a somewhat leery anticipation my next jaunt with the phantom blue Scorpion.

For the moment we got on with what we had to do here. Ornol Skobog cleaned himself up in a pretty little stream running between a fine stand of trees. We dug out the provisions they'd brought, and the archer of 1EZB, Nath the Dorvenfull, brought down a fine deer. We all ate prodigiously.

Then I went at Ornol and the others with a fine old spate of authority.

During that emotional wrangle I sent Rollo off out of it. I told him to go into lupu and contact his old tutor, Gal-ag-Foroming, and give him my sincere thanks for passing on the message. This was not just to keep Rollo out of the argument with my lads. I felt it needful to thank the Wizard of Loh. After all, I'd been pretty sharp with him.

By the time those rascals of my Guard Corps were convinced I must fly on down south alone, Rollo had not returned from the woods. So I went off after him, suddenly uneasy that he might have run into more trouble.

I found him in a small natural clearing. He was sitting down comfortably with his back against a tree. He looked up as I approached.

"Ah, Dray! I thought you would be along soon."

The voice was not that of Rollo the Runner. I knew that wheezy voice. "Deb-Lu!"

Rollo sat there, at ease, and Deb-Lu-Quienyin spoke to me through the lad.

He told me that there had been a right old furore. The two Air Service pilots were bruised but unharmed, and mighty rueful over their folly. All Vondium was buzzing with the business. "But, Jak, I do not think you will be over pleased about the outcome."

"I can guess," I groaned.

"Yes. They have been most insistent. The emperor has ordered that all of your Guard Corps who wish may volunteer."

"That means the whole flaming lot!"

"Of course." The cracked old voice, speaking to me over the miles and miles from distant Vallia, sparked with amusement.

Deb-Lu told me that Drak was content to keep his own guards. The name changes were insignificant. The PMSW—the Prince Majister's Sword Watch—would remain as a regiment for Drak's son—when he was born. The guardsmen forming the current PMSW had all volunteered into the new emperor's regiment, First Emperor's Red Jackets. At least, that solved some of the problems.

Deb-Lu went on to fill in some of the details I needed to know concerning the state of play in those parts of Kregen of immediate interest. The problem of Pandahem was being dealt with, as you shall hear in due time. My good comrade Gloag, who ran Strombor for me, hailed from the island of Mehzta. That island was under savage attack from the Shanks. Gloag, although fully assimilated into Strombor, felt he ought to take an expeditionary force to help out his birthplace. I could understand that.

"Tell Gloag to take what he wants from Strombor, always remembering to leave forces enough at home. He can contact Hap Loder. He'll lap up a chance like this. And the Clansmen ought to scare the Shanks!"

"Very well. I have no news of Delia. Seg and Inch are about affairs of state, Turko is thinking of marrying—"

"One day!"

Deb-Lu laughed. "Thinking of marrying off some of his people—"

"Oh!"

There was other news. Presently I said: "And, Deb-Lu—what of Khe-Hi and Ling-Li? I heard about the twins."

"They thrive. Khe-Hi is busy on a scheme we are concocting. I'll keep you informed. Communication has Substantially Eased."

There was a little more gossip. I finished by saying: "This bright rapscallion, Ra-Lu-Quonling—he calls himself Rollo the Runner—flunked his exams. Would you take him on?"

"With pleasure. I sense in him great potential. He just needs—as you would claim they say in Clishdrin—To Get His Act Together."

"Thank you, Deb-Lu. I think he'll turn out all right."

Rollo the Runner shifted, let out a breath, and stretched.

"You have finished, Drajak, satisfactorily?"

"Thank you, Rollo. That was courteous of you." I told him what was proposed for his future. "Deb-Lu is a fine man and a very potent sorcerer. You couldn't do better."

"As to that, I'd rather go adventuring with you as a Bowman of Loh."

"You as well!" I sighed. "It's not on, lad. Where I'm going is highly unhealthy."

For, as I'm sure you have already anticipated, I knew what my next steps must be and where I was going. And, by Krun, unhealthy it was!

"I don't see why," he began rebelliously. All that condescension I'd detected in him when we'd first met broke through again. "After all, I did save all your skins through my knowledge, did I not?"

"You did and we all give you thanks. But what lies ahead is—"

"Worse than a shuckerchun?"

"Far worse."

He remained silent.

A hint of his earlier disdain still persisted as, after a space, he said: "It does not need a genius to guess you are going up against these Shanks. I have heard the rumors. Are the Fish Heads, then, so terrible?"

I fixed him with my eye. "Yes."

He caught his breath. People who live far inland have to be educated where the sea and sailormen's ways are concerned. Once they have been indoctrinated with sea lore they can form navies as competent as an island's. The vast distances involved between what Rollo had known and the seaborne terror of the Shanks had, as I have said, inflated their reputations rather than the opposite. In all his youthful arrogance, fostered by the learning taught in Whonban, Rollo had understood that. He'd minimized the stories. Now I was coldly resurrecting all those hideous stories as facts.

"All the same," he said rebelliously, "I would still—"

"You have what is probably the most splendid opportunity afforded any apprentice Wizard of Loh to study with Deb-Lu. Vallia is marvelous. You will like it there."

"More study!"

"If you wish to advance."

"That's the rote cry. Is advancement then the only criterion?"

"Trying to make the happiest life you can for yourself and those around you is, I suppose, the main criterion. And getting on in life generally helps that ambition. But, no, you are right. There are many other factors involved, and the more advanced you get on, the unhappier you become."

"Well, then!"

I started to move off back to the fliers. "You'll just have to face the needle, Rollo. Look, give Deb-Lu a couple of seasons. See how you go."

"Oh, yes! That means you get rid of me now."

"Don't make it harder on yourself."

After that we walked in silence between the trees back to the vollers. My thoughts centered on what the confounded Star Lords were up to.

Somehow or other, after all my experience on Kregen, I just couldn't bring myself to believe the Everoinye did not know where I was. They might have not the slightest interest in what I was doing, and had no intention of employing me in the immediate future; they kept themselves informed of my whereabouts. Their messenger and spy, the gorgeous gold and scarlet raptor called the Gdoinye, would fly over and cast his beady eye upon me and my doings. Or a little reddish brown scorpion would waddle out, waving his stinger arrogantly, and tell me my fortune in picturesque terms.

Certainly, as it seemed to me, both Ahrinye and Zena Iztar must know where I was, for they'd cushioned my fall. At least, that was my supposition. Zena Iztar, possibly the most mysterious of all these superhuman folk, had her own designs. I felt strongly she was a friend. Ahrinye probably would not tell the Star Lords out of spite or contrariness. So—I was still running, still my own man, still free to follow my own plans.

Those plans, as you are aware, called for a simple next step leading to horror.

Down south in Makilorn we'd pushed Leone off the throne so that Kirsty might be queen, as the Everoinye desired. The way of doing it was beside the immediate point. Could the practical success of that plot have been enough to ensure that what the Star Lords wished to happen in the future would now take place? Their plans matured over many years. I had rescued folk for them so that those peoples' children could strut the stage of history. Why I'd saved quite a few of the men and women I had saved remained a mystery; no doubt in the years to come the reasoning of the Star Lords regarding them would come clear in some world-shaking catastrophe, or new religion, the death of a dynasty or a simple person being in the right place at the right time to influence world events.

Here and now there was no time to wait for those sweeping world movements. Here and now the Shanks were in Tarankar, and up to deviltry, and, like a canker, if they weren't stopped soon they'd spread to engulf the lands about them, and so spread further. And large though Loh might be, who would be bold enough to say when the Fish Heads would stop?

If the Star Lords couldn't see that then they must truly be senile.

Unless, of course, the whole damned shambles was just a game for them.

"By Vox, jis!" exclaimed Ornol as we reached the vollers. "You look as though you've eaten something that griped your guts rotten."

"Not eaten, Ornol. Thought."

"Ah, yes," he said, wisely, nodding. "Quite so."

And Rollo laughed.

"This young scamp is going back to Vallia. Try to see he doesn't fall out of the voller. At least, over land."

"Quidang!"

The few preparations necessary were soon made. Everyone went aboard one of the fliers and I commanded the other in splendid isolation.

A delay occurred in the other voller and I heard a few shouts and a few by Voxs! Loptyg yelled: "The Kendur said you was coming with us!" and Rollo's clear young voice, sharp with condescension: "I have decided not to go. I have things to do here." And Ornol, heavy and matter-of-fact: "You might have things to do, my lad. The Kendur gave an order and that order will be obeyed." And Coram the Flatch, a dwa-Hikdar from 2ESW: "Aye, laddie. Obeyed to the death."

This affair had best be left to my lads to sort out. Some more uproar followed, and a quantity of appeals to gods, saints and devils of various persuasions, succeeded by an uncanny silence. Shortly thereafter the voller lifted off. A row of heads appeared over the gunwale and a gale of rember-ees gusted down. I hollered the remberees back and the flier shot up into the clear sky of Kregen, dwindled to a dot in the north and vanished. I sighed. They'd be home in Vallia in no time.

Resolutely, I turned my face to the south. A touch on the controls and I was aloft.

Nine

I have said it before and, if the flint sickle of Kranlil the Reaper spares me, I shall certainly say it again. Ah! To speed through the sweet air of Kregen with the breeze in your hair and the radiance of the Suns all about! Now that is living!

On and on I urged the airboat in the sheer joy of flying. South the course headed, south to perils and horrors and death around every corner.

When I felt peckish—well, more than peckish, ravenous—I looped the bight of cord around the controls, keeping the voller on an even course and speed, and went off to rummage in the provisions aboard. My lads had done me proud. There were hampers of food, and bottles, and very soon I had the fire going on its slate bed. One has to be careful of fires aboard ships either of the seas or the air. Thinking of past adventures with Seg, I was meticulous and the voller did not catch alight.

The delicious aroma of cooking wafted up. I licked my lips. This was going to be a gargantuan meal, since it might be the last I'd get for some time. So everything went in and the succulent aromas filled the voller.

A plaintive voice said: "I declare my insides have betrayed me."

I did not turn around.

"There is a plate and eating irons," I said. "Help yourself to a bottle."

"My insides thank you, even if I find it difficult."

He sat down nursing his bottle. I said: "How did you elude my guards?" The moment the words were out of my mouth I recognized the fatuity of the question.

With all his old condescension in full space he said: "You forget. I am a Wizard of Walfarg."

He'd managed to slip overside of one voller and climb unnoticed into mine. Evidently, there was a lot more to this feller-me-lad than one might expect. He would bear closer scrutiny.

Then, Wizard of Loh or not, he betrayed the fact that he was still a youngster flying in the face of a hostile world. In a quite different voice, and a voice I will not describe as apprehensive—not quite—he said: "You show no emotion, I mean, that I'm here. I'd expect you to be angry."

"It's no good crying after you've upset the calsany."

"If that's the way of it, I agree." He changed the subject. "I hid under that canvas beside a box which, if I'm not mistaken, holds shafts. The box on the other side, I think, contains bows."

"Yes."

He swallowed. "I was wondering if I might—uh—borrow a bow." He gave me a quick sidelong glance. "If we are going where the horrors cluster as thickly as you say, a good bow and a good shot will be useful."

"Most."

"Well?"

"Take your pick."

I watched him as he opened the boxes—standard Vallian Army service issue—and chose his bow. He made a good selection. His face betrayed his joy in archery and his pride in hitting the mark. He was, in those moments, more human than he'd been apart from his reactions to the shuckerchun. I'd have to dump him the first chance that came along.

"I swore I'd go adventuring as a Bowman of Loh. And, by Hlo-Hli, here I am doing exactly that!"

He evidently wanted to prattle on and as I could sink into my own thoughts for a spot of privacy he burbled on happily for some time. I managed the occasional monosyllable in reply. Then he said: "Your guards are very ferocious. I was fascinated by them. They are clearly devoted to your person and they hold you in great awe—"

"Awe?"

"Oh, yes. But I do not think they fear you."

"Fear me? By Vox, lad, I should certainly hope not!"

"Yet they go out and die for you."

"When they do they do," I said, grumpily. Good men and women dying is a sore subject with me. So I went on: "You should see all the regiments on parade! The bands, the flags, the glitter and swing of it. Yes, that is the side of soldiering one should see and relish; but, of course, the reality is messy and unpleasant. My lads know I dislike wars. I try to keep 'em alive, and they appreciate that."

"Oh," he said with that know-all condescending air: "They appreciate much more than that in their Kendur, the Emperor of Emperors."

"And you," I said with grave solemnity, "if there's any more of that then it's over the side with you and no remberee!"

He had the grace to look away and keep silent.

Dray Prescot does not get buttered up very easily, no, by Krun!

The meal was splendid and was splendidly dealt with. As we sat back, Rollo said: "I sense something—it is interesting. Look, I would like to carry out an experiment. Would you please close your eyes."

Now there are folk on Kregen—and, by Krun, on this Earth, too—in whose presence I'd never dream of closing my eyes for a moment. Still, I felt I could trust this young Rollo the Runner. So I closed my eyes.

In no very long time I heard the unmistakable sounds of Rollo being sick.

When I opened my eyes he was leaning over the rail emptying all that beautiful meal overside.

There were water pots and towels aboard and after he'd recovered and cleaned himself up I looked at his face. It was still green. He'd washed the sweat globules off. He didn't meet my eye.

"Your experiment went wrong?"

He took a swig of water and made a face. He looked most unhappy.

"No. It was entirely successful."

"In that case, save me from your failures."

He gave me a mean look and took another drink. "I sensed, as I said, something. Now I know what it is. You have a caul."

"So Deb-Lu informs me. It is sorcery."

"It is extraordinarily powerful—" he began. Then I caught on.

"I see! You'd have made me bring my guts up if Deb-Lu's caul of protection hadn't reflected your damned spell or whatever! I see—"

"No, no. A twinge only, I assure you."

I eyed him balefully; but I couldn't be wroth with the lad. He was only doing what his nature and interests led him to do. And, anyway, he'd come unstuck. On Kregen they cannot express that kind of disaster by saying the experiment backfired. They do have a saying, expressed in a single short word, that you swung with your sword and cut your own toes off. All that is compressed into the word snizzed. Rollo's experiment had snizzed.

"H'm. Very well. Also, my lad, this means you can perform feats of magic. That could be very useful—"

"Or it could get me killed. I know."

"So be it. Now, as you are intent on flying with me, it is necessary that you learn to pilot."

He looked alarmed. "Fly this contraption?"

"Shuckerchun."

He wiped his face with the yellow towel. "Yes, I see. Very well."

To handle an airboat of Kregen and control the silver boxes that give lift and motion is not very difficult. A certain skill is easy to master. Rollo was quick and intelligent and he had the knack very quickly. It is easy enough to fly a voller. The true skill of the great pilots comes with practice, dedication, verve and sheer giftedness in the air. Some of those daredevils can perform hair-raising stunts. A top class voller pilot is greatly valued in any country's Air Service.

Landing a flier is the trickiest part of the whole flight envelope. The pilot must judge his height and at precisely the right time operate the controls which draw the silver boxes apart in their brass and balass orbits. I never forget the first time Delia showed me all this. That was a heart-stopper, on more than one level, thanks be to Opaz!

"Gently, Rollo, that's the style. Get the feel and lower down gently."

We hit the grass with an almighty thump.

"Take her up and try again. Gently."

This time the bump was appreciably less.

"Again."

This time I had to grab the controls and thrust the lever hard over so that we shot up into the air like a leaping salmon. I said: "I don't want to have to keep on asking Lord Farris for more vollers."

Rollo's green tinge returned.

"This time nice and gently, then we'll see."

He made a near perfect landing. We came down in a clearing among the trees which did not contain a circular bright green centre.

"I tell you what," he exclaimed, the successful landing already history. "I'll shoot you a round."

"Done."

So, there and then, we took up our bows, strung them, tested, and agreed the marks and ranges. He was very good. I think even Seg would have found a mite of grudging praise. For some reason I shot badly. This, I think, was that my mind kept ribbiting away at the frustrating problems of the future down south. This is, I know, unforgivable in a fighting man, and I have no excuse. The upshot was, I lost by a wide margin.

Rollo made no comment on my miserable shooting. In that, at the least, he showed a tact belonging to an older head. He might have commented that there went another Dray Prescot legend laid to rest. Mind you, most of the stories about shooting prowess were really down to Seg, as were the yarns of Dray Prescot leaping about with a great Saxon axe down to Inch.

"As you won you may have the honor of collecting up all the arrows."

The tree we were using as a mark bristled with shafts. Quite a few of mine had gone hurtling past further into the forest.

Rollo sniffed. "The prizes for marksmanship in Vallia are too generous."

"Don't," I advised him, "don't ask what you get if you lose."

"Not justice, that's for sure, by Lingloh!"

"As we made no formal wager, no reward legitimately accrues. However, as you did manage to win, you may keep the bow and a couple of score."

"Ah! Now that is more like it. I give you thanks."

He went off to collect up the shafts in a much happier frame of mind.

I wasn't fool enough to think that a man—or a lad like Rollo—could be bought with cheap and easy gifts. There would be a considerable amount of prickly disdain from young Rollo the Runner yet.

When we climbed aboard, Rollo observed the fantamyrrh, which pleased me, and he took off with great panache, sweeping us up into the sky in headlong style. A few high clouds were forming and the day was well on the wane; I hadn't much cared for the proximity of those trees where we'd indulged in our toxophily. Rollo, I was sure, had I mentioned my suspicions, would have put them down to my losing the contest. A view which may have had some truth in it, by Krun.

We spotted a nice little river winding through a valley, with clumps of trees dotted here and there. The grass was still a nice green; but not that bright a green. In the shadows of the distance the red roofs and white spires of a town appeared to float among the haze. The Suns would soon be gone.

We camped aboard the voller for the night. We stood watch and watch. Although we might well have been safer had we continued to fly through the night there were two strikes against that course. One was that, even though we were in voller-less Loh, I was not altogether sure of blindly hurtling on through the darkness. The other was that I judged the experience would severely unsettle Rollo's nerves.

As is usual during an expedition, each meal may be your last. So I made sure we ate up well. This, then, formed the pattern of the succeeding period as we sped steadily on over Loh. More and more I came to appreciate Rollo's qualities. I felt absolutely certain Deb-Lu could turn him into a first class Wizard of Loh. The weather grew warmer.

"Drajak," he said, one fine morning. "Do you intend to fly over Chem?" Now this was exactly the problem exercising my mind. Chem, tropical, clothed with jungles, fetid, stuffed with all manner of monsters, was not an inviting prospect. If we stayed aloft we should be safe, despite the certain sure presence there of gigantic flying creatures, all jaws and claws.

"If we trend westwards and fly along the coast we may attract unwelcome attention."

"Shanks."

"Aye."

"Some seasons ago I saw Las-po-Wehning just after he returned from

Chem. He'd had a good position there, for almost forgotten cities exist deep within the jungles. The folk are as ferocious and unforgiving as the monsters they combat. Las-po had a yellow skin, sunken burning eyes, thin to the bone, with the shakes. He swore by the Seven Arcades nothing would induce him to return to Chem."

"All the same, we would be flying."

"You mean, you fly these contraptions at night time?"

I gave him a brief history of the troubles we used to experience with airboats we bought from Hamal. "Now Hamal is an ally they supply good vollers."

"You mean people risked their lives in these things knowing they could break down?"

"That was in the bad old days."

I did not elaborate. Perhaps I shouldn't have said that much. The truth was, any voller might break down for a variety of reasons, however fine the craftsmanship and excellent the silver boxes. Even today.

Rollo had the habit of abruptly changing the subject of conversation. He did this with a considerable measure of skill and with purpose. He'd come back to the original subject when it suited him. Now he said: "Your guards, for all your coddling of them, were most anxious to get into the fights ahead. They foresee many battles under your command as Emperor of Emperors, Emperor of Paz. They struck me as anxious to show the world their mettle."

This young feller-me-lad, this apprentice Wizard of Loh, had an old head on his shoulders—sometimes. He saw through outward appearances.

"H'm," I said. "I'm not too sure about that. They are well aware of my views on battles."

"Of course. But if you wish to be the Emperor of Paz—"

"Just a moment, my lad! I don't want to be the blasted Emperor of Paz! My Val! Just think of what that entails. What I must do is forge alliances, friendships, between the countries of Paz. And far too many of them are at one another's throats as it is. That's not a job any sane man or woman would want, is it now?" If he could see through outward appearances, as I have just indicated, surely he could see I didn't want the rotten job?

"There are people who would leap at it."

"Makibs, the lot of 'em. Look, you have a parcel of land that two nations claim. They go to war over it, and the issue is settled until the next war. I've got to go along to them both and mediate. I've got to sort out the problem. I've got to say one nation has the land and the other does not. Or I split it up. No matter what I decide, I'm wrong. Right?"

He favored me with a little smile. "But, think of the glory, the pomp, the prestige! That would make any man's blood rise."

"It is very clear you have no understanding of me—" I began. Then I hauled myself up. That little smile played over his face, crinkling his lips. Oh, yes, he was a wise one! He was searching me out, was testing me. The truth was, he remained a Wizard of Loh. I'd offered him employment, or, more correctly, had offered to become a client. He wanted to know my feelings and my attitudes to power. As he was perfectly entitled to do.

Slowly, I said: "Have you ever heard of a Wizard of Loh called Phu-Si-Yantong?"

He lost the smile at once.

"He betrayed the most sacred teachings of Whonban. Oh, yes, he was known. Now he is dead."

"Thank Opaz. And, yet, I always searched for some good in him."

"My teachers, also, looked. I do not think any was found."

"Well, then. He stands as an example. Yet I continue to choose to believe he was not wholly evil—"

With all the arrogance of youth he snapped: "That is mere foolishness."

"Perhaps."

He turned away to stare over the side at the horizon. I felt—I hoped—my replies had answered the questions he must have answered.

I said: "I've been stuck with this job of being a high and mighty emperor. Believe you me, by Vox, the moment the job is done I'm throwing in my hand. I have other things to do—"

"Better things?"

"In certain contexts, of course. In the context of the Shank invasion, those better things must wait. It's a damned duty thrust on me."

"When we have accomplished our adventure together, I shall be happy to study in Vallia with San Deb-Lu-Quienyin."

"Dondo!" Which is a way of saying: "Good!"

Again he changed the subject. He picked up one of the arrows, twiddling it between his fingers. "It is an acknowledged fact that the best fletchings are made from the blue feathers of the king korf of Erthyrdrin." He gently smoothed the rose red fletchings made from the zim-korf of Valka. Farris knew my predilection in the matter of arrows and had stowed away these Valkan shafts for me. Brown and white feathers were more common, still, in the Vallian Army's arsenal of shafts. "These are not stained red. What is their origin? For, by Lingloh, they are very fine."

I told him, and added: "Even Bowmen of Erthyrdrin have been known to praise these over their own—sometimes."

He went on to say that the bow I'd given him was very fine, and waxed quite warm over its qualities. I didn't say that since the Archery of Vallia had been controlled and inspected by Seg only the very very best would suffice. I admit I looked forward with keen anticipation to Seg's reactions to this young feller-me-lad and his ambitions to become a Bowman of Loh.

That made me realize I'd have to be very firm with dear old Seg. There was no doubt Rollo's course in life must be steered in the thaumaturgical direction. He could be a Bowman of Loh as an avocation as much as he liked. And, of course, that brought me up all standing. What right had I to dictate what Rollo, or anyone else, should do with their lives?

Just because I was this blasted Emperor of Paz? Rather, that I might become this confounded Emperor fellow in due time.

I said: "Steer over to the west, then. We'll try a run along near the coast. Keep your eyes skinned."

"Oh, I will, I will. I don't want to be a slave of the Shanks."

"I'd have thought a Wizard of Loh could contrive something to avoid that fate."

He gave no answer as the voller curved away through the streaming mingled radiance of the Suns.

Ten

Flying at a middling height we skittered along the coast of Chem.

The twin suns continued to pour down their mingled rays of ruby and jade from a cloudless sky. When the clouds formed in this part of Kregen they did so with regularity and severity. The sky would turn black. The rain would slash down in waterfalls that would engulf Niagara as Niagara would engulf a local trout stream. The trees to larboard formed a single floor of deep green. Occasional breaks occurred among that uniform bed of foliage. The coast formed either a series of curves where sandy beaches might afford good bathing, or stretched in a straight north south line where the waves broke remorselessly.

Those trees, Rollo informed me, were probably the famous brellam trees. He'd studied natural history as one of the subjects in the very thorough Whonban educational process. That seductive witch Pynsi had a lot to answer for, by Krun!

"They grow straight up and very tall. They spread wide branches and turn up their leaves in serried masses of cups. They prevent most of the rain and suns-light from falling to the surface, holding the liquid within their cellular structure. Consequently the ground beneath is relatively bare of lesser vegetation."

"Which would more than likely be parasitic."

"Of course, here in Chem. The brellam trees are peculiar to this coast. The slaptras and syatras lie more inland."

"I," I said fervently, "do not wish to find them."

He made a grimace. "Quite."

Dots rose from the green carpet ahead of us. I peered under my hand.

At my gesture, Rollo span about swiftly and stared forward. I felt the tenseness in him that made his body stiffen into immobility.

"Now may Jallalak the Merciless be contumed!" His voice croaked. "Xichun! Damned xichun, flying to devour us!"

The flying animals swarmed up from their aerial perches. Like wind-driven leaves they were upon us in mere moments. Bodies glinted green and gold with red-edged scales, deeply curved wings beat strongly, sinuous necks and whiplike tails gave them a long menacing outline that the small heads with jaws stuffed with needle teeth perfectly complemented. These flying lizards were the kings and queens of predators among the life-forms of the forest canopy. Now they wanted us for lunch.

They were something like the xi of the Stratemsk. Iridescent wings fluttered about us. Tails lashed. Wedge-shaped heads darted forward.

Yet—our shape must have puzzled them. We had no wings. What, their lizard brains must be asking, what have we here?

They circled us, flying up and swooping down, around and around. Very soon they would dart in and seize their prey.

"Now," I told Rollo, "is your chance to act as a Bowman of Loh."

In this I was being heartless and cruel. Rollo did not know the ability of most vollers to outspeed most varieties of flying birds and animals. These xichun could probably keep up with us for a short time, and then, inevitably, muscles would tire and the voller would speed on. Still, he wanted to act as a brave adventuring Bowman of Loh. This was his chance.

I give this explanation in all shame; and add that in just about the same heartbeat I recognized that meritorious though it might be to instruct this young tearaway in the rigors of the adventuring life, that could weigh as nothing beside the far more important consideration. By the sweet teachings of Opaz! I was actually contemplating shooting, killing and destroying living creatures merely to teach a young scamp a lesson!

I tell you, in that moment, I, Dray Prescot, etc., etc., felt extraordinarily small. Tiny, by Krun!

I shoved the controls over to full speed and full lift.

We began to speed up and shoot up in the air.

The xichun must have construed that movement as threatening them, for they chose that moment to attack. With a wild hissing and a massive beating of wings, they began their swooping onslaughts.

"Here they come!" yelled Rollo.

"Take the most threatening!" I bellowed back.

He lifted his bow and let fly. He missed.

"How can you shoot straight with the wind of this contraption? Every shaft will be blown aside!"

"Allow for it. Like this."

My shaft took the leading xichun in the wingroot. He span about and immediately fluttered down to the green treetops. I felt the emotion of sorrow for him, and of elation that I'd exactly hit my mark.

Rollo shot again and again missed. I took out a second xichun and then we were racing up and away and the flying lizards beat futile wings far in our rear.

Rollo looked back. His face began to resume its natural color.

"By Lingloh! We've escaped!"

I felt it prudent not to mention what had really occurred.

And then—and then as I turned to look forward again, there they were, flying in a ruler-straight line ahead of us. Their black hulls and their squared-off upper works could not be mistaken.

In a controlled voice I said: "Have a look for'ard, Rollo. Remember what you see."

With that I thrust the levers savagely over. The voller dropped vertically through thin air. There was one chance. If we could find a gap in the brellam trees we could fly between the widely-spaced trunks out of sight of those black-hulled flying ships and their damned Shank crews.

Rollo staggered as the flier dropped and grasped the rail. He stared forward and upwards. He was smart enough to understand instantly just what we had run into now.

In a small voice he said: "Do you think they will see us?"

"They have eyesight."

His right fist clutched the rail and his left clenched on the longbow. Deliberately, forcing himself to move, as I could clearly see, he peered overside. The green forest floor catapulted upwards. "There is a gap."

"Dondo!"

"Perhaps."

I knew exactly what he meant.

Up there that drilled line of ships began to turn. The Shank flying vessels began to curve in towards us. Two of the foremost in line dipped and then dropped clear through the air. There was no doubt they'd seen us, and now they were after us.

A quick glance below showed me the gap Rollo had seen. One of the giant brellam trees had fallen. The hole in the canopy exactly matched the fullest extent of a tree's branches. There was room for our small voller to dive in.

"We will do it!" Rollo's voice screeched up the scale with released emotions. "We can go through. But the Shank ships are too big to follow!"

I hesitated for only a couple of heartbeats. Better he get the full picture right away. I said: "They will launch smaller boats."

"Oh."

"And," I added, "here come those confounded xichun again."

He stared below and aft. The flying lizards beat strongly on towards the gap in the trees. They had given up pursuit of us; now we were dropping back to where they could get their talons and teeth into us.

"We must smash straight through them." He took his right fist off the rail and reached for an arrow.

The picture presented itself to me in one of those mental flashes of vision so familiar to a watch-keeping officer on a black night off Brest. This was a problem to be solved, trigonometry in action. Of course, this was no bloodless theory, this was red-raw action; all the same, our course of action was dictated by those same laws of abstract mathematics.

The gap, a kind of locus of action, remained the focus of attention. Towards it streamed the xichun, jaws filled with needle teeth agape. Towards it dropped the Shank fliers, and soon they'd launch pinnaces and longboats of the air. Towards it we flew in a desperate attempt to slip through first.

"Come on! Come on!" I was saying to myself. My lips clamped fast shut.

Rollo kept staring forward and up at the Shanks and then back and down at the xichun. The fist that held the longbow had the finest of trembles.

The breeze whistled past. The Suns shone. The air smelled rank with the jungle smell of Chem. I thought of Delia—a stupid remark, for whenever do I not think of her?—and tried to push the control levers past their stop notches. We dropped stone-like to the green gap.

"They're pushing out little airboats!" called Rollo.

"I see." Half a dozen small fliers dropped away from the larger flying ships up there. They came down stone-like, too; I fancied we'd be through the hole in the canopy before they reached us. The question then was, would we slip through before the xichun reached us?

That question was answered very quickly in an uproar of battering wings, lashing tails and lancing heads. The xichun surrounded us as I slowed the voller down to a rate of descent that wouldn't smash us to pulp under the forest canopy. We sank down fast enough as it was, by Krun, and I had to keep one eye on the controls and the other on the xichun.

Rollo let fly, and missed, and swore, and so snatched up another shaft.

I made no move to use my bow. The voller dropped rapidly, and with a cautious nudge on the forward control lever I edged her into just the right position. A xichun got his jaws wedged into the wood gunwale under the rail. He was dragged down with us, flapping his wings in frenzy. Another of the lizards landed on deck in a great flutter. Rollo screeched a warning.

With regret I ripped out my sword—leaving the controls—leaped at him and dodging his strike cut halfway through his neck abaft that small head.

His frothing scream was chopped off. He collapsed onto the deck, untidily strewing his wings and tail over the rails. There was no time to deal with the poor creature. He was impelled to kill and eat us through force of nature; we had no such compulsions.

There was time only to jump back to the controls and swerve the voller cleanly through the gap.

Looking upwards I saw the mass of fluttering wings and licking sinuous necks and tails. They swirled crazily about the hole in the leaves; they did not follow. This fact gave me a severe dose of dire foreboding.

Rollo choked out: "Even the xichun are afraid of what lives here!"

The lizard with his teeth caught went berserk. His wings buffeted a gale across the deck. At last with enormous effort he managed to drag his head free. He left a clump of those needle teeth standing in the gunwale, the green ichor dribbling down. He flew up in a series of lurches to join his fellows out in the light of the Suns. For, down here under the canopy, the light was deep-sea green, gray and leprous, unappetizing.

The slanting mingled rays of jade and ruby from the gap revealed a different world. Here the tall straight stems of the brellam trees reached from the forest floor to the forest canopy. That was not quite all, for, indeed, there were parasitical plant growths upon those splendid trunks. Perhaps there were not as many parasites as epiphytes, and certainly there were nowhere near as many as there would have been if the brellam trees had not excluded so much of the light of the Suns.

The ground was a long long way down, sheathed in gloom.

The rank smell of a jungle was here subtly altered. Those cup-shaped leaves grew to a considerable size, and then fell to be replaced by new growth. The ground was well mulched. But there was little else to add a particular smell. Small furtive movements upon the trunks and among the vines would be tiny creatures carving out a niche in the chain of life. I had a nasty idea of what lived down here, and what so frightened the xichun.

The black boat-shaped silhouette sprang into view in the centre of the gap. Instantly it was surrounded by infuriated xichun.

I said: "If the Shanks intend to follow us they will deal with the xichun as we did. Time to go."

"We cannot go west out of the forest—"

"That is true. But we can continue south."

"What? And hope to avoid the Shanks altogether?"

"We can but try."

I realized I was not being particularly helpful to Rollo; but my mind had gone back a good few seasons to that time when Delia, Seg, Thelda and I had flown down out of The Stratemsk to cross the Hostile Territories. We'd been attacked by giant coal-black impiters, as ferocious as these xichun. Our voller had been badly knocked about and was unable to escape. We'd probably have taken a nasty beating from the impiters, even if they hadn't succeeded in eating us all, had not a swarm of tiny pink and yellow birds saved us. They had a feud with the giant impiters; they won.*

I said: "Find some strong canvas, Rollo. Drag it out onto the deck and get ready to hide under it. Don't leave any gaps."

"Do what?"

"You heard."

"But—"

"And put in some of the flying silks and furs, too."

"Very well." He'd caught the ugly undercurrent in my voice.

In the area of ground beneath the hole there would be the most unholy battle between new brellam trees and whatever other unfortunate vegetation had seeded itself there. In the end one brellam tree would win out over all the others and by denying them water and sunlight would dispose of his or her brothers and sisters. If the new area of leaves did not exactly fit the hole, adjustments would be made. These brellam trees lorded it, and they intended to keep the balance of nature that way. As for the animals of all kinds living on their trunks, these would be tolerated. I kept a sharp look out through the green gloom between those serried ranks of trunks.

This modulated deep green undersea gloom could have a profound effect on the spirits. I did not think the forest would provide adequate support for human beings to make a life here—it might, of course, humans are fiendishly adaptable—so that if we ran across any of the forgotten cities of Chem here I had the conviction their inhabitants would be a morose lot.

"The Whoorn-forsaken Shanks have broken through. They're following!"

I looked back. Two of the pinnaces flew down between the trunks, the suns light sparkling for the last time upon the weapons of the Shanks aboard. They started after us with evident evil intent.

"There will now be," I said, trying to lighten this desperate situation, "a quantity of consummate flying."

"Eh?"

"We've got to go fluttclepper flick between the trees."**

"We have to escape—"

"Keep a lookout for any swarms of small birds."

He opened his mouth, and closed it, and then said: "Very well."

He didn't know what I meant, not yet. Havilfar is the continent for saddle flyers. As far as I knew there were no birds or flying animals in Loh large or powerful enough to carry a human being and who might be trained to do so. If they were large enough then, again as far as I knew, they were intractable. We had to go fluttclepper flick between and around

---

* See *Warrior of Scorpio*, Volume 3 of the Dray Prescot Saga. *A.B.A.*

** fluttclepper flick: Hell for leather—very fast and risky speed. *A.B.A.*

the trunks and if we were caught then there'd be no more of Dray Prescot upon Kregen.

The Shanks soared along after us. We sped on ahead. I needed to calculate out the relative speeds, for I'd no way of knowing how fast the Shank's flying pinnaces could go. Farris had sent me a good voller; she was not of the finest but she had a fair pair of heels. As we sped along in that half light between the trees the Shanks gradually gained on us.

"Faster, Drajak! Faster!"

"See for yourself. The speed lever is hard against the stop."

"Then this time we are doomed—we must be!"

"This time we are doomed," I parroted him. "What kind of weak melodramatic fustian is that? If we're done for, if we're going to die, then say so, for the sweet sake of Beng Pulphan!"

"All right, all right! Tighten your scabbard!"*

I didn't reply directly to that acute remark; but I felt vastly pleased Rollo was acting so well. This kind of fraught situation would most certainly reduce many folk to abject terror. He'd wanted to go adventuring and, by Krun, he was tasting what it was like!

We roared on between those timeless trunks. The gray-green light washed us with a corpse pallor. The Shanks drew closer. Our voller would not fly any faster. The flying was demanding, swerving between the trees and lining up for the next gap and then a swift jink to avoid the trunk suddenly directly ahead. I had to give my full concentration to piloting; what Rollo was doing now was up to him. He might shaft a few Shanks before we were overrun.

The violent maneuvers at last dislodged the unfortunate xichun on the deck. He slid sideways as I jinked particularly sharply around a trunk and flopped off to tumble away below. He'd make food for the trees, eventually.

At last I saw them, up ahead.

At first I thought they were insects, a swarm of bees. They filled the aisle between the trees in a black cloud.

As we neared, for I dared not slow down, I hauled up the prepared silks and furs and draped them over me one-handed. I got the canvas up and Rollo was there, helping me.

"See to yourself—" I started.

"Now I see what you meant. Can you pilot this thing safely?"

"I don't know. I must look out ahead to avoid the trunks."

"So they'll be able to get at you—"

"Wrap yourself up and don't leave any chinks."

I didn't look back as Rollo wrapped himself up. I had a tiny gap to see

---

* Tighten your scabbard: Slang for 'Don't lose your temper', 'Don't get off your bike.' A.B.A.

through, a chink as large as one eye. Piloting was a nightmare, I can tell you! The voller hurtled on between the tree trunks.

The black cloud ahead resolved into a multitude of tiny dots. They were birds, sparrow size, with short stubby wings and long tails and beaks— those beaks! They were long and curved and sharp, sharp. If a xichun ventured down here through a gap it would be ripped to pieces. I knew.

And here we were, about to plunge into a furious flock of these ferocious little birds. I drew a breath, lined up the opening between the trees that formed a short aisle, aimed the voller, and hauled the flap of canvas across my eye.

In the next heartbeat the voller rang and resounded with the violence of hundreds of enraged little birds hurling themselves at us.

Eleven

Sharp points thrust through folds of the canvas. I felt the blasted little prickings all over my body. These little frightfuls had beaks as sharp as one of Seg's arrow points! That made me think that Rollo the Runner at this rate of punishment might never get to Vallia and stroll through the glades of lisehn trees, from which the fine Vallian bowstaves are built.

I jumped and twitched as the beaks stuck into my flesh. But the canvas and the furs held off most of the length of the curved beaks. Mostly these birds caught and ate the small living things on the trunks, and insects hiding in the cracks of the bark. As for the xichun, they could drive the big lizards mad with their torments. And, if we weren't out of it quickly, so they would us.

All this time my mental clepsydra had been counting off the passing murs. We must have reached the end of that aisle through which I had set our course. I had to take another look out. I had to throw back the flap of canvas so I could see, and that meant the deadly little birds could thrust their beaks straight into my eye. By Makki Grodno's own suppurating and dangling eyeballs! I said to myself. Not zigging likely!

The dagger I'd taken from poor old Lin snugged into my hand. I held it up before my eye, cutting edge forward. Then, with my other hand I carefully lifted aside the flap of canvas. I stared past the dagger into the gloom under the canopy and at once tiny bodies were hurling themselves at my face, crazily beating at what they saw as a threat, smashing into the upright dagger. Many of them were cut and slid aside. I had to ignore all that uproar. I had to see where the tree trunks were and where the next aisle lay. The dagger shook in my fist so great was the pressure. The trunks lined out a trifle to the right. The dagger could not be lowered. So I humped around like an Eskimo and got my left hand down to the controls and still a fold of canvas buckled above my eye so that I could see past the dagger. Lining up the voller with the aisle between the tree trunks and dropping the canvas flap back took only moments. I let the dagger sag down. I felt as drained of energy as though I'd swum the Cyphren Sea.

After that, only a short time elapsed before the sound of small bodies striking the voller died away. No more sharp little beaks thrust their tips through the canvas armor. Now I could hear a constant cheep-cheep from the deck abaft the control position.

Faintly, muffled, a voice said: "They've gone!"

"Don't take off your canvas, Rollo! Hold still!"

Just then he gave an almighty yell. I guessed what had happened.

"Wait, wait," I shouted back.

Now I could open the canvas sufficiently to see properly. No more tiny birds fluttered into my face. The aisle between the trunks petered out and I selected a new course. Then I looked back onto the deck.

The canvas hump was Rollo. A fair number of little birds had become entangled and stuck there, fluttering away like crazy. Others hopped and fluttered about the deck. The moment they flew up high enough they were whisked away aft. Rollo had thrown off his canvas the moment the main attack had ceased and one of these little fellows had stuck him.

"All right, Rollo. Cautiously. And shield your eyes, just in case."

The canvas hump moved as a sluggard moves on a Sunday morning. At last Rollo appeared, staring about, pale-faced.

I said: "Take a look aft, my lad."

He looked.

After a little interval, in which the birds fluttered and flew off, he said: "I cannot feel sorry for Shanks, after what has been said of them, no, by Lingloh! All the same—"

"All the same, these little birds of Paz have defeated a force of Shanks." This was true. The two flying pinnaces were moving erratically among the trees. One smashed full into a trunk, broke up, fell. Bodies tumbled from it. I wondered what the life here would make of a fresh fish diet.

The other pinnace curved down and went on down and vanished in the shadows of the floor among those gargantuan trunks.

"All praise to the Names!" breathed Rollo. He threw the canvas down and the last of the birds freed themselves. Those stuck in my canvas cleared off as well. We had the voller to ourselves.

"We can keep on south between the trees—until the trees stop." I eyed Rollo. "Or we can try west out to sea, or up and over the forest."

"The Shanks will be on the coast. We'll have to fly south."

I rather liked the way he'd said 'fly' so unaffectedly.

We had come through a nasty ordeal. Now we had to make the most of our chances. It would be necessary to keep an eye on Rollo in case he got the shakes. I had a shrewd idea he would not, since he regarded all this as a mere part of going adventuring. And, if he did, I had the equally shrewd idea he'd get over them sharpish.

The headlong onrush of the voller could now be eased. She cruised along sedately and there was an extraordinary amount of time to change course to avoid those solemn pillars rising to the green heavens.

Away to starboard the mingled rays of the Suns fell through a gap and made the intervening trunks dark bars, edged with color, the spaces between smoking with flittering life, hollow, fading away, on and on, into the tree-barred shadows of the distance.

Both Rollo and myself were impressed by these vistas of immensity concealed beneath a green canopy of leaves. The smell of the brellam forest remained with us in memory in after days, as I know. The many insects flittering in scintillating clouds contrasted with the tall solemnity of the trees. Undersea caverns? No, I do not think so. This strange world beneath the brellam trees' leaves formed a world of itself, a world apart, a world that owed nothing to any comparison with undersea.

Presently Rollo heaved up a sigh and said: "I famish."

Rather too brightly, I replied: "A capital notion!"

Somberness, stillness, these were the keynotes here.

We ate something or other. I'd slowed the voller well down the scale of her speed range. Usually one does not push an airboat along as fast as she is capable all the time. The general belief at the time was that if you pushed a voller hard, you would materially shorten her life. Hence, pilots cruised whenever possible at optimum speed.

When, at last, we saw we were leaving the true brellam forest and entering the rain forest proper, the jungle, I decided we had to rise. The heat was now considerable, for although Kregen's temperate zones extend far further than Earth's, the Equator is still hot. We sweated, by Krun.

Up we went, finding a gap, and cautiously entering upon the realm of the air above the jungle, we floated up into the brilliance of the Suns.

A rapid and then a second more thorough scanning of three hundred and sixty degrees revealed no distant ominous dots. We had the sky to ourselves.

"Well, now!" exclaimed Rollo. He expanded his chest and looked pleased.

"Well now, young feller-me-lad, is for us to take stock."

I raked out the strongbox Farris had placed in the voller. Whatever its contents, it would have been guarded devotedly by my lads of the Guard Corps. Now my Delia in pursuance of her mysterious errands for the Sisters of the Rose, errands which took her from me as mercilessly as the

Star Lords took me from her, had ordered the minting of a special coinage. In various sizes and weights, she had ordered produced gold, silver and bronze coins. Their difference from the normal coinage of Vallia lay in their anonymity. A vacuous face on the obverse, a blurred scene of battle and carnage on the reverse, a few profound words of the universal Kregish—'Honor that which is honorable' – and you had money you could spend anywhere without evoking comment.

As a great trading nation Vallia had access to coinage of many foreign nations. In the strongbox there would be coins from many countries beside the special Delian currency. There were also a reasonable number of Vallian talens, for people would be more likely to be suspicious of a foreign fellow without Vallian coins in his wallet. There were, I was intrigued to see, a goodly number of bronze krads, that patriotic coin minted by the Presidio of Vallia in the Times of Troubles and which formed the main part of the Vallian Freedom Army's wages. I rubbed my thumb over a krad, thinking back...

"Right, sunshine," I said, rousing myself. "We'll have a share out."

"But—" he began, and fell silent.

"You'll have to learn to handle money circumspectly. If you wish to become a freelancing adventurer upon the face of Kregen, then there are many instructions to master and lessons to learn."

"Well, I'm learning—"

"Assuredly." I was dividing the coins. I gave him half. I would have liked to have spared him more; but there were two reasons against that.

Stowing the coins away in the worn purse Farris had provided I spotted one coin so badly clipped it was shaped like an egg. It was one of Delia's special minting, what she called her 'Funny Money'. There had been a ring of dots around the edge. Milling would never deter a good coin clipper of Kregen. Coin clipping in some quarters amounted to a religious obligation.

"You are generous, Drajak—"

"Oh, no. Don't mistake me. You're going to Vallia to study with San Deb-Lu. You can shoot in your bow on holidays."

He gave his condescending half-smile. "We have not yet finished this adventure. Vallia is a long way off as yet."

I didn't choose to answer.

Steadily we flew on devouring the distance and we saw no signs of Shanks. Crossing the desert proved a simple task, so simple as to remind me of the travails the caravan with Mevancy had suffered. Truly, to fly through the air is a great boon to travel! At least on Kregen.

I said: "I do not think it would be a good idea to land in Makilorn, the capital city of Tsungfaril. We'd attract far too much attention."

"Yes, I see that. But if we land out of the way, how do we—?"

"Precisely. We can touch down on the west bank just before the suns rise, and hide the voller in one of the caves there. Then we'll have to walk in."

He made a face.

"I suppose so."

This, then, was the plan we followed. Nothing untoward happened and we stashed the voller away out of sight and marched in to the River of Drifting Leaves on which stands Makilorn. Here I stood no nonsense from the ferrymen, indicating to them that I'd been ferried across the river before and would pay only the prescribed price. Because Mevancy had been swindled on this point I called her pigeon, as she called me cabbage.

By our tunics we were clearly foreigners,* for hereabouts just about everyone wore the yellow or ochre colored gown and cloak of the desert. The heat was oppressive, lying like a leaden blanket, and wind or no wind there seemed always to be dust hanging in the air, flat on the tongue. I directed our steps to the Mishuro villa, for San Lunky Mishuro was one of us, in the conspiratorial business, even if, as a Diviner, attempting to stand aloof from our more devious goings on.

The guard was unfamiliar to me; a silver coin and a curt word saw my message passed in via the Deldar. Very quickly the Deldar returned, calling: "Pass Drajak the Sudden through. The san commands!"

So, in we went into the courtyard under the shade trees and here came Lunky, hurrying along to meet us. He did not look just the same. He had grown, filling his new office as a Diviner, fuller in the face, more assured. "Drajak!" he exclaimed, bustling forward. "Where in the name of Lohrhiang the Unfathomable have you been?"

"As to that, Lunky, I wish I knew. Although, to be sure, Tsung Tan will know." I gave him the Lahal and added: "You must ask San Chandro for the true explanation."

Now I was most anxious to know if our plotting had succeeded. I'd been snatched up by that fumble-tentacled Scorpion at the moment when we were escaping with Queen Leone, not having killed her. Now, was Kirsty firmly on the throne, the malefactors put down, everything going to plan?

Quickly Lunky sketched in the details of what had occurred whilst I'd been away. Yes, indeed, Kirsty was queen, and listened with great attention to Chandro. The fortunes of the party led by Shang-Li-Po were cast down. There was trouble in the west, out of Tarankar, and thither Kuong, Llodi and Mevancy had gone. I had half-guessed they'd be off to where the trouble lay; still, I was disappointed to have missed them.

"They have gone to Kuong's trylonate of Taranik. The queen collects an army to follow them. You will join that army, Drajak?"

He sounded wistful. I said: "Mistress Telsi thrives?"

---

* The Kregish word for stranger is autmoil. *A.B.A.*

"We are to be married as soon—" he spread the fingers of his left hand "—as soon as convenient. Affairs press hard."

I said: "You have your work here, Lunky. Fighting is not the way your life has been ordained." I did not forget the way he'd tried to protect Telsi, the way he'd ridden back for Mevancy and me.

"To the glory of Tsung-Tan." He brisked up. I made the pappattu between him and Rollo, and he went on to say that it was time for a meal. Being good Kregans, we did not disagree. We went into the villa to a very fine meal, and Telsi was gracious and charming, and I started to itch at what I considered sinful delays. A fellow has to eat, true, by Krun! But, after that, he must get down to work. I looked at Rollo the Runner in some sorrow; still, the dastardly deed must be done. One thing was sure, I didn't want him stowing away again.

All work and no play may well make Jack a dull fellow; all play and no work assuredly makes Jack insufferable.

"You will go up to see San Chandro at the palace?" Lunky handed across the silver dish of palines as he spoke.

I shook my head. "I'd like to; but there is no time even for that civility. I must get off to Taranik." I turned to Rollo. "There will be an invasion very soon, an invasion of a different sort from the damned Shanks. You are hereby appointed liaison officer. You will—"

"I am flying with you to Taranik."

"You will take care of the Guard Corps. You will explain just who Drajak the Sudden is, and why his name is Drajak."

Mistress Telsi, half-pouting, said brightly: "Why is anyone's name what it is? Why, then, Drajak, are you Drajak the Sudden?"

I laughed in a casual way, deflecting the question. "Oh, I suppose I'm too quick at times."

"Thankfully so," breathed Lunky.

"I still think I ought to come with you—"

I cut him off brutally. "What clothes do they wear over in the west?" I popped a paline. "In Taranik, say, or Tarankar?"

"Very similar to ours. Desert robes—oh, I see!" Lunky gave my tunic a stare. "Yes, that would not do."

Telsi bustled about and outfitted me and, as Zair is my witness, I thought of Thelda and her busy bustling ways, and sighed, and came back to the present. Rollo was sulking. I knew very well I would have to slip away. Well, I'd had enough practice at that game, avoiding the fanatically loyal attention of my lads in the various jurukker regiments.

Rollo's fascination with my Guard Corps did not surprise me. Any body of folk of that nature hold and demand interest.

In the course of conversation one thing Rollo said interested me. His opinion, from what little he had already seen of Tsungfaril and Makilorn, was that these people were far less apathetic than those of Walfarg. This did not cheer me up. By Zair! These people needed a sharp pointy stick applied to their rear ends to get them moving in ways outside their own obsessions with going to their paradise of Gilium. There was no secret that Queen Kirsty's army would be almost entirely mercenaries.

That sharp pointy stick would be applied—mercilessly—by the Shanks.

Lunky offered Rollo the hospitality of the Mishuro villa. "This is somewhat different, my fine feller-me-lad, from our time in Hinjanchung."

"That is due to the generosity of you and your friends. Still—" he waved an airy hand. "Still, I shall not be staying here."

I compressed my lips. Well, he would have to be dumped, that's all.

In the event that was exactly what I did. I ascertained more information about the west, brought myself up to date on what the current situation was—all of which will be related in due time—and that evening slipped quietly out of the Mishuro villa by a well-remembered back way.

Silver paid my passage across the river. I was at the cave and bringing the voller out long before Rollo, even had he realized I'd gone—which a cunning half-lie had prevented—could have followed.

With that leaping spring of a fine flier under me I soared up into the night sky of Kregen, fleeing due west in the streaming golden pink radiance of She of the Blushes.

Twelve

Through the apple green and rose pink of a splendid Kregen morning the voller soared on westwards. A voice at my back said: "So there you are!"

Slowly, I turned from the controls to look back, slowly, for the boiling fury inside me had to be contained. He stood there, not smiling and not frowning but wearing a sorrowful expression designed to cut me to the quick. His lower body shimmered and was not fully realized. His upper body seemed to float lopsidedly about and small curly blue flames lapped it in a waver of fire.

"You beastly, ungrateful, conniving hulu! You—you—" He could not go on. He was panting. His lupal projection showed that clearly enough.

The relief must have showed on my face, for just as I was about to speak he burst out: "By Lingloh! I see you are overjoyed to be rid of me!"

In a voice perhaps harsher than I meant, I said: "You have a job to do. I did not ask you to come adventuring with me. But as you have volunteered yourself for the task then you must buckle down to all of it."

"Oh, yes! I am to wet-nurse a gang of your jurukkers whilst you go flying off into wonderful adventures—"

He saw the lash of genuine anger in me as I ripped out: "So you really think I want to go flying off like this?" The bitterness in my words made his lupal projection flinch back. "Don't you think I'd far rather be at home, like any sensible person?"

He recovered himself from that blast of bitter anger. "Perhaps. Not everyone wants to skulk by the hearth—"

"You have a great deal to learn, Rollo. I just pray you stay alive to learn it."

All the same, there was truth in what he said. The trouble was not so much that I was flying off into some kind of adventure, as that I did not have Delia to share the excitements with me. That I'd never dream of taking her with me now, into the perils I foresaw ahead, was beside the point. Adventure, as I have said, is great on your own, when you can expand the chest and breathe the wonderful air of Kregen—even if down here in Tsungfaril a slick of sandy dust seemed always to film your tongue. And adventure with a few blade comrades is splendidly fine. It is the quality and intent of this so-called adventuring that dictates its values.

Maybe he saw some of that in my face, for he said somewhat surlily: "I intend to stay alive to my full allotment of seasons, thank you."

His image began to break up. As he'd admitted, his command of his own kharrna was still erratic. His kharrna would, one day, under the tutelage of Deb-Lu, become the powerful force it was in my comrade Wizards of Loh and then, like them, he could project his image in so concrete a form as to fool onlookers that he really was there.

"Remberee—" he called, and I replied as the last vestige of him winked out.

Just for a moment, when he'd first spoken, I'd thought he'd sneaked aboard as he had before. I let out a breath. Even then, even then, it would have been childish of me to have been surprised. Wizards of Loh could perform prodigies of sorcery, by Zair!

Flying on smoothly through the wine-rich Kregen air I passed over territory that looked distinctly uninviting. Now I was flying over true desert. For dwabur after dwabur rolling sand dunes stretched to the horizon in every direction. This was your genuine Sahara desert, right enough.

A touch on the controls sent the flier climbing. Higher up, that flat dusty taste on the tongue vanished, the heat diminished—although not by much, by Krun!—and conditions improved. As far as I could see the rippling dunes of unsullied sand stretched away to the horizons.

From Makilorn due west, after passing Orphasmot, the only centers of settled habitation were the oases. I flew past two in relatively quick succession, Claransmot and Hanjhin, and then the desert showed nothing until

I reached Taranik. Here I felt it necessary to descend to enquire after my friends.

The appearance of an airboat in this cut-off place aroused tremendous interest not unmixed with a quantity of religious superstition. Only for a few moments were vague fears that I might be mobbed by a panic-stricken and vindictive mob viable; then the Crebent Kuong had left in charge shouldered through the mob. He was a fine-looking man with a mop of black hair, a robe more bright yellow than ochre, and a large sword hanging at his side. His face showed the lines of care and authority. Quickly I made the pappattu and was able to give this T'sien-Fu news, for they were awaiting momentarily the arrival of the next caravan. He expressed regret that Queen Leone was dead, and in so hideous a manner, and said that he had heard of Kirsty, the new queen. He shook his head in ignorance of the whereabouts of his Lord, Trylon Kuong, knowing only that Kuong had gone to Makilorn. He'd never heard of Mevancy nal Chardaz, or of Llodi the Voice.

Although the absence of Mevancy was annoying, I felt relief that I wouldn't have to go through the same rigmarole with her as I'd had to suffer with Rollo. Crebent T'sien-Fu pressed me to accept the hospitality he could offer. As for the oasis of Taranik itself, do not imagine one of those little palm fringed water holes of the desert. The place was called an oasis because it was just that, a source of water in the desert; it stretched around a lake for something like twenty five by twenty miles. Taranik with its regular cultivated fields and herds of animals was much more like the great oases on the Silk Road of Central Asia.

In addition, and pleasantly enough, the people tended to wear brighter clothes than the utilitarian ochre desert robes. Their houses of stucco with thick walls and small windows reflected the tented dwellings of these folk when they'd been nomads. This made me think that the desert must have been the result of severe climatic disturbances. No nomads would be very happy wandering about the desert over which I'd just flown. Truly, the marvels of Kregen are never ending.

Many of the girls wore headdresses of silver coins threaded together. I gathered these were their dowries, handed down from mother to daughter. They were called, not altogether accurately, reedkhansixes, and the bright coins enhanced the bright liveliness of the maidens' faces. There was a distinctly more brisk feeling here than back in the main areas of Tsungfaril.

All the same, I felt it would be criminal of me to stay, even for a short visit. Regretfully, I declined Crebent T'sien-Fu's kind offer and climbed back into the flier, observing the fantamyrrh as I did so, thinking that this simple everyday act would help to demystify airboats for these people. With the shouts of "Remberee!" ringing in the air, the voller sprang upwards and I shot her into a steep climb towards the west.

As I have remarked before, all of Kregen is not hostile and horrible; there are friendly simple folk to be found all over that marvelous world.

The desert waste to the west became, if it were possible, even worse.

Towards evening, with Luz and Walig declining ahead of me in sheets and streamers of flame, viridian and crimson vying to paint the sky in a welter of colors, I made out on the far horizon a dark streak all across the land. At the same time I realized that to obtain this flung paint-box of color required clouds. There were clouds ahead. And, if I was not too mistaken, that dark line, rapidly broadening as I approached, must be vegetation. As though to confirm on the instant those thoughts, the declining suns touched with streamers of fire the course of a river wending from the north across my path towards the south.

The geographical situation here, then, would be a reasonably usual one. On this eastern bank of the river—whose name I had been told varied along its length and was here called She of the Sundering—the desert would form a sandy fringe; on the western bank the irrigations and cultivations would begin.

Kregen's first moon, The Maiden with the Many Smiles, lifted at my back, flushed rosy pink in the last of the sunsets. She would curve around over my right shoulder and remain shedding her fuzzy pink light so that it would be somewhat difficult to call this night a time of darkness. In view of this I decided to press on.

In addition, the Twins would soon be up, and then it would be very light indeed.

Despite this abundance of night-time illumination, any good Kregen relishes plenty of light shining upon his doings—those who do not, for various reasons, clearly do not qualify. That gave me the ironic thought that I did not always relish the searching beam of light upon my activities, no, by Krun!

So I was not at all surprised to see the dots of fire shining up from the ground beneath.

Now I had to make a decision.

I was here to do a job. Because of the perils of the situation, that task entailed the taking of risks. There was no other way—at least, that I could fathom out—in which I could do what I had come to do without a certain amount of risk.

On that somber note I nosed the voller down.

I made a good landing on soft ground encompassed by many small bushes. I sat in the voller waiting for a bur or so and after about an hour of Earthly time had passed decided that none of the folk around the camp fires had seen the airboat descend.

Wearing desert robes, with swords strapped to my sides and a longbow over my back, I set off.

Because of previous experience I fancied I had a good idea of just who the people were around the camp fires.

The direction to take had been committed to memory, for down on the ground not a wink of fire was to be seen from the camp.

Here in Loh folk were still totally unused to the concept of air power.

And, as you will readily perceive, this thought did nothing to cheer me.

They were keeping a good lookout after their own fashion. Pink shadows ran before me, the bushes thickened and clumped, and a few trees lifted above the general level. I spotted a wink of metal in one tree. I could feel a lump in the dryness of my throat.

Halting, I called out: "Llahal, doms!"

A sharp voice rapped back: "Hold still! Do not move if you value your life!"

"Oh, I value it," I called back. "Still, I trust you will not keep me waiting here long."

They rose from the ground before me. A rope whistled around my legs and before I could pitch over they'd grabbed me. Well, if you start off by taking risks, you must continue without flinching.

Carried along like a badly wrapped bundle I was hurried into the firelight where they could take a better look at me.

They were what I'd expected, and yet, subtle differences made me imagine—hope, even—that they were better than I'd expected.

They were desperadoes. That was perfectly plain. They wore old clothes, scraps of armor, were all heavily armed, men and women alike. There were many diffs among them although apims remained in the majority.

They did not share the lassitude of the folk of Walfarg, still enervated all this time after the loss of their empire, or the apathy of the people of Tsungfaril obsessed with their dreams of the paradise of Gilium. In connection with the hopes of Gilium it is worth remarking that if you had no real hope of ascending into paradise through crime you tended to be somewhat brisker than your co-religionists. This had been noticeable in the gang led by Kei-Wo the Dipensis in Makilorn. It was generally believed their hopes of salvation lay in some munificent amnesty of Tsung-Tan.

A lantern flashed in my face.

"Shove the shint up here where we can take a good look."

I was hoisted to my feet and plunked down on a bench. They crowded around, bristling with weapons, hairy, scaly, warty, the light striking menacing reflections from eyes and teeth and fangs.

"By the Healing Spittle of the True Trog Himself! He's an ugly customer!"

The woman who spoke was bold and brassy, yellow of hair, swarthy of face, with enormous golden earrings. She wore a mail shirt and carried no less than three swords girt around her ample waist. Her feet, shod in good leather boots, and her legs, bare and brown, spread in an arrogant stance of accustomed command.

"Lahal, mistress," I began politely.

"I am the Kovneva Layla nal Borrakesh and you call me my lady, or I'll have your tongue out!"

"My lady kovneva," I said, again as politely as I could.

"Well, ragamo, tell us your name, where you're from and what you want spying us. After that we'll think of a way of sending you to the Death Jungles of Sichaz."

I shook my head. Ragamo—or ragama for a woman—is a kind of general insult usually employed when you're not sure if the person you are addressing is a real shint, or just a hulu or a fambly. Insults are nicely graded in Paz on Kregen. This kovneva employed the term to make sure I understood her position and power.

I said: "Far from spying on you I walked up and called out."

Someone at the back yelled: "He did, by the Lustrous Hair of the True Trog Himself!"

I went on: "I have come to Tarankar to kill Shanks."

That stopped them dead in their tracks. There was utter silence, broken only by the heavy breathing of this kovneva woman.

Presently, she said, in an altered voice: "Then you have come to seek your death, hulu. The Shanks rule all in Tarankar."

"So I am told. In my country we have fought battles with Shanks, and defeated them, killing many and forcing the miserable survivors to flee."

Shouts rose at this: "He lies! He lies!"

"We too have fought the Schtarkins," she said when she could be heard. "We lost."

"Yet you are here, armed and armored. You are not slave."

"We have made a pact that we will all die sooner than that."

"That I well believe. But I must go on and discover things about these Fish Heads—"

"All that is necessary to know is to avoid them."

Continuing in as even a voice as I could contrive I went on speaking as though she had not interrupted.

"I need to know their strengths, their weapons, their airboats, their weaknesses—"

She gave a curt, hurtful laugh. "You mention airboats and then you prattle like a loon about weaknesses. The Shanks have no weaknesses."

"Yet we have beaten them in great battles."

"Well, they beat us in little battles."

I fixed my gaze on her, glaring into her eyes.

"Do you believe me, my lady kovneva?"

More shouts lifted at this, some for, some against. Layla nal Borrakesh sucked in a breath. "I must think on this. You will not be killed; at least, not yet."

A Khibil pushed forward, very arrogant, very superior. His clever foxy face with the bristling red whiskers was contorted into a snarl.

"My lady. Ask the shint how long ago he left the camp of Nath the Ron!"

A chorus of howls and shrieks followed this and the Khibil brushed up his whiskers in an access of self-confident cleverness.

The kovneva raised a hand and a modicum of quietness returned.

"Well, shint? When did you last see Nath the Ron?"

"Never heard of the fellow. Now, I really must—"

The uproar burst out again at this. It took no great genius to guess this Nath the Ron was the leader of a gang like the kovneva's and that the two were rivals.

The rope around me was becoming a nuisance. I took my left arm from the grip of the Brokelsh holding it and started to strip the rope away.

He tried to hit me. I lifted my left foot from the bench and kicked him— not too hard—on the nose, whereat he started a tremendous blowing and spluttering and, I am only half-sorry to report, a smidgen of blood dribbled down.

"He's escaping!" shouted the Khibil.

"I'm not, you stupid onker!" I bellowed at him.

The kovneva took a step back. The fellow grasping my right arm, a Thanko with a frizz of dark hair like a dirty mop and a long drooping nose, also stepped back, releasing me. I stretched. I looked at Layla nal Borrakesh and something of that old Dray Prescot Devil Look flashed into my face.

"Just listen, you bunch of famblys!" I used my foretop hailing voice. "I am here to fight the Shanks. I am not here to become embroiled in your petty quarrels. You can fight Nath the Ron if you wish. I cannot wish you well of it, for you and Ron Nath should join forces to help me fight and overthrow the Shanks until not a single Fish Head is left in Tarankar!"

Well, it was bombastic, boastful, things that are strange to Dray Prescot. I judged these things were needful at this time.

I suppose that just about the only thing in my favor was that I wasn't a Shank.

Indecision clouded Layla nal Borrakesh's face. Some of the others were arguing vehemently among themselves. Whatever they decided, I had decided that I would not hang about here. I'd make a run for it. Bowmen of Loh though many of them were, I'd damn-well outdodge their arrows.

The Khibil would have none of it.

He stepped forward as others stepped back, arguing. His whiskers fairly bristled up at me.

"I am Orlon Farantino, known as the Rekarder. You have not yet given your name or station. That is beside the point." He tried to keep his voice even and icily menacing but the words tended to shrill out with the force of his passionate fury. "I say you lie, shint! You lie!"

"If you wish to fight me in the Hyr Jikordur you are going to be disappointed." I spoke in a growly surly way, very contemptuous. "Keep your own station, Farantino, and don't stick your nose in where it's not wanted."

He gasped. One of his swords hissed from its scabbard. He rushed forward, face congested.

Somewhere the kovneva woman was shouting and people were yelling. The Khibil might be quick and strong; he'd certainly be clever. He tried to make a proper attack of it, holding his own anger in control so that he didn't just blindly hurl forward trying to stick me without finesse.

Very quickly I twisted and slipped that thrust, trapped his sword arm between my arm and side, reached down and grasped his throat in my other hand. I twisted his arm a trifle, and squeezed his throat a little. The face that had been black with anger transformed under the torchlights into an interesting color, of old boots, and beetroots, and moldy cheese.

I spoke directly into that remarkable visage.

"You ask my name, dom. I will tell you, so that you may not forget. Or, I shall tell you the name you are permitted to know." His mouth was hanging open, the bottom lip loose, and spittle drooled down. I gave him another shake, just to remind him. His free arm remained dangling—he was a Khibil and was clever enough to know what would happen to him if he tried to use that free arm and fist to hit me.

"I am Chaadur na Dorfu, known as Chaadur the Striker, Kurinfaril." The bench gave me height over the others and I stared around as I spoke this name, having no difficulty inventing it on the spot, as I had used the name Chaadur on previous occasions. I put venom into my voice. "You call me master, lord, lynxor, prince; you do not speak until you are given permission."

I threw him away.

Well, as I stared around at those emotion-filled faces in the lights of the fires and the torches and saw the glitter in eyeball and on teeth and fang, saw the fists curling around sword hilts and bowstaves, well, I said to myself, Dray Prescot, my boy, you've put on a good show—but is it good enough? Is this the time to run?

The question was immediately made superfluous.

A woman stumbling in her skirts ran into the firelights, screaming, screaming. "Nath the Ron! Nath the—" She tumbled forward and everyone could see the tall feathered shaft sticking up from the centre of her back.

Thirteen

The scattering of these outlaws took place in the twinkling of an eye. One minute they were clustered about me standing on the bench and the next the firelight shone upon trampled grass and camp impedimenta.

An arrow went flick! past my ear, so the time had come to depart.

As I ran away from the nearest fire the sounds of combat flowered up beyond a clump of trees ahead. I had absolutely no desire to get mixed up in this petty squabble—as I had told these people—so I angled away from the trees, making for a line of bushes.

Of course, I had chosen the bushes where Nath the Ron's Bowmen were lurking.

Half a dozen arrows flew past, for I was dodging and jinking. The situation had abruptly turned sour. By Vox, I could get myself killed here!

In the open as I was, it would be foolish to turn around and run off in the other direction. The firelight would pick me up and the shafts would unerringly find their target. I hauled out my sword, whirled it over my head—just the once, just to reinforce the image of Chaadur the Striker, Kurinfaril—then went slap bang into the bushes.

The sword flicked three arrows away in the superb discipline of the Krozairs of Zy. Now I could see the Bowmen, stumbling back through the gaps between the bushes, trying to nock arrows and shoot me at the same time they wanted to run off. I let rip a roaring brutish fantastical kind of shout, a scream of berserk anger, and charged.

The archers scampered off, and two of the famblys dropped their bows.

Quickly hauling up and looking about I saw men and women struggling past the line of bushes, rushing at one another, a maddened mob of crazies fighting in a confused melee, a crowd of mob anger.

I felt the distaste. This was no place for me. Carefully looking about, for I did not want a hidden archer to shaft me, I started to edge off out of the firelight. At one time I'd imagined these outlaws would prove of value. Well, they still might. As of now they were useless. If they did not exterminate themselves first, the Shanks would surely catch up with them. Those camp fires...

I turned about.

"By Makki-Grodno's disgusted distended guts and gouty legs!" I said to myself. "Why do I have to worry my head about them?"

The answer to that, as you will readily perceive, is obvious.

Using what skills of skulking I possess—and whilst you may not believe Dray Prescot does much skulking in the general way of things, if you have followed my narrative, you will know I am a capital skulker — I kept out of trouble. Every now and then I had to thump somebody who challenged me. Usually they had just staggered out of the fight, dazed, and were seeking their way back. I killed no one. I thumped alike the members of Layla's gang and the members of Nath's gang.

Eventually I spotted her. She was prancing about with a sword in each fist, dodging from side to side of a tree trunk. The fellow she was fighting was thin as a broomstick, tall, clad in a fantastic costume, all tassels and slashes, loops of cord and rivulets of gold lace. His face was apim, but it bore a remarkable resemblance to a cunning monkey. These two thus battled isolated from the rest of the fight. The thin fellow's hair showed a dark flash of red when a torchlight fell upon it. He, too, wielded two swords. Around and around the tree this couple went, and who was chasing who you couldn't say. There were a few bodies on the ground nearby and I hoped they were not dead bodies.

"You treacherous cur, Nath," the kovneva was panting out.

"You faithless besom," the man panted back.

"I never was!" and clink clang went the swords.

"I know. You cannot deceive me. That prancing shint Farantino—"

"Never!" She slashed with her left sword and tried to thrust with her right. Nath blocked the first blow and deflected the second. He thrust back and I stepped between them and struck up their weapons.

"What a pair of hulus!" I stared at them with a look of vast contempt, which was very easy to muster. I twirled their swords around in a swift hook and clutch and they flew up into the air, all four. "Now listen to me, the pair of you. By Chusto! I ought to put you over my knee and tan the hide off you. First of all, shout to your people to stop this stupid fight!" I bore down on them. "*Bratch!*"

They jumped.

Of course they tried to argue and I shouted at them, not forgetting to tell them to remember to call me prince or lord or they'd regret it.

Eventually after a great deal of confusion we had it sorted out.

I strutted about, waving my sword, giving orders, lining up each side between the fires. Oh, yes, I, Dray Prescot, acted like some pompous self-important numbskull of a princeling. I'd judged these people, and as I talked to them in a fierce growly way I knew I had read them aright.

They were nothing like real outlaws. Rather, they were law-abiding and had run off from the Shank invasion. They wore armor and swords without much knowledge of their use—I judged the Khibil Farantino to be the most useful fighter. Luckily for Nath's gang Farantino had been out of it, and four people only had been killed, although a number were wounded, mostly bruises, for unless you have some skill it is difficult, despite romances to the contrary, to slice someone up with a sword.

I planted myself before this tall thin lath of a fellow. His red hair showed up well in the firelight. I eyed him up and down.

"So you are the Kov of Borrakesh." I turned to his wife at his side. "And you are the Kovneva of Borrakesh. Well, by the Healing Spittle of the True Trog Himself, you are a right pair of famblys."

The sweet scent of a night bloom wafted from the bushes. The Moons wheeled by overhead, and one of Kregen's little lesser moons hurtled past like a flaming arrow across the heavens. And these two stared at each other as I left off castigating them. I finished: "For your stupid love quarrel has killed these four people and injured others. You should be damned well ashamed of yourselves. Utterly ashamed, by Chozputz!"

At that point the Khibil Farantino staggered back to the firelight. I grabbed him by an ear and ran him up to Nath. I shook the miserable Khibil.

"The lady swears Farantino is nothing. If you do not believe her I shall be forced to defend her honor as her champion and challenge you. Do you understand, Kov Nath?"

Layla's gasp was perfectly audible to me. I wondered what that gasp meant. Instantly, I understood, for she burst out: "Nath! You would be killed!"

He inclined his head. "There is no need for that, prince. I do believe, fully and completely. I was blinded by jealousy."

"Spoken like a true lord," I said. "Now we can all be friends. Is there a wet in the house?"

Someone laughed. Jugs were produced and we sat on the benches and logs to quench our thirsts. I said: "I was going to leave you. I came back to warn you that your fires are visible from the air. They can be seen for a long way. And you know the Shanks use airboats."

As they digested that, I reflected that one person, at least, of the two gangs would not be friendly to me. Orlon Farantino the Rekarder would slip a knife into my back if he had the opportunity with the best will in the world. That meant that Chaadur na Dorfu, Chaadur the Striker, Kurinfaril, would not turn his back on the Khibil.

Answering what I had said, Nath said: "How can we light fires and not have them seen by these Shank airboats?"

"This is a problem faced by any army opposed by airpower."

"We could weave leaves overhead," said Layla. "The smoke would—"

"And they'd see the light through the gaps!" Nath shook his head.

"I have no reliable method," I informed them. "I must leave the solution of the problem to you. Probably you can screen smaller fires you need for cooking. After that, use the Moons."

"Yes," said Layla. "That is one way."

After that they wanted to know about me. Now, do not imagine that the members of these two gangs, split by the lover's quarrel of their lord and lady, would abruptly forget and forgive all the hurts between them. There were still scores to be settled. More than one quarrel had to be nipped in the bud before it started the fighting again. So I was able to be casual about myself, interrupting my pack of lies by seizing two antagonists by their hair and dragging them apart.

"Prince Chaadur," said Kov Nath na Borrakesh, very formal. "I offer you my thanks for what you have accomplished. Also, and my lady concurs, we offer our services in your fight against the Shanks."

I breathed in and I breathed out.

I managed a Dray Prescot grimacing smile.

I had made a start!

Fourteen

Nath the Ron slid down from the line of bushes cresting the bank. After a last searching look along the road, I followed him.

"Well?"

"The fish convoy," he said, and his monkey-like face wrinkled up in anticipation.

"There were twelve carts, mostly pulled by mytzers or Quoffas. I counted thirty-three guards—"

"I made it thirty. That seems a more rounded number."

"There were three at the tail end, archers, hidden by the last cart who came into view after you slid down the bank."

"Ah!" He shook his head. "Truly, this banditry is a business a fellow must learn as he learns his rote lessons at school."

I didn't mention that a mistake at school might mean a flogging; a mistake at banditry could result in you being shorter by a head or dancing on air.

Away to our left past a stand of trees lay the ruins of a town and on its thither outskirts the Shanks had built a small fort. The garrison had to be provisioned, and as the Fish Heads ate mostly fish, that had to be brought up from the coast. Kovneva Layla had told me that she believed the Schtarkins either couldn't or wouldn't eat fresh fish. Here, at least, was a small chink in their apparently invincible armor. I stared upwards as I lay beside Nath and the others, waiting for the sounds of the convoy to reach us. Up there the sky hung limpid and serene with a few wispy scraps of vapor struggling to coalesce into a real cloud. The day was fine and warm, and from the bank the rich scents of rustic blooms would, in normal circumstances, have formed a happy accompaniment to a merry picnic. I looked upwards for one reason alone; to see if there were any damned black-hulled fliers circling up there. All the information we had indicated the Shanks were seriously short of airboats, and those they had were normally occupied on patrol duties. It was not, Layla indicated, in the Shanks' character to employ grand and costly airboats to ferry fish.

Now the shush and thump of hooves reached us. I looked along the line of men behind the bank. They were a vastly different bunch from the pathetic desperadoes I'd first met in the gangs of Nath and Layla. They had done this before. I'd shouted at them. We had taken in recruits. Now we commanded more than two hundred men and women of diverse races.

Of course, most of them were still amateurs. They were learning. After all, this was very much how the jurukkers of my Emperor's Sword Watch had begun. We had a few old hands. They'd explained a great deal when they told me that the professionals of Tarankar, the army and mercenaries, had fought the Shanks and had either been killed, captured or dispersed. Very few were left alive. The king and queen of the ruling race of diffs, those same riffims who had caused so much trouble for Trylon Kuong in Taranik, had been mercilessly butchered along with all the royal family. Shanks now lorded it in forsaken Tarankar.

The beautiful Fristle fifi on my other side started to crawl up the bank to the crest. I grabbed a delightfully formed ankle and hauled her down. She slid back and at once turned her face with those enormous eyes on me with a fierce look.

"Fan-Si," I said, using my best imitation of a catman's hiss, "sit still!"

"Oh, you—" she said, and an image of Mevancy ghosted into my mind. "I want to get at them! They killed my mother and father and took away my brother! You—"

"We cannot attack until they have passed the kovneva."

She flicked her silver-gray tail. She was careful, though, not to overdo the normal Fristle fifi's sense of playfulness. She did not flick me with that enchanting tail, remembering I was a prince. Ha! She went on: "And how can you tell when they have passed the kovneva?"

"By listening—if you close those pretty lips."

She pouted. "You can tell by listening?"

"When certain charming fifis allow me to, Fan-Si."

Nath broke in: "Fan-Si! *Shastum!*"

At this direct command from the kov to keep silent, Fan-Si subsided.

The creak of carts and the rolling of wheels, the thump of hooves, drew nearer. One day Fan-Si would learn how to judge distances accurately by sound. Well, they say man sows for Zair to sickle. When the noise drew abreast of me I counted in my head to a hundred and fifty. Then I said, in a very quiet voice: "Now, Nath."

"Thank the Bright Eyes of the True Trog Himself!" He stood up and waved his arms.

Instantly the whole line of men and women rose up, hurled themselves up the bank. The Bowmen picked targets and started to loose. I went up fast, took in the situation, saw a clump of Shanks between two carts and went headlong down at them. I brandished my sword, a pretty useless activity I am not prone to but one I judged effective here. Nath was with me. Shanks were falling as the long Lohvian arrows pierced them. The uproar bellowed into the sky, screams and shrieks of pain and rage. Dust smoked underfoot.

We reached the Shanks who had taken cover from the arrows. Their tridents looked sharp and unpleasant. They were shrilling their warcries.

"Ishti! Ishti!"

Apart from a few other words of command, those were the only words of the Shank language the folk of Paz understood. I heard one of the Fish Heads hissing: "Shoot the archers! Shoot the archers!"

My sword came down and thrust forward, slipping a trident, and finishing up in a fishman's guts. Instantly I withdrew, ducking and whirling, and hacking at the next. Nath was roaring and bellowing and striking about wildly. Fan-Si was there, very prettily dropping to a rounded knee and striking up like a risslaca. Her opponent dropped his trident, clasping his scaly stomach. He fell down and Fan-Si jumped on his face.

An arrow streamed in over my shoulder and a Shank with his short little bow reeled back, the shaft through one fishy eye.

At the tail of the convoy Kovneva Layla led her party in, preventing escape, and at the front the Khibil, Farantino, blocked off further advance.

Fan-Si was up again, running fleetly after a Shank trying to crawl under a cart. If he thought he was safe there he was mightily mistaken.

Nath and Fan-Si grasped a foot each and hauled him out. The Fristle fifi struck first, mercilessly driving her sword down and through the fishman's neck above the rim of his scaled armor. He flopped.

Nath was panting, his monkey-face brilliant.

"Are there any left?" I bellowed. "Look carefully, fanshos!"

We looked. No Shanks lived.

The drivers sat huddled on their seats, the reins limp in their hands.

Only two of them had been shafted, and these were both Rapas. The others, mostly apims, Fristles, Ochs, with a single Brokelsh, sat dumbly.

I shouted at them, making myself vehement. "We will not slay you!"

The Brokelsh, all black body hair and surly, called: "We were made slave! We did not volunteer!"

This I believed.

"Get up on the carts," I shouted, very commanding, very brisk. "Let's get moving! Bratch!"

Those of our gang detailed to take over the carts obeyed. The others helped turn the wagons around with much pushing and shoving, and then we all went thumping and creaking back down the road. Two dwaburs on we turned off into a narrow overgrown sidetrack. This led to the forest where we'd set up our headquarters in this section of Tarankar. We'd left the scrubby eastern areas and were now approaching the main part of the country. As we marched along these people were busily engaged in bargaining and exchanging the spoils of the recent fight. We'd collected up all the tridents as a matter of principle; it was noticeable that despite the acknowledged effectiveness of the Shank weapon, no one particularly cared to take and use a trident for themselves.

Not only those detailed to the task but just about everyone kept scanning the sky.

My harshness over proper aerial surveillance, my brutal examples of what could happen if people wandered along staring at their feet, had at last paid dividends. Now our little band was extremely airpower conscious.

As the first leaves closed over our heads and the sounds of the forest floated from every direction between the trees and the smells took on that different aroma from those of the open country, I called cheerfully: "Let's have a song or three. Larghos the Throstle! A lead, if you please."

Larghos the Throstle possessed a fine voice and he led off at once with 'The Milkmaid's Song' and we all roared the choruses. After that we had 'Happy the Day of the Shearing' and then 'The Well that Never Ran Dry'.

Catching sight of Farantino I noticed he was not singing. His lips were clamped tightly shut. The expression on his face reaffirmed my decision not to turn my back on the Khibil.

Our camp was a simple affair. We regarded the forest as home. Patrols and sentries at all times kept watch. Only twice had parties of Shanks attempted to penetrate to any depth in the forest. On the first occasion they had stumbled about for half an afternoon, found nothing, and cleared off.

The second occasion, apart from being more effective, was saddened for us by the cause of that improved performance. Human slaves, chained up like dogs, led the hunting party of Shanks. Again, they found nothing. We watched from concealment and, I confess it, I had the most extraordinary difficulty in preventing myself from rushing into a brawling hand-to-hand melee with these damned Fish Heads. We might obtain a minuscule initial advantage from a surprise attack; in a straight hand-to-hand the Shanks would murder my little band of amateurs.

So, as you can see, the old Dray Prescot might well have gone roaring into action shouting "Hai Jikai!" and got all his new friends killed.

All the same—all the same, by Zair!—I made up my mind that the next time the Opaz-forsaken Shanks ventured in here we'd shaft 'em and play 'em and torment 'em and finally, I hoped, finish 'em.

That must be for the future. As of now we marched into camp singing and looking forward to a fine fish supper.

Not that, as you know, I like fish. Still, there are some fish that are splendid: kippers and sardines, for example. The Schtarkins' convoy contained boxes of stock fish. I made a face and Fan-Si smiled, mockingly.

In the event I made do with the remnant of last night's supper and sat with my back up against a tree, brooding. This life was very fine and free and romantic. Here we were, a bunch of outlaws in the forest, living on what we could shoot or steal, annoying the Shank masters. And all this was petty, was trivial, was not encompassing enough. Although, if you have a trivial fight and get a shaft or a blade through your guts...

No. By the Divine Lady of Belschutz and the corn on her left big toe! The cities beckoned. It would take me a month of Sundays to create a full-scale army with the materials to hand using these methods.

The Kov and Kovneva of Borrakesh could be left in charge here. They could expand this gang using my methods. I'd have to travel on. There were a couple of people I'd like to take with me, Larghos the Throstle for one and Fan-Si for a second and Moglin the Flatch for the third.

They'd help me train up a new gang. That made me remember to shout at Fan-Si as she went loping by, very seductive, wearing her usual silk shirt and breechclout. She saw me and smiled and came over.

"Well, Prince Chaadur?"

"I meant to tell you, young lady. What happened to your armor today?"

She grimaced and twirled her tail. "Oh, you know I cannot abide being shut up in a leather box!"

"Next time we go into action you will wear your armor, like it or not."

Her tail twinkled down between her legs. "It's all stuffy and hot and I can't move in it! How do you expect me to stick Shanks if I can't—"

I stood up. "Armor is for your protection. I agree it may slow you down; but you exaggerate."

She pouted. She was about to say something, something tart, no doubt, when I went on: "You will wear your armor about the camp until I tell you you may take it off. You'll soon get used to it."

"That's not fair! That's dreadful! And you a prince!"

There were so many cheap answers flooding into my head that I had to turn away. I managed to say: "Dismiss!" and hurried across to the fires where the kov and kovneva were just finishing up their fish.

Without preamble, I said: "The time has come for you to take over. You know by now what must be done."

"But, prince—where will you go?"

"Where there are Shanks to fight."

They shook their heads. "They're all about."

"And you will deal with those in this section." I went on to tell them I would like to take Larghos, Fan-Si and Moglin and they couldn't very well refuse a prince, could they?

The important fact here was that I'd impressed them that I was a prince but that my real name was different from Chaadur. They accepted this with all the vivid old romances ringing in their skulls, princes in disguise traveling their kingdoms. Although, to be sure, they knew I was not of the Tarankarese ruling class, for I was apim and not riffim.

Nath and Layla, although apim, had ancient rights to their lands and titles, dating back before the riffim invasion and takeover. They had survived through the skill, cunning and groveling of their ancestors. There was nothing of that kind possible now the Shanks were the overlords.

Thinking of the peoples of other lands I knew, I had the strongest suspicions that my folk of Vallia, or Djanduin, or Strombor, would not so easily accept a fellow who came roaring in ordering about and claiming to be a prince. No, I fancy they'd be somewhat less credulous. But, then, these people had been lost, deprived of just about everything except their lives, not really knowing what to do and expressing their frustrations by quarrelling among themselves. They'd needed a prince, by Krun!

I found Moglin the Flatch painstakingly pulling an arrow through a straightener. Quality shafts were hard to come by in the greenwood; we could build our own and fletch them, we couldn't build arrows to professional quality. I thought of Master Twang and his spritely daughters, and sighed.

"Hai, Moglin!" I said, all jovial.

He replied politely, still working on his arrow. I told him that if he wished he might accompany me, for I had other gangs to train up.

He left off work and brushed up his whiskers, which were very fine. Unlike a Pachak or a Kildoi he had no tail hand. Although Katakis, who were generally detested as Slavemasters, habitually strapped six inches of daggered steel to their tails, Fristles seldom did so. This Moglin the Flatch had been known to strap a dagger to his tail.

Cautiously, he said: "I am honored, prince. Ah—is Fan-Si—?"

"Yes. I could not ask you to come with me if that meant leaving Fan-Si here. Oh, yes, she's coming along with us. Larghos the Throstle is going, and you all have dispensation from the kov."

"Then right gladly, prince. I own I wish to do unpleasant things to these Shanks. By Numi Hyrjiv the Splendid! They took Fardo the Splitter away, and he was my best friend and brother to Fan-Si." Moglin's cat face screwed up in an access of venom. His fur was a deep russet brown, and he was built like an archer, with shoulders almost as broad as mine.

"And, Moglin, tell your Fan-Si to wear armor next time we fight."

"Quidang, prince. I agree with you. But she is willful and headstrong. She laughs and scorns—"

"I know, I know. Well, by Chozputz! She'll just have to, that's all!"

"Quidang!"

I went off to tell Larghos the Throstle about our proposed trip. He was sitting on a log singing, half to himself, a little ditty about the farmer who paid ten gold pieces for a slave and married her and demanded the gold back from her owner as her dowry. This song is known as the have it and eat it song. It's title, in the obscure way of Kregen humor, is 'The Miscil Return'd'.

Larghos jumped at the chance to go adventuring, and, as he said in his modulated voice, "To even up the score a little."

His strong brown hands went methodically on as he spoke polishing up his strangdja, that feared and famous polearm of Chem with its steel holly-leaf shaped head. "Oh, yes, prince. I long to swing my Stinja down on their fishy heads."

As you know it has not been my habit to give names to my weapons. As I have remarked, a true warrior must fight with whatever comes to hand. If he relies on one favorite weapon, he is bound to come unstuck one day. Anyway, I always seemed to be acquiring and losing weapons and a name one day would be a memory the next. All, that is, apart from the Savanti swords and the great Krozair longswords.

So, everything was arranged. The next day scouts reported in that the Shanks had sent a considerable force up the road. There were carts in the procession, so maybe the fort had got their stock fish at last. All we had done was inconvenience the Shanks for a day.

That meant I had to harangue the gang with some vehemence. I used the fustian to good purpose, telling them they must think of a huge wild animal being stung by a multitude of bees. I instanced the case of the xichun and the tormenting little birds. I exhorted them to continue with pinpricks, for as the gangs grew so the pressure would grow. Their next objective, I told them, feeling the doubt in my heart, was to capture or destroy the local fort.

They waxed enthusiastic enough. Truth to tell I felt like a traitor at leaving them. Still, my mission was not to become embroiled in local guerilla operations, attractive though they undoubtedly were. My job was to find out about the Shanks and choose the weakest spot to strike.

I'd approached this gang knowing the risks I ran. What of the risks of the future when I approached a city?

"I'll send word," I promised. "When the day dawns, you will know."

The Kov and Kovneva of Borrakesh stood with the combined gang shouting the remberees as we four trudged off along the forest trail. We would take a circuitous route. We called back the remberees, and then the forest closed about us.

In that moment, my chief thought was one of great delight and anticipation at the expected reactions of my new comrades to the airboat. By Vox! They'd be far worse than Rollo ever had been.

And as for that young scamp, was he doing what he ought to be doing, or was he contriving ways and means of following me into the Shank-infested perils of Tarankar? Then Fan-Si halted so that Moglin bumped into her.

"Quiet! There is someone ahead, lying in ambush. See!" She pointed with her free hand. "There, a glint of steel in the undergrowth!"

Fifteen

"That," I said, with a stupid and rather comical attempt at princely arrogance, "will be that confounded Khibil Farantino, may the True Trog rot him."

"There is more than one," observed Larghos.

"True," I conceded in your true princely condescending way. "The rast will have cajoled his friends into helping him. He fancies his honor has been slighted. The zigging great onker!" I finished, somewhat peevishly.

We slowed down and finally stopped. My three new comrades waited to see what this braggart prince would do.

I stepped forward.

I shouted. I used the old foretop hailing voice and I put spite and venom into my words.

"Come out, you crawling creeping horror! Come on, come on. Stand up! Step out! Let's see you!"

The bushes swayed and metal clinked against metal. Larghos's bow lifted, a lethal arc, his strangdja slung over the other shoulder. Moglin's bow was held slightly down, the arrow at half draw, in that easy practiced grip of your handsome Bowman of Loh. I yelled again.

"Come on, come on! My patience is nearly exhausted."

Now the bushes were agitated. Four men and two women stepped out onto the trail. Not one was Farantino. I felt amusement at my antics. These people were roughly dressed, almost in rags. They carried an assemblage of rusty weapons, one fellow with a strangdja with a broken shaft. They had rags tied around their feet. They were two apims, two Thankos and two Brokelsh. In short, they were a miserable looking bunch.

"Why, you great pack of famblys!" I stormed at them. "So you were going to waylay us from a bush? And would you have killed us?"

"No, master, no!" cried the Brokelsh woman, her hair wound about her waist. "We have not eaten for many days—"

I gave them my hard stare and they flinched back. I told them we were on a journey and could spare no food. They should walk boldly into the camp and declare themselves. I piled on the agony. I gave them that kind of speech I had rehearsed before, designed to open their eyes to the opportunities of the future. I gave them the old patriotic fustian. Also, I told them I was called Prince Chaadur, that this was not my real name, and that on the great day when we had removed the last of the Shanks they would know my name.

All this impressed them.

Whilst they would not change from frightened and hungry fugitives to brave bold guerillas in a twinkling, the process had begun.

So, therefore, much heartened, I bid them remberee and led my three companions forward.

Fan-Si tripped alongside and, very cheekily, said: "If that had been the Khibil he would not have stepped out."

"Possibly."

"You roared—"

"Fan-Si!" exclaimed Moglin, most uneasy.

"Well, Moggers, he did! Like a pregnant Quoffa!"

"Fan-Si!"

And I laughed.

We approached the bushes where I'd hidden the voller. I said: "Treat these bushes as possibly concealing an enemy force. Quiet, now."

We'd taken most of the day to march here from the camp and now evening shadows were falling across the land. I felt the airboat to be safely hidden; there was always the chance a Shank patrol had spotted it. Then they'd do what any commander would do: they'd leave the voller there and keep watch, ready to jump on anybody trying to reach her.

We moved forward cautiously. They kept still as I'd trained them, and moved rapidly when they did move. From bush to bush we went forward.

When the voller's hull came in sight, just her prow protruding past a bush ahead, I stopped. I waited. I listened. After a suitable time, with the shadows dropping deeper and deeper, all jade and ruby, I inched forward.

Covered by three bows I reached the voller. Nothing stirred. It took only a few moments to ensure no one kept watch. The voller was clean.

Fan-Si, Moglin the Flatch and Larghos the Throstle stood in a line and stared at the airboat, their mouths hanging open.

Observing the fantamyrrh, I stepped aboard.

"Come along, come along. Get aboard."

"But—"

"Don't lollygag about down there!"

"This is a Shank bird-contraption! We can't—"

"This is an airboat and it belongs to me, for the moment. Now if you want any supper, step aboard. Otherwise I'll fly off without you."

Needless to recite the confusion, the hesitation, the trepidation.

Eventually, the three of them were safely aboard and we could see about supper.

Now it is not my intention to labor the events that followed. My task, as I saw it, was one of observation. Information was vital. We had no reliable reports out of Tarankar proper. And, to give an example of the lack of knowledge of the place held even by those as close as Makilorn—desert robes were not worn here, not in the forests and grasslands. We wore tunics and boleros, low-cut shirts, loose coats, and the predominant color was green with fawn a second favorite. So, I needed to know a lot more about the situation here before a fleet and army could be sent.

This, of course, posed the problem. To obtain that kind of information would entail close contact with the Shanks. At the moment I was attempting to build up the morale of the people, and to give them a leader now that their rulers were gone. I told myself I did this out of the best of reasons. Every blow we struck from ambush was a blow for freedom. We were forming a Liberation Army.

Well, I fancy I knew well enough the real reason why I spent time with the guerilla bands, forming organizations, training, teaching, putting backbone into them. I think I knew only too well why I led ambushes and sieges of isolated forts and dealt with the Fish Heads at that distance.

And—I could always claim what was the truth, that I was building up a dossier of intelligence on the conquerors against the day of liberation.

After the success with the gang led by Nath and Layla, we went on to organize and train and build up morale of four other gangs in various outlying districts. A range of mountains curving away to the southwest gave rise to streams. The valleys were pleasant and not always easy of access. This should be perfect guerilla country. In fact, I made the decision to clear all the Shanks out of this section and use it as the Home Base for the insurrection. Here was where the people readily accepted Prince Chaadur as their leader. At least, he knew what to do, and told and taught them. One or two self-important nobles offered a feeble resistance; my brisk manner swept all those objections aside.

In addition, my own personal band had grown from the first three to a sizeable force. In the final analysis, the voller overawed and impressed everyone, and was my ultimate arbiter.

The mountain and valley section was known as Clovang, the chief city as Clovangjin. Which prompts me to remark that the capital city of Tarankar was Taranjin. One day, I promised myself, one day...

As a matter of simple courtesy I'd insisted on my people taking proper rank titles. As to a hierarchy, they shook themselves out. Moglin the Flatch ran my archery, Larghos the Throstle my men at arms. We had practically no cavalry, for the Shanks recognized the value of draught and saddle animals and had swept so many up that the few that were left were mostly broken down. Fan-Si commanded the small nucleus of Jikai Vuvushis I hadn't the heart to prevent joining us. These three I'd dubbed Jiktars. To keep their heads from swelling too much I'd immediately added they were ob-Jiktars. A Jiktar more or less equates with a regimental commander's rank, and ob, meaning one, is the first and lowest rung of the ladder promotion within the Jiktar grade.

By the time the Shanks reacted vigorously to our activities we'd built up a nice little army formed of four gangs, plus my little band of some hundred souls, making a grand total of nearly eight hundred.

What, I could not help wondering with a deal of amusement, would the Presidio of Vallia, who loved to bestow grandiose titles on the armies we formed, make of the fellow who'd been the Emperor of Vallia and led those armies and their thousands of soldiers proudly declaring that eight hundred not very well armed and equipped folk formed an army?

Little Nikki the Lame first spotted the Shank airboats. He might have a crooked leg; he had the sharpest pair of eyes in the gang—I beg your pardon—in the Tarankar Army of Liberation.

"There they are!" he screamed down from the tallest tower in Clovangjin.

Soon we could all see them, the black hulled craft with their brightly painted squared off upperworks cruising low above the surrounding hills.

In a somber mood I counted—everyone counted. There were ten of them.

The Shanks' flying ships, strangely enough to people of Paz, were uniform. They appeared to have hit on a good design and then simply repeated that single pattern. By contrast, Pazzian vollers and skyships were of all varieties. Up there the sky smiled down, Luz and Walig sending their streaming mingled opaline radiance to bathe the world in wonder, and here foolish mortal men and women were about to try to kill one another. Still, if one couldn't talk or argue with the Shanks, then one must come to the fluttrell's vane.

The city was mostly burned or knocked down. During their first invasion of these peaceful valleys the Shanks had killed the warriors and killed or taken away the people. The city lay empty and silent when we'd marched in. Nikki the Lame after his first warning shout pulled back into the shadows of the tower's broken parapet. Everyone hiding below knew exactly what to do. If anyone showed his or herself, I'd warned them, I'd cut their ears off.

The fliers up there circled, keeping their rigid formation, line astern. The lead ship might be the flagship; she was no different from any of the others. I'd fought these beauties before. Just how many men they could carry was still conjectural, for the Vallian Air Service had met Shank flying ships crewed differently and holding differing numbers of aerial soldiers. Down below we all waited, silent, unmoving. I doubted that a Schtarkin could spot a human eyeball peering through a narrow crack from two thousand feet.

The ships acted in such a manner as to convince me they were scouting the city in case we troublesome guerillas might be here. We struck and vanished, and they must guess we had a bolthole to go to.

As though they'd made up their fishy minds to do the job right, the first fire pots came tumbling down. This was going to be unpleasant, mightily unpleasant, by Krun!

They set fire to a block of houses that had been in relatively good condition. Black smoke rose lazily, almost straight up, there being little breeze. The flames hissed and crackled greedily. Because this danger had been foreseen I'd instructed my army to hide in places that had already been destroyed. No one was being roasted in that block of houses, thank Opaz.

Moglin was holding Fan-Si's tail. The gesture appeared one of affection. I'd told him to make sure the furious Fristle fifi didn't rush out, screaming revenge, and so betray us all.

If she did rush out, Moglin's grip would tighten hard.

The so-called army was scattered about in ruined buildings and caved-in cellars surrounding a fine square, a kyro that was not the main plaza of the city, and each little group had visual contact horizontally with the next. At least, that was the theory. Theory and practice are often not even on nodding acquaintance. One must plan as well as possible, set the whole machine in motion, and then do one's personal best with everything racketing away around in the general confusion.

You may think I've been boasting away about how wonderfully I'd trained up these ragged amateurs into a professional army; of course, it wasn't like that at all. One fact, however, I'd drummed into them. The Shank flying ships were not magical. They were capable of being defeated. They were a factor in the struggle of which to be wary; not of being frightened.

I stole a look at my companions in the gloom of the cellar. There were thirty or so of us packed in. Their faces showed a tightness of lip and a drawing down of eyebrows revealing tension. I did not think I detected fear. Turning back to look out through the crack again, I saw Deb-Lu-Quienyin sitting comfortably with his back against the angle of wall, staring directly into my face. I could see him; the others could not.

"Lahal, Jak. Are you enjoying yourself?"

I smiled and both shook and nodded my head. I didn't fancy what my people would say if Prince Chaadur started talking to thin air. Deb-Lu saw that at once. He pushed his turban straight and said: "There have been delays. As you are aware, the Law of Beng Frust states that when you urgently require an article you cannot find it. In this case it seems the silver boxes chose to go black in droves." He saw the expression on my face. "I agree, Jak. This is Most Distressing News."

He went on: "Farris is moving mountains to re-equip with new silver boxes. The news is not good from Hamal—" Again he saw my face, and hurried on: "Princess Lela and Prince Tyfar are both well." I felt the drain of emotion then. By Zair! What it is to love your children!

He went on to say the Air Service was using voricas, the Vallian sailing ships of the air. "Also, Farris has negotiated with Nedfar for some of their famblehoys. We are putting an Armada together; it is taking time and it is not of the quality we at first imagined."

All the same, whatever the ships, if they carried Vallian fighting men and women, and my lads of the Guard Corps—why, then, we'd smash the Shanks!

Deb-Lu said in his wheezy old voice: "Everyone thrives here in Vallia."

His image began to fade. Expecting him to vanish I gave a tiny nod to indicate the remberee. He thickened, momentarily, for time enough to say: "Your jurukkers are so restive, Farris may have to let them off the leash soon. That young scamp, Rollo the Runner, keeps demanding troops so that he can both follow your instructions and follow you physically."

With that, Deb-Lu winked out and I was staring across the dusty flag-stones of the kyro.

As I thus looked, seeing nothing but the image of Deb-Lu in my retinas, I heard the gasps at my back.

My eyes cleared.

Touching down with elephantine grace the black hulls of two Shank flying ships settled in the centre of the kyro.

Moglin hissed: "Someone has been seen!"

"They know we're here, now," snapped Fan-Si. "That's for sure."

Larghos said: "And here they come!"

From the black hulls like ants from an anthill the Shanks disembarked and formed ranks. Trumpets pealed. They began to march straight for us, weapons glittering, scaled armor glinting, tridents all aligned and their damned fishy shouts lifting: "Ishti! Ishti!"

Sixteen

This was a moment when I'd have welcomed with the utmost fervor the sight of a couple of juruks of my lads of the Guard Corps, yes, by Vox!

As it was, we must hold to the plan and do what we could.

"Bows!" I snapped it out, harsh and flat.

One inestimable advantage we had. Our shootists were Bowmen and Bowmaids of Loh. Naturally, not every inhabitant of Loh is a Bowman.

And not all Bowmen approach even remotely the superb skills of someone like Seg—well, that is a stupidly superfluous remark. There is, in my opinion, and a not so humble opinion at that, no archer in two worlds to rival Seg Segutorio.

These rabbity old thoughts went whirling through my brain as our archers stood up and drew and loosed.

From heaps of rubble, from broken walls, from gap-toothed house fronts, the dustrectium poured in.*

Shafts, as they say in Clishdrin, blackened the sky.

I was up there, shooting in my bow, aiming at the serried ranks of Fish Heads as they trampled forward ready to break into the final charge.

Shanks were screeching and falling, toppling into the dust shafted clear through. Gaps were torn in their ranks. But still they came on. Extraordinarily hardy and tough are Shanks, fierce, merciless, determined to kill or enslave us all.

"Loose! Loose!" I bellowed, plying my bow with that steady flowing rhythm so beautifully exemplified in Seg. I could match my comrade—sometimes, not often—and on this day of such a scrappy affray I shot in such wise as I think might have pleased Seg.

The smell of blood would be rising from the bodies left in the rear of the charge, the stink of raw green ichor, the blood flowing in the veins of the Fish Heads. Their noise increased as they rushed on.

Larghos the Throstle put down his bow. He reached for his strangdja.

I agreed. I let rip one last shot that pierced a Fish Head waving a banner all green and gold, and as he pitched over onto his fishy face I snatched up the trident placed ready to hand.

The two flying ships that had landed to disgorge this bunch lifted off.

There had been, I estimated, something like a hundred and fifty Shank soldiers landed. We had wreaked fearful destruction in them. The survivors screeched on, undeterred, and in the next instant we were at hand strokes.

They tried to clamber over the rubble, to poke their tridents through the gaps through which we had shot. The stinking effluvium of rotten fish gusted over us. We held that first rush. They did not have the strength to overwhelm us in a single impetuous onslaught. We held them and drove them back, and corpses piled up before our defenses.

The instant they fell back I roared: "Bows!"

Once more the sleeting rain of death poured into them.

A swift glance up confirmed my suspicions of their next obvious step—or, rather, next two steps.

Two more flying ships were coasting in for a landing, and two more

---

* Dustrectium: As Kregen has no gunpowder, this is the word used for firepower, from bows, ballistae, catapults, etc. *A.B.A.*

were curving overhead to pass directly above us. From those black hulls the fire pots would tumble down to burn us out.

Well, that last would not be all that easy. The ruins we had chosen were pretty well destroyed, burned shells. We had to hold this next frontal attack. After that, well, I decided to wait to see if we did hold the Fish Heads—or if they swamped us.

Fresh troops disembarked. They formed their rigid lines. The wink and glitter of weapons, the flutter of green and gold flags, the racket of their trumpets—huge conch shells banded in gold—all were calculated to drive us witless with fear. I thought it apt for us to make our presence felt in other ways besides simply killing Shanks.

I roared it out, forcefully, shouting at the enemy.

"Paz! Paz!"

Others took up the cry. We hurled our defiance back in their fishy faces. Then I heard another word being yelled out, a word spurting above the noise, shafting like an arrow at the foe.

"Paz! Chaadur! Paz! Chaadur!"

Well, now...

We shot them as they stormed in again. We cut them down as they tried to get at us. We held them. Good red blood ran to mingle with the green. But we held them.

From around the Kyro arrows fleeted into their ranks. The two fliers lifted off and another two touched down. This time I judged the Shanks put out only fifty men from the two. Maybe that was it. Maybe the other four fliers were fighting ships and not troop carriers. If so, then our chances had been immeasurably increased. Surely, we eight hundred in cover ought to see off four hundred charging across the open?

But, then, these were Shanks doing the charging.

I said to Larghos and Moglin: "We have held them twice. They will come in again, probably two or three times. But they are weaker and growing ever weaker still. You will hold them. I am off to put the final part of the plan into operation."

"Quidang, prince!"

The leaders of the other gangs forming the army knew of the plan. In their heaps of rubble and their barricaded cellars they would fight and kill Shanks whilst I got on with it.

"Fan-Si!" I was brisk. "Bring your half dozen girls and follow me."

Eight of us, we climbed back through the ruined buildings. At the rear a small party under Deldar Tongo the Lash kept lookout. They reported no single sign of an enemy to our rear. I sent them all but two back to reinforce the front.

"That is one thing I've noticed about Schtarkins," I told Fan-Si and her girls as we hauled the branches and leaves away. "They tend to stick to a frontal attack, and to what they've decided. I've an idea the Shants, who are not quite like the Shanks, are more flexible."

Quickly we had the camouflage removed and I jumped up into the voller with a most abbreviated observation of the fantamyrrh. The girls followed smartly. I'd gone through the drills with them a number of times and they knew what to do.

A most careful look up was necessary. I didn't want to rise out of the ruins slap bang under a Shank flier.

Feeling the significance of the occasion I pushed the controls over and we floated up steadily until I could hold her level with the shattered top of the wall. A Shank was just flying past, going towards the Kyro, about two hundred feet above us. I let him go. There were two more being busy dropping fire pots over on the other side. We were in the clear.

Instantly I shoved the levers over to full lift and speed and up we soared into the mingled streaming lights of the Suns of Scorpio.

To breathe clean sweet air again! The stink of the battle blew away from my nostrils. The noise from below flowered up obscenely; but we flew high and fast above in the pure air.

So rapidly we rose, I was able to soar up above that Shank who'd been heading into the square. Fan-Si, very commanding, very strict, hurled the first fire pot.

"Smack in the Heart!" she exclaimed in glee. The Heart is the word often employed in archery-conscious Loh to designate the Chunkrah's Eye.

The Shanks down there were smart. Our fire pot went up and over the side; but Fan-Si's girls were hurling down more and as I drove on towards the other fliers the fellow below us began to burn.

Greasy black smoke wafted away as he turned, trying to find a place to land.

I banged the coaming. "Come on! Come on!" We sprang on, the air buffeting us, and I the only one whose hair rippled in the breeze.

Trust Fan-Si to choose all Fristle fifis for this task!

The Shanks had seen us. They began to rise. Well, now was the time to see if Farris had given me a splendid craft, or only a good one. I knew she was not of the fastest; but in a game like this, maneuver and lift were the key factors, unlike a normal airplane, more like a Harrier.

Hurtling headlong on through thin air I brought the voller across the nearest Shank as he rose. Arrows flicked up and fell away. The short Shank bows were of little use in these conditions, no matter how effective they might be from the Shank sailing ships of the oceans. The fifis dropped firepots. The second Fish Face burned.

Now we were over the kyro. Down there Shank bodies strewed the flagstone everywhere. The quick decision made, I turned slightly to get at the third Shank aloft; the two on the ground would have to wait.

I yelled: "Look around for the other ships. There should be five."

Fan-Si shrieked: "I cannot see them!"

"Well, we'll have this shint before us first." With that our voller crossed clear along the Shank from stern to stem and the fire pots burned down.

Back we turned, a slewing broadside turn in the air, and went haring back across the kyro.

The fliers down there attempted to get off. They did not succeed.

They burned.

Now we could give our full attention to the search for the remaining five Shank flying ships.

Fan-Si spotted three of them, at last, going fast and low over the ground some way off, heading away from the city.

"What in a Herrelldrin Hell are they up to?" I growled.

Then I saw. Beneath the Shanks tiny dots ran and stumbled, and fell.

One of the gangs had broken and fled. I did not know who commanded, nor did I really wish to know, not then.

"The last two!" I roared. "Where the hell are they?"

This time Finsi the Silver cried out, pointing. Yes, there they were, flying high and fast, heading northeast.

"They're running!" I exclaimed in wonder.

All I could do now was drive as fast as possible after the three fliers tormenting the Pazzians on the ground as they fled.

Many dots lay on the grass and did not move.

We soared on and I climbed up for altitude.

"Report fire pot situation."

Fan-Si, instantly, said: "We have twenty left."

Good girl! She was a capital first lieutenant!

The three Shanks ahead were rising. They circled once, and I tensed as their prows pointed towards us. They continued their swing until their sterns showed. Then they flew away.

The only explanation I could find for this odd conduct was that they'd lost their landing force entirely, and suspected there were more aerial forces on our side about to be committed. After all, we'd popped up out of nowhere, giving them an almighty shock. They'd weighed their chances. They'd lost their landing force and half their aerial force. They might be rigid and might blindly follow through a plan once committed; in this situation they had the sense to know when to pull out.

I stood at the controls, easing the speed down, and watched the Fish Heads as they flew off. I know my face bore a brooding malevolent look of intolerant determination. They might have gone for now; they'd be back!

When they did, we'd either have to be a long way away, or be ready for them.

Gently I swung the voller back to the ruined city of Clovangjin.

A lot of clearing up would be necessary. There would be pain at good folk dead. Dulled though that pain might be by our undeniable victory, the agony would remain.

Somberly I brought the voller to earth at the side of the kyro. Larghos, Moglin, a whole crowd of people flooded out, flocking about us, cheering and waving their weapons. Someone yelled: "Hai, Jikai!" and that great cry was taken up until the square rang with sound. That jubilant noise rose above the stink of blood, both red and green, over the strewn bodies, Shanks and Pazzians, soared up like a benediction.

Hai Jikai!

Seventeen

"Shank ships lie shattered, fly scattered,
over the burning land:
Fish Faces fall fear-filled
as Chaadur our Chief has planned."

Thus sang Larghos the Throstle, warbling a spritely tune for so doggerel a verse. Still, I felt his stanzas might improve with time and polishing. The most important factor was simply that these people were able to sing about their exploits. A legend was in the making.

All the same, even if this little gang calling itself an army was in the legend-fabricating business, we couldn't hang around Clovangjin much longer. If I knew my Shanks—as I did, I did, to my sorrow!—they'd be back mob-handed.

The survivors of the gang that had broken were rounded up and parceled out among the other gangs. I took pains to impress upon these folk the example thus set: "Turn your back on an enemy and you're done for." I was now deliberately bringing down the inflated image of Prince Chaadur, deflating the pompousness. I spoke hard. "You have proved you can beat Shanks. Next time you fight 'em, remember that."

So, now, we marched in the blaze of the suns, singing of our victory.

Clovangjin lay to our rear; our faces were turned towards the mountains. Had we hung around the ruined city the Shanks would surely have discovered us. This time they'd arrive in overwhelming numbers. Quite apart from the little fact that we'd all be dead or slaves, a defeat for this army now would set back my plans. To clear the entire mountain and valley area out I saw, belatedly, was for the moment beyond our strength. Patience, growing strength, more patience and then the time to strike—all very well and laudable in guerrillas.

That whole process was going to be far too slow for me.

Having got the show on the road, I turned back to the city where the voller nestled hidden in the rubble. Flying on over the column I looked down to see my little army trudging along, waving up to me, very blasé about airboats now. I smiled. Scouting ahead and keeping a most wary eye open for the first sight of tiny dots in the sky in any direction, I soon picked a likely spot for our first camp. Setting the flier down between bushes I trusted she'd be safe until I returned, then I started back for the army.

Fan-Si wanted to mock me for slogging along in the dust with them when I could have waited for them to turn up and guided them the last few ulms. Moglin tut-tutted. Larghos had stopped singing, and now he said: "My throat is drier than the Glarkie Dunes." This was one of the names given to the desert to the east over She of the Sundering. Larghos went on: "If anyone should ride in the boat of the air it should be the musical artist."

Someone threw a small pebble at him, and we all laughed.

Still, Larghos had a point.

I said: "I would gladly ferry you all in relays. But there are two reasons against that. One is that continuous flying is going to attract unwelcome attention." I stared back at the people following; none of them offered a comment. "The other is that you'll get fat and lazy if you fly everywhere. You must toughen your muscles and learn endurance."

Fan-Si's comment, I suppose, could be rendered in a very weak terrestrial play on words, so that I could report she said: "Endurance, yeah, en-durance vile."

No one threw a stone at the Fristle fifi.

We made camp just as the twin suns sank, illuminating the rocks and gulleys with a medley of greens and reds, streaming long shadows, and concealed our cook fires with slabs of rock. Sentries stood watch and watch as normal. By the morning when we breakfasted cold, everyone lay in good hidden positions. No one spoke. As the morning wore on so the tension grew. Luz and Walig scaled the Kregen sky. A few wisps of vapor coiled and disappeared. Beetles and insects scuttled over the ground.

The Shanks appeared just after the hour of mid.

Twenty-five fliers, black-hulled, purposeful, cruised over the ruined city. One interesting fact was on offer here. Some of the fliers up there differed slightly from their fellows. Not by much, true, but by enough to suggest they had been built for a different purpose. They flew a patrol circle, gradually widening the diameters, checking every inch below.

I suppose everyone of us held his or her breath when a Shank flew directly overhead. I know I did, by Krun!

So, as I thus cowered in a hole in the ground, I reflected with not a little ironic humor that the stories and legends of Dray Prescot painted him as a hero larger than life. Heroic stature, grandeur of character, nobleness of deed—oh, yes, my fine feathered friend Dray Prescot! Hiding in a hole in the ground!

All the same, all the same, by Vox! I didn't stand up and shake my sword at the Fish Heads in block-headed defiance. I stayed in my little hole.

From experience, we Pazzians knew the Shanks flew Extermination Patrols. The country of Tarankar formed a mixture and variety of prospects, from the tall mountains to the coastal plains and bluffs. Forests clothed much of the land, streams wended their ways into rivers and so to the sea. The Fish Heads kept the people they required to slave for them and the rest they killed. The country was not teeming with Freedom Fighters. There were scattered bands, and little armies like ours, and sometimes, to the shame of Paz, these forces fought among themselves. Where food is hard to come by, allegiances and loyalties tend to go to the wall. I'd managed to combine these gangs into a cohesive whole. But our strength remained pitiful.

So, thus somberly brooding, I watched the last of the flying ships wheel and depart. The last black hull vanished beyond the hills.

Fan-Si stood up, breathing deeply. "The shints!"

"Aye," agreed Moglin the Flatch, and he stood up and put his arm about her waist.

This summation accorded well with our position. The plans would have to change, to adapt to the realities, instead of being based on my high-flown ideas of what I might achieve alone.

We resumed our trek. Because the Fish Heads had found no one on this patrol did not mean they would not look again. Clovang was no longer a friendly spot for Freedom Fighters.

Over the next sennight we marched secretly. We had enough food and we found good water. I put on a brave face. By this I mean I encouraged the little army, taught them, shouted at them, told them that the day of reckoning would arrive. I did not tell them that I intended to leave very soon. We experienced one tussle, a fleeting moment of combat, in which, short though it was, we lost twenty-five people. It happened in this wise: I had taken the voller up to scout a pass ahead through a cliff wall leading to an escarpment. The Shank flier was just about to lift off from beside a grove of trees as I appeared over the crest, for I was flying low.

Fan-Si did not wait for orders.

Instantly, she had struck fire and was hurling down the firepots.

Swinging the voller back in a tight *renversement*, the second volley already ready, we crossed the Shank again. He nosedived for the ground.

Black smoke poured aft and flames blew back from his afterparts.

We could see the Fish Heads jumping off the hull like black ants. They were making efforts to douse the blaze. Fan-Si tickled them up again with expertly flung pots. A sickly stink of charring fish floated up.

Moglin, beside his fifi, drew back his bow.

I said: "You will waste arrows at this distance, Moggers. We must contain them until the army arrive."

It was perfectly clear our scouts would see the smoke and would bring on the vanguard.

When eventually our small force of outriders came galloping over the crest, the short sharp combat ensued.

The great Lohvian longbows spat their deadly shafts. Shanks fell, just as the song said. They fought back, and we lost those twenty-five good men and women.

When it was all over and the Shank flying ship had burned herself out, we discovered a single miserable apim cowering in a bush perilously close to the blackened hulk. His face was black, too, and he coughed up the smoke, his eyes streaming. Still, that proximity had saved him.

"Doms, doms!" he cried, retching, shaking. "I did not dare believe!"

We gave him water to drink and slowly he recovered his wits. He wore only a tattered scrap of dirty cloth around his loins, and his lean body was whipmarked. He said he was Winkal, known as the Horknik, and he gave us thanks and praise to the True Trog Himself for his miraculous rescue.

He explained his presence aboard the enemy flier. "They sometimes take slaves to minister to their wants. They do not much care for the land."

This accorded with what we knew of the Shanks, a sea-faring race.

His task, he said, aboard the Shank was to ply his trade. He was a fletcher.

Moglin snorted: "Aye! The damned evil shints! They know by now the power of Bowmen of Loh!"

Winkal nodded wearily. "They recognize good fletching when they see it, may Matazar the Bow rot 'em."

By this I gathered he had tried to build inferior shafts and been striped for his duplicity.

We found a secure campsite for the night and burned fires for the shortest time necessary to cook our suppers. Sentries prowled. Winkal, with a Kregan-sized meal in him for the first time in many a moon, told us of conditions in Taranjin. The tale was horrific; but not more so than we had come to expect of the devilish Fish-headed Shanks.

"They can't tell us apart," he said around a mouthful of palines. "They just keep everyone locked up in compounds. Except us tradesfolk, of course. Them poor glahbers."*

He spoke remarkably coherently after the horrors through which he had passed. He shook his head, still sickened by the sights he had witnessed. Yet he felt more sorrow for the people used as general slaves. Herded in like cattle, half-starved, beaten, they were dragged out when required. The Shanks were not stupid, in these matters as in others. Recognizing the

---

* poor glahbers: equates with 'poor devils'. An expression of pity. *A.B.A.*

superiority of the Lohvian longbow they employed bowyers and fletchers and treated them fractionally better than the common slaves. Other trades were employed – stylors, blacksmiths, hostlers. They cooked their own food.

Moglin said in his hissing catman's voice: "If they think to make Bowmen of Loh of themselves they are onkers!" He laughed, a sizzling sound of mockery. "We all know how long it takes to make a longbowman."

Whilst what he said was true enough, this was just another headache to be added to the list of migraines inflicting Paz.

I said: "Larghos—a song, an' you will."

"Right readily, prince, right readily."

He, like us all, had no love of dwelling overlong on the miseries and horrors of life now the Shanks had arrived.

He sang of the love of Ornol the Wayfarer and Vilia the Fair, and of how the village farrier's jealousy overcame him, so that this Dien-sing the Droopeyed struck Ornol the Wayfarer, struck him down in cold blood. And of how Vilia took up her father's sword, and marched the length of the village street, head up, proud, carrying the sword which was called Dalendin. Of how the villagers all peered under their hands at this beautiful girl striding down the village street with the naked brand in both hands. How she struck Dien-sing the Droopeyed so that he fell back, wounded, crying out for mercy, and of how Vilia the Fair despaired of vengeance, and kicked him away. And of how Vilia the Fair bravely put the brand to her own throat, kneeling over the body of Ornol the Wayfarer, and so sliced the soft flesh and of how the first drop of blood fell upon her love and his eyes opened and he sat up and clasped her in his arms, putting away the great sword Dalendin and her wound healed and so they remained fast locked while Dien-Sing the Droopeyed crawled away, sobbing.

When the great song finished everyone sat silently, wrapped in private thoughts. Yes, I thought to myself, yes, Vilia is a heroine of Kregen.

After that we sang a few of the more raucous ditties of Paz and managed to convince ourselves we were a rousing band of right tearaways.

Still, I thought of the Song of Ornol and Vilia, and then forced away unpleasant thoughts and joined in the chorus of "No idea at all, no idea at all!"

Then Rafe the Ponshim recited the tale of Arngalf Galfarn, a warrior mighty among men, obsessed with love of women, who was tested by his god, Schnurrdun the All-seeing. If Arngalf Galfarn would renounce the love of women for a whole year and a day, and devote everything to the worship of his god, Schnurrdun the All-seeing would reward him in a way that would astonish the world of Kregen for ever. So Arngalf Galfarn accepted the contract. His rewards in this life would be great; but the greatest gift by far that Schnurrdun the All-seeing would lavish on him was this—that after his death his body would be carried up into the heavens, and his bones and blood and flesh would receive the blessed breath of the All-seeing and become stars. In the sky, blazing for ever, would be the constellation of Arngalf Galfarn the Faithful. At this point in his tale Rafe the Ponshim paused to moisten his mouth. We all recognized the story-teller's touch of suspense.

He resumed his tale on the last day of Arngalf Galfarn's trial. On that day baleful fate decreed that the most beautiful girl ever seen in the kingdom should meet Arngalf Galfarn's eye and the two should immediately fall passionately in love, shafted by the same lightning bolt, as they say on Kregen. On the next day Schnurrdun the All-seeing summoned Arngalf Galfarn more in sorrow than in anger.

"You have failed to demonstrate that you love me more than women."

"I love you more than women, Schnurrdun the All-seeing. It was just one part of my body that betrayed me. This I swear on the grave of Nath the Graintjid whom I slew after three days of combat."

"Then instead of your entire body being a constellation, I, Schnurrdun the All-seeing, shall cast that betraying part of you up to be a single shining star."

Arngalf Galfarn smiled, for he saw generations yet unborn would point to that star and recall his name, and speak of him with awe. Here Rafe the Ponshim once more sipped to moisten his mouth. Everyone sat around, absorbed in this tale, as old as Kregen itself, so it was said.

"You smile, Arngalf Galfarn. Yes, your name will be remembered. The star will shine. I am merciful; but you failed me. I shall cast up the betraying part of your body to shine forever." The brows of the god drew together in a bar of justice. "I shall cast it up now."

The tales relate Arngalf Galfarn lived to be a very very old man.

We all looked up to see Galfarn's star shining away up there. There is a certain piquancy about this tale rather lacking, one feels, in a frozen big toe being cast up to become the Morning Star.

After a few final songs, the cups were drained, and we turned in. I found myself pondering on the song of Ornol and Vilia, very often called the Song of Dalendin. Yes, it did demonstrate the evils and the virtues of frail humanity. Quite clearly, it came from a different poetic tradition from the ancient tale of Arngalf Galfarn. Then, with my accustomed last thought, I went to sleep.

The very next day I told them.

Their dismay would have melted a heart of stone; it failed to move me. After their wailing protestations died away I stared at them, broodingly, and, I fancy, with a considerable quantity of sheer dominant arrogance. "You will fight on bravely. I am no longer needed. If you follow my precepts, seek always to hit and run, and only hit when you may afterwards run, maintain your food supplies, remain in good heart, nothing can defeat you. In the dawning of the Day I shall call you." My face bore down hard on them. "In that great Day of Calling you will be ready."

"Aye," they shouted. "Aye, Prince Chaadur, our Chief. We will!"

There was more fustian, more reassuring than bombastic, and then I said: "It is laid upon me to go into Taranjin itself—"

The uproar burst into a storm of protest. They shrieked and danced about abandoned to anticipatory fears. I saw an old lady, leaning on her spear, and the tears running thickly down her cheeks. Others were cater-wauling away. They knew that to venture into the city where the Shanks ruled was to go to death.

I bellowed over their outcry. "I shall live!" Mind you, I wasn't at all sure about that, by Krun! "There are things I must know about the Fish Faces. It is a doom laid on me that I cannot evade."

In the end they saw they could not sway me from my avowed purpose.

So, feeling suddenly light-headed, aloof, almost that dire feeling one has marching into the Arena, I observed the fantamyrrh, stepped aboard the voller and took off.

"Remberee!" I called down as the wind rush tore past.

"Remberee!" they shrieked up. "Remberee, Prince Chaadur na Dorfu, Chaadur the Striker, Kurinfaril, our Chief, remberee!"

The voller swept up into the mingled radiance of the declining suns and as the jade and ruby shadows streamed over the coaming a lambent blue fire grew about me and I stared up into the gigantic bloated shape of the phantom Scorpion of the Star Lords.

Eighteen

There was just time for me to bellow up: "You nurdling great onker! Don't drop me this time, you fumble-tentacled apology for a Scorpion!" before I went hurtling headlong into a purple-tinged mist of blue infinity.

Twice, three times, I rolled head over heels along wooden planking. Gasping, I sat up to see I was in a narrow, double-ended craft bobbing upon a blue sea under a shining silver sky.

All around stretched sparkling water. A faint zephyr blew across the deck. The boat was upflung, curved of line, with benches for a single bank of oarsmen along each side. She was similar to those swift piratical dwapri-jjers that pester the trade among the Ivilian Keys. The scent of the sea mingled with her own smells of wood and tar, and the breeze bore in the fresh tang of ozone and seaweed.

I stood up. She was some seventy feet long, and narrow with it, and I looked about for a fellow mariner and saw none. I was alone aboard her.

A voice, harsh, clanging, resonant, said: "So you have finally come to answer for your misdeeds, Dray Prescot."

I whirled about. I saw no one.

"Your get onker of a Scorpion dropped me!" I felt maltreated. "The great fumble-tentacled idiot!"

"Yet you disobeyed our express commands."

I compressed my lips. I was without clothes or weapons. I took a breath and in a more reasonable tone, said: "I interpreted your commands to prevent tragedy and to bring success. Kirsty is queen in Tsungfaril."

"It is not for you to interpret. It is for you to obey."

"I did what you wanted, you—you." I puffed out my cheeks, drew another ragged breath, and then burst out: "You wanted to murder young Leone in a most disgusting fashion! You are just a bunch of ancient murderers!"

A silence ensued.

Then: "We are well able to see your point of view. We understand. But does that alter your misdeeds?"

If that was what the Everoinye intended to harp on all the time, there seemed little chance for me. A most curious sensation grew in my inward parts, a feeling of nausea, of regret and farewell, and the overpoweringly savage desire to see Delia again, and clasp her in my arms for the last time, overwhelmed me.

Yet, I remained standing, head up, staring up into that blank and indifferent silver sky.

The boat rocked, the breeze blew, the scents twined about my nostrils. In all that vast expanse only this little boat contained a speck of life. And that poor benighted life was like to be snuffed out in the next heartbeat.

When the silence became unbearable, I opened my mouth to yell, and in that self-same instant the rasping voice spoke again.

"In our infinite wisdom and mercy, Dray Prescot, prince of onkers, we have decided to pardon you. Your crimes will be forgotten. There is work to your hands."

"I know that. I have to go to Taranjin and try to chuck those rotten Shanks out of Tarankar."

"No, Dray Prescot. We cannot permit you to throw your life away."

Whilst I was not quite dumbfounded by this remarkable statement, I admit it startled me. Once or twice the Star Lords had actively intervened to prevent me from being killed. Very few times, though, by Vox! Usually, they did not appear to care if I lived or died.

Speaking as clearly as I could, I outlined the plan. "I must get the slaves to unite. When they rise, the Freedom Fighters will move in from the surrounding country and matters will be arranged so that the armadas from

Vallia and Hamal arrive at the same time. Together, we should beat the Fish Heads."

The voice showed a casual contempt that bit like acid.

"You call that a plan?"

"All right, you supercilious bunch of—of—" I hauled up, and managed to finish unpleasantly: "What is your wonderful plan then?"

"We have placed Kirsty as queen in Tsungfaril. Our work here is done. There is a task for you in Boromir of the Ashes."

I just didn't believe this. "What of Mevancy? What of Caspar the Peaker?"

"Their tasks have been laid down."

"If we want to get rid of the Shanks what better place than here in Tarankar? We must prevent them from establishing themselves so strongly we may not have the force to eject them. This invasion is the most serious we've seen so far."

Again a break occurred in this bizarre conversation and only the shushing sounds of the sea slapping the strakes of the boat broke the silence.

A voice I could almost have sworn differed by a tone of hoarseness from the first said: "That is a point."

"We have work for him to do; if he goes to Taranjin he will die."

"He may not."

"Because he is Dray Prescot, and has the yrium?"

I yelled out then: "You don't think I want to risk my neck, do you? It's our best chance. We can't just attack blindly; we must know what we face in Taranjin."

The boat bobbed up and down. A silver fish, gleaming and magnificent, leaped in a graceful arc and plunged back into the waves.

Mind you, if the Everoinye decided I was not to go to Taranjin, I'd be the first to give thanks, joyful in my release. I wouldn't mind, in those circumstances, going to this damned Boromir of the Ashes, wherever in a Herrelldrin Hell that was.

The distant sound as of voices in an adjoining room swelled through the air. I could understand nothing of what was being said and then, at the tail end, almost as an afterthought, a voice I was convinced belonged to another Star Lord, said: "Send Strom Irvil."

Strom Irvil! I did not burst out laughing. Well, if that ferocious and cantankerous numim went, I'd wish him well of it.

"Very well, Dray Prescot. You have convinced us your argument is sound. This is a decision not lightly taken."

By the pustular nose and decayed fangs of Makki Grodno! I bet it wasn't! The Star Lords had changed their minds. They'd heeded what a mere mortal said. This was indeed a marvel.

They went on: "You may meet a man called Wulk. Listen to him."

With that the boat rose up out of the water and sailed up into the remote blaze of that distant silver sky.

Holding on grimly, dreading that the blue Scorpion would swoop down to snatch me up—and drop me—I just hoped Ahrinye wasn't around.

The boat became cloaked in mist. I felt clammy tendrils swirl about me. My breath fluttered short in my throat. It was hard to breathe.

Now the boat turned, lazily, swinging about, and abruptly, horribly, plunged downwards. Down and down we went and my ears went bang! and I clung on and a shining green sea opened beneath me. A coastline wended away to one side with a sprawling port with walls and towers, and ships floating in the harbor. I stared sickly. Shank ships!

The boat struck the sea in a long gliding motion that cleaved a clean path through the water. We surged on under the momentum of that stupendous fall. Straight as an arrow shot, the boat lanced for the entrance to the harbor, past the pharos, past the Akhram, swinging smoothly to fetch up against the quayside. I was staring at huge stones festooned with green growths, and weeds trailing in the still water, and iron bolts, and chains hanging down. Slimy stone steps led upwards. Perforce, I disembarked and climbed the stairs. I stepped boldly forth onto the quay to see squads of human slaves toiling, carrying bales, hauling ropes, and idly attentive guards using whips carelessly to drive on the hapless slaves. All the guards were Shanks.

No one took any notice of me.

As, somewhat bemused, I stood there like a loon, a glinting glance of golden and scarlet fire flew at my head. I ducked.

"You onker of onkers, Dray Prescot!"

There flew the Gdoinye, brilliant, in his coat of scarlet feathers, the golden feathers around his neck blinding in the suns light. The accipiter, messenger and spy of Star Lords, swooped about me. I knew no one else could see him.

His raucous caw mocked me. "You are invisible, they cannot see you. But if you do not move as fast as Karishmer of the Lightning Bolt... You have just five murs. Run, onker, run!"

I shook my fist at him. I wore a dingy breechclout of sorts that had once been gray and was now merely dirty. He flew up there, magnificent in his scarlet and gold, cawing down his mockery.

"All right, you Bird of Ill Omen. I'll run. And one day I'll pluck your feathers and have you for dinner."

His coarse racking caw could only have been the laughter of a raptor of the Everoinye. His wings beat and he soared aloft and vanished. I made a dead run for the warehouses lining the rear of the quay. By Zair! But this day's happenings were adding pages of information to the book I made in my head concerning the Star Lords! Pages and pages!

As I dived into the welcoming shadows I wondered if the Everoinye had lost faith in their phantom blue Scorpion. That boat, was that a Scorpion replacement?

I wished now I'd taken more notice of the craft. What, for instance, might lie concealed beneath the deck?

Then there was no time for idle reflections of great and puissant super-beings as a surly voice hailed me.

"Hey, you cretin! What d'you think you're doing, hey?"

Turning about sharply I saw the fellow, miserable and slave like me. He was a Rapa, with draggling feathers and a lop-sided beak. He rattled on: "Get away from there, onker!"

He beckoned me away from the doors. We moved further into the shadows among sacks and bales. Everything stank of fish.

"I," I said, assuming even here there would be a command structure, "am looking for the overseer." One of the Kregish ways of expressing this is, as you know, the Wielder of the Balass Rod.

"Naghan the Marbut." The Rapa sniffed through that bent beak. "Well, by Rhapaporgolam the Reiver of Souls! You won't find the shint out there."

This was a start. I'd picked up a name cheaply. We continued to walk through the aisles between the stinking bales. And then, with the force of a gut punch, I recognized and cringed at my stupendous folly. Here I was, pitching myself headlong into this hell on earth, voluntarily shoving my head into the dragon's mouth. And I needn't have done, in all, to outward seeming, honor. My little army of Freedom Fighters had begged me not to go. The Star Lords had ordered me not to go. I didn't want to go. By Zair! I wished then, in that fish-stinking warehouse, I wished with all my heart that I was out of it, that I hadn't chosen this path. I wished fervently that the Everoinye would stoop down and pluck me out of it—*now!*

I, Dray Prescot, Pur Dray, Krozair of Zy and Lord of Strombor—I dreaded the future that I had brought on myself. I wanted out. I wanted to go back to that double-ended boat and accept the other mission of the Star Lords. I felt goose pimples over my body. I felt the dampness along my forehead. I'd acted as the great and puissant superhero, the hero of myth and legend, the impossibly shining knight *sans peur et sans reproche*.

Had I then fallen under the illusion of my own legend? By the stupendous backside and stringy hair of the Divine Lady of Belschutz! What an incredible onker I was! Why should I go off and do this daft thing when I could have whistled across to Boromir of the Ashes—wherever away that happened to be—and then make top speed back to Vallia and Valka? I did not groan as I walked through that fishy stench following the Rapa. No, I did not. Not quite.

Now as you know this marvelous memory bestowed on me by the Savanti nal Aphrasöe, the mortal but superhuman men and women of the Swinging City, enables me to reproduce verbatim conversations of seasons upon seasons ago between persons long dead. That, undeniably, to a fellow trying to tell a plain story is priceless. But, mercifully, the eidetic memory shuts down at times.

I do remember horror.

I do remember, over and over again, cursing myself for the greatest fool on two planets for even dreaming of venturing into Taranjin among the Fish Faces.

I do remember that I saw things I will not mention.

I do not remember—rather, the memories are buried so deep that even ghastly nightmares fail to recall them—I do not recall much of that sojourn in Taranjin.

When we had boldly ventured into the town of Gorlki in Menaham, on the island of Pandahem, Nath the Impenitent, Seg and me, we had thought to see the final scenes of human degradation. Orso Frentar had shared our opinion.*

I'd slaved in the Black Marble Quarries of Zenicce. I'd slaved for the Overlords of Magdag in the City of the Megaliths. I'd slaved in the Heavenly Mines. I'd slaved in other places and other times. Oh, yes, Dray Prescot knew what slavery meant.

That was the later part of the reasons why Delia and I so abhorred slavery and rooted it out in our dominions and by argument and precept attempted to suppress it in the realms of our friends.

Unless slavery is worked in certain ways it leads to stagnation. The Shanks didn't care for libertarian philosophy. They needed certain tasks performed, and they used humans of Paz to do the work and if they died, what of that? There were always plenty more to be rounded up.

As to the humans themselves—they existed in holes and warrens, constantly in fear, scraping their bread off the pavements, living in the atbars of the backstreets. When they were called on to work they received a few scraps of food. I call them humans in contradistinction to the Shanks. But, of course, Shanks as intelligent living entities were humans, too. They were different from us. They couldn't tell one apim from another, one Fristle from his brother, two Rapas apart. They could tell the difference between a numim and an apim, a Brokelsh and a Khibil. Yet I know during that period of horror I forgot Shanks were a part of humanity. I wished only to see the world of Kregen rid of them forever.

Their idea of slave management sounded excellent—when a Pazzian worked for them he or she received food. There were queues at the workgates and the dockyards in the morning. The tradespeople worked independently in their smithy, or fletching arrows or building bows. They were fed according to their production. All this appeared a sound scheme.

---

* See Dray Prescot volume 37, being volume 4 of the Witch War Cycle, *Warlord of Kregen. A.B.A.*

I do remember one meeting in the atbars where I was reduced to screaming at the slaves, at folk like myself, trying to rouse them, trying to knit them into a cohesive force to resist, to rise on The Day.

The work was exhausting.

Using my skills—which Seg has honed and still mocks me for—I managed to get taken on as a bowyer. This meant I could eat on a relatively regular scale. Not so many of the slaves in the atbars. I saw people creeping along the streets, collapse and die, there in the gutter. And other folk walking past, clutching the last of their bread. Useless to give my small portion of rations away. I could not duplicate the loaves and fishes. Despite the agony of selfishness assailing me I had to eat, I had to remain as strong as I could be, so that I might go on. If I died, then what little hope these folk had would be gone.

And if you accuse me of megalomania, of imagining myself the bright shining and indispensable hero, then you are sadly adrift, my friends.

So, as you see, horror can become so great that it cancels itself out.

I do not believe even the most salacious reader could endure what I have not related.

Yet, at that time, during all that dreadful time, and despite my desire to rid the world of every last Shank blighting the face of Kregen, I still persisted in a tiny sane portion of my brain in the belief that Shanks were humans, too. They did what they did because they didn't think, didn't understand. If I could, as it were, convert a Fish Face instead of slaying him—wouldn't that be what Opaz, for one, would require?

That, I was realist enough to realize, was for the far future.

Taranjin had not been an affluent capital city. Oh, surely, there were the rich areas festooning their hills with private villas and sumptuous public palaces. The rulers, members of the riffim race of diffs, now dead and gone, had crushed all other life forms. The king's palace sprawled on a high bluff, like a lop-sided chocolate cake, grotesquely adorned. Within its lowering walls the resident Shanks now lorded it over Tarankar.

After a time the fish stinks simply became a part of the background, a part of everyday existence. People to whom I talked one day were gone, never to return, by the next. Fear stalked the streets. The compounds of the slaves continuously gave off that long low moaning of suffering that tears a person's insides out. No, this was not a happy place or a happy time.

The institution of slavery can be more abominable within one culture than another, so it is said. Dwelling on past misfortunes is, also, said to alleviate the present. I'd suffered in the Heavenly Mines, in Magdag, in the Black Marble Quarries of Zenicce. When Hunch, Nodgen and I had ventured into Moderdrin, the Humped Land, to go adventuring among Moders and Monsters, we'd been the slaves of Tarkshur the Lash. Tarkshur was a Kataki, low-browed, snaggle-toothed, with flaring nostrils and thick black hair, heavily oiled and curled. Katakis are man managers, slave masters. They have a long sinuous tail to which they strap six inches of daggered steel. You seldom see a Kataki as a slave or a mercenary or doing an honest job. They are slavers. And they are universally hated, called greeshes by the poor glahbers they enslave, torture, sell or kill.

The strange fact that when you think of someone they often turn up almost immediately is not so strange, really, given the unknown powers of the human mind. During that frightful trip down the Moder among traps and monsters I'd met Prince Tyfar and got to know Deb-Lu-Quienyin much better. So, on a raw evening when I'd slouched back exhausted from a small gathering where I'd explained what we should do, I saw the pallid figure of Deb-Lu waiting for me. He looked concerned, his face alarmed, and my heart sank.

"Deb-Lu. You look dreadful—what bad news do you bring?"

"I look dreadful! Jak! Jak! I am concerned over you—you look half dead—"

"I'll survive—just."

The tiny mud brick hut which was for the moment my home cramped in on all sides, one among rows beyond the atbars. There were rudimentary necessities needed for living. The stink of fish permeated everything—and I didn't notice it any more.

"I Remain Doubtful. Still. And, yes, I do bring some bad news."

I waited stoically.

What had happened was bad but nowhere near as bad as it could have been. The severe hold up of production of the materials for the silver boxes in Hamal coupled with the blackening of many of the boxes already installed in vollers and skyships meant a drastic reduction in aerial strength. The bad situation in Pandahem, where the Bloody Menahem continued their senseless and merciless attacks, drained aerial strength away to that theatre. A contingent had flown to Mehzta and I could not in all conscience object, for those fliers would be directly fighting Shanks.

My Guard Corps had, having become at last impossible to hold back, taken a gaggle of vorlcas and gone sailing off south.

"And there were no vollers in the fleet, Deb-Lu?"

"One. A small eight placer for emergencies."

Contrary winds had driven my lads well off course. They'd struggled back and become embroiled in a fight with a small squadron of Shanks. I gave thanks the Fish Faces were in small numbers; their black-hulled fliers could dance rings around our vorlcas, dependent as the latter were on the breeze for forward motion. The fight ended indecisively and our fleet had landed to effect repairs. They would not take long, Deb-Lu said, to get airborne again.

"So that means the armada from Hamal will arrive first."

Deb-Lu gave me their composition and numbers and I shook my head.

"This was what we did not want. Forty-five ships—h'mm. It may be needful, Deb-Lu, for you to contact Kapt Hamish ham Thanstrer." I hated what I was saying, I detested the words as they fell from my lips. "I think it will be necessary to hold off the Hamalese Armada until all our ships can strike as one."

By these words I was condemning myself to longer sennights of this hell.

And, of course, it wasn't just me. If we wanted to gather all our forces to strike together then we'd all suffer, all of us here, suffer under the Opaz-forsaken lash of the Shanks, Djan rot 'em!

Nineteen

"*Grak! Grak!*"

The hateful word cracked out over the meaty sounds of whips and cries of pain. The thoughtless cruelty all about had driven many folk insane. The survivors worked and did what was commanded—and ate.

There is quite enough cruelty in two worlds. There is no need for me to belabor the point in my narrative, no need gratuitously to add to the catalogue of horrors poor suffering mankind and womankind must endure.

When you have seen two naked women, both mothers of young babes, fighting, clawing, scratching, biting, over a rotten fish head in the gutter, then, my friend, you do not lightly talk of horrors.

The Shank guards had evidently been chosen from those Fish Faces who by threatening gesture and the use of a few words of command in Kregish could keep control of the slaves and indicate their tasks. The dominant factor obsessing everyone was food. To control a populace into doing your bidding the plan is first to weaken them so that a revolt will be doomed before it has begun and then so to keep them half-starving and subjected that they will slave until they drop for a morsel to pass between their lips.

There were many, in truth, and I saw them, who simply refused to accept the situation, refused to work and so starved to death if they were not earlier shipped off to the Ice Floes of Sicce with a Shank trident through their guts.

Having a trade in your hands in Taranjin those days was like having a passport through hell to life.

Even so, Lao-Chan the Staver was summarily dispatched because he built one too many longbows that would not shoot true.

What Moglin the Flatch, our comrade Fristle Bowman, had said remained true. I caught a glimpse, one day when I was delivering a parcel of bowstaves, of a squad of Fish Faces trying to shoot in their longbows. They were making a sorry hash of the business. Shafts stuck in the log wall at the far end of the butts and precious few even stuck in the straw targets. I kept as quiet as a woflo and delivered the staves and so scuttled back out of the barracks. The building had once been a proud palace of a riffim noble.

That was the day's work of the evening, I remember, when I called the Brokelsh, Bargrad the Pellin, the Fristle, Foke the Clis, and the apim, Nath the Rumpador, to meet in that dolorous little hut These three, it seemed to me, were the most promising.

I told them an Armada was on its way. I had to arrange for a signal to be made to the Freedom Fighters outside Taranjin. On the Day, I said, on the Day of Deliverance, we must strike.

"The people will not rise," said the Brokelsh in his uncouth way. His black body bristle looked gray. "They are broken in the ib."

"That may be true. But the Shanks are not Pazzians. Already we have discovered little ways to trick them. If they can be shown to be fallible, the people will take heart." I slammed a fist on my knee. "They must!"

"Yes," spat the Fristle. "We trick them and steal food from the warehouses. But the costs are high."

I said: "A good fire ought to help."

"Burn the shints out." Nath the Rumpador nursed a swollen jaw where the butt end of a Shank trident had smashed him. "Yes, I like that!"

We talked and argued and eventually decided to burn a certain barracks which housed a company of particularly unpleasant Schtarkins.

"It must look like an accident." I sounded heavy and tired. "If these rasts suspect it was arson, sabotage—"

"The retribution will be frightful." Nath the Rumpador nodded.

"We'll fix it," growled Bargrad the Pellin. "I'll get old Palandi the Iarvin to design a device. He's a sneaky Khibil, full of himself—"

"And much reduced, much reduced," said Foke the Clis.

"Broken in the ib," confirmed the Brokelsh. "But I will speak to him."

Having settled that, I produced a half loaf, only a little moldy, and divided it up. I'd had that off a tray going past on a wagon.

Well, we burned the barracks.

A fine hullabaloo followed; but the incendiarism was put down to accident. For the next three days it rained hard. We did no more burning for a sennight, and then we burned a smithy where arrow heads were forged. That, too, given the danger of the fires, was put down to chance.

Because the Shanks couldn't tell one person from another of the same race of diffs we were able to work some schemes that in any other context would not have been possible. I was able to join a work gang in place of somebody else. The Shanks simply counted how many of us there were in any one gang, and kept checking that number. By this means I and my companions could move about Taranjin relatively freely. We needed to get the word out and spreading that the Day was coming. And to be ready. By this means, also, I was afforded the opportunity to take stock of the Shank forces. They were formidable. Clearly, however, this was the bridgehead for an Invasion. The forces gathered in Taranjin were not of the size to resist a concerted attack delivered by even a small proportion of the strength we could muster. The problem was mustering that strength.

When I'd worked my way around to joining a group of apim armorers, I had the layout pretty well firmly fixed in my head. Shan-lao Ortyghan at first resented my presence. He ran the shop and he was well aware that if he did not produce what the Shanks required he'd get no food, or he'd be stuck through with a trident. He was a bulky apim, with a stomach shrunken away from its former protuberant glory.

He had lost the skills of Naghan the Hammer and I had to convince him I was a competent armorer in all branches of that abstruse science before he would accept me as a substitute for Naghan the Hammer. Then he became more friendly.

When I said I required a sword he just turned away.

When I persisted, he said: "Those Shank shints can count, you know."

"So we cabbage a little metal from here and from there. You, Shan-lao Ortyghan, will provide enough good quality metal that the Fish Faces won't miss for me to forge a sword."

I will not go into the details necessary in the Convincing of Shan-lao Ortyghan the Armorer. Suffice it to say that he grunted out: "Very well, Prince Chaadur, we will cabbage the metal for you. And may the True Trog Himself bless our endeavors. For if we are caught—"

"We will not be. The Shanks can be fooled. Have we not proved that?"

"Aye." He had to admit that, grudgingly. We could bamboozle the Fish Heads. It was risky; it was just about our only weapon at this time.

On a gray day of wind and rain and black clouds billowing a new rein-forcement of Shank flying ships soared in from the sea. We counted the squadrons. There were five squadrons of thirteen ships each. Also, these ships were, again, of a different style from those which we were accustomed to see flying over Taranjin on patrols.

"By the Resplendent Bridzilkelsh!" swore Bargrad the Pellin, staring up with the rain beating on his pugnacious Brokelsh face. "The shints! More of 'em. That upsets the balance, Prince Chaadur!"

"Aye."

The flying ships in their rigid lines through the bluster circled and lowered past the outskirts of the port, vanishing past the roofs, landing in the field allotted to them. This did, indeed, alter the balance.

The next time Deb-Lu contacted me, I'd have to make stronger representations through him to Drak, Emperor of Vallia, to release more vollers from the Vallian Air Service. Yes, very well, I knew they were committed and needed elsewhere. I'd just have to try to convince Drak that we needed them down here.

At this time, too, by cunning if simple appeals to the natural cleverness inherent in any Khibil's opinion of himself, I'd stiffened up old Palandi the Iarvin's resolve. In a pathetic attempt at the usual cutting superior manner of any Khibil, he said: "I have made the device, prince." He showed me the little wooden box. I was at pains to admire his handiwork.

Truthfully, the thing was a little marvel. In the box a fruit would be connected at each end to rods which held a powerful twisted cord in rest. He'd suggested a gregarian, anything of a similar nature would have done, an orange, an apple, anything that would rot away. When the fruit rotted enough it released the cord which unwound like a spring. This struck sparks from a flint and toothed wheel. The sparks fell on the prepared tinder. The rest of the box was packed with combustibles. We had, therefore, if not a time bomb, then a timed incendiary device.

"Dondo!" I said, congratulating Palandi.

"Oh, aye," he sniffed, brushing up his whiskers from which the red had faded to a dull gray. "She'll burn 'em, may Bil the Khib frizzle 'em."

The necessity was to select a fruit in the last stages of decomposition. Now, remember, food was so valuable, was so difficult to obtain, that to dedicate a whole fruit to our incendiarism was so altruistic as to be beyond credence.

"A fish head," I said, firmly. "Any fruit is beyond our powers."

"Even a stinking fish head," grumped Foke the Clis, "will be difficult."

So, and of course, in the event I donated a fish head out of a garbage pail outside a Shank barracks. You had to fight to get the garbage, too.

What with this scheme and that burning, this reconnaissance and that listing of forces, that horrendous time passed.

Through this period we discovered further ways of fooling and tricking the Shanks.

Shan-lao Ortyghan proved to be not only a fine armorer but an excellent engraver. He could produce the most wonderful patterns along a sword blade. When a party of Shank officers discovered examples of his work in a back room of the smithy they became, as Shan-lao expressed it: "Beside themselves with wonder and admiration of the workmanship." Nothing would suffice but that they must have their own swords beautifully etched with patterns of fish and ships and clouds, and the whirling Celtic lines that made a blade an artifact of art and beauty.

"I'd a' refused 'em," said Shan-lao, bitterly, "but they'll pay extra food."

"Quite right," I said.

"But, prince—?"

"You'll need acid. Strong acid. You and your assistants will beautify the swords of the Fish Faces."

Here I was piercing two birds with a single shaft.

First of all, if we could get our hands on acid, then Palandi the Iarvin could use the method of having acid bite through a membrane for a timing device instead of a rotten fish head.

In the second place, as I said to the armorer: "You will execute the most wonderful designs upon the blades of the Shank weapons. If it is to become a fashion with them, then we'll use that to our own advantage."

"It sits ill with me, prince, to pander to a damned Fish Face."

"Assuredly. You will, good Shan-lao, cut the patterns deep. Very deep. The color will conceal the depth the acid has bitten. You see?"

"Oh, aye, I see. And when the swords break in a fight, they'll march around for me and stick a trident through my guts."

"When the fight happens, we'll all be in there fighting. If we don't we don't deserve to succeed. When we've scored the victory, the depth of the acid will not be an issue. Of course, if we do not win on the Day, then little will matter thereafter."

"By the Divine Tears of the True Trog Himself! You speak sooth there!"

"Then let the acid bite deeply, Shan-lao, and curse all the Shanks down to their hellish hell."

"Quidang to that, prince!"

In a similar fashion I persuaded a lithe rascal who swore by Diproo the Nimble-fingered to go along with a scheme I'd concocted in a moment, I suppose, of divine madness.

This Luan-Chi the Flexible joined Bargrad the Fellin and myself in an argument over a suitable use to which we might put Palandi's incendiary device.

"Barracks are fine," I said. "But if we burn a food warehouse—"

Luan-Chi, a Thanko with a mop of dusty dark hair and the long and drooping nose of his race, said quickly: "That would not be clever."

"I'd burn the lot of 'em," growled Bargrad in his pugnacious uncouth Brokelsh way. "But Luan-Chi speaks true, prince. If we destroy food we reduce the amount the Bolsted-rotten Shanks will give us."

"Anyway," amplified the thief, "it is reasonably difficult to burn."

"There is a certain warehouse adjacent to the Marine Bazaar," I said in an even voice, not to be deflected. "They store barrels of fish there. The fish is preserved in oil. Oil. That will make a capital blaze."

"We'll all starve!"

"The Shanks have ample supplies of food. They deprive us to keep us in order, to keep us in chains. If they lose a warehouse of fish, they have plenty more. They go out fishing every damned day, don't they?"

"Yes—"

"Well, then. We burn the warehouse and we make sure at least one of the walls is broken down." I glared at them with all the intolerant domination of Dray Prescot. "They will order slaves to rebuild the walls."

"So we will toil to rebuild the walls—"

"We build those walls in a certain way. We arrange the courses so that a section as wide as a door can be swiftly taken down. We will enter the warehouse secretly and take away many of those precious barrels of fish. Then we will rebuild the wall section so that it looks the same. They may guard the double doors at the front; we enter at—"

"By Diproo the Nimble-fingered, prince! A scheme! It will work!"

"Aye. With care and cunning, it will fool the Schtarkins."

So, that is precisely what we did. The Shanks never did figure out how barrels of fish were short in their inventory when the doors were fast shut and locked, with guards prowling. The walls stood, firm and solid. There must be some defect in their accounting procedures.

And our people ate good fish in oil.

These were just two of the schemes we tormented the Shanks with at that time. Perhaps the greatest weapon in our armory, though, was one I did not reveal to a soul. Since my tutor Maspero in far Aphrasöe had given me that genetic pill so that I could understand Kregish, I'd understood any language. Even the hissing spitting clicking racket of the Shanks.

One day creeping along out of the way like any slave, I passed into a square where along one side the Shanks had set up a row of stakes. On top writhed the poor unfortunates condemned for whatever crime they had committed.

There were forty-seven impaled persons. I counted as I walked past. The outcries had mostly died down, and the wrigglings stilled. The smells were no more unpleasant than most of Taranjin. Slaves like myself, passing along with downcast eyes, cast a single glance aloft, and then went back to scuttling along. They were just thanking the True Trog Himself it wasn't them up there.

A few Fish Faces with shiny tridents and scale armor were lolling about by the row of impalement stakes.

"You can't believe these people," one of them was saying. This is a rough translation of the idiomatic fishy language. "Why do they do it?"

"If they become any more troublesome," spat his companion, "they will become uneconomic."

"Get rid of 'em all," said another.

Walking on past with my head lowered I almost missed the response.

"Haven't you heard? The leaders have struck a deal. By the Great Scaled One! We'll soon have these drys whimpering in fear again and back under control."

Moving on in that slavish half crouch and shuffle I realized there were a number of facts to chew on here. Not one of those forty-seven poor devils had been anyone I knew, no members of the resistance cells we were setting up, so my conscience was, relatively speaking, clear on that score. If they'd been moved to do what they did because they'd heard of resistance within Taranjin, then I decided I wouldn't hold myself responsible for that, either. Once you were committed then you took your chances like anyone else.

So what was this deal the Shank Leaders had struck?

And, too, in the tacit admission that some at least of the people of Taranjin were slipping away from control meant that our campaign had an impact.

A few days later we worked a scam on the produce being brought in from the countryside. The Fish Heads really did not care to venture too far from the sea, although, as they had proved in the past, they would do so with frightful energy if they had to. They were growing accustomed to eating land produce. So our little group having arranged substitutes where necessary went along to the Ghat Gate and watched the loaded pack calsanys and high-sided carts rolling in. Shanks patrolled, giving an occasional lick with their whips, a vicious clout with their trident butt-ends.

The scam was a simple enough affair, workable when slaves hoisted the sacks on their shoulders and trotted in lines into the warehouses. We provided a sack identical to those being unloaded from the carts and carried into the building. Our accomplice was among the carriers. At a suitable place of shadows, under an arch, just past a door, the carrier would step out of line with his sack of flour and our man would take his place with his sack of sand.

This was garsun flour ground from the massive roots of the gola-gola plant. They tried to grow corn here but the varieties were not up to much, the climate not quite right, but garsun flour made a marvelous doughy-cake in lieu of ordinary bread. We had two sacks away and then it was my turn to step into the line with my sack of sand.

Jimjim the Randell slid past, ducking down into the archway's shadows as I stepped out. His sack of garsun flour would feed a lot of mouths. My sack of sand, I devoutly trusted, would be allocated to a Shank unit. I moved on smartly following the fellow ahead and a voice, harsh, cutting, phlegm-laded with arrogant fury, lashed out like a whip.

"Grak! C'mere, you miserable apology for a slave! You think you can fool me with a hoary old trick like that! You shint! C'mere!"

I just stuck my head down, not wishing to believe, and hoping he didn't mean me.

But he did.

"You! By the Triple Tails of Targ the Untouchable! We're going to have some change around here, we're going to have discipline and slaves knowing their place. C'mere, shint."

The thick and elastic coils of a black whip snapped about my waist and I was dragged back, the sack falling to the ground and spilling yellow sand across the bricks. I stared up.

Up there a black-browed Kataki hauled on his whip, and his sinuous tail with its six inches of daggered steel hovered before my eyes.

So now I knew the deal the Shanks had struck with the Katakis.

Twenty

After the first blazing realization of the dreadful compact drawn out between Shank and Kataki, the thought uppermost in my mind was that I must not kill this arrogant and cruel bastard of a Whiptail.

If a slave killed a slavemaster, the retribution would be so frightful everything of suffering previously endured would pale into insignificance.

His whip hauled me towards him. He was a big fellow, clad in mesh, bright and bulky, well fed. His downdrawn Kataki face with the snaggly teeth and dark eyes bore down on me.

"By Koskei of the Daggered Tail! A trick that would not fool a green coy! C'mere, you cramph, and I'll stripe you!"

He expected me to try to pull back, to draw away from him. Instead I surged forward, inside the bight of the lash. My left hand freed the coil of whip about me. My right fist fastened on his tail just where the dagger hilt was strapped with leather and bright brass buckles. I yanked and then instantly thrust forward.

He was gobbling in black fury now.

There was the immediate necessity to duck a blow from his gauntleted fist. Balanced easily now, forcing the tail towards his belly, I kicked. I kicked good and hard, where it hurt, betwixt wind and water.

My toes are hard. I felt the soggy impact and he jumped under the impact. He started to double up and my left fist slashed him across that narrow Kataki jaw. He fell down and I threw his tail away.

An uproar began, slaves shrieking in mortal fear, mingled with the hoarse and furious bellows of more Kataki slave guards.

A swift look back past the shadows, past the line of slaves, showed me guards running up, whirling their whips, with the mingled suns shine glittering off their steel-tipped tails. Time to go.

Jimjim the Randell had vanished, gone with his sack of garsun flour, hurrying to one of our secret hoards. Bargrad the Fellin stood in a dark corner, his savage Brokelsh face expressing a mixture of fear and surprise. His sack of sand still rested across his shoulders.

"Drop that sack, Bargrad! Run!"

The sack went onto the brick flooring and the Brokelsh was away like a deer startled by dogs. I rushed after him, around the corner of the warehouse, down the stinking alleyway beyond. There was a certain hole in the cross wall at the end and Bargrad fairly threw himself in and through. I followed, taking a bit of skin off my elbow as I went.

The noise at our backs materially abated. We were now in a dark and narrow passageway that led past the second wall out onto Mare Street. The suns shine lay in a glitter of ruby and jade across the fish scales and bones littering the street, and a few slaves moved about carrying barrels into the next warehouse along. We had to reach and mingle with them, just two more fish among the rest.

By the time we'd slowed down and put half a dozen barrel-carrying slaves behind us, the next guards up ahead came into view. I let out a breath. They were all Shanks.

We could fool Shanks; we might fool Katakis if we had the luck of Five-handed Eos-Bakchi with us, otherwise—never!

That evening we called an emergency meeting of the Taranjin Freedom Fighters.

Those people you have met were there plus a good few newcomers, attracted to the group by our success. Everyone had a long face. The mood was grim. Little needed to be said, for we all understood the nature of the problem we faced. That problem had been intensified a thousand-fold. Katakis were man-managers and knew only too well how to handle slaves.

"Yet," I said, "we must carry on somehow."

Bargrad wanted to know when this boasted Armada would come to our rescue, when the Freedom Fighters in the country would join us.

Since I'd had no recent communication over the eerie means of the planes with Deb-Lu, I couldn't answer. I gave a rote answer, promising that the Armada would come, and saw their confidence and belief waning.

We were cramped into a tiny mud brick hut, that inhabited by Master Chan Tang Lui, with no internal lights and only the radiance of the Maiden with the Many Smiles to show up our apprehensive and lugubrious faces. Even so, the Katakis found us in secret conclave. They'd have had us all if we had not had our bolthole prepared and were able to escape out into the shadows. As it was, it was a close run thing. And this was on the first day of the Whiptails' arrival!

A few days' later, with nothing done in the way of fooling the Shanks, I had to accept the needle. Our resistance to the Shank Invasion had collapsed.

All over town in the following sennight or so all our clever scams were unmasked by Katakis, expert bastards at sussing out schemes thought up by desperate slaves. They did not discover the trick wall. One reason for that was unpleasant in its implications. Most of the Freedom Fighters were too frightened to risk it. I went into the warehouse and collected a barrel of fish in oil; but alone it was hard work. With the fish as bait I tried to re-enlist some of the Liberty Warriors; few were interested.

With their superior cunning the Katakis actually increased some of the rations doled out to slaves. This helped to reduce the slaves' willingness to chance the awful punishments meted out to those who were caught stealing.

The Whiptails did not discover the tiny little workshop where Master Palandi the Iarvin built the incendiary devices. He gave me six of them, and then indicated his unwillingness to carry on. His fear was perfectly understandable. I had six; I did not press for more.

These examples functioned through the action of acid eating away a membrane to release the twisted cord. At least, this obviated one small disadvantage of the fish-head timed examples, although I felt convinced the Shanks wouldn't notice one new rotten-fish stink among all the miasma of rotten-fish stinks in which we all lived.

The future might look dark. If I couldn't lead a great crusade of Freedom Fighters, then I must do what I could alone to whittle away at the Shank power. Accordingly, through Shan-lao Ortyghan, I obtained a position as a nik-armorer or shal-armorer to one of the Fishy Leaders. He was known to us slaves as lord, and that was all he was called as far as we knew. The rivalry between the Shank leaders to obtain the services of the most expert Pazzian slaves ought to work in our favor. I was taken on as assistant armorer and my main tasks were cleaning weapons and armor. I found myself surrounded by the paraphernalia of combat and war. In addition, the Shank lord through his Kataki taskmasters had me taken aboard his flying ship to clean and polish there. Well, now, if Dray Prescot couldn't fashion a scheme out of this situation, a scheme highly unpleasant to the Fish Faces, he didn't deserve to be the Emperor of Emperors, Emperor of Paz, no, by Zim-Zair!

In the little dingy canvas bag holding my cleaning equipment rested the six eggs of fire, as Palandi called them, for they hatched flame. The cleaning equipment, sounding grand, consisted of brick dust, oil and rags. Spittle was the other vital ingredient. So, I cleaned fighting gear.

The metal we had been cabbaging for the sword Shan-lao was to make was not sufficient. Now I was surrounded by weapons! The Shanks might be vicious and merciless killers, they were slack over managing slaves. Not so the Katakis, and a guard stood outside the armory door at all times slaves were near weapons. The door was locked from the outside. I spat and polished.

This was the period in which I learned a great deal about Shank flying ships and about the weapons of the Fish Faces.

One day it chanced that my companion slave, a little Och, Onso the Gnat, had a gripe in his guts and was absent. I was alone. I cleaned and polished assiduously. Then, in a great wave of longing and desperation, the temptation to take and hide one of these weapons swept over me.

That temptation had to be resisted. The old saw about: 'I can resist everything except temptation' had to be denied. The Katakis might unlock our chains when we worked aboard the flying ships—they remained slave drivers still. A single sword missing would be noted at once as the slavemaster counted stock. Then—I did not care to dwell on that particular then.

Just as I'd reached that somber conclusion the armory door opened and two Jibrfarils stood there, black whips trailing in grotesque counterpoint to their daggered tails. They exuded menace.

"You, apim," said one through his snaggly teeth. "Fetch your cleaning gear. You go with us."

The cleaning bag dangling from a fist, I went out with them. *Now* what had gone wrong?

This armory lay under the top deck of the aftercastle and we went along forward. I took note of the flagship. She was one of the newer large slab-sided craft and along the starboard bulwark I counted the butts of ten varters. These ballistae impressed me as being superior to other Shank artillery I'd seen; they were nowhere near the quality of the gros varters of Vallia. The ship possessed two fighting towers and a raised armored control tower. The decks were, to a first lieutenant of a Royal Navy Seventy Four, absolutely filthy.

Up forward the forecastle boasted four more smaller ballistae and a brace of catapults. This was officer country and I was shoved through a brass-studded doorway. The cabin was well-lit by mineral oil lamps. A scuttle was partially obscured by a half-drawn curtain. A smell of oil and polish reached my nostrils through the eternal unnoticed fish stink. I looked about.

When the Kataki explained why I was here I breathed easier.

The lord wanted some personal cleaning done. Like many warlords he kept up a trophy room, an idiosyncrasy of barbaric pride amusing to those who do not dwell upon their past personal victories. I speak from a private point of view; it is important that soldiers know and appreciate what their regiments have done in the past so that they maintain the tradition of duty, honor and bravery.

Rather naturally I thought of other trophy rooms I had known and particularly that of Gafard, the King's Striker, Sea Zhantil. Aboard a green swifter of Magdag he'd organized a trophy room so that he could retain possession of certain personal belongings of a certain Krozair also known as the Sea Zhantil.

By this time I was getting the hang of the Shank rank markings and the

Fish Face I took to be the Ship Hikdar was talking in a most cringing fashion to the lord. I must give their conversation in plain unadorned prose for to hear their strange splashing clicking fishy speech gave a Pazzian a most uncomfortable, not to say eerie, feeling.

"And you personally guarantee the safety here?" demanded the lord.

"Absolutely, lord. The slaves fear the Katakis. They call them greeshes, or Jibrfarils."*

As these Pazzian words clicked out from the splashing fishy words, the Katakis stiffened and their daggered tails shot up. They resented that, and they couldn't help show it. I saw there was no love lost between employer and employee in this devilish compact between Shank and Kataki.

"Place two in control at all times."

"Yes, lord."

With that the Fish Faces took their odiferous presence off. I looked about. The Katakis went over to a small table against the inner bulkhead and sat down to some obscure game involving slapping their tail daggers one against t'other. One of them growled: "Grak, slave!"

Hauling out my cleaning gear I set to work. The trophies were ranked in glass cabinets, adorned with shells and fishes and squid motifs. Many of the items were from fights between Shank and Schtarkin, as far as I could make out, between Schturgin and Shant. Also there were, to my sorrow, altogether far too many taken from soldiers and sailors of Paz. I recognized some of the blazons. A pair of shields from the Iron Legions of Hamal, a lance pennon much ripped and bloodied from Hyrklana, a helmet and a coat of mesh from a country of the Dawn Lands, a cartwheel of swords from many of the nations around the Shrouded Sea, a powerful crossbow that had once belonged to a swod in a regiment of Canops. In a cabinet in isolated splendor as I looked around, I saw half a Vallian flag. The tresh had been carefully cleaned and what was left gave my heart a thump. The regimental numbers were missing; I fancied that was from a Green Coat regiment of Vallian Spearmen almost broken in the Battle of the Incendiary Vosks.

Then, as I saw what had been carefully hung in its own glass case, I froze. Well, they didn't often venture far from the Eye of the World. Only once or twice in his lifetime would a Krozair go awandering. The roving bug might bite in the wisdom of Zair and then a few companions would seek adventure and fortune upon wider oceans. To the best of my most recent knowledge the Fish Faces had not penetrated into the inner sea of Turismond. This gear, scarlet and bronze, this great Krozair longsword, had been borne by a Krozair brother fighting for some doomed cause against the Shanks.

When I came to take down the Krozair brand to clean everything with

---

* Jibrfaril: pain lover, in the sense of taking pleasure from giving pain. A.B.A.

ten-fold meticulousness, I held the sword reverently. I saw that I was trembling. Instantly, I told myself severely and with contemptuous passion, I must hold onto reality. Swords are merely lumps of metal forged into special shapes to perform unpleasant work. A chunk of metal forged into a ploughshare is of infinitely greater worth—except, except in some special circumstances. And, by Zim-Zair, those special circumstances had dogged me all my life!

The macabre thought did occur to me that this was the work of the Star Lords. Certainly, after our most recent meetings they might very well throw me some help. Too, by thinking of an audience of the Everoinye as a meeting rather than a confrontation, I was breaking new ground. If they had indeed tossed down this Krozair longsword to my assistance then that would be a fantastic notion; but it was a credible one.

The longsword had belonged to a Krozair of Zamu. The secret marks were plain to me. She balanced perfectly—well, now, that is a superfluous observation as this perfect balance is one of the recipes for the production of the superb Krozair longsword.

"Careful with that, shint," rapped the Kataki with blue cult marks down his cheeks.

His companion snarled a sneer. "That great bar of iron? It's useless. By Takroti! I don't see why this Kiko of a Shant lord keeps the stupid thing."

"What he takes, he keeps."

"Aye."

So, I cleaned the Shant lord's trophies. The very last was a stux near the door, a hefty throwing spear with red feathers decorating the join of haft and head. Then I was finished and was shepherded out.

For my reward, when they chained me up again, I was thrown something ugly out of the refuse of the shandishalah booths along the fish quays.

Having determined to strike a more positive blow than this shilly-shallying about, I arranged with Shan-lao to take another slave's task of delivering boxes of arrows to the fleet. The impression I'd gained was that here barrels were not too easily come by, coopers being scarce, and the English system of packing arrows in barrels was not followed. Accordingly, I drove a creaking four-wheel cart drawn by two mytzers under the watchful gaze of guards onto the field. The Shank flying ships were berthed in neat rows. I delivered the boxes of arrows with due humility. Six of the Shank ships received a box containing a fire egg.

The last of the six was the lord's flagship.

As I came out on deck having stowed the boxes at the back of the magazine my two Kataki guards accosted me and in their brutal way told me to cut along to the trophy room. The lord wanted his trophies cleaned again.

As before they removed my chains and then sat down to their tail-dagger thumping game. I went to work, spitting and brick-dusting and polishing.

I'd brought a whetstone and put a decent edge on some of the blades. The Katakis merely grunted reluctant approval at this. I spent a deal of time on the Krozair brand.

The scarlet breechclout was clean and pressed—no doubt by a female slave—and the lestenhide belt supple with oils. The scabbard had been disengaged from the bronze lockets. In general there are only two styles of scabbard for a Krozair longsword, this one, the plain and unadorned krosturr style, the other being the highly decorated hyrzim fashion. Both, however, feature the device of the hubless spoked wheel.

A hubbub began outside. The two whiptails took no notice for a time and then, curiosity winning them over, crossed to the door and stood looking out.

Temptation, as I say, is a sore taskmistress.

With smooth and practiced movements I discarded the gray slave clout and donned the brave old scarlet and pulled the belt tight. That felt good!

I took up the great Krozair longsword.

The brand glittered in the light as I twirled her about. I felt the secret disciplines of my brotherhood, the Krozairs of Zy, gave me insights and understandings unimaginable to a non-Krozair—I felt just wonderful.

Reality, of course, was that I was a slave play-acting.

The uproar outside had now grown to considerable proportions. Screams fizzed into the air. Intrigued, I crossed to the scuttle and looked out.

A black hulled ship had recently landed and from her a coffle of slaves staggered along, struggling, as the whips rose and fell, rose and fell. These people had evidently recently been caught, for they wore normal clothes and they resisted still. Their guards were becoming exasperated. Dust spurted up and glinted, and red welts lashed across the slaves as they tried to fight back.

Among the glittering scaled armor of his officers, the Shank lord pointed.

"Bring those slaves up here. They will serve as an object lesson to the others." More slaves and guards were debouching from the flier.

One of his aides, a Fish Face who had a few words of Kregish, managed to convey the lord's orders to the Kataki Chuktar with the group.

This fellow, immense, banded in iron, flaunting feathers, at once protested. "They are merchandise, lord. They can be disciplined—"

"Shastum! Aboard—bring them!"

There was no arguing with the power these Fish Heads wielded. The Kataki Chuktar subsided, his face as black as the hull of a Shank ship. This lord was an objectionable bastard with a face like a cod and enough gold loading him down to sink a bullion argenter to the deepest depths of the Risshamal Deep. He held out his hand and an aide slapped a trident into his grip.

So that was what he'd do. He was going to enjoy himself thoroughly in the next few murs. He'd go along the line of miserable slaves and thrust his trident into each one's guts, and twist and pull. The filthy state of his deck wouldn't offend him in the slightest.

Sick with despair and horror I stood and watched as the line of shouting screaming Pazzians was hauled aboard. They were thrust against the bulwarks.

Unwilling to witness the horror about to occur, I started to turn away from the scuttle. The Pazzians remained defiant, having to be forcefully smashed back. I started to turn away—and then I halted. My fists wrapped about the great Krozair longsword bit and pained and knotted into grainy lumps.

So I, Dray Prescot, Lord of Strombor and Krozair of Zy, stared blankly upon my friends.

Rollo the Runner reeled back under the smash of a trident butt. His face was congested with anger, bruised, blackened, vicious. And, with him, stood Mevancy nal Chardaz, and Trylon Kuong, and Llodi the Voice. The Shank lord raised his trident. In only moments I'd have four less friends on Kregen.

I stood there, lumpen.

A great Hero? A legend? A flying figure in a scarlet breechclout wielding a glittering longsword? Me? A beaten slave?

All the passion and fury of the old Dray Prescot lashed out. No longer was I the latter day Prescot, rational, trying to be calm, hoping to achieve just ends by judicial discussion. Now I was that selfsame red raw Dray Prescot who had first landed on Kregen, savage with resentment at unjust authority, vengeful against those who did me wrong.

Even as passion flowed through me I thanked whoever it might be—the Star Lords, the Savanti nal Aphrasöe or some other greater power—who had placed into my fists the weapon with which I might redress oppression.

I moved with a suddenness I had not forgotten.

The two Katakis watching from the door were cut down by two precise blows.

I snatched up the red-feathered stux and sprang out onto the deck.

The Shank lord had degutted one poor devil of a Mionch who went down screaming to snap one of his long tusks against the deck. The lord drew back the trident for his next blow and the red feathers of the throwing spear nestled neatly between his fishy shoulder blades.

His aides and officers let out screeches of astonishment and incredulous rage as the lord toppled and fell. In a body, glittering with scaled armor, they turned to face me.

Mevancy, Kuong, Llodi and Rollo stared with enormous and disbelieving eyes.

The Fish Heads shrieked in rage, ripping out their swords and brandishing their tridents.

The stink of rotten fish suddenly assaulted my nostrils, a smell I hadn't noticed in too long a time.

Here, then, was where Dray Prescot discovered the great and final secret.

"Hai Jikai!" Redness crept in. "Hai Jikai, you murdering torturing kleeshes of Fish Faces! Hai Jikai!"

Gripping the great Krozair longsword in that cunning two-handed Krozair grip, the brave old scarlet breechclout flaming under the streaming mingled lights of the Suns of Scorpio, facing hopeless odds, I, Dray Prescot, hurled myself hurtling headlong forward.

"Hai Jikai!"

About the author

Alan Burt Akers was a pen name of the prolific British author Kenneth Bulmer, who died in December 2005 aged eighty-four.

Bulmer wrote over 160 novels and countless short stories, predominantly science fiction, both under his real name and numerous pseudonyms, including Alan Burt Akers, Frank Brandon, Rupert Clinton, Ernest Corley, Peter Green, Adam Hardy, Philip Kent, Bruno Krauss, Karl Maras, Manning Norvil, Chesman Scot, Nelson Sherwood, Richard Silver, H. Philip Stratford, and Tully Zetford. Kenneth Johns was a collective pseudonym used for a collaboration with author John Newman. Some of Bulmer's works were published along with the works of other authors under "house names" (collective pseudonyms) such as Ken Blake (for a series of tie-ins with the 1970s television programme The Professionals), Arthur Frazier, Neil Langholm, Charles R. Pike, and Andrew Quiller.

Bulmer was also active in science fiction fandom, and in the 1970s he edited nine issues of the New Writings in Science Fiction anthology series in succession to John Carnell, who originated the series.

www.ingramcontent.com/pod-product-compliance
Lightning Source LLC
Chambersburg PA
CBHW020256030726
47499CB00001B/224